BESTSELLING AUSTRALIAN AUTHOR
MARGARET WAY

MEN OF THE
OUTBACK

MILLS & BOON

MEN OF THE OUTBACK © 2023 by Harlequin Books S.A.

THE CATTLEMAN
© 2006 by Margaret Way Pty Ltd.
Australian Copyright 2006
New Zealand Copyright 2006

First Published 2006
Second Australian Paperback Edition 2023
ISBN 978 1 867 29581 5

THE CATTLE BARON'S BRIDE
© 2006 by Margaret Way, Pty., Ltd.
Australian Copyright 2006
New Zealand Copyright 2006

First Published 2006
Second Australian Paperback Edition 2023
ISBN 978 1 867 29581 5

HER OUTBACK PROTECTOR
© 2006 by Margaret Way Pty., Ltd.
Australian Copyright 2006
New Zealand Copyright 2006

First Published 2006
Third Australian Paperback Edition 2023
ISBN 978 1 867 29581 5

This is a work of fiction. Names, characters, places, and incidents are either the product of the author's imagination or are used fictitiously, and any resemblance to actual persons, living or dead, business establishments, events, or locales is entirely coincidental.

MIX
Paper | Supporting
responsible forestry
FSC® C001695

Published by
Mills & Boon
An imprint of Harlequin Enterprises (Australia) Pty Limited
(ABN 47 001 180 918), a subsidiary of HarperCollins
Publishers Australia Pty Limited (ABN 36 009 913 517)
Level 19, 201 Elizabeth Street
SYDNEY NSW 2000
AUSTRALIA

® and ™ (apart from those relating to FSC®) are trademarks of Harlequin Enterprises (Australia) Pty Limited or its corporate affiliates. Trademarks indicated with ® are registered in Australia, New Zealand and in other countries. Contact admin_legal@Harlequin.ca for details.

Printed and bound in Australia by McPherson's Printing Group

CONTENTS

THE CATTLEMAN 7

THE CATTLE BARON'S BRIDE 273

HER OUTBACK PROTECTOR 459

Margaret Way takes great pleasure in her work and works hard at her pleasure. She enjoys tearing off to the beach with her family on weekends, loves haunting galleries and auctions, and is completely given over to French champagne "for every possible joyous occasion." She was born and educated in the river city of Brisbane, Australia, and now lives within sight and sound of beautiful Moreton Bay.

The Cattleman

Dear Reader,

It is with much pleasure that I welcome you to my four-book miniseries, MEN OF THE OUTBACK. The setting moves from my usual stamping ground, my own state of Queensland, to the Northern Territory, which is arguably the most colorful and exciting part of the continent. It comprises what we call the Top End and the Red Center—two extreme climatic and geographical divisions, which is what makes the Territory so fascinating. It has the tropical, World Heritage–listed Kakadu National Park, with crocodiles and water buffalo to the Top, and in the Center the desert, the "Dead Heart"—not actually dead at all, only lying dormant until the rains transform it into the greatest garden on earth.

The pervading theme of the series is family. Family offers endless opportunities for its members to hurt and be hurt, to love and support, or bitterly condemn. What sort of family we grew up in reverberates for the rest of our lives. One thing is certain: at the end of the day, *blood* binds.

I invite you, dear reader, to explore the lives of my families. My warmest best wishes to you all.

Margaret Way

PROLOGUE

Mokhani Station
Northern Territory,
Australia 1947

ALL THE WHILE they were riding, Moira felt a stab of anxiety as sharp as a knife beneath her breastbone. She tried to tell herself not to be afraid, but it did no good. A sense of foreboding weighed on her so oppressively, she slumped in the saddle, her hands trembling on the reins. If her companion noticed, Moira saw no sign. It was another hot, humid, thundery day on the verge of the Wet, or the Gunummeleng, as the station Aborigines called it. There were only two seasons in the Territory, she'd learned. The Wet and the Dry. The Wet, the time of the monsoon, extended from late November to March, the Dry lasted from April through October. It was mid-November now. She had arrived on Mokhani in early February of that year to teach the Bannerman twins, a boy and a girl aged seven. Nearly ten months of sharing her life with extraordinary people; the ten most life-changing months of her life. Ultimately, they had turned her from just out of adolescence into a *woman*. Her great fear was she had chosen a tragic path.

Nearing eighteen and not long out of her excellent convent school, she'd craved *adventure*. Mokhani had offered it. After years of hard study and obeying strict rules, she'd been ready for a liberating experience. It was understood that at some time she had to continue her tertiary education, but if her parents hadn't exactly encouraged her to take a gap year, they'd put up no great objection when they'd seen how much she'd wanted it. As a much-loved only child, "the wonderful surprise" of her parents' middle years, their only wish was for her to be happy. The family solicitor, a good friend of her father's, had come up with the answer. His legal firm handled many Outback clients' affairs. It just so happened, the Bannerman family, pastoral pioneers with huge cattle interests in the Northern Territory and Queensland's Gulf country, wanted a governess for their children, someone of good family and proven academic ability, a young *woman* preferably, to better relate to the children.

She qualified on all counts. Her father was a well-respected family doctor. Her mother, an ex-nurse, helped out several days at his surgery. Moira had been a straight-A student, winning a scholarship to university. The Bannermans, for their part, were rich, powerful, influential. The present owner and heir to the Bannerman fortune was Steven Bannermanex-Squadron Leader Steven Bannerman, seconded to the Royal Air Force during the war, survivor of the Battle for Britain, who'd returned home a war hero. His wife, Cecily, was a niece of the South Australian governor. In short, the Bannermans were the sort of people to whom her parents felt no qualms about sending her.

The great irony was, they might have been signing her death warrant.

Moira lifted one hand, pressing it hard against her heart to stop it from bursting through her rib cage. If her companion addressed a stray comment to her, she heard nothing of it. There were too many demons clamouring inside her head. She knew she wasn't very far away from a breakdown. In a sense, it was another version of the Aboriginal *kurdaitcha* man, the tribal sorcerer, pointing the bone. Yet nothing had been said to her. Her throbbing fears were virtually without proof, but like all victims, she had the inbuilt awareness there was threat ahead.

It was deliriously hot. That alone caused profound dislocation. Temperature nearing a hundred and rising. A thunderstorm was rolling in across the tabletopped escarpment that from a distance always appeared a deep amethyst. The storm revealed itself as magnificent. Majestic in cloud volume, black and silver with jagged streaks of livid green and purple that intensified the colors of the vast empty landscape and made the great cushions of spinifex glow molten gold. Even *she* knew it was risky taking this long ride. If it poured rain, the track could become slippery and dangerous and they would have to walk the horses. But it wouldn't be the first time a thunderstorm had blown over, for all the fabulous pyrotechnics.

Nearly everyone on the station, even the Aborigines, the custodians of this ancient land, were feeling the peculiar tension the extremes of weather created. Heat and humidity. The humidity alone left one gutted. The monsoon couldn't come soon enough even if it brought in a cyclone. Not that she had ever lived through the destructive cyclones of the far north. Still she understood what the Territorians meant when they talked about going "troppo," a state of mental disturbance blamed on extreme weather conditions.

Was that it? For one blessed moment, she felt a lightening of her fears. Was she going troppo? Were her fears imaginary rather than real? No one meant her any harm. It was all in her mind. Her companion appeared almost serene, hardly the demeanour of an avenger. The heat did dreadful things to people, especially those not born and bred to the rigours of the inland.

We're white people living in the black man's land.

Steven Bannerman had said that to her when she'd first arrived, looking down at her with a strange intensity, his handsome mouth curved in a rare smile. Steven Bannerman was not an easygoing man. Many attributed that to his traumatic experiences during the war. Steven Bannerman was the symbol of power and authority on the station, as daunting in some moods as a blazing fire.

Steven!

She'd been destined to fall in love with him. Her heart leaped at the sound of his name. It resonated in her head and through the caverns of her heart. If she never saw him again, his image would remain etched on her mind, his touch imprinted on her skin. It was truly extraordinary the bearing *one* person could have on another's entire life.

She had felt it such an honor to work for a war hero. She had handled the high-spirited, mischievous little imps of twins who had seen off not one but two governesses remarkably well. Everyone said so. Particularly Mrs. Bannerman, Cecily, a benign goddess who, at the beginning, had sung her praises. Not that she had ever been invited to call the Missus, as the Aboriginal house girls called Mrs. Bannerman, by her Christian name. Steven, too, was only Steven when they were alone. At all other times, he was Mr. Bannerman.

A prince in his own kingdom; everything in the world to her. He had been since the first moment she'd looked up into his beautiful, far-seeing blue eyesthough it hadn't been revealed to her then. But each week, each month that passed, they'd grown closer and closer, learning so much about each other. Nothing had happened until a short time ago when their feelings for each other had broken out in madness.

Fate had delivered her like a sacrificial lamb right into his arms.

She had gone from innocence to womanhood all in one sublime destructive day. She was certain in her heart neither had deliberately chosen it. It had just happened, like an act of God; a flood, a drought, an earthquake, a deadly bolt of lightning from the sky. Acts of God were merciless.

The voice inside her head started up again. She let it talk. It was the next best thing to a conscience.

You know what you have to do, Moira. You have to get out of here. Leave before tragedy overtakes you. Worse, overtakes Steven. A scandal that would be talked about all over the Outback, affecting everyone, even the children.

She couldn't bear that. She had to make her decision. She had to put a thousand miles between herself and Steven. Steven had made his decision years ago before God and man. He had a wife and children. He would never leave them. Not that she'd dreamed for a single moment he would. His role had been drummed into him from childhood. He was the master of Mokhani Station. Outback royalty. She was nothing more serious than a passing affair.

Only, that wasn't true. Both of them knew it wasn't true. She had lain awake far into the night searching the corridors of her soul. There was a strong two-way connection between them, an instant bonding. Steven had told her she was his other half. His reward for what he had suffered during the war. They shared a dangerous kinship of body and spirit that opened the doors to heaven, but also to hell. Steven was passionately in love with her, as she was with him. Hadn't he told her he didn't know what love for a woman was until she'd come into his life? The admission hadn't been merely an attempt to break down her defenses; it had been wrenched from deep down inside him, causing him agony. A war hero, yet he had stood before her with tears in his eyes. Tears she understood. She too was on a seesaw.

Love and guilt. Their love was so good, so pure, yet she knew it could be equated with shameful, illicit sex. Women of other cultures had been murdered for less. When it came to dire punishment, the women were always the victims. Men were allowed to go on exactly as before. Except for the Aborigines, who meted out punishments equally.

Whether he loved her or not, Steven's marriage couldn't be counted for nothing. It was his *life*. He had married Cecily in

a whirlwind ceremony before he'd gone off to war. He'd told
Cecily he had wanted to wait. They'd been living through such
tumultuous times and he could very easily lose his life. But
Cecily had become hysterical at the thought of not becoming
his wife there and then. She'd wanted his children, and what
was more, she had conceived on their brief honeymoon. Cecily was a cousin of his lifelong friend, Hugh Balfour. Hugh had
introduced them, and then been best man at their wedding. The
tragedy was that after the horror and brutality of war, Steven
had come home a different man. So had Hugh, once so full of
promise, now well on the way to self-destruction. "A full-blown
alcoholic" Cecily scathingly labeled him. "Hugh can't cut it as
a civilian!" Cecily Bannerman, Moira had quickly learned, was
extremely judgmental, like many who had lived only a life of
ease and privilege.

But the tragedy hung over both families. She saw it clearly
the first time Hugh had visited Mokhani after her arrival. Hugh
idolized Steven. Steven in turn always welcomed his old friend,
defending him even when Hugh's own family had written him
off. Hugh had been so charming to her, offering friendship, asking her all sorts of questions about herself and her family. He'd
made every attempt to get to know her, he had even painted
her. Many times. Until, strangely, Steven had put a stop to it.
She couldn't think about that now.

Moira plucked a long strand of her hair from her cheek. It
glittered with drops of sweat. She had been so happy at first.
Lost in the uniqueness of this exciting new world. This was
real frontier country where nature in all its savage splendour
dominated everything. A city girl, born and raised, she had
grown to love this strange and violent place. It revealed itself
to her every day, this paradise of the wilds. The space and the
freedom! The absolute sense of grandeur. She loved the incredible landscape, saturated in Aboriginal myth and legend. The
blood-red of the soil, the cobalt-blue of the sky. She looked up
at it briefly. It started to spin above her.

They were heading up the escarpment, the track littered with rubble and orange rocks the size of a man's fist. The promontory overlooked the most beautiful lagoon on the station, lily-edged Falling Waters. No crocodiles were thought to swim this far inland, though they had done so in the past. Nowadays it was argued that from numerous rock slides the neck of the canyon had become too narrow. Besides, it was a known drinking place for the great rainbow snake, owner of all water holes in the vast arid inland.

She could hear the falling of water now. It grew louder, sighing, hissing, splashing. From the track, the lagoon appeared like giant shards of glittering mirror lost in the thick grove of trees. White-trunked paperbarks and graceful red river gums adorned the water hole, the sun turning their gray-green leaves metallic.

She remembered the first time Steven had brought her to this magical place. The two of them *alone*. Her heart contracted at the memory, one she would cherish until the day she died: how with a tortured oath he had pulled her body close…how her lips had opened spontaneously under his…how his hand on her naked breast had made an indelible brand. She would remember the way he'd picked her up and laid her on the warm golden sand. She had given herself to him willingly, overtaken by a great tide of passion, her blood sizzling, as he played her virgin body, his hands so knowing, so masterly, in turn demanding and tender. One could surrender the world for such lovemaking. Hadn't she? She had abandoned the tenets of her faith, honor, loyalty, cold reason. So many codes of conduct on the one hand. On the other?

Steven.

A world lost for love.

Their arrival on the plateau, heralded by a miniature landslide of eroded earth and rocks, caused a huge congregation of waterfowl to rise from the glittering waters with a thunder of wings. They dismounted. Moira removed her wide-brimmed hat, shaking out her thick blond plait. Her body was soaked in sweat, not only from the heat and exertion. Dark forces were at play and she knew it. She had gone way beyond anxiety, moving toward acceptance. She followed her companion nearer the edge, acutely aware they were keeping their distance from one another as if a contagion were upon her.

The view from the top was sublime. There was nothing, *nothing*, like the vast burning landscape. The *sacred* land. It stretched away into infinity and beyond. She could see the length of the rocky, winding corridor of the gorge, the terraced walls glowing a rich, deep red with bands of black, rosepink and ochre-yellow. The creek bed was little more than a chain of muddy water holes in the Dry, but the permanent lagoon, an extraordinary lime-green was very deep at the centre. There was an Aboriginal legend attached to it; the Aboriginals had a legend for everything. A beautiful young woman, called Narli, promised to a tribal elder, had drowned herself in the lagoon following the killing of her lover for having broken the tribal taboo. Narli's spirit was said to haunt Falling Waters, luring young men to their deaths. There was danger in being young, beautiful and seductive, Moira reminded herself. Beauty inspired obsession. Obsession inspired violence.

Half fainting, she drew breath into her parched lungs. Her tongue was dry. It tasted of dust, making it difficult for her to swallow. She wondered what lay ahead, in part, knowing she had already surrendered. The air still quivered with fierce vibrations. Not by nature timid, she'd allowed herself to be brought low by shame and guilt. She had a sudden image of Steven and her deliriously locked together, his mouth over her, cutting off her ecstatic cries. In her defense it could be said she was incapable of withstanding him.

The waterfall tumbled a hundred feet or more to the pool below, sending up a sparkling mist of spray, as intoxicating as champagne. In the rains, she'd been told, the flow that today ran like a bolt of silver silk down the blackened granite turned into a spectacle of raw power, with a roar that could be heard from a great distance. At those times, the breadth of the falls widened dramatically as it thundered down the cliff face, tiered like an ancient ziggurat to drop countless tons of water into the lake. So augmented, the lagoon broke its banks, engulfing the floodplains with enormous sheets of water—which become huge swamps that were soon crocodile rich. People and cattle had to be moved to higher ground. Afterward, the earth responded with phenomenal abundance—lush green growth and an incredible profusion of wildflowers, native fruits and vegetables. She'd been so eager to witness that sight. Now she felt she never would.

There was no redeeming breeze. Nothing swayed. No petals of the wild hibiscus scattered. All was quiet save for the tumbling waters and the heavy *thud, thud, thud* of her heart. Even the birds that fed on the paperbarks and the flowering melaleuca trees—the honeyeaters, the gorgeous lorikeets and parrots—normally so restless, were strangely silent. Moira dared to look across at her companion, who could at that very moment be settling her fate. Despite all outward appearances of calm, violence simmered just below the surface. Violence generated by perhaps the most dangerous and deadly of sins.

Jealousy.

God help me! Moira was beyond all thought of trying to escape. Escape to where? This land was hostile to those on the run. She hadn't seen her parents in many months. The tears started to trickle down her cheeks as their dear, familiar faces swam into her mind. She loved them. Why had she never told them just how much? She should have stayed at home with them where she was safe. Instead, she had betrayed them. Betrayed herself. Betrayed Cecily, who had been kind to her in her fashion. She had inspired a devouring love that overwhelmed all else. In exchange, she had inherited consuming hate. She could feel that hate everywhere, even to the tips of her shaking fingers.

Moira lifted her unprotected face to the burning sun as if there were good reason to blind herself to what was coming. If she survived this, she would have to live with her sins for the rest of her life. It she didn't...*if she didn't...*

Hadn't Sister Bartholomew, in what seemed another lifetime, said to her whenever she landed herself in trouble, "Moira, you have no one to blame but yourself!"

Slowly her companion turned away from the lip of the precipice, jaw set, grimacing into the sun. The distance between them dramatically narrowed. "I've been waiting for this, Moira," came the chilling words.

What could she answer? Words died on her lips.

There was no chance. None at all.

Moira's knees buckled under her. She was tired. So tired. The matter had to be decided. She was guilty. She deserved what was coming to her. She sank to the ground, for one extraordinary second so disoriented she thought there was someone else besides her and her companion on the escarpment. If only she could turn around...

CHAPTER ONE

The Present

RETURNING FROM LUNCH—no fun at all, she *loathed* hurting people—Jessica found a note from Brett De Vere, her uncle, summoning her to a meeting in his office. It was probably about the Siegal place, she thought, carefully hanging up her new Gucci handbag. It had cost an arm and a leg. She felt a tiny spasm of guilt, but she had decided she *must* have it.

And why not? She was single. She had a great job, a challenging, exciting life. Swiftly she took a hairbrush from the bottom drawer of her desk and ran it briskly through her long blond hair, which was naturally curly but straightened at the moment. The action freed her a little from thoughts of the upsetting lunch with Sean, who really was a thoroughly nice guy, as wholesome as rolled oats. Most girls would be over the moon having a guy like Sean love them. The sad fact was he hadn't found a way to her heart.

Jessica stowed her hairbrush away, then turned to stare out the huge picture window directly behind her desk. It offered a tranquil view of the quiet leafy street. It was the *bluest* day. A day to hold in the memory. She loved the location of their offices, the avenue of mature jacaranda trees that in November, six months away, broke out in blossom. At that time, the whole city of Brisbane became tinted with an exquisite lavender-blue no sooner spent than the great shade trees, the poincianas, turned the air rosy. She loved life in the subtropics. Not too hot. Perfect!

In the distance, the broad, deep river that wound through the city's heart glittered in the afternoon sunlight. Nature stirred her, gave her strength. Comforted, she tried to work out what she was going to say to Brett. Her uncle, trained as an architect from whence, becoming bored, had branched out into interior design, had given her the commission. She was desperate to show him she measured up, but despite her best efforts, things weren't going very well. She'd lavished a lot of time and effort on her designs for the Siegals' resplendent new river-front home. But the Siegals were proving to be rather difficult clients. At least the wife, Chic, a fixture at charity functions, was. Couldn't be her real name, Jessica suspected, though she stood by Mrs. Siegal's decision to make one up. She must have considered Chic had impact. After all, she was only five-two standing fully erect.

But it was hell trying to deal with her. The fact that her husband was a multimillionaire might have had something to do with her endless waffling. De Vere's Design Studio had a few millionaires on the books, but most of its clients staved off mini-heart attacks by having a firm budget in mind. Her uncle Brett was in his late forties and had reached the point in his career when he could handpick his clients. Such a shame, then, he'd let Chic Siegal through the door.

About ready to join her uncle, Jessica checked herself over in the long narrow wall mirror. The limegreen suit and the fuchsia-pink-and-lime camisole beneath it had cost a month's pay, but Brett was a stickler for looking good, considering it was part of the job. He, himself, was polished perfection. In her entire life, Jessica had never seen her uncle slide into sloppiness. She winked at her reflection then walked down the corridor to his office, waggling her fingers at Becky, a senior designer, and stopping at her door. Becky's desk was awash with swatches of gorgeous new fabrics she was tossing around with abandon. Turquoise, aquamarine, malachite. Jessica smiled. *Malachite* sounded much better than *olive*. As a schoolgirl hired for the holidays, Jessica had adored being in Becky's office. She still did. The space was a veritable Aladdin's cave.

Becky beamed back. "Love your suit, kid! Watcha pay for that?"

"Not telling."

"We're friends, aren't we?" Becky, fifty for a few years now, in her youth powerfully pretty and still hanging in there, peered over the top of the glasses she had finally made the decision to wear.

"Sure. I just can't get my tongue around the price tag."

"Well, you look like a million dollars." Becky gave her a thumbs-up.

"Thanks, Beck."

Jessica resumed walking, smiling left and right at staff, eight in all, clever, creative people very loyal to the firm. She had joined De Vere's Design Studio soon after completing her fine-arts degree with honors. As a result of her degree, she'd been offered a position at the Queensland art gallery, with good prospects for advancement, but she'd turned it down. A decision about which her eminent lawyer father, a pillar of society, a man who thought he had a perfect right to speak his mind at all times, had been most unhappy. "Working for your uncle is a very *frivolous* decision, Jessica. Your mother and I had high hopes for you, but our hopes don't seem to mean anything to you." Her father generally spoke with all the authority of the pope.

The fact that her stunningly handsome and gifted uncle was gay might have had something to do with it. Brett's sexual orientation made quite a few people in the family a tad uncomfortable, but she had dealt with the issue by moving out of the family home into a nice two-bedroom apartment in a trendy inner-city neighbourhood. She was able to do so thanks to the nest egg that Nan, her beloved maternal grandmother—Brett's mother, Alex—had left her. Jessica had been very close to Alex. In fact, her full name was Jessica Alexandra Tennant. Christening her *Jessica* had not been her mother's decision. She had wanted the name *Alexandra,* after her own mother, for her newborn, but such was her deference to her husband that she had given in to *Jessica* after her baby's strong-minded, paternal grandmother, a large imposing woman who wore so many layers of clothing that one never knew exactly what sort of body lay beneath. It was she who had descended on the young couple like a galleon in full sail, for frequent, unscheduled visits. Jessica's mother had once confided to her daughter that the early days of her marriage had been like living in a police state.

Jessica had been devastated when her beloved nan, with never a complaint, had died of cancer when Jessica was eighteen. She knew Brett greatly missed his mother. Nan had offered that rare thing—unconditional love. Jessica's formidable maternal grandfather, much like her own father, had great difficulty accepting Uncle Brett's homosexuality, seeing it as a blot on the family escutcheon and a major hurdle in life. The hurdle part Jessica was forced to concede had come into play; she had seen it in action. But she loved and admired her uncle, and she got on famously with his partner of twenty years, both in business and in life, Tim Langford. Tim was a sweet man, exceptionally creative, with a prodigious, largely self-taught knowledge of antiques. Tim handled the antiques-and-decorative-objects side of the business.

Brett was working at his desk, smooth blond head bent over an architectural drawing, but when she tapped at his door, he looked up with his faintly twisted, rather heartbreaking smile. Very few people saw the full picture of Brett De Vere. "Hi! How did the lunch go?"

She took the seat opposite him. "Perfectly awful! Thanks for asking. At least it didn't amount to a *scene*. Sean's a really nice person, but I couldn't let him go on thinking sooner or later we were bound for the altar. That wouldn't have been fair to him. Besides, I like my independence."

"How could you fall in love with someone like that, anyway?" Brett, who had never hit it off with Sean, asked. "He could never make you happy. He's so damned *ordinary*."

"Maybe, but it took me a while to see it."

"At least you have," Brett said dryly.

"Next time I'll go for a Rhodes scholar," she joked. "I'm not ready to settle down yet. I'm enjoying my life just the way it is."

"Until the right guy comes along," Brett murmured, sitting back and making a steeple of his long, elegant fingers. "Then you'll change your mind. Have you managed to get that truly silly woman who never shuts up on side?"

"Ever so slowly," she sighed. "The trouble with having too much money is it opens up too many options. Mrs. Siegal spends her time trolling through design magazines to the point she simply can't decide whether she wants classical, traditional grandeur, lots of drama, ultramodern or a hybrid of the lot."

"Give her pure theatre," Brett advised. "The only trouble with that is De Vere's puts its name to it. Maybe *I* should make an attempt to help her decide?"

Jessica looked at him. Her uncle was an elegant, austerely handsome man with fine features and an air of detachment. Extremely intelligent, he was inclined to be sharp-tongued, even caustic at times. His eyes were green. Like hers. His hair ash blond, again like hers. They shared the family face. Alex's face. Alex's coloring.

"Well?" he prompted breaking into her brief reverie.

"Why not? She fancies herself in love with you." Indeed Brett's air of unattainability drove some women wild.

"A lot of good that will do her," he said with biting self-mockery.

"What I don't get is they know you're not interested, yet they fall in love with you all the same."

"A bitter pill no woman worth her salt can swallow," he returned. "It's the Liz Taylor—Montgomery Clift syndrome. Women always want the man they can't have."

"Is that what it is?" Jessica swiveled a quarter turn in her black leather chair. "Be that as it may, at this point I need help."

"Surely not the talented young woman short-listed for Best Contemporary Residential Project!" Brett raised a brow.

"It would be quite a coup to win it."

"A coup, yes, but not beyond you. You're *good,* Jass," he said, giving his professional, uncompromised opinion. "I haven't handed over a client who hasn't been delighted with your services. In fact, I could say with some confidence that my mantle, when I go to the angels, will fall on you. You're developing a following with your watercolor renderings of our clients' favourite rooms. They *love* them. Single-handedly you're reviving the old genre. Oh, and remember it was *my* idea."

"Don't I always give you credit?"

"Of course you do."

It was Brett who had encouraged Jessica to turn her hobby of painting interiors in watercolors, an art project carried on from her student days, into a lucrative sideline. For the past year, she'd worked very successfully on half a dozen commissions, along with the major commission of designing the stage sets for the Bijou Theatre's *A Midsummer Night's Dream.* Maybe one day she would follow her uncle into designing stage and movie sets.

"Is that what you wanted to speak to me about, the Siegals?" she asked.

"That was the second thing. First—" Brett ruffled through his papers again, this time finding a long fax "—what do you know about Broderick Bannerman?"

"Bannerman… Bannerman…rings a bell." Jessica sorted through her memory bank. "Hang on. Don't tell me." She held up a hand. "He's the cattle baron, right? Flagship station, one of a chain, by name of something starting with an *M... M... M...* Mokhani, that's it. Bannerman always figures in the *Bulletin's* Rich List."

"The very one." Brett looked at her with approval. He leaned forward to hand over the fax, murmuring something complimentary about her powers of recall. "And he remembers *you!* He saw that interview on TV with the ubiquitous Bruce Hilton when he so easily could have missed it. That was just after you'd been short-listed for your award. Apparently he was so impressed he wants you to handle the interior design for his new temple in the wilds'temple' is how some magazine described it. Lord knows what's wrong with the original homestead. I'm sure I read somewhere it was magnificent, or at the very worst, eminently livable."

Jessica, busy concentrating on the contents of the fax, lifted her head in amazement. "I don't get this. With all the established interior designers in the country, let alone *you,* purely on the basis of the proverbial fifteen minutes of fame on a talk show, he's singled out little ol' *me* with scant history in the business and only twenty-four?"

"It would appear so," Brett replied blandly. "Obviously he's a man who can sum up someone on the spot. Remember, you're a sophisticated twenty-four with natural gifts."

"How could he want *me* when he could have *you?*" Jessica asked in some wonderment.

"How sweet you are, Jass." Brett smiled. "In addition, you're respectful. Look, just believe in yourself. Take risks. I've taught you everything you know. Between you and me and the paper bin, I'm the best in the business. If I tell you you're ready, you're ready. I'm thrilled he wants De Vere's. I'm thrilled he wants *you.* For one thing, I love you, for another, there's no way I'm heading off for the Northern Territory. The great Outback isn't my scene, splendid though it is. Parts of it are downright eerie. Tim and I were quite spooked on our trip to the Red Centre. Wandering around the Olgas was a thoroughly unnerving experience. I could have sworn we were being watched by guardian spirits none too happy we were invading their territory. It was an extraordinary feeling and I'm told it's not that unusual."

"Well, it *is* sacred ground," Jessica commented, having heard numerous tales about the Outback's mystical ability to raise the hairs on the back of one's neck. "'There are more things in heaven and earth, Horatio, than are dreamt of in your philosophy,'" she quoted. "Getting back to the cattle baron, or should I say, king? Did you know Nicole Kidman is a descendant of Sir Sydney Kidman, the original Cattle King?"

"Few of us have your mastery of trivia, Jass. No,
I didn't. Neither of them short of a bob."

"Unlike us, Nicole has a wonderfully supportive family," Jessica said. "Do you really think I'm ready for a project of this size?" she asked very seriously. The word had got around she was good, but she never thought an immensely rich Territorian would seek her services. Not for years and years.

Brett interlocked his hands behind his head, stretching his long, lean torso. "Are you doubting yourself?"

"I'm doing my best not to, but as I recall, Mr. Bannerman has a reputation for being ruthless. Who knows? Some of my designs mightn't suit him. He could turn nasty. I read an article about him a year or two ago. A lot of people interviewed weren't very fond of him, though most wisely insisted on having their names withheld. Word was, he did terrible things to them in business. His cattle stations represent only a fraction of Bannerman holdings. He's into everything."

"Don't let that worry you. As long as he's not into drugs. Then we'd have a problem." Brett straightened, shoving a file across the table. "On the plus side, he makes large donations to charity. Might help with his tax, but apparently he *wants* to, so he can't be all bad. He owns Lowanna Resort Island on the Great Barrier Reef. High-rise apartment blocks on the Gold Coast and the tourist strip in North Queensland, mining and exploration developments, foreign investments. He's loaded."

"Excessively rich clients are a pain in the neck," Jessica said from very recent experience. "We must consider he might be even more impossible to work with than Chic Siegal."

"Surely you're not going to turn the commission down." Brett shifted position, apparently trying, ineffectually, to make himself comfortable in his antique captain's chair.

"I have no intention of turning it down. I want lots and lots of commissions. Still, before I sign up, there's the small matter of crocodiles. They insist on getting their long snouts into the news." In a recent event on a remote beach in far North Queensland, one had waddled up from the water, crossed the sand and entered a camper's tent, dragging him out. All that had saved the hapless man was the incredibly brave action of a fellow camper, a grandmother in her sixties, who without hesitation had jumped on the crocodile's back, then another camper had shot it.

Brett grimaced. "It *was* a remote beach. One must treat crocodiles with respect like the Territorians do. We talk about their crocs. They talk about our traffic accidents. I don't imagine Bannerman has given crocs an open invitation to waddle around the station, anyway. Just think what could happen."

"You don't have to look so ghoulish. Speaking of which there was a big mystery on Mokhani many years ago." Jessica frowned, dredging her memory for more information. "Surely it's been the subject of articles over the years?"

"'The Mokhani Mystery,' as it came to be called," Brett said, having read a few of the articles.

"Didn't a governess disappear?"

"So she did," Brett said briskly, apparently not really wanting to talk about the old story. "It made front-page news at the time. But for years now everything about it's been quiet, though I'm surprised someone hasn't written a book about it. Horrible business, but not *recent.* It must be all of fifty years ago. Which reminds me my big five-oh is coming. Aging is not fun."

"Don't take it to heart. You've never looked better." Jessica was sincere. "Anyway, you can always do what Becky does. Birthday every three years like the elections."

"Women can get away with these things. What's the old saying? 'If a woman tells you her age, she'll tell you anything.' I look after myself and I don't smoke. At least not for years now. Couldn't do without my wine cellar, but wine in moderation is good for you. I'll be very angry if the medical profession suddenly disputes it. But back to Bannerman. You can be sure he's put up plenty of signs warning visitors about nomadic crocodiles."

"You think a crocodile may have taken the governess?" Jessica asked with some horror.

"How can one not *hate* them?" Brett shuddered. "Poor little soul. I can just see her picnicking without a care in the world beside a lagoon and up pops a prehistoric monster. There have been a few cases of that in North Queensland in recent times."

"More likely in one particular case the husband pushed her into the lagoon," Jessica offered darkly, having come to that conclusion along with a lot of other people, including the investigating police officer, who just couldn't prove it. "I can't believe you're sending me up there."

"Sweetie, you're at no risk." Brett took her seriously when she was only teasing. "I'll be very surprised if you even lay *eyes* on a crocodile. I understand the station is a good way inland."

"I hope so, but I'm sure I've read it's within striking distance of Kakadu National Park, World Heritage area, reputed to be fabulous and home of the crocodile."

"I'm quite sure you'll be safe. The very last thing in the world I want is to have my favourite niece vanish into the wilderness. I love you dearly."

"I love you, too," Jessica answered. She resumed reading the fax. "He'd like me to be in Darwin by Monday, the twenty-second where I'll be picked up at Darwin airport and taken to the station. The twenty-second! That's two weeks away." Her green eyes widened.

"I know. Doesn't leave you much time." Brett gazed past her linen-clad shoulder, a smile transforming the severity of his handsome features. "Not *more* junk, Tim?" he drawled. "You're hooked on it."

Jessica swiveled around, a big, welcoming smile on her face. "Hi, Timmy. How did it go in Sydney?" Her eyes settled with considerable curiousity on a large canvas he was carrying beneath his arm. "What have you got there?"

"My dears, you'll *never* believe!" Tim, thick black hair, deep dark eyes, extraordinarily youthful-looking and dressed casually in T-shirt and jeans, staggered through the open doorway.

"We don't *need* any more paintings, Tim dear," Brett warned.

"You're going to love this one," Tim promised, his voice reflecting his excitement. "I had one hell of a battle to get it. Some crazy old bat I swear was in costume was after it. No manners whatsoever. We nearly had a fistfight right there on the floor of Christie's."

"If you've bought some bloody *flower* painting, I'll kill you," Brett said. Tim had excellent taste but he did overly favor flower paintings.

"Voilà!" Tim rested the painting against the wall of built-in cabinets, gesturing as if at a masterpiece.

There was total silence.

Then a stunned. "My God!" blurted out from Brett.

"Where in the world did you get this?" Jessica was equally transfixed.

"I told you. Christie's auction." Tim whipped a satisfied grin over both their stunned faces.

"That's one of the most haunting paintings I've ever seen," Brett murmured, standing up the better to examine it. "The girl could be Jass."

"Now you know why I wanted it." Tim suddenly slumped into a chair as though his legs were giving out. "It made my hair stand on end."

"So everyone has a double, after all," Brett muttered. "What can you tell us about this? What's the provenance?"

"I took a chance on this one," Tim admitted, addressing his partner, the dominant of the two. Both men were devoted to each other, though Brett had strayed a few times over the years, causing much suffering. Tim brimmed over with charm and good humor, far more comfortable in his own skin than the at-war-with-himself Brett.

"No one knows anything about the artist. It's signed in a fashion in the lower right-hand corner—H.B. It came in on consignment with a batch of paintings by established artists. There was comment about its beauty, but the serious collectors only buy *names*. The old girl I'm talking about was after it, I can tell you that. She even offered me far more than I paid for it."

"It's beautifully painted," Jessica observed, making her own close inspection. "Perhaps the artist was in love with her. It has a decidedly erotic quality, don't you think? I wonder who she was?"

"No date on it?" Brett asked.

"Nothing. From how she's dressed I'd say late fourties, early fifties." Jessica, who had studied fashion through the ages, remarked. "She's very young. Seventeen, eighteen?"

"It's a particularly fine example of color and light," Brett said. He had excellent critical judgment. For some inexplicable reason he wasn't comfortable with the sudden appearance of this remarkable painting. The work struck him as decidedly odd.

"Notice the background," Jessica was saying. "It's fairly loose. No clear outlines, but I'd say it's definitely the great outdoors. Not a suburban garden. The long, curly blond hair is marvelous. So are the green eyes staring right at you. It's quite powerful, actually. Sort of mesmeric. Don't you feel that?" She looked back at the two men.

Brett nodded, turning to Tim. "How much did this set us back?"

"Twenty thousand," Tim said, looking like he was about to get up and run.

"Wh-a-t?" Brett snapped. "An *unknown* artist?"

"But plenty of panache! That old girl knew him. Or of him," Tim said defensively. "I'm sure of it. Besides I couldn't let it go anywhere else. It belongs here." His dark eyes appealed to Jessica. "*She,* the girl in the portrait, wanted me to buy it. She *moved* me to do it. You understand that, Jass. You're so sensitive. For all we know, she could be a relation."

"Don't be ridiculous. We know all the relations, more's the pity," Brett said acidly, giving his partner a sharp look.

"Well, we all agree Jessica is extraordinarily like her."

"Proving as I said, we all have a doppelgänger, nothing else. Next time you go off to these auctions I'm coming with you."

"I'd love that." Tim grinned.

"Actually, we could put it up in a prominent place in the showroom." Brett was starting to come round. "It'll certainly generate discussion."

"I thought that, too," Tim was suddenly all smiles. "Besides, what's twenty thousand? You've got plenty."

"That's because I spend little time at auctions," Brett said dryly, returning to his desk. "By the way, I can't come to terms with this chair. It looks good, but it's not kind to my tailbone. Find me something else, will you, Tim?"

"Sure. I'd remind you that I did say it wouldn't be all that comfortable, except you don't like being reminded."

"Thank you for that." Brett lowered his long, lean length into the mahogany chair. "Now, you've shown us your big surprise. Hopeless to top that, nevertheless we'll try. We've got a surprise for you."

"Do tell." Tim slipped Jessica something he'd taken out of his pocket.

"What is it?"

"Just a little prezzie." Tim smiled at her.

"If you'd be so good." Brett raised a supercilious eyebrow,

then continued. "Broderick Bannerman, the cattle baron. Hails from the Northern Territory—"

"How absolutely thrilling!" Tim broke in enthusiastically. "I know the name."

"It gets better. He's offered De Vere's a huge commission. Specifically he wants Jass to handle the entire interior design for his new Outback temple."

Tim's expression turned to one of amazement. He stared from one to the other. "You're making this up, aren't you?"

"No, Tim, we're not," Brett replied, somewhat testily this time. "Hand him the fax, would you, Jass. Bannerman saw her interview with Bruce Hilton and was so impressed he shot off that little lot."

Tim scanned the fax quickly, then looked up. "Good grief, I'm blown away. So is she going? It's a *big* job."

"One never knows what one is capable of until one tries," said Brett. "Of course she's going. There's plenty we can do to help and advise. It's a huge commission. There's bound to be good coverage and flow-ons for us."

Tim's brow furrowed. "Are you comfortable about sending Jessica by herself? She's our baby. Now I think about it, wasn't there some murder up there? Passed into Outback folklore? Remember, we found the Outback one scary place."

"Hell, Tim, don't say that to anyone else," Brett begged. "What would people think?"

"Who cares what people think?" Tim said. "On the other hand people might agree if they'd been there. Those Olgas, they were fantastic, if kinda forbidding."

"Look—" Brett tried to be patient "—forget the Olgas, okay? Incidentally, they've been renamed Kata Tjuta. A governess disappeared. A tragedy certainly, but no murder. An accident befell her some fifty years ago, but alas there was no body. Bannerman is perfectly respectable. He's one of the richest, most influential men in the country. He's not a drug lord. I'm certain Jass will be safe. I'd never let her go if I thought otherwise. She's young for such a big commission, but that shouldn't be a deterrent. She's genuinely gifted and she'll have plenty of backup. If for some reason Bannerman turns out to be straight out of a Stephen King novel, she can come home."

"You want to do this, Jessica?" Tim still looked unsettled.

"Hey, of course I do." She shook his arm. "I'll be able to brag about it for the rest of my days. Don't worry, Timmy. It should be quite an adventure." She started to unwrap his little present. "Ooh, earrings. Aren't they lovely?" She leaned over and kissed him. "Victorian."

He nodded. "I knew you'd like them. I picked them up at Maggie Reeves. She has some really nice stuff."

"You spoil her," Brett said, sitting forward to look.

"*You* should talk!" Tim shot back.

"I'm her uncle."

"And I'm her honorary uncle."

"Stop, you two. These are lovely, Timmy. Thank you." Jessica was delighted with the gift—drop earrings, peridots set in gold. She had a jewelery box filled with the little gifts Tim had given her since she was a child. Bracelets, gold chains, pretty pendants, a crystal-encrusted sea horse that she still loved and wore as a pin. "They'll go beautifully with that vintage dress of mine. The green chiffon." Sometimes she felt very sad that neither her uncle nor Tim would have children. They were loving, caring people. They had been wonderful to her.

"My pleasure, love." Tim smiled, picking up Bannerman's fax again. "They reckon there's a dark side to this Bannerman?"

"Tim, dear, there's a dark side to us all," Brett responded. "Not even *you* are nice all the time. If you're concerned, maybe you can fly up with Jass."

"Both of us? I would go, but I'm sure they don't want me."

"Not to mention how having a babysitter would make *me* look," Jessica protested. "What else do we know about this man?"

"Well—" Brett drew another piece of paper, hitherto unseen,

from the pile on his desk "—he has a son, Cyrus. His mother was the heiress, Deborah Masters. Masters Electronics."

"You said *was?* She's dead?" Jessica inserted one of the earrings in her right earlobe, remembering Tim had gone along with her for support when she'd had her ears pierced a few years back and had been a little fearful of needles.

"A riding accident," Brett informed them. "That was in the early 1990s. Bannerman remarried. A woman with a child of her own. A daughter, Robyn. Neither wife was particularly lucky. The second suffered from some rare syndrome—I don't know exactly what. She died two years ago."

"How very bizarre," muttered Tim, trying to grapple with all this. "It's right up there with the Olgas."

"Don't be silly, Tim." Sternly, Brett held his partner's gaze. "Tragedies happen."

"Indeed they do. But Bannerman could be looking for a new wife. He could fall in love with Jessica on sight."

Jessica laughed, but Brett blustered testily, "God almighty, Tim! I think you're losing it. Bannerman has to be nearing sixty."

"That's not a good answer." Tim resolutely dug in. "He could live for years and years. Aging men often turn to young women. Especially *rich* old men."

"He's hardly an *old* man," Brett said caustically. "You're nearly fifty."

"Forty-eight, thank you. Same as you. Keep it up and you'll really hurt my feelings."

"Stop it, you two," Jessica intervened again. "I'm not in the running for Wife Number Three." She took Tim's hand in hers. "Broderick Bannerman is old enough to be my father. Grandfather, if he were exceptionally precocious."

"For all we know, temptation could be overwhelming in the Outback," Tim said. "There's a real shortage of women. Besides, men never get falling in love with the young and beautiful out of their system," he warned. "I know I sound overanxious, but there's something a little odd here, Jass. You know how intuitive I am. No matter how gifted you are, you're young and inexperienced. I know you've won that nomination and you deserve to carry off the prize, but why not Brett, for instance? He's a colossus in the industry. Well, *he* thinks so."

"I *know* so." Brett was pleased to see Jessica elbow Tim hard. "For God's sake, Tim, what are you on about?" Brett was irritated that some of Tim's concern was starting to rub off on him.

"I'm not sure." Tim shook his head. "I live by my intuitions."

"And your intuitions tell you Bannerman has an ulterior motive in choosing Jessica?"

"Amazing, but true. I should join a training class for psychics. Seriously, I just had to get it off my chest. I don't actually *know* why."

"Then why are you trying to put us off?"

"I'm not," Tim protested. "I'm only trying to say Bannerman mightn't be quite the man he seems. Sounds to me like he's been struck by lightning."

"Lightning!" Brett said irritably. "How you give yourself over to the sensational!"

"Sensational?" Tim protested. "Men have been making complete asses of themselves over young women since forever. Besides, what man ever thinks he's too old?"

"Look, Timmy, I've dreamed about doing something like this." Jessica sought to calm Tim down. "You know you tend to worry about me too much."

"True." Tim's face broke out in his easy smile again. "I wouldn't mind if you were working within shouting distance, or even Sydney. But the Northern Territory! Hell, you might as well be rocketing off to Mars."

"Tim, dear, stop talking," Brett advised. "It's all fevered nonsense, anyway. Jass wants the job. I want her to have it. It'll be a considerable step up the ladder. If the slightest thing happens to cause her concern, she's to drop everything and come home."

"Hear that, sweetheart? You get on the phone right away. I'll be there like a shot. I wonder what the son's like?" Tim asked speculatively, then answered his own question. "Probably a dead ringer for his godawful father."

"Okay, enough's enough!" Brett lunged to his feet. "Where are we going to hang this painting?"

"Maybe above the console in the entrance," Jessica suggested, giving the painting a tender, welcoming look for its own sake and not because the subject bore an uncanny resemblance to her. "She'll be right at home there."

CHAPTER TWO

FROM THE TOP of the escarpment, Cy had a near aerial view of the valley floor, semidesert in the Dry except for the ubiquitous spinifex and the amazing array of drought-resistant shrubs, grasses and succulents that provided fodder for Mokhani's great herd, one of the biggest in the nation and thus the world. Today, four of his men were working flat out to round up of some forty marauding brumbies that were fast eating out the vegetation they desperately needed for the cattle until the blessing of rain. The wild horses had to be moved on. Not only that, two of the station mares were running with the mob, seduced by the leader, a powerful white stallion the men had christened Snowy. Snowy was too nice a name for a rogue, Cy figured. More like Lucifer before the fall. The stallion was so clever, it had long evaded capture, though Cy doubted the wild horse could ever be broken. He'd been close up to Snowy when they'd both been boxed into the canyon, so he knew he was dealing with a potential killer. There were few station pursuits as dangerous as trying to cut off a wild horse from its precious freedom. Ted Leeuwin, the station overseer, had lived to tell the tale of his encounter with Snowy. Just as Ted had been attempting to rope the stallion, it had closed in, terrifying Ted's gelding before biting Ted on the shoulder. Not once but several times. Vicious hard bites that forced Ted, as tough as old boots, to give up.

Cy was aware of his own excitement as whoops like war cries resounded across the valley. He knew the thrill of the chase. The men were right on target to herd the wild horses into the gorge. Two of the station hands were on motorbikes; jumping rocks and gullies with abandon, another two were on horse-back. He'd put one of the station helicopters in the air to flush the brumbies out and guide the men.

He'd have to leave them to it. His father, known as B.B. wanted him to fly to Darwin to pick up the interior designer, Ms. Jessica Tennant if you please, he was hell-bent on hiring. As usual, they'd argued about it. Any suggestion that amounted to a differing opinion caused his father rage. B.B. wasn't a man to listen. Not to his only son, anyway. Often after such arguments, his father hadn't spoken to him for long periods, by way of pun-ishment. But punishment for what? There could be a hundred things, and Cy had narrowed it down to two: for daring to cross a living legend and for being alive when his mother wasn't. He understood his father loved him at some subterranean level, but the very last thing B.B. would do was show it. Needless to say, they weren't close, but they were *blood.* That counted.

As far as this latest development went, his father had taken them all by surprise. What would a young woman of twenty-four be expected to know about furnishing from scratch what was virtually a palace? For that matter, what was wrong with the old homestead even if Livvy, his great-aunt, claimed it was haunted? He was sick to death of it all. The old story distressed him. He'd grown up with it, had been taunted about it in his schooldays. Poor tragic Moira, the governess, had most prob-ably been taken by a croc or she had fallen, her body wedged into some rocky crevice in a deeply wooded canyon, never to be found. God knows it happened. People going missing wasn't exactly a rare occurrence in the Outback. So why had journalists over the years continued to rake up the old story, when all the family wanted was to bury it? No one had ever been able to unearth any proof as to what had happened to her that fatal day.

His mind returned to Jessica Tennant. She might work for a top design studio, but surely there were many people more experienced and more qualified in that firm to do the job? He couldn't figure it out. B.B., who only dealt with the top people, never underlings, a man renowned for always making smart moves, had done something totally un-smart. He had hired a mere beginner to take charge of a huge project.

"She's coming here, Cyrus. I'm still making the decisions around here. As for you, Robyn—" B.B. had turned to his step-daughter "—I don't want to hear one unpleasant word pass your lips when she's here. Is that understood?"

In that case, Robyn had better take a crash course on man-ners, Cyrus thought. For a moment he almost felt sorry for Ms. Tennant. She would be living in the same house as a very dys-functional family. Perhaps not for long, though. Cy could still hope Ms. Tennant might decide the project was beyond her. There was no way, however, to avoid meeting her. He'd agreed to pick her up because he had business in Darwin, anyway. Otherwise, he'd have said he was far too busy, which not even B.B. could dispute. These days he ran Mokhani while regularly overseeing the other stations in the Bannerman chain. Unlike everyone else directly under B.B.'s control, he didn't toe the line unless there was substantial reason to. He had to accept his father was different. Never relaxed, never friendly, as though in doing so he would diminish his aura. The older he got, the more controlling B.B. became. Cy couldn't remember a time when he and his father had been in accord. Not even in child-hood. The precious days when his mother, Deborah, had been alive. A few years back, after a particularly bad clash, he had stormed off, thinking his absence would solve the problem of their angst-laden relationship. In the process, he'd realized he could be throwing away his chance of inheritance. But what the hell! He had to be his own man, not the yes-man his father wanted. The sad fact was that B.B. liked grinding people into the ground. He had treated Robyn's mother, Sharon, like the village idiot. His own mother, who had won the love and admiration of everyone around her, had apparently been highly successful at standing up to her autocratic husband—a man given to unpredictable bouts of black moodsbut a riding accident had claimed her when Cy was ten and away at boarding school. A *riding* accident, when she'd been a wonderful horsewoman. Cy was constantly struck by the great ironies of life.

On that last bid for freedom he'd been gone only a couple of months when his father had come after him. It'd been a huge backing down for B.B., who'd come as close to begging as that man ever could. After he'd had a chance to cool down, B.B. had seen the wisdom of not letting him go. For one thing, for B.B. to deny his own son would go down very badly in the Outback. Even he, Outback legend though he was, was afraid of that. And for another, B.B. knew that Cy was not only the rightful heir to the Bannerman empire, but he was *needed.* Cy's skills had been tested and proven. Many thought him the man of the future, serious, influential people who for years had muttered about B.B. and his ruthless practices. Things could be done right without throwing honesty and justice aside.

The conniving Robyn, though she was an excellent businesswoman and owned a very successful art gallery and a couple of boutiques in Darwin, couldn't hope to replace him. Though she'd try. Robyn *wasn't* a Bannerman, though she bore the name and fully took advantage of its clout. Robyn had a *real* father around someplace, but no one had heard of him for years. She was a year younger than Cy. She and Sharon had come to Mokhani two years after his own mother's death. Sharon had been sweet and kind. Robyn was anything but, though she trod very carefully around B.B. It was no big secret to insiders that Robyn's greatest ambition was to somehow usurp Cy and inherit Mokhani. He, the heir apparent, was the only obstacle in the way. Once, a good friend of his, Ross Sunderland, looking uneasily at Robyn, had suggested he watch his back. "Robyn likes shooting things, Cy," he'd said.

Cy had responded with a practiced laugh. The reality was he'd been watching his back for years. Right from the beginning, Robyn had been a strange one. Cy had divined even as a boy that in Robyn he had an unscrupulous rival.

But for once, he and Robyn had joined forces against B.B.'s decision to hire Ms. Tennant. His decision had been based on Jessica Tennant's age and inexperience, not her gender; his own mother, after all, had been a very creative woman. But Robyn was violently opposed to the idea of having another *woman* do the job she'd tried to convince B.B. she could do. She had reacted with the bitterest resentment not even bothering to conceal her hostility from B.B. A big mistake.

"Be careful, Robyn. Be careful." B.B. had turned on her coldly. "I have hired this young woman. I don't want second best."

Finality in action.

They were making their descent into Darwin airport when the slightly tipsy nuclear physicist beside Jessica leaned into her to confide, "We're landing."

"Yes, I know."

"Darwin airport has one of the longest runways in the southern hemisphere."

"Really? I'm not surprised to hear that." She kept staring out the porthole. The guy had been hitting on her in an inoffensive way ever since they'd left Brisbane. At one point she'd even toyed with the idea of asking the flight attendant to move her, but the plane was full. In a few minutes she'd be able to make her getaway from Mr. Intelligence.

It was not to be. He followed her every step of the way into the terminal, making like an overzealous tour guide, pointing out areas already clearly marked. He topped it all off by offering to give her a lift to wherever she wanted to go.

"Thanks all the same, but I'm being picked up."

"You never said that." He turned to her with such an aggrieved look the image of Sean floated into her mind.

"No reason to," she smiled. "Bye now." If her luck held...

It didn't. "At least I can help you with your luggage."

Drat the guy! He was as hard to brush off as a bad case of dandruff.

"So what say we meet up for a drink sometime?" he suggested. "I live here. I can show you all the sights."

"That's kind of you, but I'll be pretty busy."

"Doin' what?" He looked at her as though she were playing hard to get.

Irritation was escalating into her as much as the heat would allow when she suddenly caught sight of a stunning-looking guy, head and shoulders over the rest, maybe twenty-eight or thirty, striding purposely toward her.

It *was* to her, wasn't it? She'd hate him to change his mind. What's more, the milling crowd fell back as though to ease his path. How many men could carry *that* off?

"For cryin' out loud, you *know* Bannerman?" Her companion did a double take, his gravelly drawl soaring toward falsetto.

Bannerman wasn't Count Dracula surely? She nodded.

"He's a *friend?*"

This was starting to belong in the too-hard basket. "He's meeting me," Jessica said.

"Well, I'm movin' outta here." Her annoying companion, a full six feet, all but reeled away. "I wouldn't want to get in *that* guy's way. Good luck!"

Jessica held her breath. So *this* is Cyrus Bannerman, she thought tracking his every movement. This was as good as it gets. The fact that he was so striking in appearance didn't come as a surprise. Broderick Bannerman was an impressive-looking man—she'd seen numerous photos. Obviously good looks ran in the family. What she hadn't been expecting was the charisma, the air of authority, that appeared entirely natural. Obviously Cyrus Bannerman was ready to take over his father's mantle when many a son with a tycoon for a father finished up with a personality disorder. Not the case here, unless that palpable presence turned out to be a facade.

He was very tall, maybe six-three, with a great physique. The loose-limbed, long-legged stride was so graceful it was near mesmerizing. It put her in mind of the sensuous lope of a famous Pakistani cricketer she'd had a crush on as a child. Bannerman, as well he might be, given his lifestyle, was deeply tanned. In fact, he made everyone else's tan look positively washed out. He had thick, jet-black hair, strong distinctive features, his eyes even at a distance the bluest she had ever seen. "Sapphires set in a bronze mask," the romantically inclined might phrase it, and they'd be spot on. She knew instinctively she had better impress this guy with her professional demeanor. No contract had been signed as yet.

"Ms. Tennant?" Cyrus, for his part, saw a young woman, physically highly desirable, with a lovely full mouth and a mane of ash-blond hair springing into a riot of curls in the humid heat. Her tallish, slender body was relaxed. She had beautiful clear skin. Her large green eyes watched him coolly. Young she might be, but there was nothing diffident about her. She looked confident, clever, sizing him up as indeed he was sizing her up. They could have been business opponents facing each other across a boardroom table for the first time.

"Please, *Jessica,*" she said. Her voice matched her appearance, cool, confident, ever so slightly challenging.

"Cyrus Bannerman. I usually get Cy."

"Then Cy it is." Though every instinct shrieked a warning, she offered him her hand. It was taken in a firm, cool grip. Jessica let out her breath slowly, disconcerted by the thrill of skin on skin. "How nice of you to meet me."

"No problem. I had business in Darwin." The startling blue

eyes continued to study her. She had already grasped the fact that, despite the smoothness of manner, he hadn't taken to her. Was it wariness in his eyes? A trace of suspicion? More the pity! Anyone would think she had coerced his father into hiring her. Not that it mattered. She didn't altogether like him. She did, however, like the *look* of him. A teeny distinction.

Baggage was already tumbling onto the carousel. He looked toward it. "If you'll point out what's yours, I'll collect it. I'd like to get away as soon as possible. We're going by helicopter. Hope that's okay with you. You're assured of a great view."

So much for the big dusty Land Cruiser complete with a set of buffalo horns she'd been expecting.

They lifted off, climbing, climbing, into the blue June sky, climbing, climbing. Jessica tried to stay cool even though her heart was racing. This was a far cry from traveling in a Boeing 747. Outside the bubble of the cockpit, a mighty panorama opened up. Jessica caught the gasp in her throat before it escaped. Below them was the harbor. The immensity of it amazed her. She hadn't been expecting that. Aquamarine on one arm of the rocky peninsula, glittering turquoise on the other. She knew from her history books that Darwin Harbour had seen more drama than any other harbor in Australia. The Japanese Imperial Air Force had bombed it during World War II turning the harbor into an inferno. Every ship, more than forty, including the U.S. destroyer *Peary* that had arrived that very morning, had been destroyed before the invaders had turned their attention to the small township itself, standing vulnerable on the rocky cliffs above the port. The invasion of Darwin had always been played down for some unknown reason. The town had been devastated again by Cyclone Tracy, Christmas Day 1974. Even her hometown of Brisbane, over a thousand miles away, had suffered the effects of that catastrophic force of nature.

Today, all was peace and calm. Jessica's first impression was that Darwin was an exotic destination. A truly tropical city, surrounded by water on three sides, and so far as she could see the most multicultural city in the country. The Top End, as the northern coast of Australia was right on the doorstep of Southeast Asia, and there was a lot of traffic between the two. She was really looking forward to exploring the city when she had time. The art galleries, she'd heard, particularly the galleries that featured the paintings of the leading Aboriginal artists were well worth the visit.

The helicopter trip was turning into probably the most exciting trip of her life. As they banked and turned inland—Mokhani was a little over 140 kilometers to the southeast—just as Cyrus Bannerman had promised, she had a fantastic view of the ancient landscape. Such empty vastness! So few people! She'd read recently, when she'd been researching all she could about Broderick Bannerman, that although the Northern Territory was twice the size of Texas, it had one percent of the population. She'd also read that the population of Darwin was less than eighty thousand, while the Territory covered over two million square kilometers, most of which lay within the tropics. The Red Centre, fifteen-hundred kilometers south of Darwin and another great tourist mecca, was the home of the continent's desert icons, the monolith of Uluru and the fantastic domes and minarets of Kata Tjuta, which had thrown such a scare into Brett and Tim. She realized in some surprise she knew more about overseas destinations, London, Paris, Rome, Vienna, New York on her last fabulous trip, than she did about the Top End and the vast interior of her own country.

That was about to change. She watched the rolling savannas and the vivid, vigorous pockets of rain forest give way to infinite flat plains, the floor of which was decorated with golden, dome-shaped grasses she knew were the ubiquitous spinifex that covered most of the Outback. The great glowing mounds made an extraordinary contrast to the fiery orange-red of the earth, and the amazing standing formations, she realized, were termite mounds. From the air, they looked for all the world like an army on the march.

Silvery streams of air floated beneath them like giant cushions. At one point, they flew low over a herd of wild brumbies, long tails and manes flowing as they galloped across the rough terrain. It was such a stirring sight, the breath caught in her throat. She wouldn't have missed this for the world.

"Camels dead ahead." Bannerman pointed. A very elegant hand, well-shaped, the artistic Jessica noticed. Hands were important to her. "Very intelligent animals." Despite himself, Cy was mollified by her high level of response to the land for which he had such a passion. She was young enough to be excited, and that excitement was palpable, indeed infectious. His own blood was coursing more swiftly in response. She didn't appear in the least nervous even when he put the chopper through its paces, whizzing down low. There was much more ahead for her to enjoy. Falling Waters, a landmark on Mokhani, looked spectacular from the air. He planned a low pass over the gorge. It would allow her to see the wonderful, ever-changing colors in the cliff walls.

The flight inside the magnificent canyon, carved by countless centuries of floodwaters, was the ultimate thrill. Here below her was a verdant oasis in the middle of the desert. The colors in the cliff walls were astonishing. All the dry ochers were there, pinks, cream, yellow, orange, fiery cinnabar, purples, thick veins of brown and black and white. She felt a strong urge to try to paint them. Tier upon tier like some ancient pyramid was reflected perfectly in the mirrorlike surface of the lagoon. To either side lay broken chains of deep dark pools, but it was the main lagoon with its flotilla of pink water lilies that held the eye. It directly received the sparkling waterfall that cascaded from the plateau-like summit of the escarpment, littered with giant, orange-red boulders in themselves marvelously paintable.

"Beautiful, isn't it," Bannerman said, his voice betraying his pride in his Outback domain.

This was one lucky guy, Jessica thought. He appeared to have it all. Looks, intelligence, a vibrant physical presence, a rich if ruthless tycoon for a father, and one day all this would be his. Some three million glorious savage acres, and that was only Mokhani. She knew from her quick study of Broderick Bannerman's affairs that several other stations made up the Bannerman pastoral empire. It had to be an extraordinary experience to have millions of acres for a backyard, let alone a spectacular natural wonder like the gorge. Both sides of the canyon were thickly wooded with paperbarks and river gums; the lagoon and water holes were bordered by clean white sand.

"Can you swim there?" She pointed downward.

He nodded. "I have all my life. The pool is very deep at the centre. Perhaps bottomless."

A little frisson ran down Jessica's arms.

From the air, Mokhani Station was an extraordinary sight, a pioneering settlement in the wilds. Bannerman's ancestors had carved this out, living with, rather than conquering, the land. Jessica, with her capacity for visualization, saw monstrous saltwater crocodiles inhabiting the paperbark swamps and lagoons that were spread across the vast primeval landscape. Not for the first time on this adventure did she consider the fate of Mokhani's governess who had vanished without a trace all those years ago. It was, after all, a haunting tale that had never found closure.

The station was so large it sent a shock of awe through her; miles of open plain interspersed with large areas of dense scrub, through which she could see the sharp glitter of numerous creeks and lagoons. It would be terrifyingly easy to get lost in all that. The table-topped escarpment that towered over the canyon and dominated the landscape was another major hazard. Although she didn't suffer from vertigo, Jessica was certain one could easily become dizzy if one ventured too near the lip of the precipice. It would be all too easy to topple over. Easier still to get pushed.

I've got an overactive imagination, she thought, a strange taste of copper in her mouth. Could it be that was what had happened? A young woman, too frantic to be afraid groping at thin air, skin ripped as she bounced off rock to rock. Did Moira go into the water alive? A body carried into the deep lagoon would make a succulent meal for a man-eating crocodile. Surely no one could say for sure that one didn't lurk there....

She was rather ashamed of her lurid thoughts. There were always suspicions when no body had been found. But if she'd been pushed, it would have been murder.

She longed to question Cyrus Bannerman about the unsolved mystery, but sensed she would only anger him. Such tragedies, though never forgotten, would have resonated unhappily down the years. He could well have been the butt of a lot of taunts in his school days. Like most Outback children, he would have been sent away to boarding school at around age ten. Looking at him now, she felt, boy and man, he had coped.

They flew over a huge complex of holding yards where thousands and thousands of cattle were penned. Probably awaiting transport to market by the great road trains. Clusters of outbuildings surrounded the main compound like a satellite town. The silver hangar with MOKHANI emblazoned on the roof was enormous. It looked as if it could comfortably house a couple of domestic jets. Two bright yellow helicopters were on the ground a short distance from the hangar, as well as several station vehicles. Up ahead, across a silver ribbon of creek, she could see the original homestead, very large as even large houses go, and some distance away what appeared to be a great classical temple.

Broderick Bannerman wanted her to furnish *that?* Hatshepsut, queen of ancient Egypt, no mean hand at decorating, might have called in the professionals. Should she, Jessica, return to ancient Egypt for inspiration or settle for pre-Hellenic? Smack-bang in the middle of the wilderness, either option seemed a mite excessive, not to say bizarre. Obviously Broderick Bannerman, like the kings of old, had built his temple as a monument to himself. She wondered what role his son had played in it. There was an elegant austerity about Cyrus Bannerman that suggested *none.*

Another employee was on hand to drive her up to the house.

"I'm needed elsewhere, but Pete will look after you," Cy said, his eyes resting on her with what seemed like challenge.

"Many thanks for such an exciting trip," she responded, giving him her best smile. "I feel like I'm starting a new life."

"And yet at the end of a few weeks, you'll return to your old life." He sketched a brief salute and went on his way.

They drove past the multitude of outbuildings she had seen from the air, then topping a rise, she had her first view of Mokhani homestead. The original homestead that had withstood the fury of Cyclone Tracy, being miles from the epicenter. It was a most impressive sight, approached by an avenue of towering palms. Jessica wondered why Bannerman had wanted to build another. Two-storied, with a grand hip roof and broad verandas on three sides, the upper story featured beautiful decorative iron-lace balustrading. The extensive gardens surrounding the house no doubt fed by underground bores, were full of trees: banyan, fig, tamarind, rain trees, the magnificent Pride of India, flamboyant poincianas and several of the very curious boab trees with their fat, rather grotesque bottle-shaped trunks. Tropical shrubs also abounded. Oleanders and frangipani, which so delighted the senses, agapanthus, strelitzias, New Zealand flax plants with their dramatic stiff vertical leaves, giant tibouchinas and masses of the brilliant ixoras. The slender white pillars that supported the upper floor of the house were all but smothered by a prolifically flowering white bell flower.

She had arrived! It all seemed wonderfully exciting, dramatic really. And Cyrus Bannerman had had a considerable effect on her when she'd grown accustomed to distancing herself from any physical response to men, as it made her job easier.

As Pete collected her luggage, Jessica walked up the short flight of stone steps to the wide veranda. It was obviously a place of relaxation, she thought looking at the array of outdoor furniture. Low tables, comfortable chairs, Ali Baba—style pots spilling beautiful bougainvillea. A series of French doors with louvered shutters ran to either side of the double front doors, eight pairs in all. She hoped she looked okay, though she was well aware that her hair, which had started out beautifully smooth and straight, was now blowing out into the usual mad cloud of curls. She was wearing cool, low-waisted Dietrich-style pants in olive-green with a cream silk blouse, but no way could she put on the matching jacket. It was just too hot! Her intention had been to look businesslike, not like a poster girl for amazing hair.

Jessica hesitated before lifting the shining brass knocker with the lion's head. Wasn't anyone going to come to the door? They had to be expecting her. Just as she reached out her hand, one of the double doors with their splendid lead-light panels and fan lights suddenly opened. A tall, gaunt, ghost of a woman, with parchment skin, violet circles around her sunken eyes and as much hair as Jessica, only snow-white, stared back at her. The vision was dressed in the saffron robes of a Tibetan monk, an expression of dawning wonder on her face.

"It's Moira, isn't it? *Moira?* Where *have* you been, dear? We've been desperately worried."

The extraordinary expression on the old lady's face smote Jessica's tender heart. She took the long trembling hand extended to her and gave it a little reassuring shake. "I'm dreadfully sorry, but I'm *not* Moira," she explained gently. "I'm Jessica Tennant, the interior designer. Mr. Bannerman is expecting me."

"Jessica?" Recognition turned to frowning bemusement. "Absolutely *not*."

"Lavinia, what are you doing there?" A young female voice intervened, so sharp and accusatory it appeared to rob Lavinia of speech. "Lavinia?"

Lavinia feigned deafness, though Jessica could see the little flare of anger in her eyes. She leaned forward, clutching Jessica's hand to her thin chest and whispering into her face, "Always knew you'd come back." She grinned as if they were a couple of coconspirators.

"Silly old bat! Take no notice of her." An ultraslim, glamorous-looking young woman, with her glossy sable hair in a classic pageboy, and the long, dark brown eyes of an Egyptian queen, came into sight.

"Silly old bat, am I?" the old lady shouted. "You just leave me alone, Robyn. I'm the Bannerman, not *you!*"

The young woman cast Jessica a long-suffering look. "Excuse us. You forget, Lavinia, Dad adopted me. I'm as much a Bannerman as the rest of you. Perhaps you could do us all a favor and retire to your room. I know how much you like to read. What is it now? Let me guess. Gibbon's *The Decline and Fall of the Roman Empire*?"

"Bitch!" the old lady muttered sotto voce.

"So nice to have met you, Miss Lavinia," Jessica smiled into the troubled old face. What was it, Alzheimer's, dementia? The bane of old age. So sad. Lavinia had to be well into her eighties, though she didn't look in the least demented. More an eccentric living in the past.

Lavinia kept hold of Jessica's hand as though unwilling to let her go. "You've not come near the house for years and years," she said, looking as though she were about to weep.

"I expect I had to wait for an invitation," Jessica whispered back.

"My dear, don't you care that you put us through such an ordeal?" The sunken eyes filled with tears.

"I didn't mean to," Jessica found herself saying. Anything to calm the old woman.

"Livvy, that's quite enough!" The young woman swooped like a falcon. Her long-fingered hand closed over Lavinia's bony shoulder. "You're embarrassing Ms. Tennant. I suggest you go to your room before Dad finds out."

Lavinia threw off the hand with surprising strength and adjusted her robe. "It was Broderick who brought her here," she said. "I've never liked you, Robyn, though I tried hard. You were a frightful child and you're a frightful woman. She pinches me, you know."

"Lavinia, dear." Robyn Bannerman smiled tightly, obviously trying to retain her patience. "If I've hurt you, I'm sorry. Your skin is like tissue paper. Now, Ms. Tennant is here to see Dad. He's not a man to be kept waiting."

Lavinia nodded fiercely, setting her abundant hair in motion. "Dear me, no."

Robyn Bannerman lifted beautifully manicured hands. "She's quite gaga," she told Jessica softly.

There was nothing wrong with Lavinia's hearing. "Not gaga, Robyn. Ask me who the prime minister is. I'll tell you. John Howard. I didn't vote for him. Ask me about the war in Iraq. I guarantee I'm better than you at mental arithmetic, let alone music, the arts and great literature. I speak fluent French. I had to give up on Japanese. I'm not reading *The Decline and Fall of the Roman Empire* by the way. And it's *The History of the Decline and Fall of the Roman Empire.* I'm reading *My Early Life* by Winston Churchill. Quite delightful!"

"I couldn't imagine anything worse," Robyn sighed. "Please go to your room, Livvy. You'll be happier there."

Looking quite rebellious, Lavinia spun to face Jessica who said in a soothing manner before the whole thing got out of hand, "I'm looking forward to seeing you later, Miss Lavinia. I hope I may address you that way?"

The old lady gave her a startlingly sweet smile. "You always *did* call me Miss Lavinia. I have trouble sleeping, you know. But you always come into my dreams. I've had no trouble remembering you. Until later, then, dear."

Lavinia moved off serenely, while Robyn Bannerman stood, rather inelegantly biting the side of her mouth. "I'm sorry about that," she said after Lavinia had disappeared. "Poor old dear has been senile for years. She usually stays upstairs in her room, rereading the entire library or listening to her infernal opera. Some of those sopranos know how to screech, or it could be Lavinia. She had a brief career on the stage. She only ventures down for dinner, thank God. I'm Robyn Bannerman, as you will have gathered. Come on in. My father is expecting you." Robyn's dark eyes swept Jessica's face and figure. "I must say you look absurdly young for such a big project."

Jessica frowned and was about to respond when Robyn continued, "What you want to do is enjoy yourself for a few days, then head back to Brisbane. My father rarely if ever makes mistakes, but there's a first time for all of us. Though I must say, I'm dying to hear what you come up with."

A lot better than *this,* I hope, Jessica thought, glancing around in surprised disappointment. Although opulent, the interior of the homestead did not so much impress as overwhelm. The furnishings were far too formal for the bush setting, the drapery, though hellishly expensive—Jessica knew the fabric—too elaborate. This was, after all, a country house. It didn't look lived in. In fact nothing looked even touched. There were no books lying around, no flowers, not an object out of place.

The air-conditioning, however, was a huge plus, utterly blissful after the blazing heat outside. Jessica felt that given what she had seen so far, she wouldn't be right for the job. Not if Broderick Bannerman wanted more of this. Brett wouldn't be happy, either, unless Bannerman gave her carte blanche. The homestead had a vaguely haunted air about it, or so it seemed to her, but she could see how it could be brought back to life.

"I see you're admiring the decor," Robyn said, as though they were gazing at perfection. "I did it all a couple of years back. I hoped to do the new place, but I can't be expected to do *everything!* I practically run the domestic side of things here and I have businesses in Darwin that have to be looked after. If I do say so myself, I'm a hard act to follow."

Jessica managed a smile, but she couldn't for the life of her act impressed. In fact, she could hear Brett's voice saying, *Dump the lot!*

CHAPTER THREE

SHE WAS SHOWN into a large, luxuriously appointed study. There
was no one inside.

"That's funny. Dad was here ten minutes ago. I'll go find
him," Robyn said, giving Jessica another of her dubious looks.
"Take a seat. Won't be long.You'd like tea or coffee?"

"Coffee would be fine. Black, no sugar."

"Looking after your figure?" Robyn asked with a slightly
sarcastic smile.

"I do, but I've grown to like coffee that way."

Alone, Jessica stared around the room, thinking how one's
home environment reflected the person. It had to be the one
place from which Robyn Bannerman's decorating talents had
been banned. It certainly looked lived in. Going by the faint
film of gray on the wall of solid mahogany bookcases, Jessica
doubted if anyone was game to go around with a feather duster.
Behind the massive partner's desk hung a splendid three-quar-
ter portrait of an extraordinarily handsome man, *not* Broderick
Bannerman, though the resemblance to Cyrus Bannerman was
striking. He was painted in casual dress, a bright blue open-
throated bush shirt the color of his eyes, a silver-buckled belt,

just the top of his riding pants, the handsome head with crisp dark hair faintly ruffled by a breeze, set against a subdued dark-ish-green background. The eyes were extraordinary. Because of her own deep involvement with art, she stood up for a closer look, wanting to study the fluent brush strokes, which she had the strangest feeling she'd seen before.

"My father," a man's deep, cultured voice said from behind her. He startled her, as she felt sure he had meant to.

She turned quickly toward the voice, surprised he was standing so close to her. She hadn't heard him come in. "It's a wonderful painting," she said. "I was just going to check on the name of the artist. I've a feeling I've seen his work before and—"

"You couldn't have," Broderick Bannerman cut her off, his appraisal of her intense, as though he wanted to examine every inch of her. "The artist was a nobody. Just a family friend."

"He may have been a nobody, but he was a very good painter," Jessica said, determined not to be intimidated by the great man. "Excellent technique."

"Would you know?" His icy gray eyes beneath heavy black brows didn't shift. Had he been a horse fancier, he might have asked to check her teeth.

"I think so. I have a fine-arts degree. I paint myself. I started with watercolors, which I love, but I've moved on to oils and acrylics."

"It's a wonder you've found the time," he said. "You're twenty-four?"

"Yes, but you already know that, Mr. Bannerman." Jessica held out her hand. "A pleasure to meet you, sir," she said, though aspects of the man had already started to worry her. His gaze was so piercing, she felt she needed protection.

Bannerman took the slender hand, thinking most people had to work hard at containing their awe of him, but this chit of a girl showed no such deference. He stared into her large green eyes. Memories speared through him, for a moment holding him in thrall. "Please, sit down," he said after a moment, his voice harsher than he intended. On no account did he want to frighten her away. "Has Robyn organized some coffee?" With an impatient frown, he went around his desk, sitting in the black leather swivel chair.

"Yes, she has," Jessica answered, thinking intimidation was something this man would do supremely well. He had been born to power. Clearly, he took it as his due. Broderick Bannerman had to be nearing sixty, but he looked at least ten years younger. He didn't have his son's amazing sapphire eyes, but his icy glance was remarkable enough. His hair was as thick and black as his son's with distinguished wings of silver. All in all, Broderick Bannerman was a fine figure of a man with a formidable aura. Why in the world would a man like this choose her to handle such a big project? Brett would have been the obvious choice.

"Speaking of watercolors," he said, "my aunt Lavinia loves them. She's a very arty person, so you should get on well."

"I had the pleasure of meeting her momentarily," Jessica said, thinking it best to say. It would come out sooner or later.

"Really? When was this?" The frosted gaze locked on hers.

"She happened to be in the entrance hall when I arrived."

"Good. I don't want her to hide. Then you'll know she's somewhat eccentric?"

"I found her charming," Jessica said.

"She can be a handful," Bannerman said, with a welcome trace of humor. "Most people think she's senile, but she's not. She likes wearing weird costumes. She had a brief fling as an opera singer in her youth. Still daydreams about it.You'll no doubt get to see the costumes. Tosca's my favourite. She's a Buddhist at the moment. She's actually had an audience with the Dalai Lama. Regretfully she has arrived at the point where we can't let her go out alone, though she managed to get to Sydney recently—but I'd sent along a minder for her and she stayed with relatives. Don't be too worried by anything she says. Livvy never really knows what time frame she's in."

Wary of his reaction, Jessica didn't tell him Lavinia had called her *Moira.*

Bannerman was still talking when a middle-aged woman in a zip-up pale blue uniform wheeled a laden trolley into the room without once lifting her head. Robyn was standing directly behind her, looking very much as if one false move and the tea lady would get a good rap on the knuckles.

"Thank you, Molly," Bannerman said. "This is our housekeeper, Mrs. Patterson, Jessica. You'll be seeing quite a bit of each other."

The two women exchanged a smile, Jessica saying a pleasant hello.

"I'll pour, shall I?" Robyn asked.

Bannerman looked back at her coolly. "This is a private conversation, Robyn."

Jessica felt mortified on Robyn's account. Was this his normal behavior?

Robyn colored, as well she might. "I thought you might need a little help."

"Thank you, no."

Not the nicest man I've ever met, Jessica thought.

In the end, she poured the coffee, which turned out to be excellent. To her surprise, instead of getting down to business, Bannerman began to question her, albeit in a roundabout way, about her family, listening to her replies with every appearance of interest. One might have been forgiven for thinking before matters progressed any further she had to establish her family tree. Surely he didn't talk to everyone this way, did he? Not everyone would expect to be quizzed about their ancestors, unless they were marrying into European royalty.

In the middle of it all, the phone rang. At least *she* was off the hook for a while, she thought wryly. Bannerman turned his intense pale gray stare on the phone as though willing it to stop. Finally he was forced to pick it up. "I thought I told you to hold the calls," he boomed into the mouthpiece.

He certainly has a way with the staff, Jessica thought. That sort of voice would make anyone gulp, let alone damage the ears.

"All right, put him on."

Jessica made to jump to her feet to give him privacy, but he waved her back into the seat, launching into a hot, hard attack on the poor unfortunate individual on the other end of the line. How people of wealth liked to make lesser mortals quake! Afterward, satisfied he had made himself clear and beaten one more employee into the turf, Bannerman centered Jessica with his lancing eyes. "Look, you haven't had time to settle in and I have to attend to some fool matter. You have no idea the amount of nonsense I have to put up with. Some of my people can't do *anything* on their own. What say we met up again at four? It will be cooler then. I can take you on tour of the new house."

"I'm looking forward to it, Mr. Bannerman," Jessica said. He might be shaping up to be an ogre, but no need to call home yet.

"You're hired, by the way." He flashed her an odd look, impossible to define.

"Wouldn't you prefer to wait until I submit some designs or at least hear my ideas? They'd be off the top of my head, of course. Better, when I've had time—"

"No need," he said dismissively. "You'll do very well."

It was the first time she'd been given a commission on the basis of her looks and ancestors.

Up in her bedroom, Robyn paced the perimeter of the Persian rug, as a lioness might pace the perimeter of her cage. She was utterly enraged. For B.B. to humiliate her in front of a complete stranger left her wanting to kill someone. Though she had done everything in her power to fit into this family, she fumed, she would *never* be regarded as a true daughter of the house. Like that old witch Lavinia, who smiled so lovingly on Cyrus, had said, Robyn wasn't a *true* Bannerman. No unshakable bond of blood; the belonging was only on the surface. Scratch the surface and it was as clear today as it had been from the outset when she'd first come to Mokhani with her mother, she was an *outsider*. Her mother, not capable of getting both oars in the water, had nevertheless shoehorned herself in, always sweet and unassuming, dutiful and deferential to her rich and powerful husband.

Their marriage had been a big lie. B.B. had married her mother, an old school chum of the incomparable Deborah, only to beget more sons. But poor Sharon couldn't rise to the challenge, though she had looked like "lust on legs," as a guy she knew put it. The sad reality was that Sharon hadn't been very fertile, and her marriage to B.B. seemed to render her completely barren. Her daughter, Robyn, her only child, was her sole achievement. Needless to say, B.B. was bitterly disappointed in her mother and had all but ignored her, unceremoniously bundling her out of the master suite and into a room on the other side of the house, causing Sharon to curl up and simply fade away. B.B. had wanted a long succession of heirs, not just Cy, the son of the only woman he had ever loved, that paragon Deborah who, for all the cups and ribbons she'd won, had gone hurtling over the neck of her horse.

Robyn had sensed quickly, as an animal might, B.B.'s deep-seated fear of his own son, as though one day Cy would overshadow him, and hell, wasn't it already happening? Though she hated to have to say it, Cy was remarkable. Cy was the *future*. She didn't know anyone apart from B.B. who didn't wholeheartedly admire Cyrus. As for how people regarded B.B., they mostly feared him, called him a *bloody bastard*—but never within B.B.'s hearing. B.B. would regard such a thing as a declaration of war, then order a preemptive strike.

But he *was* a bastard, nevertheless. A ruthless bastard. It was that more than anything that kept Robyn in line. In the odd moment when she choked up on memories of her mother—she really had loved her, or at least as much as she *could*, given Sharon's single-digit IQ—she realized with great bitterness just how badly B.B. had treated her mother. Sharon had had everything *material* she'd wanted, but she had missed out totally on what she really wantedtenderness and affection. Sharon had realized from the beginning there was no way she was going to get love.

Ironically, this beast of a man seemed to inspire all kinds of women, from the innocent needy like her mother to gold diggers, to give matrimony with him their best shot. B.B. hadn't married any of them, but he certainly hadn't been celibate since her mother's death. Lord, no! There had been various affairs, all very discreet. Even with young women, who found the sexiest thing about a man was his bank balance. The one thing Robyn hadn't been prepared for when B.B. had announced he was calling in an interior designer to decorate the mansion, was that she would be so young and ravishingly pretty. Attractive would have been okay, but not a bloody aphrodisiac for men.

The shock had been ghastly. She didn't think Cy had expected it either, nor had he been pleased. But here she was among them, this Jessica Tennant.

B.B. had first seen her on national television. Robyn had missed the program herself, as had Cy, so they'd had no warning. They knew only that she was shortlisted for some big prize, which meant she had to be good at what she did, but at twenty-four she couldn't have had much experience. Add to that, she was a bloody siren. Robyn had seen the look B.B. had given the woman. It had been as rapt as a sixteen-year-old boy's.

Robyn halted in her frenzied pacing, and her blood turned to ice water. What if B.B. had it in his head this time to take another wife? Why should that shock her? He had plenty of money, after all. So what if they were decades apart in age? B.B. was a secretive man, but he didn't do anything without a reason. No one had ever seen him make a false move. Now Ms. Jessica Tennant, in the guise of an interior designer. What had seemed incomprehensible started to appear perfectly clear.

I have to protect myself, Robyn thought. *I'm no* loser *like Mum.*

* * *

A few minutes before the time scheduled for the grand tour, Jessica made her way downstairs. Best not be late, when Bannerman was famous for bawling people out. Robyn had dropped out of sight, no doubt slamming her palm against her forehead in mortification, but Mrs. Patterson, who turned out to be a very pleasant woman, had been on hand to show Jessica to her room.

There, she had changed her outfit, settling for something cool, cotton pants with a gauzy multicolored caftan top decorated with little crystals and beads over with tiny buttons down the front. Usually she did up just enough to cover her bra, but with the way Broderick Bannerman had been looking at her, she decided to do them all up.

The dazzling play of late-afternoon light falling through the beautiful leaded panes and fan lights on the front door held her immobile for a moment. The kaleidoscope of color unlocked some lovely fragment of memory from her childhood. Before she could move, the door opened, letting in a wave of hot air.

And Cyrus Bannerman. The look he gave her held her transfixed.

"Hi!"

"Ms. Tennant. We meet again."

At first glance, he could have been a particularly sexy and virile escapee from the TV show *Survivor.* His darkly tanned skin glowing with sweat and grimed with red dust gave him a startlingly exotic appearance. Red dust had thrown a film over his jetblack hair, which was tousled and fell onto his forehead. There was a stain of brownish-redblood—across his bush shirt, and his eyes seem to blaze a hole through her.

They continued gazing at one another for what seemed an inordinate amount of time. Was it the atmosphere? she wondered. The old homestead certainly had an air about it.

"Sorry," he said finally. "I must look a mess. One of the men took a bad fall off his motorbike. Head injuries. We didn't want to move him. I had to call in the RFDS. That's the Royal Flying

Doctor Service, as I expect you know. God knows what we'd do without them. They didn't take long."

"Is he going to be all right?" Only now could she take a few more steps down the stairs, reassured that an injured employee so clearly mattered to him.

"We have to wait and see with head injuries. I'm worried about him." Cy's remarkable eyes made another sweep over her. "Meanwhile, what have you been up to?"

"Why, nothing." She stopped where she was on the stairs. "Change of clothes is all," she said sweetly. "Now your father is taking me on a tour of the new house."

"I see." He pulled at the red bandanna at his throat, exuding so much powerful masculinity she felt in need of oxygen.

"That's good. For a moment I thought you'd missed something along the way. Your father *has* hired me to handle the interior design."

"Indeed he has. Forgive me if it takes a little time to get used to it." He came close to her, so commanding a presence, Jessica remained where she was, two steps above him. A dubious advantage.

"You must be extremely clever, Ms. Tennant. Dad was compelled to hire you after seeing you for about ten minutes on a TV program? Have I got that right?" He was suspicious of his father's motivation, she suddenly realized. It was emblazoned on his smug, handsome face. "You have. What's so amazing?"

"The pure chance of it." His eyes shifted to the little beads and crystals on her top and he gave a leisurely verdict. "Very pretty." He paused, then said, "Look, Ms. Tennant, I'll level with you. I'm concerned about this. I'm sure you're talented, but it doesn't automatically follow you should be given such a big commission. At this stage of your career anyway."

She leaned forward slightly, her voice mock confidential. "Be that as it may, it was your *father* who hired me, Cyrus. He's the man I have to answer to. Not you."

"Say that again." Suddenly he smiled into her eyes. Night into day.

"I'm sure you took it in the first time. Your father hired me—"

"Not *that!*" he scoffed. "The *Cyrus* bit. I really liked the sound of my name on your lips."

She knew she blushed, but she couldn't control it. "Calling you Cyrus *is* the easy bit. Getting on with you appears to be quite another. What exactly is it you and your sister—"

"I don't have a sister," he corrected.

"That's odd. I've met her."

"You've met Robyn," he pointed out suavely. "Robyn is my father's adopted daughter."

"Which surely means legally she's your stepsister?"

"Ah, you're turning into a hotshot lawyer before my very eyes. Robyn is my stepsister, forgive me. She must be. She lives here."

"Not your average loving family, then?" She forced her breath to stay even.

"Unfortunately, no."

"I'm sure there are reasons."

"There always are. Are you going to come down from those stairs?"

"Not for the moment. I like us to be on the same level." She was attracted to this man. *Powerfully* attracted. It was the very last thing she needed or wanted. She was here to do a job, not play at a dangerous flirtation.

"That would never be unless you grow a few inches."

"Or own some very fancy high-heeled shoes, which I do. Well, it's nice chatting with you, Cyrus, but I'm supposed to meet your father."

"I'm not detaining you, surely?" He made an elaborate play of backing off, his ironic smile putting more pressure on her. She felt slightly giddy as she descended the last two stairs to pass him. Something he undoubtedly noticed and chalked up as a small victory.

Her nerves were stretched so taut she actually jumped when Broderick Bannerman, a look of barely suppressed impatience on his face, suddenly appeared in the entrance hall. He looked from one to the other as though they were conspiring in a plot against him. "There you are, Ms. Tennant. I did say four o'clock, didn't I?"

"I'm so sorry—" Jessica was tempted to mention it could only have been a few minutes after four, but Cyrus intervened.

"She was chatting with me, Dad. Okay?" He lifted a hard-muscled arm and glanced at his watch. "How time flies! It's three minutes past."

"And you're back early," B.B. clipped off.

"Surely there's not a note of disapproval in that. I don't clock on and off, Dad. Eddie Vine took a bad spill off his motorbike. He's been airlifted to the hospital."

"I'm not surprised to hear that," B.B. said with a frown. "He's a bad rider."

"No." Cyrus jammed his hands into his jeans pockets. "*You're* the one we all have to get out of the way for, Dad. Now, I'm off for a good scrub. Enjoy the tour."

"We shall," his father replied curtly.

At that moment, a middle-aged attractive woman with soft gray eyes and long dark hair pulled back into a severe French twist hurried into the entrance hall. "Excuse me, B.B. I'm sorry to interrupt, but Mr. Kurosawa is on the line. I know you want to speak to him."

B.B. all but snarled. "Dammit!" Then, more mildly, he added, "Okay I'm coming, Ruth." He turned back to Jessica with a surprisingly charming smile. The many faces of Broderick Bannerman in less than half a minute she thought. "I'm sorry, my dear, this is going to take time. I'll have to postpone our tour until tomorrow."

In the background, Cyrus Bannerman spoke up. "If Ms. Tennant will give me ten minutes, I can show her around the place."

"I prefer to do it, thank you, Cyrus."

"No trouble, Dad," Cyrus insisted smoothly.

There was a silence as B.B. responded to what seemed like a challenge.

"Very well," he barked, turning abruptly on his heel.

Cyrus Bannerman stood, lean elegant frame propped against the cedar post of the staircase. "By the way, Jessica, you haven't met Ruth, have you? Ruth is Dad's secretary. Ruth this is Jessica Tennant, Dad's new interior designer."

"Pleased to meet you, Jessica." B.B.'s secretary gave Jessica a sweet, flurried smile, clearly anxious to follow her master. "I must go. B.B. might want something."

"Best not keep him waiting, Ruthie," Cyrus warned, his blue eyes full of mischief. "Now suddenly it's up to me, Ms. Tennant, to give you the grand tour."

"Why is it I'm thinking you're trying to score points in a competition with your father?"

"God, is it that obvious?" He shook his head. "Why don't you wait for me on the veranda? It's nice this time of day. I'll only be ten minutes."

"I beg you. Don't hurry on account of me."

"You should thank me for rescuing you," he said blandly.

CHAPTER FOUR

HE WAS BACK on the veranda in fifteen minutes flat. "Did you time me?" he asked. "I'm a bit late."

"Actually I'd forgotten you," she said casually, which was a long way from the truth. "I was breathing in the air and the exotic scents. It's another world up here. I've never felt so connected to the earth. It's rather a profound experience. Thanks again for the helicopter trip. It was a revelation, and one of the highlights of my life."

"I think you mean that." There was an appraising look in his eyes.

"How could you doubt me?" Jessica stood up, trying to hide the excitement he engendered in her.

"There's plenty more I can show you," he said. "How come you've never visited the Red Centre?" Something she had mentioned. "Or Kakadu, which is the jewel in the Top End crown— maybe a little off the beaten trackbut Alice Springs? It's quite a tourist destination these days. Our desert monuments, Uluru and Kata Tjuta, are world-famous."

"Maybe when you have the time you can take me." She gave him a sidelong glance.

"Jessica, we don't know yet if you're staying."

"Why does it bother you so much? My staying, that is."

"I have my reasons."

"That sounds intriguing. So what are you going to do to frighten me off?"

"Whatever it is I have to act fast." He met her eyes, a gleam of mockery in his. "No. It's going to be your decision."

"Your father's, surely," she said. They walked down the flight of stone steps together, Jessica acutely conscious of his height and pure, animal magnetism.

"He's already made up his mind," he clipped off. "My father isn't an easy man to know." His tone indicated he wished things could have been different.

She gave him a wry, understanding smile. "I can see that."

"So you can see we're not the best of pals."

"Why is that?" she asked gently.

"Long story." He glanced away.

"I can listen."

"Not right now, Ms. Tennant. Seriously, apart from my dysfunctional family, you don't have the feeling this job might be too big for you? It's a helluva place. Helluva size."

"Your father has a helluva lot of money," she reminded him dryly.

"Doing things right takes a lot more than money."

"I know that. I'm good at what I do, and I can count on my Uncle Brett for all the help and advice I need. Brett's my rock. You mustn't be so skeptical of me. I have skills to put to good use. No job is too big to handle, given ability, time and money. You have to take one thing at a time not tackle it all at once. Then it *can* become too confronting."

He shook his head. "Trouble is, there seems to be more going on here."

"Meaning what, exactly?" She was truly puzzled.

"I'm damned if I know. It's just a hunch backed up by observation. This family has a haunted past. It makes people *different*, for better or worse. No way you're not going to hear about it, if you haven't already, though it's way before your time and mine."

"You're talking about the old Mokhani Mystery?" She headed him off. "The disappearance of the governess?"

There was a decided glint in his eyes. "So you *do* know."

She nodded. "Only because I did my homework." They were walking along a lush avenue of tropical palms and ferns, on one side bounded by a fourfoot-high stone wall. Around the base of the ferns grew beautiful soft creamy lilies that gave off a perfume not unlike gardenias. *Exquisite!* She bent to pick one, twirling it beneath her nose.

"I suppose you'd have to," he conceded. "Have you met my great aunt Lavinia yet?" He held back a palm frond that partially blocked their path. "Livvy claims to have seen her, *heard* her around the place."

"The governess?"

"Of course the governess," he said shortly. "Her name was Moira. Livvy was dreaming or having one of her visions. Living in the past is so much richer for her than the present. She's got a fantastic imagination. She's always said Moira would come back one day, and we'd all have to fall on our knees in welcome. People think Livvy has gone around the twist, but they're making a big mistake. A lot of it she does deliberately. It's the thwarted actress in her. But in many respects, she's still as sharp as a tack."

Jessica laughed quietly. "I can believe that. I've met her. She greeted me at the front door. It must have been in the middle of one of her fantasies, because she called *me* Moira. I tried to assure her I wasn't, but I don't think she was entirely convinced."

He stopped dead on the path, forcing her to do the same. "Well maybe that's your trump card, is it, Ms. Tennant?"

"Trump card?" Anger rose. "You sound as though you've caught me out at something."

"I'd really appreciate it if you were straight with me," he said crisply, his gaze very direct. "You've never met my father before? Even fleetingly?"

She frowned and resumed walking. "I think I'd remember. He's not the sort of man you'd miss. *I* would have thought my trump card was the fact I'm in line to win a big award. No point in being modest. Not around you. That's quite an achievement in our business, especially for someone my age."

"Hell, I'm sure there's no question you'll win it." He was brusque. "But I'm not referring to your artistic abilities." He made a frustrated gesture. "As I said, Moira has haunted this family for over half a century. You'd swear she wanted to have some kind of vengeance for God knows what! For all the various articles and versions of events, I've never been able to find a photograph of her. The only one on record is a grainy one supplied by her parents, but then she was only a child. Someone in the family either destroyed what we had or whisked them out of sight. But I do know she was an ash-blonde with green eyes, which might explain my father's attraction to you. Livvy obviously was drawn to you, as well. My great aunt had a soft spot for Moira, so she took it very hard when she disappeared."

"Surely everyone did?"

"That goes without saying," he said tersely.

"I'm sorry. It must have been a bad time for the family," Jessica said. Suspicions, speculations, the police and newshounds coming after them.

"It's bad enough hearing about it all these years later," he said, pulling a sharp twig off a hanging branch and throwing it away. "Even her name causes distress. Can you understand that?"

"Of course I can," she said. "I'm not an insensitive person."

"I don't know yet what you are," he said. "I got hell at school until I was driven to shut my tormentors up. The entire family was badly affected. My grandparents in particular, Steven and Cecily. My dad, who was only a kid, and my dad's twin, Barbara. Aunt Barbara won't come near Mokhani except for the obligatory Christmas visit. She's married to a brilliant academic. Unforunately no one can understand a word he says—we might if he threw in some normal everyday language now and again. They live in Sydney with a magnificent view of the harbor. No children. Barbara used to say she didn't want to pass on a bad gene, whatever the hell that means. Livvy divides her time between them and us."

"I see."

Brilliantly plumaged parrots flashing an array of the most beautiful vivid colors appeared above their heads, several turning somersaults like an aerobatics display before diving into a spectacular flowering plant with huge scarlet flowers and iridescent violetstriped leaves. Jessica looked up, engrossed and entertained. "Does Miss Lavinia haunt art galleries?"

"Yup," he said laconically. "I suspect you do, too."

"I *am* an artist. Would she have attended a Christie's auction lately?"

"Ms. Tennant, I wouldn't know. Why don't you ask her?"

"I will." Who knows where such a question might lead? For a scary moment, Jessica felt as if she had entered a tortuous maze.

"What's with the *Miss* Lavinia?" he asked presently. "A bit quaint, isn't it?"

Jessica reached out to touch a prolifically flowering truss of bougainvillea somewhere between deep pink and cerise. "It just came to me. It seemed respectful, okay?"

"Respectful, certainly. Maybe contrived. I happen to know Moira called Livvy Miss Lavinia." Outright suspicion glittered in his eyes.

"Surely you don't think there's some kind of conspiracy going on here, do you?"she asked uneasily. "One wouldn't have to be the smartest person in the world to realize your family might have become a bit paranoid about Moira and her sad story. The fact I called your great-aunt Miss Lavinia means absolutely nothing. I'd feel a lot happier if you'd put it down to good manners."

"That's it, good manners?" He glanced at her as if he had considerable difficulty accepting that.

"Of course." Jessica met his gaze squarely. "I told you I came across the old mystery in the course of my research into the Bannerman family. It's been the subject of numerous articles on and off over the years. The mystery has never been solved. That alone would keep it alive."

"I hope you're not implying anything sinister there," he said, warming to the challenge.

"Certainly not." She shook her head. "It's exactly as I've told you. My desire to understand my commission led me into researching the Bannerman history. I'm sure your father had my professional credentials thoroughly checked out well before I arrived. He's since questioned me at some length about my family background."

"Obviously he wants to learn more about you," Cy said, his scrutiny, like his father's, too intense for her comfort.

"I admit I was surprised. I couldn't see what a lot of it had to do with my design skills. But I could say my family is highly respectable."

"Thank God there are a few of us left," he said acidly.

Jessica didn't bother replying. She knew he was seeking answers to what bothered him, but how could she supply them when she didn't even know the questions? But he had made her uneasy. *Was* there more to discover as to why Broderick Bannerman had chosen *her* for this project? Even Tim had found it hard to believe.

Jessica's ponderings were diverted as up several hundred yards ahead rose the soaring white edifice Broderick Bannerman had caused to be erected as a monument to himself and a celebration of his wealth.

"This is it!" Cy announced as if they'd arrived at a great circus tent. "Home sweet home! I might mention I had no input whatever so that gets me off the hook. My idea of Mokhani is the *ancestral* home of the Bannermans. I plan to keep the original homestead intact for my son. Families die out without sons. But my dad isn't circumscribed by those sentiments. He thinks Mokhani is his entirely. It isn't. A lot of my mother's fortune went into keeping it going during the hard times. We've had them like everyone else."

"It's quite extraordinary." She shielded her eyes with her hands, staring up.

"A masterly understatement. It's bizarre."

"Don't shut your mind on it altogether," she said, realizing the original homestead had great significance for him. Probably because it was not only the Bannerman ancestral home, but also the place his father had brought his mother to as a young bride. There had to be many reminders of his mother at the homestead, indeed all round the station. "You must miss your mother," she found herself saying.

He looked at her sharply, his tone cool. "At least I know what love is," he said.

"You've never been *in* love?" she asked, putting a hand to her hair as the wind gusted.

"Have you?"

"Sort of," she said smiling, "but no one I found irresistible."

"While you, no doubt, were adored."

She heard the sarcasm; responded to it. "The question is not whether I was adored, but given your need for heirs, why *you* at the very least aren't engaged?"

"Hey, ease up!" He threw up his hands. "I'm not going to do anything to jeopardize my bachelor state at the moment, Ms. Tennant, if that's what you want to know."

"I'm only making conversation." She shrugged, pausing to take in the magnitude of her commission.

"Wait until you get inside," he softly jeered. "If the Shah of Iran were still around, he'd love it."

"Good grief, it's immense." She was genuinely stunned.

"Well, I suppose it has to be big," he said carelessly. "B.B. does a lot of entertaining. He hosts many important overseas guests. Things quieted down a bit when Sharon, that's Robyn's mother, became so ill. She died two years ago. She was a good, sweet woman."

"Robyn doesn't take after her?" Jessica asked wryly.

"Well, I never!" He did a mock double take. "Are you saying Robyn's neither good nor sweet?"

She colored a little. "I only meant she isn't overly friendly. Shall we go in?"

"Of course. After you."

Just being with him was exhilarating. She felt as though she could go on talking to him forever.

They entered through a huge gabled portico supported by monumental Ionic columns that led directly to the twenty-foot-high double doors. Beyond, a space nearly as big as a football field culminated in an equally monumental staircase. After the first breathless shock, Jessica saw it as a wonderful multipurpose area. All the same, she didn't know whether to applaud or hoot. As a public building, it would have been splendid. As a private home it staggered the imagination.

"We had an army of builders and workers on site forever." Cy groaned at the memory. "They lived in row after row of tents just like on an archeological dig. Dad strode around like a pharaoh bullying and threatening. I'm only surprised he didn't carry a whip. An old quarry had to be reopened in North Queensland for all the marble—lots of columns, as you can see. B.B. loves columns. God knows what his mausoleum is going to be like."

"You're joking!" She turned to stare at him, relieved to catch a smile on his lips.

"Probably. But I can't entirely rule it out."

"This is fit for Prince Charles," Jessica said solemnly.

"Perhaps he'll come a-visiting. Do you wonder why I much prefer the old homestead? It's plenty good enough for *my* castle. It stood firm through Cyclone Tracy, though it has to be said we didn't bear the brunt of it. This place is apocalypse-proof."

"I guessed that." She stared up at the doubleheight soaring

ceiling with its great cupola letting in streams of light. "I think I'm going to need a team."

"Around two hundred might be good," he said. "I hope they enjoy living in tents. How come your uncle didn't get the commission? I don't want to hurt your feelings, but I had him checked out and he's the best. For that matter, how come he didn't want the job? From what I've seen no one is ever *too* rich."

"Isn't there something you're forgetting?" she asked, starting to pace round the huge area, staring up at the dome with its splendid yet restrained plaster work that bore the imprint of artisans.

"God, you're right. Dad wanted *you*. All we've got to discover now is why. Is it possible you remind him of someone? Someone dead these many, many long years?"

She drew a deep breath; slowly released it. She knew he was baiting her. "Oh come on, *say* it. Why beat about the bush? I made a mistake telling you your great aunt called me Moira."

"Well, she's never called anyone else that," he said, his voice flat. "Not in fifty years. Now, isn't that something that absolutely sets you apart?"

"It would seem so," she conceded. "It's certainly very unusual, but if there is a resemblance, it's sheer coincidence." Jessica walked quickly away from him to regaisn her composure, entering one of the huge reception rooms off the great hall. "Why don't we just stick to the grand tour instead of trying to figure out odd coincidences?"

"I thought we were doing both," he said blandly. "Perhaps you're Moira in another incarnation."

"Perhaps you're a reincarnation of the guy who chucked her in the lagoon," she retorted recklessly.

He frowned. "Is that wise saying something like that?"

"I usually give as good as I get." She felt anger and excitement in equal measure. "Why is it so difficult for you to accept me at face value?"

"Maybe that's it. The *face*." His tone was light, but with a sharp edge.

"I'm the interior designer your father happened to hire."

"And you haven't wondered at all why *you* in particular?"

"Maybe I have," she admitted irritably, "but unlike you, I haven't credited—or discredited him—with ulterior motives, whatever they might be. I know nothing of the situation between you and your father except what you've told me. So it's difficult? I sympathize, but don't bring me into it. As you pointed out when we met, I'm just passing through. I can handle this job. I know it's huge, but I'm not overwhelmed. If your father's ideas and mine don't mesh or he wants me to do it *his* way entirely, then I'm not the person for the job. He'll have to find someone else. While we're on the subject, why not your stepsister, Robyn? Why did he overlook her? I understand your father gave her carte blanche to refurbish the reception rooms of the old homestead."

"And have you ever seen such a disaster? If my poor mother were around she'd cry buckets." He didn't bother to keep the disgust out of his tone. "It was all done when I wasn't around. Downright sneaky, I call it. Robyn thinks good taste and wild extravagance go hand in hand. Dad gave her the go ahead— maybe to get square with me for some imagined slight—then went away on a long trip. When he got home and saw what Robyn had done, can you image the furor? Bellowing by the hour. Even great men like B.B. make at least one mistake in a lifetime. I don't want him to make another."

"He won't with me!" she answered, her voice brisk.

"If only we could be sure." He stared at her. She was as beautiful as she was potentially a threat to life as they knew it. Not that that was all good. He knew his father too well not to intuit that B.B. had a consuming interest in this particular young woman, and it wasn't for her creative skills. He'd

stake his life on that. Did she remind him of that sad little phantom of his childhood, Moira? There was no doubt his father had been deeply affected by Moira's mysterious disappearance. It was all so damned odd. Cy had all the proof he needed that Ms. Tennant had a certain fascination for his father. His father still had an eye for a beautiful women. But this one was way too young. Hell, she was five years younger than *he* was. Maybe his father's interest had been so captured when he'd seen her on that television program that he'd felt compelled to work out a way to get her here. He knew more than anyone that when his father resolved on something, it happened.

"Why don't we see what's behind this?" Her voice

broke into his ponderings. She was waving a graceful arm toward the adjoining room.

"Why not?" He followed her in, both of them moving across the space of the room. Brilliant rays of sunlight fell through the tall windows, holding her as if in a spotlight. They illuminated her very feminine slender figure, the lovely face, the cloud of ash-blond hair, setting a-sparkle all the little shimmering ornaments on her emerald blouse. Beauty like that packed a powerful punch. He had never before seen anyone that beautiful *and* sexy. He could easily imagine what it had been like for his father. A man of strong sexual appetites. Cy was reaching in

his deductions, of course. But over the years he had learned how to read his obsessively secretive father. Jessica turned her head, giving him a small sidelong glance. He was as edgy as she was. Both of them were too aware of each other and showing it. "What

are you thinking?" she asked. "You've gone quiet."

"I'm still in pursuit of answers," he said.

"Please don't continue to look at me," she begged. "The sort of answers you appear to be searching for are beyond me. I have no connection to the Bannerman past, even if I do have a passing resemblance to your father's governess."

"Which, like Lavinia, he would have seen immediately."

She reacted with an admonition. "That would scarcely prompt him to hire me to decorate all this. That's just plain crazy."

"Not just crazy, it's completely bloody insane. Look, it's entirely up to you and Dad if you stay or go," he told her. "I'm not asking to be your friend, Ms. Tennant. I've got too much else on my mind."

"When I would have treasured your friendship." She lifted her green eyes to his, not bothering to hide her interest.

He returned her gaze. "It's not mandatory to seduce the clients, is it?" he asked.

She shook her head, her cheeks flushed pink. "I'd have to be very foolish indeed to try to seduce *you!*"

He gave a cracked laugh. "You might enjoy it."

"It's a trap, isn't it?" she asked, her eyes narrow— ing. "You want me to make one big mistake."

"Damn, you're on to me," he said with a low laugh.

Then he shocked her. His arm snaked out to lock around her waist, sending streams of sensation into her body and down her legs.

"Think before you go any further." She couldn't keep back the faint tremble in her voice.

"Don't guys around you tend to lose it?" He gave her a taut smile, but he didn't take away his arm.

Unconsciously, she ran the tip of her tongue over her dry lips. "Some do. But you're just playing games."

"That's so." He pulled her in and put his mouth against her ear. "I don't get much fun around here." She stiffened in his arms, alarmed at how easily he was thrilling her. "You're going to be difficult about this, are you?" she asked sharply. Something potentially damaging to her position in this family was whipping up between them. It was like being out in a yacht in a high wind.

"Just testing, Jessica," he drawled, though in reality he was having difficulty taking his arm away. Her body alongside his made him wonder what it would be like for them to become entwined.

"Well, I'm not about to fall into the trap." She pulled back and looked at him. He was so close, if

she relaxed against him he could bring his other arm up and lock her in an embrace.

"Do you know how good you feel?"

"Stop it." She felt weak, her limbs swept by a warm languor.

"Hell, I *ought* to."

She thought he was going to release her, but instead he spun her right into his arms, bending his head and finding her mouth.

She saw stars. Other sparkling shapes. The whole world fell away to a roaring in her ears. Only sensation was left. Sensation so violent Jessica could barely stand. She had to cling to him as the only thing that wasn't moving.

When he finally let her go, she had to remain where she was, unable to move until her balance was restored. He *knew* how to kiss a woman. How many other women had he kissed? She put a hand on his chest and pushed.

"I can't believe you did that," she said.

His answer came right away, his tone not a lot different from hers. "I can't believe I did, either." His laugh held a trace of self-disgust. "I hope there aren't any hidden cameras around here."

She pushed tumbling locks of hair behind her ear. "Too bad you didn't have time to get them in place. You'd like to discredit me with your father, wouldn't you?"

He shrugged. "I'm not that kind of guy, Jessica. Truth is, you threw me momentarily off balance."

"Sorry, you're too smart for that. It's obviously much better for you if I get kicked out before I have a chance to get underway."

"Did you think I was counting on Dad turning up?"

"Weren't you?" Excitement turned to anger. She wanted to hit him.

Take that challenging look off his face.

"It scares me to tell you, Jessica, but I never gave my father a thought."

"I don't believe you!"

They were so engrossed in confronting each other, it took a few moments before the clack of boots across the marble floor penetrated. Cy turned immediately, while Jessica froze. "Talk of the devil and you conjure him up. That'll be Dad now. We both better cool down. You can bet your life he's come to check where we're at."

Her agitation increased. She was flooded by embarrassment and panic. "God, have I got any lipstick left?" She was forced to appeal to him. That kiss had been deep and prolonged.

For answer, he whipped a handkerchief out of his jeans pocket. "How could you? It's on *me*." He drew the white linen across his mouth, stuffing the handkerchief back in his pocket. "What are you waiting for? Go into the other room. Come on, *move*."

Jessica didn't need to be told twice. She'd only been on Mokhani a day and already she was waistdeep in trouble. She bit down hard on her bottom lip—it was still throbbing from his kiss—in an endeavor to color it pink. Her heart was beating a rapid tattoo—which was fast becoming a routine around Cyrus Bannerman. She knew her face was flushed. She could still feel the *heat* of that clinch all through her body. It was the most explosive thing that had ever happened to her.

"Settle down, you look great," he reassured her, crossing the room swiftly on his long legs. He lifted his resonant voice so it rang around the empty space. "This is obviously intended to be the library. Of course you and Dad might have other ideas for it. An auditorium maybe? Dad loves giving speeches."

In another second, Broderick Bannerman appeared, his nostrils flared like an animal trying to pick up a scent. "I expected you'd be a bit further along than this," he said in an accusatory voice, looking from one to the other.

"I had no idea we had to rush," Cy responded, totally unfazed. "Surely Ms. Tennant needs *time* to take in all this magnificence."

Jessica felt as nervous as if Broderick Bannerman had caught the two of them in bed. "I had no real idea of the scale of the mansion, Mr. Bannerman," she said. "The great hall is awe-inspiring."

"My father loves grandeur," Cyrus told her.

Bannerman's smile came close to a snarl. "Thank you, Cyrus. I'll show Jessica the rest of the house."

"Glad to be of assistance." Cy sketched a brief, ironic salute. "See you at dinner, Ms. Tennant."

"Please… Jessica." She gave him a quelling glance. It was obvious he liked to get a rise out of his father, and she couldn't in all fairness blame him.

"Jessica. Thank you. Feel free to call me Cyrus," he invited.

"Don't take any notice of my son," Bannerman warned after Cyrus had gone. "All he cares about is goading me. It's not so surprising, I suppose. He's always lived in my shadow. Makes it hard for him to grapple with. Our relationship is far from easy. Now, what are your thoughts so far?"

The intensity of his gaze made her uncomfortable. She could only hope she wasn't betraying the turbulence that was inside her. How could she have let Cy Bannerman kiss her? Not that she could have offered resistance—he moved so fast. She had to assure herself that's all it was. "You've set me quite a challenge, Mr. Bannerman," she said, getting full control of her voice at last. "It's a massive job. These are great architectural spaces. We'll need to separate the public from the private. The great hall could be used for any number of purposes—functions that I'm sure you have in mind. I know you're looking for a sense of luxury and opulence in keeping with the building, but I see it through the framework of the environment. I don't have to tell you that's quite unique. What we're doing is reconciling classical architecture with modern sensibilities and needs. I don't know if you want to make the public rooms a showcase for art, some sculpture… I'm sure you'll want the latest technology. Equally sure you already have it at the homestead. Why don't we continue our tour? You can tell me your likes and dislikes along the way."

They walked into another room that could be used for banqueting. "What do you think of my son?" he asked with such harsh abruptness she almost jumped.

She knew she had to play it safe. "I haven't really had the time to form an opinion." What could she say? That he was as arrogant as Lucifer and, by the way, the best kisser in the world? That would go over well.

"He's quite a catch."

"I imagine he is," she answered in a calm, composed voice.

"*I'm* bigger," he told her, with what she could only describe as fierce triumph.

CHAPTER FIVE

AUNT LAVINIA CAME to dinner in costume.

"Tosca," Cyrus Bannerman told Jessica in a swift aside, an indulgent look on his face. It was obvious he was very fond of his great aunt. They had met on the stairs. Jessica hoped her face hadn't flamed, but his voice when he greeted her had been dead casual, as though absolutely nothing had passed between them. The best way to go, she thought, matching his nonchalance. Now they watched Lavinia, not without anxiety as she tottered down the staircase, one frail knotted hand trailing along the banister. Lavinia must have been beautiful when she was young, Jessica thought. She still retained glimmerings of it.

"Tosca. I guessed as much." Jessica, an opera buff, watched the old lady's gown swish around her ankles. The navy sneakers she wore only slightly detracted from the dramatic effect. In her copious white hair she wore an elaborate high-backed ebony comb studded with pearls and rhinestones. The bodice of her gown fell flat and low due to the fact her bust had diminished with age. Some underwear was showing. Around her neck she wore a shagreen choker from which was appended a great stone that had to weigh ten or twelve carats. It couldn't be

a diamond, surely. Whatever it was, Jessica's eyes were dazzled
by the bounce of light.

"Don't you look lovely, Moira!" Lavinia called, her watery
eyes studying Jessica with pleasure before shifting to her great-
nephew. "Good evening, my darling. Didn't I always tell you
she'd come back?"

So this is what dementia is, Jessica thought sadly, feeling a
prickle run up and down her spine.

"Like my dress?" Lavinia's expression indicated there was
no possible answer but yes.

"Love it." Cyrus's smile was a little strained. "Not that I
haven't seen it a million times. And it's Jessica, Livvy. Not
Moira. Moira has ceased to be."

"Good evening, Miss Lavinia," Jessica spoke quickly to get
over a sticky moment. Lavinia continued to stand on the bottom step, posing. "Don't tell me. You're Tosca."

A big smile covered Lavinia's face. "So you still love opera!
That was one of the reasons I loved you. You *are* Moira, aren't
you? There's no use Cyrus shushing me. Turn around, would
you, dear? What a lovely, lovely dress." She smiled and nodded
as Jessica twirled. "You always were ravishing."

"*Ravishing* is too tame a word," Cyrus said, his tone sardonic.

"Miss Lavinia, I'm not Moira," Jessica insisted, thinking
she was becoming immured from further shocks. "I'm Jessica, remember?"

"Child, what's wrong with you?" The old lady, who had been
executing a few dance steps, broke off to stare into Jessica's
face, incredulous. "You can't have forgotten your name? Are
we dealing with amnesia here?"

Cyrus intervened. "We're dealing with age and submerged
grief. Come on, Liv. Give it up. It's a wasteland. Besides, you
know you'll push Dad over the edge if you start this Moira
stuff."

"His story and my story don't tally," Lavinia said.

"How could they?" Cyrus put a hand to his head. "Dad was a child."

"Broderick was *never* a child," Lavinia said, her voice sinking a whole octave. "And that's the truth."

"Oh, hell, Livvy, have a heart." Cyrus appealed to her. "Meal times are never easy, but we do have a guest. Two guests actually. Jessica and Robyn's boyfriend Erik Moore is here."

At the news, Lavinia began to beat her arms like chicken wings. "Oh, I don't like him!" she wailed. "Started up an affair behind his poor little wife's back. He always looks at me as though I should be locked away somewhere. I don't worry about that, though. If I'm so stupid, why do I know more than anyone else?" She danced a few more steps before tripping over her long velvet skirt. "Bother!"

Both Cyrus and Jessica came to her aid, each taking one of the old lady's arms. "Isn't that costume a little hot for this evening?" Cyrus inquired.

"So far so good." Lavinia gave a little laugh that turned into a cough. "I couldn't decide between it and *La Traviata*. I was such a success as Violetta." She turned her puffed white head toward Jessica. "I would have been a big name, like Sutherland. I could have had the adoration of millions, only the Honorable George Fairweather came into my life and wrecked it."

"At least you had the sense not to marry him," Cyrus comforted her.

"His dragon of a mother, a terrifying woman, insisted he break things off. His father really liked me, but he was no help at all. Mother had the power. I'm constantly astounded at the power of women."

"You can say that again!" Cyrus seconded. "A beautiful woman has all the power in the world."

The others were assembled in the opulent drawing room Robyn had spent so much of her stepfather's money on. As Cyrus, Lavinia and Jessica entered, those waiting looked up with varying expressions. Broderick Bannerman's intense scrutiny gave Jessica goose bumps. She thought he might have been seeing *through* her, then shook her head in dismay; this Moira business was getting to her. Robyn, looking very glamorous as she perched on the side of her boyfriend's armchair, showing off her long elegant legs, said, "Hi!"

Erik, so unpopular with Lavinia, smiled pleasantly and stood to attention. He was good-looking, slightly overweight, a full head of thick brown hair, hazel eyes, well-dressed. A lot older than Robyn. Married *and* divorced? Jessica wondered if he had children. Robyn wouldn't make the sweetest stepmother in the world.

"Sorry to keep you waiting," Lavinia trilled radiantly. "Don't worry. I'm safe with these two." She bestowed her sweet smile on first her great-nephew, then Jessica. "And you needn't look at me as if I've gone mad, Erik," she chided. "I love to keep my heyday alive."

"Tosca," B.B. informed Erik briefly. "You're all having a drink before dinner? Jessica, what would you like?" Again his rapier gaze swept over her face and body, taking in her cool, very pretty minidress, in layered swirls of deep pink and mauve. *Surely he can't have any sexual interest in me,* Jessica thought. If so, she might have to abandon a marvelously challenging commission. *And,* she was forced to admit, getting to know Cyrus Bannerman better.

When she glanced briefly in Cy's direction, she found his expression a touch severe. Had he recognized the sexual component in his father's stare? If he had, he bore *no* sympathy for it. Jessica shifted her gaze to Robyn, who was nursing a half-empty champagne flute.

"Champagne, if I may. That would be lovely."

"Cyrus, would you mind? Sherry for you, Liv?" B.B. asked.

Lavinia reacted with the little trill that fell so softly on the ears. "I'll join Moira in a glass of champagne," she said happily. "After all, it's a celebration. She's come back."

"'Struth!!" Robyn groaned, putting one expensively shod foot to the floor. "That's *Jessica,* Liv. Jessica Tennant, Dad's new interior designer." She'd raised her voice, perpetuating the myth Lavinia was stone deaf.

Lavinia remained oblivious to Robyn's scorn. "Why must you screech, Robyn? No one in the world yells at me like you do. That includes Broderick. I know what I'm talking about, thank you very much. *You* know, too, don't you, Broderick?"

Jessica felt herself go cold, but Bannerman's stare directed toward his aunt didn't waver. "I know you're talking nonsense, my dear," he said suavely. "That's a bit of a worry."

Oh, dear, Jessica thought. *He can't be implying Livinia is due for a nursing home, can he?*

"Ignore that, Livvy," Cyrus instructed, returning with two glasses of sparkling champagne. He gave one to Lavinia, the other to Jessica. "There's no worry. Trust me."

"Oh, I do, my darling." Lavinia's eyes flew to his after a few seconds of rapid blinking. "Every day you're alive is a miracle. The angels are looking after you."

Behind them, Robyn gave another protesting moan. "For God's sake, have we got to listen to this stuff, Dad? What Liv's got packed inside her head isn't entirely harmless. Why did you give her that glass of champagne, Cy?"

"Mind your own business, Robyn," Cyrus answered pleasantly enough. "Livvy has a perfect right to say what she likes."

Broderick Bannerman, who was standing in a cloud of preoccupation, now collected himself. "You must forgive us, Jessica. It's always a circus around here. Belatedly, I present a friend of Robyn's—Erik Moore. Erik's a property developer. I've no doubt he'll want to tell you all about his latest project. Erik, meet Jessica, who has come to take over the job of furnishing the new house. She's young, but she has a great deal to offer. I was very impressed with her ideas as we were touring the house. Off the top of her head, too, but first class."

"Delighted to meet you, Jessica." Erik didn't approach her, perhaps fearing Robyn might kick him in the shins. Instead, he executed a smooth Euro-style bow.

"Well, drink up," B.B. said briskly, throwing back his handsome head and draining the last of his drink. "My afternoon tour has made me hungry."

They ate in the formal dining room, occupying one end of the long polished table.

It was beautifully set and Jessica commented on it.

"Molly," B.B. said. "She's so much better at it than Robyn."

"I don't have to prove myself setting a table, Dad." Robyn's voice betrayed no resentment, but her eyes reflected her hurt. "The fact I'm a very successful businesswoman says all that needs to be said about me. Isn't that right, Erik?"

Erik answered the only way he possibly could. "Indeed it is, my love. You're going from strength to strength."

"She'd have been going nowhere without my support," Broderick Bannerman cut in like a master stroke. This evening he looked very distinguished at the head of the table, his jacket emphasizing his broad shoulders. Although Jessica hadn't taken to Robyn the woman had scarcely been friendly—she was starting to feel sorry for her. It couldn't have been easy growing up in such an intolerant household.

It had been the very helpful housekeeper who had knocked on Jessica's door earlier in the evening to inform her with a smile that Mr. Bannerman liked everyone to dress for dinner. There was no slacking on Mokhani.

"Not *formal,* dear. You know what I mean. A pretty dress."

Jessica had thanked her for being so thoughtful. She had an ally in Molly if not in Robyn, who had probably been hoping she would turn up in a T-shirt, shorts and thongs. She had, in fact, laid out a simple yellow dress cut like a slip, but had quickly

changed it for something a little dressier. One wouldn't want
to offend B.B.'s sensibilities.

All three men were wearing lightweight linen jackets. No
ties, but fine-quality shirts open at the throat. A concession to
the heat, though the air-conditioning kept the house at a constant twenty-four degrees Celsius. It had to cost a fortune, Jessica thought. But what was a fortune to ordinary folk would
probably be B.B.'s notion of small change.

Given the deep undercurrents, dinner went off well. The food
was delicious—Jessica vowed there and then to get Molly's
recipe for the baked barramundi for which the Territory was
famous. Chili obviously, lemongrass, coriander, Kaffir lime
peel...and what else? Thai shrimp paste, coconut cream and
some other spices she couldn't name. The bouquet of the superb
chardonnay mingled with the light scent of the bowl of white,
cerise-veined Asian lilies. At one time, B.B.'s hand touched hers
where it lay on the tablecloth of starched white damask. Inside,
Jessica froze, but tried extremely hard to convey unawareness.

Cyrus continued talking—it seemed to Jessica the conversation eddied around him—but from the blue flash in his eyes
he had seen the touch and continued to draw his own conclusions. Robyn, thankfully, was staring across the table at her
stepbrother, apparently totally focused on what he was saying.
Something about Jabiru, one of the four major mining settlements in the Territory, the other three, Ranger, Kabiluka and
Koongarra, all uranium mines, all within Kakadu National Park,
World Heritage listed. Although the Commonwealth govern-
ment imposed a high level of environmental regulation, the issue
of mining versus environment was one of bitter controversy.
It was clear from what Cyrus was saying that he was firmly
on the side of environmental preservation. Robyn, apparently,
wasn't. Neither was Broderick Bannerman, with his extensive
mining interests. Erik Moore sat uncomfortably on the fence.
Australia, the most ancient continent, was an incredibly rich
repository for valuable minerals, polarizing both sides.

"What do you think, Jessica?" B.B. asked, putting her on the spot.

No point in shirking it or trying to be diplomatic like Erik. "I'm on the side of the environment," she said quietly.

"Don't go to Jabiru and tell the miners and their families that," Robyn said, happy to entangle Jessica in the controversial issue. "Don't go to the Tasmanian forests either, and tell the forest workers to pack up their chain saws and go home."

"I understand both arguments, Robyn," Jessica said, "but I believe preserving the great wilderness areas of the world is far more important than the short-term fueling of the economy. Take Greece. Do you think farmers of ancient times realized that their olive crop, their liquid gold, was undermining a fragile ecology and turning their once-lush land barren? They didn't, but I've read that their great writers delivered stern warnings. Sophocles for one. Most trees have a branching network of roots that hold the topsoil, but olive trees don't. It has a taproot that burrows deep. Once the topsoil has gone, it can't be replaced. That was Greece's tragedy."

"That's all news to me." Robyn brushed it aside. "The olive crop is still of great commercial importance, surely."

"Of course. But what was not known *then,* or largely disregarded, is known now. We have to act on the mistakes of the past."

"That's all very noble, Jessica," Broderick Banner said. "But people and governments live in the present. Mining in the Territory is overtaking cattle. *I* should know. Now, why don't we put the subject behind us?"

"With that attitude, Dad, nothing will change," Cyrus said quietly.

Lavinia, who had over-imbibed under cover of the conversation suddenly piped up with, "Mining isn't the *worst* thing Broderick has done."

"Thank you for that, Lavinia." B.B. turned his striking profile toward her. "You'll need help to get up the stairs."

If that wasn't a dismissal, what was? Jessica thought.

Only, Lavinia wasn't going to be deflected from speaking her mind. "What did you do with all the old photographs, Broderick?"

B.B. threw down his damask napkin. "What old photographs, my dear? There are scrapbooks all over the house."

"None of Moira," Lavinia snapped back like *Take that!*

"That's ancient history, Livvy." Cyrus touched his grand-aunt's arm in a gentle warning.

Lavinia swept on single-mindedly. "Where are the paintings? The paintings Hughie did."

B.B. smiled at her. "I have emptied the homestead out my-self, Liv—which hasn't stopped *you* from foraging around all these years. There *are* no photographs. No paintings. Do you think I wouldn't know?"

Cyrus took a long hard look at his father. "But you *would* know, Dad. You know everything. By your own admission."

"Please don't try to annoy me, Cyrus," B.B. returned. "You do it so often."

"Hear, hear," Robyn raised her wineglass, her rivalry with Cyrus springing to the fore.

"You can't hide things forever, Broderick," Lavinia warned, seemingly unaware of Cyrus's continuing warning touch.

Broderick Bannerman set his two palms down heavily on the table. "Listen and listen carefully, Lavinia. You've had too much to drink." The piercing gray gaze moved on to Robyn. "So have you, Robyn, for that matter. In my view, women should stick to one drink. No more. They have no head for alcohol. I want all this Moira business stopped. If you can't or won't stop, La-vinia, I'll have to speak to your doctor about it. He might well want to put you into a nursing home for a spell."

"You call a doctor and I'll *kill* you, Broderick." Lavinia bunched her frail, knotted hands into fists.

"All right, that's enough!" Cyrus stood up. "Why bait her, Dad?"

"I'm serious," his father said. "She's getting much worse."

Any sense of shyness in Jessica, amid such a family, had to be cast aside. She understood, like Cyrus, that Lavinia had to be protected from B.B.'s wrath. "Would you like to go upstairs now, Miss Lavinia?" she asked, rising to her feet, too. "I'm feeling a little tired myself. That was a beautiful meal."

"Molly is an unsung heroine," Lavinia said. "I *am* a little tired, dear. Don't think I don't know you want me to keep my trap shut, Broderick." She shot a glance at her nephew. "There's always been too much to hide." Unsteadily, she rose to her feet, wincing a little as the blood returned to her legs.

Cyrus took her arm. "Think you can make it up the stairs, Tosca?"

Lavinia giggled like a schoolgirl. "I may be a bit slow."

Erik Moore, who looked as if he'd been hoping against hope it would all blow over, rose courteously to his feet. "Good night, Ms. Bannerman. Sleep well."

"Good night, Erik," Lavinia replied graciously. "You seem like a nice person. Unfortunately I can't seem to like you. Oh, Moira, dear, aren't you sweet! You're coming, too."

Broderick Bannerman wasn't going to suffer that. "Stay here, please, Jessica," he said, gray eyes cold. Dared she disobey? Jessica thought she could.

She stepped forward, hoping her guardian angel was right behind her. "I'll only be a minute or two, Mr. Bannerman."

"Love to you all," Lavinia caroled wickedly over her shoulder, giving Cyrus a woozy smile before Jessica came to stand at her other side.

It was Jessica who helped Lavinia undress, while Cyrus waited in the adjoining sitting room. This was more like it, Jessica thought, looking around the beautiful, slightly theatrical bedroom and what she could see of the sitting room beyond. Robyn had no hand in decorating this. It truly expressed the essence of Lavinia, even if she *had* lost much of her substance. The color scheme was the blue and white of Chinese porcelain. Filmy white draperies adorned the large four-poster bed. Beautiful blue-and-white fabric was used for the curtains at the French doors, the upholstery of the daybed and the two armchairs. An exquisite blue Venetian writing table—Timmy would love it—stood proudly in a corner. There were two lovely flower paintings on the walls, a collection of miniatures, and dominating one wall, a full-length portrait of Lavinia in her heyday dressed in an extravagantly beautiful white ball gown, clusters of pure white camellias tucked behind her ears.

Violetta, the Lady of the Camellias.

Jessica took a long, admiring look. Just as she thought, Miss Lavinia had been a beauty.

"Yes, that's me," Lavinia confirmed. "I was *glorious* in those days. No big fat diva about me. And my soaring voice! I could hit F above top C no trouble at all. Don't know where I got it from. No one else in the family had a voice unless one counts good speaking voices. We all have those. Come back in, Cyrus, darling," she called. "I'm decent."

Cyrus reentered, vibrantly male in that ultrafeminine room. "That's news to me."

"Don't be naughty, darling." Lavinia was tucked up under the covers now, her abundant white hair pulled back in a plait.

"If I had some watercolors handy, I would paint this lovely room," Jessica said. "I adore the portrait."

"Of course the artist was in love with me," Lavinia said.

"Of course," Cyrus smiled. "That was to be expected."

"You'd really like to paint my room, Moira?" Lavinia asked, motioning to Cyrus to come sit on the side of her bed. "I didn't think young artists did that anymore."

"I do," Jessica smiled. "I took it up in my student days. My uncle Brett encouraged it. I've had quite a few commissions."

Lavinia patted Cyrus's hand. "Get Moira some watercolor paints when you're next in Darwin," she said.

"No problem." The sapphire eyes moved to Jessica, standing

beneath Lavinia's portrait. "You'll have to come with me to get exactly what you need."

No second invitation needed, Jessica thought.

They were almost at the door when Lavinia said, "Don't go away again, Moira. Promise?"

Jessica appealed to the formidable man at her side. "What do you want me to say?" she whispered.

"This whole bloody thing is totally insane," he retorted quietly with intense irritation. Then, "Make her happy."

"You don't think I should stop it right now?"

"Do you *want* to?" he asked tightly.

She tried to rein in her temper. What game did he think she was playing? And how could it possibly be an advantage to her? Jessica turned her head over her shoulder. "I promise, Miss Lavinia," she said.

Cyrus lifted a hand and turned off the light. "It doesn't matter, anyway. She's asleep now. Bizarre as it may seem, Jessica, your chance resemblance to our resident ghost has brought shock waves into our already disordered lives. Time has stopped for Lavinia. Even my father seems suspended in a past only he can see."

"Well, let me assure you yet again this has nothing to do with me. We don't even know if I actually do look like Moira or if it's simply a matter of coloring."

"What I should do is conduct a hunt of my own," Cyrus muttered, almost to himself. "There are a million places to hide old photographs, even large paintings."

"But your father has denied their existence. Rather strenuously, I thought."

"Which doesn't mean he's not lying. The hell of it all is no one *knows* what happened to Moira, and your resemblance to her is keeping the whole bloody thing alive."

"Has anyone ever thought about reconstructing her last days? The last days she was seen alive?"

"For God's sweet sake, of course they did," he said, none too politely.

"Only making a suggestion. No need to bite my head off."

His eyes flashed. "Jessica, don't expect anyone around here to keep calm on the subject of Moira. She's been dead for a half a century, yet sometimes it seems like only fifteen minutes ago. Now we've had a visitation—you." His eyes rested on her face. "Can you blame me if I'm suddenly very anxious about what it all means?"

CHAPTER SIX

THE NEXT MORNING in her bedroom, Jessica had a long conversation with Brett on her mobile phone, conveying her excitement while answering his many questions. She carefully refrained from saying anything that would make him in the least bit worried, such as Great-aunt Lavinia's memory playing tricks and making her believe she was Moira. She'd rung Brett briefly the moment she'd touched down in Darwin as promised, but a scant, incident-packed day later there was so much to talk about that her side of the conversation continued nonstop.

"Then you think you can cope?" Brett asked when she took a breather. He might have been sitting in a Darwin office rather than his office more than a thousand miles away, Jessica thought. Darwin was, in fact, closer to Asia than it was to any other Australian capital city.

"I'll need help," she told him. "A lot of help. I can't carry it all. It's an immense project. Far bigger than we anticipated."

"You'll get all the help you need on this, Jass. Take plenty of photographs. I need to know the layout."

"I'll draw up floor plans. That should keep me busy. I'll need to ask Mr. Bannerman's secretary, a nice woman called Ruth if I can load them onto one of the office computers. They have all the latest technology here."

"A man in his position, with his vast interests, would need to," Brett said. "How are you supposed to get around?"

"I'm sure I'll be provided with something. A nice spirited horse, maybe a camel. There are thousands and thousands of them roaming around. Kangaroos by the millions. I never knew it but there are twice as many kangaroos in Australia as people. That means roughly forty million."

Brett laughed. "And to think I've never come faceto-face with one. Don't get burnt in that tropical sun," he warned.

"I won't. I've bought lashings of sunscreen. There are plenty of station vehicles, by the way. Helicopters, a Beech Baron and a Lear jet."

"When you're filthy rich, nothing is unobtainable," Brett said dryly.

"I prefer to think *some* things are."

"What is that supposed to mean?" Brett picked up on her tone.

"Nothing. B.B. has his own pilot, but I understand he and Cyrus are licensed to fly the jet. He goes over to New Zealand a lot. He has interests there. Apparently the jet can fly to Auckland without refueling."

"Marvelous! What else does it do?"

"I'll tell you when I'm in it."

"The son, what's he like?"

Jessica twisted a long curl around her finger. "Very lordly. His father's manner veers more to severely autocratic. Cyrus is the only one who doesn't jump at his father's command, anyway."

"Princes are like that," Brett said. "Just don't become his willing subject. What's the father-son relationship like?"

Jessica eased back on the bed. "Not good. I think they've had some terrible clashes in the past."

"That's awful!" Brett sounded appalled. "You be careful,

Jass," he warned. "Enmity between father and son is not to be dismissed. Whatever you do, don't get between them. You're there in a strictly professional capacity. Don't let the heir-in-waiting turn your head. Sounds like Tim will play a role in this. He can take a few quick overseas trips if necessary. Source out antiques."

"Good idea. Has Timmy found out anything more about the portrait he bought at Christie's?" she asked.

"Not as yet."

"She looks so much like me. Don't you think that's odd?"

"It *is* odd, but it's not like it doesn't happen, Jass. Remember the portrait we had of the woman in the red dress? She was the spitting image of the Lady Mayoress. What about the governess who disappeared? Any mention of that?"

Brett always had been on her wavelength. "The subject is taboo."

"I guess so," Brett said in a somber voice. "Can you imagine what it must have been like for Bannerman growing up? At least he had an alibi," he quipped sardonically.

"Why would he need an alibi? Why would anyone need an alibi?" Jessica felt an icy finger down her spine.

"Bannerman's father might have had an obsession with the girl, for all we know. He could have seduced her. The wife found out. The kids found out. The servants were agog with gossip. If I were writing a movie script, it would be a life-threatening situation. Listen, I have to go. Becky is signaling me. Clients have come in. Ring me every day and take care."

Broderick Bannerman insisted on coming with her while she took her photographs. Surely, she thought, such a high-pressured tycoon would have something more important to do. But no. It seemed nothing would suit him better than to walk around with her while she shot off hundreds of photographs of the exterior and interior of the new homestead, although *homestead* was far too modest a word for this modern palace. There were six guest suites contained within the main building, all with their own private porch. She would have a lot of fun decorating those. She took shots of the surrounding garden, well-nurtured by bores: sweeps of lawn like a vast green plain, towering palms and banyans, the boabs and poincianas, native frangipani that had grown into huge trees, the mango, coconut and the giant tree ferns that formed such a lush oasis in an arid land.

"We could do with a water feature," she said, removing a memory stick from her digital camera and inserting another. "The sight and sound of water is very cooling. I'd make it a focal point. Keeping to the classical idiom would be crucial. Who was your landscape gardener?" They might have to call him or her back.

"A fellow called Alan Jensen," B.B. answered, his sunglasses making his piercing gaze unreadable.

"I knew it had to be someone good," Jessica said, instantly recognizing the name. Jensen was very highly regarded in the field.

"I only deal with the best."

She took her shot, then smiled. "Then you're taking a chance on me."

"I don't think so." His deep voice was very measured, very sure.

"Well, I'm very happy about it, Mr. Bannerman."

"Broderick. Call me Broderick," he said with a smile. "I don't want B.B. or Mr. Bannerman from you. Broderick is my name. I liked the look of you, Jessica, and the way you expressed yourself on that program. I liked your beauty, your polish, your style. I like grace in a woman. My first wife, Deborah, had it in abundance. I lost her far too early. I was beside myself with grief. Then I had to put her firmly out of my mind. The Bannerman empire had to come first. The fact you're in contention for a big design award helped. The young should be given every chance."

Jessica's mouth quirked. "I'm firmly behind that." She was

touched by the way he had spoken about his wife. It showed a more sensitive side of him. It was all so sad. "Thank you for your faith in me. I'll do everything in my power to make you happy you chose me."

He looked at her standing there, flashing her lovely smile and brimming with life. The sun made a glory of her cloud of ash-blond hair, her green eyes shone like jewels, and her skin was shimmering. For a moment, he thought he was dreaming. In this young woman's presence, nothing seemed normal. "I'm not used to happiness," he said, and abruptly turned away.

Jessica stood rooted to the spot for several moments, staring after him as he headed down the path. His progress was unhurried but purposeful. There was a lot of darkness and misery in Broderick Bannerman, she thought, relieved she could now continue on her own. She didn't feel comfortable with the man. She doubted anyone would. She realized, too, Cyrus wouldn't like her calling his father by his Christian name, taking little account of the fact that she, too, preferred not to. But having been *told* as opposed to *invited* to call him Broderick, she would be giving offense if she didn't.

Robyn wouldn't like her calling her father Broderick either. Both son and stepdaughter were seeing concerns further along the track. Broderick Bannerman was still a handsome virile man. He had obviously taken a fancy to her, which was the very last thing she'd expected. Surely they all knew that. She was making her own way in life. The old rule about never mixing business with pleasure had its history in experience. Her position had already diminished, simply by allowing Cyrus Bannerman to get under her guard. She should have known better. Sexual attraction swept away good judgment. What she needed was a good shot of self-control.

Slowly, she walked back into the house, filled with a desire to capture and send just the right images back to Brett and Tim. She had already made her request to Ruth, B.B.'s secretary, for the use of a computer.

"Whatever you want, my dear, B.B. has given me my instructions."

It was abundantly clear Ruth craved her boss's approval. Jessica also had a strong sense Ruth secretly craved a lot more.

She spent until lunchtime, which Molly had told her was one o'clock sharp, getting her feel of the dimensions of the various rooms and their outlooks. She made some quick sketches of floor plans for her own benefit, having already asked Broderick—why was it such a hurdle to call him that—if she could make copies of the original house plans. The architect, not surprisingly, was of Greek extraction currently living and working in Brunei, no doubt building more palaces.

They were in fact waiting for her when she finally made it to the informal dining room situated at the rear of the homestead. It could be, and probably had been at one time, a lovely room, floor and ceiling dark gleaming timber with contrasting chalky white walls crying out for decoration. Paintings, mirrors, surely they had them? Probably Robyn had had them stored away. The hard question was, if Robyn owned an art gallery, what made her shun putting paintings on her own walls? Jessica had seen lots of superb antique silver, fine china and beautiful glittering crystal, but the house was devoid of artworks and some fine pieces of antique furniture. She wasn't thinking of all that many, but certain focal pieces from China or Japan.

Entering the room, her eye carried to the huge turquoise swimming pool in the garden beyond. She had already taken a quick look at the intricately carved ceiling of the pagoda covering it, which Robyn had told her had come from an Asian temple. It struck her, not for the first time, that the original homestead with its wonderful high-hipped roof and deep overhangs was far more appropriate to the climate and its extraordinary setting than the palatial new building, which would have looked great among the mansions of the very rich rising above Sydney Harbour.

"So sorry," Jessica made a quick, smiling apology. "The time simply flew."

Ruth, who ate with the family during the working day and sometimes at night—she had her own self-contained bungalow on the grounds—acknowledged that with an empathetic smile. Robyn remained silent. Her friend Erik Moore gave Jessica a smile full of interest. Very daring of him, with Robyn sitting by his side. B.B. gestured Jessica into the empty chair to his right. "Wondered what kept you," he said, as though that now she was present they could get underway.

No sign of Lavinia.

No sign of Cyrus. Big disappointment. Again her powerful attraction to him hit her like a blow.

Lavinia would be in her room listening to her favourite CDs of Tebaldi and Callas. Cyrus would be working hard around the station. Being a cattleman was a tough seven-day-a-week job. His father, having done it all in his time, presided at the lunch table.

"So what *were* you doing with yourself?" Robyn was in interrogation mode. She started to help herself to a very small portion of coconut chicken salad sprinkled with toasted sesame seeds and piled high on a large lime-green-and-white platter.

It looked good. Jessica found herself hungry.

"Taking photographs, mostly," she replied. "I've e-mailed a lot of them back to my uncle. He's taking a great interest in the project, which as you can imagine is a considerable coup for our firm."

"Why does everyone go in for designers?" Robyn's voice was laced with scorn. "*I've* never seen the need for calling them in. Obviously a lot of people lack self-confidence and taste."

"For which you qualify on at least *one* count," her stepfather commented in a level voice that sat oddly with the barbed remark.

Naturally Robyn protested. Jessica didn't blame her. "Oh, Dad, that's a bit cruel. *You* mightn't have been entirely happy with what I did a couple of years back, but most of our friends love it. *You* do, don't you, Erik?"

"Well, he would, wouldn't he?" her stepfather retorted before the embarrassed Erik could speak. B.B. inclined his handsome head in thanks as Ruth, having piled a plate with the delicious-looking salad, rose and set it before him.

Now that's service, Jessica thought. Ruth was not only the loyal devoted secretary; she was the hired help.

"Robyn and Erik are in partnership building an indigenous art gallery and adjoining boutique hotel on the coast a few miles out of Darwin city," Bannerman said, turning to Jessica. "At least Erik had the sense to call in a good architect, a very clever young Malaysian. Construction has only just started, but there's a chance for a good interior designer." He patted her hand.

For one shocking moment, Jessica thought Robyn would explode; instead, she threw down her fork, which bounced off the table and fell to the floor. "Ms. Tennant will have more than she can possibly chew trying to meet the challenge of the Big House, Dad."

Ruth, whose blush at being thanked by the great man still hadn't subsided, now sat so still and so quiet she might have been trying to make herself invisible.

"I hope you weren't thinking of doing the job yourself, Robyn," Broderick Bannerman said, again in that mild tone. "If so, I have to tell you, if Erik won't, you're not competent."

Robyn flushed but fought back gamely. "That's what *you* say, Dad."

Inside, Jessica applauded. *Good for you!* The nicest person in the world would have been adversely affected by a lifetime with the hypercritical, acid-tongued Broderick Bannerman.

"If you don't want to listen to good advice, Robyn," he replied, "Erik will have to. Remember, I have some stake in this."

Ah, the iron fist in the velvet glove. Jessica watched Erik surreptitiously rub Robyn's back to calm her. "You're being a little hard on Robyn, aren't you, B.B.?" he asked, keeping his tone respectful. Clearly it didn't pay to get on the wrong side of Broderick Bannerman.

B.B. suddenly looked bored. "Well, *you* can't risk the truth, Erik, can you? Erik is hoping to marry my stepdaughter," he turned his head to inform Jessica, who, had she been Robyn, would have run from the table, having first slapped B.B. over the head with her napkin. "It isn't particularly good news. Erik made his first wife—a very nice little thing—extremely unhappy. She could have had her revenge for that, but she didn't."

"Actually, B.B.," Erik spluttered, his affable face turning brick-red, "she finished with more than her fair share. Elizabeth deliberately tried to turn our friends against me. She wanted to protect her own reputation."

"Which was blameless." Bannerman gave his judgment. "God knows why Robyn is determined to have you. You won't make her happy, either." He broke off to examine Jessica's plate. "You're not eating?"

She contemplated the chicken dish before her. "Yes, I must start. This looks delicious." Dutifully she picked up her fork before she was force-fed.

"I've organized a vehicle for you to run around in," B.B. told her presently. "A four-wheel drive. You can take it out anytime you like. But unless you have company, I'd like you to keep in sight of the outbuildings and the airstrip. It would be very easy for someone like you, a city girl, to get lost. There's no need for you to spend all your time on the job. I want you to enjoy your stay on Mokhani."

He threw her another one of his rare charming smiles. If only the man would lighten up a little! Even the odd kindly word seemed to exhaust him. If only he'd show some loving kindness toward his son and his stepdaughter. Maybe kindness wasn't in his disposition, and his wealth no doubt had played a large part in solidifying his autocratic manner.

"Thank you… Broderick," Jessica murmured, keeping an eye on reactions around the table.

If looks could kill, she would have been dead in her chair.

"That's a bit presumptuous calling Dad by his Christian name, isn't it?" Robyn spoke emotionally, blindly ignoring Erik's hand at her elbow. Even the deeply reserved Ruth looked shocked.

Bannerman's voice was as dry as ash. "The fact is I *asked* Jessica to call me by my Christian name, Robyn. She isn't taking liberties. I don't hear my name enough. In fact, I don't hear it at all."

Everyone fell silent, embarrassed. Robyn, dark head bent, lifted her eyes just long enough for Jessica to see their glare.

How to make friends and influence people, Jessica thought.

CHAPTER SEVEN

JESSICA FOUND HERSELF working so feverishly on the layout of the Big House, as the family called it, she had little time to go exploring on her own or indeed with anyone else. B.B., too, was extremely busy, for which she was grateful. The very last thing she wanted was that he should follow her around. She couldn't help but be aware that she had captured his eye. Approaching sixty or no, the libido had definitely not been drained out of the man. Besides, he was very rich, and Jessica's experience of rich people told her they thought nothing impossible. Courting and capturing a woman young enough to be one's daughter might be viewed as a piece of cake.

The only time all of them met up was at dinner. As the weeks passed, Jessica had come to think of it as the time that really counted. She got to see Cyrus. Cyrus with his brilliant, mocking eyes resting lightly on her, his attentions friendly but in no way sexual. Yet when he was around, the very air sparkled, her perceptions intensified. It might have been champagne running in her blood. Only, with his punishing workload, she didn't get to see him half often enough. He was up and away at dawn, only returning to the homestead at dusk. His absence *should* have kept her in check, but it didn't. She felt him there even when he wasn't, which she concluded was one of the side effects of such attraction.

Erik Moore had long since returned to Darwin, inviting Jessica to look over his and Robyn's latest development whenever she came to town. Needless to say, Robyn wasn't there at the time he issued the invitation. Aunt Lavinia kept mostly to her room, out of harm's way. Probably that bit about the nursing home had frightened her. Which was cruel. Robyn continued to be unfriendly to the point of being rude. She seemed quite unable to say a single thing with grace. Jessica realized Robyn had convinced herself there was some mischief afoot that included her stepfather's designer. Not that Jessica could blame her when B.B. persisted in treating her, Jessica, with a gentleness and attention he bestowed on no other. Jessica might well be thought to be a rival for Robyn's stepfather's affections. Perhaps a mistress in the making? Whatever the thinking, Jessica was becoming more and more aware that her arrival at Mokhani had produced much the same effect as a bomb going off.

She tried not to let Robyn's manner upset her. Robyn clearly had problems. Although she was by all accounts a successful businesswoman, a mega-rich man's stepdaughter, Jessica had come to appreciate that Robyn's life wasn't easy. Accepted though she was as a Bannerman, she wasn't by *birth*. Jessica could quite understand how Robyn had struggled with that all her life, since blood was so important in this family. So much of her prickly manner could have its basis in insecurity. Odd she had never sought complete independence. Obviously money was the key. Robyn might find separation from the *money* unbearable. Money compelled people to stay when they really wanted to run.

Overnight, Mokhani had become the center of Jessica's world. She felt a powerful affinity with it. Every day she rose with the birds, awakened by the stupendous outpouring of song. A veritable opera she had come to think of as an homage to the sun. She lay in bed each morning, her arms stretched above her head, enthralled. The legions of birds lent the choir great power. She supposed the rest of the household was used to having the world's greatest orchestra in the backyard, but she found the depth and the volume of sound quite impossible to sleep through. And who would want to?

She longed for the weekends to come, for then she had her best chance of seeing more of Cyrus. Neither of them could turn their backs on that kiss. She supposed that's what kisses were for—to bring an attraction right into focus. Not all kisses left one with a feeling of falling into the unknown. Falling into *love?* Sometimes something he said or the way he looked at her built on her own yearnings. Other times, she told herself she was dreaming. Or simply she was far more impressionable than he was. She had never been so impressionable before.

One Saturday when she was well into her second month at Mokhani, Jessica lingered at the breakfast table, saying she'd like to pay Aunt Lavinia a visit afterward. B.B. had left the table only a few minutes before to take an urgent phone call, leaving Jessica and Robyn together. Not a comfortable situation when Robyn was in one of her abrasive moods.

"I wouldn't bother if I were you," Robyn told her shortly. "Livvy likes her own space." She raked her nails over some little bump on her arm, leaving a red weal. "Why the heck are you so bent on ingratiating yourself around here?" she asked, making no effort to hide her resentment. "Don't you think you're exceeding your brief?"

Jessica had been waiting for some sort of attack; still, she was taken aback. "Gosh, I'm certainly not ingratiating myself with *you,* Robyn. Can't we be friends? It would make life so much easier. I can't overlook your rudeness anymore. I know I don't deserve it."

"Well, you'll damned well have to put up with it," Robyn said, a glimmer of tears in her eyes.

Immediately, Jessica backed off. "You're upset. Please tell me why. I want to help."

Robyn didn't answer, but bit down hard on her lip.

"Do you see me as some kind of threat, Robyn?" Jessica persisted, trying to clear the air. "I'm no possible threat to you. How could you think it? I'm here to do a job, then I'll be gone. Out of your lives."

Robyn snorted. "As far as I'm concerned the job is simply a ploy.You're like every other female Cyrus or B.B. meet. They've all got getting bedded on their minds. Who knows? Getting bedded could be a first step to marriage."

For a moment, Jessica saw red. She counted to ten, tempted to bop Robyn in the nose. "Don't be so ridiculous," she said crisply. "If you believe that, you'll believe anything. No wonder our friendship is doomed. You couldn't be more wrong. In fact, you're downright insulting. I'm here in my capacity as interior designer. You must have missed it, but I've been working extremely hard."

Robyn gave a brittle laugh as she demolished a piece of a freshly baked roll in her fingers. "Look, Jessica, I'm the victim here, not you. Dad is paying you so much attention it's sad to see. I wouldn't care if you were one of his old girlfriends, his own age. But you're not. You're a bloody love goddess. Cyrus thinks so, too. Both of us are convinced you have a far bigger coup in mind than pulling off the Big House. *I* haven't seen anything you've done so far."

"Robyn, you haven't shown the slightest interest."

"Why should I? All the money Dad's paying you, I would have done it for nothing."

"I'm sorry, Robyn, but it's not as easy as you think. I have a lot of training behind me."

"Big deal!" Robyn returned rudely. "There's something wrong with this whole thing. Are you going to tell me?"

Jessica sighed. "Robyn, there's nothing *to* tell."

Robyn studied her with narrowed dark eyes. "Obviously,

you remind poor old Livvy of that dreary skeleton in the closet, Moira. That being the case, Dad must see something of her in you, too. Maybe *that's* the big fascination. Seeing you on that television show freed up a lot of stuff in Dad's head. Moira still stands for something in Dad's life. *I* rate a lot lower than her. I don't really matter to him, however hard I try. I'm not his blood, after all. I'm not a bloody Bannerman, I'm a lousy stepdaughter. I've been trying to get his attention all my life, yet you sashay in with your blond hair and your big green eyes and you get it right away. It must be a pleasure for men just to look at you. I see Cyrus taking his fill over the dinner table. Dad can't take his eyes off you, either. I've never seen that before. Ever! And I've been watching him for most of my life."

Jessica, staring with a mix of dismay and sympathy into the other woman's eyes, saw genuine fears. "Look, I'm sorry for all this and your problems with your stepfather, but you've just said, they started long before I came on the scene. Don't blame me for being blond, either, or for a chance resemblance to your stepfather's childhood governess, which could be very slight. What you're saying is wrong and damaging to me. Your fears are quite without foundation. Your stepfather is old enough to be my father. Don't you think twenty-four and sixty is a no-go?" Robyn stood up so violently she sent her chair flying. "Try twenty-four and sixty million!" she cried, curling her lip in scorn. "You're no different from any other female. Your big dream in life is to land a millionaire. The older the better! You won't have to wait that long to get the money."

Jessica pushed her plate away. "Speak for yourself, Robyn. I'm not another version of *you*. I haven't got anything against Erik, but isn't *he* middle-aged? You could well be chasing a father figure."

"Bitch!" Robyn smarted.

Jessica, too, stood up. "You're not the only one who can take cheap shots, Robyn. I'll go and see Lavinia now. Unlike you, she enjoys my company."

* * *

Jessica tapped lightly on Lavinia's door. Her little spat with Robyn had upset her. Her hands were shaking. She needed to calm down.

"Miss Lavinia?" She hoped the old lady would speak to her. She'd missed her, although Molly had assured her Lavinia was perfectly well. Her meals were being taken to her room, Molly always returning with an empty tray. A surprise, considering Lavinia looked as though she hadn't eaten in more than a half century!

No sound inside. Disappointed, Jessica was about to withdraw when she heard a scurrying on the other side. The door opened a fraction, a tiny face covered in thick white makeup peered out, then on seeing Jessica, the door opened right up.

"Moira, dear." Madame Butterfly showed her pleasure. "I was wondering when you were going to come and see me."

Jessica was so enchanted, she forgot to correct the old lady. "I've been very busy, Miss Lavinia, but I've been asking about you." She smiled, her eyes ranging all over the elaborate costume so completely different from Violetta's ball gown. No wonder Lavinia could stay in her room, never bored.

"Well, come in, come in," Lavinia invited happily, adjusting the wide red silk obi that had slipped from her waist to her nonexistent hips. Her kimono, red and white silk, was exquisite, the scarlet panels embroidered with white peonies. Lavinia, the purist, had arranged her hair in a loose puff with a thick topknot, various gold and pearl baubles holding it in place. "Shall I send for tea?" she asked. "I know exactly how to perform the tea ceremony."

Jessica would have agreed, only there wasn't time. "That would be lovely, Miss Lavinia, but perhaps some other time. I've just had breakfast."

"Of course you have." Lavinia tottered on her wooden clogs into the sitting room, and Jessica followed.

"Well, sit down." She waved Jessica to a comfortable armchair, taking one herself by falling back into it. "Tell me what you've been doing. I've been keeping to my room out of harm's way. I've found I can only take Broderick in small doses, anyway. As for Robyn! All she does is torment me. She was such an unhappy little girl. Never laughed, always glowering. She wants Mokhani, you know." The faded eyes, set in their violet sockets, were shrewd.

"But Cyrus is the heir?"

Lavinia wriggled in her chair. Jessica, familiar with such wriggles in the elderly, got up to push a little cushion behind her back. "Better?"

"Thank you, Moira, love." Lavinia patted her arm. "Everything fell apart in this house when Deborah was killed. Even then Broderick was a hard, strange man, but he had a horrible time trying to get over Deborah's death. He neglected Cyrus terribly. I used to think it was because Cyrus is so much like her. Not in looks, so much. Cyrus is a Bannerman, with his grandfather's blazing blue eyes, but his nature. Cyrus is a very fine young man. He's caring and thoughtful and everyone loves and respects him. They *fear* Broderick. Quite a different thing. Since he's become a man, Cyrus has shown his own brilliance. He could take over from his father any day. That's not just me saying that. The people who know agree Cyrus is *The Man*. That hardly makes Broderick happy. It must be a terrible thing to be jealous of your own son—jealous of his *youth*. Aging isn't easy, Moira." Lavinia shook her head dolefully. "Someone said—I just forget who—it was a whiplash in the face of the human spirit. I totally agree."

Jessica felt very disturbed by Lavinia's insistence on calling her Moira, but equally she felt powerless to do anything about it. "Why does Cyrus stay?"

Lavinia shrugged. "His father can't last forever. Broderick can dispose of all his other assets as he pleases, but Mokhani and the ancestral home belong to Cyrus. Even Broderick knows he has no right to deprive his son of that. Cyrus is standing in line to inherit just as Broderick inherited from his own father, Steven. My God, there was a man! But tormented, too, just like poor Broderick."

"I've admired his portrait in the study."

"Doesn't do him justice!" Lavinia delicately snorted. "As *you'll* know." She looked sympathetically into Jessica's eyes. "Madly in love with him, weren't you?"

"Oh, Miss Lavinia!" For an instant Jessica had a power- ful attack of vertigo. She lowered her head until the dizziness passed. She despaired she would never get the old lady to rec- ognize her for who she was, but she had to continue to try or slip into a similar kind of madness. "I'm Jessica, remember?"

But Lavinia's brain had an infinite number of interlocking caverns where the past and the present flowed together. She laughed softly. "It's all right, love. I was so worried about you, but now you're back. I'm not mad, you know. I know I make a lot of people uncomfortable, even my darling Cyrus. He doesn't like me talking about Moira."

I don't blame him, Jessica thought. She was feeling spooked herself.

Lavinia's tiny face contorted. "Any talk of Moira always has started such a *fuss!*" Her thin knotted hands began to twitch. "Do you know how many years have passed since you've been gone, child?"

"Moira's been gone over fifty years," Jessica said gently, leaning forward in her chair. "I must look like Moira. That's why you've made the mistake."

"Shh!" Lavinia said, holding a finger to her lips. She didn't look in the least grotesque with the white theatrical makeup plastered all over her face and her lips painted a bright red. The fine wrinkles on her face covered, she looked an echo of her far-off heyday when she had stolen an English aristocrat's heart. "Just between you and me, I think I know where Brod- erick hid your portrait," she whispered, as though her nephew were standing listening just outside the French doors. "Always said he destroyed it, but he tells lies. Have you ever been into the big storeroom?" she asked.

Jessica was galvanized by that piece of information. "The attic?"

Lavinia shook her head vigorously, setting her pearl-and-gold baubles dancing. "No, the big storeroom is a separate building. You must know it. It's at the rear of the kitchen complex, the old servants' quarters. It's where Robyn, bless her, emptied out all Deborah's things. Graceless creature! Shoved them in there. The nerve of her!" Hostility burned from Lavinia's eyes. "If you manage to get in there—it will have to be when Broderick is away—you can do a search. I failed, but *you* won't."

Suddenly a light went on in Jessica's head. "Have you seen another portrait of Moira lately?" she asked. "At an art auction, maybe? When you were in Sydney?"

Lavinia frowned, at first looking as if she didn't understand but then she responded indignantly, "Some bloody man bought it. Needless to say he was not a gentleman, because he wouldn't let me have it. I thought he would if I offered him a lot of money, but he wouldn't be persuaded, waffling on about how it was the image of a dear friend. Of course I didn't believe him."

Jessica was shaken. Very shaken. So it *was* a portrait of Moira. Moira who had disappeared in 1947. Moira, who had, in fact, looked very much like *her*. It was an incredible coincidence, the resemblance, but the sudden appearance of the portrait after half a century's obscurity surely wasn't. Was someone pulling strings and for what purpose? Had B.B. put it on the market? Maybe even his twin, Barbara?

"Did your niece, Barbara, go with you to the auction?" she asked.

"Skipped off without her," Lavinia said confidentially. "Ferris, their driver, took me in. Babs doesn't like sitting around auctions like I do. As it turned out it was a great blessing she didn't come. She'd have been tremendously upset to see the portrait, and I simply couldn't tell her about it."

No, but it set you off, Jessica thought, appreciating that the portrait had had a considerable effect on the old lady. "Do you know the name of the artist?" she asked.

"Of course," Lavinia's jet-black brows, painted in a high arch, rose farther toward her hairline. "Why are you asking me? It was Hughie."

"Hughie, of course." Jessica murmured, piecing the story together.

"He had a great deal of talent," Lavinia said, sunken eyes gazing into the past. "He painted that wonderful portrait of Steven that hangs in Broderick's study. But Hughie never had a chance. He was a pansy, you know, poor old Hughie. He tried to kill you, didn't he?"

Brilliant sunlight poured across the veranda, but Jessica felt so cold she might have been caught in an icy draft. "Why ever would you say that?" She had to force the words out.

"He was in love with Steven, of course," Lavinia tutted, "but unable to ever speak of it. There was something utterly shameful about being homosexual in those days. A man's reputation would be stained forever if he was suspected of being one. You would never pick him. Looked perfectly normal. But what did F. Scott Fitzgerald call it? An aberration in nature, that's it. Cecily was terribly cruel to Hughie, though they were cousins. Perfectly understandable. Steven was her husband. She worshipped him. People said it was the war, but I think it was poor old Hughie's forbidden love that made him drink. Killed himself in the end. I know I saw the body. I believe he intended to hurt you, Moira. He couldn't stand the fact Steven loved you. It laid him waste."

By the time her chat with Lavinia was over Jessica's brain felt fried. She crammed a sun hat on her head, shoved on dark sunglasses, then took a brisk walk around the homestead and the extensive gardens. It might calm her, though she'd gotten into the habit of taking a walk every morning after breakfast. Moving about the main compound also gave her a better feel for what she was doing. The landscaper would have to be contacted again. His work on the complex of gardens had been completed before the Big House had gone up. Now a new layout would be required to complement the classical lines of the house. She had in mind a broad expanse of fine gravel the length of the portico bordered by white marble, with perhaps a few of the wonderful upright plants, such as miniature date palms, planted into the gravel. For comparison, perhaps some rounded cushion plants. The contrast would work well.

She had no idea when she would get the opportunity to check out the old servants' quarters. She'd circled the building many times with only a passing thought as to what it was used for. Now that she *knew,* she had a mission. To find another one of Moira's portraits. What she had learned about Hughie had shocked her. Not that he was homosexual, scarcely that, but that Lavinia had thought he had wanted to kill her. For God's sake, kill *Moira,* she berated herself. Lavinia's habit of calling her Moira was really getting to her, the way a role, if taken very seriously, got to an actor.

When she returned to the homestead some forty minutes later, she found Ruth, who didn't appear at weekend meals, bustling about in the great hall. Several pieces of very expensive luggage were stacked at the foot of the staircase.

"Oh, Jessica!" Ruth's furrowed brow cleared. "B.B. asked me to find you. He's been called away unexpectedly.We're off to Hong Kong until at least the end of next week. A development B.B.'s involved in. I'm going with him. I'll be needed."

"Is there anything I can do to help?" Jessica asked. "You look a little flustered."

"I am," Ruth freely admitted. "I've often had to pick up and go at a minute's notice, but I didn't foresee this. How do I look?"

"You look fine."

"Sure?" Ruth's insecurities were deep.

Jessica smiled. "You always do." Jessica guessed Ruth was a

very efficient woman to remain in B.B.'s employ, yet she seemed so vulnerable otherwise.

A little distance off, they heard B.B.'s voice, raised in anger. Did the man ever relax? He was a prime candidate for a heart attack or a stroke. "No, Robyn. I won't let you come with me. I want you here."

Robyn's voice, wonder of wonders, sounded young and beseeching. "But why, Dad? I want to do some shopping. You've taken me at other times."

"You'll be company for Jessica," B.B. snapped. "I don't want her here on her own."

"Cyrus is here," Robyn protested. "So's Liv. And Molly. She's not alone. *Pl...ee...ze,* Dad," she implored.

"I don't want to talk about this!" B.B. strode into the entrance hall, a little startled to see Jessica standing there. "Ah, Jessica!" He recovered quickly. "Ruth's told you the news."

"Yes, she has." Jessica spoke with respectful regret, though in reality she was thrilled the household would be out from under for a few days. "I hope everything goes well for you. I'm quite okay. I have so much work to do I'll be kept very busy until your return. I couldn't help overhearing you were concerned I might feel lonely. Thank you for that, but there won't be enough hours in the day for all I've got to get through. I'm not surprised Robyn wants to do some shopping. Hong Kong is a wonderful place to do it."

For the first time since they'd met, Robyn shot Jessica a friendly look. "See, Dad? I won't take a minute to get ready." She was, in fact, already prepared, hoping for the ride but never sure of her stepfather and his unpredictable moods.

At that moment, Cyrus strode through the front door, his tall, lean body outlined against the brilliant sunshine. "Got your message, Dad," he said. "I thought I'd come in and drive you down to the airstrip."

"Very thoughtful of you, Cyrus," B.B. answered in his habitually sardonic tone.

"Think nothing of it." Now it was Cyrus's turn to be sarcastic, though initially he had spoken as a devoted son should. What deep rifts lay between father and son resided within Broderick Bannerman's complex personality, Jessica thought.

"Well, Dad, what's the decision?" Robyn asked eagerly, only to be admonished by an emphatic, "No!"

A lot of friendships must have crumbled around Broderick Bannerman. Jessica felt Robyn's disappointment. Who knew? Robyn might have become a pleasant person had B.B. been a different kind of stepfather.

"No, what?" Cyrus asked, looking from one to the other.

Robyn turned to him, desperate to enlist support. "I'm trying to cadge a ride on the jet. It's ages since I've done any real shopping. I love Hong Kong."

"So?" Cyrus shrugged. "What's the problem?

There's plenty of room."

"The problem *is,* Cyrus," Bannerman said testily, "I've told Robyn I don't want her along."

"So much for optimism!" Cyrus gave a lopsided smile. "That's a bit mean, isn't it? It's not as though she's going to bother you." He was watching his father closely, long used to picking up on hidden motivations. "We'll look after Jessica if that's what you're worried about."

It was Jessica's chance to step in. She caught Cyrus's eye. "I've already told… Broderick—" just the slightest hesitation "—I have a big job to grapple with. I don't need looking after."

"That's wonderful news," Cyrus said suavely. "Your work is your pleasure. So, Dad, can Robyn go?"

Any other father, no matter how grumpy—including even Jessica's father, not the easiest man in the world—would have said, after a beat or two, "Oh, very well!" But Broderick Bannerman was in many ways the father from hell.

Robyn on the other hand, pleasantly stunned by so much support rushed toward him to peck his cheek. She wasn't going to give him the chance to refuse. "Thanks, Dad. I'm all packed."

For a moment B.B. looked as though he would explode, but Cyrus laughed. "There's something you can do for me, Robyn, if you would. Drop in on my tailor and get me a stack of shirts. You know, smart, casual kind of thing. They know what I like by now. I'll attend to the bill at this end."

"No problem," Robyn said quite cheerfully for her, and danced off.

It was a wonder she didn't blow him a kiss, Jessica thought sardonically.

When Cyrus returned to the house thirty minutes later having seen his father off, he found Jessica, Lavinia and Molly sitting out on the rear terrace enjoying morning tea.

"When the cat's away the mice will play," he observed dryly.

"Want some tea, darling?" Lavinia asked in a wonderfully jovial mood. She had changed out of her Madame Butterfly costume into her monk's habit. Traces of white paint lingered around her ears.

"Why not?" Cyrus pulled out a chair and sat down beside Jessica. "And how's our lady interior designer?" he inquired, looking into her eyes.

He seemed to have a hundred different expressions when he looked at her, each more heart-stopping than the last. She commanded her pulses to stop racing. "Fine," she smiled. She had expressions, too.

"I'll make fresh tea," Molly said, jumping up.

"Goody." Lavinia clapped her hands. "You can bring back some more of those lovely cookies. Cyrus will enjoy them."

"Will do." Molly smiled, as happy as a kid let out of school.

"You're not thinking of working today, are you?" Cyrus asked Jessica.

Excitement soared. Hadn't she wanted and waited for this? "I should."

"Nonsense!" Lavinia broke in. "What is the weekend for if not to relax? Broderick's gone." She grinned. "Why else would I be sitting here? Robyn's gone with him. Something I was count-ing on, so there's just you two. And me, of course. And Molly. But we old girls don't count. Show her around the place, Cyrus. There's so much that's new for her to enjoy."

Me or Moira? Jessica thought, but dared not ask. "Do you ride?" Cyrus asked, looking a shade doubtful.

"In a fashion," Jessica answered, resting back in her rattan armchair. If she levered herself forward a little, she could brush his throat with her lips. She knew how warm his skin was. She knew the touch of his mouth. It seemed an awfully long time since he had kissed her and in doing so changed her life.

"Perhaps we should take the Jeep then," he said, continuing his own exploration. "I was planning a fairly long trip, and if you're not a seasoned rider you'd finish up very sore and sorry."

"No, we'll go riding tomorrow," she said blithely, rather en-joying keeping him in the dark. She was, in fact, an excellent rider, but it was plain he had branded her a city slicker.

"Don't go near the escarpment," Lavinia suddenly moaned.

"Now, now, Livvy." A flicker of irritation was in Cyrus's eyes.

"When I go there I always hear her cries."

"It's the waterfall," Cyrus clipped off in a way meant to shut Lavinia up. "I've told you that."

But Lavinia thought she had something important to say.

"Never!" She shook her snow-white head. "It could never be the cry of falling water. It's a woman. The sound haunts me, it's so piercing."

"Oh, for God's sake! If you're going to start, Livvy, I'll have to bolt."

"No, no, sit there." She reached out to detain him. "Have your cup of tea. You understand, don't you, Moira?"

"Miss Lavinia, please let it go," Jessica urged gently, and caught the old lady's trembling hand. "It's all in the past."

If only it would stay there.

CHAPTER EIGHT

IT WAS UNLIKE any other day trip Jessica had ever taken, one filled with tumultuous fun and excitement. It seemed a marvelous thing to have Cy's company, and she wondered if her happiness showed. The breadth and grandeur of the landscape was enthralling. The sky above them was a bewitching peacock-blue, the arid earth supporting little vegetation but the ubiquitous spinifex, colored a bright rust-red, which made a brilliant contrast with the sky. The heat haze ran before them in shimmering parallel lines of silver-blue, suggesting far-off lagoons. She could readily understand how the early explorers had been fooled into thinking the mirage was real.

The vibrancy of the colors—the burning reds, the bright yellows, the dark greens and all shades of the color purple—had been captured wonderfully by the great Aboriginal artist Albert Namatjira. To Jessica's artistic eye, too, they were an extravagance of inspiration. This was *her* country, too. She felt a great urge to paint it with the substances she loved: indigo, cobalt-blue, vermilion, lapis lazuli, cadmium, gold. An artist could create any color by blending the three primaries, red, yellow and blue. The whole world *was* color when touched by the miracle of light. She felt saturated in it.

They stopped many times so she could get a closer view of a particular natural feature. Once, they stopped to watch the antics of a joey only a few days out of the pouch, bounding about ecstatically on its supercharged pogo sticks of legs while its mother kept a gentle eye on it. It was like a frolicking lamb, only on a far more dynamic scale.

"Kangaroos have to breed when they can," Cyrus told her, leaning indolently against the Jeep, yet managing to convey hair-trigger alert. "They can't depend on water in the Dry. That mother has the little fella, another in the pouch and probably an embryo, as well."

"Have you ever seen such joy!" Jessica, charmed by the joey's antics, laughed aloud. Easy to see how kangaroos had evolved in a land where they had plenty of room for their fantastic bounding!

"At certain speeds, kangaroos are far more efficient than horses," Cyrus told her. "There are so many of them they're a damned nuisance, but so much part of the landscape you have to love them. They can go without water for a while, but they don't stray too far from it. There are billabongs nearby. And all those standing 'monuments' you see around us are termite mounds."

"They're extraordinary." Jessica looked out over the vast terrain where termite mounds sprang up like ancient buildings. Wide at the base, very narrow at the tip, many of them were nearly twenty feet tall. "Can we take a closer look?"

"Of course. We might even catch a piece of action."

Jessica soon found out what he meant. Fierce little lizards with forked tongues were trying on burrow their way out of one mound, almost twice Cyrus's height.

"Oh, goodness!" Jessica jumped back as several foot-long monsters clawed their way to the surface of the termite walls and clambered eagerly down their length.

"Won't take them long to reach six feet or more," Cyrus told her, amused by her reaction. "Goannas are harmless to man though I'd steer clear of the big fellas. They grow to more than eight feet and have very powerful limbs. I wouldn't want to try outrunning one."

"So they incubate in there?" Jessica asked, moving back cautiously, expecting more to emerge.

Cyrus nodded. "All goannas lay eggs. They've been in there around nine months. The mounds are the perfect protection. By the same token they present a formidable barrier when the newly hatched babies want to get out. Those walls are rock hard."

Jessica stretched out a tentative hand. She had seen the newly hatched goannas formidable claws.

"It's June now." Cyrus raised his face to the cloudless sky. "In another five months, when the monsoon comes, probably the most powerful weather system on the planet, all this—" he waved his arm "—becomes a very different place. The Wet has a dramatic effect on the landscape. Rain falls so hard our creeks, lagoons and billabongs fill to overflowing and inundate the plains. Falling Waters, the waterfall I showed you when we flew in, becomes a mighty torrent. As the rains subside, we have a glimpse of what ancient Gondwanaland—the supercontinent—looked like. Wildflowers bloom in exotic profusion, quite different to the floral carpets of the Red Centre with their endless vistas of paper daisies. These are tropical flowers. This part of the Territory, the Top End, lies in the torrid zone. And abundance of native fruits and vegetables ripen. The land turns lush and green. You get a real feel for the prehistoric past. There's a plentiful harvest for all—humans, animals, birds. We've got more species of animals, most of them unique, than Europe and North America put together. That happened when Australia broke away from Asia. The water birds have to be seen to be believed. They arrive in their millions. It's an incredible sight. The crocs don't have to swim about in lagoons fast turning to mud or do their extraordinary overland gallop to find a pool that hasn't dried out. It's paradise while it lasts. A few months.

Then the dry southeast trade winds arrive. By July, the plains will have started to dry out and all the waterways shrink. We have a few lagoons with deep permanent water like the lagoon at the foot of Falling Waters. By October, every living thing is waiting for the return of the Wet."

"Are we going to the escarpment?" She lifted her gaze to his, feeling the familiar surge of pleasure.

"If you want. We'll drive some more, then have to go by foot." He glanced up at the table-topped mesa. It wasn't particularly high, but the flatness of the giant landscape lent it considerable impact. From this distance, it glowed amethyst. "Tell me, is all the interest because of what Livvy said?" His look was very direct. "Livvy has never been exactly *normal*. Even, I understand, when she was a young woman. She has her own way of seeing things. She gets muddled up between past and present—as you know by now."

"What's normal?" Jessica shrugged.

"I suspect one can't talk to long-dead people to qualify," he said very dryly.

"I suppose not. Has she always talked about Moira?"

He sighed as though bored to death by the whole subject. "Not until *you* arrived, which in itself is quite extraordinary, don't you think?"

"I didn't plan it, Cyrus," she said, not for the first time, aware of his suspicions. "It's quite scary to be confused with someone who disappeared off the face of the earth."

"But she *didn't.*" His tone was softly vehement. "Somewhere on this land, in some crevice, in some cave, lie Moira's bones. The number of deaths in the Outback by misadventure is quite frightening. Moira wasn't a good rider or an experienced one. She had, in fact, learned on the station. The horse came home as horses do eventually. Moira didn't." His face hardened. "I find this whole business of Moira, tragic as it is, phenomenally upsetting. For a while, my entire family was under suspicion, despite the proud Bannerman name. My grandfather was a war hero. He flew Spitfires in the Battle of Britain and reached the rank of squadron leader. He was decorated. How would you like it if your grandparents were thought capable of murder?"

"They say we're all capable of murder, given over-whelming circumstances," Jessica said bleakly.

He flinched. "Let's start again. My grandparents were fine people. Highly respected all over the Outback. Everyone was fond of Moira. She loved being on Mokhani. According to Lavinia, a thousand times she said she didn't want to go home."

"Who exactly was Hughie?" Jessica asked abruptly. "What relation?"

"Look—" His brilliant blue eyes flashed.

"Cyrus." She grasped his arm. "I don't want to upset you, but this whole business, the Mokhani Mystery, has never been laid to rest. It haunts Lavinia. It haunts your father. It haunts *you,* fifty years later. There must be something more to it than the tragedy of someone becoming lost in the bush and perishing. I know it's happened many, many times over the years, but with Moira there appear to be so many suspicions. That's why journalists can't leave it alone. Now by some truly bizarre twist of fate, I'm involved in it."

"I don't disagree with that," he said somberly.

"Simply because by some freak of nature I look extraordinarily like her," Jessica went on to say.

His brow furrowed in puzzlement. "But how would you actually *know* that? You can't rely too much on what Livvy says."

"I'm not," Jessica answered quietly, turning her head away. It was about time she told him about the portrait Tim had uncovered, no doubt increasing his lack of trust. "You still haven't told me who Hughie was."

The question did nothing to ease his somber expression. "He was Hugh Balfour, my grandmother Cecily's cousin. Livvy told you about him?"

H.B., of course. "She told me Hugh liked to paint Moira."

"Maybe he did," he answered curtly, "but I've never seen anything he did outside the portrait of my grandfather."

"You're certain?"

"Of course I'm certain." Cy's temper flared. "Finding a portrait of Moira would be a major discovery."

"One has been found," Jessica said, watching him snap to full attention. "It was bought at a Sydney auction by my uncle's partner simply because it reminded him of me."

Cyrus's strong hands grasped her shoulders. "What the devil are you talking about? I think you'd better level with me."

"I'm trying to, if you let me. Tim attended a Christie's art auction a short time back. So did Lavinia, apparently without your aunt Barbara's knowledge. Tim's interest was captured by the uncanny likeness. Lavinia would have recognized it right off. Who knows seeing the portrait after all this time hasn't disturbed the balance of her mind? She didn't tell your aunt because she thought it would upset her greatly. According to Tim, he had a confrontation with Lavinia afterward. She offered to buy if off him, but he refused. Lord knows what she intended to do with it. Probably confront your father with it for reasons of her own. At the moment, it's hanging in the foyer of our design studio in Brisbane."

Cyrus's hands dropped away. He wheeled to calm himself. "What's the time frame here?" He turned back to face her, looking quite daunting. "When did this mysterious portrait turn up? Before or after Dad hired you?"

She reacted to the hard flare in his eyes. "It would have been put up for auction some time before your father offered me the job. Please don't take your anger out on me. I know nothing about any behindthe-scene machinations, if indeed there *are* any."

"Of course there are. You're not stupid." Stern blue eyes stared down at her.

She shrugged. "I admit it all seems very odd. My uncle and I were discussing the project the same day Tim returned from

Sydney with the portrait. At that time I had absolutely no idea who the subject was. Why should I? None of us did. It was simply a portrait given to Christie's for auction. Tim only bought it because it reminded him of me."

"And there's no connection?"

"Absolutely not!" She reacted sharply to his tone. "I wonder you ask. Lavinia hasn't laid eyes on Moira for over fifty years. It's coincidence, the whole thing. Chance rules our lives after all." So why, then, was she so perplexed and confused?

"Lavinia's brain might be a little skewed as to time, but she obviously recognized Moira. She would have known it was Hugh Balfour's work. *Who* put it on the market. Can you find out?"

"Tim tried, in fact, but got nowhere. A solicitor handled it for a client. The solicitor is not saying."

"I suppose we've all got a double," he said doubtfully.

"So they say. But the portrait gave us all a shock. It would shock you if you saw it."

"Oh, I will see it," he said grimly, beginning to walk toward the Jeep. "All right, I've had about enough of Moira for today."

Jessica was glad she was fit and took regular exercise, because they had to walk up the track, which was tough going but infinitely rewarding. To one side of them lay rugged bushland, to the other magical glimpses of the lagoon and the multicolored walls of the canyon. By the time they neared the high plateau, her hair was damp with sweat and her pink cotton shirt stuck to her back.

"You okay?" He stretched out a hand to her. The spark where their hands touched wasn't just a physical thing.

"Fine."

"You're doing well. Pretend a dingo is chasing you."

"I think I can make it under my own steam, thank you."

He looked back at her. The flush of exertion in her cheeks only served to enhance the flawlessness of her skin and the clear green of her eyes. She was a beautiful woman. He had to assume her lookalike Moira had been beautiful, too. Hadn't his grandmother Cecily been a little naive bringing a beautiful young woman into the household? The family had lived in such isolation, but paradoxically in close proximity to one another. Beauty made waves. It disturbed the very air. He reached down with fluid ease and lifted this maddening young woman up the rest of the way.

"We're here!" he announced, finding it nigh on impossible to release his hold on her. Her head had sunk against his left shoulder and she was moaning softly at the exertion.

"It better be worth it." Jessica straightened, laughing, until she saw the expression in his eyes. Was it desire?

The raucous cry of a bird broke the spell of the moment.

"I should have brought my camera." She busied herself retying the lace of her shoe, shocked at how quickly he could stir her body to arousal.

"We've got hundreds and hundreds of photographs."

"I'd love to see them."

"And so you shall. We can fit in quite a bit before Dad gets home."

Jessica let out a shaky breath. She started to move off toward the edge, feeling slightly light-headed.

"Jessica, *no!*" His voice cracked out, loud and urgent. He caught her up swiftly, pulling her back. "The lip could crumble at any time. Those rocks and boulders down there in the canyon have come from up here. Never, ever go near the edge."

"It's okay." She tried to soothe him. "I wasn't going to. It's a pretty vertiginous drop, anyway." His cry of *no!* had had the velocity of a bullet. "I just wanted a better look at the lagoon."

"Stay with me." He drew her back against his chest.

"You're the boss." She could have remained there forever. "It must be wonderful to preside over your own kingdom," she murmured, filled with a piercing exhilaration. "This is fantastic.

It's like we're on another planet. It's daunting, too, all that empty vastness without end. It would be so easy to die out there."

"Just you remember it," he said, the harshness still evident in his voice. "Don't go wandering off on your own. We've had seasoned bushmen get lost."

"So not everything's a mystery." The remains of the little governess could be anywhere out there in the wilderness. Moira could have been injured; thrown from her horse, lying helpless, vulnerable to the attack of wild animals. She had heard the dingoes howling at night. The deadliest snake in the world, the taipan, had its home here; marauding camels, wild horses, foxes, wild boar, feral cats as fierce as miniature lions. A massive search for Moira had been mounted. Jessica had read that in all of the articles she had sourced on the computer. The search had revealed nothing. Today, looking out at the ancient land spread before her as far as she could see, she didn't find that so strange.

Her eyes dropped to the deep lagoon. It looked so beautiful, the vegetation fresh and green even in the Dry. The waterfall, which apparently would become a deafening roar in the Wet, was tranquil today, spilling its crystal purity from the top of the escarpment whence it flowed to the water's edge. The lagoon was surrounded by aquatic reeds and grasses of a lush emerald green. The glittering water floated its cargo of magnificent pink water lilies holding their heads high above huge pads. Around the base of the escarpment grew a luxuriant tangle of exquisitely colored creepers that climbed into the stands of pandanus palms decorating their spikes. It was like looking down into an earthly paradise.

"The view from here is magnificent, but is it possible to walk the length of the canyon?" she asked him, eager to try.

He nodded. "Yes, but let's take one thing at a time. There are grottos at the base of the cliffs sculptured by the water over thousands of years. In the Wet, the high waters drown out everything down there."

"So there could be a crocodile still in residence, you're suggesting? Perhaps with a mate or two?"

"No one has sighted one," he answered, frowning at the thought. "Which doesn't mean one isn't there. Aboriginal stockmen take dips in the lagoons—those are the guys with the crocodile totem. We haven't had a fatality at Falling Waters."

One you know about, at any rate, she thought. "But elsewhere?" she asked.

"We've had a couple of stockmen taken over the years. Working dogs. Cattle. Kangaroos, of course. They never learn. This is the Territory. We have to live with the crocs. We respect them."

"No matter how great your detestation?"

"I don't detest them," he said. "I don't trust 'em either. The trick is not to stand near the edge of a river or lagoon where they're known to be. We're not that far from Kakadu National Park and the Alligator Rivers system. The person who named the East and South Alligator rivers thought the prehistoric beasts he saw lining their banks *were* alligators. Of course they were crocs. The rivers should have been named the East and South Crocodile rivers. Kakadu inspires reverence. The Aborigines worship the place. If you're lucky, we could take a trip in. It's only accessible—and then only parts of it—in the Dry. In the Wet, enormous stretches turn into waterlily-covered lagoons supporting phenomenal birdlife. A white mist hangs over the dripping canopy of the rain forest, adding to the primeval look. Waterfalls thunder. Our waterfall is a trickle compared to them. You'd swear you were back at the beginning of time."

"So why can't we pack up and go tomorrow?" She knew they couldn't, but her heart swelled at the very thought.

"Tomorrow's out, I'm afraid."

"I was only joking," she said, shaking her head. "I have a ton of work to get through."

"You've done sketches, that kind of thing?"

"Plenty," she said. "I'm getting close to what I want to achieve. I've designed quite a number of pieces that will be custom-made. The rooms are so huge, but the six guest rooms will be a piece of cake. As will the other bedrooms. I have a good idea what Broderick—"

"Did he ask you to call him that, or was it your own idea?" he cut in.

"Left to myself I'd be calling him Mr. Bannerman for the rest of my life," Jessica retorted crisply, moving away from him a little. "He asked me to call him Broderick. *Ordered* really. Arrogance runs in the family."

"You should be flattered," Cy said. "Dad's a different man around you."

"What are you implying?" Her voice rose.

"I'm not implying anything. It's a simple statement of fact. My father is a different man around you."

"Maybe you should be grateful." She shrugged. "I find calling him Broderick rather embarrassing, but I can scarcely disregard his wishes."

"Of course not," he agreed suavely.

She chose another tack. "The great hall is the biggest challenge. I have to get that right. I have a good idea what your father wants for the conference room and the telecommunications room. I'm in constant contact with my uncle Brett. Nothing will go ahead without his say-so."

"Something wrong with your judgment?" he inquired.

"Not at all. But this is an important project. I work for my uncle, as well as your father. Uncle Brett taught me all I know. Eventually, we'll need a team of people up here, as I've told you. Before that happens, I have to work it all out in my head and on paper. That includes color schemes. I work from the floor up."

"Isn't that a lot to deal with for a relatively inexperienced twenty-four-year-old?"

She knew he was baiting her. "It is. But someone's got to do it. It may seem like heresy, but I prefer the original homestead. Please don't tell your father that."

"Not unless I want to stop your winning streak," he told

her with a mocking glance. "I prefer the old homestead, too, as I've said. It looked a million times better before Robyn was let loose on it. Notice the minimalism on the walls? She solved the problem by shoving the paintings my mother had put there away. The Oriental screens and rugs were next. All the touches of Southeast Asia my mother loved and so suited the house. The porcelains and big fishbowls on carved stands. The fishbowls used to be filled with orchids. They stood on either side of the staircase. Robyn removed every vestige of my mother from the house. And my father let her."

"Perhaps he found it too painful," Jessica suggested, hearing the bitterness in his tone. "Didn't you make your feelings known?"

He grimaced. "I did, but it made no difference. I'm biding my time. I could at some time in the future have the mausoleum razed to the ground."

"Oh, don't do that," she advised. "It will have its uses. If not as a residence, than as a conference and business centre. I'm assuming you will take over your father's extensive business interests?"

"You're assuming a lot." He spoke very dryly. "My father is an extremely unpredictable man, a strange man in anyone's judgment. He's become increasingly hard and aloof as he's grown older. You've brought with you a troubling sea change. For all I know he could be planning to start another family. Sire a new heir. He could have met a woman he'd risk his soul to possess. I know he'd like to be young again. He makes no bones about it. He wants to be my age again, wants his life all over again. Dad won't ever be content with his allotted portion. He wants life everlasting. Maybe he thinks a young woman would bring it to him."

She couldn't control a shiver. "That's quite Faustian. I hope to goodness you're not looking at *me* for the job?" Jessica felt the shock break over her.

He stared into her eyes. "A lot of women, young, good-look-

ing women, would fight to the death to marry Dad. Money is
the perfect aphrodisiac, didn't you know?"

"Not for *me* it isn't." Jessica said emphatically.

"Really? That's heartening to know. So tell me, what is it
you want, Jessica? *Love?*" His blue eyes were melting not only
her limbs but her brain.

"Don't you?" she parried. "I thought love is what we all
want. And *need.* Why is it every time you mention your mother
I can hear the grief? Your father suffered from the loss, too.
He'd made a powerful emotional connection with your mother,
Deborah, then she was cruelly taken away from him. A man
could become very bitter from that experience. Your father is
a very rich man, but no one could describe him as at peace,
much less happy."

"God, no. His life has been difficult. There's no denying
that. The tragedy in his childhood—the invasion of privacy the
family suffered—was the start of his misery. He never got over
his governess's disappearance. His twin, Aunt Barbara, was
adversely affected, as well. Both of them were almost twelve
before they were ready to be sent away to boarding school. My
grandmother taught them herself. I went to boarding school
at ten. Even then the Mokhani Mystery was still alive. I guess
we'll never be free of it."

Her answer came out unconsidered and of its own accord.
"Maybe that's about to change."

"Why do you say that?" He turned on her.

"Just a feeling I have."

"You're psychic, then? That explains it?"

Tense moments ticked over. "Don't you sense that, too?" she
responded to the challenge.

His expression was dark and brooding. "All I know is, when
the past intrudes on the present, there can be unwanted consequences."

CHAPTER NINE

JESSICA REMINDED HERSELF she had to work even on Sunday.
She would have to have something fairly impressive to show
Broderick Bannerman when he returned, so she sat at her desk
working away, though with perhaps not her usual serene effi-
ciency. Her emotions were in a kind of turmoil. So many things
were happening that her life had taken on new dimensions, some
thrilling, some ominous and strange. Added to that, she had discovered within herself a certain recklessness and a taste for danger. Infatuation, falling in love, was an extreme state, after all.

Violent delights could have violent ends.

Hadn't Shakespeare said it all? She was in daily communication with Brett, speaking to him each morning on the phone,
then sending him reams of sketches and information by e-mail.
When she was ready, she would make watercolor renderings
of her proposals. She needed to take that trip into Darwin to
stock up on her art supplies. She supposed she could make the
two-hour journey on her own in the four-wheel drive B.B. had
put at her disposal. There were bound to be plenty of readable
signs, preferably the ones not featuring a skull and crossbones.
There was something very daunting about a dead straight road

that ran through endless uninhabited miles of shifting red sand blanketed with spinifex.

Over dinner, Cyrus relaxed, his heart-melting smile much in evidence as he and Lavinia recounted stories from the family's past—mercifully without the complications of the family ghost. Molly, the housekeeper, joined in, displaying her own puckish sense of humor. Cyrus and Lavinia treated Molly as one of the family; B.B. and Robyn treated her like a programmed robot. There was no question of Molly's sitting down to join them either for a cup of coffee or a meal when Broderick Bannerman was in residence. Servants had their place as far as B.B. was concerned.

Afterward, Lavinia, in high spirits, brought some of her favourite CDs downstairs for the occasion, comparing this soprano against that, turning up the volume so high the station staff in their bungalows and dormitories probably had to shout at one another to be heard. Cyrus indulged her, with only a mild "Turn it down a bit, Livvy," as criticism, but soon Lavinia was up and away, reminiscing about her career.

"I do believe I could have been as great as Sutherland," she told them, not for the first time. "Marvelous voice, marvelous technique, but oh, there was something about poor tragic Callas I adored. The *passion* in her voice! I miss that. No one else has it. I can't hear her without the tears coming to my eyes."

Occasionally, she astonished Jessica, but not the others, who had probably heard these performances many times before, by belting out a top note along with the diva on the CD. Of course Lavinia's voice was being supported by the voice singing with her, but Jessica realized she was hearing however briefly, little patches of what once had been a brilliant coloratura soprano. Molly, having produced another one of her delicious meals, poured more wine. Both ladies sat sipping contentedly while Cyrus and Jessica excused themselves for a short stroll before turning in.

That, too, proved intoxicating, though Cyrus made no move

that could have been construed as romantic. Nevertheless, an exquisite tension vibrated between them as if neither knew where or when or even how the tension would manifest itself in action. Jessica looked and listened as he pointed out the stars in the night sky and their spiritual significance to the Aboriginal tribes of the Top End. That in itself provided an element of the romance she was starting to crave. In Aboriginal life over countless thousands of years, when the people slept out beneath the stars, the moon and the stars had assumed great significance.

"They know every star in the sky," Cyrus said, his tone full of appreciation. "There's a legend to explain every origin. Such beautiful myths and legends, too. No matter how many times you hear them, you don't mind hearing them again. I used to find them enthralling when I was a kid around the campfire listening to a stockman—who also happened to be a tribal elder—telling them so soulfully. Aboriginal gods and goddesses are all too human. The sun is a woman—a beautiful woman who spreads light and warmth. The moon is a man. All the stars and planets were at the time of creation, men, women and animals. They flew up to the sky when times were bad on earth. The sky was their refuge. The Gagudju people of Arnhem Land believe a shooting star is a spirit canoe transporting a soul to its new home."

"You were blessed with a childhood out here," she said.

He nodded. "I don't know what I would do if it were taken away. Mokhani is my life."

She could hear the love and pride in his voice. She thought, as she did so often these days, how difficult it must have been for him growing up without the love and support of his mother, especially given his father's unyielding nature. He must have been wounded over and over in the past. Probably continued to be to this day, though he had grown an extra skin. B.B. seemed to be hell-bent on having control chosen the wrong man to try to dominate.

"Home is where the heart and the soul find their most comfortable place," she murmured into the starry night. "I've never seen such a glorious night sky." Her eyes were on the blue-white scintillating broad river of diamonds across the sky. The Milky Way. It shone with great brilliance and luminosity in the pure air of the Outback.

"No pollution," Cyrus explained. "No buildings, no glass and concrete towers, just the timeless land. There's the Southern Cross sparkling over us. It couldn't be clearer. The star furthermost to the south is a star of the first magnitude. It's said the ancient Greeks and Babylonians were able to see it. They thought it was part of the constellation Centaurus, so that's how much the Crux has shifted. The night sky in the Red Center is purported to be the most beautiful sky on earth. There again, it's rarified desert air and our isolation. We might be able to fit in a trip there."

"That would be wonderful." Jessica felt like a plant fast unfurling its fronds. But like tender new fronds exposed to sizzling heat, she could get burned. She had divined that the moment she'd laid eyes on Cyrus Bannerman at Darwin airport.

To everyone's delight, Cyrus returned to the homestead for lunch. Something he rarely did when his father was there, which was perfectly understandable considering the two men were often at loggerheads.

"Darling boy, how lovely it is to have your company." Lavinia sat up straight in her planter's chair. She and Jessica had been sitting companionably on the front veranda enjoying the brilliant display of strelitzias in the garden. Now Lavinia jumped up, surprisingly spry in the legs when her once-elegant hands were knotted with arthritis. "I'll tell Molly you're here. She'll be so pleased. Broderick could stay away forever, as far as we're concerned."

"Don't go to any trouble," Cyrus called after her, pitching his Akubra into a chair. "Coffee and a sandwich will do.

"So, making progress?" he asked, pulling out a chair and

settling into it "You'll have to have lots to show Dad." A lock of crow-black hair fell over his forehead and he put up a hand, raking it back. Jessica let her eyes rest on him. He was wearing his usual working gear, an open-necked pale blue bush shirt, jeans, dusty high boots, a red bandanna knotted carelessly around his throat.

He looked marvelous, so intensely vital he took her breath away. How could any woman ignore a man like that? It took a moment or two for her to answer. "You'll be pleased to hear I've been at my drawing board all morning. Mostly sketching designs for the custom-made furniture I told you about. Regardless of size and scale, the pieces must represent intimacy. It's a private residence, after all. I want to stick to the classical idiom, but obviously with a twenty-first century twist. The furnishings need to be elegant, functional, with pure, clean lines, if you know what I mean. The architecture speaks for itself."

"You're able to do that?" He looked at her as if she might have bitten off more than she could chew.

"Sure. My goal is to push myself to the limits. I have talent. I'd like to do more furniture designing down the track. My uncle Brett has won awards for furniture design. He's been my mentor."

"I'd like to meet him," Cyrus said. "He sounds a very talented guy, and obviously you love him."

"I'm sure it could be arranged. He's gay," she tacked on casually.

He cocked an eyebrow. "So? I'm not looking for a relationship."

"Just thought I'd mention it. Uncle Brett is a very clever, multitalented man. He trained as an architect, which has been an enormous help with his work."

"Tell me, do you see something embarrassing about his being gay?"

"Not at all!" She shook her head "I wanted to see your reaction, cattlemen being such macho types. I love my uncle dearly. He's been very good to me, but he's suffered in his way."

"I daresay," he answered, letting the *macho* bit go. "One can't afford to be different. But tell me about *yourself,* Jessica. I'm all ears."

She found that electrifying. "What do you want to know?"

"Everything. Go on. Give it to me. I know you're beautiful and gifted. You certainly don't lack confidence. You think you can conquer the world. I like that. I've got big plans of my own. Tell me about when you were a little girl. I bet you were adored, with your big green eyes and your blond curls."

She looked out over the garden before replying. "It wasn't quite like that," she said wryly, by now used to the way life really was. "I'm an only child. My father is a high-profile lawyer, senior partner in a firm started by my great grandfather. I think he felt betrayed when my mother couldn't give him a son. Mum always says so, anyway. There was just curlyheaded me. To make it worse, I don't look at all like him or that side of the family. I was a good student, at least, so he expected me to follow him into law. Show some ambition. Instead, I opted for a fine-arts degree, which I gained with honors. But it wasn't a degree my father thought much of. He's made no bones about the fact that as far as he's concerned I've let the family down. Especially as I went to work for Uncle Brett. The *different* factor came into play there. Dad is a great one for civil liberties and the rights of minority groups, but he's actually ultraconservative at heart. Needless to say, Brett and my father don't get on. In fact, they avoid one another, which makes it hard. Practicing law in my family is considered by all to be far more important than practicing art of any kind."

"Poor Jessica." He reached out, his palm briefly cupping her cheek. It was a gesture so unexpected, so *tender*, it nearly washed away her hidden tears. "I didn't expect to hear that. You certainly *look* very loved."

"Well, I am." She didn't fully understand why she had told

him so much, but he affected her on all levels. "Don't get me wrong. Maybe it's just not in the way I'd choose. I was very close to my maternal grandmother, Brett's mother. Closer even than to my own mother, who likes her own space. Nan was my haven when my teenage world went mad. Sadly, she died some years back, but her memory will always remain with me. A lot of the time I feel she's looking out for me. Brett and I have the same coloring, the same family face. Both of us take after Nan."

"She didn't, by any chance, have a Moira in the family?" Cy's voice had a sardonic edge.

"Good grief, no." Jessica shook her head. "Don't you think Moira would have been mentioned in passing? Especially given what happened to her? Had Moira lived she would have been a couple of years older than my nan. Someone like that would have haunted my family as much as she's haunted yours. Left alone to die—"

"We don't know *what* happened to her," he cut in, his voice hardening slightly. "I'd very much like to see that portrait of yours."

"That can be arranged. I'll ask Tim to e-mail a photograph first. Tim is Uncle Brett's partner in life and business. Once you see it, it'll be your turn to be astonished. Did you ever find out what Moira's parents had to say after she disappeared?"

He sighed deeply. "Jessica, I missed all that, not having been born. Moira belongs to another time, another world. I just wish she'd stay there. My *father* was only a child."

"But you must have heard *something* over the years," she persisted. "I mean, they couldn't just paper her over or abandon her to a deep watery realm. Moira is part of your family's history."

"I assure you there's no need to constantly remind me. All I know is her parents journeyed up here to see for themselves. I believe they were an older couple. Moira was a child of their middle years. Naturally they were filled with grief but compelled to accept, as everyone else did, that Moira had died by misadventure. Either she'd become lost in the bush, fallen from the escarpment or even drowned. Despite an intensive search, she was never found. Have you spoken to Livvy about any of this?"

"Not for now. She knows about the existence of the portrait, of course. She told me about her confrontation with Tim. She claimed he wasn't a gentleman because he didn't give it to her. I didn't tell her of my connection to Tim. Neither did I tell her I'd actually seen the portrait. She thinks there should be others, or at least one, here at Mokhani."

He groaned. "Well she would. Livvy is a creature of the theatre. She loves dramas. My father denies it."

"I recall you said he tells lies."

"Jessica, please."

She searched his face for a moment. Blazing blue eyes. Enigmatic. Maybe a little hostile.

"That's no answer." She knew he didn't trust his father. For that matter, neither did she.

"Perhaps you should ask Dad yourself," he suggested dryly. "Where exactly do you stand with my father?"

Hot color bloomed in her cheeks. She swiped her long beautiful hair over her shoulder. "I scarcely know him—he isn't an easy man to know. As for me, what you see is what you get. Why can't you accept that?"

"Too many coincidences along the way. What do you suppose was my father's first thought when he saw you on that television program? Hey, this is a young designer who could bring off decorating my mausoleum? What could be more B.B. than going with his instincts? They're so sharp they're feral. Or did the image of his former governess block out every other consideration? He may have been a child at the time of her disappearance, but that image has been kept alive. Something has to be feeding it. It's like a fairy tale by the Brothers Grimm. Maybe Hugh's paintings of her were hidden away, but given my father's temperament and his excessive persistence, he would have gone hunting for them. He's the best hunter in the world.

Maybe it was *he* who put the painting you've got on the market? It would have been too beautiful to destroy. Maybe it was a member of Hugh's family. Who the hell knows? Maybe one day Dad stumbled upon the hiding place'Nice to see you again, Moira!'"

"A bit melodramatic don't you think?" Though she didn't disagree with any of it.

"Hell, Jessica, we're all experts on melodrama with Dad and Lavinia playing the leads." He leaned toward her, unconsciously emanating tremendous male allure. "We could go on a treasure hunt together."

"We should." She was quick to agree.

Lavinia chose that very moment to stomp back onto the veranda in her monk's habit worn with gym boots. Jessica found herself wondering when Lavinia would come down to breakfast in a pink tutu. "What are you two whispering about?" she stared at them with deep satisfaction.

"I've asked Jessica to marry me," Cyrus said calmly.

"When?" Lavinia asked delightedly, turning her head to peer at Jessica, who was past being surprised by anything, however outlandish, that was said.

But shouldn't that *when* been an astonished *What!* or a *Wow!* "I've had to tell him no," Jessica said. "I won't be crowded by proposals. I'm not ready to tie the knot for years yet."

Lavinia hurried over to touch her shoulder. "But darling girl, you have to get on with your life," she protested. "You've wasted so much time already."

Jessica caught Cyrus's searing glance. "You went too far with that one," she muttered.

"You're worried I wasn't serious?"

"To be serious a man has to get on his knees."

Lavinia beamed at him. "*Do* it, Cy! Don't let her get away again."

When he moved, Jessica jumped up, placing her chair in front of her as a barrier. "This has gone far enough, thank you, Cyrus. We're joking, Miss Lavinia. Just fooling around."

Lavinia made a little birdlike cry of pain, tears welling up in her eyes. "But you're *perfect* for each other! You don't doubt that, do you, dear?"

"Miss Lavinia, I'm Jessica. Moira hasn't come back again."

Lavinia's chin wobbled. "No, of course not."

"You understand that, Livvy," Cyrus said, drawing a great sigh of relief for that chink of sanity. He regretted the fact, however, they had upset her.

"Yes, I do, darling. It's just that…" She turned and stared beseechingly at Jessica. "You *are* Moira, though, aren't you?" she whispered as though Cyrus couldn't hear.

"I'm planning to take you out riding this afternoon, Jessica," Cy intervened in an endeavor to head Lavinia off. "We should be able to find you a nice quiet horse."

"Thank you, thank you," she said sweetly sardonic. "I'm so grateful. This is the happiest day of my life."

"Yes, indeed. It's not every day a girl gets a marriage proposal," Lavinia said, yanking on her saffron robe. "Just wait until Broderick hears about it.

He won't be pleased. He wants you for himself." She cackled as though she'd said something very funny.

"The most useful thing about growing old is you can get away with saying anything," Cyrus observed, his tone a little harsh. "Although in all fairness I have to say there's been something to Livvy's revelations in the past."

"Oh, stop. Livvy's revelations are way off this time," Jessica said tartly.

"Just teasing, Jessica," he said. "I really don't fancy you as a stepmother."

"Which part of *stop* don't you understand?"

"I told you I jest. Though deep down—"

Jessica couldn't restrain herself any longer. She picked up a plush cushion and began belting him with it.

Molly, eyes bright with pleasure, came out on to the veranda at a brisk trot. "You're a one, Jessica, so you are!"

"So she is!" Cyrus put his hand very gently around Jessica's wrist and took the cushion from her, throwing it back on the chair. "I'm not used to women who play rough."

"That's hard to believe," Jessica said, "when you're the most infuriating person I've ever met."

"Now, now, my darlings!" Lavinia intervened. "It's only an excuse to kiss and make up. You were doing great, Moira. I think you scared him."

"So there it is!" he declared. "You've become one of Lavinia's incurable hallucinations."

"If you're hungry, and I hope you are, I've set up lunch on the rear terrace," Molly intervened, her cheeks flushed with pleasure.

"Oh, goody, hurray! If only there were more Mollys in this world." Lavinia executed a little pirouette, holding her arms aloft for balance. "If it weren't for you, Molly, we'd all starve."

It wasn't until later in the afternoon when the heat was less oppressive and the fiery exposure to the sun lessened that Jessica made her way down to the stables, where Cyrus had arranged to meet her. He was running a little late, so she had the Aboriginal stable boy, Seth, saddle up a lively looking filly called Chloe. Jessica had taken to the filly, one of obvious good blood, on sight. Chloe in turn appeared to like the smell, voice and touch of Jessica. They made friends over a couple of oatmeal cookies.

"That's pretty damn good." Seth grinned his approval. "Most people have to watch themselves around that one. Chances are she might throw ya."

"I don't think so, Seth." Jessica continued to stroke the filly's sleek neck, making soothing clicking sounds at the same time. Chloe was jet-black, wellgroomed, with a white blaze on her forehead.

"She got speed and she got spirit." Seth spoke with love and pride. "A real high stepper and a natural jumper, but she ain't an easy ride." He gave her a black liquid glance. "Threw Miss Bannerman, but then, Miss Bannerman got bad habits."

"Robyn?" Jessica turned to stare at him.

"Yes, ma'am. Chloe here don't like to be pushed around. She's a beautiful sweet girl when you know how to handle her right, but when ya don't..." Seth pulled a face. "Miss Bannerman don't treat the horses right. She think she got to be in control all the time. Thing is, she don't really like horses and they don't like her. Tell you the truth, the boss won't be happy you picked Chloe. He told me to saddle up Manny. A nice sedate horse. I gotta do what I'm told."

Jessica had already met Manny, a bay gelding, as she'd entered the stables. Manny was friendly, extending his silky muzzle to be stroked. She had fed him an oatmeal biscuit before leaving him in peace. "That's okay, Seth. I'll explain to him that Chloe was my choice."

"Manny is the nicest, quietest ride we've got." Seth tried to persuade her.

"I'm not surprised." Jessica smiled. "Manny's just about due for retirement. Chloe and I are a better match. Don't worry. I know how to ride."

"Thought so, seeing how you are around 'em, but Chloe can be full of mischief. Skittish, I call it. Why she has days she gallops off in all directions."

"Don't you worry," Jessica repeated. "It won't take me long to get Chloe to trust me."

Jessica was trotting the responsive Chloe around the yard when Cyrus arrived. He stood stock still for a moment watching the proceedings. "Okay, so you can ride," he observed dryly. "Why didn't you tell me?"

"I thought I'd take the mickey out of you," she responded sweetly. "I've been riding since I was a little girl."

"I can see that." He had checked her out automatically, his

mind processing all the information that told him she was perfectly at home on a horse. In fact, she looked great, a good seat, well balanced, straight back.

She brought the filly to a halt beside him. "Your automatic assumption I would sit like a sack of potatoes piqued me."

He gave a faint smile. "Oh, well, you are a city girl."

"This city girl lived on acreage. My nan, Alex, bought me my first pony when I was six. My parents didn't really want me to have it, but I was thrilled out of my mind. My father saw to it I was well taught. I joined a good pony club."

"What a piece of luck." He turned back as Seth led out his horse—a gleaming, silver-gray Thoroughbred, clearly no workhorse, but a horse reserved for pure pleasure.

"What a beautiful animal," Jessica said with appreciation. She had an excellent eye and instinct for good horses. The gray was superb.

"Monarch," Cyrus pronounced. With a nod to Seth, he took charge of his horse. "So named because there's nothing comparable in our stables. So don't bother racing me."

"I'm not that foolish. You've got the superior horse. Monarch must be a good sixteen hands high, but then, a tall horse for a tall man. Chloe is only a filly, but I can outwit you."

"You can't. I know this land like the back of my hand." He stared up at her. She had bound her long hair into a thick plait, revealing her very pretty ears. For a moment, he thought he could taste the creamy lobes in his mouth.

"So what are we waiting for?" She didn't know it, but her face was lit with such exuberance, that feeling was transferring itself to him. "Come on," she urged. "You've stared at me long enough. Let's get going. Tallyho!" She clicked her tongue, lightly kicked the filly's flanks and the spirited animal spurted into action.

She was off and away before Cyrus had time to swing into the saddle.

What a surprise packet Jessica was turning out to be! he

thought with a mix of amusement and admiration. She even put him on his mettle. She was scooting across the back paddock in a genuine gallop, approaching the white post and rail fence where a short distance off, a glossy-flanked chesnut mare was pacing with her beautiful foal.

No! For God's sweet sake, no! His heart rose to his throat as he saw Jessica lean forward, rising in the saddle as she gave the filly the signal to jump.

"God almighty!" High spirits were one thing, but you had to have nerve and confidence galore to attempt that fence. Robyn always stooped to unlatch the gate. So did most visitors to the stables.

Jessica had both confidence and nerve. Horse and rider soared, clearing the top rail with maybe an inch to spare. That the filly showed a surprisingly clean pair of rear hooves was brought to his attention. Chloe could make a show jumper. He could hear Jessica whooping with delight. He knew the incredible feeling of exhilaration and power, but his moment of fear was legitimate and had its roots in the tragedy that had taken his mother. Yet risk appeared to be a state Jessica happily embraced. Risk, to the point of recklessness. His mother had been reckless. Her dying in a riding accident had left a deep wound that would never heal.

Suddenly he felt mad as hell. Why hadn't he insisted she wear a hard hat? Because she had let him believe she was a novice who could only travel at a sedate pace.

He took off after her, urging Monarch into a gallop before he, too, flew over the fence. At least he knew what Monarch could do and what lay on the other side.

Jessica glancing back over her shoulder, saw him pursue her at a gallop. She took in a lung full of air, almost light-headed with exhilaration. Across the plain to the left of her, a great herd of prime cattle were strung out. She needed fresh territory. This was glorious! She had proved Chloe was a natural jumper. In fact, to her very pleasant surprise, the filly was flying like she was on steroids.

"That's it! Go, girl!" Cyrus would have that much more of a job to catch them. God, she loved racing!

By the time he caught up to her, he was fairly seething with anger. He came alongside, his eyes flashing. "What are you trying to do?"

"That's easy," she called back. "Beat you." Her lustrous green eyes brimmed with life, which in his agitated state he interpreted as having no sense of danger.

"Slow down, Jessica," he thundered.

"Why?"

"If you don't, we won't continue on to the canyon."

Immediately she started pulling the filly back to a fluid bounce, muttering her resentments at the same time.

When the two horses were back to a walking pace, he said tersely, "That was pretty damned risky taking the fence."

She raised her eyebrows. "I know what I'm doing. Chloe was traveling well. She *wanted* to jump the fence. She didn't take much urging."

"If her back legs hadn't cleared it, you'd have taken a tumble."

"I've taken plenty of tumbles in my time. The trick is to get right back up. Whatever is the matter with you, Cy? Why are you so upset?" Now she noticed a definite pallor beneath his deep tan.

"While you're on Mokhani, you're my responsibility."

She was a little startled by the sternness of the rebuke. "Okay, I'm sorry if you got a fright. It was stupid not telling you how experienced I am, but you're being far too cautious."

"That's the way I am." He tried to lighten up, but found he couldn't.

"Oh, God, oh no, how insensitive of me!" Jessica flushed as she belatedly recalled the great tragedy of his childhood. "I am so sorry."

He fixed his eyes on the purple escarpment that dominated

the flat landscape. A pulse beat in his temple. "My mother was reckless. Just like you."

Jessica quietly protested. "You could have that wrong, Cyrus, though I do understand how you feel. Your mother could look after herself. So can I. Freak accidents happen. No one can prevent them. For a fatalist that means your number is up." She reached across to briefly touch his hand. "You promised me we'd ride into the canyon. I hope that wasn't a ruse because I looked like giving you a run for your money."

"You'd be still nursing the disappointment." He relented enough to smile slightly. "Okay, Jessica, we'll go explore the canyon."

CHAPTER TEN

WITHIN HALF AN HOUR, they were deep inside the canyon, parts of which had been hidden from Jessica's eyes when she'd viewed it from the escarpment. No matter how beautiful the canyon had appeared from the escarpment, it was pure magic when seen from the ground. An idyllic place lost in time. The walls glowed with such intensity, the very air was shot through with rainbows of color; all the deep terra-cottas, the russets, the rose and pink, the dark purples. What was extraordinary was the way the ubiquitous, indestructible spinifex clung to every crevice in a spray of gold. Cascades of icy cold water tumbled down the tiered rock face supplying moisture to the lush profusion of plants that grew in the shade and shelter of the towering walls. Jewellike greens, tangles of blue-flowered vines, gorgeous little native hibiscus, ferns that could be quite rare, secreted as they were in this far, far away ancient canyon that few people or animals had penetrated. It was so wonderfully unspoiled. A belt of small red-barked trees with shining green foliage lined both sides of the ocher walls, interspersed here and there with what must have been some species of wattle—glowing masses of fluffy yellow puff balls gave off the all-suffusing scent of her childhood, when the lovely Queensland wattle lit up the hills surrounding her home.

Jessica walked slowly, noticing everything. The color effects and the natural beauty of the scene touched every artistic nerve. She and Cyrus scarcely spoke, but they frequently threw smiling glances at one another, each content to be in this wild and beautiful place. Small shrubs were ablaze with a heavy crop of scarlet fruit the size of cherry tomatoes.

"A bush delicacy?" she called to Cy.

"Yes, you can eat them. They taste a bit like loquats."

Jessica popped a couple in her mouth, her taste buds coming alive. They were sweet, a little bit tart. They had a sweet, tangy smell, as well. She knew there were any number of native fruits and vegetables highly prized by the Aborigines and bushmen alike. To her sensitive nostril, everything was so clean and fresh. The sand of the canyon was a radiant white in stark contrast to the deep lagoon, with its tall humming reeds and flotillas of pink water lilies, the sort Monet would have loved to paint. The waters of the lagoon were a milky lime-green in the shallows, deepest cabochon in the center where the spirit of the Aboriginal girl lived. In such a place, if one were listening, one could almost feel her presence, perhaps even hear her voice.

Jessica wandered near the edge of the pool, wondering if long ago Moira had met her fate here. No matter how beautiful, the lagoon had treacherous depths. Here, too, some prehistoric monster could have found its way through the neck of the canyon and into the lagoon to make its home. This was the Dry. What would this place look like in the full swing of the monsoon? This glittering stretch of water, at absolute peace today would the next fill the entire canyon, pounding against the rock walls and carving out the grottos before inundating the valley beyond. The beautiful pink water lilies would be torn away, scattered for miles. Falling Waters would grow and grow, immeasurably wider, thundering down the escarpment. A striking picture began to form in her head. It would be an incredible thing to see from the air, a sight never to be forgotten. She envied Cyrus his wilderness home. There was freedom to think here, to glory in nature, to get a profound sense of oneness with it. Mokhani was having such an effect on her it was difficult to believe she had another life in the city.

A shadow fell over her. Overhead, coasting low, was a powerful blue-gray peregrine falcon with its distinctive blackish-brown bars. Probably it had its nest on a shelf of the cliff face. She knew it was the fastest of all birds, able to swoop in on its prey at incredible speed. Even as she watched, guessing the predatory bird was ready for the kill, it plunged into a patch of thick vegetation and made off with its prey in a matter of seconds.

"Poor little thing!" She saw it was a small bird with azure-blue-and-black wings with flashes of bright yellow. It was slightly unnerving, the speed and accuracy of the attack, but that was nature, after all.

Much later, Cyrus called to her, pointing to the cooling blue of the sky. "Had enough?" He was a short distance down the canyon, picking up and examining some curiously shaped stones.

Jessica shook her head. "I could stay here forever. What about a swim? I'm game if you are." Of course she was teasing. Soaring on horseback over fences was one thing. Sharing a swimming pool with a crocodile was suicidal.

To her amazement, he began unbuttoning his shirt. Jessica gulped for air. This wasn't an ordinary guy from the suburbs. This was a Territorian, probably used to going skinny-dipping. She ran toward him, grasping his arms. "I was fooling, you know."

"What are you worried about?" His blue gaze was deeply teasing. "It's been many years since anyone sighted a croc around here. You feel like a dip. I feel like a dip. What's stopping us?"

She felt herself blush yet again. "I don't have a swimming costume with me."

"So you can swim without one. *I* don't care."

"Sorry, but *I* do."

"I'm amazed to hear that, Jessica, you being such an adventurous girl." He smothered a laugh. "Okay, but hell, it was definitely worth a try."

His skin in the sunlight was enriched to a warm amber. A light mat of hair, as black as the hair on his head, tapered to a narrow V dipping into his low-slung jeans. Her heart catapulted into her throat. The sight of him aroused her like nothing she had known in her life. She could feel the vital heat off his body. Her fingers ached to touch him, to stroke him, to lick the fine beads of sweat that glistened at the base of his throat…

His head snapped up. He leveled her with a blazing blue stare. Sexual tension stretched to the breaking point between them. "You want to touch me, don't you?"

"I was thinking about it," she said slowly, knowing there was a lot of ammunition in her hands. A single move on her part could lead straight into a sexual encounter.

"So what stopped you?" he asked.

"Good old common sense," she said wryly. "I have to obey the red light."

"I thought you liked risk." He covered her shoulders with his hands. Warm, light, but enflaming.

"You're too risky for me," she said in a low voice. "Also contrary to what you might think, risk hasn't been part of my life."

"It is now," he pointed out. "The two of us are quite, quite alone. No one around for miles and miles."

"Look, I'm shaken enough already!" Her laugh trembled. "What are you trying to do to me, Cy?"

"Charm you, maybe."

"You're succeeding."

His fingers caressed the fine bones of her shoulders. "Is it fate that threw us together, Jessica, or planning?"

She gave a deep sigh. "You won't let it alone, will you. Okay, it *was* planned, but not by me." She was struggling against a need so intense, nothing in her experience had prepared her for it.

"So we all dance to Dad's tune?"

"*I* don't and from what I've seen you don't, either." She tried to step free of his hands, but he preempted her movement, locking his arms around her, trapping her in a cocoon of sensation.

"No, Jessica. You're not going to get off that lightly. The last kiss we shared was so intoxicating, it left me with a driving desire for more."

She abandoned any thought of resistance. At that moment being in his arms was what she wanted most in the world.

Time stood still as he kissed her. Caution was suspended. Desire ran ahead like a flame to a keg of dynamite.

Their kiss was passionate, openmouthed, sumptuous, as though they both wanted as much as they could get in the shortest possible time.

Jessica brought up her hand, breathing hard, to sink her fingers into his black glossy hair, loving the feel of it. Her entire body clutched for his—her breasts, her stomach, her groin, hot and tingling now, her legs.

Still holding and kissing her, he moved them back into the shade of the towering cliff walls. His hand sought her breasts, pulling at the buttons of her shirt until it fell loose and he pushed it off. Immediately, he lowered his head, tonguing each sensitive nipple through the delicate fabric of her bra, so it became wet and the engorged buds strained against it.

"God, I'm *mad* for you." His free hand moved to unsnap her undergarment. He inhaled sharply as her small breasts sprang free. "So beautiful!" His hands moved over her bare skin, his lean fingers, calloused on the pads, positioning themselves over the pale creamy contours.

"Jessica!" he cried softly, and the sound was so erotic her breaths came shorter and quicker. Her heart hammered. She brought up her hand to press his over it. Couldn't he feel how her heart beat for him? His touch was exquisite, nothing rough or insistent, but masterful, and meltingly tender and loving. He took hold of her long hair to release it from its plait, wrapping it around his hand. His mouth tasted of salt. From her flesh?

When finally he lifted his mouth from hers, they were both breathing as if they'd just run a marathon. "Is this a good time to stop?" he muttered, perversely holding her closer to him so she could feel his hard arousal. "If we don't, I mightn't be able to stop later."

"So don't!" She clung to him, afraid of the ease with which he had dismantled all her defenses.

"But is it a safe time for you?"

She hid her face against his chest, but her voice didn't falter. "Yes."

"Then I'd be a saint if I resisted you." He made her lift her head, his blue eyes glowing. "And I'm no saint, Jessica. Lord, you're so beautiful it *hurts*. I should warn you I'm the kind of guy who wants it *all*. *All* is something I've never had in my entire life. I guess you could say some part of me has been deprived. I find myself wanting to drown in your body like a man might drown in waterhole out there in the desert."

"But is it *me* you're seeing?" Jessica asked, desperate to be sure he saw her as a *person* rather than the object of his sexual desire before their lovemaking went further.

"Of course it's you." He shook her slightly. "I've had to put up a struggle against you since the moment I laid eyes on you. I'm still not sorted out. Sex isn't all I want, Jessica, if that's what's bothering you. There are worse wants. I want to know everything about you."

"That will come," she said gently. "Everything I've told you about myself is true."

He relaxed his grip slightly, pulling her head back. "Except you haven't told me everything, have you?"

Her expression broke into pieces as if in pain. "Oh, Cy,

will I ever have your trust?" At last, she found the strength to step away.

"You have to admit strange things are happening," he countered, "and you're the catalyst. Dad got you here for a lot more than decorating the Big House. What's his real motivation?"

"I don't know." Her voice was very tight. "Ask him."

"I'm sorry. I'm spoiling things."

"You are."

His gaze was intense. "Because you have the power to change my world, I want desperately to believe in you. Surely you know that." He reached out a hand to her, but she drew farther away. "Why does Dad follow you around? It's been a real eye-opener for Robyn and me. What's his plan for you? A portrait of a young woman who disappeared over fifty years ago suddenly turns up in an auction room. Your uncle's partner buys it, though Livvy wants it, too. Livvy claims there are more paintings. When she looks at you, she sees Moira. She calls you Moira and you call her *Miss* Lavinia. Why should that be? Do you wonder I want to know what the hell is going on?" He stood there, gloriously handsome and very troubled.

Jessica lifted her head to stare into the brilliance of his eyes, as her own ripples of anger and confusion washed over her. "You're not the only one who's desperate for a few answers. I'm as much perturbed by your father's attentions as you and Robyn. I came up here to do a job. My expectations in life don't include marrying a man old enough to be my father. And I think there's something evil about too much money—it's such a powerful force it can start wars. I'm genuinely amazed Lavinia calls me Moira, though I have to admit Moira and I share a remarkable likeness. When you see the portrait, you'll agree."

"I can't wait," he said tersely.

Jessica's eyes were very green. "You're right about one thing. I mightn't be here long. You say you want me, yet it will probably be *you* who drives me away." To her horror, she felt like bursting into tears.

"I might have wanted to at the beginning, but I don't now," he protested. He'd been so high a moment ago, and now was plunged to the depths.

"Is that supposed to make me feel better?" The electric tension in him whipped up an answering tension in her. "Because it doesn't." Angry and suffering a feeling of humiliation, she shrugged into her shirt, fumbling with the buttons. "Let's drop this, shall we? All we've got going for us is sexual attraction."

He leaned closer, as if pulled by an unseen hand. Jessica, too, felt herself swaying into him. She might have been a stringed instrument strummed by a master.

"It's okay, Jessica." He felt the trembling that went through her body, the warring emotions that were in her. "The day isn't ruined. There's no need for you to feel threatened. I'll keep a respectful distance. That way we won't be led directly into temptation. It's not going to be easy, though, when we cued in to each other on sight. But what the hell!" He winced and moved away from her. "Shall we call a truce?" His voice had more than a lick of mockery in it.

"I've no choice," she answered, still fumbling with her shirt. "My job is at stake."

"Dad's your boss. Not me." He shrugged, watching her. Then said, "You do realize you've forgotten your bra. I know how you like to be modest."

"What? Oh, blast!" It came out in a staccato burst.

"Why don't you just leave it off?" he suggested, plucking the scrap of polyester and lace off the bush where it had landed. "You're in no further danger from lustful old me." He twirled the undergarment around his finger. "This'll fit neatly in my pocket."

"Why don't you just give it to me?" Her green eyes flashed as she stretched out a hand.

"In the old days a lady, if she were romantic, allowed an admirer to keep her handkerchief."

Jessica snatched the bra from his finger and stuffed it in her pocket. "Well, I don't have a handkerchief on me right now," she said jaggedly.

His blue eyes burned into her. "Despite that feisty rebuff I'll be seeing you in my dreams. Tonight, Jessica. I have to tell you, I think you'll be seeing me in yours."

Arrogant bastard!

It was Molly who took the news that B.B. and Robyn would be returning at the end of the week.

"All good things come to an end," Lavinia lamented. "I do so love it when they're not here."

Jessica had to throw off her fluctuating moods and get motivated. Because there was no time to make the trip to Darwin, all the art supplies she'd ordered had been flown in. She had Cyrus to thank for that, but when they came together, the atmosphere between them was so far removed from companionable she never did get a thank-you out. She had no excuse now for not creating a whole portfolio of sketches enhanced by a sensitive wash of watercolors. The last thing she wanted was strong color. The vast landscape was ablaze with it. For the interior she wanted a cool tranquillity. Pristine white with accents of aqua, turquoise, harmonizing greens and maybe a shot of fuchsia-pink in the huge living room. She and Brett had discussed antiques, rugs and artwork over the phone. She had the large, well-equipped office at her disposal, and e-mails and faxes were going back and forth daily. Brett had vetted most of her proposals coming up with some excellent suggestions of his own, which was something she had counted on. Everything was going well. It was a great comfort to know her clever uncle had such confidence in her judgment.

Lavinia took great interest in what Jessica was doing, poring over the sketched interiors brought to life by watercolors. "There's some marvelous stuff Robyn had stored away," she told Jessica, frowning. "You should get over to the old servants' quarters and have a look while you can. It's a very interesting place. Haunted, of course, but that's not going to worry you. Once Broderick and Robyn get back, they'll be following your every move. Robyn is terribly jealous and it shows. I remember some priceless things, Persian rugs, *big* rugs, dear. None of your little silk prayer rugs. Incredibly beautiful, glorious colors and patterns, a couple of floral Herats of the Isfahan type. Deborah knew how to display things. Coromandel screens, porcelains, furniture and paintings galore. Lovely mirrors in gilt frames. Robyn didn't even leave them up—she has no taste whatever, but I'm fascinated by your vision. It's most sophisticated, Moira, very polished. I had no idea you were such a wonderful drawer. Exciting things going on! We'll leave these out, shall we?" She indicated the many sketches spread out all over the table. "Cy will want to see them when he comes in. It's so wonderful to see the pair of you together. But don't forget. The two of you have to face Broderick when he gets home." She leaned forward and chucked Jessica under the chin.

Talking with Lavinia was like being detached from reality.

Towards late afternoon on the Wednesday, Jessica decided to take a great leap into the unknown. She knew the old servants' quarters were locked, but only ten minutes before Lavinia had crept up on her as she was working, dangling something hard and cold against her cheek.

"Oh, goodness!" Jessica gave a start, not knowing anyone was there.

"Sorry, dear, did I startle you?" Lavinia asked, gentleness surging into her voice. "This will solve the problem of how to get in." She twirled the large brass key, blinking coyly. "I found it in Broderick's study. I actually stole it. Oops. Did I really say that?"

"Yes, Miss Lavinia, you did, you brazen thing! Mr. Bannerman probably doesn't want anyone to go in."

"I don't care a fig for what Broderick wants," Lavinia snorted, drawing the gypsy shawl that topped off her Carmen costume around herself. It reeked of naphthalene, but it went wonderfully with all the gold medallions hanging around her neck. She passed Jessica the key. "Now push off," she said behind her hand as though someone was hiding behind the curtain. "I'd come and help you, only dust affects my sinuses. Don't say anything to Cy," she warned. "What's biting you two, anyhow? The air sizzles when you're together." Her voice dripped with interest.

"Nothing," Jessica assured her. "Cy likes to bait me, that's all."

"Works both ways, dear," Lavinia chortled. "You know, Cy hated what his father let Robyn do to the house. You never saw a boy love his mother so much. Broderick, of course, was jealous of his own son, even in those days. He craved *all* Deborah's attention, but she was a mother who loved her son. A mother, I think, before a wife. Broderick couldn't take that. He's such an extreme person."

Jessica wasn't about to argue with that.

Inside the storeroom, it took a while for her vision to adjust to the gloom after the brilliant sunlight outside. She had never done anything like this in her life before. In truth, she could have been about to open a Pandora's box, so nervous did she feel. Why hadn't she waited for B.B. to come home and ask permission? To answer her own question, she wouldn't get it. She couldn't for the life of her think of him as Broderick, and calling him that was a jarring note. If a man, however rich and powerful, was starting to develop warm feelings toward her, she'd have to start praying those feelings would fizzle out. She had no ambition whatever to become a rich man's trophy wife, even if he covered her in diamonds, rubies and pearls. It was so embarrassing and so totally unforeseen she couldn't bring herself to tell Brett.

There were several rooms, she discovered. One very large, all of them crowded with a great collection of things covered in dust sheets. She turned away to work at a catch on a window to let in more light. There! It was oppressively hot and still. All these unmoving things towering over her, and right up the walls gave her the willies. Despite the size of the main room, which she suspected had been several rooms knocked into one, she felt strangely claustrophobic.

She nervously looked under a couple of dust sheets. The whole place was drenched in an atmosphere one could almost call ghostly.

Settle down, girl!

"Drat it!" she said softly as she stubbed her toe on what was the leg of a heavy mahogany chair. She could see a stack of what looked like pictures in frames behind a gray dust sheet. She'd probably have a heart attack on the spot if one turned out to be another painted image of Moira. Sad little Moira belonged in the past but it seemed she wouldn't stay there. She lifted the sheet and was confronted by a magnficent oil on canvas of exotic fowl in the Dutch style. A glorious peacock its iridescent tail spread, its hen, a pink flamingo, a crane with a golden tuft on its head, several pheasant, and a bird she couldn't identify nesting in a branch of a tree. Such a painting had to be extremely valuable. What was it doing here in the heat? Didn't these people care? It was so big and so heavy, it was difficult to see the paintings behind it. Not portraits. Landscapes. More paintings. Chairs, marble-topped side tables. Cabinets. High up, rolled rugs. Probably rotting the whole damned lot. This was frightful! Broderick Bannerman had turned his back on what had to be a large family collection going back generations. In doing so, he surely had turned his back on his wife and son.

There was an instant when Jessica thought she heard a whispering behind her.

Mice.

What else could it be? She stood perfectly still, listening.

When the whispering became a little louder, she swung around to face it. "Is anyone there?" She moved on again, treading warily.

You feel guilty, that's what's wrong with you. You shouldn't be here.

Even that was ridiculous. Why should she feel guilty? She was absolutely certain there was a treasure trove for the Big House beneath all these dust sheets. Why buy expensive antiques, paintings and artworks when you already possessed a valuable collection? she rationalized. She ventured into the other rooms, flinging dust sheets this way and that. Why, they'd scarcely have to buy a thing outside the custom-made sofas, armchairs and soft furnishings. She didn't intend to use draperies at the double-height French doors, but white, brass-bound shutters fitted on the inside.

The whispering started again. Either she could bolt or pay it no heed. Was she going to allow a little family of mice to send her away? Even so, she felt nervous.

Her shoulder bumped against something that turned out to be a splendid eight-panel coromandel screen decorated with birds and flowers and studded with ivory and jade. What a find! She could easily place that and the two majestic baluster vases standing on the floor—both green and gold, with brilliant enameling—without any protection to the right of it. She supposed Robyn would be furious with her for entering the storerooms without permission. But she in turn was furious with Robyn for her wilful disregard of the correct storage and preservation of beautiful and valuable things. Why was such a place made inaccessible?

She patted the curly head of a life-size white marble statue of a little girl carrying a basket of flowers. "At least *you* won't fall apart."

The whispering continued.

"Go away!"

Her words had no effect. She walked toward the sound, thinking she could better cope with an apparition than a gang of scurrying mice.

After a while, hot, dusty, dry in the throat, her toe aching, she'd had enough. She recovered one of a pair of superb tall cabinets veneered with panels of marquetry and turned to leave. Still, she lingered and looked around as though something further was required of her. Finally she made her way between the mounded dust sheets, heading for the main storage room.

As she did so, the whispering increased in volume. It wasn't mice. It was more like a frantic murmur. Something was trying to get through to her. She could feel it in the very air. "Is there anyone there?" she called out again.

Nobody was. She was quite alone, her heart knocking madly. She looked back the way she'd come. Just for a moment she thought she saw a curling *shape* swirling in the dusty air. Suddenly she felt ice cold. The sudden drop in temperature raised gooseflesh on the skin of her arms. She even put up a hand to cover her eyes.

"Jessica!"

She reacted by collapsing against one of the tall cabinets.

A tall figure emerged from the gloom. Cyrus. "God, you scared me."

He walked toward her. "What the hell are you doing here? Dad says this place is off-limits." After the brilliance of the daylight outside, Cy could just make out her cloud of ash-blond hair. As he drew closer, he took in the rest of her, pale face, huge glittering eyes. "Are you okay?" He reached out to her, holding her arm as she slowly straightened up. "You look like you've seen a ghost."

"Frankly I think I have," she said raggedly. "There's something skulking around back there."

"Mice," he said shortly, continuing to stare at her, doomed to be fascinated.

"Mice whispering secrets in my ear? I don't think so."

"What are you talking about?" he asked impatiently.

"God knows! I'm not a nervous person. I don't panic easily—until today. There are bloody ghosts back there."

"Right. Let's go and take a look," he said with some decisiveness. "What's the matter? Chicken?"

"Not with you around. Even a ghost won't want to mess with you."

"Give me your hand." His tone was brisk, at odds with the way he was feeling.

"You know what happens when we hold hands."

"Any excuse will do for me," he told her dryly. "But ghosts are definitely out, Jessica. There's no such thing."

"Tell that to the people who've entertained uninvited guests. Tell me, if there's an afterlife and hundreds of millions of people believe there is, why can't a few souls go missing? For one reason or another, their travel home has been interrupted. They still have business to attend to before they can move on."

"I'm not buying it," he said firmly.

"You haven't got a spark of imagination."

"Whereas you have too much. What exactly did you hear?" He led her through the spectral dust sheets. "This is one of the earliest buildings on Mokhani. The timbers creak."

"I'm not hearing anything now," Jessica said, starting to feel a little foolish. "What are you doing here, anyway? Checking up on me?"

"I might just be," Cy said, staring around him. "I'm really angry with Livvy for encouraging you and giving you that key."

"Why shouldn't she?" Jessica retorted, standing up for herself and Livvy. "What's the big secret about this place? It's jam-packed with beautiful and valuable things. No way should they be here. Certainly not the paintings. Fine paintings should be stored at a certain temperature. I can't imagine why *anyone* would banish the treasures I've seen to a storeroom. They must have rocks in their head."

"Yeah, well you won't get any argument from me."

"Don't you *care?*"

He leaned heavily against a sideboard, giving into sheer need and pulling her taut body alongside. "Oh yes, I care," he said bitterly. "But when I was a kid, after my mother died, when I cared about something my father disagreed with I got whipped."

"You didn't!" The expression on her face mirrored her shock.

"I've still got a scar on my back. Want to see?"

"Yes." Suddenly she was extremely angry. Broderick Bannerman, what sort of man *was* he? She hated physical violence. Abuse of any kind. And on a child, a motherless boy? That was a sin!

Cy released her, pulling his denim shirt out of his jeans, one hand lifting the hem of his shirt.

His skin, even in the poor light, gleamed a dark bronze. She could see the play of muscles across his back. And the long scar that ran from one shoulder blade almost to his waist.

"Oh, Cy!" She couldn't help herself. Tenderly she traced the faintly depressed line. "This should never have happened! I'm so sorry." His pain lacerated her. On an impulse, she leaned forward and pressed her lips to the deepest part of the scar. "I'm kissing it better," she explained huskily.

He took a deep jagged breath. "Then could you do it again? You're turning my legs to jelly."

"We're starting to forget how we decided it should be."

"Relationships are like that," he said, his voice very dry.

"So we've got one?"

"You know we have. Next thing you know, I'll be back to kissing you."

"I might get in first." She slipped her arms around him, pressing her mouth to his puckered skin.

The flame of desire, ever present in him, leaped higher than the rafters. He turned about swiftly, the muscles of his arms quivering, as he caught her face between his two hands. "Abstinence isn't working for me, Jessica." His voice was harsh with emotion.

She stared back at him. "Don't you think I know what it's like to be sick with longing?"

"So what are we going to do about it? I have to tell you sexual frustration is weighing very heavily on me."

"Me, too," she sighed, determined not to say a word out of place.

"I get the feeling you're not on the pill?"

"No." She shook her head. "I wasn't expecting any sexual encounters when I came here," she said wryly, "but boy, has everything changed."

"Maybe we'd better take a trip into Darwin," he said tautly. "Meanwhile I've got protection. I want you but you have to come to me of your own free will. I would never put pressure on you."

She raised her head, giving him a dreamy smile. "You put pressure on me every time you look at me!"

"You've been pretty good at hiding it these last few days."

"I wasn't being my true self. Anyway, you're conceited enough."

"I'm not conceited at all," he scoffed. "This week has been pretty much a torment."

"You wanted pulling into line."

"What I want is to pull you into my bed." His hands ran caressingly down her back.

"Oh, I like that," she murmured. "Your father won't take too kindly to…us." She had a grim picture of what might happen.

"I can imagine," he said. "So what's more important to you? Your relationship with *him* or your relationship with me?"

She looked up to meet his eyes. "I don't have a relationship with him, Cyrus. So quit trying to extract a confession. It's *you* I care about."

"Good." He bent his head and kissed her fiercely. "Because you've got a choke hold on *both* of us," he muttered, as they paused for breath. It was incredible, Cy knew, that he could say such things to her, but the rivalry between himself and his father had been going on for years and years.

Instantly, Jessica felt animosity enter into their passion. "Don't make me another point of conflict between you," she warned. "Lavinia told me there was rivalry between you and your father for the love of your mother."

There was a distinct edge to his voice. "The rivalry was always on Dad's side. I couldn't even recognize rivalry at that stage. I had a wonderful mother. She loved me, Jessica, but she loved my father, too—or she must have at one stage to marry him. He's a striking-looking man now. How much more so in his youth? He couldn't always have been a monster, but the monster began to appear early. God knows what Dad's true nature is. I've given up trying to find out."

"I can understand that." She looked at him with sympathy. "But please don't direct any bitterness toward me. I may have some effect on your father—an aging man's fantasy—but the deep attachment I've formed is for *you,* so don't give me a hard time."

"Blame it on the difficulties of our situation," he said laconically, hauling her back into his arms. "Kiss me."

She reached up to draw down his head.

They kissed with such hectic passion, the very air around them throbbed and whirred and both of them wound up disheveled. Finally, he wrenched back. "We Bannermans are a tortured lot. You have to sleep with me, Jessica."

It was like being offered a passport to heaven. "One day I want you to talk to me about your childhood," she said. "Your precious memories of your mother. I can't imagine what else you're going to tell me about your father, now that I've seen that scar."

"Don't make too much of it." He shrugged the injury off. "I don't think he meant to go as far as he did. Dad was severely depressed for quite a while."

"Yet he remarried quite soon?" There was a subtle look of disapproval in Jessica's eyes.

He drew her down on an old Victorian settee with beautiful but threadbare upholstery. "Dad wanted more sons. One maybe more like him. It was no whirlwind romance with poor Sharon.

He didn't love her, but she, incredibly, loved him. Can you beat that? Years of being treated like a piece of furniture, yet Sharon continued to love him."

"It's a wonder he didn't beat *her*," Jessica said, deeply disturbed by what she had learned that day.

"Good God, nothing like that." Cyrus shook his head. "He'd never raise his hand to a woman. *I* was his mark. It made me grow up fast. By the time I was fourteen, I told him I'd kill him if he ever touched me again. I must have sounded like I meant it. By the time he got over the shock, he never tried it again."

"What an awful story!" she sighed with sick disgust. "How am I supposed to work for a man like that? I feel like throwing in the towel."

He replied instantly, "The only problem is, Jessica, you signed the contract, remember?"

"He pressed me into it."

Cy stroked her cheek with his finger. "You can't fight Broderick Bannerman and hope to win. Scores of people could tell you that. Dad has control of everything while he lives. I know the priceless stuff that's here. I know it shouldn't be here. This is my inheritance, too, but sometimes I think my father would like to see me miss out. This can all crumble and decay. He's not dedicated to preserving it for me. He's one of those people who think only of themselves, their own pride and place in the world. Other people aren't important."

"No wonder he's a deeply unhappy man," Jessica said. "Caring about other people brings its own fulfilment." She waved an arm around her. "I'm going to speak to him about all this when the moment is right. All these treasures lying neglected. There's a magnificent painting in the other room. The light was too bad to see the name of the artist, but I wouldn't mind betting it's a Dutch master."

"It is," he confirmed. "One of my mother's family—English originally—worked for the Dutch East India company. He lived in Batavia for many years. He acquired it there."

"So it's yours through your mother."

His expression was grim. "My mother died without a will. Anyone so young and beautiful was meant to live forever. Her premature death was never foreseen. She often pointed out what things were mine. The paintings, the jade collection, the porcelains—all her family stuff. The one time I mentioned it to Dad, he told me to go to hell. He was drunk and in a brutal mood. It was all *his* until he died, and he had no intention of dying before he reached ninety."

"Then he better start looking after himself," Jessica said. "He must have a problem with high blood pressure. He's like a pressure cooker threatening to blow the lid."

"Maybe, but he's never had a sick day in his life. Probably the bad stuff will happen all at once. He survived a plane crash, did you know? Walked away from it with only a few lacerations. The pilot was killed. Dad thinks he's invincible. He thinks he's going to go on forever. Maybe take another wife. Rupert Murdoch fathered a child in his seventies. Men do."

"Lucky old them!" Jessica said tartly, staring toward the back of the room. "Listen…"

"The mice again?" He dropped a kiss on her hair, inhaling its freshness.

"The whispering has stopped. I swear it was real enough. It was like someone trying to contact me."

"Not get rid of you?" he asked, rising and pulling her to her feet.

"Joke all you like." She shook her head. "This place has a strange aura. There's not enough light around here, either. It's dangerous in a way. Any of that stuff up there in the rafters could fall."

"Except there's no wind to move it." He lifted a dust sheet that covered a very pretty writing desk. "My mother's." The expression on his face had grown more intense. "You didn't come across another painting of our resident ghost?"

She shook her head. "It would take a month of Sundays to

sort through all this. It should have been catalogued. If there were such a painting, it could be anywhere, even up there." She pointed high up on the wall to what could have been covered paintings secured by an iron brace. "I can't explain it, but I can't help thinking there is one. There are a lot of shadows around your father. It seems to me that the more strident he was when denying the existence of anything relating to Moira, the more I thought he wasn't telling the truth."

"That's a state of affairs that's been going on a long, long time. We'd better go," he said. "And don't say anything about being inside or Livvy giving you the key."

"Of course I won't," she said indignantly. "I'll try to find another way to get in. Your father's tough, but he's not that tough."

"Not when he's in the middle of creating a fantasy." He picked up the white marble bust of a young girl. "Mignon," he read the inscription. "My mother's."

"It's beautiful." She realized just being in here and seeing his mother's things was upsetting him. She was about to turn back when a voice clearly said:

Don't go.

She almost couldn't breathe, stumbling back against Cyrus. "Did you hear that?"

"What? I didn't heard a thing, but I have to say it's a little weird in here."

She caught his hand, holding tightly to it.

He laughed, looking down at her. "I'm starting to see another side of you, Jessica."

"You're not too happy here yourself."

"Then let's get out."

They were almost at the entrance to the main room when there was a blast of wind that rushed at them with surprising force. Then a loud crash.

"What the hell!" Cy swore.

"It has to be the window I opened."

Cy strode into the main room, looking quickly around him.

"That makes no sense. No wind has blown up." He crossed to the door. "It's perfectly still outside. The fronds of the palms aren't moving."

"No glass shards on the floor, either." The window Jessica had opened was still on the hook, intact. "So what crashed?"

"Must have been the other room. We must have disturbed something. It could easily have been a pedestal or a lamp." He said it matter-of-factly to counteract the strangeness of the occurrence.

"Time to take our ghost seriously, wouldn't you say?"

"Big girl like you believing in ghosts." But he, too, felt edgy without knowing why. "That's the cause," Cy said when they saw how half a dozen paintings had come down from the wall. "The strap must have broken."

"The ghost got to it," Jessica said stubbornly.

"Doubt it." Cy dropped to his knees.

Jessica joined him, the two of them pulling the pictures from their coverings one by one. No portraits. A couple of good still lifes. A flower painting Tim would have loved, a beautiful storm scene by a famous Australian artist—Jessica didn't need to see the signature to recognize the work—a forest scene and an abstract that could have represented a star being born. The canvas had come away from the gilded frame in the fall.

"Something has to be done about these," Jessica, the artist and lover of all beautiful things, said. "Leaving them like this is a crime."

"Okay, so we *will* do something about it," Cy said, pierced by her criticisms, which were warranted. "I try to avoid major blowups with my father, but one's long overdue."

"I guess so," Jessica said, rewrapping the flower painting. "He's afraid of you, you know."

"No way!" Cy was startled.

"Oh yes he is," Jessica maintained. "You're everything he's not."

"That deserves another kiss." He put his arm around her neck and kissed the sensitive spot behind her ear.

"You're kiss deprived, that's your trouble," she said.

"I've had hordes of girls chasing me," he said, then continued his inspection of the paintings.

"You never married one. I'll leave you to rewrap the abstract, although it really should be reframed. What do you think?"

"Let's have a look," he suggested. "It's getting dark in here." He broke off abruptly, his fingers slipping down behind the canvas. "There are two paintings here," he said, sounding intrigued.

"What?"

"Take a look for yourself. There's another canvas here." Cy rested the large painting against himself while she looked.

"Push the canvas backward."

"Right out of the frame?"

"Yes. It'll be okay."

Cyrus obliged while Jessica separated the two paintings. One filled up Jessica's vision.

She rocked back on her heels in shock. "How is it possible this has been hidden for so long?" Momentarily she looked away from the newly revealed painting to stare into Cyrus's eyes. "It's Moira." She started to tremble.

"Who else!" he said in a hard, considering way. "And horror of horrors, a nude!"

"God, yes," Jessica whispered.

Moira was reclining on a couch covered in green silk, her back and shoulders propped by cushions covered in rich fabrics. Her beautiful long hair fell over her shoulders and her white, pointed breasts. She looked extraordinarily vivid yet fragile. Her skin was luminescent. Her eyes glowed. One slender leg was discreetly raised, blocking the pubic area. One lovely hand rested on her stomach, the other was twisted in her hair.

The artist in Jessica bowed low before the artistry, even if she was shocked Moira, the little governess, was the subject of such an erotic painting.

"Poor old Hugh must have been madly in love with her," Cy said, hit by a wave of arousal that had at its center the extraordinary resemblance Jessica bore to the painted image.

"That's Hugh Balfour?"

Cy bent for an inspection. "There's an *H.B.* in the right-hand corner. How did he get an innocent young girl to pose for him nude? I'm not getting any of this."

"It's a tough one all right. It opens up a whole new area of investigation. At the heart of the Mokhani Mystery, was there a love triangle? A crime of passion?" It stuck in Jessica's throat, but she had to say it. "Yet Lavinia claims Hugh was gay."

He swung his shoulders her way. "Livvy should be arrested," he said with quiet vehemence. "It's best not to believe anything Livvy says. She's outrageous, sometimes even mad. I've never heard anything about Hugh being gay."

"It was probably a big secret."

"Nonsense!" His tone was clipped.

"People were scared to admit being gay in those days. Wasn't it against the law then?"

Cy's expression was disturbed. "Look at this painting, Jessica. Doesn't it look a wee bit erotic?"

"It looks bloody marvelous," she said, suddenly wondering if the artist had painted from life or simply drawn on a fevered imagination. He could have done it from numerous seemingly innocent sketches. Would Moira, fresh out of convent school, really have posed for this? Today it mightn't have been so shocking, but fifty-odd years ago it would have been considered scandalous. And where did that leave Lavinia's claim that Moira and Steven had fallen in love? Conceivably that, too, was nonsense. Perhaps Lavinia made up stories so life wouldn't get boring. One could expect something like that after life on the stage. "Hugh Balfour was really a very fine painter," she said. "Maybe that, too, was frowned on. Painting wasn't considered a serious career, perhaps? Hugh was probably expected to do great things. Lavinia says—"

Cyrus broke in. "No one, absolutely no one, including Dad, has ever been able to get Livvy to shut the hell up." He took a calming breath, still reeling from the stunning resemblance between the painted Moira and Jessica. Of course the longer he looked, the more he could see differences. Moira appeared more fragile, a vulnerable young person. Jessica was a thoroughly modern young woman, very fit, confident, with a promising career. But the coloring, the small features, the full mouth, the luminous skin. It would appear to anyone looking from the painting to the living woman they were somehow related.

Were they? He had to wonder. More to the point, did Jessica know and was keeping it from him for some reason? Was there a conspiracy at work here? Was his father part of it? Someone had taken a punt by putting the other portrait of Moira on the market. To what end?

"Just listen quietly to what I have to say," Jessica began cautiously, anticipating an explosion. "Don't shut your mind to it. Lavinia said Hugh loved your grandfather, Steven."

He coolly scrutinized her. "My darling Jessica, I *know* that. Everyone knows that. Hugh damned near worshipped him—for what he was, for what he'd done. He was a war hero, you know. He remained Hugh's friend from the first to the last. Hugh's own family deserted him. Many men came home from the wars alcoholic. They needed alcohol to deaden the pain of their terrible memories. The world can be a pitiless place. Hugh committed suicide. He wasn't very old at all. I don't suppose anyone told you. He died here on Mokhani. My father was there when they found the body."

Jessica drew in a sharp breath. "I didn't know that."

"It's not the sort of thing one wants to talk about. No wonder Dad grew up the way he is. The events of his childhood permanently scarred him. That's why I occasionally feel pity. I don't know how Livvy came to believe Hugh was homosexual. Livvy's such a drama queen! She's known for telling howlers. God knows what she'd say if she saw *this!* The poor devil was

in love with her. She disappears. Years later, after silently grieving, Hugh finds a way out of all the pain." His voice took on a
harder edge. "You'd tell me, wouldn't you, if there's a connection between you and Moira?" He lifted a hand as she rushed
into speech. "I know you've denied it, but you could have your
reasons. I want honesty between us."

"Of course, honesty. That's all important. I've told
you nothing but the truth. There's no connection whatever.
Past or present. I expect you to believe me, Cyrus, otherwise
what have we got?" She touched his arm briefly. "It's as my
uncle says. We all have a double somewhere. If *I* look like
Moira, then so does Brett. My grandmother, Alex, looks more
like this Moira than I do. But there was no Moira in our family." Her hand dropped away as, acutely attuned to him, she felt
a residue of resistance.

He might want her. He might long to have her. But he wasn't
sure of her.

CHAPTER ELEVEN

B.B. RETURNED MUCH the same as he'd gone away. A difficult, domineering man, surrounded by shadows and given to long bouts of moodiness. At least the trip had gone well. His partners in whatever venture it was—he didn't explain—had come to heel, no doubt with words of contrition. He was, however, generous in his praise when Jessica submitted her conceptualizations for the main rooms of the Big House. He didn't go so far as Cyrus, who on seeing them had remarked they were good enough to be framed, but his opinion was highly favorable.

They were in B.B.'s study with the drawings spread out across the desk. "So you like the idea of rendering the columns that support the dome lapis lazuli?" she asked.

"I can see they'll be striking." Bannerman stabbed a finger at the excellent architectural drawing. "Who is supposed to do the fresco on the cupola?" Jessica had meant to represent a heavenly blue sky with dazzling white puffs of clouds, the edges touched with gold and pink as if from the sun. Had this been glorious Italy, she could have added cherubs for good measure, but they would have looked out of place in such a setting as Mokhani.

"I know just the man," she said. "He's Italian, classically trained. He's never out of work."

"You can't do it yourself?" His glance beetled beneath his heavy brows.

"I suppose I could, but I wouldn't have the time and I'm not as good as Primo anyway. I had been thinking that instead of paintings for the hall, we could use panels. They would go here." She quickly began to draw in several long rectangular panels. "Blue on gold. They would pick up the blue of the columns. There's so much white we need a contrast. It's a pity when the marble floor was laid the architect hadn't thought of a central design. But never mind. Do you like the library?"

"Very impressive," he nodded. "But where are we going to get the leather-bound books in those particular colors?"

"Well, we can't," she smiled, "unless we have the covers specially done. That would cost a great deal of money. Or we could have *some* of them done in order to pick up the turquoise blue. I felt the carpeting should be this very soft pinkish-red. Inviting, nurturing, but not too warm. We'll need a big important painting here." She pointed to the pale ocher wall above her rendering of an antique writing desk flanked by two splendid chairs.

"This is all very palatial," he said, his body a large physical barrier between her and the door.

"Isn't that what you wanted? A modern palace. I had to strike a balance between sumptuousness and classical purity."

"Well then you've succeeded, Jessica," he said, making no attempt to disguise the admiring scrutiny he bent on her. It went well beyond the aesthetic, Jessica thought. In fact, he was thoroughly unnerving her.

"I have some ideas for the front court," she quickly added, beginning to sketch a plan for the landscaping immediately in front of the house.

"We used to have an artist in the family," he commented, staring down at her slender flying fingers. "Name of Hugh Balfour. Ever heard of him?" He lifted his handsome head, shooting her the now-familiar piercing glance. This wasn't a man who indulged in idle conversation. He was pushing her to declare what she knew. Moreover, who'd told her.

Calmly she lay down her pencil. "Lavinia mentioned him. I think in connection with the portrait of your father up there. She's interested in art."

"Not that she knows anything about it," he scoffed.

Again she wondered if he had, through his agents, put Moira's painting on the market. To what purpose? She couldn't figure it out.

The silence stretched, uncomfortably for Jessica, during which time he continued to stare at her. Jessica thought she held up rather well. How many people actually could? Oddly, she had the impression he was not so much staring *at* her, as *beyond* her. As though Moira lived in *her* body and the two of them had metamorphosed right in front of him.

"You got to look around the station, then?" He finally shifted position, moving around the massive desk.

She could see where this was leading. "Not as much as I wanted. I needed to have these drawings ready for you. That was my top priority. I did, however, get to the top of the escarpment and later explored the floor of the canyon for a while. It was a marvelous experience, like seeing a surviving pocket of Gondwana. Before I go home I want to take lots of pictures. This is another world, the Top End. The plant life is unique. I used to think a lot of our tropical plants had their origin in the South Sea islands. Apparently it's the other way around."

He shrugged off the information as of little interest. His whole life had been addressed to making money. "You didn't go by yourself. Cyrus took you?"

She had already anticipated the question. "He was kind enough, yes," she said with a smile. Broderick Bannerman was indeed in some sort of conflict with his son, conflict that had deep roots in the past. For all she knew, Bannerman could have had problems with his own father, Steven, the man Cyrus resembled so closely. Many factors in Broderick Bannerman's early life could have been in play.

"It must have been really hard work escorting a beautiful young woman around Mokhani," he said, openly sarcastic.

Had he ever appeared in another guise, this severe, controlling man? "There was something I was going to ask you, Broderick." For the first time, she uttered his name with ease. "I understand you have many beautiful things from the family collections stored away in the old servants'quarters."

He smiled, the sort of smile that was almost alarming. "You can't use those," he said.

"I had hoped you would allow me to see them."

Bannerman leaned back in his chair, interlocking his hands behind his dark head with its distinctive silver wings. "I can't have any of my wife's things back in the house," he said.

An aura of pain was suddenly around him. Jessica stared at the handsome features drawn taut. "Oh, I'm sorry! I didn't mean to upset you." Who could begin to understand this complicated man?

"It appears I still haven't dealt with my wife's death," he said. "Perhaps I never will."

"A tragedy like that does strange things to people's lives."

"What would you know about tragedy?" he said.

"I lost the grandmother I adored."

"Ah, yes, the grandmother!"

"Why do you say it like that?" She frowned.

"You resemble her greatly?"

"Well, yes. How do you know? I don't believe I mentioned it at our first meeting, or since."

"I think you did and you've forgotten. Maybe I *will* let you take a look at what's in storage. As an artistic person, you must love beautiful things."

"That would be wonderful. Thank you. I was told there are beautiful paintings. Forgive me, but it's not wise to store them in the heat. Even the furniture will buckle. I had thought there might be a possibility of placing some pieces in the Big House. They could look quite different in such a very different setting."

He looked at her with such a strange expression on his face. "I understand what you're saying, Jessica, about the heat and humid conditions. I can see you *care*." Then, the words rolling like drumbeats, "Who's been talking to you?"

"It's been more my asking questions!" She laughed. "You must understand, I've never been anywhere remotely like Mokhani before. Do you wonder I'm fascinated?"

He seemed to relax, if indeed a hunting hawk ever relaxes. "It pleases me to hear that." He reached out, spreading his large elegant hand over hers. "Speaking of fascination, there's some magic about *you*." His resonant voice dropped low. "I'm already feeling your influence about the place. I enjoy talking to you. In fact, I've so looked forward to coming home. I haven't done that since I can't tell you when."

Jessica made no comment, not daring to inch her hand away. Well, not immediately. It wasn't the first time a male client had become attracted to her. She had begun to look on it as an occupational hazard. But this was something else again. She knew women married men old enough to be their fathers—certainly if they had severalodd million stashed away—but she thought she'd rather remain unmarried for the rest of her life than play on the soft underbelly of an aging man's weakness. Broderick Bannerman, with his formidable energy, bitterly resented growing old. He may have come to the conclusion marriage to a young woman could accomplish the impossible and keep him eternally young.

Jessica swallowed her dismay. Was it possible he was seriously considering *her*? Dear God, if true, it was a nightmare, particularly when she was head over heels in love with his son. Gently she withdrew her hand , starting to put all her sketches together.

"There's no word yet about your award?" he asked, a faint flush in his cheeks.

"I expect to hear any day now." She hugged the rolls of sketches to her. "I don't expect to win. It was an honor to be short-listed."

"So modest when you're so clever. I like that. The painter in our family wasn't a success. He was a great failure." His eyebrows jutted in a frown.

"Hugh, you mean?" Jessica's mind was racing. *Had* Balfour been gay? The family would have known. Could a gay man paint such an erotic nude? Silly question. Great painters had done it in the past.

"Rumor had it he was gay," Broderick said with a harsh laugh. "But if he were, he was very discreet. Hell of a thing to be homosexual. Maybe that's why he topped himself."

"Poor man. So he couldn't have been in love with Moira?"

The handsome, heavy head shot up. "Whatever are you talking about?"

She was almost welcoming a confrontation, but backed off. "I did a lot of research on Mokhani before I came. Many articles have been written about the Mokhani Mystery."

"I expect there'll be lots more," he grunted. "The press is conspicuous for dragging up all the old unsolved mysteries."

"They said Moira was beautiful. Was she?"

"I was only a child, my dear."

"So you never saw the paintings Hugh Balfour did of her?"

He smiled like a man who had nothing to hide. "If I did I've forgotten. I have to tell you I'm not used to being interrogated, Jessica. I can tell you Moira had your coloring. She was tallish like you and exceptionally slender."

"So you do remember some things about her?"

He studied her very gravely. "I suppose, now that I think about it. Few women in my experience have been as beautiful as Moira, though my boyish memories can't be entirely accurate. My wife was a very beautiful women with skin like a pearl. You, too, are beautiful. When I first saw you on that television program, your chance resemblance to my governess stunned me."

"Is that why you hired me?"

"You sound very anxious to know."

"Well, of course I am."

"Let me set your mind at rest," he said suavely. "I paid far greater attention to your qualifications, Jessica. You don't know me if you think otherwise."

I don't know you at all, Jessica thought.

"By the way, Robyn's boyfriend—ridiculous word, particularly as he's been married and divorced—is giving her a birthday party Saturday night at his home. I'd like you to come."

"Shouldn't I wait for an invitation?" She gave him an uncertain glance.

"You're getting one from me." He spoke as if that was all that was required. "Dress up."

"Is that an order?" On her way to the door, Jessica turned to ask.

There was a flare of amusement in his eyes. "Of course not. I confess I'm looking forward to seeing you turned out for a party. Formal is what Robyn wants. She spent a fortune in Hong Kong. That way no one gets to see her in the same thing twice."

With the master of the house back in residence, Lavinia didn't come down to dinner.

"I've told Jessica about the party on Saturday."

B.B. threw the remark at Robyn as though daring her not to catch it. "She says she won't come without an invitation."

"But she must come. Please come," Robyn said as though the invitation had been lost in the mail. "I'm so sorry, Jessica, I was getting around to it. It's going to be a big night."

"She's thirty now, you know," B.B. told Jessica. "Thinking of matrimony. We'll have to make sure there's a prenuptial agreement. No way is Erik getting his hands on my money."

"He's got money of his own, Dad," Robyn was moved to protest.

"Let's face it, my dear, Moore wouldn't have given you the time of day if you hadn't been my stepdaughter."

"I'm truly amazed someone hasn't bumped you off, Dad," Cyrus drawled. "Erik isn't the only man to notice Robyn's attractions. With or without your money."

"I'm not a very nice person, as you know, Cyrus," Bannerman said.

Cyrus lifted his wineglass in a dubious salute. "Actually I'm not all that keen on going. I think you can do better than Erik, Robyn. He ran out on his wife. He could run out on you."

"He promised me he would never leave me." Robyn was bristling and very much on edge.

"Hell, you couldn't exactly call you a loving couple. My bet is you're desperate to leave home."

Robyn gasped. "How can you say such a thing? Dad has given me a marvelous life. It's as he says, I'm not getting any younger."

"Check with Erik, he wants children," Bannerman slipped in smoothly, turning his head to capture Jessica's gaze. "Robyn could be barren like her mother."

Jessica felt herself flinch. Could Robyn be that desperate to inherit her stepfather's money to tolerate all these cruel, cutting remarks? But it was Cyrus, not Robyn, who came to Sharon's defense. "Sharon wasn't barren, Dad. She had Robyn. That, of course, was long before she met *you*."

"How you love to set me straight, Cyrus," his father answered, brushing that fact aside. Once more he addressed Jessica. "I have a little something for you, Jessica, I bought in Hong Kong. I'd like you to wear it Saturday night."

It was a startling statement that left Jessica greatly worried.

"I really think you should tell Jessica what it is first," Cyrus suggested. "Some things a girl has to refuse on principle."

Jessica felt Robyn's gaze locked on her, but her answer was weighed and controlled. "Goodness, I don't need a present, Broderick. You're paying me extremely well."

"Of course I am," he smiled, "but it gave me pleasure to buy it. I'm sure you're going to enjoy wearing it. I have it in my study. You can take a look after dinner."

"It would be so nice if Robyn and I were invited along, too," Cyrus said, contemplating Jessica's face, a decided glint in his eyes.

"This is *private,* Cyrus," B.B. said. "You and Robyn will just have to wait."

"How do you know you haven't made a big mistake?" Cyrus sat back with indolent grace.

"About what?" B.B. asked in his most aggressive fashion.

"Jessica's mother will have told her not to accept presents from near strangers," Cyrus pointed out.

"I don't think sarcasm is the answer, Cyrus," his father said.

"Of course it isn't. Jessica is shocked, in case you haven't noticed."

"That's not true, is it, Jessica?" B.B. turned to her.

She swallowed, not wishing to insult him but determined to find a way out of it. "I *am* surprised," she said.

"And a little nervous. Don't be, my dear," Bannerman patted her hand. It was getting to be a habit.

What B.B. had referred to as "a little something" turned out to be a pair of platinum earrings, each set with a half carat round brilliant cut lemon diamond and two brilliant cut white diamonds from which was appended a beautiful golden South Sea teardrop pearl of at least fifteen millimeters. Pearls of that size and shape were relatively rare, and so were much sought after by collectors. Jessica knew this from her love of pearls and her own mother's collection. Luster, the single most important factor in determining the value of a pearl, was well in evidence. The nacre was very rich.

It was quite out of the question to accept a gift like this. It was too valuable and too personal. The sooner she made that clear, the better. "Broderick, I can't possibly accept these," she said as courteously as she could.

His piercing gaze rested on her. "That alone makes you different from most women of my acquaintance." Dinner was over. They were alone in his study.

"It's extremely generous of you, but I've done nothing to warrant such a gift."

"Try them on, anyway," he said, pointing to a mirror. Broderick Bannerman hadn't gotten where he was without putting down opposition. "At least let me see them on you. They say pearls are in again."

"They should never have been out." Jessica didn't want to offend him, but she couldn't give him leverage, either. Broderick Bannerman's inch was another man's mile.

"*Please.* I don't often beg." He turned her by the shoulders, looking directly into her eyes.

Yes, she thought. Begging would be grotesque in such a man.

"If you see yourself wearing them, you might want to keep them," he said, reaching for the jewelry box.

"They must have cost a good deal of money," Jessica said. She had a fair idea how much; she looked in the windows of jewelry stores often enough. She would have thought a gift costing a hundred dollars too much, but these earrings had to be worth many thousands of dollars. There was no way she could accept. In her embarrassment, she saw it as a form of prostitution.

"What's money?" he asked, as only a rich man could. "I have all the money in the world, but it hasn't made me happy. Since you've been here, Jessica, I've felt a lifting of the spirit. Do you know what I'm saying?"

She kept her head down, not needing to feign sweet confusion.

"Put the earrings on," he urged, looking as if he wanted to do it for her. "At least give me the pleasure of seeing them on you."

She relented. "Very well." She removed her own earrings, the peridots Tim had bought her, and inserted the pearl drops.

"It was very nice of you to think of me, but I know you'll realize I can't accept such a valuable gift—the skin on the pearls appears flawless."

"Would I select pearls with the slightest imperfections when your own skin is flawless?" He came to stand behind her, an imposing-looking man. "I suggest we take one thing at a time."

Jessica vowed he wasn't going to override her decision. "Which I've done. I've shown you what they look like on."

"Perfect!" he breathed, like a connoisseur. "Push your hair back," he instructed.

Though the air-conditioning was working efficiently Jessica felt stifled. He stood back studying her, then he moved to lay a hand on her shoulder. "You can't refuse me."

To her horror, his voice had taken on what seemed to her an ardent note. This was the worst thing that could possibly happen. It would change everything, make her job untenable. With no encouragement whatsoever, Broderick Bannerman had become infatuated with her.

Patches of color stained his prominent cheekbones. "It's clear to me you're not used to accepting presents, Jessica. A beautiful young woman like you should be showered with them."

The intensity of his expression altered abruptly when a knock came at the door. The next moment, without waiting for an invitation, Cyrus entered the room, his blue eyes flashing over the fixed tableau: his father's hand on Jessica's shoulder, Jessica, her head averted, her face as pale as his father's was ruddy, her cloud of ash-blond hair pushed behind her ears to reveal exquisite drop-pearl earrings.

It was *exactly* what Cyrus had feared. His father had been struck by Cupid's arrow. A man couldn't avoid it any more than he could avoid dying. Approaching sixty—even if he didn't look it—his father was now young at heart. For once, B.B. wasn't thinking with his *brain*. He was endeavoring to romance a woman young enough to be his daughter. He should know better. That's if any man would know better with someone like Jessica around.

Jessica fell back from the blazing contempt in Cy's regard. He was so judgmental! Anyone would think she'd been caught in some odious act.

"So this is the present." Cyrus reached Jessica, standing before her. He put a finger to the beautiful drop pearl, setting it swinging. "I expect you've promised Dad never to take them off."

"Why should she when they suit her so beautifully!" Bannerman exclaimed in a mix of anger and triumph. "Is there something you want, Cyrus?" he demanded. "It's customary to knock and wait for an answer before you barge into a room."

"Sorry about that, Dad," Cyrus said. "I had a rough childhood. No mother to teach me manners. I just wanted to know if Jessica wanted to go for our usual after-dinner stroll, if that suits her?"

"It suits me," Jessica said, already removing the earrings one by one and laying them back in the satin-lined, polished walnut case. "These are much too good to wear around the garden. They're perfectly beautiful, Broderick, but I can't accept them."

"And I can't take them back. Not *now*." A deep crease appeared between Bannerman's brows. "You've worn them. Pierced ears and so forth. As I've said you'd make me happy if you'd wear them Saturday night, Jessica. I'll leave them in the safe for you. You probably didn't bring much in the way of jewelry and the other women will be dressed up. There's quite a bit of money in Darwin."

Jessica's knees were trembling as they walked down the front steps of the homestead. Cyrus was striding ahead as though he wanted to lose her.

"What's your hurry? Are you so desperate to get back inside?"

Immediately he stopped, swinging around to face her. "What the hell was *that* all about?" He towered over her.

Her temper rose to match his. "Might I remind you we're still within spitting distance of the house?"

"I'm seething, that's why." He grasped her arm, hauling her along the path. They had rounded the end of the veranda, though the exterior lights shone over the path and into several feet of the garden, ablaze with huge birdlike heliconias. "Well?"

"Well, nothing!" Jessica jerked her arm away. "Absolutely nothing. You have a very suspicious, not to say, dirty mind."

"No one has accused me of that before." He swung her back to face him. "There are certain rules of behavior—"

"Never stopped you," she reminded him sharply. "Look, Cy, I don't want to get into an argument with you. It's really your father you should be speaking to. If he sees nothing wrong in wooing a woman young enough to be his daughter, I *do*. It's so damned embarrassing."

"I agree. I told you to tread carefully around him."

"What do you think I've been doing? I've given him no encouragement at all—it simply didn't occur to me. Why put the pressure on me anyway? Go tell your father to lay off."

He laughed, though he was obviously upset. "Hell, I mightn't be seen or heard of again."

Tentatively she reached out to him, trying to read the expression on his face. His striking features, which for all the bad feelings between them bore his father's stamp, were tense. "It can't be that bad." She had a fluttery sensation in her chest as though her heart were missing beats.

"A slight exaggeration," he said in self-mockery. "I've learned how to defend myself." He walked on. Jessica followed, increasing her pace to keep up. "Dad's cracked the whip for so long, he thinks there's nothing and no one he can't get. He could exhaust any woman with his persistence and his money. Dad's not coming to the end of his sex life. It's still all systems go."

"Not with *me,* it isn't, as I've told you a dozen times. What do you think I am, an adventuress?"

"Maybe more of a temptress."

Jessica smarted. "I'd watch it if I were you. Men are all the same. Always bemoaning a woman's power over them. *She made me do it.* Rapists have sworn on their mother's lives that their victims seduced them. It all started with Adam."

"What are you going to do about those earrings? He clearly expects you to wear them."

"He can take the bloody things back. And I don't care if my swearing offends you."

"Don't worry, I'd be swearing, too. I *hated* to see my father's hand on your shoulder."

"Jealous?"

"Yes. That's what you wanted me to say, isn't it? Jealous, angry, sad, embarrassed, deeply concerned, as well. My father is a dangerous man, Jessica. A predator. It would be very foolish to trust him."

"I don't need *you* to tell me that. A little bird told me on day one—he's very cruel to Robyn. I can't help feeling sorry for her."

"So do I, now and again. Only, Robyn has picked up a few too many of Dad's traits, haven't you noticed? She reveres him like some people revere dictators. Like Dad, I don't think she'd have any difficulty resorting to drastic measures. If she could get away with it, she'd push me off a cliff."

"Are you serious?"

He forced a laugh. "If she could get off scot-free. Poor old Robyn craves Dad's love and attention. In that way *only* is she like her mother. Robyn suffered from being adopted. She's never believed she *belonged*."

"Hardly surprising!" Jessica cried. "No one acts as though they like her. Even her husband-to-be."

Cy made a little clicking sound of disgust. "They're a pair all the same. Erik's just as mercenary as she is. Dad's right when he says Erik's real interest in Robyn is the family connection. Being Broderick Bannerman's son-in-law would be great for business. Which is why I don't like him. In fact, I despise him, though he always tries to be pleasant. As for Robyn, don't think I didn't try quite hard to be friends with her when we were kids. Sharon was a nice woman who deserved better than what she got. Livvy tried hard to be good to Robyn, as well. Neither of us got anywhere. She didn't want us. She wanted Dad. Robyn is her own worst enemy. I've gone way past trying to connect with her, especially when she'd like to see me out of the way."

Jessica's whole body tingled with a sense of danger. "That's a terrible thing to say."

He shrugged. "I'm afraid it's true. Robyn believes that with me out of the way, everything would be perfect. Of course, she couldn't be more wrong. My father and I might be mostly at loggerheads, but he'd scarcely be happy if anything happened to me. At some level, in some deep dark cave, he's buried his love for me. But it's there. He's a tormented, moody, restless man. Robyn could *never* take my place. That's what she can't seem to understand. Dad never gives me a word of praise or gratitude, but he knows and I know he can't do without me. I run Mokhani these days and I've inherited his business brain. It was my mother who gave me the gift of a *soul*. Dad might have had one, but he doesn't own it anymore."

Jessica was in the office reading through a long fax from Brett, which included an architectural drawing she found very helpful, when Robyn came in search of her.

"Hi! Thought I'd find you here." Robyn actually smiled, looking a totally different person in the process. She had beautiful white teeth that showed up well against the pale gold of her skin.

What had caused this huge sea change? Since Robyn had returned from Hong Kong, she was acting much more human and likable.

"I'm so looking forward to my party!" Robyn laughed excitedly, perching on a desk and placing the envelope she had in her hand beside her. "It's going to be great! I'm very much in love with Erik."

Jessica tried her level best to look as if Erik were among the most desirable of suitors. "I'm happy for you, Robyn. Is there going to be a surprise announcement?"

"Gee, I don't know." Robyn put her elegant, manicured hands to her blushing cheeks. "Erik loves surprising me. Whatever Dad says, Liz wasn't a good wife to him. She never wanted children. Erik is a man who should have children."

"Have you discussed it with him?" Jessica's instinct told her Erik might have been lying.

"Heavens, it's understood. The truth is, I don't want to rush into motherhood. After a couple of years of marriage, maybe. Dad would adore a grandchild."

Jessica couldn't for the life of her fire off a quick answer. She tried hard to see B.B. through Robyn's eyes, but had to leave off. Broderick Bannerman would make her own crusty grandpa seem like a Boy Scout.

"What I wanted to ask you..." Robyn frowned for a moment, considering. "Have you a suitable dress? It's formal, you know."

"Your father told me," Jessica nodded. "I do have one dress I think might do."

Robyn removed some photos from the envelope. "Look, here are some possibilities. I'd like to help. You know I own a boutique in Darwin. Exclusive designer wear. I can tell you're a girl who knows clothes."

"Why thank you, Robyn. You have beautiful taste." It wasn't a white lie, for strangely enough, Robyn did with her dressing. She always looked very glamorous, nothing over the top. It was when she had attempted to be her own interior designer she had gone adrift.

Robyn passed the photographs to her. A lovely Eurasian model was wearing a collection of party dresses, all in the height of fashion.

"These are beautiful!" Jessica said with genuine enthusiasm.

Robyn leaned forward. "I had Selina put them on to give you a better idea of what the garments would look like when worn.

So much better than showing you something on a hanger. Selina is your size." Her dark eyes ran over Jessica's tallish slender figure. "What do you think? If you like one, I could have it ferried in. Evening shoes to match. What would you be? Size thirty-six, European?"

"Yes." Jessica was starting to feel a little more kindly towards Robyn. "This is very thoughtful of you, Robyn, but—"

"Dad wants you to look your best," Robyn said as though that clinched it.

"That would be my goal in any case," Jessica answered with faint irony. "But you're the guest of honor, Robyn. Not me. My own dress is very pretty."

"As glamorous as these?"

"Maybe not." She smiled. "I didn't come here expecting to be at the ready for formal parties."

"I have a faultless eye," said Robyn, obviously thinking there was nothing to be gained from false modesty. "You'd be pleasing me very much if you would pick one out. You've got a good figure, and a good back—the dresses are cut low at the back. There'll be a lot of beautifully dressed women there. All showing off. The husbands have money coming out their ears. The wives fly off to Hong Kong and Singapore all the time to do their shopping. Some have the most gorgeous jewelry. Hope I'm not boring you. You've heard of Paspaley pearls?"

"Who hasn't? They're the most beautiful pearls in the world."

Robyn gave a throaty laugh. "I know Dad called into their Darwin showroom fairly recently. I happened to run into a friend who let it slip. I suspect he chose something to mark my thirtieth birthday. Dad knows I adore jewelry. He bought my mother a few nice pieces, which I inherited, but I can't get my hands on Deborah's stuff. Deborah died without a will, but her jewelry goes to Cyrus's future wife. That's sure to be Roslyn Newman. They've been on and off as an item for years. Not Roz's fault—Cyrus won't commit. No one measures up to the adored Deborah. That's pretty much it. Cy never got over losing his mother."

"I can understand that," Jessica said.

Robyn's mouth tightened. "I lost my own mother a couple of years back. I've had to get over it. You learn to pack your feelings away in a box. You can't let them influence your thinking."

"Easier said than done, Robyn," Jessica said quietly.

"Some of us are more strong-minded than others." Robyn snapped her fingers. "So what's the verdict? I thought the green myself as you've got green eyes."

"The green is beautiful. I'm a little nervous about the price…"

Robyn laughed. "It would be a pleasure to *give* it to you, Jessica. Good advertising for me, too, if you could just drop the hint it came from my boutique. You're bound to be asked."

The fact Broderick and Robyn wanted to shower her with presents Jessica found more disturbing by the minute. "I wouldn't dream of taking it for nothing, Robyn, though it's very generous of you to suggest it. How much is it?"

"You'll accept a discount, surely?" Robyn named a price that was practically a giveaway.

"Not *that* much of a discount," Jessica said, looking adamant.

"All right!" Robyn named a price Jessica had never yet spent on a party dress. "But it's worth it."

"Done." Jessica wanted to look beautiful for just *one* man. She put out her hand, but instead of shaking it, Robyn slapped it in a bit of fun. "I'll get on the phone right away. What about evening shoes?"

"I think my own will do."

"There'll be dancing." Robyn executed a few dance steps.

"That's great!" A sexy lambada with Cyrus, Jessica thought.

At the door of the office, Robyn turned, her gleaming page-boy falling in close on her cheeks. She really was very attractive when she managed to unwind. "We must go riding one day. I'd love to show you around. You *can* ride?"

Obviously no one had told her Cyrus had taken her riding on Chloe. "Yes."

"Good," Robyn said, sounding pleased. "I don't imagine you're an expert, but I'll be able to give you a few tips. I'm sorry we didn't exactly hit it off when you first arrived—the fact you're so young was a shock—but if Dad says you know what you're about, who am I to argue? I'll leave you in peace now. Wait until you see *my* dress. It's terrific! I want Dad to be really proud of me."

Jessica was left feeling sad. Robyn measured all her triumphs and failures against what her stepfather thought. A pity when no one could call Broderick Bannerman a kind man.

CHAPTER TWELVE

THE DAY OF the party Cyrus flew them into Darwin. A stretch limousine was waiting at the airport to drive them to their city hotel. The same limo would be on call to deliver them to and from the party that evening, as Erik's house was a few miles outside the city. It was eight-fifteen before they were ready to leave, although Robyn was the guest of honor. Lavinia had kept them waiting, trying to manage her freshly washed hair. Now it stood out from her head in a pure white pompadour decorated on the crown with a great jewelled brooch. Around her neck she wore a necklace that could have adorned the neck of Queen Nefertiti: multiple strands of turquoise beads caught at intervals with diamond arrows with a large open square of diamonds as the center piece. Lavinia, Jessica had noted, was not short of stunning vintage pieces. Tonight she had abandoned her arresting operatic wardrobe in favor of a classical turquoise toga. Turquoise-and-amethyst pendant earrings circa 1930, now the rage, dangled from her ears, dragging down the delicate lobes.

"Magnificent!" Jessica applauded when they met up in the lobby. "I'm wild about your necklace."

Lavinia advanced regally, putting her arms around Jessica

and kissing her with real affection. "How I wish I'd had a grand-daughter like you, Moira. If you find my necklace attractive, it's yours. But you must keep your hands off it until I'm safely with the angels.You look glorious. What it is to be young, beautiful and in love. I've never seen you made up. Those *eyes!* Where did you get all your beautiful clothes from? I don't remember seeing any of them." Her eyes swept Jessica from head to foot.

"You know how it is. One always finds something," Jessica joked, forced to accept the fact Lavinia would always confuse her with Moira.

Looking up—hadn't she been anticipating this very moment?—she saw Cyrus quickly descending the stairs with easy male grace. He looked so stunning she thought he would take any woman's breath away. Clothes hung the way they were supposed to on his tall, lean, wide-shouldered body, but in a white dinner jacket with black tie he was so sexy it *hurt!*

"Nothing like a family party, is there?" he smiled, his blue gaze moving from his great-aunt to Jessica, where it stayed.

She bewitched him. Her exquisite evening dress clung to her, molding her body before it tapered to her delicate ankles. Her beautiful eyes glowed seagreen. Her hair was even more abundant than he had ever seen it. Magnificent hair, that rare ash-blond!

His heart bucked beneath his ribs. She filled him with such pleasure. All he wanted to do was pick her up and run away with her. Far, far away from his father, who was starting to act like Count Dracula. Of all the scenarios he had calculated had lain ahead when Jessica had first arrived, he had never considered he and his father might want the same woman. It was crazy.

"So where are the others?" he asked, managing to sound relaxed when the sight of Jessica in her finery had nearly robbed him of breath.

Jessica's own light tone covered her heightened emotions. "Your father *was* here, but he went off again with Robyn." She wanted to put out her hand to caress him. It was getting so bad she didn't think she'd be able to hide her depth of feeling for him much longer.

Look at me Cyrus. Look at me in my beautiful dress. I've never had a dress as beautiful as this. And it's all for you.

"I had trouble with my pompadour," Lavinia was explaining to Cyrus. "I washed my hair. It was so soft it kept falling down, but Moira loaned me some spray. I never knew spray made it so easy. I must get some."

"Well, you managed in the end, Livvy," he said, kissing her cheek. "It looks marvellous.You both look marvellous. I'm glad you decided to come, Livvy. I find it impossible to believe you're in your eighties."

"I know. I look splendid in my dotage," Lavinia said complacently, rearranging a fold of her toga.

"Indeed you do. Just remember one thing."

Lavinia understood perfectly. "Be on my best behavior." She rolled her eyes. "I ask you, would I embarrass you, my darling?" She turned to sweep an admiring glance over Jessica. "Doesn't Moira look beautiful?"

"*Jessica* does," Cyrus stressed, relieved beyond words Jessica wasn't wearing his father's golden pearls. She was wearing, instead, the very pretty peridots he had seen before. They were almost hidden in her cloud of hair.

"That's a seriously sexy dress, Jessica," he said, the note in his voice sending exquisite little shivers up and down Jessica's spine. "I'm extremely impressed." He made a little twirling gesture. "Turn around."

Jessica joyfully obliged. She wanted to remember *everything* about tonight. Her silk chiffon dress, strapless, in a lovely shade of mint-green, was draped closely around her body to the hips, from where the tapering hem floated from mid calf almost to her ankles. Her evening shoes—she had brought them with her on the off chance—were sexy gold heels, which gave her extra height. The plunging back of the gown showed an expanse of youthful skin as smooth as cream.

"Delightful. Delectable. Delicious." His mouth curled into a rakish grin.

"Sounds like an ice cream."

"Tell her you want her to have your children," Lavinia burst out, a tender smile on her face.

Long used to her outbursts, Cyrus didn't even blink. He replied gently, "Livvy, dear, if I come on too strong I'll frighten her off."

"No, no, no. She feels safe with you. This family made one dreadful mistake. We can't make another."

Jessica intervened quickly. Although she was pleased Lavinia was coming to the party, she was concerned about what Lavinia would say in company. It was becoming increasingly apparent Lavinia dwelled in the realm of fantasy. She had never *once* called her Jessica. Why should she start now? She touched Cyrus's arm, her heart in her eyes. "*You* look wonderful."

"Thanks." He gave a little bow. "Especially as it took me several hours to fix this blasted tie."

Lavinia gave him a tap on the hand. "It did not. When do you suppose we'll have the pleasure of seeing Robyn in her birthday finery? Pity she's got such a flat chest. Poor little Sharon was just the opposite. Top heavy. I must say Broderick looks very distinguished in black tie. Such a shame he's got a manner one wouldn't wish on a rottweiler." She smiled at them happily.

Cyrus shot her a near-despairing look. "Livvy, I hope this isn't a case of your starting out the way you mean to go on. It's very rude to criticize Dad. You've just promised me you'd behave."

"Ah, yes. I did say that. And so I shall. It's just that I'm too old to worry about a lot of things."

Jessica couldn't help wondering how long it was going to take before Lavinia's thunderbolts came down on the party.

* * *

Erik Moore's house was very much one built to survive the elements. Darwin had suffered terribly in Cyclone Tracy of 1973, so the architectural firm that had designed the Moore house had made sure it could withstand the most severe cyclonic weather. The massive two-story concrete structure was elevated high on piers to protect it from floodwaters and topped by a broad, sheltering hip roof. The piers, surrounded by beds of agapanthus, gave the impression the house was floating. Jessica looked around her with great interest as they walked to the glass-enclosed stairway, which was the entry to the house. Its solidity and clean lines were complemented by a splendid garden full of lush and fragrant tropical plants, trees and shrubs, including four floodlit soaring date palms with the trunks bent at an interesting angle.

"Elizabeth was a great gardener," B.B. informed Jessica, sensing her interest. As usual, he didn't even bother to lower his voice. Indeed it bounced off the glass walls. There were guests both in front and behind them, rich, solid, substantial-looking people with a fair sprinkling of very beautiful Eurasian women, all spectacularly gowned. "She was responsible for all this."

"That's so unfair, Dad," Robyn protested, holding up the skirt of her sleek black, silver-trimmed creation. "Erik had considerable input."

"Without actually doing any of the work," B.B. replied with a thin smile. "Erik is a firm believer in not getting his hands dirty."

Jessica cringed in case anyone overheard him, but she realized by now Broderick Bannerman simply didn't care. Such was the fearful power of having a great deal of money.

The plant-filled central atrium was crowded with people who acted absolutely delighted by their arrival. There were lots of beaming hellos, calls of admiration and an outbreak of clapping for the guest of honor, Robyn. The general opinion may have been Robyn was a vain self-centered creature who could turn nasty when threatened, but what the hell! She was B.B.'s stepdaughter and his good will had to be preserved at all costs. It was the way societies all over the world played the game. No one was going to be completely honest. Honesty didn't pay.

Many smiles even came from people who had never forgiven Broderick Bannerman for doing awful things to them in business, but the instant Bannerman passed by, the smiles changed to expressions of bitter envy and in some cases open rage.

What *had* he done? Jessica wondered. Obviously not enough to come under investigation like a couple of multimillionaires currently in the news, but then, an investigation would take a lot of digging.

It was odd, therefore, to witness the way Cyrus worked the atrium. If he'd been running for the top position in the Territory, he surely would have been elected. The women loved him, and why not? The men gripped his hand, the smiles apparently genuine. On the one hand a Bannerman who was held in some awe and deep-running hostility, on the other a man who appeared to be universally liked and admired.

The living room was so vast there were still empty gaps between large groups of people. Erik immediately broke away from his circle, coming toward them, his expression so full of warmth it could have melted the polar cap.

"Now the party can begin!" he cried expansively. "Darling, you look sensational!" He kissed Robyn on both cheeks. Lavinia grandly extended her hand; Jessica was welcomed to his "humble abode" and the men shook hands. "I know this is going to be a wonderful night," Erik continued jovially, the picture of prosperity in a double-breasted, beautifully tailored black dinner jacket that hid his slight paunch.

"Ever the optimist," said Broderick Bannerman.

The truth was, Broderick couldn't control the anger that prowled around inside him like a wild beast. Anger seemed to be destroying him these days. Was that inevitable as one progressed into old age? He hated the thought of growing old. There was so much more he had to do. So many future possibilities! An opportunity to redo the past and get wider meaning to his life. He had come to think of it as his second chance.

But she hadn't worn his gift of the earrings.

That affected his self-esteem, his whole view of himself as a winner. He'd been absolutely sure she would. Ferociously ambitious all his life, as well as enormously successful, he couldn't grasp the possibility he couldn't buy anything he wanted. Now the fact that he felt thwarted, *worse,* scorned, did nothing to soothe his jangled nerves. So many forces were at play. He was aware Jessica and his son had reached some kind of an understanding. That manifested itself in ways that caused him anxiety. What was more natural than a young woman turning to a young man—only, no one was going to be allowed to get in his way. Cyrus, especially, who these days only served to remind him his best days were over. *Unless* he could form a new intimate relationship. The fact Jessica so closely resembled Moira would allow him to put the past to rest. Perhaps make amends to a stern God. Ever since he'd laid eyes on Jessica, the possibility had presented itself. He thought of it as his time of *transformation.* He could construct a new identity.

The experiences of his childhood had shattered him. Years had passed in a kind of terror, but he had survived. Not only survived, he had raised the family fortune to new heights. As a prime mover he was a superstar. If he had an eye for a woman, he didn't worry too much about getting her—his money pulled her in. His mirror told him he was still handsome, fit, virile. People called him a dynamo even if these days they didn't fully realize how much Cyrus propped up that image. He was *exactly* the sort of rich man who deserved a beautiful young wife. Fate had robbed him of Deborah. But by God, it wasn't going to rob him of his second chance.

Bannerman felt the hot beating urgency of his own plan. He wasn't in love with her. Nothing so sentimental. Love had little place in his life. But he *wanted* her as an avid collector wanted a centerpiece for his collection. Yet her refusal to accept his gift had left him with a dreadful aching emptiness. And goddammit, his head ached, as well. It ached a lot these days. He put it down to a high level of stress, even if he *had* lived with stress all his life. And he'd forgotten to take his blood-pressure medication.

It was Moira who had brought destruction on his whole family. So beautiful, so full of innocent allure. His father, the war hero, respected by all, had totally lost his head over her, though he had never doubted his father had put up a fight. Loving Deborah as he had, Broderick understood the power of passion. The two of them had simply been carried away. But they would never have run off together. His father had been master of Mokhani. His poor betrayed mother should have sent Moira away. Sometimes his son's resemblance to Steven, his father, turned him inside out. Then there was Hugh Balfour, so tortured and torn he had to escape life.

He had always thought Moira had deserved to die for what she'd done to all of them. But now?

Jessica Tennant was her *blood.* He'd known that instinctively the instant he'd seen her on TV. She might as well have admitted it with her own lips. And she was *real,* not a ghost. That he'd even seen the program was a miracle, and he came to recognize it as fate. He remembered the instant of recognition as an explosion in his head. Then gradually he had begun to see how he could rewrite history. It wasn't difficult for a man in his position to have had gathered for him every scrap of information on her and her family. Families always had secrets. Even from one another. He hadn't been too shocked to find out theirs. After that, everything had fallen into place.

Everyone was a slave to fate. In reaching out to Jessica, Moira's kinswoman, by making her his wife and showering her with all the gifts money could buy when Judgment Day came— he still believed in one, for he'd been through hell, so correspondingly there had to be a heaven—mightn't he be judged less harshly? For a time, after Deborah had been taken from him, he'd been seriously suicidal, but he hadn't been able to go through with it for fear of what lay on the other side. Deep down inside him was a very frightened man. As frightened as a child whose mother had to leave a night-light burning in his room.

Jessica, smiling brightly as expected, was introduced to a lot of people as the clever young woman B.B. had chosen to decorate the new mansion. She could almost hear the speculation ticking in their heads. No matter how gifted she was as a designer, wasn't she too *young* to have won such a commission? Was it sheer chance she was good-looking, as well? Some reached out to her in a warm, friendly fashion; others, older, shrewd-eyed women probably one-time girlfriends of the great man, appeared cynical. The men looked at her rather too long. She might as well have arrived hanging off B.B.'s arm for all the interest she was creating. Tonight would start a lot of malicious rumors, she thought dismally, and in turn jeopardize the blossoming relationship between her and Cyrus. That *couldn't* be allowed to happen.

Robyn wouldn't like what was happening, either. Robyn in her ultrasophisticated, one-shouldered gown with a gleaming silver trim across the neckline and on the gathered hip, was wearing glittering two-carat diamond studs in her ears. She clung to Erik, who rested his hand for the most part on her taut rounded bottom. Jessica knew she would have asked him to remove it, but Robyn obviously didn't mind.

Hours on, with the party in full swing and many whispers of a possible engagement announcement, Jessica found herself worried Robyn could be in for a bitter disappointment.

She was standing briefly on her own, waiting for Cyrus to return with champagne when Robyn, smiling brilliantly, came up to her. "Oh, Jessica, this is a dear friend of Cy's and mine. Roz Newman. She's just arrived. She had to call in on a family party."

"Hi." A very pretty, dark-haired young woman wearing an

absolute knockout of a red dress, made the more so by a push-up bra, held out her hand. "It's lovely to meet you, Jessica. Robyn has told me how clever you are."

"Lovely to meet *you,* Roz," Jessica responded, looking into doe eyes that were warm and friendly. "I'm glad to hear I've done something right. It's an important commission."

"Don't I *know!*" Roz made a moue of her luscious mouth. "Everyone thought Robyn would be handling it. She did such a great job renovating the homestead, but then, she has her businesses to look after. Love your dress. One of Robyn's?"

Jessica did what was clearly expected of her. "Yes." She smiled, holding out the lovely floating skirt.

"That's Robyn. She only caters to the young and lovely."

"Make that *rich,* young and lovely," Robyn said, looking around her. "Where's Cyrus?"

"He'll be back in a moment." Jessica realized that Robyn was moving her friend right into position.

"There he is!" Roz's eyes suddenly glowed like lamps, and her smooth cheeks flushed with pleasure. "I must talk to him. We haven't seen one another since Mum and I took off for New York, my favorite city in the whole world. Cyrus!" she caroled, as though Cyrus walking directly toward them holding two glasses of champagne was visually challenged.

"I'll leave you to it," Robyn said. "My beloved is jealous of every minute I'm away from him."

"Robyn must have rocks in her head to even consider him," Roz muttered sotto voce as Robyn moved off.

"Really?" Jessica's ears perked up.

"We all loved Liz," Roz said, becoming aware Jessica was vaguely shocked. "She had it pretty tough with a philanderer like Erik. But Erik will do anything to get onside with B.B. Ah, here's my darling Cy," she said eagerly as Cyrus joined them.

Roz stood on tiptoe and kissed him full on the mouth.

Where there's smoke, there's usually fire, Jessica thought.

"Oh, boy! That was just what I needed!" Roz enthused,

tweaking his tanned cheek. "It's *sooooo* wonderful to see you! I missed you like you wouldn't believe.You haven't returned my calls." She cast him a wickedly flirtatious look.

"I fully intended to get around to it," he apologized. "But you know me, Roz. I'm always working."

"Too hard, if you ask me. Are those drinks for us?"

"Roz you look too young to be drinking," he teased, handing one glass to Jessica before giving the other to Roz.

"You know exactly how old I am," Roz said, taking a sip. "Oh, that's glorious!"

"And damned expensive," Cyrus said dryly.

"Erik wants to impress B.B.," Roz gurgled.

Jessica stared at them with a near-disembodied sensation. What did she know of his life, after all? "Look, you two have a lot to catch up on," she said brightly. "I'll see you later."

"You'll be sure to," Cyrus retorted as Jessica all but flew away.

It was the opportunity for Broderick Bannerman to move in. He reached out to grasp Jessica's arm. He was infuriated with his son. So jealous, the heat of it consumed him.

"You've met Roz," he said, powerfully proprietorial in his manner. "Scatty little thing, but she's always been wild about Cyrus. Her mother and father are here. You've probably met them. Max and Sonia Newman of Newman Industries? Max and I sit on various boards together." He drew her toward the upper balcony, which looked out on the midnight-blue harbor scattered in the moonlight, with a billion sequined dots. "Your dress is beautiful, but the earrings you're wearing spoil the effect."

"I'm sorry. I thought they went well," Jessica said lightly. "I loved the earrings you picked out, Broderick. You have perfect taste, but no way am I deserving of such a valuable, *personal* gift."

"Don't be ridiculous," he said impatiently, fighting to keep his anger under wraps. "If I think you are, you *are!*"

With her instinct for people, Jessica was aware of the terrible tensions that were tearing him apart. He was very flushed in the face. "Do you feel okay?" she asked with concern, staring into his face.

"I'm fine when I'm talking to you." He dropped his hand to close it over hers, an action Jessica was certain was seized on. "This party and the people here are boring me stiff. I don't know what Robyn sees in Erik. He'll never make a tender, loving husband."

"Maybe she's desperate for love," Jessica suggested, withdrawing her hand under the pretext of checking a stray lock of hair. "She seems to be missing out on it."

He laughed roughly. "You amaze me, Jessica. No one else says things like that to my face."

"You were wondering, and I tried to supply a probable answer. Why *does* Robyn persist if she knows you don't approve? I don't think she's in love with him, either."

"Mostly because she's turned thirty," he said dryly. "She's no different from other women. She wants a man. She wants to be married. She's had plenty come courting. *I* didn't send them away, in case you're about to blame me. *She* did. She lost every one of them with her lack of charm. Now, would you care to dance?"

"That would be lovely."

What else could she say? She had to handle this situation as carefully as she'd handle a hive of hornets.

Things didn't get better, they got worse. Roz Newman set about making up for lost time. Time and again, she attempted to chain Cyrus to her side, though to Jessica's immense relief she was far from successful.

"Ever tried saying no?" she suggested sweetly when Cyrus groaned. They were dancing.

His embrace tightened. He was a terrific dancer. "You might try doing the same with Dad."

Broderick Bannerman had continued to pay his strange court

to Jessica. Already it had set tongues clacking like knitting needles. Was B.B. looking for a trophy wife? Would she be the one? As the night wore on, B.B. wasn't the only man who made a pass at her. Serious, solidly respectable types did, too. It was as Jessica had come to accept. Men behaved badly around blondes.

There was no engagement announcement before or after the sumptuous supper featuring the superb seafood of these tropical waters. Didn't Erik Moore see that's what Robyn had pinned her hopes on? Didn't he care? Did he think B.B.'s disapproval would in the end work against him? Who could tell? Robyn's rigid expression revealed that Erik had taken a massive swipe at her ego. Jessica sincerely hoped she would dump him and afterward seriously consider charm school.

It was Lavinia, who was having a fine old time catching up with all the gossip, who brought the evening to a spectacular end. She was seated on a comfortable sofa with a few older ladies, stately stalwarts of Darwin society, when she called to Jessica from halfway across the room.

"Moira, dear! Yoohoo!" There was little hope no one heard her even in a very large room. Lavinia's voice was her splendor. It had been big enough to project to the bleachers in her prime. To add to it, she held up her hand, setting several antique bracelets tolling like temple bells. "Come and meet my friends."

The whole area took a collective breath.

Moira?

The laughter, the animated conversation turned off like a tap. They might have all been waiting for a cataclysmic announcement.

"Funny old thing!" someone said, giving a nervous giggle.

"Moira, did you hear me, dear?" Lavinia raised the decibels as if she wanted to crack glass.

Another woman muttered an obscene word beneath, her breath and her husband looked at her in astonishment. "Carole!"

"What the hell am I supposed to say?" Carole retaliated, although she wished she hadn't been shocked into a swear word. "That Lavinia frightens me to death."

"It's Alzheimer's," another woman said sorrowfully. "The family is in for a tough time."

Farther away Broderick Bannerman looked up from a discussion with a couple of his business cronies, the hectic flush on his face deepening further.

"That's just dandy," Cyrus muttered in Jessica's ear. "Frankly I don't know how we got through this much of the night."

"I better go to her," Jessica said, horrified to be the focus of hundreds of eyes. "She'll only persist."

"Yes. I guess they can hear her at city hall." Cyrus realized with a jolt that his father looked furious. But, hell, wouldn't it be fair to say it was on their own heads, bringing Lavinia? Without question, she was suffering some form of dementia, but why should she be condemned to stay at home? She was *family,* even if she was borderline nuts.

Cyrus and Jessica walked toward Lavinia as one. "Livvy, dear, perhaps we should consider making a move," he prompted gently, leaning over the sofa and clasping Lavinia's bony shoulder. "It's well after twelve. You must be tired."

"Just a teeny bit." Lavinia laughed, fighting to get up before someone helped her. "Josie, you remember Moira, don't you?" She addressed a very smart septuagenarian with beautifully coiffed platinum hair.

"Jessica Tennant," Jessica smiled at the woman.

"She's all grown-up," Lavinia said. "I've waited over fifty years."

Josie patted Lavinia's cheek. "You aren't supposed to talk about Moira anymore, dear," she chided affectionately, herself forcibly struck by Jessica's extraordinary resemblance to the missing girl. "She's dead, darling."

"No, *no!*" Lavinia's voice took on a soaring wail. "She was just hiding. Weren't you, Moira?"

"Why don't you find Robyn and Erik? Tell them we're leaving," Cyrus suggested to Jessica in a low voice, quickly getting an arm around Lavinia.

"Robyn looks so damned unhappy," Lavinia moaned. "He might have been toying with the idea of marrying her, trying to work out if it was the right move, but he won't now. Broderick is against it. Probably the kindest stand Broderick's taken in his whole life."

"We'll say our good nights." Cyrus flashed the group the charming smile that worked miracles. He expected and got their understanding. It wasn't until the very last minute the woman called Josie caught Jessica's hand.

"Poor old Liv! No wonder she's confused. You're the very image of Moira, my dear. Is there any connection? I can't help wondering."

"I'm sorry, none." Jessica said. She could see that the woman didn't quite believe her.

B.B. gestured for them to meet him in the central atrium, which was diplomatically cleared in seconds, though the partygoers were dying to stay and watch. Everyone knew the Bannermans weren't like anybody else. And old Lavinia, bless her, was good for a laugh at any time. She was what Darwin society thought of as a real character, a welcome eccentric.

"You can't be trusted, Lavinia, can you?" B.B. bore down on her, his deep voice thin with anger.

"About what?" Lavinia demanded to know, turning fearlessly toward that hard face and glittering eyes.

"Please leave it, Dad." Cyrus had an authority all his own. "At least until we get out of here. I'll take her back to the hotel. I won't be coming back to the party. Robyn and Erik won't mind."

"You don't intend on leaving, as well, do you, Jessica?" Bannerman whipped around to ask, his tone oddly vulnerable.

A strange sense of sympathy flowed through her. She could hardly claim to like him—he didn't allow anyone to like him—

but she was trying hard to understand him. "I'm only in the way, Broderick. People are talking. Robyn won't want me around."

"Don't worry about *her,* Moira," Lavinia advised, opening her evening bag and putting away her glasses. "You always were a tender hearted little thing. It will all pass like a nine-day wonder."

Robyn rushed out from the living room in a fury. "God, I swear I'm going to scream! Lavinia isn't eccentric, she's barking *mad.* I told you, Dad, it was a mistake to let her come. She's made a show of us all."

"And you're about to make another one." Broderick shrugged a powerful shoulder as though he couldn't care less.

Cyrus, however, spoke to Robyn in an undertone. "Hey, the biggest mistake is your hooking up with Moore. Leave Livvy alone. She can't help what's happened to her mind. Jessica *is* the image of Moira, after all."

Jessica's heart skipped many beats. In her ear came a long, soft sigh. She wondered where it'd come from.

Broderick Bannerman stared at his son, his formerly flushed face now drained of color. "And how would *you* know?" he asked.

"By checking. Just like you, Dad." Cyrus locked eyes with his father. "What did you think you were doing, putting a portrait of Moira on the market? What did you hope to achieve?"

Bannerman's handsome features went slack for a few moments, then he laughed harshly. "I don't have to explain myself to you."

"Maybe you could explain it to *me,* then, Broderick," Jessica said, her sympathy evaporating. "It upsets me you didn't hire me for my professional skills. I could have been puttering away in my office earmarked for failure, for all you cared."

"That's not true." Broderick looked momentarily off balance. He searched Jessica's face for understanding. "I hired you because you've achieved recognition in your profession. Look, we can't argue here. You'd better go. Please remember,

Jessica, that you signed a contract. You're obliged to finish the job. If you doubt it, you should have devoted yourself to reading the fine print."

Robyn stabbed a finger at Lavinia. "I could kill you," she cried emotionally. "You're a real witch."

Lavinia trilled aloud. "Takes one to know one," she retorted, quite unmoved.

A nerve twitched near Robyn's eye. She continued to accompany them down the stairs. "You have no business being allowed out, Lavinia."

"More of us out than in, Robyn," Lavinia told her sweetly.

"It was all destined," Broderick muttered.

"More like planned." Cyrus gave a short, angry laugh. "You've got a lot to answer for, Dad. You might have been only a kid, but you didn't escape it all. I think you know—or you learned—what happened to that poor girl."

"Yes, who did it?" Lavinia, showing her vocal range, toned her voice down to a whisper. "Did she die from a fall? Was it an accident?"

"Hello, you're *with* us, are you?" Broderick asked of his aunt, not without humor.

"Livvy, please stop." Cyrus spoke so firmly Lavinia responded by zipping her fingers across her mouth. "This conversation has to continue at another time."

"Trust me, it *won't!*" Broderick whipped out a snowy handkerchief and mopped his broad brow. "And don't take that tone with me, Cyrus." It was obvious he was barely keeping himself in check. "I *forbid* you to take Jessica."

"That's a pity, because take her is what I intend to do," Cyrus returned curtly. "It's what Jessica wants, after all. Let's finish this right now." He grasped both Jessica and Lavinia by the hand, then inclined his head toward the living room. "They must be just loving it inside. The feuding Bannermans. Have you heard what they're up to now?" He exhaled in disgust. "Let's face it, Dad. You don't inspire trust."

This charge suddenly reminded Robyn of her dearest role in life. She linked her arm through her stepfather's, chin up, eyes flashing, the picture of loyalty. "*I* know Dad better than *you* do, Cy!" she exploded. "I love him, unlike *you*. You don't deserve to be his heir. You're staying, aren't you, Dad?" She turned, imploring eyes on her stepfather, though he was standing stock-still, seemingly unaware of her. "Don't abandon me."

"Quit sucking up to him, Robyn," Lavinia advised. "It does no good at all."

That brought Broderick out of his semi-trance. "I'll stay for another hour," he said, his face impassive. "In my opinion, Erik humiliated you tonight, Robyn. But don't worry, he'll pay."

"That's right, make 'em pay, Brodie," Lavinia crowed as Cyrus and Jessica led her away. "You should get on with your own life, Robyn. The *D*-word comes around quicker than you think."

"What's the *D*-word?" Robyn frowned in perplexity.

It was possible there was great sadness in Broderick Bannerman's answering voice. *"Death,"* he said.

CHAPTER THIRTEEN

THEY WALKED TOGETHER along the waterfront with the trade
winds blowing in off the Timor Sea. The great copper moon
of the tropics hung over the vast expanse of the harbor cutting
a bright orange path from the glittering water to the sky. It was
a beautiful night with a lovely breeze that strengthened into in-
termittent gusts. It caught at Jessica's long hair and silk chiffon
skirt, ruffling the surface of the water into peaks that broke in
white ruffles on the shore.

Their minds, still frazzled by the events of the evening, they
were just trying to relax. They had finally got Lavinia to bed—
she'd been overexcited, difficult to calm—and now both Jessica
and Cyrus recognized that either this thing mounting between
them had to stop, or become a serious commitment. Nothing
this desperate stood still.

"How did you know your father had sent Moira's portrait to
auction?" Jessica asked, watching a pair of lovers blend into the
night. "You didn't tell me."

"I *didn't* know," he said wretchedly "Dad just fell into the
trap." Cyrus cursed himself for what he had to say. "You know
you can't remain on Mokhani, Jessica, no matter what threats

my father makes. I'll take care of all that. If you *don't* go, we're headed for an almighty showdown."

They were her own thoughts; nevertheless, she was devastated to hear him put them into words. "Hang on a minute. I've scarcely arrived." The fact he was urging her to go, with good reasons or not, sliced into her like a knife. She had fallen crazily in love with him. She was ready to take her chances. Now he wanted to see her off.

Cyrus caught her into the half circle of his arm, so attuned to her he knew what was running through her head. "I know. It's one hell of a mess, but it's just too explosive. You *know* it is." There was a ragged edge to his voice. "I'm worried about you and I'm worried about my father. I've never seen him like this before. He's getting like Livvy. Mixing up the past with the present. Did you see how flushed he was tonight?"

She nodded, not trusting herself to speak, she was so agitated. "He lives under such pressure," she managed to say after a while. "It can't be good for him. Now there's this problem of *me*. Something *new* is driving him."

"You don't have to be Einstein to work it out." Cyrus's voice grated. "When Livvy looks at you, she sees Moira. It seems Dad does, too, in a way. Obviously, he's never been able to forget her. Maybe he's trying to bring Moira back. God, I don't know, but I don't like it."

Jessica shook her windblown hair from her face. "Do you suppose Moira could have been murdered all those years ago?"

Cyrus's groan was eloquent of unhappiness and confusion. "She disappeared, Jessica. This mystery will never go cold."

"Is that a yes?"

"It's a *no!*" He turned her to him almost desperately. "We're talking about *my* family, remember? *My* blood."

Tension was crackling like the flames of a bonfire. "I'm sorry."

They walked on, reaching a moon-washed clearing like a small park. Her stiletto heels dug into the grass as they moved off the pathway into the deep sapphire gloom. Colors of flowers came out of the darkness. Color and heady tropical scent. She could see timber benches.

"Jessica?"

She lifted her face to him with breathless urgency, her feelings for him invading every part of her, wiping out anger. "What?"

He stared down into her shimmering face "*You*. Just you." In his world gone mad, she seemed to be the only thing he could hold on to. He bent his head, kissing the side of her satin cheek, burying his face in her neck. "You smell like a field of flowers."

The way he said it was so seductive, so utterly thrilling it went a long way toward restoring her badly shaken confidence. She wanted to beg him to make love to her, furious with Broderick Bannerman for pursuing her and thus ruining everything....

"Hey." He lifted his head. "Are you getting shorter or what?"

She held on to him with a little shaky laugh. "My high heels are digging into the grass. I'm sinking. There's a bench around here someplace." She felt she had to sit down. *Lie* down. Her breathing had changed—short, faintly panting.

"So there is." Without warning, he lifted her high in his arms as if her weight were insubstantial. The bench was set on a concrete block. He lowered her gently onto it, keeping his arms around her. "You should wear that dress always. Though if I had you to myself, I'd peel it off you."

"When will that ever be?" she asked mournfully, aware the parameters of her world had shifted. She was so much in love with him she was ready to do things perhaps she shouldn't. Cyrus Bannerman was her one great leap into the unknown.

"Can't be soon enough," he said fervently. "I want *you* no matter how much baggage keeps getting in the way."

"Why should we let it?" That golden moon hovered over them, like a pathway to heaven. She lifted her arms, drew down his dark head.

Why indeed!

When he finally stopped kissing her, it was only to mutter, "I think we should finish this in your room—or *my* room?"

"What happens when your father comes looking for us?" she asked in a voice verging on edgy laughter. "God knows he's capable of it."

"We don't answer." Cyrus was almost afraid of what he might say and do if his father pushed him too far. The idea of his father wanting this young woman he had come to love drove him crazy. Clashes with his father were one thing, but this was so dreadfully inappropriate. "Kissing you is wonderful," he murmured. "You weave such a spell. Look at this hair!" He speared a hand through the pale moonlit tresses in wonderment. "I want to see your hair spread out on my pillow. You can wear your earrings—they're very pretty, after all, but nothing else." He twisted a long coil of her hair around her throat. "You'll make an exquisite bride."

Jessica's heart rocked in her breast. "Is that a proposal?"

"Why would someone like you want to marry into my family?" he asked with near despair. "Mokhani isn't a safe place for beautiful young women. Beauty seduces. Just as in the fairy tales, it can also carry a curse."

"Don't *say* that!" She put her fingers against his mouth.

He caught them and kissed them. "A world lost for love! I see nothing. I hear nothing. All there is, is *you* all around *me*."

"I might use the very same words," she whispered. "I never want to let you go. I *won't* let you go." He stood up, pulling her to her feet. Their hunger for each other swept all before it. Tonight they were on the crest of a wave....

As they headed back to the hotel, cars whizzed back and forth, couples strolled arm in arm or came out of restaurants, laughing, ready to go on to nightclubs.

"So much we have to get to the bottom of," Cyrus said. "Dad knows a lot he's not telling."

"Why don't you try to speak to your aunt Barbara again?"

Jessica hugged his arm, thinking for all that was happening she had never been aware of such happiness.

He sighed deeply. "My aunt finds the whole subject of Moira and her disappearance too painful. Not that she'd know anything. Whatever happened would have been kept from the children."

"Unless your father saw what happened with his own eyes," she found herself suggesting, albeit in a fuzzy way. Certainly she'd made no decision to say it.

"God, no!" A convulsive shudder went through Cyrus's lean body. "He *couldn't* have been there. Dad was only seven. He would have been able to ride, of course, but he'd have been forbidden to venture too far from the main compound. From all accounts, there was a bad thunderstorm that day, as well. I've gone over and over this, Jessica. Dad couldn't have been out there."

"Could he have gone with someone who was?" The compulsion to ask these questions was worsening. She couldn't contain them.

He flinched, his arm tightening around her. "My grandmother or my grandfather?" he asked bitterly.

"I know how upsetting this is for you," she said quickly. "It was only a suggestion."

"I want a life *free* of the past, Jessica. You've affected us all so much. But we now know your coming to Mokhani was planned by my father. The great irony is I have to thank him for that, otherwise our paths would never have crossed. Dad's getting you to Mokhani had little to do with decorating the mausoleum. I don't want to offend you, but he probably didn't care if you turned out to be the worst designer in the length and breadth of Australia. He hired you to rework his *life* in some way. It's almost as though he's trying to rewrite history. But nothing makes sense. I can't begin to understand his motives. I'm horrified Dad has become fixated on you. He doesn't want *me* to get in the way.... Oh, hell, what's the use of talking about it? I don't want to talk. I want to make love."

"You shouldn't have to be in conflict with your father over me. It's not *meant* to be that way," Jessica cried. "I love *you!*"

When they arrived back at the hotel, they found Broderick waiting for them in the lobby. The minute he saw them, he heaved himself to his feet.

Cyrus swore beneath his breath. Jessica felt she could swim an ocean to get away. The unthinkable was becoming a daily occurrence.

Broderick approached, his shoulders hunched. "All right, so you're back!" He glared at his son, so cruelly young and handsome. God, if he had his time over again! he thought. Aging was a whiplash across a man's back. Jessica appeared to float, a lovely fluid motion to her skirt, her eyes brimming with emotion.

But not for *him.*

She was Moira, only different. Stronger, far more confident, knowing her place in the world. The tears would never dry for Moira. Moira lying so secret, so hidden away from the world.

"Don't do this, Dad," Cyrus muttered, between clenched teeth. "How can you sit here waiting for us like we were children?"

"I'll remind you, Cyrus, Jessica is *my* responsibility," Broderick said aloud, in a hostile voice.

Jessica noticed several other hotel guests looking their way. She squirmed inside. "You must excuse me," she said in haste. "I'm tired. I'm going to my room." She didn't fancy getting her picture in the noon papers.

"We'll all go up," Cyrus said briskly.

Broderick didn't say another word until they were in the elevator. Just the three of them in a claustrophobic space. "It may seem an odd thing for me to do, Jessica," Broderick said, apparently in an effort to apologize to her. "But your well-being is important to me."

"It's highly unlikely I'd come to any harm with Cyrus, Broderick," she said. "Besides, I can take care of myself." She didn't want to say another word, sensing they were on the brink of a terrible argument. It couldn't be good for Broderick. His color wasn't good. In the space of a few hours, he'd aged ten years. All the virility had seeped out of him.

"You know Cyrus is involved with Roz Newman?" he announced abruptly. "Am I wrong, Cyrus?" he challenged. "I rather think she's expecting an engagement ring sometime soon."

"And she's as likely to get one as Robyn." Cyrus issued a humorless laugh. "What are you on about, Dad?"

"You know damn well!" Broderick snarled. "It's for Jessica's own good."

"I'm sorry. This is my floor." Jessica took quick steps forward. "It's best if I say good night."

She wasn't swift enough.

"Not yet!" Broderick grasped her bare arm, restraining her. The door closed while they all stood arrested. "I want you to come up to my suite."

"Oh, Dad!" Cyrus groaned, shaking his dark head. His formidable father, always cold reason, seemed to be disintegrating right before his very eyes. "What's going on with you?" He began to wonder if dementia was going to overtake the entire family.

"What do my actions possibly have to do with you?" Broderick said through gritted teeth.

"I'm your son, remember?"

"So maybe I want your support, not your opposition."

"To do *what?*" Cyrus appealed to him. "Can you let us know what's on your mind?"

"I don't trust you, Cyrus," his father snapped.

"Around Jessica, is that what you mean?" Cyrus watched the high color flare into his father's face. "I take it that's a yes," he said quietly.

They had arrived at the top floor where Broderick had his

suite. Still clutching Jessica's arm, he stepped out into the empty hallway, Cyrus right behind. Broderick turned Jessica to face him. "I thought you liked me, Jessica." Incredibly he spoke like a suitor who having been led on, was left bitterly confused and disappointed.

"Of course I like you, Broderick," Jessica said, sick with pity and embarrassment. "But first and foremost you're my client."

Their voices were hushed, but the atmosphere couldn't have been more intense.

"That's the only reason I got you to Mokhani," he explained, never taking his eyes off her. "So we could get to know one another."

Jessica dropped her head, quite unable to meet his gaze. He had placed her in a terrible position. "I can't talk about it anymore. I had no idea your thoughts were running on those lines. You actually got me to Mokhani under false pretenses, Broderick. I was so excited to get such a commission, too. I've done so much work already. All for nothing! Cyrus is right. I must go home."

"Go home?" Broderick's eyes flashed with shock and rage.

"You don't leave her with much alternative, Dad," said Cyrus. "There can't be any relationship between you and Jessica." He stretched out his hand to his father in sympathy.

But Broderick ignored the gesture. "You envy me, Cyrus. Envy fills your heart. Envy of one's father is a terrible thing."

"It's the other way around in our case," Cyrus said with weary sadness. "I don't envy you at all. You may have achieved a great deal in your life, but you're not a happy man. You've given everyone, including yourself, such a hard time. Let's end this discussion. Call it a night. You can't expect Jessica to want to stay on when you're starting to harass her."

"Harass her?" Broderick spat. "How dare you!" He shook his head like some sovereign of old, ready and able to put his own son's head on the block. "How dare you say such a thing! It's not *right!*" He twisted his body, shaking his head from side to side.

Tears were forming in Jessica's eyes. "Please stop, Broderick," she begged, laying a restraining hand on his arm. "You don't look at all well. You must see I can't stay."

Arrogance flooded Broderick Bannerman's expression. "My son is acting like he's trying to protect you. He really just wants you for himself."

"And you have a big problem with that, don't you, Dad?"

"You've always hated me, Cyrus."

Cyrus's handsome face contorted in distress. "God, Dad, we're *family*. The wonder is I *don't* hate you. You've always treated me like the enemy even when Mum was alive. You seemed to see me as a rival for her love and attention, isn't that right? You turned your back on me when I was just a kid. You didn't change even after she was dead."

Broderick's head shook as though he had palsy. "You can't know how desperately unhappy that made me."

"You could have turned to me, your son." Cyrus got a grip on his father's shoulder. "But that didn't cross your mind. You set out to bring me to my knees. I might have been another man's son. That really worried me when I was a kid, do you know that? I seriously considered I might have been a bastard. That would explain your behavior. But I look like you, don't I? I also look like my grandfather, Steven. I'm the Bannerman you rejected."

His father looked a bit mad. "With good reason. You're the—"

"Broderick, *stop*." Jessica put herself between the two men. "Somewhere deep down, Broderick, I think you hate yourself."

It was a statement that seemed to strike Broderick Bannerman like a blow. He closed his eyes as though he were in terrible pain and slumped as if pierced through with a sword. "I do. You're right, I do," he muttered.

"Let's go, Jessica." Cyrus reached for her.

But like a man possessed, Broderick changed suddenly from passive to violent.

"Cyrus!" Jessica shouted the warning, but it was too late.

With a look of savage hatred in his eyes, his fist clenched, Broderick Bannerman launched himself at his son, screaming, "Do you understand what you've done to me? *Do you?* Treason—"

Almost without volition, Cyrus swung a defensive punch. It sent his father sprawling back against the wall, from there to the floor, where he slumped into a posture of defeat.

Immediately Cyrus felt an overwhelming disgust for himself. He stretched out his hand. "Get up, Dad. I shouldn't have done that. Neither should you."

His face marred by a look of terrible bitterness and defeat, Broderick allowed himself to be pulled to his feet. "Damn you to hell!" he swore.

"I'm sorry I hit you." The words were flat.

"We've got nothing to say to each other," his father snarled. "Take her if you want her. She's not who she says she is, anyway. She's Moira back from the other side."

It was meant to be a deadly parting shot, only Broderick staggered, clutching at his head with his two hands.

"Aaaaaaaah!"

"Dad!" Cyrus cried in alarm.

"Go to hell," Bannerman said, still clutching his head.

Cyrus turned to Jessica. "Call an ambulance," he said urgently, moving to his father to physically support him.

She needed no prompting.

CHAPTER FOURTEEN

OVER THE NEXT few days, the family fielded innumerable questions from the media about Broderick Bannerman's condition. Finally Cyrus had to take the phone off the hook. Their stock answer had been the same as the spokesman's for the Royal Darwin Hospital. Mr. Bannerman was resting comfortably. He had not suffered a heart attack or a stroke. He would be in hospital a day or two, undergoing tests.

A media crew drove all the way from Darwin to the station, but got turned back by stockmen acting as security guards. A media helicopter flew over the main compound, taking aerial shots, but the pilot wasn't about to risk landing. This was the Territory and strangers didn't come onto a man's land without an invitation. B.B. especially had to be treated with respect.

What Broderick Bannerman was really suffering from was a tumor growing in the right posterior temporal region of his brain, dangerously close to the brain stem. This information was not released to the press. The tumor would most certainly paralyze him, cause deafness, blindness, in short, kill him if not removed or treated by chemotherapy, which he refused. Broderick

Bannerman had elected to take his chances with an operation. His doctors gave him only a fifty percent chance of survival.

It seemed the family had found the explanation for the patriarch's frenzied behavior.

"So this is when we say goodbye to Broderick," Lavinia announced, crossing herself in a rare moment of religious fervor. "Who would ever have thought I might outlive him? I'm old, old, old. A nuisance to everyone, including myself. He was a beautiful little boy. Steven's heir. We all thought he was going to be fine. It's what happened to Moira that tore the family apart. Even now Barbara won't come to Mokhani, although she visited the hospital." Lavinia was seated in her favorite planter's chair on the front veranda. Jessica had taken a chair near her, holding the frail hand with its knotted fingers. The skin around the contours of Lavinia's eyes was a murky violet, but the eyes themselves were bright. Jessica had the idea Lavinia played a lot at being batty. "You should ask him before it's too late," Lavinia said.

"Ask him what, Miss Lavinia?" Jessica tried to smile into the old lady's face.

"What they did with you, of course."

That blew the notion of not being batty out of the water.

A little distance off in the trees, a bird sang one beautiful heart-piercing note.

Jessica stood up. "I think I hear the phone. It could be Cyrus." Cyrus was in Darwin meeting with the eminent neurosurgeon who was to head the team to perform the very difficult and risky operation on his father.

It wasn't Cyrus. It was Brett, saying he couldn't leave until the weekend, but he and Tim were coming up to join her and take her home.

"You need to be looked after, Jass," he told her, his voice filled with concern. "You sound unhappy."

"I seem to have been through a lot." A lot she hadn't told him.

"It's scarcely your fault, sweetheart." Brett tried to console her. "The tumor has probably been growing for years. Cyrus will probably want to continue the project at some point, but that will be the last thing on his mind with his father so ill. And right in the middle of it, you win the award. You have to show up for the ceremony, you know. Life goes on, no matter what. We have to celebrate it. I'm very proud of you."

Robyn was taking her stepfather's illness very badly. In fact, she looked like she was coming apart, lost in silent, secret, desperation.

Jessica no longer doubted Robyn loved her stepfather. She was not prepared, however, for Robyn's anger. "He doesn't want to see me anymore!" she screamed at Jessica, having sent Lavinia rushing to her room as though she couldn't lock the door fast enough. "I'm nothing to him. *No one.* I never have been."

"He doesn't want to see Cyrus, either," Jessica tried to point out. Facing death, Broderick had turned in on himself. "He's not clear in his mind."

"No, he's not." Abruptly she changed topics. "So who are you really?" Robyn stared at Jessica with her deep-set dark eyes.

Jessica sighed. "Not a ghost, Robyn. It's all gone far enough, this Moira business. Your stepfather has an excuse. He's been diagnosed with a brain tumor. Lavinia's excuse is—"

"She's mad as a bloody hatter," Robyn interrupted bitterly. "God, why doesn't the old bat die? Oh no, she's got plans to stick around for Cyrus's wedding when it's just possible he won't get married for years he's so bloody choosy. Look, I've got to get out of the house. Why don't we go for a ride?"

"If you want to," Jessica agreed, not really wanting to, but realizing Robyn was suffering in her own way.

When the stable boy led out Chloe, Robyn turned abruptly. "I don't like that horse. It's bad-tempered. Take her back."

"It's for Miss Jessica," the boy said. "She rides him."

Robyn stared at Jessica with something like outrage. "Since when?"

"Since Cyrus took me to the escarpment," Jessica said, having second thoughts about accompanying this volatile young woman. Robyn delighted in baiting Lavinia about her eccentricities. Was it possible Robyn was bipolar? She certainly had huge mood swings. "It was when you were in Hong Kong."

"Congratulations. So how did you manage to stay on?" Robyn gave a twisted smile, laced with challenge.

"She's better than you," the stable boy piped up, digging his hands into his jeans.

"Oh, shut up." Viciously Robyn flicked her whip at him but he moved out of range with natural agility. "Who's asking you?" she growled.

"Only tryin' to help." Unperturbed, the boy gave Jessica a big white grin.

"Don't worry, Robyn, I'll keep up," Jessica said. "I don't think we should go all that far. Cy is due home late afternoon."

"You're involved with him, aren't you?" Robyn swung her leg over her mount, a big gelding. Her tone was despairing, as though she could prevent nothing.

Jessica turned the question aside. "Cy's thoughts are only for his father."

An hour and more later, they were lost in the vastness that was Mokhani.

"Somewhere around here that blasted Moira's life came to an end." Robyn sat her horse, one hand on the reins, the other indicating the primal wilderness surrounding them. "I suppose if the truth be known, someone killed her. I can just see it happening. She was very pretty, from all accounts."

Jessica shuddered. "Do you really believe someone in your family was capable of murder?"

"Not *my* family!" Robyn gave a bitter laugh. "I have something to be grateful for, it seems. My poor mother was a saint.

She put up with Dad, who treated her like dirt, just a possible brood mare Dad could never get his adored Deborah out of his memory. He even turned on Cy, his own son. I ask you, is that crazy or what? Anyway, there's been some haunting in this family. The legend of bloody Moira has survived the test of time."

"She ought not be *bloody* Moira, Robyn. She was a victim and so young!" Jessica stared out over the immense primeval landscape. Its extraordinary mystique was palpable. It wasn't just the wonder of nature, the vastness or the savage beauty. It was the *antiquity* of the Timeless Land, the oldest continent on earth.

They were taking shelter beneath the branches of the loveliest of all the Outback trees, the slender white ghost gums. A grove of six or more were growing luxuriantly out of the sand, highlighting the rust-red of the soil, the golden grasses that sprung out of it and the burnt siennas of the boulders strewn about like discarded devils' marbles. To the northeast, the purple escarpment stood out ruggedly against the brilliant cobalt sky. She marveled that she had actually been right to the summit. She'd walked the length of that magical canyon with its rainbow walls, caught the spray off the waterfall, pondered the mysteries of the deep dark green lagoon where the spirit of a beautiful *lubra* had made her home.

"It's easy to see how Moira could have disappeared." Jessica spoke her thoughts aloud. "Someone who didn't know the bush would be in a lot of danger out here."

Robyn's expression was chilling. "Easy to bury the body. We have cases of disappearance right now in the present. That English tourist—they'll never find him."

"What a great grief for his family." Jessica drew a deep sigh. "Moira's family must have been devastated. I don't think they could have faced the notion she might have been murdered. They had enough of a nightmare to contend with. I've never asked you about what happened to *your* mother, Robyn. You must have loved her dearly."

Robyn hunched forward in the saddle, frowning. "I did. She comes to me in my dreams. But when she was alive, she was little use to me. She was completely dominated by Dad."

"How did she die?" Jessica asked again, very gently.

Robyn's face, inexplicably, became distorted by anger. "Curious, are you?"

"I'm sorry." Jessica hastened to apologize. "I was actually trying to help. Sometimes it lightens the load if you can share it with someone. You haven't had an easy time, Robyn."

Robyn's eyes brimmed. "Don't feel sorry for me. Feel sorry for yourself. Cyrus is only using you. You're nothing in the scheme of things. Just a passing affair. He doesn't give a damn about you, really."

"I don't think you're in his confidence," Jessica said. She trusted Cyrus. She knew she was right to trust him. This was a clumsy attempt to undermine him.

"I know this much." Robyn looked at Jessica, hardeyed. "He's going to marry Roz Newman. He doesn't need you. He needs Mokhani . He's there in Darwin pouring out filial love, but he's too late. Dad will see I get what I deserve."

"You can't be implying he'll make you his heir?"

Robyn gave a convulsive laugh that petered out. "Cyrus hitting on you was a disastrous move. It upset Dad greatly. From that moment, things started going well for me."

"I thought you wanted to marry Erik Moore." Jessica endeavored to follow Robyn's reasoning.

She shrugged. "Dad was right. He isn't worthy of me. Liz did try to warn me."

Jessica shook her head. "Don't you think it strange your stepfather doesn't want to see you now? Perhaps he was building up your hopes, Robyn, only to knock them down. A tumor affects the sufferer's behavior, sometimes in a disastrous way. I would say even before that, your stepfather liked to pull the rug out from under people."

"He's famous for it," Robyn confirmed. "People have warned

me a thousand times but I was blind. Dad seemed like a god to me when I was a kid. My judgments were all wrong. I picked the wrong Bannerman to be my champion." Robyn sank in the saddle as though all the air had gone out of her body. "Cyrus tried to bond with me, God knows he got precious little love from his dad, but I shut him out. You know why? There's something dreadfully wrong with me. I'm even *happy* in a way that Dad's dyingput him out of his misery. He's said some rotten things to me. If there is a heaven, which I seriously doubt, Mum will be there. Dad, I'm thinking, is heading straight for hell."

The sun sank in a blazing ball of fire toward a horizon brushed with great sweeps of pinks, golds, indigo and grape. The mauve dusk settled in quickly. They didn't seem to be getting anywhere. How was it possible for Robyn to get lost? She'd grown up on Mokhani. The horses were tired and sweating, especially the filly, Chloe.

Robyn ripped off her Akubra and smoothed her shiny black hair in agitation. "Listen, I have to go for help. You stay put. You'll just be holding me up."

"You don't expect me to stay here by myself, do you?" Jessica looked nervously around her, amazed that the Outback-bred Robyn seemed as disoriented as she was.

"You're not scared, are you?" Robyn taunted.

"I think anyone in their right mind would be. It's pitch black at night. There's no water. We haven't seen any dingoes, but I'm sure they're about. What about snakes? Are you sure you're not doing this deliberately? You want to punish me for some reason? You said yourself there's something wrong with you."

"Don't be so bloody stupid," Robyn snarled. "Cyrus will be home. He'll be expecting us back. All you have to do is stay put. That's the first rule in the bush. When someone knows the area you're in, you stay there. You don't move off. I'll ride back as fast as I can. I can cope a lot better without you and the filly tagging along. She's tired. She doesn't have the stamina of the gelding. Cyrus will be only too happy to come back for you. You might even rate a night under the stars. Make the most of it. It's all you're going to get."

Robyn arrived back at the homestead to a very hostile reception.

"Explain yourself, Robyn. And fast." Cyrus's voice carried the strain of their wait. "You rode out together. Where's Jessica?" Cyrus generated such anger it was like a fire had been lit inside him.

"Yes, where is she?" Lavinia ran at Robyn raining blows on her. "Don't lie to us, you wicked girl. Where's Moira?"

Robyn ground her teeth with fury. "It's *Jessica,* you crazy old bat. You should have been locked up long ago. Jessica is where I left her. It's all her fault, wanting to wander around on her own, taking no notice of the time. She could easily have ridden back with me if she'd tried, but she's just a soft city girl. She's out by Wirra Creek. At least that's where I left her. I told her to stay put."

"You better not be lying to us, girl." Lavinia stared up at Robyn, wild-eyed.

It *was* a lie. Robyn had long felt she was under no obligation to tell the truth. All her efforts these long years, her bids for love and respect proved futile.

"Why the hell would I? You're nuts!"

Lavinia shook her head grimly. "You're not so sane, either."

Cyrus's voice cut them off like the crack of a whip. "Livvy, you'd better go up to your room. I'll come and see you the minute I get back with Jessica. Robyn, I'd advise you to leave Livvy well alone or you'll answer to me."

"I will, will I?" Robyn shouted, her face twisted with bitterness. "Let's have it. Dad's told you you're his heir?"

"He hasn't said a word." Cyrus regarded his stepsister with contempt. "And if I am, that's as it should be. You're not going to get anyone to disagree with that. But take heart, you won't be left out. I'll take the helicopter. You made Jessica understand the importance of staying where she was?"

"What do you think I am?" she asked with weary disgust. "Of course I told her. She mightn't have listened."

"You'd better be telling the truth." Cyrus was nearing the end of his tether.

"Yeah, yeah. Go to her," Robyn yelled. "It's pretty damned dark out there."

Overhead, waterfowl, myriads of them, were flying in formation, squadrons of them at various heights, darkening the already fading sky. Jessica kept looking until they disappeared from sight. They were heading for water. Without water, all creatures died.

I can't sit around waiting for help, she thought. *I have to get myself settled in case I'm stuck here for the night.* In her saddlebag she had a canteen of water, a couple of teabags, two crisp Granny Smith apples, and a few little packets of dried fruit— sultanas and apricots. She had even found a box of matches right at the bottom of the saddlebag, though she hadn't put them there. Maybe one of the stable boys stealing a quick smoke while he was out exercising the filly.

Food and fire, at least. A cup of tea. No milk. No sugar. She didn't care. Her throat felt parched, a combination of heat and panic. Hot during the day the desert, she knew, could turn freezing at night. What could she use for warmth? She was wearing jeans and a cotton shirt, a bandanna around her throat. If the worst came to the worst, there was Chloe's saddle blanket. She didn't fancy that around her, but then it was still light and the temperature was only beginning to drop.

She found herself a stout stick just in case a couple of dingoes came calling. Beautiful-looking animals, she knew they could and did kill humans. She had to be ready for that sort of violence.

What a fool you are trusting Robyn.

Robyn had big problems, which she frequently demonstrated. Like today.

Jessica felt a bursting sensation in her chest. She had the dismal feeling she had walked right into a trap. But what had Robyn hoped to achieve? Had she simply wanted to give her a good fright? A miserable night spent alone in the wilderness, communing with the guardian spirits. With Moira perhaps? Poor little Moira, who had disappeared without trace. Jessica had no fear of Moira's shadowy ghost. Moira didn't threaten her. Moira was a friend.

You are, aren't you Moira?

She spoke exactly as if the young governess were standing near her. One needed a friend at such times, even if the friend existed in another dimension.

As she worked to collect enough firewood, Jessica cast her mind back over Broderick Bannerman's parting shot. *She's not who she says she is.*

Had he found out something about her family? Something no one else knew or about which no one had ever spoken? It had nothing to do with her beloved Alex, her nan. Virtually every minute of Nan's life had been well documented. Nan had been the only daughter of a prominent family.

Yet it was such a strange thing to say. If not Nan, who? Someone who had handed down the family face. Her great grandmother, Margo. Margo had gained quite a reputation for being "difficult." She had run off to Europe at one stage and her parents had had to go chasing after her. She'd been at that time engaged to an upstanding young man who'd been devastated when she'd taken off without a word of explanation. The miracle was he'd taken her back and married her. Nan always told that story, an odd expression in her eyes.

Jessica got the fire going without too much trouble. Fire was beautiful and terrible. Tonight it was beautiful, wonderfully comforting. She made herself a cup of tea. Again, absolutely delicious, and she wasn't a tea drinker; it slicked the dry patches in her throat. She was hungry, so she started on a packet of raisins. Good source of iron.

In no time at all, it was dark, except for the orange-gold flames of her fire, which, as she piled on the kindling, rose higher and higher. She couldn't let it go out. She'd collected a good amount of fallen branches, dried leaves and grasses. Ordinarily, she wasn't frightened of the dark, but then, she'd never spent a night in the vast desert where nocturnal animals were on the prowl. She had Chloe to protect her. Or maybe she was supposed to protect Chloe, she wasn't sure. Chloe wouldn't be hungry, at least. She'd had her fill of the golden grasses, and Jessica had given her some of her own water.

All they had to do was sit tight and wait for Cyrus.

Cyrus!

Just to say his name sent a thrill of warmth through her. Images of her other loved ones kept coming.

If you're up there, Nan, now's the time to make the stars come out.

They did.

As she watched with bated breath, the stars came out in all their glory, spreading their brilliance across the sky. There was Orion, the mighty hunter striding across the sky, his faithful hunting dogs at his heels. The Southern Cross beamed its magic down on her. Even the night wind sang a song to her. Not mournful but shivery sweet. The rapidly cooling air was incredibly fragrant as the desert plants released their aromatic oils which blended subtly with the perfume of a little carpet of wild flowers, like a mauve mist that covered the sand nearby.

One by one, several kangaroos approached the fire. They remained there, standing upright on their powerful back legs, ears pricked, their large soulful eyes seeming to ask her what she was doing there and was she all right? It was clear they meant her no harm and expected no harm from her, but when Chloe wheezed, they bounded off into the night, their great sinewy tails pounding the earth. She was sad to see them go.

Time went slowly. The cold air acted like a drug on her tired body. It was almost possible to nod off....

At one point, she thought she heard a whirring sound. It grew louder. Had she really dozed off? She must have. Her eyelids were heavy and she was freezing! Her fingers encountered gooseflesh all over her arms.

She leaped up, staggering a little.

It was a helicopter.

"Cyrus!" she yelled like a madwoman, a loud melancholy wail. She began to leap around the fire like a dancer at an Aboriginal corroboree. Something skittered across her vision. She peered across the mounting flames where someone who looked very like her had joined in the dance. How was that possible? She had to be hallucinating. She fought to reassert logic. The cold had sapped her brain. "Is that you, Moira?" she cried confusedly. "Do you know this place?"

Moira disappeared with a little wave.

Jessica told herself everything would be okay. She was being protected. She didn't know how she knew that. She just did.

And now, she could see the welcome lights of the helicopter beaming over the rough terrain, coming over.

Had Robyn lied? Why? But then Robyn basked in lies, Cyrus told himself, even now scarcely crediting she had done such a seriously twisted thing as abandon Jessica in the desert. He could be heading miles in the wrong direction given that it was Robyn who'd told him where Jessica was. Nevertheless, he made a low pass over the area around dried-up Wirra Creek. It was as he was circling he spotted the glow of a fire several miles off.

Thank God.

His relief was enormous, sweeping from his head to his heart. *I'm coming for you, Jessica. Hang on.*

All he wanted in this world was to gather her in his arms. To tell her how much he loved her and wanted her to be with him forever.

* * *

So, it was time to face the music, was it?

Robyn heard the helicopter before she saw Cyrus put down on the home grounds. Him and his easy skills. Not a bloody thing he couldn't do. She stood at the French doors watching the rotors slow to a stop before he jumped out, disappearing around the other side of the chopper from where he emerged into the strong wash of exterior lights with a bundled-up Jessica tucked in his arms. He loved the bitch, Robyn realized now. She had seen the very real fear in his eyes when she had returned to the homestead alone.

He hadn't trusted her to tell the truth, of course. Never had. Very wise.

Her head ached. Her stomach cramped with nausea. She couldn't do a goddamned thing right. The bitch was back. Not that she'd really believed Cyrus wouldn't find her. Cyrus knew she'd been lying her head off since she was a kid, hell-bent on trying to get him into trouble. But what choice did she have, then or now? Nobody loved her. Well, her mother had, but her mother had passed through life without causing a single ripple. By rights, she should have hated B.B. if only because of the callous way he had treated her mother. Instead, in accordance with her perverse nature, she had singled him out as the one person in life from whom she wanted love and attention. That longing had taken on obsessive proportions. But then, she'd been an extraordinarily distressed and needy child. She had been drawn to Erik because he was something of a father figure.

"I'm a natural-born victim," she said aloud. "It's bleedingly, blindingly, bloody obvious!"

Her head spun. Why not? She was drunk. Her poor mother had turned into a real lush.

Robyn pulled back the opulent covers on her bed—fit for Cleopatra—then slipped beneath them. Turning groggily to look at her bedside clock, she was startled to see it was only seven-thirty. Little kids stayed up later than that!

But what the hell! She wasn't going to endure any tongue lashing from Cyrus, so madly in love with Jessica, who looked like bloody Moira...pardon me, *Moira*. There was always the chance Jessica and Moira were somehow related. If they were, B.B. would have found it out, B.B. the super sleuth. She'd locked her bedroom door. Cyrus could pound on it all he liked. Her entire existence could be summed up in one word.

Failure.

Robyn pulled her iridescent violet nightgown around herself. She'd shelled out a fortune for it. She'd intended to wear it on her honeymoon. Turn Erik on, though it would've been blood hard, damn pansy. Yawning helplessly, Robyn allowed her troubled spirit to sleep.

CHAPTER FIFTEEN

IT WAS A silent house they returned to, although enough lamps were blazing for a Christmas party.

"Robyn's not here, waiting for us," Cyrus commented, his tone grim. "I bet she locked herself in her room the minute she heard the chopper. Her pitiful little scheme—God knows what she hoped to achieve—foiled. It's about time Robyn was forced to stop and take a good long look at herself and what she's become. Dad was a terrible influence on her."

"Not tonight, Cyrus," Jessica begged. "I don't think she meant any real harm."

"How little you know her," Cyrus said. "How are you feeling now?" He looked down at her anxiously. She had stopped shivering. He had given her a brandy at the rescue scene which had quickly warmed her, then had wrapped her in the mohair rug. At the very least, he had expected and wouldn't have been surprised by a few tears. It was a pretty scary experience for anyone who wasn't used to the wilderness to be left alone in it. But she had been aglow with welcome, literally dancing into his open arms, wanting no fuss, even if she was chilled to the bone.

"What you need now is a hot bath," he told her. "I'll run it for you. Then I better tell Livvy you're safe and sound. I know she'll be worried."

"We'll both tell her," Jessica said, feeling utterly warmed by his embrace. "I can wait another few minutes. But I *am* hungry."

"I'll take care of that, as well." He dropped a kiss on her up-turned mouth.

Lavinia threw open her door at the sound of Cyrus's voice. She emerged in a crumpled pink nightie and a magnificent brocade full-length evening coat fit for Boris Godunov. "My darlings!" She threw her arms around Jessica and kissed her. "We couldn't lose you a second time. That bloody Robyn! She's a criminal. We ought to turn her in to the police."

"Have you had something to eat, Livvy?" Cyrus asked quickly, anxious to get Jessica settled.

"Molly brought me a tray. She's such a comfort. I hope Broderick has left her a tidy sum in his will."

"He's not dead yet, Livvy," Cyrus reminded her bleakly.

Lavinia sighed and touched his face. "It has to happen, my darling. What other ending can there be? Now, why don't you take Moira off and feed her? She must be hungry stuck out there in the bush, though I suppose she's accustomed to it by now. Good night then, my darlings." She made to shut the door. "You've got no chance of waking up Robyn. She's quickly falling a victim to the wicked booze like poor Sharon. At lease *she* had an excuse. Only, Sharon liked vodka, I think."

Jessica took a long time over her bath, letting the warm, scented water ease the tiredness and take the chill out of her bones. Afterward she didn't bother getting dressed again. She slipped on a nightdress, then covered it with the silk robe her mother had bought for her on her last trip to Hong Kong. It wasn't as magnificent as Lavinia's rich brocade coat, but it was very pretty. Pretty enough to wear out, considering some of her friends attended functions in what looked like their underwear.

She found Cyrus in the kitchen giving his attention to a meal. "Omelets?" His blue gaze enveloped her.

"Sure you can make them?" She smiled. She went to him and slid her arms around his waist, resting her head against his broad back.

"Of course!" He stood perfectly still, in case feeding her didn't get off the ground at all. His heart was on fire. "You sure you're okay?"

"I'm fine. Don't fuss." Even now she was reliving the blissful moment when he had found her, swooping her into his arms, holding her so close their hearts had thudded as one.

That's what a man's arms were for, she thought. To hold a woman. To make her feel cherished. She had felt all that and more. She had felt a profound sense of homecoming.

"So come on," he said lightly, holding himself on a tight rein. "I'm going to feed you and *then* we're going to bed together."

"Sounds like the most wonderful destination in the world," she murmured.

He lifted her hand and pressed it to his lips.

He cared not at all if they ate but tried not to show it. "Two eggs or three?"

"Three please. You need three for a good omelet." She sat down at the table, watching Cy with a sense of wonder. There were oranges, lemons, grapefruit in a bowl. She picked up a lemon and put it to her nose savoring the smell.

"Where's Molly?" she asked belatedly. She had expected Molly to be around.

He picked up a handwritten note and passed it to her. "She's gone over to stay with Ruth for the night. Ruth is tremendously upset."

"I know. She loves your father." She read the note, put it aside.

"Some women love men who treat them badly. Probably some syndrome. She's worked for him for twenty years, but he's never noticed her as a woman. Poor Ruth, wasting her life like that! She should have gone off, met the right bloke and had a family."

"The right bloke isn't easy to find."

Their eyes met and clung. "Then isn't it nice you've found him?"

Arm in arm, her head resting lightly on Cy's shoulder, they went around the house turning off the overhead lights, leaving only a few wall brackets glowing.

"Thought about what room?" He kissed her light and fast, setting up all sorts of aching expectations.

"I'm too distracted."

"Then mine." He wrapped her closer. "I've dreamed about you in my bed."

"Have you?" She was fathoms deep in love with him and falling farther.

"Oh yes. I was drawn to you from that very first moment. Now I'm absolutely sure you're the woman I want to share my life with."

Outside the open French doors, millions of stars patterned the sky. He carried her to his bed, her hair spread over his shoulder, his head bent, his lips kissing and tasting her lovely soft skin.

Cy lay on the midnight-blue quilted silk, poised over her, an arm to either side. She was so beautiful. The most beautiful thing in his loveless life. He could never let her go. He could never allow anyone to hurt her.

A combination of soap and body lotion wafted up to him, deliciously citrusy and fresh. There was a trifle of lace showing at the neck of her robe. Slowly, he pulled the silk sash and the robe parted.

"Jessica." He was trying to steady himself, not give in too soon to the tremendous weight of desire. "I'm going to undress you, okay?"

She looked up at him with tender, trusting eyes. "You'll have to. I don't think I could get my fingers to work."

"Allow me."

The robe came off first, falling from her shoulders. Ever so gently, he turned her, tugging a little so it slithered out from under her. His breath was coming shorter and deeper. Hunger for a woman could be an agony. He had to hold her up so he could pull her nightdress over her head like a child. A groan came from the back of his throat as he saw her for the first time naked.

Her skin seemed to radiate light, and blood shot to his head. He had to regain his composure just to go on. His hands caressed her shoulders, silky skin and delicate bone, moving slowly over her, deepening his sense of touch and heightening his pleasure. His hands moved back up to her breasts, so beautiful, so perfectly formed, dusky-pink-tipped. It was a kind of agony just to look at them, hold them, take their tender supple weight.

Jessica let herself go with it, excitement roaring through her bloodstream like the most potent drug. The more he caressed her, the more she needed. Sensation ran so high she had to press back against the pillows, her eyes closed against the galvanic surges, like sails caught in a high wind. Didn't he know he tore the heart from her? His ministrations continued, unhurried but intense. She had to clamp her lips shut so her little rasping breaths wouldn't escape her and turn into moans.

Cyrus understood perfectly the feelings that racked her. He was astonished at the depth of passion between them, long imagined, now finally being delivered. He was entranced by the slender perfection of her body, the curves, the long lines, the creamy whiteness of her skin. He let his mouth travel her body as though following a map that utterly absorbed him. Her little moans were both agonized and joyous, urging him on. Once, in a bout of intensity, her whole body bucked, then fell back onto the softness of the bed. She was reaching for him, inflamed into taking action.

She tugged at his shirt. Tore it loose. Next the waistband of his jeans, thrusting her hand inside, giving him so much pleasure he cried out.

"I want you right next to me," she commanded. "Your skin touching mine."

He stood up, stripping off his clothes, a lean, powerful living sculpture of a man, his skin in the glow of the lamps a dense gold.

The sleekness and strength of him! Jessica sat up in the bed reveling in his manhood. She thought she might catch fire when he touched her. She threw out an imploring arm, secure in the knowledge she had made it her business to start on the pill for protection. "What's keeping you? I *want* you."

"How much?" He approached the bed, the planes of his face taut with passion.

"Let me show you." She was maddened by even the smallest distance between them. "I never knew it was possible to feel like this."

He wanted to cover her right then and there. Bear down on her. Make her his. Instead, he rose above her bracing his weight on his arms. "Then we have to do something about it."

"Let *me* start." This time she did the seducing. Her hands took hold of his fully erect shaft, scorching him with pleasure. She stroked and stretched the velvet skin until he grew too weak to withstand her.

"What are you trying to do to me?" He grasped her head to kiss her beautiful mouth. She tasted of whitefleshed peaches. It was amazing!

"Don't talk," she ordered. "I want to make you *feel*. I want you to experience the same rapture I do."

She moved over him and he covered his eyes with his hand, drawing in the ecstasy.

The intimacy between them continued to gain pace and intensity, the tenderness changing to the faint violence of passion bent on release. Delirious tears streamed down her cheeks. She and Cyrus were coiled around one another like vines, one ascendant, then the other, anything permissible between them because of the love they felt for each other.

"It was meant to be like this from the beginning." He pressed his mouth to hers, rapidly approaching his climax but waiting for her to catch up.

"I love you. Cyrus, I love you." She knew such a thing only happened once in a lifetime.

"Then come with me." He was determined to hold back until her climax seized her.

She held on to him for dear life, pressing her mouth to his shoulder tasting salt. Her body was filled with such heat....

And then it began. Ripples gathered in the pit of her groin. They gained strength, spreading to all levels of her body like molten lava. Her eyes were tightly shut so she could lock in the incredible sensations. She reached down to where their bodies joined. He was moving against her, very slowly like a sleek, powerful big cat. Up and down. Deep. Deep.

Her whole body seemed to be quaking, as though something inside her was about to gush open.

"Now!"

Did she shout it? She was beyond caring.

Robyn denied everything. Her head was pounding from a hangover. She looked so ill that Jessica, despite everything, felt very concerned. Jessica herself was looking as radiant as a bride on her day of all days, still trailing the glory of the previous night. She was ready to forgive anyone, anything. Even Robyn, who undoubtedly would never be her friend.

Cyrus wasn't feeling anywhere near so magnanimous. He was deeply perturbed by what his stepsister had done. Robyn needed help and he came straight out and said it.

"Are you talking about a shrink?" she gasped, looking panic stricken.

"I'm angry enough to tell everyone what you did unless you make an appointment to see one."

"But everyone knows me," she protested. "I'd be the talk of the town."

"Don't be ridiculous! You know all about doctorpatient confidentiality. I'm serious, Robyn. It's important you get professional help. It could be one of the smartest things you've ever done in your life. Obviously we can't discuss this any further today. You're hungover. You can count your lucky stars I didn't believe you, and Jessica found matches in her saddlebag and was able to start a fire, otherwise this could have ended rather differently."

"Whereas it ended just the way she wanted," Robyn responded bitterly, hell-bent on driving everyone away. She jumped up precipitously, winced as her head threatened to split. "I don't know why I'm sitting here. I should be in Darwin with Dad."

Cyrus sighed. "If you're determined to go, Robyn, why should I stand in your way? You'll be better there than sitting around the house plotting some fool mischief. You're welcome to go to the hospital. I happen to know Dad's given instructions—no visitors. That means us. Bad sign in a man, don't you think, when he doesn't want to see his family?"

Robyn gave a snort. "Maybe I can get him to change his mind."

"Good luck, then. You might as well stay in Darwin while you're at it. The operation is scheduled for 9:00 a.m. Friday."

That got Robyn's full attention. "Dad would have made sure his will is in order?"

Cyrus's voice was dry. "I'm sure you've been well looked after."

"Well, I *am* his adopted daughter. Can I get Bill Morris to take me in the chopper? I can't face the long drive."

"Sure." Cyrus nodded his permission. "I'm going out to have a word with the men so I'll tell him now. When do you want to leave?"

Robyn fixed her stepbrother, then Jessica, with a hard stare. "As soon as possible. I'm sure you two lovebirds don't want me around. Say, eleven o'clock? I have to do a few things first."

"Like sober up?" Cyrus grunted. "I'll tell him." He looked across at Jessica, who had sat silently through the exchange. "What about if I come back for you then, Jessica? We can spend the day together."

"I'd like that," she said quietly. Despite what was happening, joy that would not be denied welled up in her heart.

"Course you would!" Robyn's laugh cracked. "With Dad out of the way, we'll have to drop to our knees and worship at Cyrus's feet."

"Dad's not dead yet, Robyn," Cyrus reminded her. "Now, I'm out of here." He turned away, crisply businesslike. "Be ready at eleven sharp, Robyn. I actually need Bill today, but I recognize you're in no state to drive into Darwin."

"Thanks a bunch." Robyn suddenly scooped up the delicate cup and saucer that held the rest of her morning coffee and flung them to the floor. They shattered into pretty pieces, the black coffee staining the rug.

Broderick Bannerman had been on the operating table for four hours.

They all sat in the waiting room, Cyrus, Lavinia, Jessica and Robyn, their backs aching, their expressions betraying their strain. Robyn stared fixedly and, Jessica suspected, sightlessly, at the television, though Cyrus had insisted it be turned down. Robyn actually looked like she needed a hospital bed herself.

They all looked up as Barbara Nicholls, Broderick's twin, who had arrived from Sydney, came back into the room carrying a cup of coffee and a cell phone. "Nothing?"

"Nothing," Cyrus confirmed. "Babs, why don't you take

Livvy back to the hotel? You're only ten minutes away. This could go on for hours yet. I'll call you the minute we have news."

Barbara Nicholls, with the same handsome features as her twin, but much less severe, stylishly confident, beautifully dressed, sank into a chair and sighed deeply. "I don't feel good about this."

"Better to die than finish up in a wheelchair or lying in a nursing home, Babs," Lavinia said. "That wouldn't suit Broderick at all."

Barbara shook her dark head. She had the same distinctive silver wings as her brother. "No," she agreed quietly. "Don't feel bitter, Cyrus dear, but he let me see him for a time." She laid a comforting hand on her nephew's. "Please don't hold it against me. Probably I'm the only person who can get inside Broderick's head. I'm his twin, after all. Broderick has always been his own worst enemy. Keeping you away from him, especially at this time, is part of his defense mechanism. You must understand that. You're so much like our father, Steven. For some reason that has always upset him. It takes him back in time. Then there was the damage left in Moira's wake. Of course, Broderick being Broderick found out I put that portrait of Moira on the market."

That hit Cyrus with stunning force. "*You* did? I didn't even know you had it. You've never said. I thought it was Dad."

They were all focused on Barbara now. Jessica reached out to take Cyrus's hand, seeing his agitation. Even Robyn dragged her eyes away from Oprah Winfrey for a moment, even though an extraordinarily slim Oprah was offering everyone in the studio a free car.

"I've had the painting in storage for years and years," Barbara said. "It was too beautiful to destroy and too upsetting to display. No, I was the one." Barbara looked at her nephew. "Your father never told you?"

Cyrus shook his head. "I accused him of it. He didn't deny it."

"That's Broderick all right," Barbara said heavily. "I did it on impulse. It was Hughie's anniversary. I always feel badly around that time. I feel cleaner, freer, bringing his portrait of Moira out of hiding. The tragedies of our childhood left terrible wounds. Wounds that were concealed, but never healed. I knew Broderick would find out what I'd done.There's nothing much that happens inside the family—and out—he doesn't know about. He knew how I felt about the portrait. He knew I had it. He knew I unravel around Hugh's anniversary—he does, too. I suppose he was waiting for me to let it see the light of day. He's uncanny like that."

Cyrus's handsome face was baffled. "What else have you and Dad been hiding all these years, Babs? We found another portrait, Jessica and I."

"Where, in the storeroom?" Barbara made an informed guess. "One could hide anything there. So much was concealed, you know. My mother couldn't bear to hear Moira's name. It was all so very painful. Brutal as it sounds, making all trace of Moira disappear was the only way we survived as a family."

"Oh man!" Cyrus turned away, sighing deeply.

"Hugh was a wonderful painter," Barbara said. "He could have made a name for himself, only his whole life ran off the rails. What was this painting of?" she asked.

It was left to Jessica to reply. "A nude. A very beautiful rendition."

"What?" Barbara gasped. "No, no, that's impossible."

"Nothing's impossible, dear," said Lavinia, looking worldly-wise.

Robyn sat as if struck dumb by all they were saying.

"A very erotic portrait," said Cyrus, searching his aunt's face.

"Moira didn't pose for it." Barbara spoke with absolute certainty. "Okay, I was only a child, but I *know.* A portrait of Moira in her prettiest dress was one thing. My parents allowed that. Moira nude would never have happened."

"No, it wouldn't!" Lavinia shook her forefinger energetically.

"Hughie must have seen her like that in his *mind.* An erotic fantasy as it were. He was an artist, after all."

"Bloody odd, if you ask me," said Lavinia. "Wasn't he a pansy?"

Barbara was thoroughly rattled. "No, he was *not,* Livvy. Where did you get that idea? Look, I don't know how this happened, but there was nothing between Moira and Hugh."

"As far as you know," Lavinia piped up.

Barbara flushed. "Of course he could have fallen in love with her, but Moira certainly didn't love him. All Moira could see was—" She broke off abruptly, dropping her gaze.

"Steven," Cyrus supplied grimly, as if this were the piece that was missing.

Silence from Barbara, but a look of extreme gravity.

"We're all human," Lavinia pronounced. "Human beings fall in love." She reached out to pat Jessica's hand. "That's what Cecily was afraid of. He loved you."

"Livvy, will you stop that?" Barbara exclaimed in horror, rising to her feet. "This is *Jessica,* for heaven's sake. I have to admit, I got a great shock when I first saw her. The resemblance is uncanny, but sheer coincidence. We were talking about Hugh. I've always thought something terrible happened to Hugh. Something he would never talk about."

"Unrequited love?" Cyrus suggested, continuing to regard his aunt closely.

Lavinia frowned at him. "No, no, my darling, Hughie was in love with Steven. Not that Steven had a clue."

Barbara was visibly trying to keep control. "Livvy, sometimes you sound quite mad."

"And sometimes I don't," Lavinia returned darkly.

"If Hugh had been in love with anyone, it was Moira. I'm sure Hugh wasn't gay."

"Gay?" Robyn's voice came out so loudly it made everyone jump.

"He was, too." Lavinia stuck to her guns. "It explains everything."

Cyrus held his head in his hands. "If it does, I'm missing it."

"*Everything* has to do with what happened to Moira," Lavinia insisted. "I expect if Broderick doesn't die, the police will come and arrest him."

Robyn gave a contemptuous snort. "If anyone should be arrested, it's you, Lavinia. You're long overdue for the giggle house."

"And you should be coming with me," Lavinia told her tartly.

Barbara acted. "Darling Livvy, I think we should go back to the hotel for a while. You need to lie down."

"You'll stay with me?"

"Of course." There was great confusion in Barbara Nicholls's gray eyes and the glint of tears.

Shortly after they'd left, Erik Moore made an appearance.

On seeing him, Cyrus straightened, his gaze challenging. "What are you doing here, Erik?"

"Yes, tell us." Robyn actually switched off the TV. "After my lousy birthday party, I vowed never to speak to you again."

Erik searched her face, looking for understanding. "You've no idea how I've missed you, my darling."

"That's the reason you came, is it, Erik?" Cyrus stood up, towering over the other man. "To tell Robyn you've missed her?"

"That and to find out about B.B." So confronted, Erik sank strategically into a chair. "It was B.B. who warned me off, Robyn. He let us get to the stage of talking marriage, then right out of the blue he told me to butt out of your life. That was the very night of your birthday party, when we should have been deliriously happy. I had the ring. I still have it."

"You didn't dump me?" Robyn stared at him, apparently poleaxed by the disclosure.

Cyrus exhaled in wonderment but never said another word.

His conscience was clear. He'd tried all he could with Robyn. None of it had worked.

A look of dawning wonder put life into Robyn's pale face.

"Would I dump the love of my life?" Erik asked, apparently always at the ready no matter what life dished up.

Robyn's look of shock had been replaced by hope. "Dad did that to us?"

Erik nodded, letting his head drop as in deep regret.

Obviously he was smart enough to know when actions spoke louder than words, Jessica thought cynically, not taken in by what she saw as a performance.

"Why didn't you tell me?" Robyn went to him, half kneeling so she could get a closer look at his face. "Why bother?" he said forlornly. "B.B. means everything to you. I knew you wouldn't go against him in the end."

"The *end?* Now that, I think, is highly relevant," Cyrus cut in. "Your goddamn brain is always ticking over isn't it, Erik? Dad mightn't pull through. I bet you've got your sources inside the hospital who gave you a complete rundown on his condition. Many people survive brain tumors, however."

"Of course they do!" Erik heartily agreed. "I'm hoping and praying that will be the case with B.B."

"So who told you it was a brain tumor? We never gave out that information. It could be stomach cancer, for all you know."

Robyn was thoroughly roused from her stupor, apparently dead set on standing by her man. "Erik is a highly regarded member of the community, Cyrus." She ran a loving hand down Erik's cheek. "It would be easy for a man like Erik to be given certain information. After all, everyone knows we're as good as engaged."

"Really? I thought it was all over Darwin you'd broken up," Cyrus said with weary sarcasm. "So if Dad doesn't survive, Robyn will never know if you're telling the truth, Erik?"

"Robyn knows her father." Erik shook his head ponderously.

"Her stepfather," Cyrus corrected curtly.

"Robbie, would you like to have a cup of coffee in that little place across the street?" Erik said quickly, rising to his feet. "The coffee here is deplorable."

"I'd love to!" Robyn all but sprang to the door.

"Is that okay with you, Cyrus?" Erik asked before joining her.

"Sure," Cyrus drawled. "Thanks for coming."

Erik totally missed the sarcasm. "No worries. We'll be back."

They sat in a stunned silence for a few moments after Erik and Robyn had gone.

"Sweet Jesus, can you believe that guy?" Cyrus sighed.

"She fell for it, hook, line and sinker."

Cyrus nodded. "He got the inside story. He knows just how bad Dad is. Obviously with Dad out of the way, he's home free. He can control Robyn and her money. And I'd say we're talking a lot of it."

"Reparation for not treating Robyn very well?"

"Probably." Cyrus shrugged. "I don't mind. Dad did adopt her when she was only a child. She's entitled. Erik is prepared to take his chances. That's how he runs his businesses."

"He's in big trouble if your father pulls through."

"I don't think the world holds any more appeal for Dad," Cyrus said, an expression of resignation on his face.

Broderick Bannerman did not pull through, however great the combined skills of his surgical team.

As the neurosurgeon, Dr. Jung, who headed the team came toward them, Cyrus and Jessica stood up, their hands clasped tightly together for mutual support.

Something in the surgeon's expression alerted them the news was far from good.

"I'm so very sorry," he said, looking first at Cyrus, then Jessica. "Mr. Bannerman has gone. We did all we could, but we lost him. Please, let's sit down a moment."

Dr. Jung sat with them, explaining the various reasons why

everything had started to go haywire. "I think your father had already decided he didn't want to live," he told Cyrus gently. "He was such a strong personality, such a powerful and influential man, he found it extremely difficult to consider the possibility of a greatly changed life. We had discussed every possible outcome of the operation, of course. He went into it with his eyes wide open. If there was a chance, he was going to take it. I wish things had turned out differently. I understand how deeply distressed you are. We did all we could."

But it hadn't been enough.

"So who *was* the last person in the family he saw?" Cyrus asked after the surgeon had gone. Despair and a deep hurt were in his voice. "Whose face did he light on last? Not me, that's for sure. Not poor unwanted Robyn. But Babs, his twin. Sons and adopted daughters don't count. You, the young woman he became so infatuated with. In the end he shunned you, as well."

"In his mind, I betrayed him," Jessica said. "He was living a fantasy. I was no *real* part of it, Cyrus. Barbara was his twin. She loves you and she knows much, much more about your family's history than she's ever let on. Except maybe to her brother."

"That's obvious," Cyrus said harshly, pulling out his cell phone to start making the necessary calls. "Well, it doesn't matter now. Dad's gone. The secrets he'll take to the grave are probably too shattering to know, anyway."

Later, as they were about to leave the ward, a tall distinguished-looking man in his late fifties came toward them. He was wearing a clerical collar.

"Mr. Bannerman, Cyrus Bannerman?" he asked, putting out his hand. His voice had a soft Irish lilt. "I'm Father Brennan. I was with your father last night. I've just been told he passed away. I'm so sorry. Please accept my deepest sympathies."

Though stunned by the revelation—his father had been anything but a religious man—Cyrus responded courteously, shaking the clergyman's hand. "Thank you, Father. This is my friend, Jessica Tennant."

"Miss Tennant." The priest's dark eyes wandered to her distressed face.

"You're a Catholic priest, Father?" Cyrus asked, trying to grasp what the man was saying. Clergymen had freaked his father out.

"Yes. I heard your father's last confession," the priest said in a perfectly calm voice.

"But we're not Catholic, Father." Cyrus forced himself to speak quietly when he was agitated and upset. Just when he'd been thinking there were no surprises left, up popped a Catholic priest.

Father Brennan smiled. "Your father and his twin sister, Barbara—is that right?—were baptized in the Catholic Church. I understand there was a tragedy in the family many long years ago and the faith lapsed, but your father called for me, as a matter of fact. He wanted to see a priest."

Cyrus shook his head as if to clear it. For the moment, he had to rely on the man's word, but he saw nothing but truth and dignity in the clergyman's eyes. "Father, I have to tell you I'm stunned."

"I can see that, Cyrus. May I call you Cyrus?"

"Of course." Cyrus stared into the quiet, focused face.

"If it gives you comfort, I can tell you your father was a peaceful man at the end. Strangely happy, accepting of his fate."

"You gave him absolution?" Did a man automatically get it? Cyrus wondered.

"Certainly," the priest confirmed gently. "You probably have some clergyman in mind for the funeral service. If you haven't, if I can be of help to you, you have only to let me know. I'm at St. Mary's. God bless you both." He lifted a hand in a gesture that was both a blessing and a salute.

CHAPTER SIXTEEN

BRODERICK BANNERMAN WAS laid to rest according to his wishes in a closed ceremony with only his family and a handful of life-long associates present. Because of his status in life, a memorial service was to be held in Darwin at a later date when it was expected a huge crowd would attend.

Like most great Outback stations, Mokhani had its own cemetery. The graves of five generations of Bannermans were arranged within a large enclosure bounded by a tall black wrought-iron fence and double gates, and shaded by massive banyan trees that spread their long weeping branches over the graves. In a far corner, removed from the intersecting concrete pathways, was a species of cassia in gorgeous display. It caught Jessica's artistic eye. It was the only bright spot in that quiet place; the spent golden blossom covered the built up mound beneath it.

How beautiful! The long perfumed sprays moved like floral arms, even though there was scarcely a breath of air. Cyrus had spoken to Father Brennan, who presided at the service in the calm dignified manner Jessica remembered. If Broderick Bannerman had called on a priest at an extreme moment the same priest ought to bury him, Cyrus had decided when the family had discussed it. He'd met with no opposition from anyone. From now on, everyone would defer to him as head of the family.

Broderick Bannerman's last will and testament had already been read. Overnight, Cyrus had inherited the bulk of the Bannerman fortune, making him one of the richest men in the country—and thus one of the most eligible, though no one, not even Robyn, made reference to it. Robyn might have been cut out of all Bannerman business operations, including the pastoral empire, but what she did get was splendid enough for her not to rock the boat and had Erik Moore talking wedding dates.

Barbara, already a rich woman, was made a whole lot richer, not that she cared, and that was that. For a notoriously tight-fisted man, B.B. had been extremely generous. His longtime secretary, Ruth, who had loved him from afar and was crazy with grief—she'd had to be sedated when she'd been told of his death—wouldn't have to work another day for the rest of her life. A godsend for most people, but looking at Ruth, anyone could see she would much rather have had Bannerman back. Handsome bequests were made to various longtime employees, including Molly, who had gone so far as to burst into tears and start planning to join her widowed sister in Tasmania. Charities had a bonanza. Hospitals, medical research centers, an educational institution to be set up in Darwin, also a park—B.B. had owned the land—bearing his name. A huge monetary gift was made to the city. The list went on and on. No mention whatever of Jessica, for which she was greatly relieved. She couldn't have handled even a tiny bequest. Nothing about her stay on Mokhani had been *normal*.

After the funeral, Jessica had made the decision to go home and give Cyrus breathing space. She had thought about it long and hard. Cyrus needed time to clear his mind and focus on his future. Whether in the light of momentous events she was going to be part of it, she still had to give him space. For all the bitterness Broderick Bannerman's behavior had engendered in his son and nigh on everyone around him, Cyrus *was* grieving.

Brett and Tim were due to arrive on Saturday, which was two days off. They would take a look around Darwin, make a quick courtesy visit to Mokhani to meet the new master and take a look at the great folly Broderick had caused to be erected in his honor. Indeed a mausoleum. It was up to Cyrus now to decide what would be done with it. Had it been a timber structure, Jessica thought Cyrus would have burned it down. Her own idea was it should be turned into a huge conference center with every facility. As Cyrus was to take over all of his late father's business concerns, which spread to Southeast Asia and New Zealand, such a center made sense.

They hadn't discussed it. Broderick Bannerman's death and the events leading up to it had cast Cyrus into an inevitable state of depression. He wasn't immune to grief, sadness for what might have been, and quite starkly, the knowledge that at the end he had been met with rejection. What extraordinary place he had held in his father's mind. His heir and, quite simply, his *rival.*

It was late afternoon before everyone left after a subdued reception at the homestead. Barbara couldn't avoid staying over at the homestead even if she wanted to. Her husband was at a conference in London, where he was a guest speaker, and had been greatly relieved he wasn't required to return home. Barbara had been staying at the same Darwin hotel the family favored. It was obvious Lavinia was very fond of her niece—after all, Barbara had had Lavinia stay for years on end—so to humor the old lady and offer some comfort to her nephew, Barbara had agreed to stay over at Mokhani, the Bannerman ancestral home where Barbara felt she no longer belonged. She didn't think she would ever get over the desolation of her childhood, she'd confided to Jessica. The *loneliness,* the internal struggles. Hitherto inseparable, overnight her twin had been shut off from her. Her mother had changed into someone else. Her wonderful father had never been the same. After Moira had disappeared, they hadn't worked as a *family*. For years, her mother had gotten all choked up if anyone so much as mentioned Moira's name. Her father had looked as though he had lost something irretrievable. Uncle Hughie, who was the nicest man in the world, had killed himself on the station. Something had caused him so much pain, he couldn't go on living.

Small wonder Barbara seldom visited her old family home.

Strangely, Barbara didn't appear to have those feelings now that her twin was gone. Was it because there was no more Broderick with his stinging tongue? Broderick, always trying to wrong-foot everyone. And his secrets? Broderick had been her mother's favorite. Their mother, Cecily, had loved him far more than she had her daughter. Broderick had been on the receiving end of all Cecily's attention. That had incensed and alientated Barbara right up until the time she had married and made a new life for herself.

Because everyone felt terribly sorry for Ruth, the woman was pressed into staying, instead of going back to her own comfortable bungalow.

"You don't need to be alone, Ruth," Cyrus told her kindly. "We all know how devoted you were to my father."

"Head over heels in love with him more like it," Lavinia the irrepressible piped up.

"What of it?" Ruth countered, distraught. "I'm not ashamed of it."

Barbara's voice was soft and sad. "You have no need to be, Ruth. Loving someone can never be wrong."

"What about Moira?" Lavinia asked, adjusting her monk's robe, which she had worn to the funeral, along with blue socks and sandals. "I mean, loving the wrong man must count as one of the worst things you can do in the world."

"Certainly one of the most painful." Barbara put a hand over Lavinia's in an effort to quiet her. "I told you, Livvy, dear, I didn't want to talk about Moira."

Lavinia did a double take. "But she's sitting right opposite you, love."

Robyn threw down her linen napkin. "The only bloody difference between Lavinia and Zelda, the mad old bag lady in Darwin no one seems to do a thing about, is occasionally the authorities have to lock Zelda up."

"How unjust," said Lavinia. "She does no harm, but she does go on a bit about *sin*. The reason you don't like me, Robyn, is that I see through you. I think Broderick's leaving you all that money was a dreadful mistake. Erik will only glom onto it, mark my words!"

Barbara's eyebrows shot up like birds' wings. "Livvy, it's scarcely the right time for all this."

"There are only two kinds of times," said Lavinia. "The good times and the bad. Let's drink to Broderick. He up and died on us and left my darling Cyrus with all his problems."

For the first time in days, Cyrus laughed. "Don't worry about me, Livvy. I can handle it."

"That's right, my darling!" she encouraged him. "Build a new life with Moira." Her bright eyes moved to Jessica. "I don't know that there's any better color for a beautiful ash-blonde than black. No news, I suppose, but that's my expert opinion."

It wasn't until much later in the evening that Ruth came out onto the veranda to speak to Cyrus. He and Jessica were sitting out there talking quietly.

"Sorry to interrupt!"

"No problem, Ruth. Can I help you?"

Ruth's eyes filled up again with tears. "You're so good to me, Cyrus. I must thank you." She shifted her gaze to Jessica. "Don't think I don't appreciate how nice you've been to me, Jessica, since you arrived." Although she was obviously sincere, Ruth spoke in a flat monotone. She was clutching a padded bag in her hand. "Your father asked me to give this to you, Cyrus, should anything happen to him," she said. "I've been so desperately upset, it all but slipped my mind, so I'll give it to you now."

"What is it?" Cyrus made no move to take it.

"A video." Ruth passed the package to Jessica, who was nearest, and Jessica in turn passed it to Cyrus. "Your father wanted to speak to you."

Cyrus stared down at the package. "He could have done that very easily, Ruth," he said, making no attempt to extract the video from the padded bag. "I waited for hours on end at the hospital."

Ruth shook her head. "You know your father was a very strange man, Cyrus, but in his own way he loved you. Remember, I knew him well. He suppressed so many of his true feelings."

"Wouldn't it have been easier for all of us if my father could have shown a shred of appreciation, let alone affection?"

Jessica could feel Cyrus's tension. The knuckles of his lean, tanned hands were white.

"I don't believe he knew how to, Cyrus. That was the cross he carried. You should thank God you're like your mother."

"I do, Ruth. I do." Cyrus slowly withdrew the video. "You have your job, Ruth, if you still want it. I'd never find anyone else as good as you. For that matter, you know more than I do."

Ruth looked amazed. "You're serious, Cyrus?" The flatness in her voice turned into an emotional quiver.

"Perfectly," he said. "My father found you indispensable and he was a hard taskmaster. Of course you'll need time to think it over. Time, too, for a holiday. Something to look forward to. Let me know."

Ruth pressed her hand to her agonized breast. "Where else would I go, Cyrus? I'd be honored if you'd give me a chance."

Cyrus leaned forward. "Get some confidence in yourself, Ruth," he said gently. "Somehow my father stole it. You're absolutely first class at what you do. I'll *need* you."

He couldn't have hit on a more powerful argument if he'd tried.

"Oh, thank you," Ruth said in a heartfelt voice and fled back into the house.

"So what am I going to do with this?" Cyrus asked Jessica, looking down at the package in his hands.

"What do you suppose it is?" Jessica felt a bit fearful.

He sighed. "You can bet your life it's not to tell me how much he loved me. The strange things he was doing—the intimate connection he was trying to make with you, Moira's double, calling in a priest, making his confession, I'd say it was an extension of all that. I don't think I want to know."

"I don't blame you. Still, it would be unthinkable to throw it away. You've lived through bad times. You can handle it. Perhaps at the end he wanted to explain himself. He could even be asking forgiveness."

"So." Cyrus let out a sigh. "Where do we see it, in the study? Somewhere private anyway."

"Are you sure you want me?" Jessica asked, very sensitive to his grief. "These are probably your father's most private thoughts. I wouldn't blame you in the least, Cyrus, if you wanted to see it on your own."

Cyrus stood up drawing her to her feet. "You love me, don't you?"

Her voice broke a little at the expression on his face. "With all my heart."

"Then from this moment on we do everything together." He cupped her face in his hands, looking directly into her eyes. "I've been waiting for you my whole life, Jessica. I can't let you go. All right, you can leave with your uncle—I'm looking forward to meeting him—but that's only to go back and see your family. I'll need to meet them. They'll want to look me over. I love you, Jessica. I want to marry you. Not at some hazy time in the future. I want it to be right away, but that would be seen as too soon. Besides, I want our wedding day to be wonderful.

I want to see you as a bride. I want the memory of that day to stay with us forever. Say you'll marry me?"

"You've got it all planned?" She smiled through her tears, believing herself to be truly blessed.

"Within seconds of meeting you," he confirmed.

"The miracle of love at first sight." Her eyes luminous with love, Jessica put up her arms and drew his dark head down to her in a long, loving kiss.

Cyrus was her life. Mokhani was her home.

Together they would bring it back to the light.

CHAPTER SEVENTEEN

BRODERICK BANNERMAN WAS seated somewhere that looked like a law office because of the legal tomes in the bookcase behind him. He was directly facing the camera. Just for a moment both Cyrus and Jessica forgot he was dead. He looked very much alive. He addressed himself to his son: "The best son a man could wish for!"

"Dear God!" said Cyrus. "I actually heard that, did I?"

Jessica, seated close beside the man she loved, held his hand, understanding Cyrus took great comfort from her presence. All that passion with tenderness and need, besides! Sublime sex wasn't all that connected them, but rather the *depth* of their connection, the perfect matching. They were truly meant for each other.

There were points along the way when Cyrus had to stop the video to get up and pace around the room. Jessica sat, head bent, appalled by Broderick's tale told in such a matter-of-fact tone. *Some people put more emotion into reading a grocery list,* she thought with some wonderment.

Bannerman's voice never faltered, not once, during the telling of his harrowing story.

Uncle Hughie and I followed Mom and Moira at a safe distance. They didn't keep to the usual trails like we thought they would. They ventured out into the wilderness, heading toward the escarpment. The weather was terrible, hot and thundery with the sky piled up with clouds. I knew Uncle Hughie was worried. He didn't have to say anything. I just knew. Once or twice, I'd overheard a couple of the stockmen sniggering about Dad and Moira. The father I worshipped and my *governess?* It didn't seem possible. Babs and I really liked Moira.

Mum was mistress of Mokhani. But Moira was a servant. There was a huge gulf between the two.

Uncle Hughie and I waited until Mum and Moira reached the top of the escarpment, then we followed using the scrub for cover. Mum began speaking angrily to Moira. My mother could be really scary when she got angry. Moira fell to her knees. Mum told her to get up. I remember every word like it was yesterday.

"Adultery is a sin, Moira. A terrible sin. No

decent young woman in her right mind would allow herself to be seduced by a married man. Unless she's the sort who seduces men. And what about Hugh? You want him as well?"

I've never believed, like poor old Livvy, Hugh was homosexual. Maybe he did have a sexual encounter with Moira. Who would know? Lovely little Moira turned out to be a slut anyway. She had to be guilty because she did nothing to defend herself even when my mother began to hit her. Mum sounded like she was going out of her mind. That's when Uncle Hughie broke cover, yelling at Mum to stop. Maybe Hugh did love Moira, but it was my father Moira had set her sights on.

Mum was shocked when she knew we were there. The words she threw at Uncle Hughie were so ugly I had to cover my seven-year-old ears. I didn't even know Mum knew words like that.

"Sins have to be paid for, Hugh."

That's when Moira asked very quietly, even sorrowfully, "Is love a sin then?"

Mum whirled about and slapped her, struck her so hard Moira went reeling.

"Marriage is sacred, you wicked little bitch. Sacred, you hear? You'll never break up my family. Destroy my marriage."

That's when I knew what I had to do. A son fights for his mother's honor even if he's only seven years old. I was big and strong. We were all standing close to the edge. What could be easier than pushing Moira off the cliff? She deserved what was coming to her. No way was she going to be allowed to break up my family. So I ran, propelled by hate and the need for action, my mother's agonized cries ringing in my ears: "No, Broderick, no! Stop!"

It was impossible to stop. I evaded Uncle Hughie easily. Poor Hughie, he was sobbing like a woman. Moira just stood quietly with her face turned toward me as though accepting her fate. She only had time to get out a few words, but I've never forgotten them.

"I'll always be here, Brodie. You'll see me."

Sure enough I have.

Appalled and in thrall Cyrus and Jessica listened as the voice droned on with the same peculiar lack of emotion.

Afterward, wrapped so tightly in my hysterical mother's arms she could have broken bones, we watched as Uncle Hughie went down into the canyon. There wasn't the remotest chance Moira could have survived. We all knew that. But surely no one would blame me? A child of seven couldn't be held responsible for the outcome of his actions. It was a terrible accident. I hadn't meant to push her so hard. Except I *had*. I knew precisely what I was doing. I was the Bannerman heir. The family honor was at stake. I had chosen to send Moira to her death.

Of course the whole business turned Uncle Hughie's mind. That and the booze. He buried Moira under cover of night. "Out of sight, but in a sacred place," he told us, not that Mum and I ever wanted to know. Poor man! It was my mother who locked him and me into living a lie. She was the strong one. *She* made up the story. We had to get it straight. Moira had gone out riding alone. It had been drummed into Moira not to venture too far from the main compound. For some reason she had anyway. The horse came home. Moira didn't. She was never seen again.

My father turned into a madman instigating a mighty search. My mother aged overnight, but she never broke her silence. All that mattered was that I be protected. No one thought to question me. Not my father, not the policeman who traveled from Darwin to the station. I was a child, heir to Mokhani. My family was powerful, well respected. The mysterious disappearance of our governess joined Outback lore. Another tragedy of the bush, people said.

Only as it turned out no one could protect me from my memories or the apparitions. They ruined my life, twisted my soul. The whole story should have come out at the beginning. Perhaps the truth might have saved me. They could have locked me away in a home for the insane, and I wouldn't have cared. But my mother insisted I could never do anything so dangerous as to tell. My father would never understand.

"He would hate us, Broderick. Could you stand that? Your father would hate us. It was never your fault. How many times do I have to tell you? It was Moira's. She got what she deserved."

Did Moira really deserve such a terrible fate? These days, of course, I'd say, no. She was so very young and love is madness. Of late I've contemplated making my confession to a priest. My mother had been born into the Catholic faith. Babs and I had been baptized. What I so desperately need is absolution. God knows I've long repented yet, I often dream of the gates of Hell opening for me, then shutting me inside.

There was more. Jessica knew there had to be more. She placed a hand over her mouth as Bannerman explained the rest of the secret he had unearthed. There had been no stopping him once he'd laid eyes on Jessica's face in that interview. It was Moira's face. They had to be related by blood. Such a resemblance was too uncanny to be mere coincidence, though such things happened.

Before her marriage, Broderick's image said, Jessica's young and beautiful great-grandmother, Margo Townsend, had had an ill-fated affair that resulted in the birth of a baby girl. Her parents, knowing Margo was engaged to another, had been shocked out of their minds. Such disgrace would taint the whole family. Something had to be done and done quickly. Word was deliberately put out that Margo had gone off alone to Europe, and her parents were obliged to go after her. In fact though Margo spent her confinement on a remote farm in central Queensland. Her baby daughter was given up for adoption hours after the birth to two good people—he was a doctor—who hadn't been able to have children of their own. They named their baby Moira, never speaking to her of her adoption. Margo and her mother waited until Margo was fully recovered before they returned home. Margo's fiancé, genuinely puzzled by it all, still wanted her, and they were married a few months later. A year after that, their daughter, Alexandra, Jessica's grandmother, had arrived to a fanfare of joy.

* * *

Jessica and Cyrus were still sitting stunned in front of the television long after the tape had come to an end and this extremely tragic story had sunk some way in.

"So it turns out Moira was murdered, after all," Cyrus groaned, and passed a hand over his eyes.

"Could anyone hold a seven-year-old child responsible?" Jessica asked, as appalled as he was. "It must have been unbearable for a small boy watching his mother so furious, hitting out at Moira, screaming that she wasn't going to be allowed to break up the family. Her actions incited the child. Cecily would never have meant what happened to happen, but what your father did on that day tortured him for the rest of his life. It made it impossible for him to like himself. He was right. It all should have been brought out into the open. Brodie should have had counseling."

Cyrus shook his head. "My grandmother would never have allowed that, for Moira would have *won*. The marriage would have broken up. She took on the responsibility. Only, they all suffered, no one more than her own son. Even Hugh found a way out."

"I feel strongly that Hugh *did* love Moira," Jessica said.

"Those paintings surely lent credence to that." Cyrus's eyes leaped to the portrait of his grandfather. "God knows where Livvy got the 'pansy' bit from."

"She mistook the nature of Hugh's love for your grandfather. Probably Hugh had never found a girlfriend. But who knows what goes on in Lavinia's mind?"

"She was right about implying Moira's disappearance was not an accident," Cyrus pointed out bleakly. "How could my poor father show love when he believed himself a murderer? I won't accept that he was, no matter what he says. He couldn't have understood the full consequences of his actions."

"I think I know where Hugh laid Moira to rest." Jessica stared down at her clasped hands.

"A sacred place? That could be anywhere." Cyrus was in despair. He began thinking of all the Aboriginal sacred sites on the station. "That poor girl was hardly more than a child herself."

His words brought tears to Jessica's eyes. No wonder she had felt such a bond with Moira; the bond of blood was impossible to ignore. "Hugh buried her in the family cemetery," she said with an amazingly clear belief in what she had said.

Cyrus's face betrayed his shock. "Jessica, sweetheart, how could you say that? There's nowhere—"

"Yes, there is," Jessica said in a quiet sad voice. "Beneath that beautiful golden tree, the cassia, in the far corner. I was drawn by the way it captured all the light. I'm sure that's where Hugh buried her, then planted the tree. Sacred ground, not out in the wilderness—he loved her too much to do that. Cecily must have begged Hugh to keep quiet, probably appealed to him on bended knee. Hugh must have thought lying about what happened was a gift of mercy to his cousin and to his lifelong idol, your grandfather. They were protecting Broderick and the family. Only, Hugh couldn't live with the lie. The guilt and the grief were always there."

"Poor Hugh," said Cyrus, not wanting to think of the anguish that had led to his suicide. "So how do we lay Moira's ghost to rest? Start the whole sorry business up again?"

"Why don't we ask her?" Jessica said. "We'll go out there together and call to her."

"Jessica!" Cyrus stared at her, his love and need for her spilling out of his eyes. He stood and drew her into his arms. "Out of all this suffering, I have to bless my father for bringing you into my life."

Jessica lifted her head to kiss the sculpted line of his jaw. "I think all Moira wanted was for us—you and I—to know what really happened to her. She wasn't looking for vengeance, but recognition. I acknowledge her as my great-aunt. I am happy to do so. We can turn that area of the family plot into a garden of remembrance with a seat beneath the tree where one could say a prayer. I'd like that. Instead of living inside our heads, Moira can be set free."

Cyrus's somber expression brightened. "I'll say a simple amen to that, and goodbye to all the heartbreak." He bent his head and kissed her long and lovingly. "I'm almost afraid to be so happy with you, Jessica. I'm not used to such happiness."

She smiled up at him radiantly. "Well, you'd better get used to it, because we're going to have a lifetime of it ahead."

Cyrus enfolded her in his arms, speaking into her beautiful cloud of ash-blond hair. "Everyone I have, everything I am, is yours!"

Early the following dawn, they walked hand in hand to the family cemetery, paying their respects first to Broderick Bannerman, who finally lay at peace, before moving to the corner of the enclosure where the cassia bloomed in all its glory.

"It blooms for months," Cyrus murmured gently as the tree spilled blossom and soft perfume on them like wedding confetti. "Like a beacon."

"We'll think of it as Moira's tree," Jessica said.

It might easily have been a trick of the rising sun dappling the light green leaves and the pendulous branches of bright yellow, but looking up, Jessica fancied she glimpsed a smiling young face. A face very much like her own.

An illusion or Moira bidding farewell?

* * * * *

The Cattle Baron's Bride

CHAPTER ONE

BY THE LIGHT of the stars alone in a situation fraught with difficulties and dangers Sunderland and his tracker Joe Goolatta led
a traumatised jackeroo missing since late afternoon the previous
day back through dense tropical jungle to the safety of the savannah. The forest floor was alive with activity. All sorts of nocturnal creatures, some with malevolent eyes, pounced on prey
or scuttled under foot hunting for food. Forest debris crashed to
the ground as the countless legions of possums with their thick
pelts ripped up leaves and twigs or made their prodigious leaps
from tree to tree sending down a hailstorm of edible berries and
nuts. Huge bats hung upside down assuming the appearance of
vampires. Other dark forms flapped over head. Monstrous amethyst pythons growing to twenty feet long wrapped themselves
around branches close over head, while the brown snakes and
their brothers the deadly black snakes moved slowly, sinuously
through the trees guided not by sight but smell as they stalked
sleeping birds. Now and again a night bird shrieked an alarm
at their presence as they trekked through the forest galleries.
Giant epiphytes clung to the buttresses of the rain forest trees,
staghorns and elkhorns; all kinds of climbing orchids glim-

mered in the starlight. Now and again Sunderland slashed at
something. Probably the Stinging Tree. Brushing up against the
leaves could inflict extreme pain. Sunderland and the tracker
scarcely made a sound. They might have spent their whole lives
living in this overwhelming stronghold of Nature among the
community of rain forest animals. Ben Rankin, the jackeroo,
seventeen years old moaned and groaned, his every movement
jerky and slow as he stumbled over thick woody prop roots
and fallen branches, vines that grew in wild tangles, letting out
high pitched nervous cries to rival the shrieks of the night bird.

"Get a hold there, Rankin," Sunderland clipped off, not impressed by the lad's behaviour. He grasped the boy's arm for
perhaps the hundredth time giving him a helping hand. "We're
nearly there."

How could he possibly know? Ben marvelled. The Boss's
night vision was awesome.

Finally they emerged into a clearing having walked unerringly to the very spot where a station jeep was parked. *Who
would believe it?*

"Made it!" The old aboriginal stockman spoke with satisfaction. "Must be four, thereabouts," he growled, looking up at the
lightening sky. "Not far off sunrise."

"Almost time to start work again," Sunderland said wryly,
pushing the hapless jackeroo into the back seat of the jeep where
the youngster collapsed into a heap. Ben's whole body was shuddering. He was physically and mentally spent now his ordeal
was over. "Oh God, oh God!" he sobbed, covering his head with
his hands. "I'm such a fool."

"Too right, little buddy!" the old aboriginal said, making
his disgust clear.

Sunderland showed no emotion at all as though it were a
sheer waste of time. He put light pressure on the boy's shoulder. "You've had a bad experience. Learn from it."

"Yes, sir." Ben's breath came out like a hiss his jaw was

clamped so tight. "Kept thinking a bloody great croc would get me."

Goolatta snorted.

"We're nowhere near the river. Or a billabong for that matter," Sunderland pointed out matter-of-factly, not having a lot of time for the boy's distress either. Rankin like all the other recruits had been obliged to sit in on lectures regarding station safety. He had been warned many times never to hare off on his own. Most had the sense to listen. Territory cattle stations were vast. Some as big as European countries. It was dead easy to get lost in the relatively featureless wilderness. Obeying the rules made the difference between living and dying. A few over the years had disappeared without trace.

"When you realised you were lost you should have stayed put instead of venturing further into the jungle," Sunderland told him. "We would have found you a whole lot quicker."

"I'm sorry. Sorry," the jackeroo moaned, appalled now at his own foolhardiness. "What a savage place this is. Paradise until you step off the track."

"Remember it next time you fell like pulling another daredevil stunt." Sunderland told him bluntly. "Joe and I won't have the time to come after you. You'll have to find your own way home." Sunderland raked a hand through his hair, looked up at the sky. "Let's move on," he sighed, listening carefully to something crashing through the undergrowth. A wild boar? "You can rest up this morning, Rankin. Back to work this afternoon. That's if you want to hold onto your job."

The jackeroo tried desperately to get a grip on himself. To date he had never found anyone better. Action. Adventure. A fantastic guy for a boss. A real life Indiana Jones. Sunderland never showed fear not even in the middle of a stampede that could well have been Ben's fault though no one blamed him. Well maybe Pete Lowell, the overseer. Not too many chances left he thought, his heart quaking. "Yes, sir. Thank you, sir," he muttered. The last thing he wanted was for Sunderland to get rid of him. All the same it had been terrifying his endless hours all alone in the jungle. The ominous weight of the *silence* that was somehow filled with *sound*. He had actually *felt* the presence of the *mimi* spirits greatly feared by the aboriginals in this part of the world. Not that he was ever going to tell anyone about his brush with psychic terror. It had seemed so real. All that whispering and gibbering, ghostly fingers on his cheek. He would never be such a fool again. He just hoped Sunderland would never find out about the bet he'd had with his fellow jackeroo Chris Pearce.

"Want me to drive, boss?" Joe asked quietly, as always looking out for the splendid young man he had watched grow to manhood.

Sunderland shook his head. "Grab forty winks if you can, Joe," he advised, slinging his lean powerful frame behind the wheel. "It's going to be one helluva day and I have an appointment in Darwin tonight."

"The photographer guy? Big shot."

"That's the one. A showing of his work. I've actually seen some at a gallery in Cairns. Wonderful stuff. Very impressive and very expensive. The asking price for many of the prints was thousands. He was getting it too. Photography is supposedly so easy especially these days but I've never seen images quite so extraordinary or insightful. It must have been difficult trying to get the photographs he did. Difficult and dangerous in untouched parts of the world, waiting around for the precise time and conditions, hoping the weather will stay fine."

"So what's he want to do now? The Top End?"

"Why not? The Top End is undoubtedly the most exotic part of Australia. It is even to other Australians a remote and wild world, frontier country, a stepping stone away from Asia. The Territory is the place to wonder at the marvels of nature. Kakadu alone would keep him busy. It's a world heritage area, of international significance as are the cultural artworks of your people, Joe. I don't know if he wants to get down to the Red

Centre, Uluru, Kata Tjuta and the Alice but if it's the whole Territory he intends to cover then the Wild Heart is on his itinerary.'

"Nobody could be that good they'd capture *my* country," Joe Goolatta said, fiercely proud and protective of his heritage.

"I guess you're right, Joe," Sunderland said.

They swept across the rugged terrain the jeep bouncing over the rough tracks heading towards North Star homestead. The first streaks of light lay along the horizon, lemon, pink and indigo prefacing dawn. Soon the little Spinifex doves would start to call to one another, music from thousands of tiny throats and the great flights of birds would take to the skies.

"Think you'll help him out?" Joe asked, after a pause of some ten minutes. He was leaning his head, covered in the snow white curls that contrasted so starkly with his skin, against the headrest. He was bone tired, but well into his sixties he was still hard at it.

"Don't know yet," Sunderland muttered, still toying with the idea. "His first choice for a guide was Cy." Sunderland referred to his good friend Cyrus Bannerman of Mokhani Station. "But Cy is still in the honeymoon phase. He can't bear to be away from his Jessica. Can't say I blame him." He saluted his friend's choice. "It was Cy who suggested me."

"Couldn't be anyone better," Joe grunted. "However good Cy is and he *is* I reckon you're even better."

"Prejudiced, Joe." A beam from the head lights picked up a pair of kangaroos who shot up abruptly from behind a grassy mound, turning curious faces. Sunderland swerved to avoid them muttering a mild curse. Kangaroos knew nothing about road rules.

"Thing is whether *you've* got the time," Joe said, totally unable to fall asleep like the kid in the back who was snoring so loudly he wished he had ear plugs.

"If I did go I'd take you with me," Sunderland said glancing at his old friend and childhood mentor.

"Yah kiddin'?" Joe sat up straight, an expression of surprise on his dignified face.

"Who else will take care of me?" Sunderland asked.

Joe's big white grin showed his delight. "I was afraid you might be thinkin' I'm getting too old."

"Never!" Sunderland dropped down a gear for a few hundred metres. "You're better on your feet than a seventeen-year-old. Besides, no one knows this ancient land like you do, Joe. Your people are the custodians of all this."

"Didn't I teach you all I know?" Joe asked gently, thrilled their friendship was so deep.

"It would take a dozen lifetimes," Sunderland said, his eyes on a flight of magpie geese winging from one lagoon to another. "But we're learning. This land was hostile to *my* people when we first came here. Sunderlands came to the wild bush but managed to survive. As cattle men we recognize the debt we owe your people. North Star has always relied on its aboriginal stockmen, bush men and trackers. Elders like you, Joe, have skills we're still learning. I only half know what you do and I'm quite happy to admit it. In the beginning my people feared this land as much as it drew us. Now we love it increasingly in the way you do. We draw closer and closer with every generation. There's no question we all occupy a sacred landscape."

"That we do," Joe answered, deeply moved. "So you think you *could* go then?" Now that he knew he might accompany the young man he worshipped he was excited by the idea.

Sunderland's smile slipped. "I'm a bit worried about leaving Belle at home. She's had a rotten time of it. I can't just abandon her, even if it's only for a couple of weeks."

"Take her along," Joe urged. "Miss Isabelle is as good in the bush as anyone I've seen. She could be an asset."

Sunderland shook his dark head. "I don't see Belle laughing and happy any more, Joe. Neither do you. I know your heart aches for her as well. My sister is a woman who feels very deeply. It'll take her a long time to get over Blair's death. She's punishing herself because his family, his mother in particular, appeared to blame her for his fatal accident."

"Cruel, cruel woman," Joe said. "I disliked that woman from day one." He stopped short of saying he hadn't taken to Miss Isabelle's husband either. Good-looking guy—nothing beside Miss Isabelle's splendid big brother—but as big a snob as his mother—aboriginal man too primitive to look at much less to speak to. No, Joe hadn't taken to Miss Isabelle's dead husband who had died in a car crash after some big society party. Miss Isabelle should have been with him but the awful truth was they had had a well publicised argument at the party before Blair Hartmann had stormed out to his death.

"Dad and I never took to her either," Sunderland sighed. "Incredibly pretentious woman. But Blair was Belle's choice. You know what she was like. As headstrong as they come. Blair was such a change from most guys she knew. A smooth sophisticated *city* guy, high flyer, establishment family, glamorous life style, family mansion on Sydney Harbour."

"Dazzled her for a while," Joe grunted. "But that wasn't really Miss Isabelle."

"No," Sunderland agreed with a heavy heart. "I expect she was acting out a fantasy. She was too young and inexperienced and he was crazy about her. So crazy he practically railroaded her into it. I somehow think she'd never choose someone like Blair Hartmann again though she won't hear a word against him. I don't think I could convince her to go although I know she can handle herself. Hell she was born to it but on principle I don't like women along on those kind of trips. Most of them are trouble. They can't handle the rough. They put themselves and consequently others at risk. It makes it harder for the men."

It took another few minutes before he came out with what was really bothering him. "If Langdon suggests his sister comes along I'm walking."

"Langdon? That's the photographer right? And the sister was the bridesmaid at Cy Bannerman's wedding?" Joe flashed him a shrewd glance. Joe had never met the young lady but unlike everyone else Joe found it easy to read the man he had known from infancy. "I thought you took a real shine to her?" He chuckled and stretched but Sunderland refused to bite.

"How would *you* know?"

"I know." Joe smiled.

"Pretty weird the way you read my mind. You're a sorcerer, Joe Goolatta."

Joe nodded. "Been one in my time."

"Think I don't know that."

Joe closed his eyes.

The memory was seared into his brain like a brand.

The first time he laid eyes on Samantha Langdon she was running down the divided staircase at Mokhani homestead one hand holding up the glistening satin folds of the bridesmaid dress she had just tried on. He and Cy had picked that precise moment to walk in the front door after a long back breaking day. He'd been helping Cy out with a difficult muster, riding shot gun from the helicopter to frighten a stubborn herd of cleanskins out of the heavy scrub. That's what friends were for. He and Cy went back to the toddler stage. He was Cy's best man. Cy would be his if he ever got around to getting married. The floating apparition—that was the only way he could describe her—was a close friend of Cy's bride to be, Jessica, a beautiful young woman, clever, funny with something *real* to say. Samantha Langdon was the chief bridesmaid. One of four. They were to have a rehearsal later on after the men had washed up and had time to catch a cold beer...

The vision laughed, spoke, the words tumbling out as if she were unable to help herself.

"Oh goodness, we didn't think you'd be back so soon!"

She spoke the words at Cy, but rather looked at *him* as though he possessed some kind of uncommon magnetism. He remembered he just stood there, in turn, mesmerized. In the space of a few seconds he was overcome by feelings he had never experienced before. Hot, hard, fierce. They swirled around him like plumes of smoke. The sweat on his body sizzled his skin. It wasn't just her beauty, so bright he felt he had to shield his eyes; it was the way she *moved.* Grace appropriate to a princess and something more. Something that arrested the eye. He supposed ballerinas had it. He wanted to reach for this gilded creature. Close his arms around her. Find her mouth, discover the nectar within.

Then all at once he pulled himself together, regaining his habitual tight control, shocked and wary at her impact. Lightning strikes didn't feature in his emotional life. Why would they? He knew what sorrow a man's obsession bred. He couldn't trust a creature as fascinating as this. The lovely laugh. The teasing voice. The grace and femininity she used to marvellous effect. Not after what had happened to his family. He and Belle had been devastated by their parents' divorce. Their much loved and revered father had never recovered. The wrong woman could destroy a man. He had long assured himself it would never happen to him.

The vision came towards them in her lovely luminous gown, the power to captivate men probably born in her, a creature of air and fire. Her shoulders were bare, her hair a glorious shade of copper streamed down her back. She had beautiful creamy skin, the high cheekbones tinted with apricot almost the colour of her heavy satin gown. He had to tear his eyes away from the slope of her breasts revealed above the low cut bodice. This was a powerful sexual encounter. Nothing more.

"It's Ross, isn't it?"

Not content to hold him spellbound her charm and breeding was about to reduce him to an oaf.

Cy smiling, started to introduce them with his engaging manner. He on the other hand must have appeared an ill mannered boor by contrast, stiff and standoffish. A consequence he knew of his strong reaction A man could drown in a woman's eyes. Large, meltingly soft velvety brown eyes with gold chips in the iris. He knew the colour in her cheeks deepened when he looked down at her. *Stared* probably, not doing a good job of covering his innate hostility. He remembered he made some excuse about not taking her hand, standing well back so the dust and grime off his work gear wouldn't come into contact with her beautiful gown. He knew he looked and felt like a savage. He found out later there was a dried smear of blood on his cheek bone.

She had endured his severity well. Right through that evening and the great day of the wedding. It was all so damned disturbing. He wasn't usually like that. Looking back on his behaviour he cringed, cursing himself for his own susceptibility. It was a weakness and it pricked his pride. Maybe the Sunderlands weren't fated to have happy emotional lives. His dad, then Belle. The very last thing he needed was to be enslaved by a woman. The secret he was convinced was never to lose sight of himself.

"Hey, where dja go?"

Joe's voice broke into his troubled reverie, sounding a little worried.

"Just thinking."

"About that girl?" Joe studied the strong profile in the increasing light.

"About Belle." He had no trouble lying.

Joe took it Ross didn't want to talk about it. "Hell, man, better Miss Isabelle don't mope about the homestead," he said. "Is she gunna go with you tonight?"

Sunderland shrugged as if to say he wasn't sure. "My sister at the great age of twenty-six has reached a crisis point in life. I'm just grateful she chose to come home. It was bad enough losing Dad the way we did. Two years later Belle loses her husband."

Joe wondered as much as anyone else what exactly that last

argument between husband and wife had been about. Miss Isabelle hadn't just been grieving when she returned to the Sunderland ancestral home. She was and remained in a deep depression which led Joe to remembering what a glorious young creature she had been. The apple of her father's eye, Ross his great pride. The Sunderlands had become a very close family after the children's mother, Diana, who had been a wonderful wife and mother to start with fell in love with some guy she met on a visit to relatives in England. In fact a distant cousin. Within a month Diana had decided he meant more to her than her husband back home in Australia. She'd had high hopes of gaining custody of her children but they had refused to leave their father. Ewan Sunderland was a wonderful, generous, caring man. An ideal husband and father. He had idolised his beautiful wife. Put her on a pedestal. At least it had taken her all of fourteen years to fall off, Joe thought sadly. Such a beautiful woman! She laughed a lot. So happy! Always bright and positive. Wonderful to his people. Then all of a sudden put under a powerful spell. Love magic. Only this time it was *black magic*.

All these years later Joe's eyes grew wet. Her defection had severed Ewan's heart strings. The children had suffered. Three years apart. Ross, twelve, Isabelle only nine. Joe still couldn't fathom how Diana had done it. The cruelty of it! Now Ewan Sunderland lay at peace struck down by a station vehicle that got out of control. A bizarre double tragedy because the driver, a long time employee had died as well, a victim of a massive heart attack at the wheel. The shock had been enormous and none of them had really moved on. Ewan Sunderland was sorely missed by his son and daughter and his legion of friends.

Isabelle woke with a start. For a moment she couldn't remember where she was. The room was dark. There was no sound. Her heart hammering she put out a hand and slid it across the sheet. Nothing. No one. A stream of relief poured through her. *Thank God!* She pressed her dark head woven into a loose plait back into the pillow, her feeling of disorientation slowly evaporating. She lay there a few minutes longer fighting off the effects of her dreams, so vivid, so deeply disturbing she felt like crying. The same old nightmares really. She could feel the familiar fingers of depression starting to tighten their grip on her, but she knew she had to fight it. No one could cure her but herself. There were still people who loved her—her brother most of all—but she had to solve her problems on her own. Another approach might have been to talk to a psychologist trained to deal with women's "problems" but she was never *never* going to tell anyone what her married life had been like. The truth was too shocking.

Her bedroom was growing lighter, brighter. Soon the birds would start their dawn symphony. Did those wonderful birds know how much emotional support they gave her. The beauty and power of their singing cut a path through her negative feelings, the grief, the anger, the guilt and at bottom the disgust she directed at herself.

Determinedly she threw back the light coverlet and slid out of bed her bare toes curling over the Persian rug. A glance at the bedside clock confirmed what she had guessed: 4:40.

Oh God! So early, but there was no way she could go back to sleep. In her dreams Blair slept with her, a hand of possession on her breast. That's what she had been to him. A possession. Some kind of prize. He put a high value on her. Her looks and her manner. He had even insisted on coming with her to buy her clothes. Only the best would do. Roaming around her, viewing back and front, giving his opinion while the saleswoman beamed at him, no doubt fantasizing what life would be like with a rich handsome loving husband like that.

If only they knew!

Fully awake now, she tried to shrug off the memory of Blair's voice. It still had the power to resound in her ears. So tender and loving, so full of desire. That alone had filled her with trepidation. Then as predictably as night followed day, full of a white hot fury and the queerest anguish, berating her. His hand against her throat while she froze in paralysis.

You make me do this. You just don't understand, do you? What it's like for me. You cold neurotic bitch! What have I got to do to make you love me? What, Isabelle, tell me. I can't put up with any more of your cruelty. You will understand, won't you? I'll make you!

Then a blow that made her double over. Who could have dreamed such a charming young man could be capable of such behaviour? Cushioned in normality, the love of her father and brother and then Blair. In a single day everything changed.

What have I got to do, Belle, to make you love me? For all the very public displays of loving and remarked generosity Blair was what her grandmother would have called "a home devil." Correction. Blair *had been* a home devil. Blair was dead and a lot of people blamed her. Probably they always would. Certainly his family, especially his mother, Evelyn, who had bitterly resented being ousted as the number one woman in her only son's life. But then, she was to blame. How could anyone think otherwise? Maybe things in her own past—her mother's destruction of a marriage and the childhood trauma she had suffered had played a part in the calamity of Blair's death. Maybe her mother had passed on her destructive genes to her? This feeling was especially strong in her. A sense of guilt. Yet it could be argued she was being very unfair to herself. She used to be such a positive person. Not now. Being with Blair had poisoned her. She had never told a soul of his psychological cruelties, the little mind games, much less the unpredictable rages when he had resorted to physical blows, trying to pummel her until she found the courage to fight back. Sometimes it happened he came off second best. She reminded herself she was a Sunderland. She told him it had to stop. It was so *demeaning*. She wouldn't tolerate it. She would leave him.

No joke, Blair, she told him when he began to laugh, swinging around on him, picking up a knife. *No joke!*

Something in her eyes must have warned him she was in deadly earnest. After the confrontations, the usual deluge of apologies. Van loads of red roses. Exquisite underwear and nightgowns he loved to tear off. Blair down on his knees begging her to forgive him. He idolised her. She was everything in the world to him. He despised himself when he lost his temper. *Hated* what he did to her. But didn't she realise it was *her* fault she made him so angry? She deliberately provoked him, always trying to score points like a skilled opponent with an inexperienced adversary. It hurt him desperately the way she flirted with other men. People talked about it.

How could they? She never did...

And why did she have to go on about a *baby* for God's sake? Wasn't he enough for her? She had already stopped talking about a baby. Honest with no one else—her damnable pride again, her blind refusal to admit she had made a terrible mistake—she was honest with *herself.* The days of her marriage were numbered. Almost three years on, she wondered how she had married Blair in the first place.

Well, she had paid the price. Far better that they had never come into one another's lives. She knew Ross thought she had been in deep mourning these past months. Well she had in a sense. Mourning the waste of a life. What might have been. It was her failure to be able to mourn Blair's removal from her life that was the problem. She hadn't deserved his treatment of her—no woman did—but she did deserve her crushing feelings of guilt. It was what she had said to Blair that last night of his life that had sent him on his no return journey to death.

Isabelle showered and dressed then went downstairs to prepare breakfast for her brother. The best brother in the world. She loved him dearly. When she thought about it they had never had a single fight right through their childhood and adolescence which wasn't the norm in a lot of households. Ross's aim had been to love and protect her just as it had been their father's. Both men in her life had tried their hardest to make up for the painful loss of a mother. They couldn't bear to see her cry and after a while she had stopped. She was a Sunderland.

So many losses she thought. Mother, father, husband. Losses aplenty. Plenty of bad memories. Plenty of scars.

She heard Ross come in and moved into the hall to greet him, wiping her hands on a tea towel. "Find the boy?"

He nodded. "I don't think he'll pull that stunt again. Had some bet with young Pearce he could make it back to camp on his own. The only thing is he headed in the wrong direction."

"Easy enough to do if you're stupid." Isabelle gave a half smile. "Ready for breakfast?"

"In about ten minutes okay?" Ross needed a shave and a shower. Out all night he showed no signs of strain or tiredness. "You don't have to get up this early, you know," he turned back to tell his sister gently.

"My sleeping habits aren't what they used to be," Isabelle answered. In truth she was immensely grateful to sleep alone.

Her brother heard the sorrow behind the words and misconstrued it.

Isabelle let him make inroads on a substantial breakfast, sausages, bacon, eggs, tomatoes a couple of hash browns, toast, before starting any conversation. She smiled at the enthusiasm with which he attacked his meal. She couldn't fill him. Never could. A big man like their dad. Six three, whip-cord lean with a wide wedge of shoulders. His down bent head gleamed blue black like her own. His fine grained skin was a dark gold. His eyes like hers were a remarkable aqua. Their mother's eyes. Otherwise they were Sunderlands through and through. When they were just little kids people had often mistaken them for twins, but Ross grew and grew while she stopped at five-eight, above average height for a woman.

"So have you made up your mind about tonight?" She poured them both a cup of really good coffee—a must—hot, black and strong the way they liked it. None of that milky stuff.

He didn't answer for a moment, absently chewing a piece of toast. "I don't know."

"Hey, they're expecting you," she reminded him, knowing full well he didn't like to leave her. "Cy and Jessica will be there. After all, Jessica was the one who arranged it all. It's Robyn's gallery." Robyn was Cy's rather difficult stepsister married to a big developer. "You'll see Samantha again."

His lean handsome features tautened. "Who said I wanted to?"

"Sorry. I don't mean to pry." Isabelle considered for a moment. "She got under your skin didn't she?"

"Yes," he said bluntly. "I don't like women getting under my skin."

It was no revelation to his sister. "We've paid heavily for our past, haven't we?"

"Sure have." His eyes reflected the grimness of his thoughts.

"The past can spoil relationships."

"I know. It's all patterned and planned and destined." He looked at her. Always slender Belle was close to fragile. There were shadows under her eyes from many hours of lost sleep and probably bad dreams but she was indisputably *beautiful*. That was the main reason Hartmann had wanted her. For her beauty. It had woven a spell around him. With so many other things about Belle to appreciate and admire, her intelligence, her talent, her sheer *quality* Hartmann had seemed to ignore all that. If indeed he even saw it. Poor Belle! She had rushed in to a marriage that probably wouldn't have endured even if Blair had lived.

"Talk to me, Belle," he found himself pleading. "I'm here to listen. Tell me what went so terribly wrong in your marriage?"

"I'm a tough nut like you. I keep it all locked up." Isabelle stirred a few more grains of raw sugar into her coffee.

"It might help to talk don't you think?"

What could she say? Good-looking, softly spoken, Blair had been abusive? What an upsurge of rage that would arouse! It was *unthinkable* to tell her brother, just as she had never been able to tell her father. It was all *so* demeaning. Both Sunderlands big strong *tough* men living a life fraught with dangers and non stop physically exhausting work, would have cut off a hand before lifting it in anger to a woman. Her father had never so much as given her a light slap even when she got up to lots of mischief. Ross was intensely chivalrous. An old word but it applied to him and a great many Outback men who cherished women as life's partners and close friends. Blair could have considered himself done for if she had ever told her father or brother of her treatment at his hands. But for all his insecurities, cunning Blair had known she would never expose him. In exposing him she would be devaluing herself. Pride, too, was a sin. There was just no way she could tell her brother her terrible story. He would wonder if she had been in her right mind not seeking her family's protection.

"Well?" Ross prompted after a few moments of watching the painful expressions flit across his sister's face. "He adored you, didn't he? I mean he was *really* mad about you. It might seem strange but Dad and I never thought he plumbed the *real* you. Was that it? Terrible to speak ill of the dead and the tragic way he died so young, but Blair gave the impression he was extraordinarily dependent on you. Needy I suppose is the word. You couldn't walk out of the room ten minutes before he was asking where you were. Who you were with. You don't have to tell me but I know he was terribly jealous. Even of our family bond. Did it become a burden?"

She couldn't meet her brother's eyes. "We had problems, Ross." She concentrated on the bottom of her coffee cup. "I imagine most married couples do, but we were trying to work them out."

"What problems?" Ross persisted, knowing there was a great

deal his sister wasn't telling." I know you wanted to start a family. You love children. Every woman wishes for a baby with the man she loves."

Only I didn't love him. Blair was the baby. Blair wanted a real baby to stay away. His mania was her sole attention.

"There's no point in talking about it now, Ross," she sighed. "I feel terrible Blair had to die the way he did. Such a waste of a life!"

His brows drew together in a frown. "Surely you mean you find it unbearable to be without him?"

"Of course. We both know what it's like to lose someone we love."

"But you can't despair, Belle. You're young. In time you'll meet someone else." Someone *worthy* of you, Ross thought. "I realise the fact the two of you had an argument before Blair left the party is weighing heavily on you. His mother's attitude didn't help but she was so intensely possessive of her son she would have blamed any woman who was his widow. Grief made her act so badly."

By and large Evelyn Hartmann was right. She had sent Blair to his death.

"Evelyn wasn't the only one to assign the blame to me. Blair's whole family did. A lot of our so called friends looked at me differently afterwards. There was a lot of talk. I couldn't defend myself. I was the *outsider*. Everyone looked on Blair as the most devoted of husbands."

"But *wasn't* he?" Ross asked, hoping he could get to the truth. Did the truth set you free or make matters worse?

"He adored me just as you say, Ross." Isabelle spread her elegant long fingered hands. "I know you're trying to help me but can we get off the subject." *Stay away from it entirely.* "Samatha Langdon now. I'd like to meet her. I missed out on Cy's and Jessica's wedding. Impossible to go under the circumstances."

"Cy and Jessica understood," Ross assured her. "If you really want to meet Samantha Langdon why not come along with me tonight? We'll take the chopper into Darwin late afternoon. You'll need to book an extra room at the hotel. I think it might do you good to get out of the house."

Would it? All the hurtful rumours and she supposed she hadn't heard the half of them had given her a strong feeling of being *separated* from other people. Her problem—early widow-hood and ugly spate of rumours—wasn't *their* problem, thank God. She knew all the gossip would be doing the rounds of Darwin but then she wouldn't be on her own. Nevertheless she said: "It's just that I don't think I can, Ross." She began to gather up plates remembering how Blair in one of his moods had smashed their wine glasses, deliberately dropping them on the kitchen tiles, then laughing as she shrunk back wondering seriously if he were mad. Certainly there had been a demon in him.

"Look Belle, I'm not pressing you but I know there's a heck of a lot you're not telling me. Just remember, you're not alone. A lot of people love you. You're my baby sister. I'd lay down my life for you."

Tears rushed into her eyes and she turned away.

"So it would mean a great deal to me if you made the effort to come. Jessica likes you a lot."

Isabelle had composed herself enough to turn back. "We've only met a couple of times but Jessica is a lovely person and Samantha is a close friend. Would Jessica have a friend who wasn't a nice person?"

Ross stood up, shoving his chair beneath the table. "I never said she wasn't *nice*." God, nice hardly described her. "It's David Langdon we're there to meet anyway. Say you'll come, Belle."

"You need protection?" She gave a glimmer of a smile.

"Nope." He moved his wide shoulders restlessly. "Getting hooked on a woman like that would be as dangerous as catching a tiger by the tail."

CHAPTER TWO

THEY SLIPPED INTO an animated crowd, most with champagne glasses in hand, and waiters circling with delicious looking finger food. There was a buzz of a hundred voices. Isabelle spotted Cyrus Bannerman first because of his commanding height and presence. Half hidden by the breadth of his shoulder was his beautiful wife of several months Jessica, her magnificent mass of ash-blond hair radiant in the bright fall of skylights. The interior of the gallery was divided into three spacious rooms interconnected by wide arches. The lights were trained on a large collection of photographs, most colour some black and white that took on a rivetting quality to rival paintings. Someone had taken the trouble to hang the prints *perfectly* on the white expanse of walls.

Jessica looked up and waved, a lovely welcoming smile on her face. Cy turned around to follow his wife's gaze, beaming too. They watched him glance back at the group he was with, obviously making their excuses, before he tucked his hand beneath Jessica's elbow steering a path towards Ross and Isabelle who were also being greeted on all sides. The big cattle families were outback royalty. The Sunderlands were as well known as the Bannermans though the late Broderick Bannerman, an immensely wealthy man had not scored anywhere near the late Ewan Sunderland's high approval rating. Mercifully both sons and heirs were held in high regard.

"Hi!" The women brushed cheeks, smiling into one another's eyes. The men, looking very pleased to see one another settled for affectionate claps on the shoulder.

"I'm so glad you could come, Isabelle," Jessica said with complete sincerity. "You look absolutely beautiful."

"Thank you. So do you." Isabelle, who appeared so poised was actually quaking inside. She was grateful for the compliment. Jessica's warmth and friendliness steadied her. It was a long time since she had ventured out. Blair's death had put such a contagion on her.

Jessica smiled. "It's a brilliant collection." She turned her head over her shoulder. "I know you'll both love it. David is being feted in the next room. Sam is with David's assistant, Matt Howarth. A very pleasant guy. Come and meet them. David is an extraordinary man. You'll like him, Ross. We know he's very keen on meeting you and hopefully having you for a guide."

"Piece of cake!" Cy assured his friend.

"I don't know that I've made up my mind, Cy," Ross said, sobering a moment. *Sam was with Matt Howarth?* What did that mean? What do you think it means he thought a hard knot in his stomach.

"You want a break. You work too hard," Cy urged him, forging a path through the throng.

"*You* should talk."

"It's not like it's going to be for long. Belle would *love* it." The *old* Belle, Cy thought. Knowing her from childhood he recognised and understood Isabelle's fragile state of mind.

Jessica made a little surprised gesture, looking towards Isabelle. "What a marvellous idea!"

"I couldn't, Jessica," Isabelle said quickly, touching the other woman's arm. "I beg you, don't say anything."

"Of course not!" Jessica promised hurriedly seeing the tension in Isabelle's face. She knew Isabelle's tragic story and she was full of sympathy. How did a woman cope with losing a beloved husband? Jessica found herself giving an involuntary shudder. Her own days were filled with ecstatic fulfilment. To lose Cy would be like a descent into hell.

Someone came out of the crowd, a stylish, sweet faced woman in her fifties who grasped Isabelle's arm. "Isabelle dear, what an extraordinary surprise! I'd heard you were home."

"Mrs. Charlton, of course." Isabelle's face lit up. She allowed herself to be detained. "I'll catch up with you," she called to the others.

Ross relaxed when he heard the comfortable note in his sister's voice. He didn't know the woman, although he was sure he had seen her some place. So many of Isabelle's so called friends had betrayed her taking the opinion she somehow had played a role in her popular husband's death.

The next room was even more crowded. A lion of a man with a large handsome head covered in thick tawny waves and strongly hewn features was holding court. The several women around him were staring up into his face, magnetised, their expressions buoyed up, obviously excited.

Jessica laughed a bit, "Starstruck."

"Extraordinary guy," Cy answered. In fact very few in life had that impact he thought.

But Ross saw no one but *her*. The same galvanising jolt passed through him as the first time he'd laid eyes on her. A sensation he had tried—how unsuccessfully—to erase from his mind. And then, tensing, the man standing too close at her shoulder. Early thirties, slight of build, thin sensitive face, nice smile. Matt Howarth. It had to be. His attitude, the way he was standing flashed an unmistakable message. They shared a relationship, or at the very least an understanding. Surely he hadn't imagined she would be unattached. A beautiful creature like that! Hell he couldn't even allow himself to think of her, but the knowledge he wouldn't succeed was there.

Tonight she was wearing a slip of a dress of a golden hue that complemented her colouring. High heeled gold sandals were on her feet. Her beautiful hair was centre parted falling like a bolt of bright copper satin down her back. Even her skin looked gilded. He could actually feel its smoothness under his hand. Cool and satiny when the very thought of touching her heated his blood.

You want her. You know you do.

He heard that inner voice, the voice that wouldn't be silenced, whispering in his ear.

Their eyes met. He realised with a sense of crushing mortification he'd been standing once *again* transfixed. *Hell!* Acting foolish wasn't his style. He found himself wondering if the others had noticed he was rooted to the spot. Yet she too, seemed shocked, her beautiful doe's eyes widening, as if electrified by the intensity of his hunter's gaze.

Immediately he was seized with the fierce desire to turn around and leave. This woman was temptation. The sort of challenge any smart man would step free of it. No way could he guide this expedition if Samantha Langdon was to go along. He hadn't the slightest desire to allow a woman to play him like a clown. Woman magic. Sometimes he thought he could never wipe away the bitter taste of his father's betrayal at the soft hands of his mother. That's what lay behind everything he thought, abruptly sobering. A man could be shackled by adoration. His beloved father had gone about his life but both of his children had known inside he was shattered. That's what women were capable of. Leaving a trail of destruction.

He looked away at the brother, David Langdon, thinking with a vague sense of astonishment he liked the man on sight. Brother and sister shared a resemblance—not as marked as his and Belle's—mostly the colouring. She looked very delicate beside him, ultra feminine. Long, light beautiful bones. The brother was a big man, well over six feet like himself, but strapping rather than lean, very fit and strong looking. His hair was a tawny mix of dark blond to bronze, his eyes a pronounced shade of topaz. Both had generous well defined mobile mouths.

Cy introduced them. The two men shook hands then Langdon speaking easily—he exuded charisma—introduced his assistant, Matt, who regarded Sunderland somewhat warily as if he thought this was someone who could turn dangerous and he was already aware of it.

"I'm looking forward to us all having dinner together," Langdon said after a few minutes of exchanging social pleasantries. "Meanwhile I hope you enjoy the showing. I have to circulate, it seems." Cy's stepsister, Robyn, the owner of the gallery, looking very glamorous in black and white was beckoning to him pushing forward a distinguished looking elderly man. "Excuse me, won't you?" Langdon's manner was so warm and charming Ross thought the man would have no difficulty selling heaters to the nomads in the desert. David Langdon had every appearance of a man you could trust with your life.

They all began to study the remarkable array of photographs, moving about the room in procession. Ross listened to the comments of his friends as they talked. Jessica, the creative one, was very knowledgeable. She was just right for Cy he thought. Lucky guy! He wondered where Belle had got to. Ah, there she was, standing with a red-haired woman, seemingly at ease. He stopped for a moment to read a CV of Langdon's work. Very impressive. He'd spent time in the war zones, East Timor, Afghanistan, Iraq. He was very widely travelled. A great deal in South East Asia. Thailand, Cambodia, Indonesia, Malaysia, Papua New Guinea. Ross had seen his marvellous impressions of that little known country although it lay on Australia's door step. Separated momentarily from the others—so many people wanted to meet Jessica—he studied the shots of the Great

Barrier Reef and the glorious tropical islands. Langdon must have spent hours and hours flying around trying to find the exact spots. Probably in a helicopter or a light plane, door open, strapped in tightly so he could film. Perfect crystal clear waters, cobalt skies, pure white sand ringing jade islands.

He wouldn't mind a few weeks on a tropical island. He could almost feel himself there. His eyes dwelt with pleasure on a magnificent shot of the Outer Reef shot from the air. The deep channel was a deep inky blue, the waters a deep turquoise, with channels of aquamarine. The fantastic coral gardens were in the foreground, an anchored boat and a group of snorkellers swimming off the reef wall lending perspective. Moving on, he recognised Four Mile Beach at Queensland's Port Douglas, the purple ranges in the background, luxuriant palms and vegetation wrapping the wide beach, sun worshippers like little colourful dots on the sand. A marvellous, marvellous shot of a small sand cay covered with nesting crested terns, the deep turquoise waters rippled with iridescent green like the heart of a black opal. He felt like he was in the middle of the ocean.

"These are good," he found himself murmuring aloud.

"You sound surprised?"

He straightened and turned slowly before answering, giving himself time to suppress the involuntary electric thrill that flared along his nerves. As a consequence his voice came out in that strange arrogant fashion. "That wasn't my intention. Your brother is more than a fine photographer. He's an artist."

"He is," Samantha said with complete conviction, her cheeks flushing a little at the curtness of his tone. Her powerful attraction to this man shocked her. Not Mr. Nice Guy that's for sure. Formidable. "I run the Sydney gallery for him. Of course you know that. We're thinking of opening another one here in Darwin."

"And what do you suppose Robyn will think about that?" Incredibly in his imagination he was pushing her low necked dress down from her shoulders. She had beautiful breasts. She had teased him with their beauty at the wedding, smiling into his eyes, provoking him to dance with her. Of course he was obliged to. They were after all chief bridesmaid and best man.

She was shrugging lightly as if to show she was unfazed by his scrutiny and the challenge of his comment. "There's plenty of room for another gallery. Robyn specialises in paintings and sometimes sculptures. Hopefully one gallery will be a spin off for the other. There are always a great many tourists in town."

"Yes," he agreed briefly, feeling as though he was drunk on some rich potent wine. That was the effect she had on him. But no way, *no way,* was he about to fall to his knees.

She was returning his gaze equably, so gracious when he always acted the complete boor around her. He suspected she was doing it deliberately.

"I'm wondering why you don't like me, Ross?" she inquired softly. "No, don't throw up your head." Which he did in that high mettled way. "Don't deny it. We both know it's true. Remember how it was at the wedding?"

As if he had forgotten.

"I didn't imagine your...what can I call it? Animus, antagonism? Was it something I said? Something I did? I seem to have gone over it many many times in my head. But it's still there tonight. The thing is, David and I are so hoping you'll act as our guide. It would be awkward if there remained *difficulties* between us."

He frowned, giving her a look that both smouldered and sparkled. "You intend to go along then?"

"I've never seen a man with aquamarine eyes." She was so unnerved she didn't answer his question, but said the first thing that came into her head.

"It runs in the family." He returned carelessly. "Lest you deflect me, I'll ask again. Do you intend to go along on this trip?"

There was no mistaking the opposition on his hard, handsome face. "I'm thrilled David wants me," she said, feeling the friction between them like a burr against the skin. "I don't know if you've noticed the little texts beneath the photographs. I was responsible for them."

It was a reflex to compliment her. He had thought they were Langdon's; a few lines, often poetic capturing the very essence of the scene. "Very good."

"I don't think you know—I made such a poor impression on you at Cy's and Jessica's wedding but I write and illustrate children's stories as well as managing the gallery. They're for children with vivid imaginations. They're starting to do very well. Jessica and I took a Fine Arts Degree together, but I'm not nearly so gifted as she. It won't be too long before Jessica gives an exhibition of her paintings. She not only fell madly in love with her Territory Man, she fell in love with the Territory. So far David hasn't photographed the Top End or the Red Centre which has been widely covered of course. He likes to capture his subject matter in a new light."

"And it works." He tried hard to lighten up but that was difficult when he was standing less than an arm's length from her. "You realise a trip into Kakadu wouldn't be a picnic?"

She tilted her chin, hoping her eyes weren't betraying her reactions. This man attracted and daunted her in equal measure. "I know it's a great wilderness area."

He nodded, his black hair sheened with purple highlights like the sky at midnight. For a cattle man used to working gear, off duty he was very stylishly groomed. Dark cream linen suit. White shirt with a brown stripe the top button casually undone. Silk tie with alternating white and brown stripes. Sexy enough to take her breath away.

"Have you ever got up close and personal with a twenty foot croc?" he asked with light sarcasm.

"I'd make sure *you* were in front of me." She tried to joke.

"It's no joke," he told her, his lean features taut.

"I'll have you know I'm serious." She looked directly at him, feeling on her mettle. "What is it, Ross? Have you written me off as a bimbo? Someone who'll turn into a quivering liability?"

"I have to tell you I wouldn't be happy to take you," he said bluntly.

"Samantha," she prompted. "That's my name. Sam, if you like."

"*Sam* is just *too* quaint." Anyone less like a Sam he had yet to see. He gazed into her dark doe eyes, bright with little golden motes.

She could have hit him. Damaged her hand. *Herself.* "Actually I was hoping your sister, Isabelle—she's *so* beautiful— might be persuaded to come along with us. Station bred she'd be an enormous help to me."

He could only warn her off. "Belle wouldn't be interested, I'm afraid. She lost her husband not so long ago."

Samantha dipped her head, her nerves tightening. "Jessica told me. I'm so very sorry. She's so young. Mightn't it help her to get out though, don't you think? Nature is a great healer."

Very deliberately he cut off that line of thinking. "Thank you for sharing that with me, *Samantha.*"

The effect of her name on his lips was extraordinary. How strange it was to be excited by a man and thoroughly disconcerted at the same time. "Don't be like that," she pleaded.

"Like what?" He was sizzling with sexual energy. A male aggression that appeared to possess him in her presence. Chaos threatened when he liked order.

"Arrogant, actually," she told him quietly, feeling a twist of desire deep inside her and nothing she could do about it. "Unpleasant as well when Cy thinks you're the greatest guy in the world."

"Maybe I'm a lot more used to dealing with men than women. I'm sorry. I apologise."

His sudden smile made her suck in her breath. It bathed his

rather severe handsome features in dazzling light. "That's not what I've heard either," she found herself saying.

"Meaning what?" He shrugged, a surprisingly elegant movement.

"There are a lot of girls hung up on you I was told. I suppose that's a good sign. Then again a lot of women are attracted to men who have little use for them."

"And you're assuming I'm that kind of man?"

The colour of his remarkable eyes was a source of wonder. "Aren't you?" Her every instinct had warned her this man was trouble yet she plunged ahead angered by his resistance, almost dismissal. It wasn't something she was used to.

"I love my sister," he pointed out.

"You certainly should. You had to stick together."

His expression tightened. "Cy told you my life story?"

"What's wrong with that? I was interested. He filled me in a little way. I know your parents divorced when you were twelve and your sister a few years younger. Don't feel overly bad about that. Our mother and father split up when I was still at school and David had already left home. Both of them are re-married. David and I have two stepbrothers—my dad's. Things like that."

He was surprised. He had thought her the most cosseted of creatures. Daddy's little princess. A most beautiful little girl. But there was a sudden haunting in her eyes. "You can't quite cover up the fact you'd been praying they'd stay together?"

"Absolutely, but they'd hit a very bumpy ride. In fact it's put me off marriage."

"True?" He let his smile loose again.

Another thrill. That alone shouted a warning. "I've already decided *you* have a lot against it."

"Really?" He looked down his straight nose at her. "You don't know me." *Even if you are trying to lead me on.*

Her heart gave a wild flutter. She couldn't believe the arrogance of his manner could be a seduction. But it *was*. "I'd like to know you better," she said, something she'd discovered the moment she'd laid eyes on him.

"So you can dig out my weaknesses?" He *willed* his blood to stop racing. There was a tremendous exhilaration in this sparring. It was like being caught up in an electrical storm when at any moment danger could be inflicted on a man.

"I didn't imagine for a moment you had any," she answered with faintly bitter sweetness.

"As many as the next man." He shrugged. "But I work hard to keep them under control. I had the impression you and your brother's assistant were close?"

A flare of something, was it anger? deepened the apricot colour in her cheeks. "Now how on earth did you arrive at that conclusion?"

"Are you telling me it's not true?" Sad if he was giving *himself* away.

"I'm not telling you anything," she said crisply, knowing with every passing minute getting involved with this intoxicating man would be a terrible mistake. "I'd like to see you less sure of yourself and your opinions."

"And you're the one hoping we can be friends?" he scoffed. *Think, Sam. Try to clear your head.*

Yet all her pulses were drumming in double time. "Not *friends* so much," she successfully mustered her poise. "I don't believe we could ever be friends, not unless you undergo a radical change, but colleagues of sorts. I know you'd prefer Men Only, women being such nuisances, but I'd endeavour to keep out of your way."

"Fine," he drawled, staring down at her mouth with her small teeth like prize pearls. Her lips were full, luscious, incredibly tempting. He'd like to crush their cushiony softness beneath his. Teach her a lesson. "But not exactly easy if we had to share a tent?"

She battled the shock wave. "We wouldn't have to do that. *Would* we?"

For the first time there was genuine amusement in his jewelled eyes. "Not your idea of fun? It could get worse."

She was still seeing them sharing a tent. "Like dodging crocs and pythons that devour you at a gulp?"

"Lady, there's so much I'm *not* telling you." It came out with a flicker of contempt.

Use your head. Go!

She had to make her escape before she said something she would regret. Ross Sunderland was dynamite. Exciting yes, but one of the dangerous men of this world. He drew her so much it was scaring her badly. "Anything to put me off," she managed lightly. "I think I'll have a word with Isabelle if I can find her. *You're* a terrible man." She half turned away.

"Knowing that at the start will save you a lot of trouble," he called after her.

"To be frank I knew it the instant I laid eyes on you." She turned back to confront him, long silky hair swirling, flame bright in the strong lights.

His mouth curved in a challenging smile. "Then you know we're not fated to be *friends*."

"That sounds so much like a *dare*?"

They were caught in a tableau, neither moving until a very pretty brunette dressed in show stopping red broke it up by rushing between them, ignoring Samantha as though she weren't there. "Ah there you are Ross, darling!" She grabbed his arm. Held on for dear life. "I didn't think this was your scene. Mum and I have only just arrived. Come and join us. We were just saying we should have a good party. It's seems like *ages* since we got together." She began to pull him away.

Samantha didn't wait to see them move off. She was cursing herself for allowing Ross Sunderland to get to her. No way either was he going to block her path. Her company and contribution were important to her brother. She was determined not to be left behind.

* * *

David Langdon took a long slow breath then decided to catch up with the woman he'd spent so much time watching. Albeit out of the corner of his eye. *A beaute fatale.* Of course he had known she was beautiful. In fact she was more beautiful in the flesh than she was in the photographs he had seen in the papers and the few times they had captured her on television always hurrying away, head bent, one hand trying to cover her face like the tragic Princess Diana. For a while the media had hounded her. That must have been a bad experience. He knew who she was of course. Isabelle Hartmann, Blair Hartmann's young widow. She couldn't be more than mid-twenties and her beauty hadn't even reached its zenith. She still looked as though she was hurting badly.

David hadn't even told his sister how much he had learned about this near notorious young woman over the past months. Mostly from people supposedly in the know. Little of it good. It seemed to him a shocking thing to condemn her out of hand. Who knew exactly what went on within a marriage? Closer to the truth he'd been seized with a fierce desire to protect her which was quite odd since he had never managed to meet her. Not that he wasn't in and out of Sydney all the time but he made a point of avoiding the big social functions unless they were in aid of charity. His deep seeing eyes, *trained* eyes, had divined the torment in her.

A lot of the rumours and gossip had their origins in plain jealousy. He'd come to that conclusion. Men he'd found were far more reluctant to put any blame at all on her though all were in agreement Blair Hartmann had been a nice easy going guy, maybe a little light weight, spoiled outrageously by his wealthy mother. Everyone knew that. It was women, especially Evelyn Hartmann's circle, fuelled by envy and resentment and fearing to cross such a formidable figure in society as Isabelle's ex-mother-in-law, who claimed Isabelle was an altogether different person from the one who appeared in public. For one thing she had been near arctic to the husband who had adored her. There was even talk she had refused him a child no doubt to preserve her willowy figure, selfish creature. She was terribly vain they reported, obsessed with herself and her clothes.

At least they couldn't say she had married Hartmann for his money. The Sunderlands were a highly respected pastoral family wealthy in their own right as the press had easily uncovered. The fierce argument between the two, husband and wife had of course found its way into print. Speculation had been rife. Something Isabelle Hartmann had said had caused her late husband so loving and appreciative of her, to storm out of the party. Worse, perhaps caused him to be careless of his own life.

Whispers still followed her. He had overheard a few this very night. Blessed or cursed by such physical beauty she was bound to be a cynosure of attention. But no one he had noticed had been so careless as to give rein to gossip with her brother in earshot. Ross Sunderland was a man with fire in his remarkable eyes. Even the way he stood near his sister, sometimes with his arm carelessly around her, told the world not to be surprised if he retaliated on his sister's behalf. Langdon had been told and had since witnessed the two were very close. My God, didn't he feel the same about his own little sister, Samantha, nearly seven years his junior who had borne the brunt of their parents' undeniably bitter break up with Sam the pawn in the middle. On his world travels at the time he had since done his level best to make it up to her.

Seeing Isabelle Hartmann alone for a moment that beautiful face cool, passionless as a statue, he made his way towards her, gesturing with a smile he'd get back to a couple who surged across the room to gain his attention.

"Good evening, Mrs. Hartmann. I've been meaning to introduce myself for some time. David Langdon."

She turned to him quickly, staring up into his face. "Of course, Mr. Langdon." Some emotion stirred in her, swiftly crossed her face, then disappeared. She gave him her hand, silky soft, slender quite lost in his bear grip. He fought down the powerful urge to carry it to his lips.

"My pleasure." She smiled, finding something incredibly mesmeric about this big, dynamic man. "And it certainly has been. I've so enjoyed your showing."

"I'm glad." Was it his imagination or was she trembling?

"I'd have met you much earlier only I got caught up by friends who haven't seen me for a while. You've been so much the centre of attention I didn't want to intrude." The fact was both Cy and Jessica, then a little later Samantha followed by Ross had insisted they introduce her—it was high time—but for some reason she had made the excuse she would wait a while until all the adulation died down. It still hadn't stopped.

"The gallery shuts its doors at ten." He glanced over her satin smooth dark head. She wore her hair in a style he particularly liked if the woman could get away with it. A classic chignon that emphasized her enchanting swan neck. "I sincerely hope you're going to join us at dinner?"

She pressed her fingers to her temple.

"Please don't claim a headache," he begged, smiling into her eyes. "I promise you you're going to enjoy yourself. I've already met Ross, of course. I feel already he's just the right man to lead our expedition."

She allowed her eyes to appraise his height and his broad shoulders. A gentle giant but she had no doubt he could be incredibly tough when he had to be. "You don't strike me as the sort of man who needs anyone to lead him."

He gave her another charming smile. "As much as I hate to say it I'd definitely need an expert to guide me through Kakadu. This is your part of the world."

"Yet you've visited other extremely remote places. Very dangerous places as well."

"And I've counted on good people who know what they're about for survival."

She braced herself a little. He was very close, towering over her. So big, so solid, but marvellously nonthreatening. She had made a horrendous error in judgment with Blair but she knew in her bones this man would always deal with women gently. "I'm not exactly sure Ross has made up his mind, Mr. Langdon," she warned him.

"David, please."

"Isabelle." She spoke almost shyly, her creamy white skin colouring slightly. It was enormously appealing. Rumour had painted her a vain self centred creature who lived only for her own pleasure and conquest. He saw none of it. Perhaps tragedy had destroyed her confidence.

"It suits you," he remarked, his voice deep with more than a polite veneer. If he had to visualise Shakespeare's Dark Lady of the Sonnets, it would be Isabelle Hartmann. He surprised within himself not only fascination but a curious tenderness for this young woman with the purity and loveliness of a lily. She was wearing white to enhance the effect, one shouldered, a fluid column, no jewellery except for pendant earrings. Lustrous South Sea pearls appended from a diamond cluster. She wore no rings on her long fingered hands. No engagement ring. No wedding ring. Pearl painted nails. There again a puzzle. Would a woman so recently widowed remove clear evidence of her marriage? What did it say? She had gained no comfort there?

His topaz eyes glowed like a cat's without giving anything away, but Isabelle was aware he was noting every last little thing about her. Extraordinarily she welcomed it. One of the paradoxical facts of life. As big and masculine as he was, he didn't *threaten* her. Rather she felt in the presence of some powerful creature who for his own reasons had taken her under his protection. She had already noticed there was something distinctly leonine about him even to the tawny mane. She realised she too was taking stock, wondering how those thick waves would feel beneath her hands. To grasp them! To tug gently. It would be quite wonderful.

My God, she had to be mad!

"That's great! You two have finally met."

Each was so engrossed in the other they actually started when Samantha appeared at her brother's side, smiling her pleasure. She glanced at her watch excitedly. "Ten minutes to go then we can all get to know one another better. I have to admit I'm hungry. What about you, Isabelle?"

It was her moment to say she had a slight headache and would be returning to the hotel only someone as radiant and friendly as Samantha Langdon was hard to resist. David Langdon said nothing, quietly waiting for her answer. She was forced to admit the fact he was going to be there had a huge bearing on her decision. She couldn't bring herself to ask why. Better that way.

"Perhaps a little," she smiled. "But I warn you. I'm not going to talk. I'm going to *listen*."

They all sat round a circular table, paired off as if it would have been obvious to an onlooker that Isabelle and Ross and David and Samantha were closely related. David's assistant Matt had a previous engagement to meet up with a friend staying at the Holiday Inn so the numbers were even. The restaurant was nowhere near as opulent as the restaurants Isabelle had frequented with Blair and their circle of friends. *His* friends really, part of the Establishment, grown up together, gone to the same schools and University, but the food was every bit as good. Over the last dreadful months it had been difficult just trying to swallow enough to stay alive but tonight sitting between David Langdon and her brother Isabelle found herself surprisingly hungry. Even the air around her had taken on a different quality. Maybe sanity wasn't staying away from people but joining them.

They all had different things for an entrée, though she and Jessica shared a range of appetisers, crudités and quails eggs and a beautiful Haloumi that came from Kangaroo Island and was much better than the imported. Samantha had sea scallops wrapped with bacon with a red wine sauce, David, pan fried prawns in potato waistcoats, Cyrus decided on abalone with shiitake and young salad leaves served in its beautiful ovoid shell and Ross stayed with one of his favourites, rice noodle cannelloni stuffed with the superb blue swimmer crab meat.

It was difficult not to mellow under the influence of such beautiful food and the excellent chilled chardonnay that accompanied it. Seafood figured heavily for the main course, magnificent lobster caught that very morning, coral trout off the Reef, and the superb eating fish barramundi for which the Top End was famous.

Ross glancing across at his sister found it deeply heartening to see her eating with apparent enjoyment, smiling frequently at something David Langdon said to her, obviously at ease with him. It was almost as if he had brought her to life. There was colour in her cheeks. She looked very beautiful but still dangerously vulnerable. Well, Langdon was a kind man. He could see that. A gentleman. He was also very amusing, very knowledgeable, and Ross had had ample evidence women found Langdon extremely attractive. David Langdon had to be one hell of a catch. It didn't occur to Ross that people said exactly the same thing about him.

Dessert was out of the way—the men had wanted it—the women protested they had to mind their figures but Langdon persuaded Isabelle to try a lime and ginger crème brulee. Coffee after that, and the *real* discussion began.

Here it comes Samantha thought. He's going to make it perfectly plain he doesn't want me along. The Great White Hunter on his men only expedition. Men she had to admit had a special camaraderie. In the space of a couple of hours she could see her brother and Ross Sunderland had made a good connection. Something she could hardly say for herself and that complicated man. It was easy to see both men would get along indeed all three men had a lot in common, essentially men of action living their lives outdoors for most of the time. Of course women formed extraordinary bonds but in different ways and usually it took longer. She and Jessica were long time close friends but she could see she couldn't intrude on Isabelle's space no matter how much she liked her. Isabelle had lost her adored husband and she was wrapped in sadness. Nevertheless it was lovely to see her responding to David's gentle masterly hand. Her big brother was simply *the best*. There had been women in his life of course, but apparently nothing so intense it had made him want to enter into marriage. Marriage didn't always culminate in happily ever after anyway. Before their parents had been divorced they'd become bitter enemies. Two bitter enemies who had together created herself and David. When did a marriage go wrong? What happened to the spoken vows of love and commitment? In the end the only thing possible was for each to release the other. A sane person would stay away from marriage entirely.

She moved on to Ross Sunderland who knew all about parental marriage bonds broken and the grief that attended it. Certainly he was relaxing his guard. In fact he was showing himself to be excellent company but when his eyes fell on her she couldn't miss the challenging glint that sent tingles chasing down her spine. That in itself was unsettling. How could one be attracted to a man with an irresistible need to snap one's fingers at him at the same time?

Talk of Kakadu, the great national park brought the men alive. Twenty thousand square kilometres of crocodile infested rivers, low lying flood plains, rocky outcrops, waterfalls rain forest and woodlands dominated by the magnificent buttress of the Arnhem Land escarpment that ran for six hundred kilometres across the tropical Top End, one of the last great world wilderness areas. It had been established aboriginals had inhabited Kakadu for fifty thousand years. Neighbouring Arnhem Land was still inhabited by large numbers of Australia's indigenous people indeed Kakadu was under the custodianship of the traditional owners.

Ross and Cy were telling David about the world famous rock

galleries of Nourlangie and Ubirr estimated at around twenty thousand years old and of great archaeological importance.

"Most of the paintings at Nourlangie are in the X-ray style," Ross said, leaning towards David like a man on a mission to sell the Top End. "Two phases descriptive and decorative. Extraordinarily these X-ray drawings depict the subject's internal anatomical features. Ibirr is another treasure house you'd need to see. You'll find the *Mimi* spirits depicted there. The aboriginals believe they live in the caves, even in the little cracks and crevices."

"To them, the *Mimi* are terrifying creatures," Cy eased in the comment.

Ross nodded. "Namargon, the Lightning Man is represented, stone axes growing from his head, arms and knees to strike the ground. He appeared when the region first experienced the great electrical storms of the Wet. The rock art is the region's major cultural heritage. It can't be missed."

"Take me there," David smiled. "I'm sold."

They got through almost another hour talking. David Langdon asked a great many questions. Cy and Ross answered them, taking turns, sometimes speaking together their enthusiasm was so great. Isabelle sat back quietly. Jessica smiled lovingly at her husband, Samantha inwardly was on tenterhooks. She couldn't bear to think for once she would lose out although Sunderland hadn't as yet agreed to act as their guide. His purpose on the whole seemed to be that of an arm chair guide, pointing out the very special areas of interests, the sacred sites, the extraordinary land forms and the spectacular escarpment country and the various hazards along the way which included the immensely dangerous giant saurians of the Alligator River, North and South, and the numerous billabongs and wetlands. Both he and Cy maintained if you treated the crocodiles with respect and didn't intrude foolishly on their territory no harm would come to you.

Samantha took that as a very good reason for being allowed to go along. It wasn't as though she was planning to come within patting distance of their hideous snouts. They weren't cuddly koalas, though even koalas being wild animals could inflict a lot of damage if they felt threatened.

David gave a satisfied sigh. "So are you going to be free to take us?"

For one dreadful moment it looked like Sunderland was about to say, no, only Samantha breathed a sigh of relief when his sister caught his eye and smiled. Isabelle knew he wanted to go. Ross loved being out in the wilderness. There were a few pressing commitments he would have to attend to before he went. Afterwards for the space of a few weeks of the trip he could delegate. Their overseer, Pete Lowell, was a good, dependable man. Their father had trained him.

"All right," Ross agreed, returning his sister's smile with some wryness. "I'll take you. That would be Matt, your assistant and yourself, I take it?"

Well you take it wrong, Samantha thought smartly, catching *her* brother's eye.

"I was hoping, Ross, Samantha could come," David said sounding thoroughly persuasive.

It was quite clear that didn't work on Sunderland. The animated expression on his lean handsome face changed abruptly. Samantha *willed* him to give in but he shook his head. "That would well and truly be bending the rules, Dave. It will be far from easy getting to the places you'd want to get your shots. I've seen your work. I know danger entices you. It's the same excitement as a safari only we don't get to kill magnificent wild animals as they did in the bad old days."

"What if we established camps?" David suggested, seeing Sunderland's point of view.

"And leave your sister on her own?" Sunderland's black brows shot up.

I'm not even Samantha, Sam thought. I'm "your sister."

David's topaz eyes moved to the silent Isabelle. "What if Isabelle came along? For all her lilylike appearance I expect she's a woman who could handle herself in the bush."

Yes, oh yes!

Samantha, mindful of what Isabelle had said to her, managed to hold her tongue but instead of shrinking away from the idea, Isabelle glanced down, her long lashes dark and heavy on her cheeks. She knew Ross had made it clear he didn't want Samantha on the trip which in all fairness she had to admit was in the wildest least explored area of the continent. On the other hand she could see Samantha had a positive yen for adventure.

She glanced up and caught David Langdon's golden eyes on her. Her pulses gave a mad little jitter as though he had actually touched her lightly. "Do I have to answer now?"

Her brother stirred restlessly. "Belle, would you really want to go along? You know as well as I do, it won't be any party. I think Samantha's initial enthusiasm for such a trip would be short lived. I can't keep my eye on her one hundred per cent of the time which means I can't guarantee her safety."

"Maybe David has the answer," Cy intervened mildly, thinking it was a bit of an awkward situation. "Make camp in a safe area. If there was any danger involved when David was taking his shots, the girls could stay together. That's if Isabelle consents to go."

"Come to think of it I'd like to go myself," Jessica gave her husband an arch look.

"No chance of your going without me," Cy grabbed her hand playfully.

"Doesn't that prove what I'm saying?" Ross asked. "Taking the women would slow us down too much."

"Come on, Ross!" Isabelle's eyes suddenly flashed giving a glimpse of the high spirited girl she had been. "You're telling me *I* couldn't keep up?"

Ross sighed. "You don't have the same level of fitness you

used to have, Belle. In fact you look like a stiff breeze could blow you away."

Isabelle stared at him, outraged. "I do *not!*"

David Langdon broke in, holding up a large hand. "You honestly believe this trip could become too rough for the women, Ross?"

Ross nodded, giving Samantha a long speaking look. "I've already worked out the areas I'd want to take you. For that matter I'd bring along my own man. Cy knows him well and can vouch for him. His name is Joe Goolatta. He's a full blooded aboriginal elder, a fine man and a great bushman and tracker. He won't be a follower. He'll lead with me. This is *his* country. The crocodile is *his* totem. Believe it or not the crocs seem to recognise this. They sure don't with anyone else."

"Incredible!" David commented, having seen strange things himself in various primitive parts of the world. "The reason I wanted Sam to come along—apart from the fact I believed she would thoroughly enjoy it—is that Sam usually writes the text. She's very good at it."

"I agree." Ross nodded, moving an impatient shoulder. "Going on tonight's exhibition but couldn't she just as easily write the text from the finished product?"

"I'd be missing the *immediacy*." Samantha gave him an incensed glance. "I wouldn't be frightened if you left me alone back at camp. I'm not a wimp. Of course it would be wonderful if Isabelle could keep me company," she murmured, brushing back a silken slide of hair.

Only a fool let himself be manipulated by a woman. "Do you know how to shoot?" Sunderland asked her brusquely, watching that copper hair slide forward seductively again.

The challenge in her seemed to evaporate. "You mean a gun?"

"Certainly a gun," he clipped off. "A rifle. A .22?"

"No, sir!" Samantha glanced across at her brother for support. "I've never even seen a gun up close let alone handled one. I hate guns. They're horrible."

"And necessary if you're trying to protect yourself in the bush." Sunderland studied her as though she really belonged in kindergarten. "What do you do if a wild boar goes on the attack or a croc abruptly surfaces out of a pool and comes at you at speed. Aim a stone at it? What do you do when some member of the party inadvertently treads on a taipan? Throw a stick at it?"

Colour stained Samantha's cheek bones. "Would *you* mind not taking a chunk out me? I get your point, Mr. Sunderland." She really *loathed* this man.

"Well that's a first."

Watching the electric exchange Isabelle entered the fray. "But *I'm* good with a rifle," she said. It wasn't just women sticking together. What else? "Dad taught us both well."

Her brother looked like he thought the conversation had gone far enough. "Don't let your sense of derring-do get the better of you, Belle. Really think about it."

It was David who brought it to an end. "Perhaps that's the answer. Why don't we let you and Isabelle talk it over, Ross? I understand your concerns. I daresay in your position I wouldn't be prepared to take the risks either, but if Isabelle steps in, it sounds like we could reduce the risks considerably. Sleep on it. Maybe we can meet tomorrow in the morning seeing we're staying at the same hotel. Or did you want to get away early?"

"I ought to." Ross gave a slight frown. "But the morning will be fine. Belle can have a sleep in. I've agreed to be your guide, Dave, and that will stand. I know Samantha is angry at me but she doesn't actually know what she could be in for."

"Sleep on it, friend," David advised.

There were much fewer guests now. People had begun to leave. Cy stood up, holding his wife's chair. "On that note, we'll say good night. I have a feeling it will all turn out well. Jessica and I had best be off. We're staying with Robyn and her husband. They're sending a limo to pick us up, so I'd say it will be waiting out the front."

"We had a wonderful time," Jessica said, rising gracefully. "I loved your showing, David."

David also on his feet now, bowed slightly. "Great seeing you again, Jessica. And thanks for all your help." With one hand he held Isabelle's chair, catching her elusive, very beautiful perfume as she rose to her feet.

"Marvellous food!" Cy put in, sending David a friendly grin. "You can't do better than Ross for a guide," he added, throwing a glance at his friend who was starting to move back. "Isabelle's not bad either."

For a female Samantha started to say, then thought better of it. No point in angering Ross Sunderland until he'd made his decision. She took a precipitous step away from the table without looking, then realised with a pounding of the heart she'd all but bumped into him.

On a reflex his arm swiftly snaked around her waist holding her steady.

"Sorry!" she breathed, shocked by the sensation. "You're a very fast mover."

"I guess I am." His eyes locked into hers. He could feel the warmth of her body through the thin fabric of her dress. He soaked it up hungrily, tempted to spin her into his arms. He might have been fool enough to do it had they been on their own. And damn the consequences. He knew it by its name. *Temptation*. At least the others were momentarily distracted saying their goodbyes.

Samantha glanced back over her shoulder, her blood coursing at his closeness. Against his bronze skin his blue-green eyes were startling. His sculpted mouth wasn't all that far away. She only had to lean back further. She wondered what it would be like to have those clean cut lips pressed against hers. Deep and passionate. For he was a passionate man. She was sure of it.

"You can let me go now," she said tautly. His hand was singe-ing her flesh.

"Sure," he drawled, slowly withdrawing. "The last thing I want to do is unsettle you."

Male arrogance was in his very stance. "What makes you think you have?" she asked sharply.

He smiled, but didn't answer, malicious laughter in his spar-kling eyes.

CHAPTER THREE

USED TO A predawn start Ross woke at the usual time even though he'd had what for him could only be described as a bad night. Mostly he was so dog tired after a hard day's work on the station he fell asleep the instant his head hit the pillow but here in this quiet air-conditioned hotel room his mind kept revolving around the problem of Samantha Langdon. And she was a problem. A *big* one.

Go away. Damn you!

Hell, it was almost a prayer.

Too late for that, Ross, old son. The inner voice answered. *She's got to you.*

That didn't mean he had to surrender.

He and Belle had talked well into the night, Belle arguing strongly for Samantha's inclusion on the trip. He told himself the thing that had clinched it was Belle's surprise desire to go. It was the first real interest she had shown in anything since she had come home after the loss of her husband. That in itself was encouraging but what, he wondered, had prompted the big upsurge of interest? It had to be something to do with the near instant connection she had made with David Langdon. Whatever it was it had energised her. He had seen with his own eyes the harmony that had flowed from one to the other. Langdon was a very motivated, very self-disciplined, powerful sort of man. He was also, as might be expected of an artist, a man of sensitivity, finely attuned to women. Belle liked him. Hell, he liked the man himself.

But Samantha?

He couldn't stop his body stirring. He could even *sense* her presence.

Why are you rejecting her, Ross?

He had tried to give Belle an answer but he knew she saw through him. The answer cut into the most primitive part of him. Part of his and Belle's unhappy past. Yet for all that he had finally agreed to take both Belle and Samantha Langdon along. The beginnings of a friendship was flowering between the two women. He couldn't say the same for himself and this copper haired woman. All bright things in nature could be dangerous. Dammit all he was *hurting*. He knew now he'd been hurting since he'd met her. That's what was making him so stubborn. Obdurate if you like. Up until now he'd negotiated easily enough through emotional entanglements—he'd had his share of girlfriends—but he simply couldn't do it with this woman. He'd hate to fall in love. *Really* fall in love. To want so much. To be left...*wanting*. Belle knew what a lot didn't. Underneath he was a pretty passionate guy. Passionate guys had to take care....

He braced his hands beneath his dark head going back over Cy's wedding. He'd had a little bit too much to drink. It was, after all, a very grand and happy occasion. Cy was over the moon, madly in love with his beautiful new bride, Jessica. He felt great for him. Cy was his pal. As best man he'd given a good speech and it had gone well. A mix of remembrances, mostly good, one or two touching, but on the whole leavened with humour. People had laughed even until tears came to their eyes.

The other three bridesmaids had accepted him completely as scion of a well respected family, Cy's best friend and someone nice to know. Very pretty girls, all three, who'd enjoyed flirting with him. With his senses exquisitely sharpened he had flirted back when all he'd really wanted was his arms around *her*. The urge was so powerful and persistent that in the end he had surrendered to it. Besides, it was his *duty* to dance with the chief bridesmaid. It would have been a serious breach of etiquette not to.

She had looked like a man's dream come true. The smooth naked shoulders, the half naked back. The heart shaped dip of her strapless neckline revealed the creamy swell of her breasts and the shadowed cleavage. The material of her gown was something called *duchesse* satin. He understood that meant the fabric was thick, lustrous, supple. The colour, champagne with a blush of apricot, was perfect with her colouring. She didn't wear her hair free as she had done the first time he had seen her running down Mokhani's staircase. It was pulled back from her face, like the other bridesmaids and arranged in some full upturning roll at the back of her head, one beautiful silk flower to match her gown tucked behind her ear.

When he went to her, her face brightened. "Oh, Ross!"

"My dance, I believe." He put his arms around her, his need too great to be suppressed. She was heartbreakingly beautiful in her wedding finery, wearing Cy's gift to the bridesmaids, a drop pearl pendant on a fine gold chain around her long slender neck. Hers was an unusual gold with a single sparkling cognac diamond above it. Her earrings matched the colour, the pearls dropping from a series of tiny winking diamonds. He wondered if Cy had bought them as well or they were her own? What man wouldn't love to give her jewellery he thought. Cover her naked body with it.

"I really thought you didn't want to dance with me." Her expression was sweetly anxious as she looked up at him.

"Why wouldn't I want to dance with the most beautiful bridesmaid?" he had countered in that voice that was all wrong.

She'd smiled in a poignant way. "For one reason you've been having the most wonderful time with the others."

"That isn't the reason," he said.

Sparklelike tears rose to her eyes, heightening his desire for her that was growing beyond measure. Many eyes were following them. He was fully aware of that. She turned her head to acknowledge the smiles and nods from either side. "I'll remember this day forever," she said. "Jessica as radiant and beautiful as a bride should be. Cy so splendid and so much in love with her." She'd looked up at him. "I loved your speech too, Ross. It made us all laugh and cry."

"Is that why you've got tears in your eyes now?" He knew his grip had tightened on her. He could feel her trembling as though unprepared for what might ensue.

She blinked her damp lashes. "I didn't know I had."

"Well it's a time for high emotion after all." He was disgusted with the vaguely taunting way it had come out but unable to rein himself in. He wanted to cup her breasts; lean in to kiss her lovely mouth.

"Ross, what *is* it?" she had asked as though she could no longer cope with what was happening between them.

He hadn't answered. What could he say? *I want to take you to bed. Now!* Instead he began to dance her fast down the full length of the room, while the other guests laughed and clapped, standing back to give them a free path, thinking it all such glittering, good fun.

He remembered her lovely flush afterwards, her hand to her heart, and her carefully hidden agitation. She understood the strange ambivalence in him.

Blood was rushing through his entire body. He was conscious of his hard hurting erection. He couldn't continue to lie there thinking about her. He groaned and pushed up. He was tired of his own thoughts. Tired of being haunted by a woman with doe's eyes. Now he'd have to spend *weeks* with her.

Bronze brolgas struck a pose in an idyllic setting. In the luxuriant gardens that surrounded the hotel's swimming pool tropical plants abounded, gardenia, oleander, hibiscus, ginger, bougainvillea, beautiful orchids and bromeliads with their brilliantly coloured rosettes. Magnificent palms soared overhead shading an area that was perfect for swimming and light sunbathing. No one wanted to be exposed to the full force of the tropical sun even at this early hour. The turquoise pool looked wonderfully inviting, plenty big enough for a serious swimmer. Better yet, there was no one around. She would have it all to herself. She had plenty of time to do her usual laps before returning to her room to shower, shampoo her hair and get dressed.

Samantha dropped her hold-all on a teak recliner lavishly upholstered in broad bands of turquoise lime and aqua, then pulled her floaty caftan over her head. It matched her bikini, both in a vibrant botanical print. An expensive outfit considering the cover-up was see-through and didn't reach her knees and the bikini was so flimsy if it hadn't been guaranteed shrink proof she wouldn't have dared to expose it to water. Still if you had it you might as well flaunt it as her girlfriend, Em, always said at some point in their work-out at the gym. Samantha didn't take her slender figure for granted. She worked at keeping her body in excellent shape. The right food—not too much of it—except the occasional breakout, two nights a week at the gym, a run around the marina near her harbourside apartment every other day, surfing at the weekend at one of the beautiful beaches, Bondi, Tamarama, Bronte close by.

Oh that water looked good! She approached the deep end of the pool and dived in, not even surfacing until she had swum one hundred metres. There was a time at high school when the coach had tried to talk her into having a shot at the Australian Institute of Sport. She was good—she had even won a couple of Junior State titles—but she knew she didn't have the tremendous dedication that was needed to make it as an elite swimmer. Besides she had other goals. Mostly creative. It had come as a surprise to many of her friends when she had turned to writing and illustrating children's stories. They had thought she would try to make it into television but that wasn't her goal either. One day when she had enough maturity she would try her hand at adult fiction. One review of her last children's book suggested with her ability and "rich poetic voice" she would soon turn to something beyond her present scope.

Hopefully. That was all in the future.

She put a hand to her hair—she had woven it into a plait—ready to kick off again when she froze. Ross Sunderland was walking down the side of the pool dressed in shorts and an open casual shirt, with a towel over his shoulder. Just when she thought she would have the pool to herself! It was only a matter of time before he saw her. He was heading her way, his every movement filled with tantalising male grace. It was a daunting aura he exuded in her presence but she knew it was only a mask. She'd seen how sweet and gentle he was with his sister. David had really liked him—thought him remarkable—and her brother was a good judge of men.

Samantha kicked off again, determined not to allow him to upset her. She thought nothing of doing fifty laps, but not today. Her arms sliced through the water, while her legs scissored beneath the turquoise waters not making a splash.

Finally she had to stop at the shallow end to do something about her hair. It had come out of its plait, floating around her like a mermaid.

"How long are you going to keep it up?" he asked her.

She glanced up but the sun was in her eyes. Nevertheless she could see his wide shouldered outline. He had gone down on his haunches beside the edge of the pool.

"This is only a little paddle, okay?" She pressed her hair back with her two hands.

"You'd have fooled me," he mocked. "I thought you were going for Olympic gold."

"Don't worry, I could have made it." She indulged in a bit of wishful thinking.

"Amazing!"

"Well I won a couple of Junior State titles." She turned her head out of the direct line of the sun. Now their glances clashed. Brown velvet and blue-green ice.

"I bet in record time." Those shimmering eyes were moving over her face and the line of her shoulders just above the water.

"As a matter of fact, yes." She grasped the coping and pulled herself out, anxious to get her towel. As always his gaze made her giddy.

"Oh, Miss Langdon." He came to his impressive height, effectively blocking her way. "I'm sorry. Surely I haven't frightened you away?"

"No, I've got better things to do, that's all," she responded tartly. She had never been so conscious of her own body though he wasn't looking at her in any offensive way, rather with cool male appreciation. A connoisseur of women, which doubtless he was.

"Wouldn't it be an idea to race me?" he surprised her by suggesting.

"Good swimmer that I am—I'm sure you thought the best I could do was splutter and drown—I just *know* I wouldn't stand a chance," she replied.

"Why not give it a go just for the hell of it? You're very good. Very fast. I'm not nearly so efficient on the turns. Yours are quite professional."

"They ought to be. I spent enough time practising them." She moved her slim, shapely legs towards the recliner vowing there and then not to get into any competition.

"So is it a race or are you going to chicken out?" he called, feeling that edgy desire slice through him. It never went away. She had the most beautiful skin all over. The cream in the sun deepening to honey. Or as all over as he could see which happened to be a lot. "Who knows if you impress me I might just want to change my mind about the trip."

In the act of towelling herself down Samantha broke off. "I think you're hooked already." She might never be able to bring this man to his knees which she'd absolutely *love* but she knew enough to gauge he was powerfully attracted. It was something he also found unacceptable.

"What is that supposed to mean?" He came towards her so purposefully for a mad moment she thought he was going to pull her to him.

"Sad you're so aggressive." She had to make a real effort to steady her voice.

"I'm not usually." A faint smile touched the chiselled lips. "You've managed to tap into that vein."

"Why I wonder? Do I remind you of someone? A romance gone wrong?"

He measured her with those cool sparkling eyes. "Don't feel guilty on that account. I don't go in for failed relationships."

"But you are seeing someone aren't you?" she asked with growing provocation. "I couldn't help noticing the little brunette in the red dress last night. Not that she noticed *me*."

"Oh, she noticed you all right!" There was amusement in his expression. "But Julie is just a friend."

"Hoping for a whole lot more." Who could blame her for all she'd have to put up with?

"As is your Matt," he slotted in neatly.

That rattled her. "I though we'd settled that. Matt and I are not romantically involved."

"That's good, because I'd have grave misgivings about that."

"You're joking." She tossed back her hair. It was already drying in the heat.

"I'm not." He shrugged. "I don't believe in mixing business with pleasure." He half turned. "So are we going to race or not?"

Would it go better for her if she did? "On one condition."

He started to peel off his shirt, then the shorts, quite unself-consciously, incredibly fit, incredibly lean. "I'm sorry, I'm not going to give you a start."

Damn if he didn't have the most marvellous body. She couldn't miss the perfectly honed musculature, the straight, strong legs. He was every inch a *man*. She had to swallow and glance away. "I don't think I need one. What I was going say was, if I win, you'll take me along on the trip?"

"And if you *lose*?" He looked at her with such intensity her heart leapt in her breast.

"I'll still be a good sport. And I'll still want to come."

His mouth compressed. "Oh, well, while we're at it, why don't you make a list of what you want me to do?"

"Well, you could be a little more, um, *friendly*?" she suggested sweetly.

"I might find that too exhausting. Are you ready?"

She slicked her hair back from her face. "I will be when you take your eyes off my legs."

Again he flashed that elusive white smile. "You can't wear a bikini like that and expect a man not to get excited. One hundred metres, two hundred, your call?"

Two hundred involved more turns. Valuable time could be lost at the turns even with top swimmers. "Two hundred," she said loftily, securing her plait with a band she fetched from her bag.

"Do you mind if we shake hands?"

"Of course not." Surprised she offered her hand, then saw his eyes. Eyes that sparkled and glittered with sardonic amusement.

She tried to withdraw her hand, only he caught her fingers with his own. A charge like dynamite rocked through her. She drew in her breath and jerked away. "Right, this has gone far enough."

"We were only holding hands."

"Yes, well…"

"Freestyle, I take it?" He helped her out.

"I can do the lot," she clipped off. "Freestyle, backstroke, butterfly, breaststroke. Take your pick."

"Why don't we stick to freestyle. That's *my* best stroke. On the count of three."

They hit the water together, sending up jets of spray. Samantha stayed underwater as long as she could before breaking into her stroke. Out of the side of her eye she could see him churning away, but she let him, keeping to her plan for a strong finish. It was *true*. She was better than him at the turns. At the one-fifty she was matching him stroke for stroke. They went down the pool together, slick as dolphins. She started to pick up speed, putting all her competitive spirit into it. Still she was racing an incredibly fit *man,* a good swimmer with a far superior reach. For an instant she thought he was dropping back, maybe letting her win. That made her angry. Then less than fifteen metres to go he shot past her like a torpedo, pulling his lean powerful body out of the water just as she touched the wall.

End of story.

He stretched out a hand. "Congratulations, Miss Langdon. I had to work hard to shake you. You're pretty good."

Her blood was pounding. Her heart was racing. She *had* to accept his hand. "That would have been my personal best," she admitted coming up out of the water in one graceful flowing movement.

"Truth is I used to swim for the team at University."

Her brown eyes flashed. "Dammit, don't you feel guilty not saying something about that at the beginning?"

"No." He smiled, the pool water still streaming over his darkly tanned, gleaming skin.

"You won because you're a *man.* A big man. I could have beaten a little guy," she pointed out.

"You could have beaten a guy *not* so little," he said wryly, wanting to pull her to him. Demand she forfeit a kiss.

"So are you going to let me come?" She looked appealingly into his eyes.

"You *lost,* remember?"

"Where's your sense of adventure?" Appeal turned to disgust. "I promise I'll keep a safe distance."

"Like now?" His eyes pinned her, held her in place.

"What do you mean?" She felt an instant's panic like some creature of the wilds caught in a high beam.

"Let's face it." His eyes moved lightly over her. "You've practically got no clothes on."

She shook her hair out of its plait. "Isn't that normal when one goes swimming?"

"Hey I'm not complaining." A smile touched his lips. "You're absolutely beautiful as I'm certain you've been told at least a thousand times. I'm only saying the kind of trip we're planning is no place to show off your sexual allure."

She recovered fast. "I'll be happy to wear dungarees," she said tartly.

"Not so great in the hot humid weather."

Samantha let out a long breath, preparing to move off. "I need to shower and wash the chlorine out of my hair before breakfast."

How he'd love to help her out!

And to think women had never been his problem! He watched her stalk off on those long golden legs, her colourful caftan doing nothing to hide the curves of her body. He began to ask himself yet again if he were mad.

Probably a bit.

While Ross and Samantha were trying to outdo each other in the pool David Langdon was renewing his acquaintance with the city of Darwin which he'd only visited in transit for some years. Long gone was the old Darwin of pioneering cattle kings, pearl trawlers, buffalo shooters, crocodile hunters and all kinds of adventurers, but the exotic *feel* to the place remained. Indeed it was difficult to compare the Territory's capital with any other city of Australia. It had the feel and smell of Asia. Asia was close enough, across the Timor and Arafura Seas. Darwin's full-on tropical climate and the city's rich racial mix—the Chinese remained the largest non-European population as well as the dominance of exotic Asian food made it unique. Loping teen-agers passed him, drinking milk from coconuts. A police car cruised by. The constable in the passenger seat waved casually. He waved back. He'd decided on making for the forty hectare Botanical Gardens. He knew it housed a range of tropical plants unequalled anywhere on earth. It certainly looked splendid, a luxuriant belt of green giving on to the turquoise waters of the huge harbour.

All around him were the signs of prosperity. The old isolated outpost, the centre for the gold rush of the 1870s, had grown enormously into a thriving capital. Tourism was now second only to the giant mining industry. The city had a very clean modern appearance due to the fact it had been rebuilt after Darwin had been destroyed in the 1974 Cyclone Tracy disas-ter. A new beginning had to be made virtually from scratch. Few buildings had survived consequently the present buildings had been built in contemporary style and designed to resist fu-ture cyclones. He sincerely hoped they would because another major cyclone would surely come again.

He realised he was impatient for their safari to begin. Champ-ing at the bit really. He had photographed ancient ruins in the jungles of South East Asia, the beautiful stone temples of An-gkor Wat and elsewhere, Thai kings palaces, the wonderful temple ruins of Borobudur in Indonesia, built by the Buddhist rulers the Sailendras in the 700s. He had photographed the great hardwood forests of Borneo and Java, teak and ebony, but he had never ventured into his own country's greatest wilderness area, Kakadu, the jewel in the Top-End crown and the giant among Australia's great national parks. The park was jointly controlled by the traditional Aboriginal owners and Parks, Aus-tralia. He also knew controversy had long raged between the conservationists and those wishing to exploit the incredibly rich reserves of uranium and other valuable minerals in the area. Ranger Uranium Mine and Jabiru, one of four major mining settlements in the Territory lay within the boundaries of World Heritage listed Kakadu. He'd like to gain access to both Jabiru and Ranger. He was relying on Sunderland to get permission from the mines' management. He knew they had to go through the traditional owners to visit certain parts of Kakadu and its sacred sites. No doubt about it. He felt *inspired*. To some extent he knew the expanding euphoria had to do with meeting a certain woman. He had allowed himself to yield to it. Yet she was a mystery woman who had become the subject of cruel gossip. A sexually exciting woman who could play on a man's deepest emotions. Sympathy for her came all too easily for him but he had to concede he had no real knowledge of her to rely on.

Jump in and you might find the water's too deep.

He was about to cross the broad esplanade that ran parallel to Bicentennial Park when he saw another group of teenagers, with spiked black hair—dressed in T-shirts and colourful board shorts—cutting off the progress of a young woman he recognised even from a distance as Isabelle. She would be impossible to miss in a crowd.

Immediately his protective instinct went into overdrive. This wasn't just any woman although he would have made it his business to see what was going on. This was a woman he had related to on the deepest level. A kind of primal thing.

And don't you forget it!

Were they teasing her, annoying her, threatening her. What? She was a beautiful young woman on her own. There weren't all that many people about at that hour and it was the weekend. Stern faced he made short work of closing the distance between them while the youngsters broke off what they were saying to stare back at him in perturbation judging from their expressions.

What they saw was a *big* man, with powerful shoulders, his movements expansive and totally balanced. His tawny hair glowed in the sun. Clearly this was a man not to be trifled with. For that matter he looked like a lion full of pride coming to the defence of its mate.

"Anything the matter, Isabelle?" He stopped beside her, towering over the group as he checked her expression.

She looked up at him. Exposed to his mellow, charming side she now saw the combative daunting male. Well it was a long time since a man had had such concern for her, outside her own brother. "Nothing, David," she answered quickly, seeing how it might have looked to him. "These young people are my friends. I've known them since they were children. Say hello to Mr. Langdon, kids. He's a famous photographer. This is Manny and Jimmy and Charlie Chun Wing." As she spoke she laid a gentle hand on each boy's shoulder.

"Hello there. It makes us very happy to meet you." The eldest, Manny, the spokesman gave a big toothy smile, while the others executed modified bows that looked quite natural.

"I'm so sorry if I startled you," he apologised, his expression lightening. "I rather jumped to the wrong conclusion. I should have realised, Isabelle, you would know a great many people in Darwin."

"You thought we were annoying her?" Manny asked as if that were the last thing in the world they would do.

"How wrong I was, Manny. I can see none of you would do such a thing."

"Never!" Manny shook his jet black head gelled into upstanding spikes. "Nobody could be as good to us as the Sunderlands. Miss Isabelle's father set up Mum and Dad in our shop. My grandma and my Aunt Sooky used to work at the house. That's where Nan met my Grandpa. On North Star."

"So you see, David, we go a long way back," Isabelle glanced up at him with a little smile. "Please tell your parents I'll call on them soon, Manny."

"I know they would *love* to see you," Manny who was maybe sixteen responded with great dignity.

"Nice kids," David murmured, after the youngsters had gone on their way with much waving.

"Yes, they are. Manny's very clever. He plans to be a doctor."

"Marvellous, a success story," he said gently.

"I hope he makes it." She started to walk with him, recovering her head and shading her face with the wide brimmed straw hat she had dangled in her hand. They moved together through the entrance gates of the park, the dark green background of magnificent tropical trees animated by shafts of golden sunlight. Beautiful and welcoming as the Gardens were they also performed the practical task of providing a huge area of shade and protecting the city from much of the buffeting winds and torrential rains during the Wet.

Isabelle breathed in the air that wafted from the gorgeously perfumed shrubs in bloom. It was as powerful as any aphrodisiac. "There was a time when Manny's family was desperately poor. Cyclone Tracy wiped out their farm. Their uncle Frankie was killed, poor man. They were such hard workers Dad thought they deserved a helping hand, so he bought them a shop. Fruit and vegetables. They're experts at growing and selling."

"And the conditions would be much like Southern China," he commented. "Your father must have been a generous and kindly man."

Tears stung her eyes. "His good deeds were legendary. Ross is carrying on the tradition."

"You and your brother are very close." Though he dipped his head, he couldn't see her clearly. Enchanting as that daisy decked hat was, the wide brim did a good job of shielded her beautiful face from his view.

She let him have a glimpse of her aquamarine eyes. She was slightly flushed and not he thought from the mounting heat of the day. "You're bound to find out sooner or later, if you don't know already, David." Her tone implied he did. "Our mother left us when we were children. Neither of us thought it possible our parents would ever split up. They seemed so happy. We were *all* happy. A united family. Dad worshipped her."

"What happened?" he asked quietly.

She bit her lip and shrugged. "I suppose it was all meant to be. But after that I was never quite sure how my own life was going to turn out. Badly as it happens. My mother was visiting another branch of the family in England and fell in love with a distant cousin. It must have been something quite overwhelming. Something that robbed her of all control. My mother was not the frivolous type. Far from it. I remember her once saying nothing was better than a stable marriage. My God!"

"There's a lot of pain in passion, Isabelle."

She looked away at a great circular flower bed flaming with colour. "You don't have to tell *me!*"

So she had been madly in love with her husband.

"But, we have choices in life, David. There must be a moment when we can pull back. My mother didn't. She gave in to the feelings she had for this man. He ruined any hope she would come back to Dad although she wanted custody of us. Or at the very least me, the girl. Ross was the heir. Males are always on the inside track, especially when it comes to running the family business."

"You felt some resentment about that?"

She shook her head. "No, not at all. Just a simple statement of fact. The fact is I couldn't run North Star. You have no idea what's involved. One really does need a *man,* a strong man to handle most of the problems. Ross was reared to succeed Dad. No one could have stepped into the role better. Actually Ross feels even more strongly than I do about our mother's defection. No way would he have gone to her. How wildly unfair that would have been to our father. We were tied to him through love and blood and pride in our pioneering family and the land. A judge from the family court talked to us privately. We told him we would never leave our father. We loved him and wanted to stay with him. We didn't in fact want to see our mother."

Her voice was expressionless, hiding he felt sure a torrent of emotions she had locked away.

"I understand your feelings at that time, Isabelle, but do you *never* miss your mother?" After all he and Sam knew a whole lot about hurt.

She lifted her head, her expression brooding. "If I were honest, I'd tell you I've missed her every day of my life, but that doesn't change the fact I regard her as a traitor. I believe treason is punishable by death."

"You wanted her dead?"

She turned her slender back to him but he could see her shoulders trembling.

"I'm sorry, Isabelle." He had to ball his hands into fists lest he place them on her shoulders...those smooth fine boned shoulders.

"Of course not." She turned back, but her eyes were very bright. "Just a figure of speech. I'm really rather a damaged person, David."

He considered her gravely. "Aren't you being a bit hard on yourself?"

"No harder than the gossip." She laughed, but the flowering colour left her cheeks.

It wasn't possible not to reply. "You mean that things weren't well between you and your husband?"

She nodded. "You got it in one. The best way, I suppose, is to ignore it. I suspected you might have my history at your fingertips."

"Why would you think that?" he asked and waited.

"People talk wherever they are. Sydney, Darwin. Nothing too obvious last night, not with Ross around, but enough to cloud people's once good opinion of me."

"So what are you going to do about it? Put them straight?" He stared into her beautiful, black fringed, eyes.

"David, I don't much care. I am what I am. I've never tried to present myself as something different. Anyway, I was talking about my mother. You're too good a listener. For years she wanted me to come to England for the holidays—Dad wouldn't have stopped me—he loved me too much, but I refused to go. For Ross and for me—more so for our father—it was a grief so deep nothing, not even time, could heal the scars."

"So you learned to live without her?"

They walked on, keeping to the golden-green shade. "It wasn't easy but I had a wonderful father and a wonderful brother."

"And a wonderful husband?" He realised he shouldn't have asked her but he couldn't stop himself.

That was his *public* image anyway. "I can't talk about him, David." At least that was the truth.

"Forgive me. That's understandable. It's been such a short time. I've no wish to upset you."

She could admit one thing however. "I rushed into marriage," she said. "Maybe it was the loneliness we Outback women endure. So much of Dad's and Ross's time was taken up with station affairs. I did my bit. I ran the domestic side and I handled a lot of office work, but I was on my own for much of the time."

"You could have left?"

Her beautiful eyes slanted up at him. "Of course I could but I wasn't fully *free*. My love for my family made up for a lot. I would have gotten around to it, if it hadn't been for Dad. He was bereft without the woman he'd made his life. I like to think I gave him emotional support even when he told me straight out I wasn't to sacrifice my life for him."

So she was far from selfish. She had a heart. "How did you meet your husband?"

"Why d'you ask?"

He captured her in profile. "I confess I want to know." In fact it seemed to matter greatly.

She took a long moment before she answered. "I was visiting a friend in Sydney. Her family was always on the social circuit. I'd only arrived that very day. Tanya was going to some big party hosted by Blair's mother at their palatial harbourside home. Blair's stockbroker father died of a massive heart attack a few years before. Tanya asked if I could come and Evelyn Hartmann said yes. It was there I met Blair. A fairy tale beginning without the fairy tale ending. Of course I failed to notice that Evelyn didn't like me from the start, but Blair fell in love with me. I was dumbfounded how quickly."

"So for you it wasn't love at first sight?" he asked after a bit, somewhat shamed by the feeling he was glad that wasn't so.

"I'm afraid I missed that experience, David." It wasn't a completely honest answer given her extraordinary reaction to *him*. For that she felt guilty as though she had broken a serious rule, almost a taboo. So recently widowed in the worst of circumstances, she had no *right* to be drawn to another man.

"Do you have someone you…care about?" He could be living with someone for all she knew.

"No." He answered simply. "I have quite a lot of women friends. I like women. I enjoy their company but to be honest I've spent much of my time travelling the world, particularly South East Asia. I studied architecture as you probably read last night. I have an architectural degree but I only practised for a couple of years before I moved on. I wanted to see the world and I did. In the course of seeing the world I found my first love. Photography. I've been lucky. I'm able to do something I love and get very well paid for it."

"You've been to the war zones as well."

He nodded, terrible memories suddenly crowding in on him. "The horror you've heard about and see on the television isn't exaggerated. The reality is far worse. I had to pull out of it for a while. The sheer scale of the human suffering became unbearable and I came to realise I was highly likely to get killed which wasn't going to help anyone. This breathing space is in the nature of therapy. It's impossible not to witness humanitarian disasters without coming away unscathed."

"I would think so," she said quietly. "The television coverage is disturbing enough."

He sighed deeply. "We're truly blessed living in Australia. From all I've seen it's something to celebrate." He paused and looked around him, deciding to change the subject. "It's remarkable to see how Darwin, not so long ago a frontier town, is booming."

"Yes, it's made a huge leap," she said, a proud Territorian. "Strategically it's become very important. Our Defence Forces are stationed here. The victims of the Bali bombing too were flown straight to Darwin Hospital. I'm sure the close proximity and the skill and dedication of Darwin's doctors and nurses saved lives."

"Absolutely," he agreed. "That rocked us, Bali, so close to home. The shock waves haven't gone away any more than 9/11. It's a deeply troubled world."

"On top of all that the tsunami."

"Yes indeed." His strongly hewn features tightened. "My heart bleeds for the people and the places I came to know and love. I spent a lot of time in Thailand and Indonesia. I've holidayed in Phuket many many times, journeyed through Indonesia, visited the Maldives like so many other Australians. I could have even been there. The wrong place at the wrong time." He released a sigh, glanced at his wristwatch. "I suppose we should go back."

"Good heavens, is that the time?" She glanced at her own watch in amazement. Time had flown. "I've enjoyed our walk. And our talk."

"So have I," he said lightly. No way could he allow himself to show his private feelings. "Has Ross made up his mind do you know?"

"To take Samantha?"

"She'll be bitterly disappointed if she can't go along," David said. "Sam can handle herself, but of course I don't want to go against Ross's wishes. I appreciate we're on the verge of the Wet. It would be a matter of getting in and getting out."

"And quickly, taking our signals from the land and the sky. Joe Goolatta will be invaluable there. He's positively uncanny, but this is his land. Filming in far North Queensland you must know what it's like on the verge of the Wet."

"Of course. Some years back I took a helicopter flight from the bauxite town of Weipa in the Gulf to a mineral survey camp near Cape York. It was absolutely extraordinary. One of the great trips of my life. To see that prodigal wilderness from the air was fascinating. Great sluggish rivers twisting back on themselves like the Great Rainbow Snake of aboriginal legend. Hundreds and thousands of birds in the swamps many miles long. The Top End of the continent is still a no-man's land to most of us. Remote, barely accessible, certainly not in the Wet."

She nodded. "It's a pity, tourists, unlike the locals, never see this part of the world at its most spectacular when the wilderness bursts into fruit and flower. The billabongs and lagoons swell to overflowing with the rushing flood waters. Trickling waterfalls turn into mighty torrents. The wetlands abound with birds and I have to say crocodiles. The plains turn a lush green. It's Nature at its most powerful. But the tourists are back home by December before the deluge begins. It's all about picking exactly the right time. Which is what you're try-ing to do. We've already had a few spectacular lightning storms which will increase. But obviously around now is when you're going to get your most dramatic results. We've come to believe as the aboriginals do the Wet and the Dry is an oversimplifi-cation. The aborigines recognise at least six seasons, maybe seven signified by the flowering and fruiting patterns of food plants and the migratory and breeding patterns of birds and other animals. They are so attuned to the land they understand it as few white people do." She lifted her head to ask, "You use a digital camera?"

"Just about everything is digital these days, but a lot of the time I prefer to use film. A large format panorama. I've agreed to let Matt, my assistant, take some shots for part of the book so he'll be coming along all going to plan. I'd like to help him out. He's a good photographer but he needs to develop his 'eye.' Sam will do the text. Now she really does have an eye. Her children's books—they require a flight of imagination—are marvellously entertaining and her illustrations quite magical. She's very talented is my little sister. One day I believe she'll make a name for herself."

"She's already started." Isabelle smiled. "All right, David, I'll put you out of your misery. Ross and I counted up all the risks and at the end of it I managed to convince him it might be a very good idea to take two women along. In fact I'll make it my business to see Samantha has the loveliest time. It will do me good too to get out of the house. I've done so much brooding I sometimes feel I'm going mad. This is Gunumeleng by the way. The trip couldn't be contemplated if we wait much longer for Gudjeuk when the Wet is really unleashed. It won't be anything out of the ordinary if a cyclone or two blows in. But nothing on the horizon so far." She lifted her head, seeking his expression. "So does that make you happy?"

"That you're coming?"

The way he said it, the look in his topaz eyes made her catch her breath. Telltale colour spread along her cheekbones. "That *Samantha is*."

Smiling, he took her elbow as they crossed the broad street. "Isabelle, I'm happy on *both* counts."

CHAPTER FOUR

THINGS MOVED VERY quickly after that. By midafternoon Monday they were all assembled on North Star ready to make their journey into Kakadu the next morning. They were to approach the great national park from its western side.

The land baked under a peacock blue sky but each afternoon there had been an ominous build up of cloud heralding spectacular electrical storms with lightning so bright it wounded the naked eye. Their trip had to be fitted in to the brief period before the rains came in earnest and the plains were inundated.

That night they dined in rural splendour in the homestead's formal dining room which these days Isabelle told Samantha as they prepared the evening meal together was rarely used. She and Ross always ate in the breakfast room off the enormous kitchen. No wonder! Samantha thought. The size of the homestead and its interior spaces obviously reflected the pioneering cattle man's idea of his castle in the wilds where wide open spaces were both expected and respected. The dining room was *huge*. Ideal for anyone planning a wedding banquet. As it was they sat at one end of the mahogany table which Samantha had set using beautiful buttercup yellow line and lace place mats with matching napkins. Isabelle had let her choose from a dizzying array of table linen bought over the years, loads of it never taken out of its cellophane packaging. Samantha had been in and out of many beautiful houses back home in Sydney but none so steeped in the pioneering tradition. She could settle down here she thought quite seriously. Love of Nature and this was Nature on the grand scale was an important part of her.

On arrival she had found the white-washed homestead built of stout timbers enormously picturesque. She could see herself sketching it in her mind's eyes, little aboriginal spirit imps with big liquid black eyes peeking out of all the trees in the luminous green jungle that surrounded the house and protected it from the winds. Buttresses of monster shade trees supported staghorns and elkhorns the likes of which she had never seen. Beautiful orchids thrived out in the open or burst out of the trees. Vivid vandas and dendrobiums, cymbidiums with spikes six feet long and the showiest of orchids the cattleyas in myriad varieties. Terrestrial orchids too popped out of fallen tree trunks or the fallen bark that was piled up beneath the trees. Her eyes were dazzled by the blazing bougainvillea; the familiar purple cascading from every trellis and fence but closer to the house there were other colours, the modern hybrids, white, pink, orange, bronze, crimson and violet. The vibrancy of the colours set the timber house a-shimmer.

Mangoes, their cheeks blushed with colour, the size of small pumpkins, were scattered beneath the trees. Dozens had rolled out onto the pathways that crisscrossed the home gardens. It was, she was told, a bumper year.

Standing on the gravelled drive way staring up at the homestead she was roused to say: "This is *amazing*, Ross. It's like some exotic film set."

"Glad you like it." He was hurting not to lean down and kiss her. She looked radiant in the humid heat, her long copper hair pulled back from her face in a pony tail. Her lovely, touchable skin was flushed with colour. Her eyes glowed, her expression dazzled, maybe overcome. He liked that. Her reaction to his home.

For the homestead was lovely. Two storied, set in some ten acres of gardens that formed the main compound. Basically a rectangle, deep verandahs extended across the front of the house on both levels, running down the sides of the house. Mahogany shutters protected high arched doors that marched in pairs down the lengthy expanses of the verandahs. Inside the high and handsome ornately carved double doors the entrance hall was revealed to Samantha's fascinated eyes.

"Wow! This is bigger than my apartment. What would it be like to actually live here?"

"I don't know. I've never lived anywhere else. You have an apartment?" He gave her his sardonic glance.

"Did you think I lived in a back alley?"

"You could live at home with mother," he suggested mildly, nodding at Isabelle who was showing David and Matt into the house.

She took a deep breath. "Mother has never asked me to move in with her. She has remarried. I don't like her husband." In fact she loathed her mother's second husband—she never would say her *stepfather*. He was an enthusiastic toucher so much so that when they met up she torpedoed past him so he couldn't grab a hold.

"Hard to describe love isn't it?" Ross mused, momentarily lost in his own thoughts. "What *is* it?"

"What you feel for your sister and I feel for my brother," she suggested.

"I'm talking about romantic love."

"An utterly crazy longing. Mostly for the wrong person."

"At least on that we agree," he said crisply. "So when was the last time you had this utterly crazy longing?" He stood watching as she moved gracefully around the hall, placing a gentle finger to the large Cambodian tapestry that hung on one wall.

"The last time?" She considered. "That's easy. To beat you

in the pool." There was a circular library table holding a large
eye catching arrangement of a giant tropical leaves, palm and
monstera, setting off the living fire of the exotic bird of paradise, with sprays of ginger and heleconia, Samantha guessed
must have come from the garden. It was easy to comment on it,
thus changing the subject. Beyond a wide arch was the staircase
with a tall lead light window above the first landing. Multicoloured rays poured through it. She moved to get a better look
at this work of art, her own head on fire as the sun's beams fell
directly on her.

What was depicted was a lagoon of water lilies, edged by
reeds. Glorious blues and greens and amethysts were used, with
the contrast of rose pink and liquid silver for the glinting water.
It was a jewelled canvas of glass.

"Art Nouveau?" She turned to ask him then drew in her
breath sharply. He was a lot closer than she thought.

"You're more in touch with all that than I am," he shrugged,
too busy admiring the effect of the sunlight on her glorious
hair. He found himself thinking at least one of her children, if
she had them, would inherit that copper hair. "Right period.
It's the work of a Japanese artist who happened to be a pearl
diver on the side."

"Art Nouveau borrowed Japanese stylish features," she commented. "It's very beautiful. How do you protect it during cyclones and torrential storms?"

"It's boarded up. The shutters, obviously, are on the outside.
Want me to show you to your room? It's already been prepared
for you by Mrs. Lowell. That's our overseer's wife. She keeps
an eye on the house when we're away. We used to have a permanent housekeeper but she left after my father was killed. It
was all too much of a shock for her."

"I imagine it would have been," she said gently, the weight
of his own grief coming at her.

Samantha preceded him up the stairs hearing her brother's
deep cultured voice from somewhere at the rear of the ground

floor. She gave into a simple impulse and waltzed into her allotted bedroom, not quite sure if she wasn't in the middle of a dream.

"Oh this is lovely. Thank you." She looked around her with evident delight.

"It's not mandatory to like everything, Samantha." He stood in characteristic pose, handsome head thrown up, one hand speared into the pocket of his jeans. She had a way to her all of her own. As if a ring of light surrounded her.

"I can't help it," she exclaimed, going to try out the springs of the bed, like a child, checking its bounce. The bed was hung with billowing pale yellow mosquito netting that matched in colour the drapes at the arched doors. A big ceiling fan shaped like a flower whirred overhead, cooling the air and ruffling the filmy curtains. An antique cabinet faced her, an elaborately carved chest at the end of the bed, carved chairs with aqua cushions. She spread her hands on the duvet, a cool shade of lime-green covered with tropical blossom. The bed skirt was aqua. A life-size ceramic brolga stood in one corner, an Asia folding screen in another.

"This is absolutely beautiful!" she said. "The pity of it is I'm only here for *one* night."

Which ought to have pleased him, but it didn't. But then she had many spells at her disposal to cast. "Well make the most of it," he said crisply, discovering the sight of her poised so gracefully on the bed, slender arms to either side of her was unsettling him. "You could be spending quite a few in pouring rain."

She stood up as though she divined his odd mood. "You're not a bit of fun are you?"

"Whereas you're hell bent on being an adventuress. No, I'm the serious type," he mocked her, supporting his long lithe body with one arm propped against the solid antique cabinet.

"Then I'm sorry I'm annoying you with my girlish chatter." She looked about her. "Is it all right if I explore? This is all so glamorous!"

"Sure!" He gave a shrug, then surprised himself by saying, "I have to make a last minute check around the station in about a half an hour. You can come if you like."

Her expressive face lit up. "Hallelujah! So there *is* a nice part of you?"

"The bumpy part will come later." He crossed to the door, turning to flick a searing glance over her. "Don't wear the shorts."

She gave voice to mild exasperation. "What is it with you and my clothes?"

"I apply common sense. What else? There isn't a plethora of gorgeous looking leggy females around here. I don't want my men getting all steamed up."

"Bless you!" She looked back with bright challenge. "It's not like I could do the same for *you*?"

He narrowed his eyes. "My dear Miss Langdon, I run from trouble. I'm dedicated to North Star."

"Until you sort yourself out?"

"I beg your pardon?" He drilled her with a long stare.

"Sometimes I speak without thinking."

"So I've noticed." He proceeded on his way, throwing over his shoulder. "I'll have your things sent up. Meet me in the hall in around twenty minutes."

"Right, boss," she answered smartly.

"Don't push it."

"I wouldn't do that. Not to *you*." *You arrogant so and so.*

"It seems to me you like living life on the edge." He turned to face her. "Another thing."

"I'm all ears." She pantomimed the act.

"Leave Matt alone."

She took that as censure. "Come again?"

"You heard the first time."

"You mean I'm not to speak to Matt at all? He's my friend. You've got to be joking."

"I don't know whether you've noticed, but I'm not one for jokes. I just don't want to bump into you locked in his arms."

She could feel the colour flood her cheeks. "Funny I can think of worse things like—"

"Don't say it." He shook his head warningly. "You can talk all you like. Just remember to put off all thoughts of romance until the end of the trip."

Her face, always an animated mirror of her emotions betrayed temper. "You must be one of the biggest wowsers on the planet."

"Well of course I am!" He laughed, his blue-green eyes asparkle.

The whole effect couldn't have been more sexy, but Samantha determinedly ignored it.

"The fact you're not all that interested in Matt doesn't mean he isn't anxious to make it with you. Forewarned is forearmed as my dad used to say."

"I've got another one for you," she answered tartly. "All work and no play makes Ross a dull boy. But thank you anyway. I promise I'll take to heart everything you've said."

But she wasn't counting on what life on safari might offer.

They were well underway by midmorning of the following day. Samantha had never been so close to Nature. This magnificent wilderness had to be one of the most beautiful places on earth. It was a wild paradise simply teeming with life. She rode in the lead 4WD with the Boss Man as she had taken to calling Ross Sunderland to herself. He certainly looked the part in khaki bush shirt and hard wearing khaki trousers, a tan leather belt slung around his waist, a cream Akubra with a crocodile skin band on his dark head.

A commanding presence.

And don't you forget it!

She could scarcely walk by him without wanting to drop a mock curtsy, except he might take it as his due. Joe Goolatta, one of the most engaging characters she had ever met, rode in the back, the two men keeping up non-stop commentaries solely for her benefit. Between the two of them it was all marvellously entertaining and educational as it was meant to be. It both surprised and pleased her enormously to see how fond of the old aboriginal the hardhearted Boss Man was. He made no bones about it. It was equally clear Joe Goolatta worshipped Ross Sunderland without being in any way subservient. The two men fenced lightly, Goolatta teasing from time to time, which incredibly Boss Man took. Joe had known Sunderland since he was a child and it showed in his relaxed affectionate attitude. She began to think about what Sunderland would have looked like as a little boy. Not a shy nervous kid that's for sure. A haughty little prince.

She found herself laughing a lot listening with aesthetic pleasure to the cadences of the men's voices. The Boss Man's clipped, dark timbred, educated, the older man's basso deep and wonderfully melodious.

As they drove deeper into the great national park Samantha looked all around her with a sense of buoyancy and privilege. Some kilometres back they had passed a Top End safari taking a break.

"Only for the young and fit," Ross commented. "No more than nine a trip. Back packers love it. Young people looking for adventure. Those safaris are no sight seeing tours. It's a learning experience and as I said they have to be young, fit and strong. They have excellent guides."

"So what do they do? What do they see?" Samantha asked.

"Much of what we're going to do," he shrugged, "only we'll explore further a field. Go where no man has ever gone before, in Star Trek speak. That lot back there are on their way out of the park. I'd say it was one of the five day tours. Camping out under the stars, bar-b-ques around the camp fire, long bush treks, cooling off at any number of the park's falls. No crocs. There are some seventeen permanent water falls even in the Dry. Jim Jim plunges two hundred metres in a single drop. They'd have seen the estuarine crocs from a boat as we will. We have a boat on standby. That's all been arranged. For certain they would have taken in the beautiful ancient aboriginal rock art at Nourlangie and Uburr. Much of it is well in excess of twenty thousand years old, priceless to man for its spiritual and cultural significance. Joe can tell you all about the Dreamtime and Mythology of the sites. Joe is a tribal elder. The origin of Kakadu in case you don't know is a breakdown of *Gagudju* the name of the aboriginal tribe who lived in the area for more than fifty thousand years."

"It beggars the imagination." Samantha turned her head to smile at the aboriginal elder. "I'm so looking forward to seeing these magical sites with my own eyes, and with such authoritative guides. This is a marvellous experience for me. I'm picking up so much inspiration from *everywhere!*" She waved a hand. "I write children's books, Joe."

"So Ross told me," Joe answered in his deep tones.

"Do you want to see what I can do?"

"Sure." He laughed warmly, having taken to this beautiful, friendly creature who appeared to have no pretensions at all. A far far cry from Miss Isabelle's cruel mother-in-law.

With no more ado, Samantha reached into the hold all at her feet, extracted a sketch pad and a charcoal pencil and went to work.

"No looking," she warned Sunderland.

"Right!" He gave an amused grunt. He made a brief check in his rear vision to see their back up vehicle driven by David. It was holding to their speed, a short distance behind. So far the trail was broad and easy to follow but it wouldn't be long before the countryside became rugged with grasses growing ten feet tall. The black soil plains were relatively park like with large stands of pandanus, vast grassy expanses and sculptured stone outliers that had been separated by time and erosion from the mighty Arnhem Land escarpment.

A few minutes later, Samantha tore off a page and passed it back to Joe who took it in his weathered hand.

His grin faded. "My, my, Miss Sam. You've done what no other person has even done. You've drawn me."

"Like it?"

He broke into a sardonic chuckle. "I don't look as good as this."

"Show me." Sunderland put up his left hand to take the drawing.

"I could have done better," Samantha said quickly. "The track is a bit bumpy."

Sunderland held the wheel and cast his eyes down. "You don't need excuses."

"What *do* I need?" She fixed her eyes on his strong handsome profile.

"Why ask? Congratulations, of course." He threw her his rare devastating smile. "This is Joe to a T."

Samantha blushed at the sincerity of his tone. "Why thank you," she said jauntily. "Do you want one of you?"

He turned his dark head. "Don't you want to wait until you know me better?"

There was that glitter in his eyes that thoroughly unsettled her, but she managed to keep her voice even. "Okay, I'll wait. You can give that back to Joe now."

"I reckon you should have that framed, Joe," Sunderland laughed, passing the sketch back over his shoulder.

"I will," Joe replied, quite seriously. "You're an artist, Miss Sam," he offered homage.

"I'm getting there," Samantha answered modestly. "Would it be *suitable* do you think, Joe, for me to try to interpret aboriginals legends in my stories. I would never want to offend your people."

"Can't see how you'd do that, Miss Sam," Joe replied after a minute or two's consideration. "I think you're a very sensitive young lady who might well be able to see and understand our magic. I have many many myths and legends I can tell you. So much is being lost. Maybe you can save a little bit of my culture."

"That's a very great compliment, Miss Langdon," Ross said, intrigued by the whole thing. Miss Samantha Langdon was far from being just a pretty face, she fell into the multitalented category.

"And I'm duly mindful of it." Samantha returned his sidelong glance, accepting the fact this man thrilled her to her core. Did he know it? She hoped not. She had to be very, very careful he wouldn't latch on. But oh, he left her shaken. Just being beside him produced a degree of sexual arousement hardly imaginable with anyone else. Nothing much she could do about it either. Her body was releasing a whole host of biochemicals causing this tremendous rush of sensations she rationalised. It mightn't have been love at first sight given the curious sexual hostility both had experienced when they'd first met—but it was something momentous. She'd had her share of boyfriends, some good, some not so good, but never had she felt this *intense* attraction. Even intense didn't come close. Knee buckling was better.

She had to set her mind to something else. Why not a Dreamtime series of children's books? That seemed like a good idea. Her style was particularly adapted to magical themes.

Matt Howarth, his hazel eyes like stones, was sitting in the back seat of the second 4WD cursing his luck. This wasn't going a bit the way he intended. Up front Dave and Sunderland's beautiful iceberg of a sister were working their way through a whole range of subjects, Dave's travels, his shock encounter with a drug lord, her encounter with a ruthless tycoon who gave every appearance of wanting to separate her from her husband but definitely wasn't Robert Redford, what was happening around the globe, what governments were going to do about it, Dave even told her stories from when he'd started out as a photographer filming interiors for which he'd been in great demand, then gardens, even food. He'd done a stint for a well-known gourmet magazine. They appeared to be getting on famously, whereas he was locked into a sickening bout of jealousy. Being separated from Sam was like a slap in the face to him.

From time to time they tried to include him in the conversation but his responses were such they must have concluded he was finding the humid heat enervating. Dave's glance was even a bit *anxious*. Dave was a kindly guy, but then he had seen and photographed so much human suffering. It had had its effect. Dave championed the underdog, the underprivileged, the downtrodden. Just when he thought he'd been presented with a marvellous opportunity to launch his campaign for winning Samantha over, along came the Great White Hunter with his bloody commanding height and film star good looks. And those assessing light eyes. Who had eyes that colour apart from his sister? Matt had the distinct impression Sunderland was trying to split him and Sam apart. Did he want her himself? The very thought turned his stomach.

The whole thing looked like being intolerable. The dynamics were all different having Sutherland along. Matt's resentments festered. He'd confidently expected he and Sam would be sharing the back seat instead just as Sam went to slide in beside him giving him the most delicious shivers of anticipation, Sunderland had cut in coolly, without waiting for her reply:

"You're riding with me."

Arrogant bastard!

His reaction had been so violent it had winded him. This was no ordinary guy like he'd been expecting. Tough, yes, but a bit of a bush whacker. No such luck! The cattle baron was upper crust. Everything had to be done *his* way. Lived like lords these cattle barons. It made his skin prickle with heat. They didn't act like *normal* people. They were *nobles,* no less. What they were doing was important. Anyone would think the country couldn't survive without them. So they had pioneered the Never Never. Who cared? They were rich enough weren't they in their bloody great homesteads. He wasn't going to lose Sam to any cattle baron. No, sir! He was in so deep he could never ever look at another woman again.

He'd known Sam now for a couple of years, but despite his best efforts, and reading up surreptitiously all the right things a guy should do, he was still no more than a friend. He couldn't possibly push it with Dave around. Dave doted on his little sister. Just a handful of times she'd accepted his invitations, a rock concert, cricket match, football final, race meeting, things like that. Open air, crowds, nothing remotely romantic. But he'd managed to kiss her lovely lips. Nothing more, but he'd lived on it. Was still drunk on it for that matter. She was an angel with that glorious exuberant mane of hair. But Sam seemed to place a higher value on him as a friend and her brother's assistant than a would-be suitor. What would she think if she knew he had taken hundred of photographs of her? Most of them when she didn't even know he was around. Some people might think he was a stalker but he wasn't. He was deeply in love with her. The last thing in the world he meant Sam was harm. Why the walls of his apartment were decorated with beautiful shots of her, walking, talking, laughing, pensive, huge blow-ups of her lovely face, so ripe and alive begging for him to touch her. She had such a luscious mouth under that small pert nose. Technically he supposed the woman in the front passenger seat, the Great White Hunter's sister, was more beautiful, but her features had the remote perfection of a classical statue. The black hair and the ice-aqua eyes only served to complete the picture. Give him Samantha's ever changing expressions, her wonderful *bright* colouring every time. For all her nice manners and upper class voice he thought the rumours about Isabelle Hartmann were bound to be true. Her husband was reputed to have been a very nice guy not some dissolute playboy. You wouldn't have to look too closely to see she was a cold bitch underneath. He knew from experience women found Dave absolutely charming. He could *reach* them somehow. He was certainly getting a response from the Snow Queen.

Buy hey, *he* was attractive to women too. Don't let's forget that. He dressed well, worked out, was nice looking, mannerly, thoughtful. He'd had a pretty lousy time of it going back a bit, but he was climbing the ladder. He was no loser. He could have lots of girls if he wanted but the truth was Sam had ruined him for the rest. His mother—he took good care to keep away from *her*—always said he had an obsessive nature as though that was something for her to worry about. Why not obsess when you had something to obsess about? It meant he was wonderfully *loyal*.

He had a lot of time for Dave. Dave was a good bloke. He'd been very good to him, very supportive after his layoff—a slight breakdown actually—call it what you like. They'd overworked him at the TV channel not that he'd shed any tears over getting the sack. Pompous old McCutcheon had a spot of abuse coming. He had explained it all to Dave who gave him a chance. He had a B.A. in photography not that he was one to boast. Surely Dave would welcome him as a brother-in-law? He would love Sam as she had never been loved. Work hard to keep her safe. She was so lovely, *lovely*. With Sam he knew he could become as steady as a rock.

CHAPTER FIVE

FROM LONG EXPERIENCE Samantha knew her brother would go to any lengths to get the shots he wanted. He was the *true* professional dedicated to his craft which he had turned into *art*. She also knew he took no account of fatigue, hunger, intense heat, even personal danger. Over the next two days she and Isabelle were left alone for hours while the men went in search of sites Ross Sunderland and Joe Goolatta brooded over before pronouncing it too arduous a trek for the women especially in the steamy heat.

"He's treating us like cream puffs," Samantha fumed.

"Maybe a little bit," Isabelle conceded. "But you wouldn't enjoy trekking through the mangroves which is where they're heading today. The mozzies are merciless. They'd *love* your skin. And mine. Don't forget it's a place where the crocs still attack but they'll be extra careful. Joe has a thing going with the crocs. That's his totem. Don't fret. We'll see plenty."

"I've already seen plenty," Samantha responded, suddenly repentant. "In fact I'm immensely grateful I'm here. And it's all due to you. Your dear brother would never have taken me."

Isabelle smiled at the sarcasm. She could see the way Ross

and Samantha struck sparks from each other and she wasn't unhappy about it. "I think you've shown him you're made of the right stuff." A little pause. "Would it be presumptuous of me to ask if you and Matt have a history?"

Samantha gasped. "Honest answer?"

"Please."

"No." Samantha slapped at an insect. "I've known Matt for as long as he's been David's assistant. He lectures at an adult learning college at night and he does private photographic work. Weddings, studio portraits that sort of thing. David told me Matt had a breakdown a few years back. Overwork, lost opportunities, hassles with his superior at work. Matt doesn't talk about it. Especially not to me. He likes to present himself as a guy who's getting it all together."

Sitting beside Samantha beneath a shade tree a little distance from the camp, Isabelle turned to her. "You know he's in love with you?"

Samantha groaned. "Oh, don't say that!" Isabelle was quite right and she'd have to face it.

"Surely you know?" Isabelle asked quietly, alerted by something in Matt's manner. Something secretive. Something hidden. She knew all about manic upsurges in men. Matt harboured resentments, though on the surface he tried hard to be pleasant. "He never takes his eyes off you." Isabelle made the judgement from the depths of her own bitter experience.

Samantha sighed deeply. "That sounds like a warning, Isabelle. I haven't given Matt any reason to believe we could become more than friends."

"Does he need a reason?"

"Probably not being what we are. Is something worrying you, Isabelle?" For that matter Samantha had noticed Matt never looked at Ross with liking though his responses were courteous enough.

"D'you think he's becoming a little jealous?"

Samantha flushed. "Of Ross?"

Isabelle nodded. "He's very edgy when Ross is around. They're so different in style. In fact a complete contrast. Ross and David had instant rapport which has only grown, but it's not the same with Matt. It seems to me he's increasingly looking for conflict where there is none. He has to be *needed*. Some men are like that." A remembering chill struck her bones. "I could be overstating it but it seems to me Matt's starting to act as if he's being left out."

Spot on. "And you think it's because of me?" Samantha asked unhappily.

"Well you're the one he cares about. He was very peevish wouldn't you say last night when you and Ross dropped the sparring and carried on the conversation in perfect accord." In fact to Isabelle's discerning eyes jealousy had been coming off him in waves.

Samantha made a little grimace. "Well for all our little clashes, I agree with Ross about so many issues. However, I did notice Matt had his nose out of joint. I don't know what I can do about it though."

"Be on your guard," Isabelle suggested. "I don't mean to suggest for a minute Matt could present a danger, but maybe a little problem. Being included in David's book is important to him, I know. He wouldn't want to do anything to jeopardize that." She leant forward to retrieve the coffee mugs she had laid on the ground. "What about if you and I do a little exploring on our own, this afternoon?"

"And risk the Boss Man's ire?" Samantha asked blithely.

"So that's what you call him?" Isabelle looked across with a smile.

"And don't you dare tell him," Samantha said, scrambling to her feet. "I haven't got a way with your brother, have I?"

"Really?" Isabelle raised an arched brow. "I thought you *had*."

Which was precisely what was putting Matt Howarth's nose out of joint.

* * *

The afternoon's rigours gave Samantha a hearty appetite. The men returned full of the day's exploits. Or rather Ross and David talked as if they'd had a glorious time, thoroughly successful, while Matt's chief concern was his mosquito bites which were giving him noticeable gip.

"You'll have to stop scratching, Matt, you could get a secondary infection. I've got a good hydrocortisone cream I can give you," Samantha tried to console him. "As a matter of fact I'll get it now. See any crocs today?" she asked, as they walked to the tent she and Isabelle shared.

"Plenty," he grunted finding it difficult to control his feelings. "I couldn't wait to get the hell out of there." He gave a genuine shudder, his terror still not evaporated. "Sunderland dragged us through the swamps. They're overflowing with everything. Dank and steamy with awful muddy soil, snakes and all kinds of insects and tree roots that are only there to trip you up. By the time it was all over I could have yelled bloody murder."

"But isn't that what David wanted? The swamps may be difficult and dangerous but they're the central element in the coastal ecosystem. I bet he took some wonderful shots. I know my brother. He comes up with something entirely different from the pack. That's why he's famous. It's the special way *he* sees things."

He grasped her arm, detaining her. "David is *my* friend."

Samantha disengaged herself, feeling dismayed. "Of course he is. What's the matter, Matt. We're only a few days into the trip yet you seem right out of sorts. I thought you were really going to enjoy this trip. I'm loving it and we've travelled a long way for it. It's not too late to go back if you feel so strongly. I daresay we can manage with one vehicle."

That she could say such a thing caused him physical pain. "Is that what you want, for me to *disappear*?" To his horror, his voice broke.

"Listen, Matt, today upset you. I can see that. But you'll have to settle down. Ross is looking this way."

"To hell with Ross!" Matt exploded, his heart thumping wildly. "Is that supposed to make me cringe?"

Samantha walked on, anxiety flooding her. "I don't want to see you lose control, Matt. I thought you were going to be as excited about this as the rest of us."

"Excited?" His tone leapt. "You wouldn't feel so excited if you'd been eaten alive by mozzies. They're as big as helicopters."

"I'm sorry. So sorry," Samantha said gently. "Wait here a moment and I'll get the cream."

Instead of waiting as she asked, he pushed into the tent behind her. "What was really exciting me, Sam, was the opportunity for you and me to be together."

Studying his tormented face Samantha felt the last thing she could do was humiliate him. "Matt, dear, aren't we comfortable being friends?"

"You know I want more," he said passionately, reached out for her arm.

Why have I realised too late where all this was going, Samantha thought wretchedly. "Friendship is all I can offer, Matt," she said with great compassion.

Incredibly he began to laugh. "It's Sunderland isn't it? I've got eyes. I can see. The two of you keep up the sparring, but it's only a smoke screen for something else."

"You're talking nonsense, Matt," Samantha took a step backwards. This was a Matt she had never seen.

"I think not." His eyes were liquid with emotion. "Just don't forget in a very short while he'll be out of the picture altogether, the arrogant bastard."

Samantha counted ten before she answered. "I think you're mistaking a natural superiority—he is after all, a high achiever—for arrogance. You see him with Joe. Would an arrogant white man treat an aboriginal employee like *family*? I don't think so. Anyway why don't you take it up with him, Matt?" Samantha swooped on the cream which mercifully was to hand and passed it to him. "I hope this helps."

He realised too late he had overplayed his hand. His only option was to act out remorse. "I'm sorry, Sam." He hung his head contritely. "Of course I'm not being fair. He's Someone, even I can see that... But if you could just give me a chance?"

Samantha stood there pitying, but adamant. "You're my friend, Matt. I'm sorry, but I can't offer anything else. The others will be waiting for us. We'd better go." She went to brush past him but he startled her by caching her around the waist.

"*Please,* Sam."

In the blink of an eye he felt like he *hated* her.

Sensing something was not *right* Samantha twisted away.

"Everything okay here?" a vibrant voice asked.

In the opening of the igloo like tent stood a tall, muscular figure caught in a freeze frame. Ross ducked his dark head and stepped inside, the glow from the gas lamps throwing his shadow high on the nylon mesh side. In that confined area— roughly one hundred square feet—generous enough for a two-person tent, he appeared quite dramatically larger than life.

Samantha had never been so glad to see anyone. "We were just coming," she said, taking a few swift paces towards him like he was her saviour. "I gave Matt some cream for his mosquito bites."

Sunderland continued to stand with his tall shadow on the wall. "They wouldn't have been nearly so bad, Matt, had you used the spray I offered you this morning." He stood aside so Samantha could exit the tent. "Next time you'll use it."

A seething reply rose to Matt's lips, but he bit it off. Much as he disliked him, Sunderland wasn't the man to tangle with. Matt too left the tent, stalking off towards where the others were seated around the camp fire. Fury at Sunderland's reprimand was burning in his chest.

"What was that all about?" Ross asked, letting his flashlight play along the ground ahead of where they walked. They were using a small petrol driven generator out of the back of one of the vehicles to cast additional light on the site, but the bush was blacker than black at night.

Samantha didn't want to tell him. She had to *think*. "He's a bit upset. He's a sensitive soul, Matt."

Sunderland just laughed. "Don't you think it's time for him to grow up?"

"Don't be impatient with him. He hasn't had your upbringing. His skin is quite fair. I've seen the bites. He must feel on fire."

"Well I'm sorry about that," Ross said, not even bothering to disguise the impatience in his voice, "but I'm afraid Matt pointedly chose to ignore my advice this morning when David and I were sensibly giving ourselves a good protective dousing."

Samantha walking at his shoulder, was vividly aware of his physical *presence*. It was something that could not be ignored, or locked away for when she was on her own. *I've regressed to adoring teenager with an almighty crush.* "I can't understand why Matt was so foolish. He's not usually like that."

"Are you sure you really know him?" Ross asked, his voice dry. "Or just vaguely?"

"I know him well enough." It wasn't the right answer. She only *thought* she knew him.

"You'd tell me if he started to bother you?" He paused as they came within the perimeter of light. It was marvellous the way she kept so shiningly clean and fresh even when tramping through the bush in the humid heat. "Certainly you would tell David?"

Her eyes remained focused on him as though she were unable to look away. Her whole being seemed to be *melting* so powerful was his attraction. "Matt won't do anything to wreck his chances with David. Matt's not really a man of action, I suppose." She sounded distressed. "Being out of his element has made him feel inadequate, but he'll pick up."

"So how come *you* don't act helpless?"

"I want to impress you," she said lightly when she was speaking the exact truth. "Prove what I can do. Stuff like that."

"You're managing to get away with it too," he commented dryly as though admitting to a weakness. "As for Matt, he knew what he was in for surely?"

"Give him a chance, Ross," she pleaded.

God, the use of his name packed a punch. He clenched his fists before he surrendered to the dangerous impulses that powered through him; to pull her into his arms. Every minute he was with her, the desire to do so grew. Tonight that feeling was tremendously strong. Still he managed to keep his tone businesslike. "Certainly I'll give him a chance, if only because you champion him so sweetly." He made sure she heard the sarcasm. "I don't want to get on his case, but I have to tell you after today David isn't too far off telling him to straighten up his act." He avoided saying Howarth had never let up whining for most of the afternoon until at one point he nearly gave into the urge to chuck him in the swamp. He knew Howarth had problems. Even his devotion to Samantha was a little creepy in character. He changed the subject to something less stressful. "So you and Belle went hiking this afternoon?"

She looked up at him with a smile. "We had a wonderful time. It's very powerful country and it's having its effect on me. Isabelle is an excellent guide in her own right and such good company."

"She says the same of you. I'm very grateful you and Belle are getting on so well. She's had a great grief to cope with but she's got the courage to rise above it given enough time. *I* was the one who got it wrong. Your coming along as it turns out, Ms Langdon, was a great idea."

"Momentous words!" she crowed. "See how *easy* it was to say them?"

"Well I'm not suggesting you move into my tent."

Her heart jumped. "Don't you play your games with me."

"Oh?" He sent her a sizzling glance. "It hasn't crossed your mind?"

"Oh, all right it has, but I'm not about to admit to it. Mercifully I can control my feelings."

"But you've just admitted to having them?"

"Which is more than I can say for you. You're *deep,* Boss Man. Impossibly deep. In fact you're a dangerous man."

"Now how would *you* know?"

How beautiful he was! She could sit and stare at him for ages.

"I know." She said with fervour.

"Do you now. I would never hurt you. Your boyfriend is more likely to do that than me. I have to tell you I'm keeping a watchful eye on him."

"Hold on a bit." She was dismayed. "I can handle Matt. Okay? It's *you* I can't handle."

He stared down at her. She was wearing a cool little top with a gauzy flowered skirt that had an uneven hem that was undoubtedly the rage. Her beautiful, oh so feminine hair was pulled back into some arrangement of plaits he found very attractive, even when he wanted to set those plaits loose. "When men collapse around you like soufflés?"

Perversely she was amused and charmed. "Well not *collapse* exactly. I think you've got me down as *dangerous* as well."

He answered without hesitation. "It so happens you're *right!*"

"Do I *look* dangerous?"

"I've no intention of flattering you."

"I'd be very surprised if you did. Like you, I want reasons. You must have made some kind of decision that involvement with a woman you perceive to be unsuitable would be akin to a rope around your neck?"

Dismal scenes from his memory bank flashed up. He even remembered the way at night time his father used sometimes take the hair brush from his mother as she sat at her dressing table and proceed to draw it through her beautiful long hair, his face wearing such an expression of love. "Not to mention a giant leap into the unknown," he replied with unnecessary harshness. "Heaven for a time then a detour to hell."

She regarded him with trepidation. "You confuse me. You tell me one thing, the next you speak as from bitter experience?"

I don't want this, he thought. *I'm in thrall to this woman and I don't want to accept it. Hadn't he learned the hard way? Hadn't he been warned?*

"The moment I saw you…" He stopped dead before she prised it out of him.

"Yes?" She caught her breath as if on the brink of a revelation.

There was a recklessness in his blood he knew was getting the better of him. *Calm down,* he exhorted himself, on the fine edge of frustration. She was with him every waking minute. She had insinuated herself into his dreams. Certainly it was witchcraft.

In a way it was like being locked in silken chains.

He looked at her through the mask he affected. "I knew then I'd have need of protective armour." He turned away, knowing he was leaving her baffled. Why not? He never meant to say half the things he was saying. "We'd better join the others. Joe's the chef tonight."

"That's right change the subject." She had to near jog to keep up. "I'd love to know what you were really going to say."

"The fact I even said it, makes me wonder."

"It would be really something to see. *You* losing control."

"Well you're not going to see it tonight," he answered bluntly. "Tomorrow, who knows? Joe is taking Dave and Matt out on a trip of his own while I take you and Belle somewhere you'll enjoy. Maybe a swim. I know just the spot. We can get most of the way in the 4WD then we'll have to trek. A little reward for being good and not doing too much complaining."

Her dark eyes slanted up at him. "You are *such* an enigma, Ross Sunderland."

"And like a woman you're desperate to solve the mystery. Are you going to say thank you?"

"Give me a moment." She touched her temple. "It's odd to be in your good books. I'll say please *and* thank you just for good measure. In fact I appreciate the thought so much I'm nearly on the point of tears."

It was then he shocked her into absolute silence. "I can almost feel them on my tongue."

. The seductive note in his voice roused her so much he might have suddenly begun to trail a hand over her body. She could feel the blood flushing her cheeks and her neck. He had to be the most perverse man she had ever known.

Dinner was freshly caught barramundi on a bed of basmati rice spiced up with ginger and chilli and a splash of lemon, served with considerable panache by Joe. It was a simple meal that became a taste sensation because of the freshness and superb flavour of the giant perch, one of the world's great eating fish and a symbol of the Territory. It really was like being on an old-style safari Samantha thought, hungry and utterly under a spell. This trip couldn't be long enough.

They ate around a collapsible table covered each evening with a fresh linen cloth and matching napkins. No plastic plates for them. Isabelle had sorted all that out at the homestead. They had good china, good stainless steel cutlery and fine wine glasses at their disposal. Peaches and cream out of tins for dessert. Good wine. Good coffee. Tremendous good will which was grating terribly on Matt's already strained nerves.

Afterwards they sat around in comfortable deck chairs that creaked as they moved, conversing lightly, enjoying the night.

How different it all was in the wild bush, Samantha thought. Like a dream. The sky over this marvellous mystical country was incredibly clear. She lay back in her chair staring raptly at the sky. The stars were like glowing windows through which poured the dazzling light of Heaven. Over the tip of a grove of spiky pandanus hung the Southern Cross. The air was blessedly cool after the heat of the day, the light breeze carrying myriad scents from the abundant wild flowers and fruits that appeared almost overnight from the heralding storms. She sniffed in the fragrance. There was a definite high note of wild gardenia and something else, not jasmine, but musky blossom. It was everywhere…so soporific…. She was a woman, enchanted. Liberated from the everyday world.

"You're drifting off," a voice close to her ear brought her out of her reverie.

Samantha's eyes flew open. She stared up at Ross, fantasising what it would be like to be here with him alone. She was already in love with him. Had been from the moment he had pinned her with those extraordinary eyes. It owed nothing to the time or the place though that added to the magic. She knew beyond all possible doubt this was no easy thing. She could be badly hurt. "Now you know I don't snore," she covered the fierce spasms of yearning with the mundane.

He lowered himself to the rug at her feet, drawing up his long legs. "No, but you talk in your sleep."

"What?" She leaned over the better to see his handsome face. "You've really heard me?"

He made a soft, scoffing sound. "Actually it's more like a mumble."

"So you've been spying on me? Is that what you're saying?"

"Do you want me to spy on you?" He glanced up at her.

"I'd never feel safe."

"Well relax. I check on the tents and the perimeter of the camp last thing at night before I hit the hay myself."

"Oh." She relaxed. "You had me going for a minute. Clearly you have your responsibilities." She lay back, her hands behind her head, feeling so *wired* it was a wonder she wasn't lit up. "You know what I'd *really* like to do?"

Even in the semidark she could see the sparkle of his eyes. "Join me on the rug?"

He was doing it again. Trying to throw her off balance. It shouldn't be allowed. A blush rushed over her skin. "I'm much too cautious to do that."

"What do you think might happen?" *I mightn't be able to get enough of you?*

"Absolutely nothing," she responded to his half derisive tone. "And just to prove it." She lowered herself onto the rug, but keeping a foot away from him. "Besides, the eyes of the world are on us."

"Really?" He turned his dark head. Joe was moving about, obviously making preparations for the morning. Matt was nowhere in sight. Gone off to bed in a huff without saying goodnight? David and Belle were sitting companionably side by side, David's tawny head bent to Isabelle's sable, as he passed some remark which was met by a soft burst of laughter. They shared an affinity which was plain to see. Belle was glowing, absorbed. She seemed to have thrown off the grinding grief. Beyond that Ross could think no further.

"No one's taking the slightest notice of us," he pointed out. "We could disappear into the jungle if we liked."

"To do what?" Excitement moved in with a great rush of wings.

He trapped her gaze. "I think it would be fair to say, Samantha, I was attracted to you from the start." Why deny what was in the very air? If he admitted the attraction he might be able to head it off.

The admission had her incandescent. "Someone should have told me. You acted like you disliked me on sight."

He reached out and grasped her hand, that now lay at her side, lightly twining her fingers through his own. "That's a lie, Samantha." The urge to pull her closer was so overwhelming he almost forgot where he was, who he was, *everything!* He'd tried so hard to fight this feeling of losing himself. He was too accustomed, too comfortable with control. His male territory. Except since he met her he was a different man.

No wonder men went mad about women, he thought, for the first time totally comprehending his father's dilemma. She was staring at him with her large eyes, her bright copper hair now unconfined, splashing over her bare creamy shoulders and curving to her breast. Her woman's fragrance, fresh, natural, hauntingly sweet all around them, flooding him with desire. He could feel the heavenly softness and texture of her skin. It was like satin against the roughness of his work hardened hands.

"Ross?"

His mouth twisted. He released her hand, grateful in a way he could still do that. "You sound like a little girl frightened of the dark."

"I'm more afraid of *you*." She continued to look directly at him, trying to reconcile the barrage of contradictory messages he was sending. "What is it you're trying to do?"

"God knows!" His voice cracked. "Lose myself for a while." *Pin your warm, beautiful, living body to the ground. Kiss your lovely mouth. Unbutton your shirt. Let my hand find your naked breasts. Immerse myself in you.*

Hot blood was like a swirling darkness before his eyes. The force of his desire for her was getting worse with every passing day. Lord knows he had tried to put up defences. They didn't work. Somehow without his wanting it, she had slid in behind his heart. He had learned the worst way possible there was terror in wanting a woman so much. Did that tearing, violent, disruptive desire last or slip away? It had lasted with his father. He had the underlying conviction it would last with him.

Was that a blessing or a disaster? Though he would never act with the quietness and resignation of his father. He had a far more combative nature. He'd have gone to England and dragged his wife home. Kicking and screaming if he had to. Vows were vows. Marriage wasn't a sport, a recreation. Marriage was total commitment. The children of a marriage had to

be protected. Did his mother have any *real* idea of the suffering she had caused or was she now full of regrets? I hope so, he
thought with anguish. What she had done deserved punishment.

Watching him Samantha shivered. "You look so grim. What
are you thinking?"

He bowed his head. "A hell of a long way back."

"Do you want to talk about it?"

"No," he said bleakly. "It's not as though you could come
up with a solution. It's all gone well beyond that." He stood up
resolutely, giving her his hand. "A reasonably early night might
be a good idea. I'll have a word with David before we turn in."

Once on her feet, she had a sudden hysterical desire to wrap
her arms around him; lay her head against his chest. But she
had her pride. "Does Isabelle know we're going with you?" she
asked quietly.

"I'm sure David has told her by now." He had returned to his
clipped tone. "It was meant to be a surprise, but there's such
accord between them."

"Aren't you glad?" she asked gravely.

A muscle jumped along his clean sculpted jawline. "As far
as it's going, yes."

"Isn't that a matter for them?"

"Belle is mourning her husband, Samantha."

Samantha had qualms she couldn't even put her finger on.
"I know. Forgive me if I sound insensitive. I'm not suggesting
for a moment it could be easy, but Isabelle has to survive the
terrible blow that life inflicted on her. Her husband has gone
and no amount of crying will bring him back. The agony must
be extreme. She told me she's been numb with it. But she's so
young and so beautiful. Isabelle has decades and decades in
front of her. You wouldn't want her to be *alone*? It can't be easy
for a woman alone. Moreover a woman who has no children. I
have learned from Isabelle she loves kids."

"Do *you*?" His face was in deep shadow but his voice was
intense.

"I know exactly how many children I want. I want four."

"*One* husband?"

"Of course one husband. Isn't that what every woman wants when she goes into marriage?"

"I hate to remind you your parents divorced."

She sighed deeply. "They had to. It was too painful for them to remain together. Actually it was my father who was unfaithful. He was the real culprit. Divorce was the last thing my mother wanted, but after all the cruelties and humiliations, no longer loved, betrayed, rejected, she became so bitter and angry I think she wanted to kill my father. And his mistress."

Your poor bloody father is trying to recover his lost youth!

Her mother had never run out of that explanation.

Samantha shut down on her old memories. She was very good at it from long habit.

"It's a mean old world out there," Ross said. "There are some wounds the soul can never recover from."

Samantha looked up at the blossoming stars as though seeking answers. One blazed down the sky leaving a trail of white fire. She made a wish. That she would be granted the priceless gift of finding her true love. Her soul mate. "Perhaps if one is patient and lets the anger go instead of holding on to it," she suggested, and surprised herself by taking his arm. She wasn't rejected. He drew her close to his side. "I believe recovery *is* possible, Ross. In the meantime we have to take comfort where we can. Somehow David is shielding Isabelle from the worst of her sorrow. We can only be grateful for that."

They were settled comfortably for the night before Isabelle whispered into the semi-darkness. "You're happy about going off on your own with Ross tomorrow?" In the course of talking over the following day's itinerary, between them they had come up with a change of plan that seemed to suit everyone. Isabelle was now to join David's party. Samantha was to go with Ross.

Samantha levered herself up onto one elbow. Happy? The

truth of it was she was ecstatic. "I'd say it's shaping up to be one of the highlights of my life," she whispered back. "You engineered it, didn't you, you designing woman?"

Isabelle cut her laugh short. The night was so *quiet* and voices carried. "I have to confess seeing you both together has aroused my matchmaking talents."

"What? You're not joking?"

"Oh, Sam, I have eyes. Besides, I know my brother. I know the flash of his eyes. Underneath the formidable exterior he's passionate and emotional."

"With me, he's mostly an enigma," Samantha sighed, lying back and settling her head into the small pillow. "It's scary being struck by lightning."

"Is that what it feels like?" Isabelle asked gently.

"It's a wonder I haven't been hospitalised," Samantha remarked wryly. "I'm way out of my depth here, Isabelle. Your brother is very very suspicious of me."

"Hang in there," Isabelle advised in a sisterly way. "It's not surprising you know given our history. Our mother bolted. She didn't set a good precedent for the female sex. For what it's worth, there's no one I'd rather see my brother taking such an interest in. It's just that Ross over the years has become accustomed to being the man in control. He's very disciplined. That means he doesn't lose his head over women and he's had a lot literally throw themselves at him. I've seen it with my own eyes. Even when he's been with another girl, they take no notice. Shameless. Ross has seen a lot of failed relationships. So have I. So have you. You suffered similarly when your parents divorced and that must have been very hard. Ross worshipped Dad and Dad had such pride in him. Ross is extremely hostile to our mother for what she did not only to us but mostly what she did to Dad. It's made him very wary because if he weren't he could star in a replay of Dad's life. You know about emotional wreckage. God knows I do. Ross had been programmed to fight becoming enmeshed with a woman who really got under his skin and you pretty much have."

Samantha turned her head to where Isabelle was lying. "You wouldn't say that if you didn't believe it."

Isabelle just smiled. "And why not? You have a lot going for you."

"We both do. You and me. But I can't hide the fact I feel very vulnerable where Ross is concerned."

"We're all vulnerable," Isabelle reminded her, backing away from dangerous ground.

"He could forget me in a week." Samantha mused, gazing at the big copper moon through the screened window in the side of the tent. There was one opposite allowing cross ventilation.

"Could *you* forget him?"

Samantha was lost for a moment trying to think how she could adjust to a life without Ross Sunderland in it. "Not if a thousand years went past."

"Well then!" Isabelle smiled in the darkness.

"So are *you* happy going with David's party?" Samantha asked, buoyed up by Isabelle's approval.

"Yes of course." Isabelle tried to convey no more than easy acceptance when each minute in David's company she was re-awakening to the richness of life. "Actually I'm not completely responsible for the change of plan. David wants to include me in some of his shots."

"The human figure in the vast landscape?"

"Yes. He's wanting shots of you as well."

"I have to get the text right. That's important and my head is already swimming with ideas." Samantha gave a light yawn, finding the scent of the woodsmoke from the fire intoxicating. "The ones David's taken on the digital camera are great. I can't wait to see the film scanned. I'm going to have my pick of the digitals blown up to whatever size I want in Darwin. By the way, what happened to Matt? He just disappeared."

"He sat for a while," Isabelle murmured, quite at peace.

"Then he announced rather shortly he wanted to crash. I don't think anything is working in the way Matt wanted. He's very tense and he's really feeling the heat."

"Obviously he doesn't like life stripped down to essentials," Samantha lamented. "Matt's a city person."

They both knew that wasn't the cause of Matt's ill humour.

"Belle?" Samantha whispered as Isabelle turned on her side.

"Yes?"

"Thank you for everything. You're wise and kind. I'm really glad we met. When it doesn't hurt so much to talk about what has happened to you, I'll be around to listen."

Tears stung Isabelle's eyes at the touching note in Samantha's voice. She swallowed down a sudden flare of pain. Not a lot of people had been kind to her since Blair. She knew for some bereaved people talking would be a release. But there was no talking about her marriage. The very last thing she wanted was to go back.

CHAPTER SIX

STILL SMOULDERING IN silent fury over Samantha's lack of trust in him, Matt assumed a nonchalant demeanour, strolling over to where she was down on her haunches re-arranging her pack.

"Hi, all set?" She looked so beautiful it broke his heart.

"Just about." She looked up and tried a warm smile. She knew Matt well enough to know he was feigning good humour. He didn't look well. The dark shadows beneath his eyes gave him an exhausted look as if he weren't getting enough sleep. "I hope you get the shots you want today. I can't wait to see them," she added, injecting enthusiasm into her voice.

"So far so good." He shrugged. "Of course I haven't got Dave's masterly skills. The stuff he's done so far is going to be pretty damned marvellous."

"You haven't had David's experience," she said kindly. "You're a very good photographer, Matt. You're exceptionally lucky to have Joe along with you. He knows this place like the back of his hand. Incredible to believe his people have lived in this region for more than forty thousand years ago."

"They can have it," Matt was sufficiently derailed to say.

Samantha stood up. "You can't mean that? It's marvellous

and we've only experienced a little. I can't wait until we get to see the rock art. It's considered to be without parallel in all the world."

"Yes, yes, I know." Now Matt's irritation was barely disguised. "Whose idea was it for you to go off with Sunderland?"

Samantha tried to rein her temper in. "I'm tempted to say mine, Matt. Actually Ross was to take Belle and me but David wanted the human element in some of his shots so he invited Belle along. Surely you know?"

He didn't even attempt an answer. "You two get along well?"

"Belle and I?"

"She doesn't strike me as the grieving widow," he said in a bitterly sarcastic voice.

Tenderhearted Samantha was greatly distressed. "What a rotten thing to say."

"Is it?" Matt's brown head was poised curiously like a cobra's about to strike. "Word is she drove the poor man to his death."

"Oh Matt!" Samantha dropped the tin mug in her hand. It hit the ground and rolled away. "That I do *not* believe. I'd advise you not to listen to cruel rumours. A woman as beautiful as Isabelle is always the target for vicious gossip. That's the way of the world. Usually it's other women. Not *men* so much."

"Okay I'm sorry." Matt dropped his head, pretending shame. "But take a look at her when she's laughing with Dave. I'm convinced she's got him lined up as her next."

"We need the Davids of this world," Samantha said sharply. "Lucky for you he was around when your life was in the doldrums. Isabelle is suffering. David is trying to ease her pain. I don't know what's got into you, Matt. Your health doesn't seem so good. Since we left Darwin you seem to have lost your sense of well-being."

"Why not!" he exploded, yearning to show her how much he loved her. He'd fight a duel over her if he had to only that bastard, Sunderland, would win. Sunderland, the natural born leader accepting adulation as his due. "Everything has turned out so differently from what I expected," he said. It made him furious. He hated it. "I'm trying. I'm trying the best I can. What would be really great is if you and I could get to spend a little time together. That would be wonderful, just the two of us."

Samantha wanted to end this, but was torn by pity. "We share breakfast and dinner, Matt. We get to relax around the camp fire. It's *you* who doesn't want to join in."

Matt set his fine white teeth together. "I'm talking about spending a little time *alone,*" he ground out. "You're spending the day with the Great White Hunter. Why not me? No one could enjoy your company better. We've always had a great time when we've been out, haven't we?"

"Of course we have. We're friends. If you don't see it that way, I've told you, Matt. I can't offer anything more."

"Because you've fallen for Sunderland," Matt muttered like he had a score to settle.

"How come you know more than I do, Matt?" Samantha tried to take the heat off Ross. "You know the way it works. Ross is our guide. And he's coming this way. It's about time we all got going."

Matt's hazel eyes held hers, something desperate in his thin face. "All I want from you is only what you're prepared to offer. I care about you, Sam. Remember that. All I'm asking of you is to come with me while *I* take a few photographs. I'm far more interested in photographing you than the scenery. Is that so much to ask?"

"No of course not!" Samantha tried to mollify him.

"Great!" Matt smacked his fist into his palm, a triumphant look on his face.

Ross and Samantha drove across flood plains rejuvenated by the tropical storms that had already started. Mostly they occurred in the afternoon, short lived, maybe thirty or forty minutes, but spectacular enough. It was the late night thunderstorms that turned on the most awesome displays of Nature's unmatched power. Once the Wet really got underway, January was the worst month, access to many areas of the park became too dangerous to attempt. As it was these same plains they were travelling over would be inundated and the Park's innumerable water lily covered lagoons and billabongs would become home to the legions of beautiful wading birds that returned from Asia to the lush grasslands.

Ross pulled over under a magnificently gnarled paperbark, scattering the masses of brilliantly coloured parrots that were resting in the willowy, iridescent branches. Birds and birdsong was everywhere all over the Park. Parrots, cockatoos, lorikeets, galahs, corellas, rosellas, warblers, honeyeaters. There were even plenty of the great flightless bird, the emu.

He cut the ignition. "Right!" His sparkling gaze swept her, the large velvety eyes, the creamy skin the flushed cheeks. With her beautiful hair bound up in plaits she looked about sixteen and crying out to be kissed. "Our trek starts here. Still up for it?"

She answered readily. "I'm game if you are, Captain."

"Yes, well, we haven't started yet."

"Give me two seconds." She opened out the passenger door and slid to the ground. "Tell me where we're heading. Point it out," she challenged, well and truly on her mettle.

His amusement was apparent. "See that small range?" he walked around the back of the vehicle to join her.

She almost reeled. "Gosh, I could hardly miss it." Her eyes travelled to a flat escarpment washed with purple against the smouldering blue sky. "It must be twenty miles away."

He made a soft jeering sound. "That's a lousy guess. It's closer to five. No more than my daily constitutional. Anyway, you said you wouldn't miss this for the world."

She looked up at him, heroic figure that he was. "Okay let's make a start," she said briskly, easing the straps of her backpack.

"This is the *easy* bit," he assured her.

"It's time I showed you a thing or two!"

It was all he could do not to seize her and demand she prove it. "I sure am willing to learn."

"You don't think much of women, do you?" she called over her shoulder, stepping off.

His mouth twisted in a cynical smile. "Believe me I know how powerful you are. Maybe not in the physical stakes."

"That's why women last a heck of a lot longer than men." She retaliated.

"You're not killing me off, Samantha, thank you very much. What was Howarth griping about this time?" He caught her up easily, so they could walk side by side.

"Aren't you jumping to conclusions?"

"No," he answered flatly. "You *have* to tell him he has no chance with you."

"Why don't you tell him," she challenged. *He won't listen to me.*

"He's madly in love with you." He shook his dark head in disgust.

"There must be worse things in life," she said tartly.

"Not for your friend, Matt. I could be wrong but he strikes me as a man on the verge of a break-down."

Samantha let out a long sigh, thinking there was something in what he said. "That's a bit extreme, isn't it?"

"He has the signs all over him."

She had taken note of the fevered tension. "I have told Matt I can't offer him more than friendship."

"Even that's too much," he said rather curtly. "It gives him hope."

"So what do you want me to say?" She stopped so abruptly she almost slammed into him. "I'm having an affair with you?"

His eyes gleamed, pure aquamarine. "Well, aren't you?"

"Give me a break!" she spluttered. "You're arrogant beyond belief."

That made him smile. "Don't get too steamed up. Save your strength for the trek ahead."

She stared fixedly through the lace work of trees. Most were tall palms, stands of pandanus, paperbarks, an understorey of blossoming grevilleas, native hibiscus, cassias which produced colourful scented flowers, luminous green mosses, surprisingly delicate ferns, long trailing vines, a lot bearing trumpet like flowers in cerise and purple with bright yellow centres. Not so bad. She could go a mile or two in bush like this. The land was level pegging. "Look why don't we cut this battle of the sexes short. I can do this on my own. At least to the escarpment. I've been bush walking plenty of times. You must have noticed by now how fit I am?"

They were walking so close together, their hands were almost brushing. "We're not talking a delightful stroll along a State Forest track. You're in the presence of the greatest wilderness on the continent except maybe for tropical Queensland's Cape York. Even David arranged for a guide."

"You think I'd get lost?" she asked tartly, his superior male attitude doubling her determination.

"I *know* you would."

"This isn't jungle. It's relatively open woodland. All I need to do is follow my nose to the escarpment. God knows it's smack bang in the middle. I'm determined to do this, Ross."

"What if I don't let you?" He moved with catlike grace to bar her way.

"Excuse me. I was brought up in a feuding family and survived."

He glanced around them. "Ah well, if that's the case, I might sit down for a half an hour. Give you a headstart." He eased his lean powerful body onto a large boulder, one of a rocky outcrop, that was so much a feature of the landscape. Its base was framed by emerald spear grasses. "Do you want the rifle?" he asked.

She gave an involuntary shudder. "What would I do with it? Set my sights on you? I don't even know how to hold it. No, I don't want the rifle. As long as there aren't any crocs trying to waddle up on me, I'll watch where I plant my feet."

He tilted his Akubra further down over his eyes. "All right then," he said in a relaxed accommodating fashion. "Off you go. If you're feeling disoriented or you run into any trouble just yell like hell. I'll come running."

"I'd prefer if you came driving. At top speed."

"No can do." He crossed his long outstretched legs at the ankle. "One thing you *look* the part." His eyes swept her from head to foot. She was wearing good solid walking shoes, cotton shirt and cotton jeans. On her head she wore a big floppy natural straw hat that dangled chiffon folds she could tie around her neck and even over her face in case of an insect attack.

"Well so long," she said crisply, trying to look like a professional safari goer. "See you in a couple of hours."

"Take your time," he responded pleasantly, easing off his backpack as though *he* had all the time in the world.

For more than an hour she wandered rather than tramped through the wilderness always keeping the table topped summit of the escarpment in sight. The huge diversity of flora was amazing; the great variety of fruits and nuts and gourds which almost exclusively had made up the aboriginal diet. Up ahead she could see the distinctive ghost gums with their shimmering white trunks. Joe had told her Kakadu had species of eucalypts which had never been found elsewhere. She was longing to get to the wetter areas of the park where gorgeous waterlilies wove a carpet across the dark green waters. That was a classic image of Kakadu, the great sheets of water floating their cargo of huge lily pads and exquisite blooms.

The ground cover was becoming heavier, the vines sometimes tripping her up. She saw many many birds but no mammals. They had to be asleep in their hollows. The sun wasn't too hot beneath the trees. Richly scented flowers cascaded some thirty feet down a bush giant, scarlet with cream centres. She stopped to take a closer look but didn't touch. The main reason being she didn't know what sap was poisonous and what was not. Legions of lizards scampered through the fallen tunnels of leaves. Looking up she saw, for the first time, colourful bean shaped pods growing down the barks of certain trees. Edible? She wasn't game to find out. One plentiful shrub dangled small fruit not the usual yellow, orange or bright red, but an incredible indigo blue. She wondered what it tasted like. Walking on, she tried to imagine the place when it was teeming rain. Even now it was warm, humid and *green*. Green smelling. She lifted her head to a branch of a slender tree alerted by a flash of colour.

A kingfisher with a poor little frog in its mouth. There had to be pools of water nearby. Remnants of the last flood topped up by recent storms. The kingfisher's plumage was glorious. A rich violet, bright orange breast, scarlet beak. A fallen tree probably from a lightning strike blocked her path. She would have to go around it. Now and again she had the sensation Ross Sunderland was watching her, but however swiftly she turned, eyes keen, she saw nothing. Not even a swaying frond to betray his presence. Nevertheless she had no feeling of fear or apprehension. She felt certain he was somewhere close by even if she couldn't see him.

Of course she regretted her independent stance. They should be walking through this paradise together.

Dry leaves crackled underfoot as she circled around the decaying trunk that was covered in rich fungi. She was still heading in a straight unimpeded line for the flat topped purple range. This was really the first time in her life she'd been up close and personal with a tropical wilderness. No real predators. No lions and tigers. She hadn't come to the crocs or the wallowing buffalos that did so much damage to the environment. She realised the deadly taipan lived in the Park but hardly anyone saw it. Snakes kept to themselves.

Blithely she continued her walk, imagining how marvellous it was going to be to go swimming at the end of it. Mineral springs. No crocs.

Out of the corner of her eye she saw a long black shadow detach itself from the cover of the trees.

She stood dumbstruck too petrified to move. Then, "Get. Get out of here!" She lifted her arm warningly.

The perentie, the giant goanna, fully eight feet long sheafed in speckled black and yellow chain mail ignored her, holding its frightening stance. She could feel herself shaking as if it were a crocodile. The monitor had such powerful limbs and a strong thrashing tail. Its sharp claws were dug into the track, its purple tongue extended. She knew it could run as fast as a race horse and she knew it could inflict serious wounds if threatened.

She battled to give voice to a cry, but her throat was closed and dry. Where the hell was Sunderland when she needed him?

"Get!" she croaked.

She was wasting time. A split second before the goanna decided to charge Samantha ran, heart pounding. She heaved herself up a tree, fearful the giant lizard would come after her. They climbed trees didn't they? She was mumbling to herself, inching across the branch, adrenalin pumping, hoping to God the limb would hold steady under her weight.

As she drew a tortured breath there came a sound that was stunning in the silence of the forest. A rifle shot tore into the earth a few paces from where the goanna was raised on its powerful legs, ready for battle. A second shot struck a sunken rock ricocheting away harmlessly.

Ross was beneath the tree making a furious hand signal to her to stay put.

As though she was about to disobey!

The goanna needed no more prompting. Alarmed it took off at high speed, crossing the track inches away from where Sunderland was standing, like a gun dog hell bent on retrieving a fallen bird for its master.

"You can come down now, Samantha," he called, cool as a cucumber. "Our friend has moved on."

To *joke! How dared he!* She was deaf in one ear from those

shots. From being frozen with panic Samantha was incandescent with rage.

"Fall I'll catch you," he suggested, holding out his arms.

"Will you just." She launched herself through the air as though she wished to attack him only he caught her, whirling her around and around until she gasped, "Stop!" she yelled at him, kicking and lashing at him with her hands, causing them both to topple over.

She was absolutely *livid*. She wriggled on top of him, straddling him, straining to hold him down. "You rotten, mean, nasty, arrogant son of a bitch! You just stay where you are." She started to pummel him, her breath sobbing in her chest. "You *knew* chances were I might run into that monster."

"Look I'm sorry." He was absorbed in fending her off without hurting her.

"Sorry's not good enough. I've been waiting to do this for ages, you brute. You were behind me the whole time. I mightn't have been able to see you but I knew you were there."

"Top marks for having the sense to scale a tree." He caught her flailing wrists. "You did it in excellent time."

"Ross Sunderland I *hate* you!" The little gold flecks lit up her eyes.

"Let's see if you do." His look of amusement was abruptly extinguished. With one deft movement their positions were reversed. He had her pinned to the ground, looking down on her trembling body.

"Don't you dare touch me," she warned, her senses heightened to the point of pain.

He controlled her easily with one hand, but the distress in her face made him hold back the loud clamour of his own needs. Her straw hat had long since fallen off and one of her copper braids had come undone. "Now that soft growl would have done justice to a lioness," he scoffed, understanding he had to rein himself in.

"That was horrible, horrible." She shuddered. "The bloody thing was ten feet long."

"More like eight," he corrected. "They're harmless to humans unless they're threatened. She might have laid eggs close by. I'm sorry, Samantha. Really sorry. I'll let you up."

"I'll get up when I'm good and ready," she said perversely, the sensuality within not in keeping with her tart words. She studied the curve of his lips. What a beautiful mouth he had, the edges so clearly defined. She lived in hope he would kiss her the hateful beast.

"Yes, ma-am." He looked down at her, achingly aroused, but unprepared to force a response from her which he knew he could surely do. The curve of her breasts showed through the neck of her crisp blue cotton shirt. A button had come undone in their tussle, another strained to come loose. She was wearing a bikini top beneath the shirt in a much darker shade of blue. Her flesh looked so soft and creamy it begged to be fondled. He could feel the delicate weight of her breast in his hand. What it was to be filled with desire and unable to satisfy it.

"You've got no right to scare me." Her whole body was vibrant with nerves.

"Poor baby!" He wondered if the craving was showing in his eyes.

She saw it and her heart tumbled over inside of her. The unexpected tenderness brought her totally undone. Tears sparkled in her eyes.

"Don't *do* that." A muscle twitched just under his skin. His self-control had its limitations. Surely she knew? The magnetism that drew them together could be their downfall. As ever, unhappy memories were sharp and jagged in his mind. Maybe they would be there forever. Love for a woman was wonderful. And treacherous. Who could blame him for being so deeply apprehensive? This beautiful young woman was not only getting under his skin, she was cutting close to his heart. He couldn't seem to do anything to shield himself. She was the *only* one

who had been able to bring the whole protective edifice down.
It set off the roar in his ears and his harsh breathing. God, how
he wanted her!

Samantha heard the little puff of violence in his tone; recognised the sexual hostility, that was somehow incredibly erotic.

"Let me up. It's the heat. Perspiration in my eyes." Her own
fear of defencelessness made her act.

He stood up instantly, pulling her to her feet. "Maybe this
time we can stick together."

"Great idea." She dusted herself off, fixed her plait and
looked around for her straw hat.

He retrieved it, passing it to her. "Give me your pack."

"It's okay. I can keep up."

"*Give* it to me."

She surrendered, not all that gracefully. "Whatever you say,
Boss Man."

He slipped his own pack over his shoulders. "I know you
call me that."

"How do you know? I've never breathed a word."

"I can read your mind," he said crisply. "Have you anything
sweet in this pack?" He began to look inside.

"Some packets of walnuts and raisins," she told him. "Why
are you hungry?"

He made a quick examination of the pack, found the little car-
tons of dried fruit and nuts. "I'm a little concerned about *you*."

"Boy, is that a good feeling," she mocked. "Don't be too nice
to me, Ross. It will go to my head."

"Okay I'll ignore you." Perversely he gave her a glance that
was blindingly sensual. "Let's just get to the falls okay? I need
to cool off."

CHAPTER SEVEN

CLOUDS OF BEAUTIFUL butterflies acted as scouts.

They were passing through an area thick with shooting grasses, pandanus showing fresh new growth and spiky low growing palms of a light green glowing colour. Yellow purple-fringed lilies and their tall upstanding leaves grew as a ground cover, so exquisite Samantha tried her level best not to step on them. It wasn't easy. The plants grew profusely. Through the light scattering of trees was the fascinating spectacle of free standing sandstone pillars, almost like people, quite different from the wedge shaped clay termite mounds she had already seen decorating the plains.

Up ahead a small tree was lit up like a beacon with large pet-alled flowers of a dazzling yellow. She would love to pick one.

"Listen!" Ross took her arm suddenly.

"What?" She stood perfectly still, unsure of what she was listening for. Then she heard it. "The song of the falls." She looked up at him with a beautiful smile, her face flushed, her eyes a-sparkle. "What do you call them again?"

"Ngaru. We're coming to the Ngaru lagoon, hence the birds."

He pointed to the sky, as a flight of magpie geese caught the airstream. "We're almost there."

She sighed blissfully. "I can't wait for a swim. It'll be absolute *heaven!*" Though she had made no complaint—indeed she had been too enthralled with their Nature trek to think of it—she was happily exhausted. A sweat had broken out all over her, dampening her hair and causing her shirt to stick to her. She was glad now she had a fresh t-shirt rolled up in her pack which he was still carrying like it was a paper bag. He on the other hand looked like the six million dollar man. Indefatigable. Not the slightest trace of weariness. He'd have made a great explorer.

Ross took the lead as the vegetation rose up in front of them more luxuriously, parting long luminous grasses like reeds for her to tread through. Used to finding the appropriate words, she thought the wild beauty of their trek was beyond her. She had all but forgotten her encounter with Nintaka, the perentie, better known as a goanna, though there were other less fearsome animals along the way. Once a frilled lizard thinking it had to defend itself, its mouth wide open its neck extended in its characteristic striking "umbrella" had nearly frightened the life out of her but she had managed to swallow down a cry. Kangaroos were more friendly. They stood up on their powerful hind legs staring at them with mild curious eyes; a pair of superb looking golden dingoes moved with complete confidence through their wild habitat, totally ignoring them.

"Plenty of those through the park," Ross told her. "Generally they're pure bred. They hunt alone or maybe two together. You don't see them that often in groups."

"So what do they feed on?" Samantha, like every other Australian had heard the terrible, tragic story of Lindy Chamberlain's baby being taken by a dingo near Uluru.

"Small animals," he told her. "Birds, reptiles. Its not our native species we have to worry about, it's introduced species like the buffalo. They roam wild in the Territory particularly in the region of the Adelaide and Alligator rivers where they do great damage."

"Like what?"

"They wallow in the billabongs turning them into mud pools. They trample the vegetation. That's only the beginning."

"How did they come to be here in the first place?"

He checked a little so she could catch up with him. "They were introduced in the early 1800s from Timor to work the farms. When the settlements died out the bullocks were turned off to run wild. They flourished so much nearing the end of the 1800s they were hunted for their hides and horns. The market didn't decline until the mid '50s. The meat's dreadful by the way."

"But I thought the buffalo was a symbol of the Territory?"

He shrugged. "Well they've gone down in our folklore, I suppose, like the introduced camels in the Red Centre, but regardless both are large-scale destroyers of our fragile environment. Buffalo really are bulls in a china shop. Make no mistake. It isn't just the wallowing and trampling. They eat out the protein grasses our native herbivores depend on. Even the birds are affected by their presence. Don't start me on buffalo. As a cattleman I'm all for culling. They spread bovine disease. That alone threatens our beef industry. Feral pigs create similar problems. We have brumbies on North Star but they're a more limited problem."

"What about man?" she asked quietly. "The mines must have a big effect on the sensitive environment."

"Whatever *I* think," he said, "the fact is the mines are *there*. Ranger, Jabiluka, Jabiru, Koongarra. All we can do is work to minimize the adverse ecological *and* social impact."

"You feel very strongly about it."

"Of course I do. Don't you? This is one of the last remaining great wilderness areas in the world. This is my *home*."

"Well you're a very fortunate man." Her breath was a little laboured.

He stopped quickly and stared down at her. She was fit and she was strong but she *was* a young woman. "This has been a bit too much for you," he said, carrying on his inspection.

"Oh, I'm a bit puffed, that's all. I've been loving it."

His tone combined concern and anger directed against himself. "It's my damned fault," he frowned.

She struggled to stand perfectly upright, shoulders squared. "Ross, relax. I can puff once in a while, can't I? I'm perfectly all right."

"Well we're within spitting distance." He grunted and reached up to hold a low branch away from her head.

"I never knew you were such a fuss pot," she muttered, realising he was genuinely anxious about her.

"I have to blame *you* for that," he returned acidly.

For answer because she was getting to know his ways, she linked her arm companionably through his. "I think you must definitely like me."

He was faintly smiling. "You have heard the saying, she grew on me?"

"Well we do have a lot in common, don't you think?"

"Like what?"

She smiled at him sweetly, her velvet eyes glowing. "Both of us love a swim. What else?"

The sound of the waterfall grew louder. Moments later they were converging on a beautiful stretch of water the milky green of an opal.

Samantha pulled off her straw hat and began to fan herself with the wide brim. "This must be the Garden of Eden," she said with conviction.

"Not an apple tree in sight." Not that he needed any tempting.

"I think that biblical apple tree was more likely to have been a fig tree," she mused. "Look, plums, wild plums," she said excitedly, pointing to a clump of dark purple fruit. "Wild pear as well. I've never seen such a beautiful peaceful spot in my whole life."

He walked across the sand. "There are many like this in the region. Much more spectacular falls like Jim Jim which can only be viewed from a helicopter in the Wet."

"Thank you so much for bringing me." She gazed across table topped rocky outcrops where water swirled and eddied in a series of small crystal clear pools to the deeply furrowed cliff face of the escarpment. It glowed a bright orange in the sunlight with stria of white, yellow and black ochres. Foaming white waters cascaded across the summit and tumbled into the cool palm fringed lagoon below. "I consider it a real privilege to see this. I couldn't possibly have found it on my own."

The peace and the quiet of the place was remarkable; apart from the song of the falling waters and the clear, far carrying call of the birds.

"So, you want a swim?" He glanced at her expressive face, aware the heat had got to her. Despite that, her joyful responses were giving him immense pleasure. City girl she might be but she had a natural deep feeling for this ancient land. "Do you need to change?"

She shook her head. "I've come prepared. Where can we leave our packs?"

"Over there." He pointed to the widest section of sand, scattered with boulders so polished they glittered in the sun.

"Lovely!" Her heart beat speeded up. This was too fabulous to believe in. To be here in this paradise with *him*. Quite alone. She was light-headed with the excitement of it.

A minute more, she saw the long muscles of his sleek darkly tanned back. The narrowed waist. His jeans came away and she saw his strong straight legs, then the taut low line of his swimming briefs. She was half hypnotised by his male beauty. He was a beautiful sexy man. She coloured and felt something like static electricity pass through her body.

"Well?" He glanced back at her with an arched brow.

Her blush deepened, her heart racing as it did whenever he appeared. "I won't tell you," she said. "You're vain enough already."

"Now *that's* funny."

"You must know what you look like."

"Men don't spend their time staring into mirrors."

"Some men do. I know a guy who can't pass a mirror without checking himself out."

"God!" he said with droll disdain.

"So, let me get undressed." Suddenly overcome by shyness she waved him away.

He rolled his aqua eyes heavenwards. "I've already seen you in a bikini that wasn't a bit less revealing than necessary. I've seen your bra top through your shirt."

"This is a more cover-up version," she said, beginning to unbutton her shirt. "You're not going to spring any crocs on me, are you? Because I'll freak out."

"You and me both!" He flicked a derisive smile at her and started to move off. "Don't keep me waiting."

Swiftly she started peeling off her cotton jeans. She couldn't be that close to him. Not all day, without something happening.

They waded into the water that quickly became deep underfoot. It was surprisingly cold considering the heat of the sun was full on it. Samantha sucked in her breath and began splashing water over her face and head so it began streaming water.

"Oh this is what I wanted!" she explained, turning her face up to the golden dazzling sun. "I'm going to swim across to the waterfall, okay?"

"Go for it!"

They both dived together, stroking strongly. It was a marvellous, exhilarating sensation being in the water after the long, hot trek. They swam together towards the falls that up close pounded rather than tumbled into the lagoon. Then they were right inside it, treading water. Samantha laughed with sheer bliss, reaching up to cup the sparkling water in her hands.

"Wonderful!" she shouted from the depths of her exalted state. She felt the energy of the cascading waters crackling deep inside her.

"You can say that again!" He was savouring this just as much as she was, his pleasure in their swim increased many times over by having her with him.

For almost an hour, they sported like a couple of dolphins, gliding through the opal waters, lying on their backs so they could look up at the waterfall. The beneficial effect of the water was acting like a powerful therapy on Samantha's tired limbs. She felt reinvigorated, engulfed in physical and mental pleasure. She had the most wonderful of companions. So in harmony with her surroundings, she began to sing, a lovely old ballad she had learned long ago with the school choir, her voice soaring, pure and true.

He applauded thinking her voice had reached his heart, chasing away all the shadows, lighting up the darkest place in his soul. He couldn't remember when he had had such pleasure in a song, the lilting voice. Even the birds had joined in the chorus.

The song over she was calling to him. "Fancy having *this* in your backyard!" She threw up her arms, staring up at the illuminated cliff face.

The sky was cloudless; the deepest blue. They might have been alone in the garden of Eden complete with waterfall and deep lagoon.

Finally because they were hungry, they made for the shore, the sandy beach a pristine gold carpeted here and there with some kind of aquatic plant with frilly little yellow flowers in bloom.

Samantha pulled the pins from her hair, shook it out, then combed it away from her face with her fingers.

"You've had enough sun, you know," he warned, his muscles rippling as he ran a towel briefly over his body.

She replied with a languorous wave of her hand. "I'm wearing sunblock."

His slanted over her. "No arguments. Sunblock is not enough. We'll eat over there in the shade."

"Okay, boss." She'd brought with her a length of gauze, bright purple printed with huge white hibiscus which she tied sarong like around her waist. It wasn't much of a cover-up, but it would have to do.

"Feeling a bit better?" he asked. He had pulled on his jeans but left his darkly tanned torso bare.

"I feel great," she said, a little huskily, suspended between exhilaration and trepidation in equal measure. They couldn't have been more alone. She dropped her eyes to his backpack. "What have you got there?"

"Fruit," he clipped off, partly because he, too, was on a fine knife's edge. "Apples, bananas, some sandwiches Joe made for us wrapped in a cold pack. Couple of cokes, likewise. A packet of biscuits and a slab of chocolate in with the sandwiches."

"A feast in other words." Her pulses were beating like moths around a light. They were moving towards something momentous. She couldn't step back from it. She kept her eyes down, hoping her lashes veiled the sexual excitement that throbbed through her in waves.

A long swathe of her drying hair fell across her face. Pure copper. Her cheeks had the colour of peaches. Her mouth looked luscious. Had she looked up at that moment she would have seen him openly desirous. The driving need to make love to her had grown into an obsession, but from long habit Ross retained some control. He opened out the packed sandwiches, then pushed them towards her along with a crisp, red apple.

"I think I'll start on the apple first," she said, unaware the upward sweep of her glance was burning through all his defences. She bit into the crisp flesh with her small perfect teeth. "Delicious!"

The shocking thing was the *force* of his need for her. The

muscles of his arms were quivering with emotion. A trickle of apple juice dribbled down her chin and she brushed her creamy skin with the back of her hand.

That set him off. He moved as swiftly and powerfully as a big cat, reaching for her, one hand at the back of her head, the other grasping her around the waist. "You *know* this has been coming. Eve with the apple."

Her heart shook at the expression in his eyes. Their colour was a shock of pleasure every time she looked into them. She had no thought of protest even if she could have induced him to release her. She had *fantasised* about this. Now it was actually happening.

"My God, look at you," he groaned, her hair on fire in the dappled sunlight. "You're as beautiful as an angel."

Playing the angel was totally beyond her. "I'm a *woman* Ross. I don't want to be an angel." Angels didn't have desire moving in a rippling motion right through their body. Angels were chaste, far removed from earthly passions. She stared up at him, letting him draw her more fully into his arms. Her body was trembling, locked in a spasm of excitement as he gathered her in.

She couldn't speak. Instead she buried her face against his neck, aware of the wonderful male scent of him, the warmth of his skin, as she gently gripped his lean hips.

"Show your face to me." He nudged up her chin, with his thumb beneath, desperate to find her mouth; feel her lips give under the weight of his. Above all he wanted her to *feel* as he did.

His heart seemed to slip from behind his rib cage. He bent over her as she clung to him, kissing her for a long time, tasting, tongueing, exploring. That lovely soft, full mouth. Two minutes, three, four? Who was counting? It was ravishing beyond belief, mouth upon mouth, breath on breath. It was a form of expression that gave him heart-stopping pleasure yet soon it wasn't enough. It seemed to him they mated perfectly as though they had prior knowledge of each other. How was that possible?

There wasn't the slightest brush of awkwardness, but instant magic as though their bodies and perhaps their souls were familiars in perfect accord.

Soon he drew back to stare at her, asking what he desperately wanted to know. "How far can I go, Samantha?" There was a hint of desperation in his voice. His hands stroked and slid across her skin hungrily, though he was still walking a tight rope. God only knew if he could regain full control. Maybe he would have to retreat to the tingling waters of the lagoon.

Samantha was shaking so much she couldn't get a word out. Her hair had tumbled to frame her impassioned face. She wasn't a virgin. Her first taste of sex at seventeen had been no wild adventure, just an odd disappointment with a boy she had known all her life. A nice boy who thought she had been as transported as himself.

"What if I never see you again after we leave this place?" she asked with a hint of melancholy.

"Maybe I won't let you go." His hands clenched on her shoulders. "I'll lock you up in the homestead. I'll never let you go back to the city."

"I must know what it is you want of me?"

"Your trust," he said ardently. "We can learn together." Powerless not to, he disengaged her bra top, hearing the catch snap with a faint twang. Her small perfect breasts were revealed. Creamy roses with a wine-red centre.

He lowered his head to her, his heart pounding so hard he might have had a raging beast caged inside of him.

Samantha bit so hard into her bottom lip she almost drew blood, arching her back as he took her budded nipple into his mouth. Ripple after ripple of sensation was rushing into her groin. She could have wept with the force of it. "Be gentle, Ross," she begged, excitement worryingly swamping her.

"Is it against the rules for me to suckle your breasts?" Shivers of pleasure were running over his whole body. He might have been some love-starved fool wanting more and more of her.

He needed to explore her beautiful woman's body, her naked, flesh, her secret places. He was almost beyond thinking now. There was nothing but *sensation.*

"How can I say no to you," she muttered, turning her head this way and that, her eyes tightly closed so she could shut in the ecstasy of his caresses. "But then you know that."

He groaned harshly, lifting his head. "I would never take a defenceless woman against her will. I would never hurt you, Samantha. I speak of *trust.*"

She opened her eyes then to discover a stricken look on his taut handsome face. "Trust there is, but you don't *love* me."

So why was this the greatest rapture he had ever known? "How can I love you when you won't let me?" he accused her.

"But I love *you!*" The words were ripped from her like a rending of flesh. Once said, would she live to regret them?

His face took on a daunting expression. "You don't mean that," he said flatly as though she'd been making a joke instead of declaring her heart.

Something painful heaved in her chest. "Does my loving you make you feel trapped?"

His gaze was turbulent. "If you made a commitment to me I'd *never* let you go. I don't know if you fully realise that."

"You're worried I might *want* to go?" she asked incredulously.

His eyes brooded on her highly charged face. "Why wouldn't I worry," he countered in a sombre voice. "This could all be an adventure for you. Great for a time but could you possibly settle into my kind of life?"

"Some things you can't entirely know, Ross. Life itself is a gamble."

"As far as marriage is concerned, no gamble," he told her bluntly. "Marriage *is* for life."

"So you're thinking more of an affair?" she asked emotionally, aching at that brooding expression.

"Does what we're doing mean so little to you?" he demanded.

"I want you so much I just could damn myself forever. Ah, what's the use!" He hauled her to him, crushing her soft breasts against the hard muscled wall of his chest, revelling in the physical contact. A man would do anything for this.

"Don't turn against me," she begged.

"I think that's impossible," he said in a near despairing voice. He made one last effort to keep control, something inside of him continuing to fight her woman magic. "Is it a safe time for you or could I make you pregnant?" He stared down at her, eyes intent.

He could make me pregnant any time she thought wildly. She *ached* to one day give him a child. Children. Children who would all have his startlingly beautiful eyes. "It's a safe time," she flushed. Was any time completely safe? But the clamouring that beset her were too powerful to be denied. She threw up her glowing head, meeting his steady, questioning gaze. "I'm in love with you, Ross Sunderland, and no other man will do."

His emotions overflowed. "Say it again," he ordered, holding her captive for a moment before laying her on the rug. Her beauty filled his eyes. He looked at the tantalising triangle of blue lycra, all that was left to cover her naked body from his gaze.

"Dare I?" she whispered, transfixed by his expression which seemed to her to be beyond desire.

For answer he began to kiss her, his upper body curved over her, listening to her little moans as he moved lower and lower, the tip of his tongue savouring the silky texture of her skin.

"You're so beautiful," he whispered reverently and lifted her so he could remove the last remnant of clothing that separated her from his loving mouth and his hands.

After hours of driving around in search of potential sites David might want to capture, then more hours filming under a sapphire-blue sky, suddenly they came across some remarkably shaped rocky outcrops too low to be called hills. The surrounding savannah was covered in waving waist high dark golden grasses and beyond that a pocket of luxuriant tropical vegetation, an irresistible oasis.

"We can take a rest here," Joe said, looking across at David. They had taken it in turns to do the driving. Now Joe was at the wheel.

"A cup of tea would go down well," David smiled, each man easy in the other's company.

It was the bloke in the back who set off the alarm bells in the highly perceptive Joe. Something's wrong with him, Joe thought, listening to the warning voices in his head. Made a big deal out of the least little thing. Jealous of Ross, of course. Wanted the young woman, Samantha. Take a lot more than that fella could offer to win such a woman.

He found a parking spot in the shadow of a crouching sandstone monument and cut the engine. "I'll get the billy going," he said.

"Thanks, Joe," David said gratefully. "I can't give you high enough marks for looking after us."

"Long as you're happy," Joe showed his dazzling white teeth in a smile.

"How are *you* holding up, Isabelle?" David opened the rear door and helped her out, while Matt exited the other door in a somewhat stony silence, wandering off.

"Let's say I'm fine and hope to be for many, many years," she answered lightly, not daring to raise her head to him. The very last thing she had been expecting after the terrible trauma of Blair's death was to find another man—and *such* a man! The look of him, the sound of him, his laughter and the warmth of his deep voice—his kindness and his gentlemanly gestures. All this she found powerfully attractive. She might have *dreamed* him up so intense were her feelings. When he was driving she had sat up front beside him, torn between a kind of euphoria and despair that she could feel this way. There was a price to be paid for forbidden longings. The improbable had happened,

she thought with fatalistic acceptance. She had fallen headlong
in love with a man who was almost a stranger. But how could
he be a *stranger,* when he seemed to know things about her she
wouldn't even admit to herself.

A faint melancholy descended on her which David remarked
with a clutch of the heart. He could sense she was upset about
something and he found himself wanting to rock her tenderly
in his arms. The rumours had been utterly wrong. This beautiful young woman was in mourning. She wouldn't thank him
for any action on his part that could be interpreted as intimate.
Intimacy couldn't happen even if she had such a dangerous fascination for him. At such a turning point in her life she needed
her own space.

Sheltered by the sandstone outliers that surrounded it was
a chain of small pools of an entrancing smoky blue that in the
Wet became one large deep billabong. Now while it awaited the
full onset of the rains the fresh water billabong had dried out
to four shallow waterholes some distance apart. Rocky ledges
formed a natural amphitheatre around the banks, the sandstone
studded with chips of quartz that sparkled like semi precious
gemstones in the sun.

Such a lovely place to rest! The ubiquitous pandanus lent a
wonderfully cool feeling to the site. Many of the trees had sent
down prop roots deep into the water. Others fanned their picturesque spikes over the ancient stone benches softening the
contours of the weathered rock. Elsewhere flowering grevilleas, hibiscus and delicate eucalypt flowers stood out brilliantly
against the rich greens of the vegetation and the curious blue of
the water that nevertheless was so clear it was easy to see the
sandy bottom scattered with more chips of quartz.

Joe got the billy going in no time while Matt prowled restlessly around the area trampling bright displays of little pink
and white storm flowers under his heavy boots. At intervals
he stood staring off into the wilderness with a rather fierce
expression on his face. What was he thinking? At one point

David went over to speak to him. Isabelle sat quietly observing without appearing to, watching Matt's thin face break into a smile. He shook his head at something David had to say and Isabelle found herself reluctantly empathising with Matt's position. Clearly he was very much in love with Samantha, a feeling Samantha definitely did not share. She wondered how Samantha's trek with her brother was working out. Well she hoped. She thoroughly approved of Samantha.

In some strange way Matt reminded her of Blair. Blair had that same *tension* inside him, the fear of being a failure, of being passed over. Blair had been plagued by a manic jealousy which culminated in violence. She just hoped nothing would happen to mar their trip. Not that Matt stood a chance of asserting himself over Ross or David. That would be like comparing a cub with two full grown lions. It was tenderhearted Samantha he might threaten. He only had to get her alone.

Isabelle breathed a sigh, watching David return. He made directly for where she sat on the stone ledge, making a sweeping gesture with his arm.

"I could be here a year or more and never run out of sites," he said with the greatest satisfaction. "Everything is progressing so well. I have high hopes for this series." He moved back to sit beside this beautiful creature who would have made the most common place surroundings seem like heaven. "Thank you again for sitting *and* standing so patiently while I photographed you. It couldn't have been all that easy, especially not in the humid heat though you always look as cool as a lily."

"Well thank you, David." She dipped her head. "But goodness I'm used to it. I was born here. I'm a Territorian."

"And it shows. You're so much at home here. Yet you left it for the city. I can't imagine it was easy to replant you. Then again you were embarking on a new life."

"Yes," she agreed quietly, knowing he was desperate not to hurt her by saying the wrong thing. "At the beginning I settled in well." Blair had not revealed his true nature until much later.

"It was a very social life. We were out pretty well every night of the week." Hadn't Blair been hell bent on showing her off like some trophy? "I wasn't used to that as you can imagine, having spent my life on North Star. After a while I have to say all the partying became wearisome. A lot of it was quite meaningless. People can be very insincere. Then again I seemed to antagonise my mother-in-law and because of her Blair's whole family. I know Mrs. Hartmann had already picked the right girl for Blair to marry."

"One no doubt she could manipulate and control," he answered rather grimly.

She looked at him in surprise. "It sounds like you've met Mrs. Hartmann?"

He shook his tawny head. "I have to admit I've heard a lot about her."

"Then you've also heard a lot about me." She had to accept it.

He smoothed over this. "Listening to gossip isn't high on my list, Isabelle. I've told you that."

"Nevertheless I fear you've heard something. You've been so nice to me, David. Going out of your way to comfort me."

"I'd do anything to help you, Isabelle. When I first met you, you seemed to be just coping with the pain. Nowadays you appear stronger."

"I feel it," she said. "I was like someone frozen, but the sun has warmed me through." The sun and *you*. He was always calming her in his powerful benign golden presence. Somehow he had given her back a sense of her own identity. Not Blair Hartmann's abused wife. Isabelle Sunderland as she had once been.

His sense of urgency grew. Could she intuit his powerful desire to hold her close? Day after day it got harder not to take her in his arms. He had never with his passing lovers experienced such a rush of emotion.

For a moment Isabelle felt almost transparent under his topaz gaze. As if all the agony with Blair she had kept so secret, so hidden, might be there for him to see. Somewhere close a bird called. It seemed to be the only sound in this paradise. "I find myself very anxious to correct any false impressions, David," she said. "Your good opinion means a lot to me."

"Hello?" He couldn't help himself. He caught the point of her chin with his finger turning her beautiful poignant face towards him. "Don't you know you've got it."

Of their own accord tears glistened in her eyes. "I've already told you my marriage wasn't working out, David. At least the gossips were right about that."

"And you're blaming yourself?" Reluctantly he dropped his hand.

Her eyes were fixed but blurred. How much could she expose of herself? She felt such shame. Would he feel disgust? "It seems to me I *am* to blame," she said sadly. "Small wonder Blair's mother hates me."

He stepped up his defence. "You had *nothing* to do with his death."

"I know that with my head." She touched a hand to her temple. "In my heart there's a lot of guilt. Blair turned out to be different from the man I thought I'd married. Sometimes I think he only married me to spite his mother."

He frowned at the absurdity of that. "Surely not. I've been told he was passionately in love with you."

"Not me," she said quietly. "Not the *real* me. I, in turn, was quite different from the woman Blair thought he had married. There was a lot of pain in our marriage. Especially towards the end."

"You sound like you felt *trapped*?" He studied her closely, trying to see through the layers and layers of defences she had set up to protect herself.

"I was trying to find a way out of it."

Suddenly she sounded greatly determined causing him to hesitate. This wasn't what he had thought. It was more in keeping with the general view. Her husband had adored her. She had denied him her love. *The Ice Queen* was the label that had been thrown around. Was it *possible*? For all her beauty and charm something about her sent the message not to reach out and touch her. "You never spoke to your father or Ross?" he asked.

His eyes rested on her like a warm golden glow. "The damnable sin of pride."

Pride and vanity. He had seen little evidence of it.

"I've shocked you." For a moment her very soul was naked.

"Hardly shocked, Isabelle," he said. Something far less certain and subtle. An inclination to question. Get to the bottom of it but he had no right. "Unhappy marriages aren't terribly unusual."

"You're doubting that I tried?"

Those appealing eyes couldn't have been more alluring. "I'm sure you did. Nevertheless you've been allowing your feelings of guilt to grow."

"Now why did I start on this?" she asked, a tremor in her voice.

He caught her hand and just barely stopped himself from carrying it to his mouth. "Obviously you need someone to talk to. I think you've learned to trust me."

"In a remarkably short time." Her voice was barely above a whisper.

"And what you might tell me you've never told another soul?"

She winced. "You make it sound like I have terrible secrets."

"*Do* you?" It was worse not knowing. He had to remember she had been abandoned by her mother as a child. That had dire consequences. A replay of the pattern? She had grown up in an all male household albeit a loving and protective one. Her husband, her lover, had failed her. She had failed him. How?

"I daresay all of us take some things to the grave." She looked up as a flight of pure white corellas landed in a stunted acacia covering the branches like so many large floppy flowers.

"I don't think you could have experienced anything *that* bad?"

Misery that only ended with Blair's death. Misery she found she couldn't possibly share. Not even with David. She had to hide the things Blair had done to her though they would stay with her forever. A normal person would consider her either a masochist or a coward. She was neither. Put simply, it was just she had been in such a state of shock, of denial, to cope with Blair when he turned on her.

David could see her withdrawal to a quiet place in her own soul.

"I have to deal with things by myself," she said, turning her head and looking into his eyes. "I have to start a new life. I *have* started. I'm much better being active. This trip is working its own magic. I'm glad I came. I'm honoured you wanted to put me in your photographs. I think I was a little more than the subtle human element, wasn't I?" She couldn't help but know he had used her as a *focus,* the element that drew the eye rather than a background figure.

"Ah, so you noticed!" His deep voice was self-mocking. "You're a very beautiful woman, Isabelle. The camera loves you. Plus you have close ties with this landscape. In fact I'm mesmerised by the way you move about in it. The easy grace and the confidence. The way you *listen* for sounds. Sounds of danger, sounds of pleasure. When I asked for a certain pose today—not easy when you're not a professional model—your concentration was absolute. You worked with me to get the best shot possible. That means a lot. You even consented to wearing this outfit." He raised a fold of her skirt slightly so the sunlight shone through it making it shimmer. Desire closed in. He had to grapple with that like he had to grapple with a monster. "Not your usual safari gear," he commented lightly. He hadn't wanted that look, but something flowing and feminine which still blended with the wild environment. She had chosen wonderfully well. An ankle length skirt and a matching loose top that nevertheless clung to the contours of her body and showed the beautiful shape of her breasts. The material was semi transparent when the sun shone through it, the fascinating black, brown and burnt umber design on the sage green fabric had aboriginal motifs which were outlined in dots of yellow. On her feet she wore ethnic type sandals with the thin straps wound around her elegant legs to mid calf. With her long centre parted raven hair tumbling down her back he couldn't have had a more stunning subject.

Isabelle's blood raced and her heart tingled. He had perfected a lightness and calmness when he was with her but she knew in her heart it was carefully cultivated. Perhaps he felt *exactly* as she did? "And less hot." She smiled. "But the sandals aren't good for tramping. Are you going to shoot more film today?"

"More of the sunset," he said, waving back at Joe who was signalling all was in readiness. "They're unbelievably brilliant up here in the Top End. There's something very exciting in the lighting. I'm awaiting my opportunity to capture a midnight thunderstorm."

She smiled at his enthusiasm. "You sound like you have an endless love for your work."

"Love is the poetry of the senses." He gazed down at her for a moment, before taking her by the hand and leading her the short distance over the sand to the waiting afternoon tea.

Maybe one day in the weeks ahead, as they grew closer, she would confide what troubled her and what had caused her to rebel so violently—and she *had,* for all her reticence—against the confines of her doomed marriage. Only then was he going to do what was in his heart.

CHAPTER EIGHT

GREAT FLIGHTS OF water birds, glossy ibises and pied heron passed to the east of them, boring into the swamps, that were ideal sanctuaries. They were out on a broad tributary of the Alligator river, misnamed by an early explorer who mistook the far more dangerous crocodiles for their less ferocious brothers. Samantha was brimming with bravado and it had to be confessed, tingling nerves as though one of these monsters could attack the launch. During the morning's trip up river she saw for the first time in her life, basking in the hot sun, the giant prehistoric reptiles that had outlived the dinosaurs. Their pale yellow mouths were open even though they were at rest, showing their fearsome teeth.

"That's to reduce the effect of the heat on their brain," Ross told her. "It's called thermo-regulating. It's how they retain a body temperature of around thirty, thirty-two degrees C."

He was talking quite nonchalantly, but he was avidly aware of her as she was of him. *Passion* hummed like a wire stretched taut between them. The rapture of the lovemaking they had shared at the waterfall was the powerful current that fused them together. It kept them awake at night, separated, each in their respective tent, as their bodies longed for release from the never ending pressure of sexual desire.

Now Ross steadied her by the shoulders as she shied back instinctively. "It's okay. We're quite safe."

"I'll have to take your word for it."

He just laughed. As a Territorian he had lived with the presence of crocodiles all his life. Indeed they inhabited his back yard, hidden away in the deep and mysterious lagoons on North Star. No hot and weary stockman out on muster would dream of plunging into one though a visitor in the early 1920s had and paid for it with his life. From time to time horses and even stray cattle had disappeared on the station and the blame was always laid at the jaws of a croc. Kangaroos with their small brains had never learned not to drink from the swamps, lagoons and rivers consequently they often fell prey.

He lifted one hand from her shoulder and pointed as a "big fella" well over twenty feet long began its muddy slide into the water.

"Oh my God!" She shuddered, staring at the huge muscular body with its distinctive gnarled skin. "It's *black* isn't it? I thought they were grey?"

"Grey, dark brown, close to black like that old-timer."

"I've never seen anything so frightening in my life. Imagine being taken by one. It would have to be worse than being taken by a shark."

"You can take your pick up here," he said laconically. "The crocs, the estuarine crocodiles, the salties have no predators outside man. They're feared by all creatures."

"Which doesn't come as a surprise." The crocodile she was watching and David at the front of the launch was filming had submerged. Only its yellow eyes and its high ridged nostrils were visible above the surface of the water like some reptilian submarine. "Easy to see how they sneak up on you." Samantha was experiencing both horror and fascination.

"They float, keeping just the right degree of buoyancy to remain hidden," Ross explained. "Among reeds, water lilies and their pads, any floating debris. Then they spring with astounding speed for so cumbersome an animal."

"And eat you on the spot?" She let out an involuntary moan, thinking of the cases she had read about in the newspapers.

"No. Crocs only eat about once a week. They drown their prey in the famous death roll, dismember them and store them away underwater to eat later."

"How gruesome."

"There's a black side to Nature," he said. "A dark side. Magnificent as the Park is, it has it. In the old days crocs were aggressively hunted for their skins. Handbags, shoes, luggage, whatever. These days they're protected though God knows there are enough of them. I'll all for a controlled cull. I think you'd find most experienced bushmen are."

"So where does the expression 'crying crocodile tears' come from? Do they actually cry?"

He lowered his head closer to her ear, relishing the fresh scent of her. God only knew when they could be alone again. It couldn't come soon enough so urgent was his need. "Only when they've been out of the water for a long time, like in the Dry. At night in the relative cool they race overland from one dried out pool to find another with more water. As a sight, it's extraordinary. They cover the ground with incredible speed, holding those log like bodies up high on their short stumpy legs. Their 'tears' are only a fluid produced by the glands to protect and lubricate the eye. They're not emotional hence the saying. It's the breeding season right now until about April."

"But we're going on land. Surely that's a huge hazard?"

"Don't worry. We'll pick the right spot and the right time. During the breeding season the crocs just like the perentie you encountered become quite aggressive. Dominant males kill other males or badly injure them. The females attack one another as well. Dads are known to eat the eggs or their hatchlings if they can get to them but the female guards her nest well. The much bigger males back down just as a big man can be intimidated by his little wife."

She gave a soft, breathy laugh. "How extraordinary! Praise be there weren't any crocs in our beautiful lagoon. We could have been death rolled."

His voice was dry. "I hate to tell you this, my beautiful Samantha, but saltwater crocs can and do live in fresh water."

"You're joking!" She spun around to face him, meeting his gleaming, teasing eyes.

"Never! It's a myth saltwater crocs are only at home in salt water. There have been many many sightings in fresh water. A lone croc will stake out a lagoon or a billabong for himself at the end of the wet season especially if it has a good supply of barramundi and God help any young male croc who tries to come into the marked territory."

"You're not telling me there could have been a croc at the falls?"

"Would I put the woman I'm crazy about in danger?" He slid his hands around her waist, drawing her back against him.

"Ross…" she murmured.

"It's like a fever isn't it?" he said, his chin resting on her hair. "I want you so badly I'd take on six crocs. I have to find a time we can be together, even if it's only to kiss you. But first we have to lose your boyfriend," he tacked on sardonically.

"It'll be a challenge!" Her eyes moved to the front of the boat. Everyone else was preoccupied, but Matt, was staring their way, his expression masked by the deep brim of his hat.

A trickle like an icicle slid down Samantha's back. This was getting to be ridiculous. Anyone would think Matt was a rejected long time lover instead of a friend she had shared casual outings with. Why hadn't she taken note of this infatuation sooner? Like a blind fool she had drifted thoughtlessly into the path of trouble. She had no wish to hurt him.

Ross, his back to the other man, missed Matt's concentrated

stare entirely. It might have made him call something challenging back. Samantha was all for avoiding confrontations.

In the heat of midafternoon, when the crocodiles indulged their love of a snooze on the banks, the skipper of their charter boat, a wiry little man nicknamed "Goldy" because he had once mined a fair sized nugget on the Queensland goldfields, pulled alongside a timber jetty that looked like it would collapse as soon as the next strong breeze hit it. Ross sprang out of the boat with the rope to tie the motor launch up. Large patches of spiked rushes grew around the bleached grey-white of the splayed jetty legs, the golden tips waving with the motion of the wavelets caused by the wake of the boat.

"All right, ladies and gentleman," Goldy announced, standing on the salt stained deck, feet apart, hands behind his back. "I'll be here, drinkin' until around five-thirty at which time I'd like to depart. Which reminds me, Rossie, darlin'. Didn't yah tell me you'd have a bottle of whiskey for me next time you saw me?"

"A promise is a promise, Goldy," Ross called from the jetty. "I'll give it to you before we leave. No use looking for it either."

"Spoil sport!" Goldy grinned. "Watch where yah put your feet now. See yah all later."

The picturesque pandanus leaned at extraordinary angles the cause of which was the prevailing winds. They stood out black in silhouette against the dazzle of light from the sun and the white sandy beach which was ringed heavily with dark green vegetation overhung by the lacy canopy of trees.

On their trek through the trees the women were flanked by Ross and David, while Joe and Matt brought up the rear. Joe's trained eyes moved everywhere. Along the ground and through the foliage checking out the possible presence of snakes not that they weren't more frightened of humans than humans were of them. But here beside the river, the vegetation was more markedly tropical. The eucalypts that were dominant in the woodlands gave way to cottonwoods and myrtles that soared a hundred feet and more. Great buttress roots impeded their progress, the whole area covered with lichen, mosses, ferns and vines.

They had travelled some distance before they came on a welcome clearing where great banyan trees whose massive bulk could withstand the fiercest monsoon spread their giant arms over a wide area offering shade and a good camp site.

Samantha gave a little exclamation of pleasure. "Aren't they magnificent?"

"According to my people, the Gunwinggu, our 'mother' Waramurungundji created the banyan tree at the very beginning of Creation." Joe supporting himself with a stout branch spoke up. "Our legendary ancestors came from across the sea by canoe from maybe the direction of Indonesia," Joe continued, knowing how eagerly this young white woman received and soaked up the legends and oral traditions of his tribe.

"Hasn't science arrived at similar conclusions," David asked.

Joe grunted wryly. "When Moses led his people out of Egypt, *my* people had been occupying this region of the Alligator Rivers for more than twenty thousand continuous years. We are the *first* Australians."

"No argument there, Joe." Ross turned his head over his shoulder. "Tell Samantha about the adventures of Waramurungundji's husband."

"How I like the way you roll that off your tongue." Samantha was impressed. Some aboriginal names were very difficult. "She had a husband?"

"Wuragag." Joe nodded. "But she wasn't his only wife. He had many wives, wicked old man. Many adventures. At the end of his earthly life he was turned into a high rocky hill which you will see sometime soon. It dominates the plains north of Oenpelli. A lot of white people call it Tor Rock. We call it Wuragag. There's a smaller rock beside it that's his favourite young wife, Goringal."

"And the Oenpelli region is where we'll find much of your great aboriginal artistic heritage, Joe?" Samantha asked.

"Our *major* heritage," Joe answered. "Arnhem Land is very rich in our culture. It houses outstanding rock galleries of great antiquity."

"And we have you to interpret them for us, Joe," Samantha smiled back at him, receiving a beaming acknowledgment in return.

Many hundreds of feet of film had already been shot and packed up ready for processing in Darwin. Almost as many more shots on the digital camera had been printed off allowing them all to see work in progress; David's powerful and often moving evocations of a unique region. The rain forests, wetlands and woodlands, its remarkable flora and fauna, the magnificent bird life, the innumerable species of water birds alighting on lily covered lagoons, the brilliantly coloured parrots and parakeets with their long green and blue tail feathers, the honey eaters, the colourful Gouldian finches, the blue winged kookaburras and the sacred kingfishers, as well as the birds of prey, the eagles, falcons and the osprey.

Today was the crocodile's turn. Ross carried the rifle as a necessary precaution, Joe had a lethal looking hunting knife thrust through his belt. Even Isabelle in safari gear like Samantha had some sort of knife in a sheaf strapped to the tan leather belt around her waist Samantha noted without surprise. Isabelle who was as elegant as any top fashion model was equally at home in this wild bush setting. But then she had been born to it.

"So what's the plan? Where are we going?" Samantha asked, her face vivid with excitement.

Ross shook his head gently. "Not *you,* Samantha. Not this time."

She came back to earth with a great thud. "What do you mean? Isabelle's going."

"Belle *has* offered to stay." Ross turned his head briefly to where Isabelle was passing some piece of equipment to David. "She's made countless forays into the bush in the past. Dad and often Joe used to take us from when we were children. She's had a lifetime of experience. You haven't."

"So I'm disqualified on that count?" She looked at him, temper ignited by deep disappointment.

"Don't take it like that." He gave her the sudden smile that so illuminated his face. "The very last thing I want is to put you in any danger. It's obvious the crocs freak you out and David wants to film their nests."

"He must be mad," she said, fuming at being excluded. "I might have a word with him."

Ross shook his head. "It would do no good. We've discussed it. Neither of us wants to risk taking you. You're very precious."

"Precious be damned!" She stared up at him, more affected than she should have been. "You're fobbing me off. You never wanted me here in the first place."

"Ah, Sam," he groaned.

"Don't 'Sam' me," she said, flushed and hurt.

"It *is* your name. I don't think I've heard David call you Samantha once."

"David's my *brother*. You've had this whole thing planned. You knew on the boat, yet you never told me."

"Hang on," he said firmly. "I should have known you'd have quite a temper." Her hair in fact was a fiery corona in the sunlight. "You've been in on just about everything. This particular trip has been ruled out for a very good reason. For one thing we'll be moving with the utmost caution. Crocs take great exception to anyone approaching the nest. A goanna frightened the living daylights out of you. I can't risk your letting out a scream if you spotted a python, a feral pig or even another perentie. There are plenty of them about. You just don't see them for much of the time. It would be risky to even make a peep where we're going."

"You're making out I'm an absolute idiot."

She went from fire to ice very quickly. "No such thing. All I'm saying is, you're inexperienced in the bush especially in this kind of situation. Think about it, Samantha."

"But I *want* to go," she insisted, not yet able to control her disappointment.

"You're not going and that's the end of it," he said firmly. "I'm sorry. I'll make it up to you. If it's any comfort, we won't be gone long. You can be sure of that. David will have to work very quickly in a dangerous situation but he's well used to that."

She blinked back hot tears, embarrassed they were there. "And just what am I supposed to do while the rest of you have gone adventuring? Sit under the banyan tree and sing calypso songs."

"Why not?" he asked with humour. "I've heard you sing. In fact I'll never forget it. You have the sweetest voice."

"I'll stay right back." She tried a last time, fixing her eyes on his face.

"*No.* You're too used to getting your own way. This one expedition has been judged too dangerous. Please don't take it personally."

It was hard to realise this was the man she *loved!* "Well I *am* taking it personally," she announced, the knot in her stomach working its way up into her throat. "You're such a hero you could carry me on your shoulders."

He studied her with his startling eyes. "You'll have to get your weight down by at least twenty kilos."

She was shocked into incoherence. "Whh-aa-t?"

A smile curved his lips. "A joke, *Samantha.*"

"Well it hasn't cheered me up." Her shoulders slumped. "All right go off and leave me."

"Don't sulk. I only want the best for you."

"Now isn't that fine and dandy. For your information I am not sulking. I am hurt and disappointed. Some days, Ross Sunderland, you remind me of a really big bully."

"When I'm trying to look after you? Have a heart!"

Isabelle who had been watching this mild confrontation and knowing what it was all about, crossed the clearing to join them. "You're disappointed, Sam?"

Samantha tried to rally but found she couldn't. "Well I'd planned on coming, Belle."

Isabelle touched her hand consolingly. "I've been on these trips before. They can get scary, I promise you. No one is doubting you're game for anything but something might cross our path to give you a fright. No one could blame you if you cried out."

"*You* wouldn't react?" Samantha asked, trying to see it through Isabelle's eyes.

Ross cut her short. "No she *wouldn't* Samantha. Accept that."

"Anyway I'm staying with you." Isabelle made the swift decision.

Matt who had been eavesdropping all the while saw his golden opportunity. Oh my, oh my, to get Sam on her own! Wasn't this what he'd been waiting for? He straightened his shoulders, put a winning smile on his face and wandered up to join them. "Did I hear you offer to stay with Sam, Isabelle?" he asked, refinding his old charm.

"Really I'll be quite all right on my own," Samantha protested, knowing Isabelle was only being kind. She really wanted to go.

"You don't have to be," Matt was the picture of supportiveness. "David doesn't need me right now I'm relieved to say, so I'm free to keep you company."

A slight frown crossed Ross's face. "That's nice of you, Matt, but Belle doesn't mind."

To pique him Samantha succeeded in hiding her true feelings. "I don't want Isabelle to miss out on account of me," she said.

"I'm not *that* keen to go, Sam," Isabelle assured her, wary of the way Matt could change his persona in the blink of an eye. Hadn't she seen it all before?

"What's the problem?" Matt turned up his palms, looking

innocently around the group. "Sam and I have shared many a pleasant hour. We're used to being together. We can settle back and relax while the rest of you go in search of where the crocodile makes his nest. As far as I'm concerned it's healthier here."

"So that's settled," Samantha said, making a great effort to appear bright and accepting and actually achieving that end. "Matt and I will remain here until you get back."

David who had finished assembling his equipment came their way. "I know it's not what you want, Sam, but I'd feel much happier if you stayed in camp. Isabelle has agreed to keep you company."

"There's been a change of plan," Samantha gave him an easy smile. "Belle's going. I know she wants to. Matt has kindly offered to stay with me."

Something flickered in David's golden eyes. "Who decided this?"

"*I* did," Samantha lied smoothly before Ross was allowed to break. "You'll only be gone an hour or two. Matt and I can do our own exploring."

"I'd rather you didn't," Ross clipped off.

"It would be best, Samantha," Isabelle offered, more gently.

"We'll be quite happy here," Matt intervened, his expression suggesting he thoroughly agreed with Ross and Isabelle. "A couple of hours will pass in no time at all."

"Better them than us," Matt said. The hunting party had long gone and they had finished exploring their immediate environment without venturing too far. "Crocodiles are too gruesome for words."

"I just hope one of them doesn't decide to go walkabout while their mates are asleep," Samantha said, moving over to the shade of a mighty banyan. It had a great central section of some hundred of trunks and scores of small trunks slender as saplings ringing the perimeter of the trees' branches where the birds had dropped the seeds and the sprouting seeds had taken root.

"Isn't this a fantastic tree," she said, not much liking being stuck with Matt but determined to make the best of it. These days he seemed to be two people. The old Matt she thought she knew and the *other* Matt, a far less pleasant character.

Matt looked up just as the fig like fruit of the banyan dropped to the ground. "Indian, aren't they? I remember a photograph Dave took of one in Sri Lanka. I wouldn't worry too much about crocs going walkabout around here. At least Macho Man knows what he's about. He's bound to have picked the right time and the place to find a nest or two." Matt lowered himself to the sand beside her, thrilled they were on their own at last with no one to disturb them. "I can't imagine why you wanted to go, Sam or Isabelle for that matter although Dave's the big attraction, not the crocs. For some reason she's trying to get her hooks into him."

"And it only took you a half a second to figure it out?" she said in a voice that should have warned him.

"Pretty much." He chewed on the side of his thumb. "I saw how she was with him that first night at the showing. People pressing in on all sides wanting to talk to him but she managed to find his ear."

"I'm not surprised. Isabelle is a very beautiful woman. Men tend to seek out beautiful women. Bachelor that he is, my brother is very susceptible to beauty."

"Well he's bending double to please her." Matt grunted, not bothering to hide his disapproval.

"Why don't you like her, Matt? You're so ready to condemn her when she's so charming and understanding."

"She has a *history,* Sam, remember?" He unsheafed his expensive sunglasses and shoved them on his nose. "Consider the events of her life. The lead up—the broken home. Mother going off. Inevitably that sort of thing has its effect. Hence, the bad marriage. You know the old saying there's no smoke without fire. I don't want to bring this up again, but I think you should be concerned. I know how much you love Dave. You wouldn't want to see him hooked by a woman like that. Women who chew a man up and spit him out."

"That, actually, is your very jaundiced opinion. Are you sure you're not referring to something in *your* past?"

"My past was quite ordinary," he lied. His parents had been too busy battling each other to bother about him. But he had survived them both.

"Anyway, David can look after himself better than anyone I know," Samantha said, intensely irritated by this line of talk.

Matt gave a sceptical shrug. "You said yourself Dave is highly susceptible to beauty. I have to admit she's a looker if you like the type. I see her as a cold shallow person, untouchable, no real feeling or emotion there, yet she's a manipulator of men. Dave's a strong guy, but you should have seen him the day they spent together. The time and trouble he went to, to photograph her. Forget the scenery, it was Isabelle he focused on."

"And it will come out wonderfully," Samantha said loyally. "For the record, and I happen to have met quite a few people in my life plus the fact I'm supposed to be 'highly perceptive' according to one book review, I think Isabelle is simply beautiful. In every way."

"You don't know her." He gave a short bark of a laugh. "Or her brother. There's something about those two. They're heartbreakers. Believe me too many people were of the opinion Hartmann was a nice guy, willing to give her *everything* he loved her so much. It couldn't have been enough. Word is she told him she was going to leave him. I ask you! A couple of years of marriage and she wants out. Sunderland is the big he-man, the macho figure, the bloody cattle baron with a homestead much too big for ordinary people and jammed packed with stuff most people could never afford. Don't get too close to him, Sam. I feel it my duty to warn you. Like his sister I have him pegged for a callous breaker of hearts."

"Could it be you're jealous?" she asked bluntly, not caring

if he was offended. She wondered how far the party had gone. She could run after them.

"Jealous?" Matt repeated the word. "Hell it's more like being flayed alive seeing the two of you together. You'd be better off without someone like him in your life, Sam," he said turning to her urgently. "He'd make a bloody awful husband, arrogant bastard. I care so much about you can you blame me if I feel the greatest concern?"

"Don't do this, Matt," she said.

"I *have* to. These days I rarely get the opportunity to speak to you alone."

Her nerves grated. "It's never occurred to you I can handle my own life? That includes the men in it."

"*Most* men, Sam," he emphasised. "Not this guy. He's different."

"He is indeed."

He took it badly; the soft expression on her face. "I'm only trying to warn you as a friend, Sam. Please don't take it the wrong way."

"So what do you think could happen? Tell me?" she challenged, her warm, musical voice slightly harsh.

He looked back at her, eyes concealed, his thin face colouring up a little. "He's working on you like his sister is working on Dave. He's not married. Why not? He must be thirty or thereabouts? Perhaps he prefers affairs?"

"A lot of men do even when they're married." She said dryly. Her own father among them.

"That wouldn't be *my* way," he said and caught her fingers. She had beautiful hands. He could see one of those slender fingers wearing *his* ring. "You're so beautiful, Sam. I couldn't bear to lose you to someone like Sunderland."

She dragged her hand away, thinking she should get up and run. Why oh why had she acted as if she were quite relaxed about staying with Matt? Because she had wanted to flout Ross. She had wanted to let him know he couldn't control her. "Matt, knowing me as long as you have," she asked with exaggerated patience, "have I *ever* given you reason to believe we could become something more than friends?"

"A man can catch a star, Samantha," he said. "Hold it in his hand. You're not serious about anyone. I've seen them come and go. At least not serious until you had the misfortune to run into Sunderland. You could have any guy you wanted. They were all standing in line but you chose to come out with *me*. You know why?"

"No, Matt, I don't," she lamented.

"It's because you know you can *trust* me." He whipped off his glasses and stared into her eyes. "Can you really and truly say you *trust* Sunderland? He's a wild card. Just look into *his* eyes. Spooky eyes, I reckon. He's a dangerous guy. This trip is nearly over. Dave isn't going on to the Red Centre. He's concentrating on the Top End. He has to be in Brunei early next month anyway."

"I know that. David does discuss his itinerary with me."

"Well then, you know the trip is nearly over. I know he wants to photograph the Arnhem Land escarpment and get to see all the rock art but he's more for evoking the moods of the land. He's already said when the Wet really gets underway he wants to come back and do a lot of filming from a helicopter. Much of the place, the wetlands, will be inundated and the major waterfalls will be inaccessible by land. Dave likes filming things in a completely different way."

Samantha glanced around the broad clearing not quite knowing what she was looking for, but taking stock. "I know my brother's work, Matt. I *sell* it. I've even sold yours."

"Of course you have," he said immediately. "No one better. You do a marvellous job of running the gallery. You must want to go back to it?"

"Anyone can sell, Matt," she pointed out.

"That's not quite true. Not all that many are as good with

people as you are. That's a gift. *I* couldn't do it. I couldn't charm visitors to the gallery into buying."

"David's work sells itself, Matt. I think you're overestimating my powers of persuasion. I could find someone to take over from me. In fact I know someone who could make a change over a smooth transition. I actually want to *write.* Not just children's stories which I enjoy but mainstream fiction. At least I'd like to give it my best shot."

"Good for you!" Matt smiled at her delightedly, looking for a moment his old amiable self. "You need to stretch yourself to the limit. You need to travel. I can see the two of us wandering the world." His hazel eyes lit up. "I know you're attracted to Sunderland now. God knows he's a handsome devil, and he wants as much as he can get of you, but you'd be a plain fool to lay your emotions bare. He'll use you, then when you're gone, he'll pick up with someone else and begin all over again. One day he'll get around to marrying—some suitable girl from a rich pastoral family—someone who understands life on the land. That's the way it goes, isn't it? They marry their own. It won't be *you,* Sam. You couldn't survive the life. You'd wither and die. You're too bright and beautiful—you have too much to offer—to be stuck in the wilds with all your dreams trampled on. You can't have missed he's a domineering bastard."

That really stirred up her anger. "Well he's certainly the dominant male but *domineering,* no," she said forcefully. "I didn't stay back, Matt, to listen to your bitter criticisms of the Sunderlands. I think them unfounded."

"Lordy, Lordy me! Don't get angry. It's because you don't *want* to believe them, Sam."

She made one last attempt to turn him off his line of thinking. "Matt, can't we drop the subject or I might have to take a hike." Surely she could walk a little distance. She could take a stout stick like Joe or maybe pick up a rock for protection. There were plenty of them scattered about.

But Matt wasn't about to be deflected. He wanted to get it all off his chest. "God, weren't you humiliated when he told you to stay put like you were a child?" He sneered.

"This is what's called ear abuse, Matt," she said shortly. "Ross told us to stay put for a very good reason. Both of us are out of our depth in this kind of environment."

"There were nicer ways of saying it," Matt protested, suddenly seizing hold of her wrist.

"Matt, that hurts!" She jerked away, rubbing her skin.

"I could never hurt you," he said, shaking his head from side to side. "I love you. You're magic. I've wanted you ever since Dave introduced us. I've learned to be patient. I have photographs of you all over the walls of my flat."

"*Me?* You *can't* have."

Her lovely face registered not surprise and pleasure but utter dismay. "*Beautiful* photographs," he insisted, stung by the repudiation in her voice. "The thrilling part was you never even knew I was there."

A moan escaped her. "Matt, that's sick."

"Don't spoil anything, Sam." He stared at her with a peculiar gleam in the depths of his eyes. "How do you define *sick* anyway? How do you define love?"

She tried to push up but he pulled her back. "Matt, you're getting right out of line here," she said sharply. "You'd better reel yourself in. The last thing I want to do is tell David you're starting to harass me. I don't think he'd like that." She didn't like to think how Ross would handle it either.

Matt shut his eyes, his expression deeply offended. "Tell me what I have to do to convince you I love you. *Tell* me. I'll do anything."

"Right!" Samantha seized the moment and stood up. "Go jump in the river. It will cool you off."

"It's no joke, Samantha." He stood and took a few threatening steps towards her. "You're mine, Sam. Forever mine. He stole you."

"You're not trying to scare me, surely?" She stared at him, willing him to regain control.

"Be *nice,* Samantha," he begged, giving her the sweetest smile. "Otherwise I might hurt you. I wouldn't want to but your little jabs are coming close to my heart."

"You're losing it, Matt," she warned him. "If I were you, I'd get some professional advice."

"Would you now?" The attractive mask slid off. He came at her at a lunge, determined to knock some sense into her as his father had to do to bring his mother under control, but the little bitch turned on her heel and ran.

"Samantha!" he yelled. "What the hell! Come back."

She stumbled. Fell over a prop root and crashed to the sand.

He was on top of her, his skin paled to a curious grey patched with red. "Samantha what are you doing?"

"What are *you* doing, more like it!" she yelled. "Get off me. Have you gone quite mad?"

"Mad, yes." He struck her across the face, stealing her breath away. "He's had you, hasn't he?" He grasped her long hair, tugging it back painfully as he lifted her face to him. This wasn't working out at all like he expected. *Nothing* was.

Nightmare time Samantha thought, her heart quaking, her voice full of fury and outrage. "How *dare* you hit me. How *dare* you!"

Incredibly he began to mumble. "Oh I'm sorry, sorry. Forgive me, Sam. You made me so angry. It was your fault. You shouldn't do that. Just let me kiss you and make up." He forced his mouth down over her, his teeth grinding against hers, which were clenched tight against the invasion of his tongue. His fingers dug in to prise her jaws apart.

"Planning to rape me, Matt?" she gritted, struggling for all she was worth. She would never have believed Matt was so strong. "Try that and there's nowhere you can run."

He scarcely heard her, trying to fight his old demons. The

black anger that wouldn't die. It was stirring within him, egging him on.

Take your medication and you'll live a normal life, Matt.

He had, with or without it. Until *now.*

The eyes staring back at her were empty. Samantha knew he couldn't get his will to obey him. Let someone come, she prayed, knowing no one was going to come. She had to brave this out. Get through by herself. She had to *fight.*

Silence was so thick and heavy around them their harsh breathing sounded almost inhuman. She feigned surrender, allowing her body to sink back into the sand. His demands were only going to increase.

I won't let this happen. I won't!

She'd have to hit him with something. A rock. A rock big enough to control him. They were all over the place. She spread-eagled her arms as if she were in ecstasy, her fingers searching...burrowing...while she sucked in air between his vile kisses.

Oh, let it stop!

She writhed further sideways pretending emotion was swamping her. He must have been convinced because he began crooning her name, his hand fumbling with the buttons of her shirt, spreading it open.

He lowered his head and she rolled a little more, her body near rigid with horror and loathing. Her fingers continued the search. She felt no inclination to cry. She felt an overpowering urge to immobilise him.

A stone large enough for her purpose miraculously found its way into her hand when she was certain it was a way off.

How had they ever thought this unstable man was *normal*?

Because he had acted normal, that's why.

His primal jealousy of Ross was the catalyst to set him off.

Somewhere a bird shrieked as though there was need for loud protest.

God forgive me! Samantha thought as she struck out.

Out of the corner of a delirious eye Matt Howarth saw her hand rise. He saw the rock in it. Pain burned through him. She had been pretending after all. His heart broke as she struck him midway between his ear and his temple.

He swayed a little, crumpled on top of her, then as Samantha pushed him off violently, he toppled to the sand.

At first she couldn't stand. She was in shock. She tried again. Fell to her knees. Stood up again. Her face was smarting where he had struck her. The corner of her eye was sore.

Get up, Sam.

A voice inside her head gave the order. Strangely it sounded like her beloved Grandad, long dead. Grandad had been a hero who had gone into a neighbour's burning house to save their small child. As a child, herself, he had been wonderful to her.

Get up, Sam. Run. I'll be with you.

I haven't killed him? Please tell me I haven't killed him.

He's not dead.

Matt was breathing. She brushed her long mane from her hot swollen face. "I'm too weak to stand. Too sick."

Who was she talking to?

No you're not! You'll be fine. Go to the boat.

CHAPTER NINE

THEY CAME UPON a nest down stream in the primal fastness of dense green scrub. It was a good distance from where king tides could sweep the structure away. David set to quickly, photographing the rotting pile of dead leaves, grasses, reeds and other dank vegetation. The mound, some three feet high in the middle was shaped like a pyramid, the circumference of the nest a good thirty feet.

As soon as David was ready Joe parted the pungent rotting vegetation that was generating a considerable amount of heat. He dug down carefully, while Ross kept a watchful eye in case the female crocodile decided to make an early return to the nest. Normally there was a certain excitement in these expeditions but today there was a feeling of restlessness, call it anxiety, about everyone and everything. He for one couldn't wait to get back to the camp. Though he seemed harmless enough Ross didn't have a good opinion of Matt Howarth.

The leathery looking eggs, some fifty or more, about three times the size of a large hen's egg, lay in a rough circle. A good many it might seem, but fewer than 1 per cent of eggs laid resulted in mature crocodiles. Muttering in his own language, very slowly and very carefully Joe prised open a shell already cracked and immediately a tiny little monster, exhibiting all the fierce characteristics of the adult began viciously snapping at his hand.

"Savage little beggar, aren't you!" Joe said fondly, handling the little creature gently. He got his thumb and forefinger behind the neck to hold the belligerent little head still for his photograph. "Stay little fella," he cautioned. "I'll put yah back in the nest soon. Mumma will be back."

David gave a snort of wry laughter and took his shots.

"We should pack it in, David," Ross warned a short time later. "Got all you need?" His waves of anxiety weren't altogether connected with fear of their being overtaken by a man eating croc.

"One more, that's it!" David too had been working under pressure, something gnawing away at him about leaving Sam. Not that there was any real reason for concern. Matt would look after her. He doted on Sam. Nevertheless he, like the others weren't feeling the usual exhilaration. They all wanted to get back to camp.

They broke out of the deep green vine shrouded jungle to an empty clearing where the sun had a pellucid brilliance. Everything glittered in the light. The sandy earth, the rocks, the shining leaves on the banyan trees.

No sign of Samantha or Matt.

Anxiety built up quickly, especially when there was no response to Ross's loud bush call. Only wild duck flew overhead in their curious V shaped formation.

"Where could they be?" Isabelle asked the obvious question, her womanly intuition never to be taken lightly going into overdrive. She knew far too much about needy men. The time bomb ticking on the short fuse. Her heart started to thud against her ribs. "Surely they can't have gone far?"

"Sounds travels. They should have responded to my call. It's rough country out there and its swarming with snakes. I told them to stay put." Ross's light eyes glittered beneath the brim of his akubra.

Joe had walked off studying the flurry of imprints. There was a newly roughed up area, deep depressions in the sandy ground. Within seconds he called to Ross who was already heading towards him. "Two lots, boss," he said quietly.

"Man and a woman moving away," Ross muttered grimly. "They're heading back into the rain forest. *Why?* Surely not to the boat?" His face tightened as his nerves began to jangle. "They would have had the sense to stay put."

"Y'd think so." Joe continued to track ahead, eyes scouting around, even his acute sense of smell coming into play. Towards the line of wild bush the sandy loam hardened, the whole area liberally carpeted with twigs, small and large stones, ankle deep fallen leaves.

"No use wasting time talking." Ross muttered, fighting down an unfamiliar sense of panic. If anything had happened to her! He knew he would barely cope with that.

David and Isabelle joined them, both looking ready for a search. "Looks like they've headed back to the boat," David said, his broad forehead pleated in a frown. "Why the hell would Matt allow it? For that matter Sam has too much common sense. To travel with a guide is one thing but Matt's no bushman. He can't even navigate around Sydney."

"Joe and I will track them down. Don't worry," Ross assured him, feeling a great burden of responsibility.

"Easier said than done, Ross. We'll come too," David was caught up in the general feeling of urgency though Samantha and Matt could wander back at any moment.

To a hot reception he thought as relief inevitably turned to anger. "I've found my way through the jungles of Indonesia," he said, looking grim.

"We can't just stand here," Isabelle said briskly, ranging herself alongside David. "You and Joe take one route, Ross. David and I will take another."

"Co-ee if you find them," Ross instructed her, knowing she would do it anyway. "I can't believe Howarth would be fool enough to go back. And why? They were told to stay put. Anyway let's get cracking. We have to find them while there's sufficient light."

Twenty minutes later he and Joe following signs they were trained to see caught up with Matt Howarth. He was staggering around in a circle, within a bamboo enclosure, obviously disoriented and weary to the bone. It wasn't until they were almost on him that they saw the bloodied caked mess on the side of his head.

"For God's sake, Matt, what happened?" Puzzled, Ross moved swiftly, grasping him by the shoulder with fingers like steel. He wanted to yell what the hell did Howarth think he was doing, but with difficulty he restrained himself. Instead he studied the man's injury. It probably looked worse than it was but for some reason Howarth appeared barely recognisable as though his usual persona had vanished. "Where's Samantha? Where is she?" he asked urgently. "Speak up, man. We're worried sick."

"Stupid bitch!" Matt startled them by saying. He was shivering like he had a fever, cursing incoherently to himself.

Ross couldn't help himself. He rammed the other man against a tree, pinning him to it. "Did you have an argument? Is that it?" he asked fiercely. "Did she go back to the boat?"

Matt braced himself as though expecting to be punched to a pulp. Sweat slicked his entire body. "Little fool hit me." He put a hand to his bulging temple, his hazel eyes dull as stones. "Struck me with a bloody rock."

In the one hundred degree heat Ross's blood turned cold. He made a deep growling sound in his throat, battling a powerful rage. Samantha wouldn't have done such a thing unless Howarth had frightened her. *Threatened* her. His free hand clenched into a fist. The other continued to hold Howarth captive.

Joe jumped a large fallen branch to get to his boss. "Steady, Ross, steady." He put a restraining hand on Ross's shoulder feeling the powerful waves of emotion that were running through his body. "Leave the bugger. Push him out of your mind. We're wasting time. We know Miss Samantha passed through here up to this point."

Suddenly the wild bush looked forbidding and inaccessible. A barred prison to a young woman gently reared in the city. Ross stood rigid beneath the old aboriginal's calming hand. Slowly he pulled himself together. The red tide of rage receded. Every second counted.

"Stay where you are," he snarled at the shaking Howarth in a voice that had to be obeyed without argument or question. "We've marked this spot. Don't move if you value your life."

Matt broke into a spasm of wild laughter, sinking to the vine covered forest floor that was actually alive with insects.

"We're going after Samantha," Ross spoke so harshly Matt's laughter ceased abruptly. "You'd better pray she's okay. If she *isn't,* I just could shoot you, you weak, snivelling coward."

Matt lifted his head, his eyes strangely tragic. "Shoot me. You might as well."

"You're not worth wasting a bullet on." Ross spat out.

They all converged on the river bank within minutes of each other, their journey swift and hard in the oppressive heat.

"No sign of anyone," David yelled. "No Sam. No Matt." He thought they must have missed them completely. God knows any set of tracks would be as good as indistinguishable with so much debris on the forest floor and the undergrowth beneath the forest canopy so thickly screened.

"She's been through here," Joe muttered, knowing exactly how and where to look. "She's no fool. I reckon we'll find her on the boat."

Ross let out a harsh pent up groan, dreading that she might

have come to some harm. "Oh God, I hope so, Joe." He felt another terrifying spasm of rage. "If she *is,* she's going to get a good talking to. What the hell went on back there?" His blood burned and he turned away from his old friend abruptly.

"We will see. We will see," Joe soothed him, knowing the terrible upset behind the words of anger. Ross Sunderland had finally found *his* woman.

They all moved towards the jetty, silently praying Samantha would appear on the deck of the boat.

"I think I'll kill Howarth if anything has happened to her." Ross shook his head with a feeling of impotence. "We found Howarth," he called across as the others drew near. "Jabbering to himself in the jungle. Almost incoherent."

"What on earth happened?" David's tongue was like lead in his mouth.

"Samantha must have run away from him." Ross turned, his light eyes blazing. "He pursued her. He's got an almighty lump on his head for his trouble. Apparently she hit him."

David let out a great oath while Isabelle suddenly bent over as though in the sudden grip of severe pain.

Already perturbed, David got an arm around her, supporting her slight weight. "Isabelle!" His voice was a dead giveaway, betraying the depth of his feeling for her. "We travelled too quickly," he groaned. "Isabelle!"

She managed to straighten just as Goldy appeared on deck.

"She's here, she's here!" Goldy yelled, realising how distressed they all were. He waved his arms, beckoning them in. "Where's that bastard, Howarth?" he called. "That's what *I* want to know." Disgustedly Goldy spat on the deck.

"If he's hurt her I'll feed him to the crocodiles," David promised.

Hearing their voices Samantha struggled up from the bunk. She had to think. What could she say? Matt tried to rape her? Something less violent, knowing how they would react to that.

Matt had tried to make love to her? Things were getting out of control so she hit him on the head? They wouldn't believe her. Why should they? She had seen the sick passion in Matt's eyes, his mad yearning for her that was almost a blood lust. He had been determined to have her no matter the consequences.

Her hair was streaming all around her, little bits of twig and dried leaves were still caught in its web it was so thick. She had a red graze on her cheek, numerous little bleeding cuts on her arms from her flight through the forest, the beginnings of what would be a colourful black eye from when Matt had struck her.

You've got to face them, Sammy. You are no way to blame.

Grandad again. He'd always called her *Sammy*. Hadn't he shown her which way to run?

When she made it on deck they all stared at her as though rooted to the spot.

"My God!" Ross paled beneath his tan, a hard glitter in his eyes, his face a graven mask.

"Oh, Sam," Isabelle who had been expecting something bad, nevertheless burst into heart broken tears, realising as only an abused woman could what Samantha had endured.

"Samantha, sweetheart!" For a big man David closed the distance between them as nimbly as a cat. He drew his sister into his arms, hugging her thankfully to him. "You're okay? Tell me," he whispered, shutting his mind against the worst.

"Yes, yes," she reassured him quickly. "A bit knocked about."

"He's going to pay for this," he gritted. "How could I have taken such a viper into our midst?"

Ross did his best to comfort his distraught sister. Belle had been so stoical right through her own tragedy, yet the sight of a battered Samantha had unleashed an uncontrollable tide of grief. A delayed reaction? Fellow feeling?

Hearing Isabelle's pitifully sobbing, Samantha entirely forgot her own woes. Gently she broke away from David's embrace moving across the deck to her friend's side. "Belle, dear,

I'm okay. Really I am." After one brief searing glance, Samantha averting her eyes from Ross standing on the other side of Isabelle, so tall and dauntingly remote. "I'm so sorry I gave you all such a fright." She put her arm comfortingly around Isabelle's narrow waist, herself upset by the misery that contorted Isabelle's beautiful features. "Come with me, Belle. We both need rest."

Isabelle, still sobbing, went willingly.

The men watched in silence for a while. "Well she's safe," Ross muttered finally.

"Howarth still has to be dealt with," David said. His strongly hewn face took on a disquieting cast.

"I'll go back for him," Ross said.

"Risky the way you feel." David gave a grim smile.

"I'll go with you, Boss," Joe, on the point of exhaustion, volunteered.

"I'd rather you stay here, Joe," Ross said, gripping his old friend's arm. "I think you've done enough for one day."

"No matter." Joe shook his snow white head.

"If you're worried I might harm him in some way, I give you my word I won't. Or not much."

"I'll come with you," David said decisively. "We can keep a brake on one another. Besides, you'll need another pair of strong hands, Ross. Sam's okay. I can tell. She always was a feisty little thing. It's Isabelle who appears to be in the greater pain."

"I'll watch over them Boss," Joe promised. "I'll see they're both all right. You watch over yourselves, okay?"

"S'truth! I need a drink," Goldy said hoarsely. "I hadn't counted on this. A beer for you, Joe?"

Joe nodded. "I reckon."

Ross and David swiftly exited the boat, pounding down the jetty. What it was to be young and strong as a bull buffalo, Joe thought. He'd been like that in the old days. He watched as they disappeared into the olive green line of wild scrub. Whether

Howarth was going to cop a few punches or not Joe knew he wouldn't want to be in the sick bugger's shoes.

Nothing was the same any more. That one ugly incident changed everything. They all returned to Darwin. Ross and David took charge of the disgraced but queerly unrepentant Matt Howarth, dropping him off at the hospital where he was subjected to a thorough physical and mental evaluation. On no account had Samantha wanted to press charges. Not for Matt's sake—he deserved no consideration—but for her brother's and her own. The story would inevitably make the newspapers. She couldn't have that. She wanted to blot the whole thing out. Matt would never come near her again. She prayed he would never harass another young woman but his fixation appeared to have been solely with her.

As it turned out Matt had a medical record going way back. He had been diagnosed bipolar in his late teens, a diagnosis reaffirmed after he'd had his nervous breakdown. According to his own account he had been on and off his medication ever since, citing negative side effects he couldn't tolerate. The only problem was he had difficulty controlling his behaviour when off it. How he had sustained his injury—which Samantha was grateful had proved not all that serious—was skirted over. He had become disoriented in the bush, remembered falling over, crashing into something hard. Maybe a rock. In the absence of a conflicting account, his was accepted.

David despite his intense anger and feelings of self blame waited around Darwin just long enough to see his flawed protégé out of hospital, complete with medication and into a motel where he was left to get on with his own life.

"So you never want to see me again. Is that it?" Matt, incredibly, appeared to think of *himself* as the victim.

"Much better that way, Matt," David told him, keeping his face expressionless when so much anger, disappointment and disgust, was upon him. "You abused Samantha's trust. My trust.

It could all have ended very badly only my gutsy sister was able to limit the damage. I wouldn't show my face around the Territory again. Get your things together and clear out. Take good advice. Stay on your medication. This is Sunderland's part of the world. No way has he forgiven you. In fact we've decided it's safer if he doesn't come near you. Come anywhere near Samantha again and you'll answer to us both."

It was Joe who drove Isabelle and Samantha back to North Star while Ross and David turned the film already shot in for scanning and tied up a number of loose ends. No way could anyone pretend they had the same enthusiasm for the project. Matt's brutish behaviour had shocked them all. They needed to mark time for a while. Perhaps when David came back from Indonesia where he had a long-time commitment.

A big perhaps!

Samantha had the dismal feeling Ross would never consent to her joining another expedition. In fact it seemed like it was all over for them so withdrawn had he been in the wake of Matt's attack. No words of comfort for her. He *couldn't* be blaming her for what had happened.

Isabelle had tried to console her. "How could you think such a thing, Samantha? I think it struck my brother hard, if anything had happened to you...!" She left the rest unsaid as though Samantha only had to open her eyes wide enough to see the reasons for Ross's seemingly perverse reactions.

After almost a week the men returned home while Isabelle and Samantha, closer than sisters, ran together to greet them. Samantha went to her brother first who slipped an arm around her waist and hugged her. They had spoken daily, sometimes twice daily on the phone so she was up to date on everything that was happening.

"Ross?" Finally she turned to him, her eyes searching his darkly handsome face.

"Hi." He acknowledged her. No smile, but a piercing, comprehensive gaze, noting no doubt how quickly she had healed. "How are you?"

"Fine."

He nodded approval. They went forward to the front steps of the homestead.

Behind them David reached out a long arm for Isabelle who seemed to float into what could only be interpreted as an embrace. He couldn't prevent himself. He kissed her cheek, inhaling the lovely natural fragrance of her skin and immediately drew back. This woman affected him like great music affected him. She touched his heart and his mind and his soul. "I didn't like to be away from you both," he told her quietly. "You were so terribly upset before we left. How are you now?"

"Much better." She smiled up at him, recognising and accepting she loved this man. Whatever the outcome. It wasn't something she had asked for, or something she felt she deserved. It was Fate. Just having him beside her was enough. He was so powerful yet so gentle. She revelled in his bearing, so close to *regal* it didn't matter but absolutely natural. If only such a man had entered her life before Blair! *If only...if only.* The journey through life was paved with *if onlys*. But what an enormous difference that would have made. She would have been spared so many ugly experiences. She would have been able to act more openly. Often over the last few days she had come to the brink of telling Samantha of the brutality of her short marriage but at the last moment drawn back. Why heap all that on Samantha's graceful shoulders? Samantha was carrying her own burden and carrying it well.

Without thinking Isabelle caught David's large handsome hand linking her fingers through his. He looked down at the beautiful face at his shoulder, drawing in a sharp breath. This one small gesture he found terribly important like a long awaited message. On a wave of elation he bent his tawny head over hers saying in a low, telling voice: "God, I've missed you."

"I've missed *you*." She let out a long fragmented sigh, the

faintest flicker of *fear* could it possibly be? in her luminous upward glance. He couldn't understand it, but whatever it was it
was unbearably moving.

He lifted her slender fingers and kissed them gently. If there
was a direct way to this woman's heart he was going to find it.

They ate dinner in the breakfast room, carrying their steaming
fragrant coffee out onto the rear terrace where the great copper
moon of the tropics lit up the garden and illuminated the seat-
ing area with its attractive rattan furniture. David and Isabelle
kept the conversation going. Ross from time to time joined in.

The great talk of the Outback at that time was not just the
death of a legendary Territory figure and cattle baron, Rigby
Kingston, but the shock distribution of his will. All the Territory knew there were skeletons in the Kingston closet; Kingston's elder son and heir had been killed a decade or so before
in a light aircraft crash which for a time had caused murmurs
and it now came as a shock that Kingston's granddaughter Alexandra had been nominated chief beneficiary. Overnight she
had become an heiress and a prime candidate for one of the
most eligible young women in the country. Still it was impossible for most people to imagine a slip of a girl would be able to
take over the running of a vast station like Moondai, much less
want to if she was anything like her social butterfly of a mother.

"Daniel's not going away in a hurry," Ross said briskly, referring to Moondai's highly rated overseer, Daniel Carson, Kingston's former right hand man and not yet thirty. "He'll hold the
fort until a good professional manager can be found. That's if
Daniel doesn't want to stay on."

Isabelle nodded agreement. "I remember Alexandra as a little
girl," she said with warmth. "She was a great little rider, won
quite a few prizes, something of a tomboy, her father adored
her."

The subject of the Kingstons was gradually dropped; another
picked up. Ross launched into a story about the "man with the

Midas touch," another rich Territory tycoon called Moreland. Samantha was reminded how the Outback seemed to breed men that were larger than life. Small wonder she thought. Such men were the descendants of the early pioneers and settlers; men who had overcome every obstacle the vast, dangerous, inspiring and heartbreaking Territory, the last frontier, could throw at them. Against all the odds they had not only survived but gone on to found dynasties.

She rested her head back, conscious nostalgia mixed with a strange exhaustion was working its way through her veins like a drug. She knew Ross was deliberately maintaining a front, but that wondrous tangible connection that had been between them appeared to have been broken. David and Isabelle on the other hand radiated a *togetherness* that was quite striking. They didn't have to tell her they were in love. That was as plain to see as the moon that sailed above them. She couldn't really see how Isabelle had fallen deeply in love so soon after the death of her husband. Obviously it wasn't something Isabelle had *wanted*. As had happened in her own case both of them appeared to have surrendered to a kind of biological demand. Nevertheless she was very happy for Isabelle and her much loved brother. They seemed to have been made for each other. As for her and Ross? She had chosen a far stormier path.

David's voice drew her out of her reverie.

"...well we can pursue the possibilities," she heard him say. "What do you think, Sam?"

"I'm sorry." She had to clear her throat. "I must have drifted off. What was it you were saying?"

"It doesn't matter, pet," David said kindly.

She touched her hand to her temple. "I have a slight headache. It's the heat."

"We're due for a storm," Isabelle predicted. Certainly it was on the air. Already clouds were ringing the moon.

"If it's okay with you all, I think I'll have an early night." She was apologetic.

Ross glanced over at her. "Why don't we go for a walk?" he suggested. "The night air might shift it. It's much too early to turn in." His glance cut sideways to David, certain David wanted desperately to be alone with Isabelle.

"Okay," she answered gracefully, determined not to run away from him.

Ross put out his hand. She let him take it. No way was she going to allow him to upset her. She had to speak to him. Draw him out into the open. Only then would she know what she had to do.

No sooner were they on the path than he let go of her hand.

"What's wrong between us, Ross?" She plunged right in. "Clearly something is."

"Well if that doesn't take the prize," he groaned, his vibrant voice was strained. "Howarth bloody near raped you and I'm supposed not only to let him get away with it but forget about it?" Couldn't she understand how a man felt when his woman was attacked? It had torn the heart out of him and caused such a harsh reaction. But that was him. His love for her had drawn him in too deep.

"*I* have to," Samantha protested. "So how is it *my* fault?"

"I never said it was your fault," he answered curtly, his nostrils flaring. Inside he was lit up with an enormous rage, powerless and frustrated that he wasn't able to make Howarth pay for attempting a crime he could have got away with. He was angry with Samantha too for giving him the greatest fright of his life. She had only stayed with Howarth to pique him never dreaming Howarth would try to hurt her. He had to shut out that dreadful scene as he had imagined it, before it drove him mad.

"Well you've retreated from me, haven't you?" Samantha was saying. "You've gone away. Do you do this often? Get a woman to fall headlong in love with you. Fall in love yourself but can't sustain it."

"Stop talking nonsense," he said bluntly, feeling absolutely hellish.

"I'm talking commitments, Ross," she retorted, flaring up. Both of them were incredibly on edge. "That's not nonsense. I thought what we had was *real*. Very serious."

He stopped in the middle of the path, his lean muscular body in silhouette against the moonlight. "When the woman you love is attacked by another man it cuts into the deepest most primitive part of you. Surely you can understand that?"

She stared up at him, aware of his tormented expression. "I do. I *do*, Ross. It was terrible what happened but it could have been so much worse."

"Isn't that what I'm saying," he retorted bleakly and continued walking. "You never have said just how far he got?"

What had been hazy was now clear. "Ah, Ross, are you doubting my word?"

He was wracked with powerful emotions. "I just don't think I could live with it."

Hot tears sprang into her eyes. "Would I have lost my value?" Her tone spoke volumes. "I'm sullied. I'm spoiled? Is that it?"

"You don't know what you're saying, or I'm not communicating what I feel," he gritted, feeling like he was shut in a cage and couldn't get out. "I can't come to terms with Howarth getting away with it. The punishment should match the crime. Or the attempted crime. He was on the brink of it when presumably you hit him?"

"I had no option, Ross," she said. "You got a few punches in, I believe." David had told her.

"So I did. Do you blame me? The sick bastard had absolutely no remorse. It was as though he had a *right* to do what he did. I know a guy who suffers from bipolar disorder. A nice guy. A hard worker. No way would he act like that. Howarth is plain crazy."

"So what did you want to do, *kill* him?" she asked raggedly, her emotions getting the better of her.

His face hardened. He turned away from her. "Very much so, except I'd have to come down to the level of the beast. Sometimes it's hard fitting into the dictates of civilised society, Samantha."

Her heart ached so much she felt like weeping. They were drifting so far apart. "I'm so sorry, Ross."

He let out a frustrated breath. "Your being sorry makes no sense. You were the *victim*."

A breeze loaded with ozone floated around their heated bodies, but it didn't damp down the fierce emotions. "He got no further than some awful slobbering kisses and he touched my breasts," she confessed, painfully, aware he was desperate to *know* the extent of the attack. "I *had* to act passive. I *had* to let him until I found some kind of weapon. Even though he was trying to do the unthinkable I didn't want to kill him. I wanted to disable him so I could get away."

"You were very brave." She had earned his respect. But he was still angry with her as though she had failed some test. What was the matter with him, for Chrissake! She was the innocent victim. There were always men like Howarth. He was sickened and horrified even when he wanted to treat her so tenderly. He could see the glint of her tears.

Love was terrible.

He couldn't think of a life without her. Yet his anger was driving her away when he should have been embracing her. He had to be insane.

"I wasn't brave." Samantha shook her head in denial. "I was charged with adrenaline. I don't like being the powerless female."

"I think we can now all safely say you're not." He sighed deeply in the darkness. "You're telling me the truth about this? All of it?"

She waited a moment to compose herself, a dismal melancholy well and truly descended upon her. "I'd be a truly remarkable woman had I been damaged further and was still able to function the way I have since. My whole heart goes out to rape victims. It's an unspeakable ordeal. The fallout goes way beyond a violated body right to a woman's soul."

He groaned in empathy. "Which was *precisely* why I felt like killing Howarth. His lack of remorse was the most unforgivable part. I can't help wondering if you should have pressed charges?"

Warily she looked at him. "Would you have wanted that?"

"I would have stood by your decision," he said firmly. "It's like I've said. These sort of crimes—intended crimes in his case—shouldn't go unpunished."

"Ross, I had to make the decision I thought in the best interests of us all. I wanted to avoid the notoriety." Her voice cracked. "Besides, the deciding factor was, I got away."

He laughed angrily, frustration a knife in his guts. He knew it had been a bad, *bad* idea to leave her. "What a miracle that was. Not only did you get away from Howarth who in his manic state was hard cnough for David and me to control. You found your way through the jungle. I mean you know *nothing* about the bush. Inexperienced stock men sometimes get lost."

"My Grandad showed me the way," she said, praying he wouldn't reject such a notion scornfully. "Grandad was always there for me when my dad wasn't. Grandad was talking to me the whole time."

"Samantha!"

The sudden solicitude in his voice brought the tears to her eyes. He wasn't openly sceptical. He merely sounded…indulgent. "He really did," she said. "Grandad reaffirmed what I believe. Death isn't the end for us. We move on to a different dimension. I wasn't hysterical. I realise you might think that. I was sick and shaken but I had my goal firmly in mind. I did what Grandad told me. I made it back to the boat."

He let out a long suffering sigh. He had relived her flight through the jungle many times. Marvelled she had found her way out. It looked as though she had had help. "Well incredible as it may seem we have your Grandad to thank for that."

"You don't believe it?"

He gave the ghost of a smile. "Maybe. What's important is *you* do." He put out his hand in reconciliation but for some reason she couldn't begin to explain to herself Samantha went into retreat. She jerked back, too close to disintegrating. "The old servants' entrance is over there, Ross," she said, turning her head. "I really do have a headache. I'm going to bed."

David and Isabelle lingered on the terrace, in their armchairs, each basking in the glow of happiness the other gave them. Isabelle for her part felt like she was emerging like a butterfly all velvety and new from her spent cocoon.

"Ross is pretty upset," David remarked eventually. "The whole incident with Howarth shocked him to the core. Not that anyone could blame him. A man would do *anything* to protect and defend the women he loves."

She fixed her eyes on the arching sprays of some flowering orchids. How beautiful they were. How serene. "Not all men are like that," she said. *Don't panic. There's absolutely nothing to panic about. This is David.*

He wouldn't be judgmental.

Her tone was so serious he seized on it. "You've known someone like that?" He turned his chair slightly, so he could face her directly.

She was done with pretence. This was the man she loved. She had to be entirely honest with him. "I was married to one," she told him as quietly as if she were talking to herself.

"Isabelle!" He reached out and took her hands. "What are you saying?"

She gave a sad smile, staring down at their locked hands. "Nothing thousands, maybe millions of women couldn't say. I was in an abusive marriage, David. That's why I went to pieces when I saw what Howarth had done to Sam."

"My God!" His expression turned stony. No wonder Ross had been boiling with rage. All set to pummel Howarth into the ground when he had urged some restraint. "Do you want to tell me about it?"

"I have to."

"Come here to me." He saw the stricken look on her face. He stood; gathered her up like a defenceless small girl and carried her back to the huge bucket chair where he could cradle her.

She placed her head in the hollow of his chest, drawing heavily on the comfort he gave her. "I've never been able to tell anyone else—not my dear father nor my brother. I was too ashamed. Too worried what they might do. You see how Ross has reacted to Samantha's trauma. He's traumatised himself. I trust you, David."

"You're *right* to," he said, kissing her hair. He was enormously grateful she had decided to liberate herself from her dark secret. And with *him*.

"In a way you've healed me." She curled into him like a long lost rescued child. "I know I don't look like a woman who would tolerate physical and mental abuse but I'm ashamed to say I was. At least for some time. It didn't start until six or seven months into our marriage then everything started to go wrong. No one could have been more jealous or possessive than Blair. We were out practically every night of the week. He acted like he adored me, but I couldn't do a thing right. The abuse started the moment we set foot inside our door. The first time he hit me I was shocked out of my mind. I couldn't believe it. I was married to a batterer. Who could believe it? He'd been so charming, so loving and considerate throughout our courtship. He didn't *look* like a man who could abuse his wife. Most people thought I was extremely lucky to have married him."

"My God!" David had heard all those stories. Had even given them credence.

"Afterwards—after these episodes—he appeared to be genuinely sick with shame. He showered me with presents. Promised he'd never do it again. Of course he did. Gradually I began to hit back. It was all so degrading."

"My poor Isabelle!" he groaned, feeling shame for his own sex. Men *were* the aggressors. It was a miracle she hadn't wound up dead. And to think Hartmann had fooled everyone with the Mr. Nice Guy persona. There was a parallel with Matt. Some men really did lead double lives.

Isabelle lay against David's powerful muscular chest, hearing the rhythmic thud of his heart. "He told me if I tried to leave him he would kill me."

"What miserable cowards these men are!" He released a long breath. "Isabelle, you really should have told someone. Your father or after he was gone, Ross."

"I'm *never* going to tell Ross," she shuddered. "He wouldn't believe I couldn't turn to him for help. Think how upset he is about Sam. I was too proud, David. Too unwilling to admit I'd made a terrible mistake. Another thing, I'm not going to burden Ross with what happened to me. I love him too much. But I can't pretend with *you*." Her voice trembled with emotion.

"Because I'm going to be your lover, your husband?" he said with a sense of the inevitability of it all. This woman was infinitely precious.

"Do you want to be?" She couldn't look at him. She had to *feel* his response.

"Want to be?" he echoed, the longing he felt for her welling up. "I've waited this long. Not a second more. Kiss me, Isabelle," he said, masterfully. He lowered his head, his blood *glittering* there was so much passion, unerringly finding her lovely upturned mouth.

Desire took his breath away. Desire mixed with a kind of agony. How much horror had she endured, this exquisite creature? The reason why she had dissolved into heart breaking sobs on the boat was fully explained.

Nothing remotely like this had ever happened to Isabelle before. The boldness, the sweetness, the flavour of real passion. She had grown used to Blair calling her frigid. Kissing had never been like this with Blair, even at the best of times before they were married. Even the early on sex didn't come near it. This was sensual bliss, for the moment all-consuming.

They held each other as if drowning in a sea of rapture, each unable to get enough of the other. Kisses without pause. Sublime kisses when two lovers passed into a brand new world of their own.

"Will you?" David's strong hand trembled over the curve of her breast. "Will you marry me? I know it's not long since... since." He found himself unable to speak Hartmann's name he felt such repugnance. "You deserve happiness, Isabelle. No waiting. No fake mourning period. You *escaped*. You deserve the right man to love you. I swear I'll spend my whole life making it up to you. I love you, Isabelle. Something momentous happened to me the moment I laid eyes on you."

"And me." She placed her hand along his cheek, close to weeping with joy.

"You'll come to Indonesia with me?" he urged, looking into her beautiful eyes.

"I'll come to the ends of the world with you," she said simply.

"My *love*," he answered, profoundly moved.

"Stay with me tonight," she begged, taking a few shallow breaths just to calm herself.

"Is it what you truly want? You're not saying it to please me?"

"To please *me*." She gave a broken laugh and spread her fingers lovingly along his strong jawline. Her David. Her lion. "I love you, David," she said, speaking with her whole heart.

"What have I done to deserve you?" he swiftly countered. "What was it you told that cowardly cur you married that sent him storming out of the party?"

She drew a jagged breath. "I was cruel."

"Don't!" He rejected that entirely. "You couldn't be."

She shuddered. "I told him that I was leaving him that very night. I wasn't coming home. I'd made arrangements I would never come back to him and if he threatened me I'd go to the police, his boss, his mother, his family, everyone he knew and tell them what sort of man he really was. Something about me must have convinced him I really meant it. Had I told him when we were alone in our home I'd have risked my life."

His heart contracted at a possible truth. "Instead you started to get your life on track."

"With Blair out of the way, yes. I'm as sure as I can be, he didn't intend suicide," she said. "I've thought and thought about it. He *had* to live to fight another day. Such was his tormented nature he wasn't going to give me up. We were both destined to live in a dark, dangerous secret world. His death was an accident."

"And you're asking me to keep what sort of man he was a secret?" He tilted her chin, made her raise her eyes to his. "I don't know if I can do that, Isabelle. My role is to protect and defend you."

"But Ross would know," she said sounding distressed about it.

"Ross will internalise it and understand," he said firmly. "You had found the courage to leave Hartmann. Personally I'd like to shut a few people up. For a start that appalling woman Evelyn Hartmann. No one is going to spread false rumours about my wife. You have to leave it to me now, Isabelle. Will you?"

In the half light his eyes glowed golden. "Yes, David," she said.

CHAPTER TEN

THE STORM BROKE with tremendous power some time after midnight. Such was its savagery Samantha felt a shuddering wave of panic. Storms could be extremely destructive leaving people to not only mop up their homes but their lives. She rose from her bed where she'd been tossing and turning fretfully, to go to the high arched doors that led onto the verandah. She literally jumped as thunder rolled across the heavens then broke asunder with a tremendous cracking noise like forest giants being felled. The tall pier mirror behind her turned a blazing silver, reflecting the electrical power of the lightning bolt that drove through the highly charged atmosphere to plant its spearhead in the shuddering earth.

She padded out onto the verandah in her bare feet, drawing back almost instantly as the rain came down, suddenly chilling and remorseless. Its deep throated roar seemed to her excited imagination like an army on the march. The wind *shrieked* above it. The force of it almost took her breath away. She couldn't imagine what it would be like in a cyclone. Terrifying! She dared not go near the balustrade. Rain enveloped the immediate world. Driving walls of water that almost immediately began to challenge the guttering of the huge roof. It didn't seem possible the guttering could handle such a massive volume of water. She had a nightmare moment when she thought the roof could collapse.

The hem of her nightgown, lifted, fluttered, whipped around her body, already soaked. Not that she cared. The power of the storm was so mesmerising even as she trembled before nature at its most frightening and majestic she continued to stare out in thrall, her vision periodically seared by the great jagged flashes of lightning. This side of the homestead had to be exposed to the worst of the lashing. Sheets of water drove across the verandah intimidating her to the point where she fell back against the shutters. She didn't want to close them against the spectacular theatre of the storm, but she would have to before the rain entered the bedroom. It was utterly black out there. Black and silver. To be out in the storm's fury!

"Samantha?"

Even through the cacophony she heard his voice. She wasn't dreaming. She turned her head in its direction, her heart heaving a great surge of elation at the sight of his tall hard muscled figure striding along the verandah towards her. All she had wanted was for him to come to her.

Yet his manner was far from loverlike. "What the hell are you doing?" he demanded, gathering her up and drawing her back forcibly into the shelter of the bedroom. "Don't you know when a storm is in full swing you can be struck by lightning?"

"What?" she asked dazedly. "It comes in under the roof?"

"You bet your life it does. Lightning can reach you if you're standing in front of a window *inside* a house. I just knew you'd be out here lapping up the pyrotechnics."

"Well, they're pretty impressive aren't they?" Her nerves were screaming like the wind. Excitement whipped up in her at a tremendous rate, fraught with sexuality. She had him all to herself, quite alone in her lovely bedroom. She had to make the most of it. She had to get through to this complex man that she *loved* him. That no secrets were hidden from him. They could make a good life together.

"You're wet." He ran his hands in a near frenzy down her slick arms, his proximity to her rendering him as weak as Samson shorn of his mane.

"So are you," she stood on tiptoe to whisper into his face. "Who cares?"

"I have to close the shutters," he said tersely, turning his dark head, a man drunk on beauty. Dazzled by it. "At least for a while. We'll have to make do with the ceiling fan."

"You're going to *stay* with me? I thought you'd decided it was time for me to get out of your life?"

"Don't start," he gritted, already on razor edge. She shouldn't tease him when he felt this way, strung out with yearning, his blood roaring in his veins.

"Don't close them yet," she begged. "Let's watch."

"Then I'll hold you." His hand closed tightly over her shoulders as a fierce white light lit up the world. Rain streamed across the broad verandah. "A minute more." He couldn't help but understand her excitement. Her excitement was his. And much more. It was a provocation, almost a directive to action he couldn't ignore.

"Just the two of us together." She smiled back up at him, a smile that drew him like the moon draws the tides.

"Didn't you call me?" he challenged tautly, doing as desire commanded. He turned her fully into his arms, pressing her wet body against his, consumed up by his own arousal.

The stimulation was *violent*. His blood heated to sizzling point. There she stood within his embrace, near naked except for a froth of silk. Wet silk he could so easily rip from her. The passion for her he had been holding under such tight rein broke loose like a wild stallion that would not be controlled.

The rain was heavier now. Deafening. He groaned softly, feeling the answering tension in her body, painful, *sublime,* tension as great as his own. She seemed to have lost weight since her ordeal. He could feel her nipples flooded with blood hard as berries against the palms of his hands. Her breasts were smaller he thought taking their delicate weight. The heat in his body rose to a fever. He could feel her ribs through her satin skin. He let his hands slide down to her narrow waist, over the curve of her hips and thighs unable to stop himself from directing his caresses to the heart shaped apex of her body.

"Do you want me?" she whispered, drawing a shuddering breath.

"I want to keep you forever," he muttered almost fiercely into her neck. "I'll *show* you!"

Energy seethed and snapped around him like blue burning electricity. The storm was forgotten. He was bewitched. With one movement he pushed the wet nightgown down from her shoulders, letting it pool at their feet.

An elemental flash of lightning picked her out like a spotlight. She looked *exquisite*. Lovely luminous face. Beautiful small breasts, rosebud nipples, tapering waist, delicate hips, sex hidden by wisps of gold, slender sculpted legs, high arched feet.

"Samantha," he breathed, lowering his mouth to hers while she swayed into him, twining her arms around his waist.

Passion poured into her so she felt her legs would give way. She clung to him as though he was all there was in a rocketing world.

"My most beautiful Samantha."

Her breath caught. How the passion and the tenderness in his voice worked on her! The bloodrush to her extremities!

His tongue was filling and exploring her mouth. She opened it wider to receive such ecstasy.

"You want to torture me, do you?" he muttered strangely.

"Never! I want to *love you.*" She felt weaker and weaker, sinking deeper into his embrace. The fierce tug of contractions began deep in her womb. The pain and the pleasure. His mouth was taking her very soul.

Roughly, his movements spurred by his desperate passion and

all the little exciting sounds that issued from her throat he lifted her effortlessly and walked back to the bed and deep shadows. In sheer abandon he threw her onto the tumbled bed watching her roll away from him across the coverlet.

That would never do. He wanted the two of them together. Fused. As one. He wanted her to open her heart and her mind and her body to him.

Another clap of thunder bombarded the house. They heard it but it didn't distract them.

"Why have I got my clothes off when you've got yours on?" She lifted herself onto one elbow. "Come close to me, Ross. Please come. I want you so badly. I hate it when you're angry with me."

How shamed he suddenly was. "Not angry with *you*. Angry with myself. I've had demons to fight."

"Then let me help you." She held out her arms.

"You're a sorceress!" Her body was glistening like a pearl.

"*Your* sorceress. No one else's."

"Then you'll have to prove it," he said a little raggedly. He stripped off his shirt and sat on the side of the bed.

She was eager to help rid him of his clothes, coming behind him and laying her heated face against the breadth of his back. Not satisfied she inched closer spreading her slender legs to encircle his hips. "I love you madly." She rained kisses on his velvety skin, loving the very smell of him, the glowing masculinity.

"Aaah!" His breath seeped from him in a long voluptuous sigh. He threw back his head back, revelling in her attentions. After a moment she rose up onto her knees, leaning against him. "Do you love me? I know at first you didn't. You didn't even *like* me."

He turned his head so their mouths could meet. "Liking didn't even enter it," he told her moments later when she was lying across his lap. "I wanted you from the moment I laid eyes on you. As well you know."

"Do you remember our first kiss?" She would remember it for centuries.

"I'm still marvelling," he exclaimed as he stood, turning her over onto the bed. He was seized by the desire to be as naked as she was. "You don't think I'm going to let you tease me all night?" he asked, staring down at her.

"I love to tease you." Fever flooded in. Sweet intoxicating fever.

"Well I've *come* for you," he said. Swiftly he stripped off the rest of his clothing and stood before her, a marvellous looking man his erection full and hard.

"Now's *my* time," he murmured in the deepest, most seductive voice. He sank onto the bed, pulling her in his arms, immersing himself in her fragrance. "Oh God, that's *so* good," he groaned. "Just to touch you is to solve all my problems in one swoop. I love you, Samantha," he said with boundless tenderness.

Her heart jumped into her throat. "Repeat that please."

"I love you." His tone was even more darkly erotic.

"And I love *you!*" She hugged him closer, insides melting, her joy was so extreme.

"Go on," he commanded. "Tell me. I'm your perfect mate."

"You *are!*" She let her hands move luxuriously over him in perfect freedom. "No other man in the world will do."

"That's good, because I cannot, *will not,* share. You're mine."

He held her face to him and Samantha's eyelids fluttered then closed.

It seemed to him he was *starving,* ravenous for sex with this *one* woman favoured above all others. All other thoughts, all the impotent rage that had given him hell all week fell away. They were *together.* That was all that mattered. The world was washed clean.

His hungry mouth began a long voluptuous slide down over her body, opalescent in the semi-dark. "Trust me, do you?" Quickly he raised his head.

"With my life." Her fingers sank into his thick curling hair. Emotional tears sprang to her eyes, as all her senses heightened into an exquisite, excruciating awareness.

"That's good, because I want you for life," said he tautly. "I've struck gold, Samantha, with you. I'll never give you up."

"As long as we both shall live?" She put all pretence aside.

He was still for a moment, his face resting against her thigh. "Yes." It was said very quietly but it resonated like a vow.

"Then that's all I could ask."

Outside the tumult of the storm grew less and less. The distant roar of thunder began to fade away. Every tree, every shrub, every flower to the blades of grass glistened and glinted with rain. A crush of scents entered the room. Petals, aromatic herbs, exotic fruits.

Out of love and need, their courtship continued to undeniable delight and it had to be said, growing frustrations. Spread eagled on the bed, Samantha couldn't stifle her tiny, high pitched moans. The teasing was so exquisite it was quite simply an agony. Once she tried to speak but instead exhaled deeply, the hollow of her back arching up from the bed as he tongued her most secret place.

Sensation flared into flames miles high.

"If anything happened to you I don't think life would mean anything to me." He lifted a face taut with passion. "Do you *know* what that's like for a man?"

"But how could I replace you?" Samantha spoke up, though she couldn't seem to get her voice above a whisper. "I've told you what you are. You're *everything* to me."

"Then we ought to get married." He stated what he so fervently wanted.

Samantha's eyes went wide. She lay there, stunned, speech for the moment beyond her. Then a tremulous query, "Ross?"

"I thought I was making that clear, my dearest heart," he said gently. "I'll make it formal. Will you marry me, Samantha Langdon? Will you become my beloved wife?"

She repeated the wondrous words like they were the lyrics of the most beautiful love song every composed.

"Yes, marry." He laughed at her reaction, rising up so his powerful torso was suspended above her, supported by his strong arms. "You're not allowed to say no."

"Would I dare?" She gave a little broken laugh, rapture pulsing through her making her entire body glow.

"Not if you're longing for more love making, you won't!"

"Then it's yes!" Everything about her bespoke her delight. "Yes, yes, yes."

"Perfect." He allowed himself to collapse full length beside her, turning again on his side to face her. "Then that's settled."

"Not yet," she whispered. "Continuing to make love to me was part of the bargain."

"Which of course I intend to honour." He wound her long hair around his fist. "So…first your face—" he caressed, stroked, kissed her face all over "—then your neck….no, I'm rushing things…your lovely mouth…" Long moments later… "Your breasts…how the nipples flare to my touch…the curve of your stomach, so smooth…" More kisses that moved downwards. Exquisite. But they soothed her not at all.

"Come to me," she begged, her limbs flailing in mounting ecstasy.

"Don't cry."

"I'm not crying." But she was. "Please…" Her voice trailed off as he took hold of her body and entered her powerfully.

Two bodies. One flesh. A ritual when performed with love that is indeed a consecration.

Outside in the rain washed sky the moon made its reappearance from behind a bank of clouds as if on cue. It shone far into that enchanted night. On Isabelle and David, asleep now after making love with such tenderness and mutual adoration. Isabelle on her side, her dark head pillowed on his shoulder, David on his back with one arm draped protectively around her.

On Samantha and Ross lost in the magic of their passionate coupling.

Fate had brought them all together. Their entwined futures were thus laid out. The moon, a fabulous illumination in the dark wind tossed night, was witness to that.

* * * * *

Her Outback Protector

CHAPTER ONE

Darwin Airport
The Northern Territory
Australia

INSIDE THE DOMESTIC terminal Daniel surveyed the swirling crowd. A full head and shoulders over most people he had an excellent view over the sea of bobbing heads. He was confident he'd spot the girl, technically his boss. There were tourists galore. Most were probably headed for the World Heritage listed great national park, Kakadu, but many of the faces in the crowd were familiar; Territorians returning from a stint in the big coastal cities of the eastern seaboard; business, pleasure, maybe both. Striding along to the check-in counter, where his charge had agreed to be, a booklet on the Northern Territory in hand, he constantly exchanged waves and friendly calls. He was a familiar figure himself after nearly six years of working for Rigby Kingston, a pioneer cattleman recently deceased. His allotted chore for the day was picking up Kingston's long estranged granddaughter, Alexandra, and ferrying her back to the station.

She could have flown to Alice Springs. That would have been a lot closer to Moondai. It was a bit of a haul from Darwin in the tropical Top End of the Territory to Moondai in the Red Centre but he'd managed to kill two birds with the one stone, dropping his leading hand off at RDH, the Royal Darwin Hospital, for a deferred minor op and picking up the girl who had made the long trip from Brisbane. But surely even a city girl would appreciate the magnificent spectacle of great stretches of the Top End under water? That was what she was going to see. Vast swathes of floodplains teeming with nomadic water birds; chains of billabongs floating armadas of exquisite multicoloured waterlilies; the western fringe of Kakadu, the North, East and West Alligator Rivers snaking through the jungle. That stupendous panorama, especially the endless vistas of waterlilies and the thundering waterfalls of the Wet were to him as much an enduring image of the Top End as were the crocodiles.

They were into March now. The Wet, the *Gunemeleng* as the aboriginals called it, was all but over. Two cyclones had threatened the tropical North, one extremely dangerous. It had put Darwin, destroyed in Cyclone Tracy in 1974, on high alert. Mercifully cyclone Ingrid had taken herself off into the Timor Sea, but not before dumping torrential rain over the coast and the hinterland. That same deluge, more than they had seen in decades, had brought life-giving water to the Red Centre. The Finke, the oldest river on earth, ninety-nine per cent of the time dry, was now flowing bank to bank. These days it thrilled him to fly over it rejoicing in all the waterfalls that ran off the ochre coloured rock faces into serene green gullies.

Born in tropical North Queensland not far from the mighty Daintree rain forest he had become used to the desert environment. It was very, very special. Maybe the girl would think so, too. After all she had been born on Moondai and spent enough years there to remember it.

"Dan!" A voice boomed.

A passenger off the Brisbane-Darwin flight, a big affable

looking man, pushing sixty with keen blue eyes threw out an arm. It was Bill Morrissey, a well respected member of the Northern Territory Administration.

"How are you, sir?" Respect and liking showed in Daniel's face.

They shook hands. "Hot and tired." Morrissey wiped his forehead with a spotless white handkerchief. "What brings you into Darwin?"

No harm in telling him. "I'm here to pick up Alexandra Kingston and deliver her to her family."

"Lordy!" Morrissey put a hand to his fast thinning hair as though to check it was still there. "Wouldn't like to be that poor child! Not with those relatives. Rigby's will would have totally alienated his son and grandson and let's not forget the second wife, Elsa. I have to see it as an angry man's last response. Rigby cut his family out of the main game even when it's a fact of life dynasties die out without sons to take over. Daughters tend to walk off with some guy out of the family field."

"True," Daniel acknowledged, having witnessed that scenario first-hand. "But in all fairness to Mr. Kingston, Lloyd and Berne aren't cut out to be cattlemen. Maybe Mr. Kingston made demands on them they simply couldn't cope with, but they have no taste for the job on their own admission."

"Well, they could never be carbon copies of him," Morrissey replied. "A lot of rich families produce at least a couple of offspring who have no head for big business. Now the girl's father, Trevor, *was* shaping up to be a chip off the old block. Tragedy he was killed. It happens in our way of life. You're still going to be around, though, aren't you, Dan? Can't see how they could possibly do without you. You might be young, but you're up there with the best."

Daniel heard the sincerity in the older man's voice. "Thanks for the vote of confidence, sir. I'm committed to one year at least under the terms of Mr. Kingston's will."

Morrissey clamped a hand on his shoulder. "Trust Rigby to

ensure the transition would be smooth. With you at the helm, or guiding the girl into getting a professional manager they might be able to get by. How old are you now, son? Twenty-seven, twenty-eight?"

"Twenty-eight." Sometimes it seemed to Daniel he had to be at least double that age, he had seen so much of life.

"Do you have any idea how well regarded you are?"

Daniel gave his very appealing, crooked grin. "If I am I'm very glad. I've worked hard."

"That you have!" Morrissey agreed, knowing the full story. "Rigby certainly thought so and we all know how demanding he was."

"He wasn't loved, that's for sure!" Daniel agreed wryly, "but I always found him fair enough and willing to *listen*. One of the things that made him so successful I guess. He never had a closed mind, even for a relative newcomer to the game like me. Besides I've learned to love the Territory. It's my home now."

"And the Territory needs young men like you," Morrissey said, comfortable with the mantle of mentor. "Young men of brains and vision. You've got both." He thrust out his hand for a final shake. "Best go now. Can't keep the chauffeur waiting. When you're next in Darwin come and see me. When your twelve months are up I guarantee I'll find you something to suit your talents."

"Might hold you to that, sir." Daniel grinned.

Morrissey began to move away, then paused, looking back. "By the way, Joel Moreland has expressed a desire to meet you. Not for the first time I might add. The Big Man's heard about you. Now he wants to take a good *look* at you. You could be in luck, there, my boy. Moreland is a Territory icon. I'll set it up for lunch. Just the three of us."

"That's great!" Daniel was surprised and deeply flattered. It never hurt to have friends in high places he thought as he strode off. Joel Moreland was known in the Territory as the man with the Midas touch. Not one of his many ventures stretching back forty years and more had failed. Not that the man with the Midas touch hadn't known his own tragedy. Moreland's son and heir, Jared, had been killed in a freak accident at an Alice Springs rodeo well over twenty years before. Apparently he had put his own life on the line to save a cavorting teenager from a maddened bullock. The Grim Reaper no more spared the lives of those rolling in money than he did the poor.

Well *he* knew all about being poor but strangely he'd never developed any lasting complexes about it. He was a fighter. He'd spent much of his childhood fighting for the honour of his pretty little mother and the good name some callous guy had stripped from her without looking back. People didn't label the illegitimate *bastards* any more. It was politically incorrect. When he was a kid growing up in a small, redneck Queensland town, they didn't give a fig about that.

From very humble beginnings he had made something of himself. He'd had help. Everyone needs a little help. Even the strongest couldn't do it on their own. A Channel Country cattleman called Harry Cunningham had given him and his mother that helping hand when they were so down on their luck he'd been filled with fear his vulnerable mother would resort to taking her own life. Harry Cunningham had been their saviour, the man behind his education.

"You've got to have an education, Dan. You're smart as they come, but education is everything. Get it. Then you can pay me back."

Well he had paid Harry back, reviving the fortunes of Harry's run-down station only to have Harry's daughter, his only child, sell the valuable property within a month. Some sons-in-law proved themselves to be eminently capable as substitute sons but as Bill Morrissey had pointed out this particular daughter had married a city slicker who had shied away violently from the prospect of taking on a cattle station. Far easier to take the money and run.

It was Harry's glowing recommendations that had come to

the ears of his late employer, Rigby Kingston. That's what had gained him a job on Moondai, rising to the rank of overseer. It was *he* Rigby Kingston had looked to. Not his remaining son, Lloyd, or Lloyd's son, Bernard. It wasn't often a man bypassed the males of his family to leave the bulk of his estate to a grand-daughter, moreover one who had been banished. What was his reasoning? Did Kingston secretly want his heirs to *fail*? Having been robbed of his favourite son, Trevor, the girl's father, the rest could go to hell? Rigby Kingston had been a very *curious* man. Yet tyrannical old Kingston had left him, Daniel Carson, a nobody, however dramatically he had risen, a handy little nest egg of $250,000, on top of his salary, on the proviso he remain on Moondai as overseer for a period of twelve months after Kingston's demise.

It was all so damned *bizarre!*

It didn't take him a minute more to spot the Kingston heiress. All five feet two of her. Her slight figure, standing brolga-like on one leg, was a few feet from the check-in counter, booklet on the Territory in hand. He didn't know what he had been expecting. An ultra smooth city girl in expensive designer gear. There were plenty of them about. It surely wasn't *this!* A cute little teenager—okay she was twenty, nearly twenty-one, but what the heck, she didn't look a day over sixteen and she was showing at least five or six inches of baby smooth skin between the end of her T-shirt and the top of her tight jeans. He took in the delicate coltish limbs, jeans sinking on nonexistent hips, the T-shirt blue with a silver logo on the front of her delicate breasts, gentle little rises beneath the clingy fabric. She shifted one hand in her hip pocket, apparently searching for something but as he closed in on her she raised her cropped head and literally *jumped.*

What the hell! He wasn't such a dangerous looking character, *was* he? Maybe his hair was overly long. It was very thick and it grew at a helluva rate and there weren't too many hairdressers around Moondai. He had lived with his image so long he couldn't really tell how he presented. Perhaps seen through those saucer eyes staring at him he looked a touch wild; eyes that were so big and radiant a blue they dwarfed her other small features. Except maybe the mouth. Not a trace of lipstick so far as he could see, but then makeup was a mystery to him, but beautifully shaped. He had a notion he was staring back, but she was *such* a surprise packet.

Obviously she didn't agree with the notion that a woman's hair was her crowning glory, either. Hers was cut to within an inch of its life. Buttercup-yellow, curling in the humid heat into a cap of pretty petals. A few escaped onto her forehead. What was the definition of sexy for God's sake? Against all the odds Miss Alexandra Kingston, looking like she wasn't all that long out of school, fell into that category.

He collected himself enough to tip a jaunty forefinger to the brim of his black akubra. It felt like he *towered* over her all the more so because he was wearing high heeled riding boots. He scrutinised her shoes, soft moccasin kind of thing. "Ms Kingston?" he asked, trying to keep all trace of dryness out of his voice and not succeeding all that well.

"Sandra, please." She cleared a husky throat. "No one calls me Ms Kingston." Her hand rose defensively to her neat little skull as though to check on an unfamiliar hair style.

Probably just cut it, he thought. Unceremoniously with a pair of nail scissors like an expression of rebellion.

"I *am* an employee," he pointed out.

"Hey." She shrugged. "I said you can call me Sandra."

"How very egalitarian. Dan Carson." He introduced himself. "I'm your overseer on Moondai and your chauffeur for the day. I'm here to transport you to the station."

"Transport?"

He saw her gulp. "Now why make it sound like you're going on a road train?" he chided gently. Road trains that transported anything from great numbers of cattle to petrol were an awesome sight on Outback roads.

"I was worried about the word, *transport,*" she said smartly.

Her voice all of a sudden had an unexpected *bite* to it, an *adultness* that had him re-evaluating her. "Set your mind at rest. We go by helicopter," he told her. Could there be a trace of *hostility* in those bluer than blue eyes? "I had to drop my leading hand into RDH for a minor op so it was convenient to pick you up and bring you home."

"How kind." The expressive voice turned sweetly acid. "Only Moondai's no home of mine, Mr. Carson."

"Please—Daniel." He dipped his head. "I'm not in *my* element with Mr. Carson."

"Great! I'm glad we've got that sorted out."

So it *was* antagonism.

"Actually I thought Christian names might be beneath you." She was desperate to cover up the fact she felt as if she'd been struck by lightning. Daniel Carson, her overseer, was a marvellous looking guy with Action and Adventure emblazoned all over him. He'd make the perfect hero in some epic movie, she thought. Dark, swashbuckling good looks, splendid body, commanding height. The aura was *mesmerising,* but his manner was definitely nonthreatening.

"Nothing so old-fashioned," he mocked gently, looking towards the luggage carousel. It was ringed by passengers all staring fixedly towards the chute as though willpower alone would cause the luggage to start tumbling through. Every last one appeared to be in a desperate hurry to be somewhere else. "The baggage hasn't started to arrive as yet," he commented, unnecessarily, just making conversation. "How many pieces do you have?"

"Just the one," she murmured, so overloaded by his presence, she transferred her attention to the milling crowd. Multiracial. Multilingual. English predominated; a variety of accents, Aussie, Pommie, New Zealander, American. Lots of backpackers.

A group of handsome Germans, speaking their own language, which she had studied for four years at high school; Italian, Greek, Scandinavian, ethnic groups from all over the South-East Asia region.

As the gateway into Australia, Darwin, named in honour of Charles Darwin, the famous British naturalist, was a real melting pot; a far more cosmopolitan city than her home base, Brisbane. In fact it had the *feel* and even the smell of Asia. Hot, my God, how hot and such *humid* air! Almost equatorial but somehow vibrant, the scent of jasmine, joss sticks, spices; beautiful golden skinned Asian girls, dead straight shining hair sliding down their backs, strolling by in little bra tops with tiny shorts, a trio of older Asian women wearing gorgeous silk tunics over trousers.

She saw her overseer, Dan Carson, pause to smile at an attractive flight attendant who came over all giggly and flushing. Who could blame her, Sandra thought, wanting to put an instant stop to it. "Hi, Dan!"

"Hi, Abby!" His eyes eventually moved back to Sandra's small censorious face. Mentally he began to rearrange his first impressions. Young she might be, but she was as sharp as a tack. "You believe in travelling light?"

"Surely it's one of the great virtues," she told him loftily, shocked by that irrational flash of jealousy. Where in the world had *that* come from?

He digested this by compressing his quirky mouth. "Not especially in women. They generally travel with mountains of luggage."

"You'd know, would you?" Another haughty look as like a replay, two more attendants smiled and wiggled their fingers at him while he grinned back, saluting them with a forefinger to the broad brim of his hat already tipped rakishly over his eyes. Not only her overseer but a playboy of sorts though there was something almost mischievous in those grins.

"I'd say so." He turned back to her.

He used that flashing, faintly crooked white smile like a sex aid she thought looking on him sternly. "Well I'm not staying long."

"How totally unexpected." He couldn't keep the mockery out of a baritone that flowed like molasses. "Seeing you've inherited the station and all."

Sandra's eyes glowed the blue of a gas flame. "So what are you saying, that's *amazing*?"

He shrugged. "No more than if you said you'd climbed the Matterhorn on your own. Still, I'm sure your grandfather had his reasons."

She gave a cracked laugh. "He did. He hated me. Now he's gone he wants Moondai to go to wrack and ruin. Then again, my grandfather never could miss an opportunity to cheat the family out of their expectations. How did he come to hire *you*?" She met his eyes squarely, not bothering to conceal the challenge. "Surely there's Uncle Lloyd and cousin Bernie to take charge?"

"Both of whom prefer a different lifestyle," he returned blandly. "No, actually the job got dumped on me."

"You don't sound as though you expect to lose it any time soon?" she cut in.

Pretty perceptive! "Now this is the tricky bit," he explained. "Under the terms of your grandfather's will I can't check out for at least twelve months."

"What?" She rammed both hands into her jeans pockets. Her waist was so tiny he knew he could span it with his two hands.

"You didn't know about it?" The way she tossed her head reminded him of a high stepping filly.

"My mind went blank after the first few minutes of hearing the will read."

"Pays to listen," he commented briefly. "Ah, the baggage is starting to come through. Let's go." He grabbed hold of her soft leather hold-all and slung it over his shoulder. "You can point out which suitcase is yours when it arrives. Or is it a backpack?"

"It's a designer case," she said flatly.

"Sweet Lord!" Try as he might he couldn't prevent a laugh. "Envious?"

"Not at all."

"You'll be happy to know it's not mine," she said waspishly. "A friend of mine lent it to me."

"That surely means your friend likes you?" he asked, amused by their disproportionate heights. She was a *tiny* little thing. He could fit her into his back pocket.

"He *loves* me." She stared straight ahead, almost trotting to keep up with him and his long, long legs.

"Loves you?" he repeated, as though amazed she was ready for romantic love. "Would this friend be your fiancé?"

"He's gay," she said quite patiently, considering how she felt. Outside, all mock toughness and tart banter. Inside, a throbbing bundle of nerves.

Daniel took up a position beside the carousel as the throng miraculously parted for him like the Red Sea for Moses.

"He's nearly eighty," she continued, trying to keep her attention on the circling luggage when she felt like flopping in a heap. It had been a long, long trip from Brisbane. Another one faced her. She was terrified of light aircraft and helicopters. With good reason. "He has his Abyssinian cat, Sheba, and he has me. We're neighbours and good friends."

"So where do you live?" he asked mock politely, lifting a hand to acknowledge yet another enthusiastic wave from the far side of the luggage carousel.

All these women trying to communicate with *her* overseer, instead of getting on with their business. Sandra fumed. She didn't feel in the least good humoured about it. An attractive redhead this time, who seemed to have peeled off most of her clothes in favour of coolness. It was irritating all this outrageous flirtation.

"You don't need to know," she told him severely. "But I'm desperately missing my flat already."

"Like the older man do you?" he asked, rather amused by her

huffiness. It was fair to say she didn't *look* like a considerable heiress. She didn't dress like one, either. She was definitely *not* friendly when he was long used to easy smiles from women.

"The older the better," she said with emphasis. "You seem awfully young to be overseer of a big station?" She eyed him critically. He radiated such *energy* it needed to be channelled.

"I grew up *fast*," he answered bluntly. "I had a very rough childhood."

"That's hard to believe." He really was absurdly good-looking. Hunk was the word. Stunning if you liked the cocky macho male always ready for the next conquest. "You look like you were born to the sound of hundreds of champagne corks popping...already astride your own pony by the time you were two."

He smiled grimly. "You're way off." He watched the expensive suitcase tumble out onto the conveyor belt, getting exactly the same treatment as the most humble label.

"So there's a story?" Why wouldn't there be? He looked anything but dull.

"Isn't there always? *You've* got one." He pinned her with a glance and a rather elegantly raised eyebrow.

"Haven't I just." There was a forlornness in her eyes before the covers came down.

He hefted her heavy suitcase like it was a bundle of goose down. "Listen, how are you feeling?" he asked, noticing she had suddenly lost colour.

"Quite awful since you ask!"

Such a tart response but he didn't hold it against her. "Did you have anything to eat on the plane?"

Dammit if he didn't have a dimple in one cheek. "A big steak," she answered in the same sarcastic vein. "Actually I had an orange juice. Plane food lacks subtlety don't you think? Besides, I hate planes. I thought I might throw up. I didn't really want to precipitate a crisis."

He pondered for half a second. "Why don't we grab something to eat now?" he suggested. "There are a couple of places to grab coffee and a sandwich. Come to think of it I'm hungry, too."

She didn't bother to argue. He was used to taking charge as well. He didn't even consult her about what she wanted but saw her seated then walked over to the counter to order.

Two waitresses, one with a terrible hair day, sped towards him so quickly, the younger one, scowling darkly, was forced to fall back to avoid being muscled aside. No matter where you were good-looking guys managed to get served first, Sandra thought disgustedly.

Macho Man returned a few minutes later with a laden tray. "This might help you feel better," he said, obviously trying to jolly her up.

"Thank you." She tried to fix a smile on her face, but she was feeling too grim.

He placed a frothy cappuccino with a good crema in front of her, a plate of sandwiches and a couple of tempting little pastries. "We can share. There's ham and whole grain mustard or chicken and avocado."

"I don't really care."

He rolled his eyes. "Eat up," he scolded, exactly like a big brother. "You're not anorexic are you?" He surveyed her with glinting eyes. "Not as I understand it, anorexics admit to it."

"I eat plenty," she said coolly, beginning to tuck away.

"Pleased to hear it." He pushed the plate of sandwiches closer to her. "What did you do to your hair, if it's not a rude question? Obviously it's by your own hand, not a day at the hairdressers?"

To his consternation her huge beautiful eyes turned into overflowing blue lagoons.

It made him feel really bad. "Look, I'm sorry," he apologised hastily, remorse written all across his strongly hewn features. "You have a right to wear your hair any way you choose. It actually looks kinda cute and it must be cool?"

She dashed the back of her hand across her eyes and took a gulp of air. This big macho guy looked so contrite she had an urge to tell him. A spur of the moment thing when she'd barely been able to speak of it. "A little friend of mine died recently of leukaemia," she said, her expression a mix of grief and tenderness. "She was only seven. When she lost all her beautiful curly hair, I cut mine off to be supportive. Afterwards the two of us laughed and cried ourselves silly at how we looked."

He glanced away, his throat tight. "Now that's the saddest story in the world, Alexandra."

"You just want to die yourself."

"I know."

The sympathy and understanding in his voice soothed her.

"But your little friend wouldn't want that," he continued. "She'd want you to go on and make something of your life. Maybe you even owe it to her. What was her name?"

"Nicole." She swallowed hard, determined not to break down. She could never ever go through something so heartbreaking again. "Everyone called her Nikki."

"I'm sorry." He sounded sad and respectful.

She liked him for that. It was oddly comforting considering he was a perfect stranger. "The death of a child has to be one of the worst things in life," he mused. "The death of a child, a parent, a beloved spouse."

A sentiment Sandra shared entirely. She nodded, for the first time allowing herself to stare into his eyes. He had the most striking colouring there was. Light eyes, darn near silver, fringed by long, thick, jet-black lashes any woman would die for. Jet-black rather wildly curling hair to match. It kicked up in waves on the nape. Strong arched brows, gleaming dark copper skin, straight nose, beautifully structured chin and jaw. For all the polished gleam of health on his skin she knew his beard would *rasp*. She could almost *feel* it, unable to control the little shudder that ran down her spine. He was the sort of guy who looked like he could handle himself anywhere, which she supposed would add to his attractiveness to women. A real plus for her, however, was that he could be *kind*. Kindness was much more important than drop dead good looks.

"I know what loss is all about," he said, after a moment of silence, absently stirring three teaspoons of raw sugar into his coffee. "There are stages one after the other. You have to learn to slam down barriers."

"Is that what you did?" Her voice quickened with interest, even as she removed the sugar. Obviously he had a sweet tooth and too much sugar wasn't good for his health.

"Had to," he said. "Grief can drain all the life out of you when our job is to go on. So how old are you anyway?" He tried a more bantering tone to ease the rather painful tension. "My first thought was about sixteen," he said, not altogether joking.

"Try again." She bit into another sandwich. They were *good*. Plenty of filling on fresh multigrain bread.

"Okay I know you're twenty." He concentrated on her intriguing face with her hair now all fluffed up.

"Nearly twenty-one." She picked up another sandwich. "Or I will be in six months time when I inherit. If I'm still alive, that is. Once I'm on Moondai and at the mercy of my relatives who knows?"

He set his cup down so sharply, a few heads turned to see if he'd cracked the saucer. "You can't be serious?"

"Dead serious," she confirmed. "My mother and I left Moondai when I was ten, nearly eleven. She was a basket case. I went into a frenzy of bad behaviour that lasted for years. I was chucked out of two schools but that's another story. We left not long after my dad, Trevor, was killed. Do you know how he was killed?"

"I'd like you to tell me." Obviously she had to talk to someone about it. Like him, she appeared to have much bottled up.

"He crashed in the Cessna."

He sat staring at her. "I know. I'm sorry."

Her great eyes glittered. "Did your informant tell you the Cessna was sabotaged?"

"Dear oh dear!" He shook his head in sad disbelief.

"Don't dear oh dear me!" she cried emotionally.

Clearly her beliefs were tearing her to pieces. "Sandra, let it go," he advised quietly. "There was an inquiry. The wreckage would have been gone over by experts. There was no question of foul play. Who would want to do such a thing anyway?"

She took a deep gulp of her coffee. It was too hot. It burnt her mouth. She swore softly. "You may think you're smart—you may even *be* smart—I'm sure you have to be to run Moondai, but that was a damned silly question, Daniel Carson. Who was the person with the most to gain?"

He looked at her sharply. "God, you don't think very highly of your uncle, do you?"

"Do you?"

"My job is to run the station, not criticise your family."

Tension was all over her. "So we're on different sides?"

"Do we have to be?" He looked into her eyes. A man could dive into those sparkling blue lagoons and come out refreshed.

"I don't *want* Moondai," she said, shaking her shorn head.

"So who are you going to pass it on to, *me*?" He tried a smile.

She sighed deeply. "I'd just as soon leave it to a total stranger as my family."

"That includes cousin Berne?"

She put both elbows on the table. "He was a dreadful kid," she announced, her eyes darkening with bad memories. "He was always giving me Chinese burns but I never did let him see me cry. Worse, he used to kick my cat, Olly. We had to leave her behind which was terrible. As for me, I could look after myself and I could run fast. I bet he's no better now than I remember?"

"You'll have to see for yourself, Alexandra." He kept his tone deliberately neutral.

"I won't have one single friend inside that house," she said then shut up abruptly, biting her lip.

He didn't like that idea. "I work for you, Sandra," he told

her, underscoring *work.* "If you need someone you can trust you should consider me."

She continued to nibble on her full bottom lip, something he found *very* distracting. "I certainly won't have anyone else. I wasn't going to offload my troubles onto you, not this early anyway, but I'm a mite scared of my folks."

He was shocked. "But, Sandra, no one is going to harm you." Even as he said it, his mind stirred with anxiety. The Kingstons were a weird lot, but surely not homicidal. Then again Rigby Kingston had left an estate worth roughly sixty million. The girl stood between it and them. Not a comfortable position to be in.

Frustrated by his attitude, Sandra dredged up an old Outback expression. "What would you know, you big galah!"

He choked back a laugh. "Hey, mind who you're calling names!"

"Sorry. Galah is not the word for you. You're more an eagle. But surely you realise they must have been shocked out of their minds by the will. Uncle Lloyd would have fully expected to inherit. He wouldn't want to work the place. He'd sell it. Bernie would go along with that. Bernie disliked anything to do with station work. You must know that, too. Where do you live?" she asked abruptly.

"I have the overseer's bungalow."

"Roy Sommerville, what happened to him? He was the overseer when we left."

"Died a couple of years back of lung cancer. He was of the generation that chain smoked from dawn to dark."

"Poor old Roy! He was nice to me."

"Anyone would be nice to you." His response was involuntary.

She grimaced. "I don't recall Uncle Lloyd ever bouncing me on his knee. His ex-wife, Aunty Jilly, used to dodge me and my mother all the time. No wonder that marriage didn't work out. Bernie was always so darn nasty. Now they must all think I'm the worst thing that ever happened."

He couldn't deny that. "What was your grandfather like with you?" he asked, really wanting to know. "Any fond memories?"

"Hello, we're talking Rigby Kingston here!" she chortled. "The most rambunctious old son of a bitch to ride out of the Red Centre."

He shook his head. "When you'd melt any man's heart." A major paradox here when Kingston had left her his fortune.

"I don't *want* to melt men's hearts," she exploded, the blood flowing into her cheeks. "It's all smiles and kisses one day. Rude shocks the next. I don't like men at all. They don't bring out the best in me."

He held back a sigh. "I think you must have had some bad experiences."

"You can say that again! But to get back to my dear old grandpop who remembered me at the end, I do recall a few pats on the head. A tweak of the curls before he was out the front door. I didn't bother him anyway. He was happy enough when my dad was alive. After that, he turned into the Grandad from Hell. He seemed to put the blame for what happened to my dad on my mother."

"How could *she* have been responsible?" he asked, puzzled.

"Uncle Lloyd blew the whistle on a little affair she had in Sydney," she told him bleakly. "Mum used to go away a lot and leave Dad and me at Moondai. Uncle Lloyd said she was really *wild,* but then he was a great one for airing everyone else's dirty linen." She broke off, staring at him accusingly. "You must have heard all this?"

Why pretend he hadn't when an unbelievable number of people had made it their business to fill him in on Pamela Kingston's alleged exploits? Lloyd Kingston wasn't the only one who liked airing the world's dirty linen. Apparently Sandra's mother had been famous for being not only radiantly beautiful but something of a two-timing Jezebel. There had even been gossip about who Alexandra's father really was. Alexandra didn't look a bit like a Kingston which now that he had seen her Dan had to concede. The Kingstons were dark haired, dark eyed, *tall* people with no sense of humour. Pamela had routinely been labelled as an absentee wife and mother who spent half her time in Sydney and Melbourne living it up and getting her photo in all the glossy magazines. Dan knew she had remarried eighteen months after her first husband's death. Wedding number two was no fairy tale, either. It too had gone on the rocks. Pamela was currently married to her third husband, a merchant banker with whom she had a young son. It seemed Sandra had moved out fairly early. He wondered exactly *when*? Not yet twenty-one the combative little Ms Sandra Kingston gave the strong impression she had looked after herself for some time. And possibly after her mother, the basket case. Hell, he knew as much about female depression and the various forms it took as the illustrious Dr. Freud.

"All right, what are you thinking about?" Sandra cut into Dan's pondering.

"I was wondering when you left home?"

At the question put so probingly she began to move the salt and pepper shakers around like chess pieces. "To be perfectly honest, from which you might deduce I'm given to telling lies— I'm *not*—I've never really had a home."

"You and me both," he confessed, laconically.

Instantly she was diverted from her own sombre thoughts. "So there's more?" She leaned forward, elbows on the table, all attention.

"If you think I'm about to share my life story with you, Ms Kingston, I'm not!"

She shook her head. "Is that a hint *I'm* communicating too much?" she asked tartly, slumping back in her chair.

"Not at all. It strikes me you've spent a lot of time alone?"

She sighed theatrically, then stole one of his sandwiches. "That's what happens when your mother has had three husbands."

"One of them was your dad," he pointed out.

She nearly choked she was so quick to retort. "That son of a bitch Lloyd challenged that at least a dozen times before I was ten.'"

The muscles along his jaw tightened. He knew all about labels. "He's not a very nice person," he said shortly.

"He's a bully," she said. "And I'm going to prove that. He really *really* upset my mother. I know she wasn't the woman to exercise caution but don't you think she would have been completely insane to try to put one across my dad let alone my fearsome old grandpop. My dad always knew I was his little girl. He used to call me 'my little possum.' He told me every day he loved me. I think he was the only person in the entire world who did. Then he went off and left me. I was so sad and so angry. My mum and I *needed* him. It's awful to be on your own." She dug her pretty white teeth into her nether lip again, dragging them across the cushiony surface, colouring it rosy.

"So a man does come in handy?" he asked.

She looked into his eyes and he saw the sorrow behind the prickly front. "A dad is really important."

Hadn't he faced that all his life? Even a bastard of a dad.

"Getting killed was the very last thing your dad *wanted,* Sandra. Unfortunately death is the *one* appointment none of us can break. I'm sure your mother loves you. Your grandfather too in his own way."

"God that's corny!" Now she fixed him with a contemptuous glare. "In his *own* way. What a cop-out!"

"He made you his heiress," he pointed out reasonably. "Do people who hate you actually leave you a fortune? I don't think so. Your grandfather bypassed his son, your uncle, and his only grandson who is older than you by three years."

"I can count," she said shortly, hungrily polishing off another one of his sandwiches. "I actually got to go to university. I was a famous swot."

"Head never out of a book?"

"Something like that." She shrugged, picking away a piece

of rocket. "In a locked room. My stepfather, Jeremy Linklatter, IV, developed a few little unlawful ideas about me."

He who thought himself unshockable was shocked to the core.

"You can't trust anyone these days," she said in a world-weary fashion. "Certainly not men. There should be a Protection Scheme for female stepchildren."

"Hell!" he breathed, hoping it wasn't going to get worse. "He didn't touch you?"

Her expression showed her detestation of stepfather Jeremy. "Not the bad stuff." How was she confiding all this to a stranger when she had never spoken about it at all? There was just something about this Daniel Carson.

"Thank God for that!" He released a pent-up sigh. "The guy must have crawled out from under a rock. So when did you leave home?"

She shrugged, licking a little bit of avocado off her finger-tip. "I went to boarding school. Then I went on to uni and had on campus accommodation. It proved a lot safer than being at home."

"Did your mother know what was going on?" Surely not. That would have been criminal.

She sighed. "My mother only sees what she wants to see. She can't help it. It's the way she's made. Besides, Jem was pretty adept at picking his moments. I was always on high alert. Occasionally he got in an awful messy kiss or a grope. Once I pinched his face so hard he cried out. Then I took to carrying a weapon on my person."

He could picture it. "Don't tell me. A stun gun?"

"Close. A needle with a tranquillizer in it."

"You're joking!" That was totally unexpected. And dangerous.

"All right, I am. But I was desperate. I took to carrying my dad's Swiss Army knife. You know what that is?"

"Of course I know what it is," he said, frowning hard at the very idea of her needing to carry such a thing as a weapon. "I have one, like millions of other guys. It's a miniature tool box."

"You don't have one like mine. It's a collector's item," she boasted. "An original 1891 version."

"Really? I'd like to see it."

She laughed. "And I'd enjoy showing it to you only I couldn't bring it on the plane."

"I wish I could meet up with this Jem," he said grimly.

"No need to feel sorry for me." She tilted her chin. "Nothing catastrophic happened. He's such a maggot. He just had all these urges. Men are like that."

"Indeed they're not," he rapped back. "Evil men give the rest of us ordinary decent guys a bad name. It's utterly unfair. There's something utterly disgusting about a predator."

"That's why I like my gay friends," she announced, wiping her hands daintily on a paper napkin before brushing back the damp curls at her temple.

"How long was your hair?" he asked, his eyes following the movement of her small, pretty hands.

"That's a funny question, Daniel Carson."

He gave his dimpled, lopsided smile. "Oh, I dunno. I'm trying to visualise you as the girl you were."

"If you *must* know, I had a great mop of hair. A lot of people thought it was lovely. Say, those sandwiches were good. I think I must have been starving. I might even have another one of those little pastries. Oh, it's yours!" she observed belatedly.

"Take it," he urged. "You're the one paying."

"What?"

"Just a little joke," he said. "My shout this time."

"Which reminds me," she said in quite a different voice. "I want you up at the house."

His eyebrows shot up. "You can't mean living there?"

"I can mean and I do mean." She sat back, fiddling with her thumbs.

"Just forget about it," he answered flatly.

"Might I remind you, Daniel, I'm the boss. I want you about two steps up the hallway from me. I don't know you very well, but I'd find having a great big guy like you around—especially one with a Swiss Army knife—reassuring."

He frowned direly. "Sandra, your fears are groundless."

"Sez you!" she responded hotly, sitting up straight. "Do you know how many people get killed over money?"

"There could only be one in a million who don't finish up in jail," he told her in a stern voice.

"A few more than that filter through," she struck back.

He studied the flare-up of colour in her cheeks. "Listen, Ms Kingston, if you're under the impression your family would agree to that, you're very much mistaken. Both your uncle and your cousin would see me gone only neither of them can do my job. It was your *grandfather* who hired me. It was your grandfather who gave me so much authority. As you can imagine your uncle and your cousin bitterly resented that fact, even if they didn't want to take over the reins. After twelve months I'll have no alternative but to quit."

"You *won't* quit while I need you," she told him imperiously. "And you *will* shift your gear up into the house, if you'd be so kind. I may have been only ten when we were kicked out but I do remember it was so big you needed a bus to get around it."

"Just leave it for the time being, won't you?" he asked in his most reasonable voice. "See how the family reacts."

"In that case, Daniel, you better be present," she said. "So where did you come from anyway? Are you a Territorian?"

"I am now, but I come from all over."

"You're worse than I am," she sighed. "Could you be a bit more specific?"

"Maybe not today."

She looked at him searchingly. "So what about a compromise? Where *precisely* did you learn to manage a cattle station. You're what?" Her blue eyes ranged over him.

"You want me to produce a birth certificate? I'm twenty-eight, okay?"

"Most overseers aren't off the ground by then," she observed, impressed.

"Then I must be the eighth wonder of the world. As it happened, I learned from the best. My mother and I lived like gypsies moving around Outback Queensland until we came to rest in the Channel Country when I was about eleven. A station owner there, a Harry Cunningham, offered her the job of housekeeper after his wife died and there we stayed until he died some years back. His daughter sold the station almost immediately after. Something that must have the old man still swivelling in his grave. But such is life!"

There were a hundred questions she wanted to ask, but the first was easy. "So where is your mother now?"

His handsome face instantly turned to granite. "I'm like you, Alexandra. I'm an orphan."

"I'm sorry." She saw clearly he had no more dealt with the loss of his mother than she had the loss of her father. *Orphans*. Hadn't her mother been lost to her the day she married that rich, worthless scumbag, Jem?

"Not as sorry as I am," he said.

"What happened to her?" She spoke as gently as she could, fearing she was about to be rebuffed.

"I think we'll just leave it," he said.

CHAPTER TWO

HE TOOK HER on a journey that filled her with fascination. The landscape beneath them was so vast, so timeless in character Sandra found herself awestruck. The first hellish minutes, just as she expected, had been taken up with fighting down her fears. She would never be cured of them. Not just of helicopters. In a chopper one couldn't look out on a fixed wing, causing not only in her, but in many people the sickening sensation the aircraft might simply drop out of the sky. She feared *all* aircraft. She'd been battling that particular phobia since she was a child and the family Cessna had taken a nosedive into the McDonnell ranges, not far from Moondai, with her father strapped into the pilot's seat. That was the start of it.

He did it, Sandy. Your uncle Lloyd. He caused it to happen. He'd know how. He was always jealous of your father. He couldn't let him inherit.

Some words are scorched into the memory as were some scenes, like her mother sobbing out accusations...

He did it, Sandy. He couldn't let your father inherit.

So where did that leave her, her grandfather's heiress, all these years later? No way was she sitting pretty. Just like her father she was a target. But unlike her trusting father she had learned the hard way to always be on red alert. It helped too to have backup. Small wonder she'd decided, very sensibly, to shift her overseer into the homestead for a time. Daniel Carson had an aura that made a woman feel safe. She suspected there was more than a hint of Sir Galahad about him. She even liked the way he stared down at her from his towering height, though occasionally it had made her feel like toppling backwards.

He was an excellent pilot. He was handling the helicopter with such confidence and skill she was actually approaching a state of euphoria, where she believed nothing bad could possibly happen. Phobias were only there to be licked! The ride was so *smooth!* She gave herself up fully to the pleasure and excitement of the flight.

The immensity, the primeval nature and the remoteness of the landscape, lit by the brilliance of a tropical sun left an indelible imprint on the mind. This was a land unchanged in aeons. It appeared far more splendid than she remembered as a child. Of course there was no better way to see it than from a helicopter with its three-dimensional visual effects. She felt as free as a bird, wheeling, skimming, darting across the glorious cobalt sky.

Great inundated flood plains glittered below them. She stared out eagerly. Rivers extended wall to wall in numerous spectacular gorges. Such places were inaccessible in the Wet. They could only be seen as she was seeing them, from the air. A foaming white waterfall was coming up on the right. It crashed over the towering stone escarpment, throwing up a white haze like a great curtain. In contrast, the walls of the canyon glowed like a furnace, a throbbing orange-red streaked with bands of iridescent yellow and pink. Millions of litres of water were being delivered into the turbulent stream below, although the rains had abated some weeks back.

Gradually as the inundated land began to settle there would be an abundant harvest. The animals and the birds would begin to breed. Wildflowers would open out, going to work to form a prolific ground cover over the warm, receptive earth. All the varieties of palms and pandanus would put out new fronds. The golden and crimson grevilleas would bloom, the hibiscus and gardenia would spread their scent and colour across a background of lush greens. Mere words couldn't prepare a visitor to the Top End for the sight. Suddenly after years in the city, Sandra felt the tremendous pull of the great living Outback. The Outback had fashioned her. She had been happily content as a child. Maybe she could be again?

Beneath her mile after mile of lagoons filled to the brim with beautiful waterlilies swept by. She knew the species: the sacred lily of Buddha, the red lotus, the pink and the white and the cream, and the giant blue waterlily with flowers that grew a foot across. The master of the waterways was down there, too. One could never forget that. The powerful salt water crocodile. She shuddered at the very thought. Moondai in the Red Centre was a long way from the crocs though according to the magnificent aboriginal rock drawings on the station they had inhabited the fabled inland sea of prehistory.

Daniel turned his handsome head to smile at her with a real depth of pleasure in his eyes. She smiled back, both of them in perfect accord; both captive to the space, the vast distances, the sunlight and the colours, the incomparable beauty of nature. Here was the very spirit of the bush. The air was so *clear,* it was like liquid crystal. By now, Sandra was so enthralled she'd completely forgotten how initially she had wanted to turn back. She felt happily content to fly with Daniel, an almost telepathic communication between them. It struck her he was really her kind of person. One knew these things right away.

It dawned on her very gradually their air speed was slowing. Steamy heat was rising from the waterlogged soil.

"Everything okay?" She turned to him, an alarmed croak in her voice.

His profile was set in stone. "We're losing power. Sit tight."

Instantly Sandra jerked back in her seat. Panic surged through her chest, near driving the breath from her lungs. All illusions of safety were abruptly shattered. Her worst nightmares appeared to be coming true. They were in trouble. Didn't trouble follow her around? The helicopter was losing power *and* altitude. She craned her head. Beneath them lay a forest of paperbarks with their slender trunks standing in who knows how many feet of water. At least she could swim. She thought of the crocs. Their bodies would provide a nice feed. Troubled though her life had been she felt a sharp nostalgia for it. She wanted a *future!*

Okay, time to pray. What was the point, a dissenting little voice said. Her most fervent prayers hadn't saved Nikki from a tragically early death. She would pray all the same. She couldn't afford to get on the wrong side of God. Maybe *her* time was up? Hers and Daniel Carson's. Maybe that was why he didn't feel like a stranger? They were going to die together.

She was suddenly indignant. There had been *enough* trouble in her life. She deserved a break. She couldn't submit to her fate without paying strict attention to their plight. Not that she could do anything, basically, but try to help Daniel spot a place to set the chopper down.

Sandra stared fixedly at the magnificent landscape beneath them that had abruptly turned hostile. Daniel would have no other option but to force land.

Tell him something he doesn't know.

But where? The vast terrain was covered in glittering swamps with a canopy of trees growing so close together if they were monkeys they could scamper across it. She even had a fevered thought if the worst came to the worst, they could bail out, land in the water then if they were lucky spring up a tree with a pre-historic monster snapping at their heels.

If there was one thing Daniel had learned it was to stay cool under pressure. Even immense pressure like this. They were a few kilometres into a big, flooded paperbark swamp. The manifold pressure had dropped off and he was losing power and RPM. Air speed was declining as well. He knew the girl was only too aware of it and the consequent danger, though he was so focused on what he was doing he dared not turn his head to look at her or even speak.

Seventy knots to sixty and bleeding off fast. No matter how he wished otherwise he had Alexandra Kingston with him. A girl whose father had been killed in a plane crash.

He couldn't lose another second. He used his radio to report a mayday, giving his bearings. What could be causing this failure? He scanned the control panel which was going haywire. Something was screwing the system. The helicopter was regularly serviced as a matter of course. Only he flew it. And Berne.

He stared down, the muscles of his face rigid. There were huge paperbarks all around them fringed on the outer perimeter by pandanus.

Fifty knots.

God almighty! Was this the way it was going to end? A life span limited to a few decades? What a bloody mess. Adrenaline kicked in, flushing through his system. He was a good pilot, wasn't he? A very good pilot. Now was not the time to be modest. He was *lucky* as well, which was almost as good. He had the girl with him and she deserved a life. They had to survive. He had to land the chopper safely even if he clipped the rotors which was a strong probability. He could sense the girl beside him was sitting rigid with fear, but she wasn't screaming. Thank God for that! Many would be yelling their heads off at this point, when they were on the brink of a crash. She was, in fact, pointing frantically to a pocket handkerchief-sized clearing at the same time he spotted it coming up.

He lined the chopper up. The clearing was shaped like a playing field with its boundaries set at one end by a stand of pandanus, at the other by four paperbarks, their foliage iridescent in the sunlight.

Hell he almost loved her. She was far from stupid and she had kept her head. He had to applaud that.

Okay. It was now or never!

The swamp was rising to meet them with crocs in it for sure. Didn't you just love them? He had to judge the tips of the branches of the trees by centimetres. He could feel the tremendous rush of adrenaline through his body, even the thrill of extreme danger. Paradoxically it gave him a weird feeling of excitement as well as fear; a buoyancy he had experienced before in tight situations.

Ten metres above the water, the surface was quivering and shimmering like a sea of sequins, then it churned into waves by the strong down draught. He couldn't run the chopper on in case the skids got hooked onto the arched root system of the trees. If that happened, the chopper would flip over. A rotor tip only had to clip those trees. He could hear a hissing sound clearly. The clearing seemed to be lit up, preternaturally brilliant. It could signal the end but he took it as a good omen. He hovered, shutting everything out of his mind but the need to set the machine down safely. The will to survive transcended fear...all the blades were at the same pitch...

That's it. Hold it still. Praise the Lord!

At the last moment, Sandra shut her eyes, her small hands clenched into fists. Death was always waiting in the wings. She didn't want to see it coming. If she was going to die she was going to die. There was not much anyone could do about fate. But if anyone could save the situation this guy might. Sweat was pouring off her yet her blood was running ice. They could drop like a stone. The chopper would be hurled around like a piece of debris before it went up in flames... It only needed one false move.

Though she waited in limbo for the moment of impact and probable annihilation, the chopper seemed to come down in ultra slow motion as the rotor blades set up a whirlwind. The machine didn't *hit* the water, rather it seemed to Sandra's bemused mind it came down as lightly as a brolga on its tippy toes. She felt the skids sink and held her breath in case the probing skids got caught up in the trees' root systems and tossed the fragile aircraft around like a child's toy. Dread paralysed her limbs. This was a nightmare!

Only slowly, so slowly, the skids settled on the swamp bed. She couldn't believe it!

Sandra's eyes flew open. The chopper was bobbing on the surface of the swamp, the body surrounded by streams of bubbles. There was a gurgle of water somewhere but they were stable.

Eureka!

The aircraft gave a groan that was almost human. Daniel killed the engine. The beating rotors, main and tail, gradually stopped their thundering.

All was still.

Sandra couldn't even turn to face him. Whole moments passed while her racing heartbeats slowed to normal. Then she turned to him whooping triumphantly, unaware her face was milk-white with shock. "Carson, you have to be the coolest cat on the planet!"

"Supernatural!" he agreed wryly, tasting blood on his bottom lip.

They hit an exultant high-five.

"Which reminds me, you idiot! You could have killed us."

"I look on it more as a truly great save." Daniel stared at the control panel. "The person I should really kill is whoever's been tinkering with the chopper."

"What are you saying?" She heard the shrill note in her voice.

"Nothing. Absolutely nothing." Daniel backed off, removing his earphones and unbuckling his seat belt. "I have to get out and take a look. You stay here."

The very idea made her break out in a sweat. "You didn't think I was just going to jump in? There must be crocs in there."

He shook his head almost casually. "The water around us

isn't deep. It's already begun to subside. Nevertheless we could become waterlogged even supposing I can fix whatever problem we have. The good thing is we're not far out of Darwin. Air Rescue will scramble another chopper in no time. I'll send you back with them. You'll have to be winched up. I'll stay with the chopper until we can get it airborne."

"So who's going to pinch it around here?" She resorted to sarcasm, not wanting to let him out of her sight. "The crocs? And don't tell me they're not lurking out there in among the reeds because I happen to know differently. I was born in the Territory, remember?"

"The *desert,* sweetheart," he jeered, not even aware in the stress of the moment he had called her that. "The Red Centre is completely different to the Top End. Desert and tropics, both in the Territory. Moondai might as well be a million miles away from the crocs."

"And I couldn't be happier about that," she retorted. "But shouldn't you stay put? You could come to a grim and gruesome end. I think I'd hate that."

He merely shrugged. "You don't happen to know how to handle a rifle?" He sounded extremely doubtful.

Sandra snorted. "Do I ever! My dad taught me how to handle a gun. I'm sure I remember. It's like learning to ride a horse."

Daniel studied her in amazement. "He must have started you off early?"

"Because I wanted to *learn,*" she replied tartly. "Bernie could shoot. I had to be able to shoot too in case he planned a little accident. Grandpop used to think becoming a good shot was character building. So what do you want me to do?'

He frowned. "I'm going to make a full circuit of the chopper. It's a miracle we didn't sustain any damage to the main rotor. We're centimetres from the trees. What I want you to do, if you feel up to it, is cover me just in case we have a nosey visitor. Just don't shoot *me,* okay? Want to have a run through first?'

She unbuckled her belt and stood up though her legs were still wobbly. "Might be an idea. Where's the rifle?"

He moved to collect it from where it was stashed, broke it open to load it, snapped the action shut, then passed it to her. "Think you know what you're doing?"

"I'd prefer a dirty great cannon," she muttered, making her own checks and feeling it all coming back. "But I do know which end of this thing shoots." She swung up the rifle and took aim through the chopper's reinforced forward windshield. "If there really is a croc out there where do I shoot him? Right between the eyes? They've got tiny brains haven't they?"

"I've never had the pleasure of finding out. Just don't miss or it will come right after me."

"Then me." She slicked stray tendrils off her forehead. "I'm ready if you are."

"Then let's *do* it!' he said.

He plunged straight down into the water which only a week before would have been over his head. "Fuselage appears to be unscathed," he called to her eventually, his eyes scanning the waxed, glinting sides. "I want to check the shafts of the tail rotor. Keep your eyes peeled for ripples in the water."

"Struth, what's with you? Of course I will. We're dinner otherwise. They're there. I know they're there."

"Yeah? Well I'm the guy in the water." Daniel moved about near soundlessly in the swamp stirring up the mud on the bed so the shining water turned dark and murky. Sandra followed him from one side of the helicopter to the other, her keen young eyes focused on the surface.

"Skids are in a web of roots and vegetation," he yelled to her. "That's the danger. They'll have to be cleared."

"I bet there are leeches in there?" Her voice was level, her face pale but resolute.

"Too right. The little buggers are stuck to my legs."

"Oh how vile! You can't *do* anything, can you?" she called.

His voice came back to her sounding perfectly in control.

"I'm going to use my old faithful Swiss Army knife. I have to clear that vegetation. Just cover me."

She watched him plunge beneath the muddied waters coming up with coils of vines and gnarled roots that he tossed away across the swamp.

Only now could she smell the stomach-turning odour of mud and rotting vegetation. "Finish soon, Daniel," she begged him. Her whole body was vibrating with tension and the rifle felt very heavy.

"Doing my best!" he grunted and plunged again.

A brilliant sun burned down on the small clearing, the paperbarks and pandanus standing all around like sentinels. Sandra had never felt so exposed in her life.

Hurry, hurry, Daniel.

She saw his sodden dark head decorated with trails of luminescent green slime emerge at the very moment she spotted thirty feet beyond him an arrowhead of ripples across the stagnant surface of the swamp. Then at the apex of the triangle nostrils and behind that twin blackish bulges about twenty-two to twenty-three centimetres apart.

Eyes, that glinted gold!

She was so panicked for a moment she felt she might pass out. It was coming at surprising speed for such a great cumbersome creature. It was *surging* towards the challenger in its territory ready to dismember it limb from limb and stash the feast for a week later.

Horror was as sharp as a drill. "Get out!" she yelled. "Daniel, get out. It's a croc."

His lean, muscular body shot out of the water, his strong arms lunging at the body of the helicopter towards the open cockpit, hauling himself up.

Sandra took aim down the sights of the handsome bolt action rifle which had been fitted with a small telescope to make distant targets appear closer. Her whole face was pinched tight with control while she waited for the *precise* moment the giant reptile's brain, situated midway between the eyes, would be dead centre in her range. God help them if the action jammed!

Now!

She held her nerve. Her finger that had been holding steady on the trigger, squeezed… The butt plate kicked back into her shoulder as the firing pin struck the rear end of the cartridge.

The noise was deafening in the torrid, preternatural quiet of the swamp.

"I've killed it. I think I've killed it." Her voice was ragged. There were runnels of sweat running down her face. "Did I?" she called to him for confirmation, "or did I just nick it?" Now the crisis was over she was shivering. "I should have had an M16."

"Sorry, they belong to the armed forces." Swamp water was streaming off him, as he stood within the chopper, his boots oozing mud. Leeches were feasting off him. "No worries, you got him all right," he assured her. "Didn't you see his yellow belly as he rolled?"

"Hell I'm good!" she congratulated herself. "I hope he's not just playing dead? Maybe he wants both of us to think so until it's time to make a leap into the cabin."

He shook his head. "What do you want, a tooth for a trophy? You got him, Sandra. Good and proper. I would never have guessed you could shoot so well. You turned into Annie Oakley right before my eyes."

She staggered away to sit down. "Who's Annie Oakley anyway? One of your girlfriends?"

He moved to the edge of the doorway, beginning to remove the brown and black leeches with the help of his Swiss Army knife. "Hell, Ms Kingston, none of my girlfriends can shoot like you. You could give a lot of guys lessons. Annie Oakley, for your information, was a famous American markswoman. Supposedly Buffalo Bill's girlfriend though I believe she married someone else."

"Maybe it was a sore point she could shoot better. Uugh!"

she shuddered, watching him remove the bloodsuckers with no show of revulsion. "How's this for adventure? What are you going to do to top it?"

A lock of wet raven hair flopped over one eye. He tossed his head to dislodge it. "I could carry you on my shoulders across the swamp?"

"No thanks."

"Changed your mind about going back with me?"

She hugged herself, rocking back and forth. "What do you reckon went wrong?"

"Too early to say." One leg was clear.

"You seemed pretty sure it was tinkering before?"

He kept silent, concentrating on the sickening task to hand.

"Do you mind answering?"

"Maybe I was a little too quick off the mark back there. The chopper will be checked out. Accidents happen all the time."

"There's nothing Uncle Lloyd and Bernie would like more than to see me dead," she said.

And I'd be a bonus, Daniel thought.

CHAPTER THREE

SANDRA AWOKE WITH a start. She ached all over. That's what happened when you had to be winched into a helicopter. She rolled over onto her back, throwing an arm across her eyes. She was in a hotel room back in Darwin, waiting for Daniel to make a reappearance. He had remained with Moondai's downed chopper while Air Rescue had ferried her back to Darwin. She really ought to get up, take a shower, tidy herself up. Everyone had been very kind to her, smoothing her way. She knew people would have been just the same had she not been Rigby Kingston's heiress.

It was night outside. Darwin throbbed with life but inside the hotel room all was quiet save for the hum of the airconditioning. It was a very nice room; thickly carpeted, nicely furnished, the decor suited to the tropical environment, softly lit, a beautiful big waterlily print behind the bed. She slid her bare feet to the floor, sat a moment, then walked over to the corner window looking out. Floors below her, the city was all lit up. A big yellow bus crawled along the main street, taxis whizzed up and down, a couple was turning into the hotel's entrance. Pedestrians crossed at the lights.

Where was Daniel? He seemed to stand alone as an ally. Their shared ordeal had established quite a bond, as such hair-raising incidents tend to do, although she'd been feeling quite kindly disposed towards him even before that. She knew he viewed her as a young person who needed looking after. A loner. An orphan. He seemed to identify with that. Her lack of height—she was five-two—had never helped. Actually she was very good at fending for herself. A result of having a mother like Pam who really loved her but somehow had never been able to demonstrate it as a parent should. Not that her mother hadn't had her own harrowing time. Losing her husband the way she had, then being thrown out of Moondai had caused huge psychological trauma.

Her ever present memories began flashing through her brain again. She let them roll like a video clip. There was her mother lying on a bed, an arm thrown across her swollen, tear-streaked face. There was she, a bewildered, grief-stricken child, standing beside the bed, her hand on her mother's shaking shoulder, trying to make sense of a world that had been turned violently upside down.

I loved your father, Sandy. Our marriage would have survived if only he'd come away with me from Moondai. Moondai killed him. Moondai and your uncle Lloyd.

Uncle Lloyd said I'm not Daddy's. Is it true?

Would our marriage have survived if you weren't? Of course you're Daddy's little girl. Your uncle would say anything—anything at all—to try to discredit me.

Then how come Grandad threw us out? How could he do that if I'm his granddaughter?

Her mother's answer was always the same. *His grief was too powerful, Sandy. In a way he started to believe your uncle. But never, never doubt. You are Daddy's daughter. I swear to you on my life and his memory.*

Well, her doubts had persisted. It was only years later she had learned to thrust them aside. That was after her mother had married Jem—the second guy didn't count. Then she was truly on her own. She had never let her mother know what a sicko Jem really was. Her mother seemed happy with a man who liked to impose his will on everyone else, and now they had their son, her stepbrother, Michael, whom they both adored. Didn't she love Michael herself? Spoilt rotten Michael, despite the bad parenting was a nice little kid. And she was now an heiress who could have anything she liked. That's if she managed to survive the next six months. She would officially inherit on her twenty-first birthday in August. Her mother had interpreted that as Rigby Kingston trying to buy redemption.

How could her grandfather buy redemption when he hadn't had a soul?

Twenty minutes later she was showered, shampooed and dressed to descend to the hotel restaurant. She had scrubbed up rather nicely she thought, splashing out on makeup, a pretty dress, and a couple of squirts of perfume to give Daniel Carson a bit of a jolt. She was a *woman,* not the coltish youngster he thought he had taken under his wing. That attitude had set her a challenge and she liked challenges. She liked Daniel. He had saved her life. How could she not?

So where was he? Surely he'd be back by now, whether they'd been able to restart the helicopter or not. One thing was certain, a team of sharpshooters couldn't stick around in that swamp at night. It was crawling with crocs. A mechanic with the rescue team had been winched down to him. Maybe together they could get the chopper back in the air as they hadn't run out of fuel. It had to be some mechanical defect.

The digital clock said 7:23 p.m. She was hungry. All she'd really had all day was hers and Daniel's sandwiches and a cup of coffee. She was starting to worry about him. She didn't want to go ahead and eat without him. Even as she thought it, the phone rang. She reached it at speed.

"Ms Kingston?"

Mysteriously her heart leapt. Was that significant? "Daniel, where are you?" She hoped she didn't sound too needy. She wanted to project the weight of maturity.

"Keep calm. I'm down the hallway. Isn't that what you wanted? Your overseer close by."

"You bet. What happened about the chopper? Did you get it out?"

"It took a lot longer than expected. It's grounded for a complete inspection."

"So what was the problem?" She caught her reflection in the mirror, all pink cheeked and bright-eyed as if they were having a cosy chat.

"You wouldn't know if I told you."

"Just tell me this. Should we contact the police?"

"No way," he said.

He had such a sexy voice on the phone. It was sort of like being *caressed.* She took a deep breath. "Listen, we can't talk on the phone. I'm hungry."

"Aaah, yes, I remember your appetite. Give me ten minutes okay?"

She'd probably have given him an hour.

She was *full* of surprises Daniel thought in some amazement. So much for the immature, just-out-of-school girl without a scrap of makeup! What he saw in front of him was a dead sexy little buttercup blonde of at least twenty. She was wearing a swishy blue dress that doubled the impact of her violet eyes. Even her hair seemed to have trebled in height and thickness. For a few crucial moments he couldn't take his eyes off her. He damned well hadn't expected this transformation. Even her delicate breasts had perked up an inch or two. He was so astounded he had trouble hiding it, which didn't gel with his usual cool.

"Well good evening." He tried to smile his way out of it.

"Have a problem with the way I look, Daniel?" she asked

sweetly, pleased at his readable reaction. Maybe she wouldn't take her little blue dress off.

"No, ma'am." He half shrugged. "You look different that's all.'

"*You* don't." She surrendered to the impish urge to put him in his place.

He winced. "So, you don't want to be seen with me?"

"I was only being a smart alec," she confessed, kindly.

He glanced down at himself. "I did try to order a dinner suit but they didn't have one in stock. I had to make do with what I've got on."

She made a business of looking him up and down as a prospective employer might the new chauffeur. What, she wondered, wouldn't he look good in? He was wearing what was obviously a new open necked shirt, white with fine beige and blue stripes and new denim jeans. "And those ridiculous boots?" she said, staring down at his feet. "You're towering over me."

"Yeah, well, most guys would. What was I supposed to do, buy a pair of loafers? This lot cost enough. My gear was ruined by the time we were finished in the swamp."

"Lose no sleep," she said loftily. "You'll be properly reimbursed."

"Thank you, ma'am." He bowed slightly.

"And you needn't be cheeky."

"I didn't know I was. I thought I was being respectful as befitting my position."

"Now that sounded sarcastic, Daniel," she warned, looking back over her shoulder for her clutch. "Where are we going?"

"Somewhere cheap," he said.

"*I'm* paying."

"That's different," he smiled, the dimple deep in his cheek. "I hope it suits but I've already made a booking at a little Vietnamese restaurant a short walk from here. I know the owners. The food's great."

"It's not noisy is it?"

"Not so it'll damage your ears." He studied the small face that had within a few short hours blossomed from a furled bud into full flower. "What's the problem, a headache?"

"I'm sick with nerves, Daniel, if you must know." She walked back to pick up her purse.

"I promise I'll lay down my life for you." He said it lightly with a grin. Then it struck him. He had just said something he actually *meant*.

She paused in front of him, wide-eyed. "Promise?"

Daniel felt the need to swallow. "No one will so much as tweak a hair of your head," he said, trying to fight out of a daze.

"My hero!"

If he weren't shocked enough, she upped the ante by going on tiptoes and landing a kiss on the point of his jaw.

The food was as good as he had promised and more. The restaurant was small but fully booked. Only Daniel was clearly a favourite they would regrettably have been turned away.

"How come everyone likes you?" Sandra asked, tucking into prawns in a delicious spicy sauce.

"It's my sunny nature," Daniel explained. "*Not* everyone likes me, however. My boyish charm doesn't work on your uncle Lloyd or Berne. Berne and I often have words."

"What about?" she asked with interest.

He shrugged. "Just about anything sets Berne off."

"So he hasn't changed," she said dryly.

"I never had the great pleasure of knowing him when he was a kid."

"He was the biggest pain in the arse in all the world. Pardon the language." She glanced around hoping no one had heard her. Mercifully they were all too busy eating.

"You obviously feel strongly," he remarked, underlining the *strongly*.

"I apologised, didn't I? So, did you find anything suspicious? You can tell me now."

"Nothing we could pin on anyone." He shrugged. "If you really want to know it was like this." He launched into a detailed account of their preliminary findings until she held up her hand.

"Sorry. Like they say, that's way over my head. The real question is, are you game to charter another chopper and fly back to Moondai? More to the point, am I game to go with you?"

"It's the only way I know to get there, unless we walk." He forked another sea scallop.

"Do I need to remind you I'm an heiress?"

"No, ma'am."

"You're not going to keep calling me ma'am are you?" she asked crossly.

"I thought as you're my boss, I should. You don't seem to like Ms Kingston."

"What if dear old Uncle Lloyd is right and I'm *not* a Kingston?" she asked waspishly, then resumed eating.

"You must be. You remind me of your grandfather."

That set her beautiful eyes asparkle. "Do you want to hold on to your job, Daniel?"

"I've got nothing better at the moment," he said, calmly returning her stare.

A fraught moment passed. "Tell me about yourself," she invited, seemingly able to assume a cajoling voice at will. *"Please."*

"You really want to know?"

"Would I have asked if I didn't? To be honest, after surviving today's little mishap I feel we're meant to be friends." To prove it she solemnly took a scallop from his plate.

"Then I wouldn't lay it on you."

"That bad?"

Relaxed and smiling a minute before, he suddenly looked grim. "Absolutely awful. Your own childhood couldn't have been a dream?"

"It was okay until we lost Dad. Then everything changed. He used to call out from the front verandah, "Hi, my little darlin', I'm home." It wasn't my mother he was talking to. It was me. Sometimes I think both my parents needed their heads examined getting hitched."

He nodded. "Another case of if only I knew then what I know now. It makes me very wary of having a passionate affair."

"Now that I can't swallow." She threw him a look of disbelief. "Meaning what?"

She shrugged a delicate shoulder. "I imagine there's no end of women willing to go orgasmic—is there such a word?—over you."

"Sandra, for that you need a good spanking."

"Please," she moaned. "Don't you dare talk down to me."

"I didn't mean to." Frankly he was at a complete loss how to treat her. It was easier before when she looked like a little damsel in distress, but now? Just looking at her made him gulp for air.

"That's okay then." She nodded briskly. "I'm twenty, soon to be twenty-one. I've led an adventurous life. Some might say *seedy.* I think *I* would in my place."

His tongue got the better of him. "So why am I convinced you're a virgin?" As soon as he said it he could have bitten his tongue out because street smart as she claimed to be she coloured up furiously.

"Daniel Carson our relationship does *not* extend to discussing subjects like that." She tilted her head, looking down her small perfect nose. "What do you mean anyway? When I had all my hair and I was six kilos heavier I was *hot!"*

He couldn't help himself. He laughed aloud. "You'd set off a few smoke alarms right now." He hadn't missed the appreciative glances coming her way especially from one guy who might need sorting out. "Better get cracking then and put back those six kilos. Would you like to consult the menu again?" he asked helpfully.

"Are you having a go at me?" Her expression was sharp.

"Would I dare?" He raised his black brows. "There's actually nothing I like better than to see a girl with a healthy appetite."

She shrugged. "Maybe dining with you wasn't a good idea. All I've had all day was those sandwiches at the airport. Besides I can afford it remember? I'm an heiress. Except I don't want to be and I don't want Moondai."

"I think you can be persuaded to change your mind. Moondai is a wonderful place."

"Well it makes *your* eyes light up," she commented. "*You're* not hoping to marry me, are you?" She cocked her head to one side. "Because I have to tell you I'm not an easy target. Being an heiress attracts scores of guys."

"I wouldn't be a bit surprised if you finished up with several hundred suitors," he retorted, watching the waiter approach with their main course, chilli baked reef fish.

"Daniel Carson, you're *priceless!*"

"No, I'm one of those guys who like to make their own way in life, Alexandra."

"You'd better point out another if you see one," she returned breezily. "Oh goody, here comes the waiter! What about dessert?"

"You can have dessert if you want," he replied. "They do a delicious coconut dish with gula melaka syrup and another ginger one that's very good. I'm going to have one."

"How could they ever fill you?" She was in awe of his height and superb physique.

"My sweet little mother used to say that to me nearly every day of the week. *How am I going to fill you, Danny?*"

Some tender note in his voice, the poignant expression on his dynamic face tugged on her heart strings and made her close her eyes.

"Hey what are you doing?" he asked in alarm as a teardrop ran from beneath her thick lashes and down her cheek. "Sandra?"

She opened her eyes and choked back a cough. "Something went down the wrong way," she lied.

"Here, have a glass of water." He began to pour one.

"Thanks." She drank a little, looking up brightly as the Vietnamese waiter arrived at their table. "Ah, this looks sensational!" She smiled.

He was out of it—after all it had been quite a day—when the insistent ring of the phone ripped him out of the enveloping clouds.

"Daniel? Get down here fast," a voice hissed.

Instantly he was on red alert. "Sandra?"

"Someone else you know?" she asked sharply. "There's some guy at my door. He keeps tapping and asking, 'Are you in there, blondie?'"

"I'm on my way." Daniel was already pulling on his jeans. This was just the sort of thing the attractive blond women of this world had to put up with, he thought wrathfully. He shouldered into his shirt, not bothering to button it. Sandra was several rooms along from him down the corridor. He was at the very end of the hallway.

Outside in the passageway, he caught the back of a heavily built guy, not tall, striding purposefully towards the lift. At that hour—it was 2:30 a.m.—there was no one else about. Daniel recognised him immediately as the guy in the restaurant who'd been giving Sandra looks Daniel hadn't cared for. "Hey," he called, lengthening his own stride. "Hold it there, fella!"

"You talkin' to me?" The man swung round, on his face an expression of challenge.

"You see anyone else nipping around at this hour?" Daniel closed the distance between them. "You staying at this hotel?"

"Sure I am," the guy blustered.

"Name and room number, please?"

"You security or somethin'?"

Daniel was reminded of a cornered bull. "Right on," he clipped off, daring the other man to question him further. "I've just had a phone call from a hotel guest saying some idiot was tapping on her door, wanting an invite in. Could that possibly be you?"

The guy swore. "Look I'm lost, okay? Had a bit too much to drink with a couple of my mates. Probably on the wrong floor."

"So what's your room number, Mr.?" Daniel pressed his body forward slightly so the other guy had to back up.

"Three Fourteen and it's Rick Bryce."

"Well I agree with you when you say you've had too much to drink and you *are* on the wrong floor."

"Listen, mate." The guy started his appeal. "I don't want any trouble."

"Then you won't mind if I escort you to your room? Management might have a couple of quick questions."

Minutes later when Daniel tapped on Sandra's door, softly calling her name, she opened it a fraction peering at him with huge eyes.

"Come in." She made a grab for his shirt, trying ineffectually to pull him through the door.

"We're going to have a conversation then?" He made it easy by stepping inside. She was wearing what looked like a flirty mini but was probably the latest in nightwear. Her small face was distressed. He knew distress on a woman's face when he saw it.

"Was *he* the guy?" she asked. "I peeped out and saw you talking to him. You had him backed right up against the wall like you were going to give him a good biff."

"He won't be bothering you again. Count on it."

"Is he staying in the hotel?"

Daniel nodded. "Several floors down. His name is Rick Bryce. He claims he had a bit too much to drink and got mixed up with the floor."

"Rubbish!" she said fiercely, shaking her head. "Why does this stuff happen to me?" she moaned, crossing her arms over her delicate breasts.

"What stuff?" He watched her suddenly take off on a rage around the room.

"Men knocking on my door." She threw her arms wide. "Men trying to get in. Stop asking me questions."

"Sandra, settle down," he said soothingly. "You don't have anything to worry about. I promise."

She exhaled noisily. "I felt like he could break in. I knew he couldn't, but I felt he could." Her eyes were swallowing up her face.

"You should have rung management immediately." He looked back at her intently. Suddenly remembering the things she had told him, the little pieces started to fall into place.

"I rang *you* didn't I?" she cried. "I knew you'd be here in a few seconds. I trust you, Daniel. I don't trust anyone else."

"Gee that's sad," he said quietly, running a hand through his sleep-tousled hair. "So, are you going to go back to bed? We have a big day tomorrow."

"Sure." She looked sheepish all of a sudden and a tad ashamed. "Thanks a lot, Daniel. Sorry I had to wake you up."

"That's absolutely no problem at all. You're certain you're okay?" She looked very pale and agitated.

"He gave me a fright, that's all. Don't you ever get a fright?" She turned roundly on him.

"So what's this really about?" he asked, his voice quiet and reassuring. "The odious stepfather?"

Colour swept her pale cheeks. "Don't be so stupid, Daniel," she raged. "I've been over that for years." She swung away from him, her exposed nape, her delicate shoulders and the fine bones of her shoulder blades like little wings so vulnerable to his eyes. The fabric of her nightdress was gossamer light. For a little space of time he could see through it as she moved into the glow of the bedside lamps. The outline of her young body was incredibly erotic. Emotions assailed him, very real and very deep but he thrust them vigorously away. He was her knight in shining armour wasn't he?

"That's a *yes,* Daniel," she burst out, turning back to him.

There was a little vein beating frantically at the delta of her throat. "I hated... I *hated*..."

Images sprang to Daniel's mind that gave him a chill. "He must have been a real sick, sad bastard, your stepfather. I'd like to meet up with him. As for your mother!" His face was dark with disgust.

"Leave her out of it, okay?" she said fiercely. "She did her best."

"Some best!" Daniel threw himself down into an armchair. "Do you want me to wait here until you fall off to sleep?"

Her beautiful eyes quieted. A passing ripple of expression told him she liked the sound of that, but she looked at him coolly, the twenty-year-old with attitude. "Kinda kooky isn't it, Carson?" she challenged.

"Not at all." He shrugged, lifting his arms and locking them behind his head. "You're not all grown-up until you're twenty-one. Why don't you just hop into bed and close your eyes. I promise I won't leave until you're fast asleep."

"Can we talk for a bit?" She slipped beneath the coverlet, her body so ethereal a man would have to shake the sheets to find her.

"No," he said firmly. "Plenty of time to talk tomorrow. Close your eyes now."

She sat up briefly. "Will you tell me something, Daniel?"

"If I can." Sometimes she sounded so darn endearing.

"Wouldn't you have liked a younger sister?"

He thought of his early life the way it was. No place for a little sister. "There was only room for me and my mum."

"You'd have made a lovely brother, too." She sank back again, sounding young and wistful.

"*Good night*, Sandra," he said pointedly.

"All right, all right." She plumped up the pillow, irritable again, then punched it. "By the way, thanks. Did I say thanks?"

"Yes, you did."

"One more request. Do you think I can have a glass of water?"

"Okay." He stood up, wondering briefly and wildly what it might be like to join her. "After that, you promise to be good?"

"I promise." She gave him an utterly beautiful smile.

He walked into the ensuite, filled one of the glasses with water, then returned to the bedside. "Here." He put the glass into her hand.

She took a couple of quick gulps then passed the glass back to him. "I'm so glad you were here tonight. You're really dedicated to your work, aren't you, Daniel?" She stared up at him as though he just might give her a brotherly peck on the forehead.

Instead he gave her a quick glance with silver eyes cool. "Yes, ma'am." He put the glass down on the bedside table, then turned off the lamps, leaving one burning in the ensuite. He moved well away from the bed, resuming his seat in the armchair. Once there, he threw back his head and started to snore.

"It's all right, Daniel. I've got the message." She giggled softly at the sounds he was making, snuggled up to the pillow and closed her eyes.

"Don't worry about a thing," he murmured, letting his own eyelids drop. "I'm here."

CHAPTER FOUR

IN THE END Daniel was able to get them aboard a nine seater charter flight bound for the Alice. The station helicopter remained grounded in Darwin undergoing a more thorough inspection than the one hurriedly carried out at the swamp site. All Sandra knew was it had something to do with mechanical components in the tail rotor that had worked their way loose.

It was almost noon before the twin engine Cessna landed on Moondai, depositing them on the station strip before taking off on the last leg of the flight into Alice Springs. The Alice as it is affectionately known is located almost in the very centre of the continent and the town that most symbolises the legendary Red Centre. Sandra had memories of going with the family to the annual fun carnivals the town put on. There was the annual Henley-on-Todd regatta when teams raced in leg-propelled, bottomless boats across the dry bed of the ancient river. Everyone, locals and tourists alike, delighted in the ridiculousness of it all. Then there was the Alice Springs annual rodeo with big prize money. Her father had often competed in that. But the festival she had most loved as a child was the riotous Camel Cup Carnival also raced in the dry bed of the Todd River. Those memories, mostly fond, reassured her if only slightly. She was extremely nervous of meeting up with her dysfunctional family again. Why wouldn't she be? Her grandfather's will had left her immeasurably better off than them.

She looked around this remote world that was now hers. She had almost forgotten the size of the place, the primal *stillness* like a great beast sleeping. The fiery colours of the earth contrasted wonderfully with the deep cloudless blue of the sky. "What, no welcoming party?" she quipped.

"Amazingly, no." Daniel picked up her luggage and piled it into the back of a station Jeep that was parked with the keys in it. "Did you want one?"

"It's all too late for that, Daniel," she sighed with resignation. "You know and I know they hate me."

"Win them over," he advised.

"Don't joke, I'm *serious.*"

"So am I. Just give yourself *and* them a chance."

"Right!" She pulled a face. "I'll have them eating out of my hand."

"Like me," he said, dryly.

She felt a flush of heat run right through her body. That had sounded so *nice!* "So what do you suppose Grandpop was thinking when he left the lion's share to me?" she asked, trying to act cool.

"Reparation?"

"Maybe." She raked her fingers through her cropped hair. "What's the worst they can do to me, do you reckon? Carry on bitterly resenting me, or move right on to hatching *more* plans to get rid of me? And *you,* for that matter. I can't wait until we get the final report on the chopper. It seemed very convenient to get downed in a crocodile infested swamp. I mean tiny ole me mightn't have made much of a meal, but *you* surely would have."

"Well it didn't happen. You turned into Annie Oakley right before my eyes. Anyway, you can bet your life there'll be nothing to *prove.* The chopper held up for the flight from Moondai to Darwin. Anyway there's no point in speculating. Let's wait and see. Don't be afraid."

"It takes courage to act unafraid," she said quietly.

"You've got it," he said. She had proved that at the swamp.

"How can you say that after what happened last night?" She frowned into the shimmering distance. The desert mirage was at play creating its fascinating illusions. Today it was long ribbons of lakes with vigorous little stick people having a corroboree around the shores.

"Hey, don't look so worried." His tone was light. "*What* happened exactly? I stayed with you until you fell asleep which was almost immediately. I'm not so insensitive that I can't understand what living with that stepfather of yours did to you. Besides you're not alone in your fears of being on your own in a hotel room with some drunken oaf pestering you. It would upset most women."

"You think he'll do it to someone else?"

Daniel opened the passenger door for her. "I've had a word with a couple of people and they in turn will have a word with others connected to the hotel business. They'll be on the lookout for him."

"He kept calling me *blondie!*" Sandra took her seat in the station vehicle.

"Forget it. It's over." Daniel climbed behind the wheel beside her, turning the ignition.

"Stay by me, Daniel," she urged.

The drive up to the homestead seemed to go on forever. She'd forgotten about all the *space!* They passed numerous outbuildings which all looked solid and cared for, painted a pristine white. Colourful desert gardens thrived around the married staff's bungalows and the bunk houses for the single men. It all presented with so much character and appeal it could have been the setting for some Western movie.

"Someone is doing a good job around here," Sandra said with approval as they approached the walled home compound.

"Thank you, ma'am." Daniel took credit where it was due. "It makes me happy to hear you say that."

"It'd make me a lot happier if you wouldn't call me ma'am."

He gave her an ironic glance. "Don't take it personally. I'll call you Sandra when we're on our own. In front of your family and the staff I'd like to leave it as ma'am or Ms Kingston. Take your pick. Think about it, Sandra. It's more respectful and it will make for fewer waves. I couldn't imagine taking liberties with your grandfather and calling him Rigby. He was always Mr. Kingston."

"He was more than seventy!" Sandra pointed out scornfully.

"Well until you're approaching seventy I think I'd better stick to calling you Ms Kingston."

"How would you like it if I called you *Mr. Carson*? For that matter are you sure Daniel mightn't be considered too familiar?"

He shook his head. "No, Daniel's okay. Your grandfather called me Dan. I should tell you now what you would have learned had you paid attention to the reading of the will. Your grandfather left me $250,000 on top of my normal salary providing I stayed on for a period of twelve months."

Her mouth fell open in astonishment. "Was that the *only* way he could get you to stay?"

"You don't think I might have earned it?" He glanced at her with glinting eyes.

"Now that's a stupid question. I'm *sure* he made you earn it. It's just so unexpected. Did Grandpop find his heart at the last minute or was he counting on *you* to prop *me* up?"

"Absolutely!" His voice sounded amused. "That's until you make a decision, Ms Kingston."

She swung her head. "I don't see anyone in the back seat."

"A little practice will make Ms Kingston come easier," he told her reasonably. "I might have been in your grandfather's good books, but that's where it stopped. Lloyd and Berne bitterly resented my influence with him. Berne went ballistic when he heard about my legacy."

"When it had nothing to do with him," Sandra said crisply. "They got plenty. They can stay in the house for as long as they like."

"That will make it hard all round."

"You bet!" she said drolly.

They were driving through an avenue of venerable old date palms with massive trunks. It was all coming back to her. Beyond the eight foot high wall smothered in a bright orange bougainvillea she would get her first glimpse of the homestead from which she and her mother had been banished. At least the tall iron gates were wide open in some sort of welcome, launching them into the home gardens.

The light dazzled. The wind caught boldly coloured blossom and sent it whirling to the ground. Native trees soared, all manner of eucalypts, acacias, casuarinas, a few exotics that had survived the dry conditions, clusters of the beautiful ghost gums she loved, underplantings galore, jasmine clamouring everywhere scenting the air.

This is all mine!

She spoke aloud in wonderment. "Can you believe it? I own all this."

"Lucky you!" Daniel said, giving her a sardonic look. From apprehension she had gone to excitement. The big question would be, did this place speak to her? Had she really come home or would she stay a while then put it on the market? He'd had experience of that. He knew had he been born to a splendid inheritance he would have used every skill he possessed to build it up further and hold it for his heirs. But fate was a fickle thing. Rigby Kingston had amassed wealth and a pivotal role serving his country as a big beef producer. He had lost the one son who might have been able to assume his father's mantle but neither his remaining son nor his grandson had what it took to be a cattleman or to even play a significant role in the running of the station. How could Moondai fare better with a young woman at the helm? The cattle business had always been a male-orientated concern for obvious reasons. It was a hard life, too tough for a lone woman. Had Rigby Kingston mapped out a plan he hoped might work?

The Kingston heiress was addressing a question to him, bringing him out of his speculations. "Just what do Uncle Lloyd and Berne do with themselves all day? They surely can't sit around the homestead?"

"Your uncle has his all consuming interest, botany."

"Still at it, is he?"

"I understand his knowledge of the native flora is encyclo-paedic. No small thing. Berne works around the station. Nothing too stressful."

"That must make it difficult for both of you as you're not friends?"

"Not even remotely," he assured her, "but I try to give him space. Your uncle involves himself in the business side of things from time to time, though Andy Fallon—he's an accountant and a good one—runs the office. Do you remember him?"

Sandra shook her head. "He must have arrived after we left. What about Elsa? She might have been Grandad's second wife, but Mum always called her *The Ghost!*"

"Well she does move around the place very quietly," Daniel said, thinking that was pretty well the way he too pictured Elsa. "She bothers no one." Daniel was still wondering how Rigby Kingston had ever married such a socially inept woman, especially after the idolized first wife, Catherine, who had died fairly early of cancer. "Lloyd and Berne hardly acknowledge her, which is pretty sad. Meg is still the housekeeper. You must remember Meg?"

"Of course! Meg stood on the front verandah tears pouring down her face as we were being driven away. She was always very kind to me, looking after me when Mum was away on her city jaunts."

Is that what Pamela had called them, Daniel thought cynically. City *jaunts*? He had heard so much about Pamela he now felt a lot of the bad stuff had to be true.

"We're almost here," he said, casting her another quick glance. In the baking heat she looked as fresh as a daisy, her skin as smooth and poreless as a baby's. She wore a neat little top almost the same colour as her hair and navy cotton jeans that were chopped off midcalf. The feisty look on her face, the angle of her small, delicately determined chin, were only self protection. He knew she was thrumming with nerves.

And he was right. Sandra stood out on the broad paved circular driveway looking up at the house that had figured so frequently in her dreams. Now she was the *owner,* about to inspect the premises and renew her troubled relationship with her family. Not that she had ever considered Elsa, *family,* which was really odd given Elsa's status. But Elsa had never involved herself, standing curiously aloof from them all. Her mother was right. Elsa had acted more like a visitor than mistress of Moondai. Strange behaviour from a woman who at one stage had run an Outback charter company with her first husband, a confirmed womaniser. Pamela always said divorce from that first philandering husband had dealt a blow to Elsa's psyche from which she had never recovered.

"So what do we do now?" Daniel looked to her for further instructions.

"You come up with me," Sandra said. "Every girl needs a Daniel when she's walking into the lion's den."

Moondai homestead was built of beautiful golden limestone, arcaded on both levels, the ground floor open, the upper level bordered by white wrought-iron balustrading. Tall, graceful vertical French doors set off the horizontal mass of the impressive façade. The shutters to the French doors were and always had been painted a subtle ochre to complement the golden limestone. The entrance hall was guarded by beautifully carved tall double doors with brass fittings that gleamed from many years of frequent polishing.

As Sandra peered into the cool interior a tallish, thin figure suddenly appeared, ankle-length skirt flapping, as if caught in a draught.

"It's Elsa, Sandra," Daniel prompted, in case there was any confusion. Elsa Kingston had aged a great deal even in the time he had been on Moondai.

"Gawd!" Sandra breathed irreverently. This wasn't the Elsa she remembered. Elsa had been a handsome blonde woman showing her German heritage in her bone structure and colouring. Not only had she aged she'd lost stones in weight.

Elsa approached, holding out her arms. "Alexandra! Welcome home, my dear."

Sandra responded at once. "Forgive me, Elsa, I didn't recognize you for a moment."

"I dare say I've changed a lot." Elsa not only hugged her, but she kissed Sandra on both cheeks.

"I suppose *I* have, too," Sandra answered tactfully, dismayed by Elsa's appearance and trying hard not to show it. "Thank you for the welcome." As a child Elsa had never ever so much as patted her on the head. Why now the affectionate greeting, even if she was grateful for it?

"Let me look at you!" Elsa stood back, staring at Sandra with eyes that had faded from their clear, striking light blue to almost colourless. Her once fine-grained skin was a maze of wrinkles. Clearly she hadn't cared for it in the Outback sun. Her long thick blonde hair, once her best feature, she had allowed to turn a yellowish-grey. Today it was bundled into a thick knot with stray locks flying loose. She wore no makeup to brighten her appearance. Her clothes could have been bought at a Thai street stall. The whole effect was one of eccentricity. Sandra felt a deep stirring of pity. This shouldn't *be!* Elsa looked as if the life had been drained out of her.

"You're still the image of your mother," Elsa was saying,

"though you're so thin. I can't catch even a glimpse of your poor father."

"Nevertheless his blood runs through my veins," Sandra said, determined not to become upset. "Daniel will be staying in the house for a while, Elsa. I intend to learn as much as I can about the operation of Moondai in the shortest possible time. I want my manager on hand."

Elsa didn't look like she was about to argue. "Just as you say, dear." She nodded. "It's a very big house. There's plenty of room. What about the west wing?"

"I'll look around first," Sandra said, softening it with a smile. The west wing was about as far away from the main bedrooms as one could get. She endeavoured to move forward, but Elsa seemed oblivious to the fact she was blocking the way. "Where's the rest of the family?" Sandra couldn't prevent the touch of sarcasm.

"They're waiting for you in the library," Elsa said in a voice that conveyed disapproval. "I should have asked immediately, forgive me, but how are you feeling after your scare? Lloyd told me about the mishap to the helicopter. Such dangerous things, helicopters. *All* light aircraft!"

"We survived, Elsa," Sandra answered dryly.

"Thank God," Elsa responded with what sounded like genuine fervour. "Do you *want* to stay at the house, Dan?" She turned to Daniel uncertainly.

"I'm here to do whatever Ms Kingston wants," Daniel replied in his courteous voice. "Mr. Kingston trusted me to carry out his orders."

"You weren't afraid of him, were you, Dan?"

Daniel looked unsurprised by the question or the bleakness of Elsa's tone. "I didn't see anything to *be* afraid of, Mrs. Kingston."

Elsa's gaze went beyond him, as if looking into the past. "He was a hard, *hard,* man. No heart, no compassion."

"He did live through a terrible tragedy," Daniel offered quietly.

"Where's Meg?" Sandra sought to break up the sombreness of the exchange. She looked about her. The black and white marble tiles of the entrance hall gleamed, the woodwork shone. A beautiful antique rosewood library table stood in the centre of the spacious hall, adorned by a large bronze urn filled with an arrangement of open and budded blue lotus with their seed pods and open and furled jade coloured leaves. Everything with the exception of Elsa looked *cared* for.

"She has a few more jobs to do, Alexandra," Elsa said. "You'll see her soon."

"Good. I'm looking forward to it. Probably at lunch. You want lunch don't you, Daniel?"

"A sandwich will do me fine." Daniel shrugged off lunch with the warring Kingstons. "Like Meg I have plenty of work to do."

"Shall we go through to the library?" Elsa asked, long thin hands fluttering like birds on the wing.

"Actually, Elsa, I'd like to freshen up first." Sandra lifted her head to the first floor gallery that was hung with pictures. "Which room have you given me?"

Elsa's gaze dropped as if to consult the marble tiles. "I thought your old room...perhaps you might want another... Meg said you should choose... I wasn't sure..."

"Thank you," Sandra said. "I'll look around before I decide." Her family had kept her waiting. Now they could wait for her. "You can bring up my luggage now, Daniel." She gave the order, mock lady of the manor.

"Yes, ma'am." There was an answering wicked light in Daniel's eyes but Elsa, still fixating on the tiles, didn't notice.

"So what have you in mind?" Daniel asked, after they had negotiated the divided staircase and were several feet along the east wing.

"Not the master suite that's for sure," Sandra said. "I bet Uncle Lloyd has moved in there already."

"I wouldn't know."

"Let's check it out!" Sandra rushed ahead. The hallway was still carpeted with the same valuable Persian runner.

She threw open her late grandfather's bedroom door, gasping a little to see it was indeed occupied by her uncle. Books spilled everywhere. A pair of glossy riding boots stood near the massive bed and a magnificent silk dressing gown was thrown carelessly over a deep leather armchair. "Right! Uncle Lloyd in residence. I doubt very much if it's Bernie. I don't want it anyway. I'll have my parents' suite. *You* can have my old room, Daniel. That way you'll be near me."

"Does it have a dear little bed?" Daniel asked sarcastically, wondering how he could be remotely comfortable living up at the house let alone in what had been a small girl's bedroom.

She turned her head over her shoulder. "I trust you. You trust me. You can have any furniture you want, Daniel. Just don't interfere with my plans."

"Yes, ma'am."

"We're alone, aren't we?"

"Your ancestors are on the wall." He cast a glance at them.

"Arrogant looking bunch aren't they?"

"Don't mistake arrogance for iron determination," he said. "The Kingstons and others like them pioneered an industry. They pioneered what is still in many ways wild frontier country."

"I stand corrected, Daniel," she said, mock repentant. "Are you sure your dad wasn't a cattleman?"

His gaze had the cool intensity of a big cat's. "Ms Kingston, I'm not sure *who* my dad was," he said bluntly.

The colour in her cheeks went from soft pink to crimson. She put out a tentative hand. "Daniel, I didn't mean to hurt you."

"You haven't," he assured her crisply. "Let's get you settled."

"Right." She surged forward. "It's along here." She pointed and Daniel followed with her case. "You're over there."

"God, Sandra. It's opposite yours."

She raised haughty brows. "So what's so disturbing about that? It's not as though we intend playing little seduction games."

"Indeed no!" he said sternly.

"Oh come off it, Daniel. I couldn't care less where you sleep as long as it's close by. You can get someone to help bring up your things."

"I'm not happy about this," Daniel said, shaking his head.

"And I understand. But, Daniel, I *need* you. I'm not asking you to move in with me so quit pulling those anxious faces. I'm like a soldier who needs backup in a combat zone. Think of it like that."

They found Lloyd Kingston and his son Bernard, sitting in splendour in the library—an *enormous* room—which housed thousands of books and maps which no one to Sandra's knowledge had ever read, or even attempted to read outside herself. As a child she had loved climbing up and down the moveable ladder, pulling out books on the adventures of the early explorers, crying over their deaths in the desert. Uncle Lloyd had always kept his huge collection of botanical books quite separate from the library. For one thing her grandfather, if he hadn't exactly ridiculed his son's consuming interest in plants, was extremely irritated and disappointed by Uncle Lloyd's lack of interest in the cattle business, or indeed business in general. Bernie too barely tolerated his father's passion for wildflowers, herbs, native plants and the like but he, no more than his father, had enjoyed station life. What they both enjoyed was reaping the benefit of Rigby Kingston's success. Finding "enlightenment" her grandfather had called it when her uncle Lloyd took off on his field trips.

So far it didn't look like he had found it. Though Rigby Kingston's will had left them both rich, neither Lloyd nor Bernie had made the slightest attempt to vacate the family home. Likewise Elsa who was still nipping at Sandra's heels wearing the long-suffering expression of an early Christian martyr.

"Sandra, my dear." Lloyd Kingston rose to his impressive feet, with quite an air of bonhomie. He came towards his niece as though he too, like Elsa, meant to catch her into a bear hug.

"Uncle Lloyd! You haven't changed a bit." Sandra suffered the hug which was mercifully brief. "You're as handsome as ever." As indeed he was. Tall, dark haired, eyes so dark they were almost black. He hadn't gained weight in midlife though his upper torso had thickened somewhat lending him more substance. Lloyd turned his head. "Berne, come greet your cousin." Narrowed eyes swept over the silent Daniel. "You may go now, Daniel." The politeness of the tone didn't conceal the order. "That was a terrible business with the helicopter. And so awful for Sandra! What exactly happened again? You did tell me when you called."

Daniel gave him a direct look. "It's being thoroughly checked over, Mr. Kingston. I prefer we wait on the full report. It might take time."

"You're the only guy I know who could have landed it." Berne Kingston moved to join the group, giving off an aura of aggression plain for all to see.

"Maybe someone wasn't counting on it," Sandra said. "How are you, Bernie?"

His mouth twisted but he made no attempt to touch her nor she him. "Long time no see." He examined Sandra carefully from head to head. "You're so like Aunty Pam it hurts," he said finally. "Except Pam would have made two of you. You've scarcely grown. And what's with the hair?"

"Nothing terminal," she answered, "so don't get your hopes up. I didn't expect to see you here, Bernie. Were you waiting around especially to welcome me home?"

"You can't honestly believe that?" he asked flatly.

"I don't."

"You've one hell of a nerve. I'll say that for you." He gave a brief laugh. "Always did even as a kid. I don't know what Grandad was thinking of—he always was devious, but Moondai should have gone to Dad, not you, and me, before you. You were last in line."

"The last shall be first."

"Oh, funny!" Berne sneered.

"Bernard, do you think you could stop," Lloyd Kingston appealed to his son, before directing a sharp glance at Daniel. "Daniel, I said you could go."

Daniel didn't move, but there was a coolness in his eyes. "No offence, Mr. Kingston, but I work for *Ms* Kingston."

"I prefer Daniel to stay for the moment, Uncle Lloyd," Sandra broke in. "I mightn't have been here today only for him."

"Quite so, quite so." Lloyd Kingston gained control of himself quickly. "But this *is* family business, after all. Please, come and sit down. Elsa, you'll join us?"

"Thank you," Elsa said in a stilted voice.

Berne followed suit. "So what are your plans?" he fired off at Sandra. "You're going to sell the place?"

"What does it matter to you, Bernie?" Sandra asked, sinking into a deep leather armchair.

"It matters a lot. You seem to have forgotten Grandad gave Dad and me the right to remain here for as long as we want."

"Elsa, too," Sandra reminded him, turning her head to smile at the other woman. "I didn't think you'd want to stay, Bernie. Unless you've changed a good deal you hate station life?"

Berne's face so much like his father's darkened. "Don't tell us you intend to keep the place going? As if you could!" he added scornfully.

"Maybe *I* couldn't on my own, but Daniel can until such time I put a professional manager in place. That's if Daniel doesn't want to stay."

Berne gazed from one to the other. "You're pretty cosy aren't you? Daniel this, Daniel that."

"Oh, do get a grip on yourself, Bernard," his father implored. "You can't waste your life like I have. Sandra is right. You're no more suited to station work than I am. Dad knew that."

"That is no reason why he should have left Moondai to Sandra," Berne responded hotly, his thin cheeks flushed. "What the hell does *she* know? Less than either of us. It's all so unfair. We can't even contest it. Dad's lawyer told us it'd be a waste of time."

"Have you ever known your grandfather to get legal matters wrong?" Lloyd asked very dryly. It appeared, unlike his son, he was in a conciliatory mood. "Dad spent a lot of time in Brisbane in the months before he died. He meant then to cut us out. Trevor's daughter was to get Moondai. Trevor, after all, was his favourite son. *I* never did measure up."

"I didn't think *I* did, either," Sandra said. "Grandad's will was as big a shock to me as it was to you."

"I bet it wasn't a shock to Daniel here," Berne's handsome face was twitching with pent-up anger.

"Meaning?" Daniel's powerful, lean body stirred restlessly.

"You know exactly what I mean," Berne exploded. "You, after all, were in my grandfather's confidence. He had such faith in you. You were damn near the grandson he never had. Was he hatching some plan, do you suppose? The cogs and wheels never stopped turning. Sandra was his heiress. *You* were the sort of guy who could take over the reins. You've proved to be very successful running Moondai and while you were at it, running rings around me, deliberately showing me up. Dad's an old dinosaur. All he wants to do is study his stupid plants."

"So what *are* you saying, Berne?" Lloyd Kingston broke in testily.

"I'm not a fool, Dad," he exploded, showing no respect for his father at all. "I've gone over and over this. Either Grandad expected that without him the whole place would go to wrack and ruin or he could fit Sandra up with a suitable husband. A lot of people in the know seem to think Daniel here is outstanding. He's a real go-getter. He never stops working to impress. Yet he's a nothing and a no-one. Dirt poor until Grandad gave him a leg up. For all we know, Grandad could have extracted a promise from Dan to look out for Sandra. *Marry* her. Take on the Kingston name. It's been done before today. He certainly felt no woman could run Moondai. Sandra's not even a woman. Just look at her! She's hardly grown since she was ten."

"I have, Bernie," Sandra assured him. "I don't apologise for being petite. You know what they say. Good things come in small packages. I'm all grown-up, *unlike* you. Just so you know I graduated with honours from university with a B.A. majoring in psychology among other things. Consequently I find this theory of yours of considerable interest. Daniel is signed up to be my hero. Is that it?"

"Doesn't look like you're too uncomfortable with it," Berne snorted.

"Well *I* am," Daniel said, his eyes luminous with anger. "You're talking drivel, Berne, but then you seldom talk anything else. I fully expected Mr. Kingston to leave Moondai to your father who could have hired top management to run the station had he wanted. My windfall turned out to be at least as big a surprise. Mr. Kingston never once mentioned his granddaughter to me."

"You expect us to believe that?" Berne was the picture of outraged disbelief. "You always had your heads together. Every time I saw you, you were going into a huddle."

"You don't run a station this size sitting on your backside, Berne." Daniel didn't bother to hide his disgust. "Your grandfather always had areas of concern for me to address. They were *all* about station management and business. Which reminds me instead of standing here listening to wild scenarios I should see what's been happening in my absence. The men like to have their duties for the day laid out."

Sandra tried for eye-to-eye contact, failed. "But you haven't had anything to eat, Daniel," she reminded him, loath to see him go.

"Don't worry about me." He gave her a brief salute and turned on his heel.

Sandra made no apologies to the others. She went after him, catching him in the hallway. "I'm sorry about all that, Daniel," she panted. "Bernie has always been a jealous, resentful creature."

"And he talks a lot of drivel. I'd advise you not to listen."

"You're angry?" Carefully she approached him, touching his arm. It was rigid with tension.

"You bet I am!" He stared down into her face. "This isn't going to work, Sandra. I want to help you out, but I'm not going to cop the likes of Berne. Your uncle's arrogance only adds fuel to the flames."

"Why put them before me?" she retorted. "I need help, Daniel. I need it from *you*. Please tell me I have it?"

"Hell!" Daniel was grappling with her potent effect on him. All this woman magic shouldn't be allowed.

"You're more than a match for both of them put together," she cajoled him, giving him a soulful look.

"No need to pour it on." He stared back challengingly into those blue, *blue,* eyes, his own expression somewhat grim. "The *real* question is, Ms Kingston. Am I a match for *you!*"

CHAPTER FIVE

IT WAS A dismal lunch though the food was good. Meg, looking almost exactly the same, but a little plumper, had come to the library door all smiles. Sandra had no hesitation going into her arms.

"Sandy!" Tears brimmed in the housekeeper's eyes. "It's wonderful to have you back."

It wasn't possible to say, "Wonderful to be back," instead Sandra settled for, "It's wonderful to see you, Meg. I've never forgotten you or your kindnesses to me and my mother."

"I wrote to you, dear."

Sandra shook her head, frowning slightly. "I didn't get any letters."

"I didn't think you did." Meg sounded unsurprised. "Anyway, you're back and I'm thrilled."

"Do we have to listen to any more gushing?" Berne burst out. "I'm hungry."

"You must try to do something about yourself, Bernard," his father said, regarding his son with disappointed eyes. "You'll never get what you want out of life if you continue to be so belligerent."

"And *you* have, Dad, I suppose?" Berne scowled.

Sandra waited for another reprimand, but none came.

Meg had set up lunch in the breakfast room which had a high beamed ceiling and a lovely view of the rear garden with its stands of lemon scented gums. Roast chicken was on the menu, cold cuts, potato salad and a green salad enlivened by a Thai chilli dressing. Sandra had deliberately not chosen the carver at the head of the mahogany table which could seat ten. She guessed correctly her uncle had laid claim to that. She sat to his right with Berne opposite her and Elsa way off at the other end of the table though Sandra had tried to coax her to sit closer. It was clear Elsa had made an art form out of staying near invisible when she could easily have kicked over the traces and spent the rest of her time travelling the world, first class.

It soon transpired Uncle Lloyd was set on his course of reconciliation—or the appearances thereof—but after a limited amount of time spent on pleasantries—including kind enquiries about Pamela, once so dreadfully maligned—Berne began to worry away at Sandra's inheritance and her future plans like a dog with a bone.

"Obviously you've got some idea what you intend to do with Moondai?" Fiercely he stabbed at a small chunk of new potato.

"Give me a break, Bernie," Sandra said. "I've only just arrived."

"Wonder of wonders!" He rolled his eyes.

"You can say that again! Only Daniel's such a good pilot or I could be dead or in hospital in a coma. As I've already said, I had no idea Grandad would make me the major beneficiary in his will. After all, he sent Mum and me packing, remember?"

"He should never have done that." Elsa startled them by offering the stern comment.

"No, he shouldn't!" Sandra showed her own deeply entrenched resentments.

"Come off it, Sandra." Berne's smile was acid. "Your mother was a real tart! No offence."

His father broke in. "This has gone far enough, Bernard. I insist you keep a civil tongue in your head. Apologise to Sandra right now."

"Dad, you must be joking!" Berne sat back astounded. "Aren't *you* the one who called Aunty Pam every dirty name you could think of? So now you're going to make nice?"

Colour stained Lloyd Kingston's strongly defined cheekbones. "That was in the past, Bernard. I was only teasing anyway."

"Teasing?" Berne shouted with laughter that held no trace of humour.

Sandra for her part felt a swift surge of anger. "My mother suffered from your taunts, Uncle Lloyd. So did I. Now, if *I* am willing to let bygones be bygones I hope you'll do the same. I didn't make myself Grandad's heiress. Grandad did. I have no idea what was going through his mind—"

"Boy, that's rich!" Berne lounged back. "I gave you a reason. Every time I came on Grandad and Daniel they were locked into deep conversation. He'd turned his back on Dad and me. We didn't measure up. He *knew* Dad would sell Moondai like a shot if he got his hands on it. I would, too."

"What about Elsa?" Sandra asked, looking in Elsa's direction. "Elsa is Grandad's widow."

Berne looked stunned. "Elsa could never take over. She can't even handle the dinner menu as I'm sure she'll agree. Meg runs the house."

"Why are you speaking like this, Bernie?" Sandra asked. It was so unkind and disrespectful.

"It doesn't matter, Alexandra!" Elsa said, waving a thin hand.

"But Elsa it *does* matter," Sandra said. "Anyway Meg *is* the housekeeper. Before you married my grandfather you were a successful businesswoman. Didn't you miss it?"

Elsa seemed to shrink in her carver chair. "That was a lifetime ago, Alexandra."

"Does one truly lose one's skills or the need to use them?"

"My cleverness has diminished with the years," Elsa said. "I know you mean to be kind, Alexandra, but nothing Bernard says affects me."

"Is that so?" Berne intervened with heavy sarcasm. "If the truth were known, Elsa, you *lost* it the day you married Grandad. Grandad didn't want a career woman with a mind and a life of her own. He wanted a woman who would know her place, not a business partner. That's when you set about turning yourself into a piece of furniture."

"Really, are you any better?" Elsa asked, piercing him with her colourless eyes. "You strut around doing next to nothing while Daniel runs everything. Gutless young men like you disgust me."

Berne's face was a study. "Well what do you know?" he chortled. "She *can* talk."

"Rudeness is what you employ, Bernard, instead of brains," Elsa said gravely. "I have never wished to talk to you."

"Ditto!" Berne retaliated, dark eyes flashing. "I'm lighting out of here as soon as I'm ready. Who am I anyway? *No one!*"

Sandra, amazed by the exchange between Elsa and Berne, felt a sudden rush of empathy for her cousin. "Look, I'm sorry, Bernie," she said. "I'm sorry Grandad cut you out. I'm sorry he did the same to Uncle Lloyd. He was a very strange man."

"He was that!" Elsa pulled more wisps out of her bundle of hair. "He should have been had up for mental cruelty."

"Struth!" Berne dug his fork into a piece of chicken like he wanted to spear someone. "Don't be so ungrateful, Elsa. Grandad's life may not have centred around *you,* but he made sure you were kept very comfortable in your quiet corner. He did leave you rich if not merry."

"Which was only fitting," Sandra murmured.

"If I could I'd send it back to him in hell," Elsa told them bleakly. "It wasn't *money* I wanted from Rigby. It wasn't *money* the rest of you wanted from him, either. It was love and attention. There were only two people Rigby loved in this world.

Catherine and Trevor. The rest of us amounted to a big fat nothing."

"Well thank you for sharing that with us, Elsa," Lloyd said suavely. "I must say I too have been missing the sound of your voice. Perhaps Sandra's arrival has brought it back?"

"Why not?" Elsa nodded her head. "I was fond of her father. He was very different to you, Lloyd." Her colourless gaze shifted to Sandra. "It's a great burden you've taken on, Alexandra. This place killed your father."

"Oh for pity's sake!" Lloyd Kingston fetched up a great sigh. "Please don't start on that, Elsa. I won't have it."

"My mother believes to this day my father's death wasn't an accident," Sandra found herself saying although she hadn't intended to.

"And what do you believe, Sandra?" her uncle asked while Elsa turned her head away, looking extremely distressed.

"Can you truly say you weren't my father's enemy?" Sandra looked directly into her uncle's hooded dark eyes.

Lloyd Kingston's face flushed a dark red. "I'm going to forgive you for that, Sandra. That's your mother talking. You were a child. Your mother filled your head with terrible stories. It was a way of getting back at me for the things I'd said about her. A lot of which was true by the way. I loved your father, my brother. I looked up to him. He was everything I wasn't just as Elsa so kindly said. And he had a *heart* which Dad never had. I never regarded Trevor as the enemy. That's blasphemy. I don't regard *anyone* as my enemy."

"Not *me,* Uncle Lloyd?" Sandra asked, quietly.

"Especially not you," he answered without hesitation. "You're Trevor's child."

"Sure about that, Dad?" Berne asked in a taunting voice. "If I were Sandra I'd be worried about what lay behind your sleek mask. No one in this family ever tells the truth."

"How very true," Elsa said in a heartfelt voice, brushing long fingers through her hair. "It is only justice you inherited Moondai, Alexandra. It would have gone to your father."

Sandra bit hard on her lip. After a moment, she rose from the table, saying quietly, "Please excuse me. I'd like to look around this afternoon. I'll take the Jeep out the front if that's okay?" She pushed in her chair, holding the back of it while she got out what she had to say. "I've asked Daniel to move out of the overseer's bungalow and into the house for a while."

As she expected, there was a stunned silence. She might just as well have said the authorities had handed over to her the most dangerous felon in the country to be housed.

Berne finally broke the silence. "You've *what*?"

"Sandra, is that *wise*?" Lloyd asked with less intensity, but he too looked shocked.

Sandra shrugged. "Elsa has no objection. Daniel can have my old bedroom. It's only until I bring myself up to scratch on station affairs. He'll be a big help there as Grandad intended. I'll move into my parents' old suite."

"I'm quite happy to move out of the master suite," Lloyd Kingston offered. "You have only to say the word."

"Sandra isn't going to say it, Dad, just as you were counting on. What you *weren't* counting on was that Sandra is no fool. She wasn't easily fooled as a kid, either."

Sandra was surprised by his support, if indeed that's what it was. She decided to hold out an olive branch. "I don't suppose you'd like to drive around with me, Bernie?"

For the first time he looked uncertain of himself. "You can't want me surely?"

"What's the sense in us not being friends? We're cousins. We can adapt."

Berne considered that one, in the end succumbing to his overload of resentments. "Not overnight we can't!" He shook his head sharply. "Thanks for the offer. It's beyond me right now to accept."

* * *

In the kitchen she spoke to Meg about room arrangements asking Meg to make up some sandwiches for Daniel's lunch. Meg too looked surprised when told Daniel would be staying at the house for a time, but in no way did she appear dismayed. Rather she appeared firmly onside.

"What is it, love? Are you nervous?" she asked shrewdly, long used to the warring Kingstons.

Sandra gave a wry laugh. "I have powerfully bad memories of this place, Meg. Daniel is a big dependable guy. I'd like him around. Besides, it's quite true I'll be relying heavily on him to teach me what I need to know about the station."

"Well he can do that," Meg said, slicing off some ham. "Towards the end he was your grandfather's right hand man. You could say your grandad treated him as more a grandson than he did Berne."

"That must have been awful for Berne?" Despite everything she felt twinges of pity for her cousin.

"It wasn't good." Meg shook her head. "It's time for Bernie to make a life of his own. He's got no direction. It's my belief, excuse me, Sandy for saying this, but inherited wealth is death to ambition. Most times anyway."

It was amazing how quickly it was all coming back to her. Sitting tall behind the wheel of the Jeep Sandra drove out of the home compound taking the broad gravelled drive that wound past the neat and comfortable staff bungalows and bunkhouses. Station employees materialized out of nowhere, roughly lining the track. She began to wave. They all waved back. There were mothers with little children, groundsmen, stockmen, what looked like station mechanics going on their oil stained overalls. Finally she stopped the Jeep and climbed out.

"Hi! Lovely to see you all. I'm Sandra, back home again."

Her youth, the diminutive size of her, the smile on her face and the friendliness of her tone instantly broke the ice. People surged at her, delighted and determined to meet the new boss personally. They had all known she was coming. Mr. Kingston's will—what they knew of it—had been discussed at great length and gasped over. What was going to happen to Moondai, to their jobs? They all knew about the forced landing of the station helicopter in the swamp. Daniel had spoken to his foreman as well as Lloyd Kingston up at the house. The foreman relayed the news to the crew. In a small closely knit settlement like Moondai news travelled faster than an emu at full gallop.

Rigby Kingston had been one thing. His granddaughter was proving to be very much another. Instead of leaping briskly out of the way or averting their eyes if their former Boss was about in one of his dark moods, his granddaughter was happy being surrounded by smiling faces. Some faces Sandra remembered and greeted by name. Others, the young wives and the small children were newcomers to Moondai. Sandra found herself nursing babies, which she loved, accepting invitations to morning tea and paying a visit to the schoolhouse where all the children on the station under ten were offered an education by a well qualified teacher. With these open-faced smiling people around her Sandra felt safe.

By the time she drove on she was feeling quite cheerful, not realising friendliness and a genuine interest in the people around them was a side of the Kingston character that had seldom emerged since her father's day.

I could almost build a life here, she thought. That was the voice of her heart. But what of her head? These people liked her at any rate. Drat her family.

One of the station hands had told her Daniel's location. He was out at the crater, a natural amphitheatre caused by massive earth movements hundred of millions of years before. The family had always used that name for the grassy basin which was almost enclosed—save for a broad canyon—by low lying rugged cliffs of reddish quartzite and sandstone. It was quite possible to climb to the highest point which their Kingston forefather had named Mount Alexandra after his wife. The same Alexandra Sandra had been named for. Of course it wasn't a mountain at all. More a hill, but it *reared* out of the vast perfectly flat plains so its height was accentuated. The climb to the summit was a stiff hike too and dangerous with all the falling rubble, but the view from the top Sandra could still remember.

Her father had used to sing to her that they were sitting on top of the world, his arm around her sheltering her from the strong winds.

Why did you go and die on me, Dad? Why? Why did you leave me? It was hard. So hard. Do you know the things that have happened to me? How frightened I was without you to protect me? How much I hated Jem?

She often found herself talking to her father. Not out loud of course, but in her mind. Sometimes she thought he answered. She talked to her little friend, Nikki, too, asking her what it was like in the kingdom of Heaven. Was it all it was cracked up to be? If anyone deserved eternal joy it was Nikki and the children like Nikki who had been so brave and cheerful it had put her own troubles into perspective.

Her father hadn't wanted to die, either. She couldn't forgive her uncle, for all she had said about letting bygones be bygones. Life didn't work that way. The past could never be buried so deeply it couldn't resurrect itself at a moment's notice. All it needed was the requisite trigger.

The light was dazzling. She pushed her akubra further down over her eyes, congratulating herself she'd had the foresight to buy one from a Western outfitter in Brisbane. It had been hard getting one her size especially when she no longer had her mop of curls to help prop it up. Best quality lens sunglasses sat on her nose, though in the heat they were continually sliding down the bridge. She remembered this extraordinary dazzle of light, blinding in its brilliance, the cloudless skies, the golden spini-fex and the blood red sands the wind could sweep into the most beautiful and fascinating delicate whorls and patterns. She remembered the way the desert bloomed in profusion after the rains; the great vistas of the white and yellow paperdaisies she particularly loved; the magnificent sight of the burning sun going down on the Macdonnell Ranges that were always over-hung by a hue of grape-blue. These ranges of the Wild Heart were once sand on the beach of the inland sea the early explor-ers had searched for in vain. She loved the way the wild don-keys came out to graze at sunset and whole colonies of rabbits popped out of their warrens keeping a sharp lookout for any dingoes on the prowl. Around Moondai all the dingoes had been purebred. A wild dingo in prime condition was a splendid sight, but one always had to remember they were killers by nature.

A big mob of cattle was being walked not far from a water-hole where legions of budgies and perky little zebra finches were having a drink, indifferent to the presence of a falcon that coasted overhead making itself ready for a leisurely swoop. Kill and be killed, she thought. There were always predators, always victims. Her mind returned to the question of what had caused the mechanical components in the tail section of the helicopter to work their way loose. Daniel had explained it but it hadn't been all that easy for a nonmechanically minded person like herself to take in. Had someone deliberately interfered with the control system, or had it simply been another case of mechani-cal failure? So many people over the years had been killed in the Outback when helicopters or light aircraft crashed either soon after take-off, or attempting to land. Some plowed into rugged ranges while others took a nosedive to the desert floor. Flying was a risky business especially over the heated unpre-dictable air of the desert, but given the vast distances flying was no luxury; it was a way of life.

It was the greatest good fortune that Daniel was such a good helicopter pilot. He had to be equally good with fixed-wing al-though she understood flying a helicopter was quite different to flying a fixed-wing aircraft. Daniel was licensed to fly both as was Berne. She wasn't sure if her uncle flew the helicopter, but he had always held a pilot's licence as had her father and grandfather. It occurred to her it might be a good idea for her to start taking lessons. She had to overcome her fears if she really intended to stay on Moondai. Maybe in the process she would unveil a new aspect of herself?

The drive through the broad canyon was an experience in itself. The walls presented an extravaganza of brilliant dry ochres, fiery reds, russets, pinks, yellows, stark glaring white with carved shadows of amethyst. High up in every available pocket of earth the hardy spinifex had taken root. Because of the recent rains many clumps were a fresh green, most a dull gold. The sandy floor of the canyon was as red as boiling magma, giving vital clues to the mighty explosion that had formed the crater aeons ago. To either side of the canyon long tranquil chains of waterholes already beginning to dry out sparkled in the sun. In the gums nearby, preening or dozing amid the abundant fresh olive foliage were great numbers of the pink and grey galahs who made sure they were always in the vicinity of water. She had grown up with all this even if she had lost contact over the years. Only love of this ancient land was in her bloodstream hence her deeply felt response. Time and distance had not altered the old magic.

The crater, secret to all save the aborigines for tens of thousands of years was a miracle of nature. It attracted massive flocks of birds and wildlife. It was wonderful to look out over the giant bowl of the crater with its protected grasslands then up at the rounded curves, peaks and swells of the surrounding rim.

That afternoon the natural amphitheatre was thickly carpeted in grasses that were liberally strewn with the wildflowers and spider lilies that thrived in the semi-desert environment. Her favourites, the everlastings which didn't wilt when picked, were by far in the majority. In one area she drove through to get to the holding yards they were pink, then a mile or so on, bright yellow interspersed with long trailing branches of crimson desert peas, native poppies, hibiscus, fire bush, hop bush, salt bush, emu bush. There were so many she couldn't begin to name them. She had to leave that to Uncle Lloyd who loved every living thing that grew in the earth far more than people. Cataloguing all this floral splendour was his passion. The ranges at their back door harboured a great wealth of wildflowers, making them an exciting hunting ground for a man who was both amateur botanist and excellent photographer. She remembered her father saying with admiration how his brother, Lloyd, had an encyclopaedic knowledge of the flora of the Red Centre and Queensland's Channel Country where he had spent a lot of time. Did a botanist, passionate about wildflowers, morph into a murderer? It didn't seem possible.

She brought the Jeep to a halt a little distance from the pens. To one side she could see a calf cradle, a ratchet locking device that restrained the calves due for earmarking, branding, dehorning and castration. She slid out of the Jeep and stood with her back against the passenger door watching Daniel stride towards her. Back in the city any guy that looked like him would be mobbed on a daily basis she thought with wry amusement. She had never seen anyone so young exude so much authority. It was strange to think Daniel didn't know who his father was. He had to be a six footer plus, strikingly handsome. From which parent had come those extraordinary eyes? They were the colour of sun on water.

"Hi!" He sketched a salute, forefinger to the brim of his cream akubra.

"Hi, Daniel," she replied, not a whit disconcerted by the way he towered over her. Authority emanated from Daniel, never menace. "When you stalked off, you missed lunch so I brought you some sandwiches."

"Now aren't you kind." He smiled at her, wondering if her beautiful skin was as cool and soft as it looked. "The men are about due for a break. I'll get Nat to make us a cup of tea. You can meet the men in the break."

"I'd like that," she said, following him over to an area of deep shade. The thick stubby grass that surrounded the tall gums was studded with the all embracing wildflowers, their pretty faces brighter in the refreshing shade. The men had looked up at her arrival, but when she looked back, they had their heads down, hard at work.

Nat turned out to be a wiry jackeroo of around twenty whose duties included making the billy tea for the men when they were out on the job. He had recently perfected an old-fashioned camp fire damper which he offered to Sandra spread with lashings of jam. She accepted tea and the damper with a smile not about to tell him she rarely drank tea and never ate jam. Somehow she'd choke it down.

She and Daniel made themselves comfortable beneath the shadiest tree, Sandra thinking there was no one she'd rather share the moment with. How did one reach such a point so early in a friendship? she thought in some wonderment. All she was absolutely certain of, was, she *had*.

Daniel, oblivious to her soul searching, opened out his packet of sandwiches kept fresh by cling wrap. "These look good," he said appreciatively, getting a kick out of the fact she had thought of him. But then she was thoughtful. And very kind. He remembered her little friend Nikki and the sacrifice Sandra had made of her crowning glory.

"Eat up!" she said happily.

His smile was beautiful. The towering gums were beautiful, the crush of wildflowers at their feet were beautiful. The cooling breeze was beautiful, the aromatic smell of the camp fire. *Everything* was beautiful she thought ecstatically.

"You must be hungry?" She stretched out a little, revelling in the vast landscape.

He held a protective hand over the package. "I'll just down a few of these before you start to pinch them."

"It's okay. I had lunch."

"How did it go?" He shot her a sidelong glance thinking her profile was like a perfect cameo.

Sandra swallowed a mouthful of tea, finding it surprisingly good. "Uncle Lloyd was in a conciliatory mood. Bernie was Bernie and Elsa made a few surprising comments that struck home. As a child I couldn't make her out. I can't now. She's so *quiet,* but I have the feeling a lot is going on in her head."

"Well it can't be *good.* She looks positively haunted to me." Daniel picked up another sandwich, deriving a great deal of pleasure in the company of his new boss. Even in the heat of the afternoon she was as bright and fresh as the daisies that ringed them round. She had a tiny beauty spot high up on her right cheekbone just beneath the outer corner of her eye. It emphasized the porcelain perfection of her skin and the natural darkness of her lashes and brows. Quite a contrast with the buttercup coloured hair that clung to her beautifully shaped skull. Not many could look so good with so little hair.

Sandra, while endeavouring to appear not to, was intensely aware of his leisurely inspection and was just as intensely satisfied. She *wanted* him to notice her. She was actively *willing* it. "Why are you looking at me like that?" she asked.

He laughed. "May a cat not look at the queen?"

"I suppose so if it gets the opportunity. This damper is very good but I don't actually eat jam. Would you like it? Then I can have one of those sandwiches."

"Which one?" he asked with an amused look on his face.

"Oh any! I couldn't get my tongue around lunch although I was hungry. Bernie was shouting and shoving his chair around. It put me off."

"I don't want the damper, either," he told her, passing a ham and mustard sandwich and looking Nat's way. "I'll eat just about anything when I'm hungry but *not* damper. It sticks in my chest."

"You'll have to eat it," she said. "We don't want to offend him."

He shook his head carelessly. "He'll get over it. So did you tell them you want me to move into the house?"

She tossed her head back. "I said you'd fit in like you belonged there."

"Like hell I will!" he muttered beneath his breath.

"No matter, you're doing *me* a great service. Elsa took the news with great equanimity. She can't have much fun with Uncle Lloyd and Bernie who, predictably, had serious misgivings."

He drained his mug of tea. "Please don't tell me on a beautiful day like this."

"It *is* a beautiful day, isn't it?" She gave a voluptuous sigh, looking utterly relaxed. A gorgeous butterfly drifted by just to add to her happiness. "You can smell all the wildflowers!" She inhaled. "I used to love Moondai when I was a kid."

"Why wouldn't you? It's a part of you." He was entranced and entertained by her ever changing expressions. She might be small but there was a lot of life in her.

"I know that now. Daniel, why do you suppose my mother thought Uncle Lloyd wanted to get rid of my dad? Uncle Lloyd is a passionate botanist for God's sake."

"I can't imagine him killing anyone, Sandra." While Daniel didn't have a lot of time for Sandra's uncle, he had to say what he believed.

"He wouldn't have to do it himself," she pointed out.

"No." He was deeply sceptical. "Your uncle isn't the most likable man in the world. He's an appalling snob, but not, I think, a murderer."

"Who then?" she asked. "Bernie has more hang-ups than I have, but he was just a kid. Elsa? I can't imagine Elsa turning into a homicidal maniac. Marrying Grandad had to be one of the worst decisions she ever made. She mustn't have wanted a man who would play around like her first husband. Sex creates tremendous problems."

Daniel leaned back, the more to study her. "When it's good it beats most things," he offered casually.

"I beg your pardon?" Her heart started to make wild little flutters in her chest.

"You don't agree?" One eyebrow shot up sardonically.

She coloured up. "You keep waiting for me to make a slip."

"I do." He looked at her with a mixture of gentle mockery and indulgence.

"Well you're not ever going to hear it," she promised.

"And here I am the soul of discretion," he said. "Your secrets are safe with me, Alexandra. Anyway we were talking about more momentous things. Who hated your dad enough to want to see him dead? We already know yours is a highly dysfunctional family but I think you'd have to rule them out. It was an accident, pure and simple. Now you're a woman as opposed to the child, you have to accept that. Your mother would have been in a highly emotional state. She probably hated your uncle as much as he hated her."

"He was right about her behaviour when she was away from us," Sandra stared down at the tea leaves at the bottom of her tin mug as though the random arrangement held answers. "Mother was a bad, bad, girl. She's highly susceptible to male admiration to this day. I didn't see it then of course. I heard what Uncle Lloyd was saying but I couldn't understand what he was getting at. Heck, I was only a kid. What I *did* take in was the way he questioned whether Dad was my father or not."

"Now that's really wicked." Daniel gave his judgment. "And just plain wrong."

"Sometimes I wanted to attack him with a meat axe," Sandra confided, watching the beautiful butterfly, a marvellous blue, make another circuit of their heads.

Daniel ran his thumb along his lean jaw. "You're a bloodthirsty little thing. I just hope I never fall out with you."

She jabbed him in the arm. "You must never, *never,* do that, Daniel."

"Even if it's a lot to ask?"

He didn't smile. He appeared to be taking her seriously. "Even then." She nodded as though she could see into the future. "You've signed on for another year. I won't be twenty-one until August. A journey of six months. You have to stick around for another six after that."

"Will do. Hey, sit still," he urged in a hushed tone.

"What is it? What's the matter?"

He sat up straight. "A butterfly has been hovering around. It's alighted on your head. Probably thinks it's a chrysanthemum."

"Oooh!" She drew in her breath and held it. "Is it still there?"

"Want me to catch it?"

"You might damage its wings."

"No, I won't!"

He sounded very sure. Still she shut her eyes. When she opened them again, their heads were very close together, the sable and the golden yellow. "All right, ready?" he murmured.

"Ready."

He opened his hand slowly, revealing the butterfly in all its beauty. It clung to the skin of his hand for barely a second, brilliant blue, yellow and black wings with a glinting yellow body, before it flew off.

"Surely that's a good omen," she whispered, staring into his eyes. They were so close she held her breath. This man was *beautiful!* He made her insides ache.

"I'm sure it is," Daniel said just as softly.

Something in his eyes, in his voice, made a thousand tingles run up and down her spine. Neither of them moved—it was as though movement was impossible—then Daniel pulled back, casualness falling over his intense expression.

Sandra followed his lead, though the tingles hadn't gone away. She sat back, her shoulders pressed against the trunk of the tree. "By the way, Grandad didn't approach you with any deal, did he?" she asked after a moment.

"What sort of deal, Ms Kingston?" He was all crisp attention.

"Oh forget it," she said, taking swift note of the crease between his brows. "Just me being paranoid. Bernie took one hell of a crack on the head when he was a kid. Fell off his horse. Maybe that explains why he too is wandering around in an emotional fog." She broke off, as the stockmen started coming around for their afternoon tea break. "Time to meet the men," she said.

"Right you are, ma'am." Daniel stood up, offering her his hand. "Some of them were around when you left."

"I've already met quite a few people on my way out here," she told him. Now the tingles spread from her spine to her hand, to *everywhere!* "I loved the babies. I've been invited to a getting to know you morning tea. The schoolteacher wants me to look in on the lessons. I mean to meet everyone on the station. That includes the aboriginal people who pass through on walkabout."

"Seems more and more like you intend to stay?"

"Who knows!" She took a very deep breath. "One thing I do know with certainty. My life has changed forever."

CHAPTER SIX

DANIEL HAD BEEN expecting a bedroom modest in size—or as modest as the rooms at Moondai homestead could get—and furnished in a way that reflected the taste of a very young girl. Maybe not lots of pink, painted furniture, decorations, a collection of dolls and so forth, given Sandra's self confessed tomboy qualities. What he got was the stuff of dreams. Ms Alexandra Kingston's childhood bedroom was very large and very grand. So large in fact she must have been lost in it.

"Think you can get used to it?" She circled the huge four poster bed with its draped canopy, giving the beautiful embroidered silk cover several good thumps while she was at it. "Dressing room adjoining, the bathroom pretty small for a big man but it will do."

"I'm sure." He looked about him with the same sense of wonder he had once felt wandering around an Adelaide art gallery. The bedroom walls were hung with paintings. Not any old paintings. He had a naturally good eye, or so he had been told, but art works as good as the ones he was looking at immediately declared their quality. A magnificent antique chest stood at the foot of the bed. She could easily have hidden in it as a child. Maybe even now. A splendid crystal chandelier hung above his head.

"Baccarat," Sandra said nonchalantly, as he tilted his head.

"Of course, Baccarat!" he mocked. He'd never seen anything like it before.

There was a big comfortable cushion laden sofa upholstered in the same gold silk as the bedspread, two armchairs to match and a wing back chair covered in a bold tapestry obviously designed for a man. "I had the wing back chair brought in especially for you," she explained, moving to grace it.

"Not many people have a bedroom like this," he said, brushing long darkly tanned fingers across the pile of a cushion.

"I didn't want my bedroom to look like anybody else's," she said.

His mouth twisted. "You certainly got your wish. What is extraordinary is, you wanted all this when you were what—?"

Sandra rested her bright yellow head against the striking tapestry, the fabric a complementary mix of golds, bronzes and deep crimsons. "Around eight, I guess. I asked my dad if I could have a look around the stuff in the storeroom and he said, 'I'll come with you.' We picked the furniture together. I spotted the chandelier in a big box. Dad had it repaired and in no time at all it was up."

"Where was your mother when all this was happening?" he asked thinking her father's sudden death must have left a tremendous void in her life.

"Oh around," she said vaguely. "Mama said my taste was unbelievable."

"It was very exotic for a small girl."

"That's exactly what I wanted. Exotic, like the old travel books I read in the library. Something from an Arabian bazaar or Aladdin's Cave. Don't you just love the Persian rug under your feet?"

"Don't tell me." He moved backwards so he could study the central medallion and the floral arabesques. "It flies?"

"No, no," she said, laughing. "It's a late nineteenth-century Isfahan. My great-great-great-grandmother, Alexandra, was a rich Scottish lassie who was the big collector in the family. That's her portrait over there." She pointed to a large painting of an aristocratic looking young woman with a thick mane of bright red hair, narrow green eyes, very white skin and a pointed chin. She wasn't a beauty, her features were too sharp, but she was certainly striking as was her richly decorated dark green velvet dress.

"Nice to have ancestors," he said dryly.

"Have you never tried to find out who your father was, Daniel?" she asked, hearing the darkness in his tone. "I thought you could find out anything these days."

"Did you now?" he said, turning away from this young woman who was right out of his league. Outback royalty no less. Even the ancestor looked impossibly classy. He moved closer to inspect a gilt framed equine painting of a magnificent white Arabian stallion in a half rearing—neck bent stylised pose. In the background beneath a darkening turquoise sky was its dark skinned handler, with a bright red fez on his head. A fine horseman and a great lover of the most beautiful of all animals this was the one painting he coveted.

"French," Sandra said seeing his interest. "Late 1800s. I absolutely love it. Do I take it you tried but got nowhere?"

"Nowhere at all," he said briefly, turning back to face her. Her eyes were like precious gems, so dark a blue in some lights and depending on what she wore, they were violet. Did she know she looked like a painting herself framed by the antique armchair that all but swallowed her up?

"I'm sorry, Daniel," she said, those huge eyes sad and serious.

"I've dealt with it," he said brusquely, wanting yet not wanting her sympathy.

"How?"

"You ask too many questions." He began to prowl around restlessly.

"What happened to your mother?"

He picked up a silver object, put it down again. "She just died. I don't like to talk about it."

"Maybe you should. I hoped you would talk to me. After all I know a lot about death. Your mother must have been very young?"

"She was," he said sombrely, wanting her to leave it alone. "But I can hold on to her memory."

"Yes, you can," she agreed, turning her face more fully towards him. "I remember as clearly as though it were yesterday the afternoon my father was buried. All the Kingstons are buried on Moondai."

"I know." He was familiar with the family cemetery where Rigby Kingston had been buried alongside his first wife, Catherine, who had died of cancer, his favourite son, Trevor, not far away; his ancestors around him. His mother's ashes he had tossed on a desert whirlwind for that was what she had wanted. No trace left.

"Of course, you were *there*," Sandra realized. "My grandfather obviously didn't want me at his funeral. Maybe he was trying to spare me something Lord knows! But I held his hand the day my father was buried."

"Did you?" Daniel took a seat on the huge carved chest to listen to her tale. He had never before he met her considered he might fall under the spell of Ms Alexandra Kingston. She was his employer for one thing. She was too young, unattainable to the likes of him, but everything about her gave him immense pleasure, the more so every time he saw her. "Why not your mother's hand?" he asked, really wanting to know.

"Mama went to pieces," she explained. "She was crying all the time. I remember someone I didn't know was standing beside her holding her up."

"Man or woman?"

"What do you think?" Her response was laconic. "I remember his glossy black shoes. I held Grandad's hand and he let me even though he didn't like holding hands. Everyone was in black but I wore my best dress, the one Dad liked. It was bright yellow. I tied my hair back with a yellow ribbon. When they lowered the coffin I wanted to jump in with him. I know Grandad wanted to jump in, too. He nearly broke my fingers he held them so tight. Mama was crying buckets, but Grandad and I saved our tears for later."

"What about your uncle Lloyd? Can you remember what he was like that day?"

Sandra shut her eyes tight the better to summon up the memory. "He didn't cry, either, but he looked terrible. He threw something in. Some little leatherbound book. I threw in a letter I wrote and the gold cup I'd just won at a riding competition at the Alice. Mum threw in a red rose. It made Grandad very angry but he never showed it until later."

"That must have been a terrible day for you, Sandra."

She pressed a hand to her fragile temple. "Maybe that's one of the reasons I trust you, Daniel. We both know about terrible days. And we both lost a dad."

"You can't miss what you never had." Daniel shrugged, which was a lie. "At least you were blessed with your memories of him." He stood up abruptly, tall and strong, suppressed emotion in his eyes.

I'm starting to get very good at reading Daniel's face, Sandra thought. Underneath the calmness, the quiet authority and the humour was a passionate man. "Want to see my room?" She whipped herself into sudden action.

"Now that's an offer! I can't refuse." He caught the fresh scent of her as she all but danced by him, light and graceful as any ballerina.

"I want to do lots of things to it," she confided. "It's much too staid. I bet you thought you were going to sleep in baby bear's bed?"

He laughed. "I never thought for a minute you'd let me into anywhere so grand."

"I need you to be happy, Daniel," she said seriously, walking through the open doorway of her parents' old suite while Daniel followed, keeping a few paces behind.

The suite was massive, very traditional in design with a colour scheme of bluish-grey and cream. A few paintings hung on the wall—nothing like the eclectic collection in Sandra's room but a beautiful, eye catching Chinoiserie screen stood beside the white marble fireplace. Over the mantle hung an oil and pencil drawing of a lovely little girl around five years of age with huge blue eyes and a cascade of golden ringlets.

"Recognise me?" she asked.

For a moment he said nothing, seized by a violent rush of tenderness that caught him unawares. He wanted to reach out and touch it, study it up close. There was a magical quality about such sweetness and innocence.

"Daniel?" she prompted. He'd had more than enough time to make a comment.

"Let me look at it properly." He stalled for time. "Who painted it?"

"A very clever friend of Dad's who was visiting us. He's a famous architect now. He lives in Singapore."

"It's lovely," he said, after another pause. "And I get to see your curls."

"You can see them better here." She lifted a silver framed photograph off a small circular table which held a collection of other framed photographs and passed it to him.

"This is Nikki?" he asked quietly.

"Yes." Her voice turned husky.

"Thank you for showing it to me." There was a lump in his own throat. He stared down at the recently taken glossy black and white photograph. In it, Sandra's small face was more gently rounded. She was smiling radiantly. A great cloud of blond hair framed her face and tumbled over her shoulders. Her arms were locked around a little girl obviously in the final stages of the childhood leukaemia that had robbed her of life. The child had huge sorrowful dark eyes but a big smile. She was wearing a beanie to cover the cruel effects of chemotherapy.

"How sad can life get?"

Sandra swallowed on a tight throat. "As soon as my affairs are finalised, I'm making a grant to the Leukaemia Foundation for research on paediatric leukaemia."

"You should," he agreed gently. "How did you come to meet Nikki?" He set the framed photograph carefully back on the table.

"It was my last year at uni. A medical school friend rang me one day to ask if I'd consider joining their little group. A few of them entertained sick kids in hospital, played games with them, read to them, sat with them, sang to them, played guitar, anything to take their minds off their suffering. I went along and listened as dying kids poured out their hearts." She broke off a minute to compose herself. "For some reason they wanted to *talk* to me. I think it had something to do with my blond hair and blue eyes. One little kid around four asked Anthony, my friend, who always dressed as a clown if I was an angel. Some of our group cracked up it was all so gut wrenching but I couldn't walk away. The very same day this photo was taken, Anthony shaved off all my hair when he didn't really want to. He was a little bit in love with me. I've got a photo of that as well with all of us laughing and crying at the same time."

"Well now isn't this cosy?" A voice rife with sarcasm shattered the moment of closeness. "I haven't seen so much togetherness in a long, long time."

Daniel threw back his head, his striking face taut but before he could speak Sandra cut in. "I'm not surprised, Bernie," she said, turning towards her cousin. He was smirking and boldly wagging a finger. "Togetherness isn't something I associate with our family. Do you want something?"

Irritation broke over his face. "Call me Berne," he protested. "I was Bernie when I was a kid. I'm Berne now. I prefer it."

"Berne it is," she said crisply. "I was just showing Daniel his room."

"In case neither of you have noticed, this is *yours*," he said, acidly, somewhat stunned by the obvious rapport between Moondai's overseer and his cousin.

"So it is," she returned sweetly. "After all, Uncle Lloyd has taken over the master suite."

"Why not? He's the rightful master after all," Berne retaliated.

"Grandad didn't seem to think so."

"No, he was too busy scheming with Daniel here, mornings, afternoons, evenings, you name it. Heads together. Black and silver. Grandad always did cut a fine figure. I always thought—"

"Spare us, Berne," Daniel said, his face strangely impassive. "Your thoughts are way off beam. Your grandfather knew he was dying."

"He told you?" Sandra and Berne spoke together,

Daniel nodded in a matter of fact way. "Yes, he did. I was to say nothing to no one and I didn't. It was his wish and his place to tell his family and anyone else he wanted to know. Some days I suppose he thought he mightn't even last until the morrow. But there were orders to be carried out, decisions to be made. He wasn't going to be around to be in charge. Consequently there was a lot to talk about."

"By God you've kept a lot to yourself." Berne hurled the accusation. "My grandfather was good to you. Why?" he demanded, unable to hide his mountain of resentments. "You got paid well enough, so why the quarter of a million?" More than a touch of challenge had entered Berne's voice. "Was that the dowry price? You could have asked a hell of a lot more."

His intention was clearly to goad Daniel into speaking out and perhaps revealing too much but Daniel had assumed a different guise even as Berne spoke; detached, businesslike, official, pretty much like Rigby Kingston had been as boss. "Maybe I'd better leave. I just know you're going to talk absolute drivel."

"Am I now?" The hot blood rose to Berne's high cheekbones, but something in Daniel's body language sent him back to the doorway where he turned for the final word. "Makes sense to me. Think about it, cousin." He shot a glance at Sandra who was balancing some bronze object in her hand as though she meant to throw it. "Make sense to you? Of course you won't get anything out of Daniel on the subject, but denials. But how many girls want to believe their future husbands were bought for them?"

"You don't think the plan a bit tricky, Berne? As far as I'm concerned marriage is the kiss of death. More than half of all marriages today end in divorce. Quite apart from that, how could Grandad possibly imagine he could so easily manipulate two people? Hypothetical question as I don't believe for a minute there's even a grain of truth in your theory."

"There isn't," Daniel confirmed with quiet contempt.

"Don't believe him, cousin," Berne warned, pleased to have stirred up a hornet's nest. "Listen to your inner voice. See it my way and it all starts to make sense. Didn't Grandad love playing God?'

"That he did," Sandra said, wondering if she could possibly be blinding herself to what she didn't want to see. After all, it did happen. She raked a hand through the silk floss of her hair, wanting to cling to her natural instincts to trust Daniel.

Berne nodded, as though he had won an important point. "You said it. This whole thing smacks of a deal…a marriage of convenience?"

Sandra stared at him while Daniel clenched his fists, looking like he was struggling hard not to lash out. "I'm not bothered by what you think, Berne. Ms Kingston's trust, however, is important to me."

Sandra spoke up. "There's no need to call me Ms Kingston at *any* time, Daniel, I know why you're unwilling to call me by my Christian name in front of the family and staff but it simply doesn't matter to me. I need guidance and I'm willing to take it from you, Daniel. I trust you." For some reason she felt very close to tears, but no way was she going to allow them to fall.

"That's a mistake." Berne frowned fiercely, jealous of her taking sides. "You're a Kingston. *You* own the station. *He's* an employee."

"An indispensable one Berne, lest you forget. I don't have a problem with Daniel calling me Sandra. The *one* person who knew exactly what he intended when he left Moondai to me, was Grandad. Have you bothered to consider he might have wanted to make reparation. After all, he did kick us out."

"With a trust fund," Berne was driven to shouting. "You weren't chucked out into the snow. Grandad didn't want to lay eyes on you and your playgirl mother but he made sure you were provided for."

All trace of colour left Sandra's cheeks. "You're lying."

"Lying? Why would I be lying?" Berne gave her a weird look. "It's easily proved. Grandad wasn't going to let you starve. You went to all the best schools didn't you? I know you were kicked out of two. You went on to university. Where the hell did you think the money was coming from? Come on tell me. You're supposed to be so bright."

Daniel intervened, holding up his palm to Berne so Sandra could speak. "Did your mother never tell you this, Sandra?"

She shook her head wretchedly. "I was *ten,* Daniel. We always had money. I never knew any other life. My mother told me it was my father's money. I accepted that. Why wouldn't I? When she remarried she married money. That was her way. I had part-time jobs all the time I was at university so I wouldn't be too much of a burden. I never thought Grandad was continuing to look out for us."

"Well he was," Berne said, sounding equally wretched.

"Your mother should have told you, Sandra," Daniel said. "She had a duty to tell you."

"Shameless bitch!" Berne muttered. "Never did tell the truth.

All she was ever interested in was herself. Dad was right about her. You should think about it instead of blaming Dad."

"I love my mother, Berne," Sandra said, unable to disentangle herself from the ties that bind.

"Fine!" he fumed. "I know you can love someone and be disgusted with them at the same time. Why did Grandad bypass me for you? Sons and grandsons always have the inside track."

"I know they do," Sandra acknowledged. "Maybe Grandad knew I was the most likely to try to hold on to our inheritance. The Kingston inheritance. Kingstons are buried here, Berne. Do we walk away from Moondai and leave them here?"

Berne gave a strangled laugh. "They're *dead,* Sandra. They're gone forever. They don't know and they don't care."

"But *I* care," Sandra said. "I want to be loyal to my ancestors, to my dad and my grandfather, harsh though he was to us. I don't want to betray them."

"You're too young to be such a sentimental fool," Berne said in disgust. "The dead are dead. No way do they care about our actions. As for Daniel here—" he shot Daniel a glowering look "—he's a fast worker. I'm betting he was offered the deal of a lifetime on a silver platter. He gets Moondai but you're part of the package. He couldn't have imagined such a scenario in his wildest dreams. But a word of caution."

"Okay, let's hear it, Berne," Daniel clipped off, looking like he was more than ready to hear it and deal with it if needs be.

"It's for my *cousin,* pal," Berne emphasized, predisposed to hating Daniel Carson for so many reasons; showing him up without even trying, relating so easily to his grandfather when Rigby Kingston had produced awe, fear and a great deal of anxiety in him and everyone else, and just to compound the problem, it appeared very much like Daniel had Sandra sold on him on sight. It tied Berne in knots and made him doubly aggressive. "We don't know anything much about you, do we, Dan?" he charged. "You're a dark horse if ever there was one. Grandad accepted you on the word of a fellow cattleman. So you did a good job in the Channel Country? I guess you've always been hell-bent on climbing the ladder. Personally I think you should be investigated. Most people have things to hide. We know nothing about your background for instance. Sandra should make it her business to find out."

But Sandra was reeling from Berne's disclosures. "You think Grandad didn't check Daniel out?" she asked, staring at her cousin.

Berne shrugged. "It was different with Grandad. No man had power over him, but from what I can see Daniel has power over *you* already."

"He must if you say so, Berne." She looked at her cousin with acute distaste. The charge stung like a whip because it was *true*.

"Look how you treat him for God's sake!" Berne wheeled a half circle in his rage. "You've installed him in the house. It would never have happened in Grandad's day. Dad certainly wouldn't have allowed it. Daniel is *staff*. He's got the overseer's bungalow. It's good enough for him."

Sandra noted the sharp shift in Daniel's lean powerful body. She moved to stand between them. If there was any physical confrontation she knew Berne would come off second best. "Let's say I want Daniel on call, Berne. Not a good distance away. Yesterday we crash landed in a crocodile infested swamp. Incredibly Daniel was able to bring the chopper down in a clearing the size of a bathtub. The sad thing is, it's my *family* I don't trust. There's a great deal at stake here. You and Uncle Lloyd did handsomely out of Grandad's will as you should, but you're filled with bitter resentments. I understand that. I got the lion's share. But I think most people in my position would find themselves with a few more fears than they started out with. I've made a judgment in regards Daniel. I've elected to trust him."

"More fool's you!" Berne's voice trembled with anger. "It's just as I said. He's got to you already. Just be careful, cousin. That's all I'm saying."

"What have *I* got to gain from something happening to Sandra, Berne?" Daniel asked in a voice that would have brought anyone up short.

"Not now. Not yet," Berne said obscurely, turning to go.

"If you've got concerns why don't you go to the authorities?" Daniel began to move towards him.

"Daniel, please." Sandra grasped his arm. "I will be careful, Berne. I don't need you to tell me. My mother has always believed the Cessna was sabotaged when Dad was flying it. That means someone got away with a crime." Even as she said it Sandra felt shame. Berne had had nothing to do with it even if he had been an awful kid, jealous, resentful, always spoiling for a fight.

"That's your stupid mother talking," Berne rasped, his tanned skin turning white. "You might have a little chat with her. You talk about untrustworthy? You can't go past her. Uncle Trevor wasn't supposed to make that trip anyway. It was Grandad." He punched the words out, turned on his heel and stomped off down the hall.

For a moment Sandra couldn't catch her breath. Confusion was growing at such a rate of intensity her mind was in turmoil. "Could that possibly be true?" she managed eventually. "Have you ever heard it?" Her legs felt so wobbly she had to sit down.

"Never." Daniel's voice was rough with concern. "And I've heard plenty of talk. Don't upset yourself, Sandra. You've gone very pale."

"Why would he say it?" She searched those silver-grey eyes.

"God knows." Daniel could see the shock in her. There were far too many revelations for her to handle all at once. "He's been making a lot of wild accusations."

"So that's it, wild accusations?"

He saw the doubts that brushed her expression. Doubts that made something flare deep in his eyes. "So who should you believe, Sandra?" he asked in a dead-serious voice. "Because it's *you* who has to decide."

CHAPTER SEVEN

IN THE DAYS that followed Sandra had plenty of time to mull over Berne's revelations. Had it really been her grandfather and not her father who was to have flown to the Kingston outstation that fateful day? Her grandfather had long been accustomed to flying off on regular inspections, often without notice because he took pleasure in catching the staff on the hop. On numerous occasions he had taken her father along with him. As the heir apparent, her father was being groomed to one day take over the reins. Berne had sounded so *sure.* She struggled to understand how, if that were so, her mother had been able to maintain her silence.

She had lost no time ringing her mother in an effort to set the record straight. Just as she feared, immediately she broached the subject, her mother became highly emotional. That was Pam's way of protecting herself from being questioned too closely. Pam invariably resorted to controlled hysteria. She swore she knew nothing of the change of plan. When asked about where their money had come from after they left Moondai, she had flown into a fit of defensiveness saying she had never spoken to Sandra about financial matters because they simply weren't her concern. Whatever lines of credit Rigby Kingston had made available, it was his duty to do so. He was a hateful man. Pam was overjoyed he was dead. Sandra deserved everything that had come her way. Moondai would have gone to her father in any case. Sandra should not upset her like this. That part of her life as a Kingston was long over. Besides, Mickey had chicken pox and needed her attention.

All in all the phone call had been a stomach churning disaster. Her mother had even been crass enough to call her stepfather to the phone to say a few affectionate words, but Sandra had all but hurled the phone down, thinking though she loved her mother Pam was a fool. It made life so much easier if one didn't have to look truth in the face.

The upshot was Sandra felt desperate to get confirmation from her uncle. Daniel had urged her to do so, but somehow she always baulked at the last moment. If Berne's claim was true and not made up on the spur of the moment, it would open up an entirely new avenue of thought. Her grandfather had made enemies over the years. He had never been what one would call popular. In fact a lot of people wouldn't have been upset by his demise. But surely his son wouldn't have conspired against him? Her father had been without question, the favourite, but by no means had Rigby Kingston closed the door on his younger son. Though Lloyd's consuming interest in cataloguing the native flora had been a mystery and an irritation to his father, Lloyd had been allowed to make his numerous field trips and tour the country at will. They all lived in what most people would consider, splendour, all financed by Rigby Kingston, notoriously miserly in some areas and surprisingly generous in others.

Mystery piled on top of mystery. It was those closest to Sandra she felt she couldn't trust. Not even Elsa who lived on the periphery of everyone's attention. In some ways Elsa was like a resident ghost, forever hovering about without really being seen or heard. Whatever had happened to the handsome, hardworking, businesswoman of yesterday? Happiness had passed

Elsa by. But what had actually happened to cause her to pass from one state to the other? Certainly her grandfather had been an autocratic man but one would have thought Elsa in her mid-forties when they married would have been able to cope with him? There must have been attraction between them for them to have married in the first place. Instead Elsa had turned into a watcher, not a doer as hollowed out inside as if she'd been gutted. That in itself was a mystery. The empty shell of her marriage was now over, but still Elsa made no move to get on with a new and better life.

Sandra on the other hand made a good start on learning about the running of Moondai. As the weeks went by Daniel was able to spend more and more time with her though the amount of time was determined by his own heavy work schedule. She was grateful he was loosening up his routine in order to be able to show her the ropes. It had taken no time at all to discover his workload was considerable. He was on the job at sunup, not returning to the homestead until well after sunset. Consequently she never saw him at breakfast or lunch, meeting up maybe an hour before dinner when they retired to the office. There they read through piles of memos, invoices, letters and documents that Andy, the station accountant had arranged in batches for inspection and signature where necessary. Whatever decisions Daniel came to regarding the business side of running the station he explained the reasons for it, going into quite a bit of detail and not fobbing her off or treating her as if her opinion at this early stage had little value. He treated her like the intelligent person she was. She liked that about him. Her uncle invariably talked down to her. Sandra had never thought of herself as a businesswoman in the making, but she was finding learning about all these financial matters far more interesting than she ever supposed.

"Your grandfather has left you one of the finest cattle stations in the country and the fortune to keep it intact," Daniel told her. "It's important you understood how everything works. You have a good mind. Now's a great opportunity to use it."

To that end she and Daniel continued their learning sessions for a couple of hours after dinner. Even dinner had turned into a routine with some degree of normalcy. Her uncle solved the problem of Daniel's presence at the table by addressing the odd civil remark to him but concentrating on his niece. Sandra who had no great knowledge of the desert flora but had always been filled with wonderment at the phenomenon of the vast desert gardens began to avail herself of her uncle's extensive knowledge.

"Don't start him off for God's sake!" Berne had warned when she first started to show an interest.

"You're incapable of appreciating the beauties of nature, Bernard," his father responded, finding he was warming to his niece now that she had become an adult. Sandra had been a very precocious little girl as he recalled. Something both his father and brother had encouraged no doubt to counter Pamela's single digit IQ.

But it was to Daniel Sandra always turned for advice and instruction. It was getting so she couldn't hide her feelings. From herself at least. She prided herself she had the sense not to allow Daniel to see how important he was to her. That might have put him in a very awkward position. She knew she was more than half way in love with him—hell, madly in love with him—which might have been precisely what her grandfather had in mind. Just thinking about it all was interfering with her sleep and her thought processes. To counter her increasing need for him and his company she upped her businesslike manner. The last thing she wanted to do was put pressure on him. A girl had her pride. Daniel was there to give her protection, to be her friend and mentor, so that when his year was up she could step into his shoes albeit with the help of a professional station manager they would select together.

End of story or the start of a great adventure?

It was only when she lay in bed at night, thinking about him, she wondered if he were fooled by the briskness of her manner. She was so *aware* of him, every word he spoke, every inflection, the way he laughed, the way he walked, the gleaming glances he sent in her direction, every gesture he made. When their hands brushed, whilst passing documents to one another, little electric shocks zapped through her. There was such a *buzz* around him. No use pretending. She was in *deep.* It amazed and alarmed her, causing her to wonder if her own susceptibility had overtones of her mother? She had seen too much of vulnerable women. She had no intention of becoming one.

It took six weeks before they received a full report on the helicopter crash.

Daniel stood by the window in the study reading it, a frown of concentration between his brows.

"Well?" Sandra couldn't stand the suspense.

He broke off to look at her. "Nothing much new."

"Damn, are you sure?"

He shoved that errant lock of hair off his forehead. "Of course I'm sure. You can read it in a minute. It's much the same as the preliminary report. Mechanical failure. There's no blame laid, no criticism of the maintenance of the aircraft. In fact a little pat on the back for me for pilot skills."

"Is that all they came up with?" Sandra felt angry and frustrated.

He sighed. "Don't get upset. We survived. The failure of mechanical components is well documented, Sandra. Now we have the chopper back, I'll have the hangar, attended by day and locked up at night. It's never been done before."

"So we drop the whole thing?" Sandra showed her dissatisfaction.

"Nothing else we can do." Daniel shrugged in acceptance. Nevertheless he quietly went about putting new security measures in place.

It didn't take long for a steady stream of visitors to start to call; station people and business people from Alice Springs who wanted to welcome Rigby Kingston's granddaughter back home. Most were good-hearted, Outback people simply wanting to wish her well. A few busybodies came to size her up. Gossip was rife Moondai might very well come onto the market. The wheeler-dealers wanted to be there on the ground floor. Even would-be suitors came to call; some overconfident, dressed nattily, some afflicted by stammering shyness that was painful to behold. None of them fortune hunters exactly—they were all from established families—but young men looking for a suitable wife and future mother for their brood. Sandra's enviable financial standing made her a prize candidate.

The consensus of opinion was made available by way of the grapevine. Alexandra Kingston would make some lucky bloke the perfect wife.

"The word's gone out," Daniel told her, a dry note in his voice. They were sitting atop a fence watching a mob of around thirty brumbies being drafted. For wild horses they had surprisingly well developed muscles and came in varied colours, bay, iron grey, black, big, medium, compact sized, some showing station blood. One liver chestnut beauty was trying its level best to bite a stockman on the shoulder.

"What word?" She turned on him so precipitously he had to grab her to prevent her falling.

"Why your beauty of course, Ms Kingston." His eyes beneath the brim of his hat mocked her.

"And you're the expert?" she asked tartly, to cover the strain of sitting next to him without being able to touch him. Every single day she was reacting more *bodily* to him. Lord help her she wanted him to crush her in his arms. Envelop her. A great thing had happened to her. She was head over heels in love. Then there was the other thing which might or might not have significance but she had to find out from him.

Among the visitors who wished to renew their acquaintance

were station people called McAuliffe accompanied by their only daughter, Alanna. Sandra vaguely remembered Alanna, although Alanna was several years older, a vibrantly attractive brunette with a shapely figure and unusual coffee-coloured eyes.

Memories of that afternoon kept coming... After partaking of afternoon tea and complementing Meg on her cooking, Alanna stood up with an appealing, "Do you mind if I go off and find Daniel?"

Sandra had been shocked at her own reaction. She'd wanted to tell Alanna to back the hell off. She was *jealous,* when she had vowed never, never to become a jealous woman.

"I need him to confirm something," Alanna explained. "Would you mind if I borrow the Jeep?" she asked prettily, casting her eyes over the Jeep that Sandra kept parked in the drive for her own use.

Again Sandra couldn't for the life of her wring out a "Please do."

"There's a ball coming up." Alanna looked back, big eyed. "Daniel has promised to be my partner. He's just so much in demand, I'm thrilled out of my mind it's going to be me."

"Lana's absolutely *crazy* about him," Mrs. McAuliffe piped up, just in case Sandra had missed the message. "Daniel's enormously popular with the girls. There's something about him that makes the knees buckle," she gushed, turning quite pink cheeked herself.

"We're kinda hoping something good might come of it," Mr. McAuliffe tacked on, cracking his knuckles.

Over my dead body!

"Prickly little thing aren't you," Daniel interrupted her recollections, amused by her feisty expression. "It just so happens I *like* it. You must have known you were going to attract every last bachelor from eighteen to eighty in the Territory and beyond."

"I'm relying on you to put it about I'm very bad-tempered," she said shortly.

She had taken off her akubra and damp golden curls clung to her nape. Her hair had grown so quickly Daniel thought, resisting the powerful urge to fluff the gilded halo that had replace the short petalled look. No wonder the little kids at the hospital had mistaken her for an angel. But she was more spicy than sweet though she had her sweet moments. A man couldn't ask for more he thought. But it wasn't going to happen to him.

Forget it, Daniel.

The words dropped as dull as stones.

"Unfortunately temper doesn't put a man off," he said. "It's the really *nice* girls who tend to get overlooked."

"That certainly doesn't apply to your friend Alanna," Sandra retorted, sharper than she meant. *Be careful. Be careful. Don't give yourself away.* "Now there's a sexpot if ever I've seen one. Are you going to the ball with her?"

He laughed, an infinitely attractive sound to her ears. "Though tempted I had to turn her down."

She turned her head to stare at him. He was worth staring at. He had a beautifully structured chin and jawline. She wanted to trace it with her hand. She was painfully aware of the excitement that was throbbing inside her, wishing and wishing she could pass her excitement on to him. "She told me you had *promised.* I'm surprised at you, Daniel. You shouldn't break a promise."

"As it happened, I didn't." He whistled at a hostile horse with a star-shaped white blaze on its forehead. The horse amazingly quietened, ears tipped forward. "Alanna thinks if she wants something badly enough she'll get it."

"And she wants you. Mamma and Poppa made that clear. You better remind her you're working for *me.*"

"Yes, Ms Kingston." He tipped a tanned finger, eyes sparkling. "Anyway what's not to want?" he quipped.

"I suppose. You're very likeable, Daniel," she said kindly. "What are you going to do with your life? You're so clever and capable."

"You forgot popular." His glance seemed to mock her. "Trying to get rid of me already?"

She wanted to say, you can stay forever but was worried about frightening him off. How could you stop yourself from giving your heart away? It just happened. "The truth is I'm coming to rely on you more and more, Daniel," she said. "Do you suppose—I don't want you to take this the wrong way—but do you suppose Grandad had some master plan in mind?"

Sunlight made a dazzle of his eyes. "For you and me?"

His tone was so highly sceptical she was stopped in her tracks. "Well we all know it wouldn't work. I am resolved not to get married anyway. But I keep wondering why he arranged things the way he did. Berne stirred things up as he meant to. There's got to be some logic to it. Grandad was nothing if not logical. Did he assume in throwing the two of us together some magic might happen? Or more likely did he think we'd see it in materialistic terms? What would undoubtedly advantage you would advantage me as you could successfully step straight into Grandad's shoes. You'd maintain authority and style. You said yourself it made a kind of sense."

His mouth twisted. "Where would I get style from, Sandra?" he asked as though he was burdened by some terrible legacy. "I have no family, not a lot of money but enough to get started somewhere on my own and I didn't get to go to university, like you. But a good man made sure I got the benefit of a fair education. He would have let me continue but I was too determined to pay him back."

"That was Harry Cunningham from the Channel Country?" she asked with care.

"You've done your homework. What else have you found out about me?" His tone was astonishingly clipped.

"Don't get mad. It was Vince Taylor who told me," she said, trying to sound casual when she'd really been pumping foreman Vince, for information. "Mr. Cunningham must have been a good man."

"The best," Daniel confirmed.

"Obviously. He trained you. As for style, as far as I'm concerned, style is innate. It's knowing who *you* are, not who your dad was; what *you* are. You've got good blood in you, Daniel."

"The hell I have!" It came out like a soft growl.

"Oh, you've got good blood all right," she insisted. "You'd be at home anywhere."

He gave her a smouldering glance. "Your family doesn't seem to think so. I'd be lucky if your appalling snob of an uncle addresses two words to me over dinner."

"I wouldn't have a nervous breakdown about it," she said dryly. "Uncle Lloyd is worried *you'll* ask him something he doesn't know. Think about it. Exactly what does he know about? He's spent his whole life on Moondai but he couldn't possibly run it. His towering achievement is becoming an amateur botanist."

"Well that in itself is something," Daniel said with unexpected approval, given Lloyd Kingston's patronising manner with him. "I'm like you I'm finding the whole area fascinating. I've even taken to looking out for the exquisite little plants tucked away in the canyons. Botany is a legitimate career. Your uncle would have been a much happier man had he struck out for himself. The same goes for Berne."

"It hasn't occurred to you both of them are bone lazy?" Sandra said, marvelling that it was so.

"Now that you mention it, yes. Listen, much as I'm enjoying the break, I must go. I have to do some bull catching this afternoon with a couple of the men. The tallest and the fittest."

"So they can lift the steel panels for the portable yards?"

"Right on." He gave her a little nod of approval. "You might only have been ten when you left but you haven't forgotten much. It's great you've kept up your riding, too." She was, in fact, a natural born horsewoman. He took great pleasure in watching her ride, knowing she loved horses as much as he did.

Daniel swung himself off the fence in one lithe movement, without thinking, holding up his arms for her.

Yes, yes! She craved those strong arms around her, those tanned hands holding her, his hard muscled chest against her cheek.

"Catch me!" she invited, joyous as a child. She threw out her own arms launching her feather light body at him.

But it wasn't a child who landed in his arms. It was a woman who was growing more lovely, more sexually exciting by the day. Just holding her was dangerous. Her skin was perfection even in the strong sunlight. Her buttery curls swept up from her graceful neck. Her full tender lips were curved in a smile but it was her eyes that drew Daniel in. So deep and so sparkling a blue he wanted to drown in their lagoon-like depths.

A woman's beauty and sexual allure was a powerful weapon to render a man helpless. A weapon he couldn't risk putting into her hands. There was no way he could reverse their station in life. She was the Kingston heiress; he was the overseer. He had to hold tight to his pride though he realised had they been on their own and stockmen weren't around, all it would have taken was to tighten his hold on her and lower his head.

Desire swept through Daniel's body like a dark rushing river. He couldn't step back from it. It was on him. All of his senses were astonishingly *keen*. Sight. Sound. Smell. Touch. They were far too close, their heads bent to one another, both of them seemingly fearing to speak. He could savour the fresh scent of her; feel the heat off her body. She was the very essence of femininity. He could almost *taste* her on his palate.

For one long precious moment he allowed himself to be held in thrall. He couldn't even think straight; just standing there, holding her, drenched in a yearning so powerful, so evocative of something just beyond his reach, it was causing him *pain*. He wondered with an unfamiliar surge of panic what more lay in store for him. What could happen from this point on? This was no fleeting attraction. It was something over which he was losing control. Yet getting her to fall in love with *him* wouldn't be so difficult. He had enough experience to recognise that. He could see the little electric flame in her eyes. What burned her burned him.

Only it wasn't *right*. This was far more than a momentary indiscretion; it was as good as forbidden. She was quite alone. Her family wasn't much use to her. She relied on him; she trusted him. Sometimes she seemed *so terrifyingly* young and innocent. He couldn't possibly hurt her or betray that innocence which he knew instinctively she retained for all that predatory stepfather who deserved to be pummelled into the ground.

Daniel made his decision. Falling in love was not only a powerful emotion, it could come as a body blow. One false move could spoil everything. They were friends. They could never be lovers. He stepped back abruptly, dropping his arms.

"I do believe you've put on six or seven kilos?" He rallied sufficiently to make a joke.

"I'll be a butterball in no time," she said, herself faring quite well in regaining her balance. As he turned away she called, "Do you think you could spare me a full hour tomorrow, Daniel?"

"Sure, what for?" He stood in a characteristic pose with his two hands on his lean hips, long fingers pointing down.

She took immense pleasure in his dynamic male aura. "I want to learn how to ride a motorbike," she told him with feigned casualness.

His expression was comical. She might just as well have said she wanted to learn to drive the bulldozer and start ripping up new tracks for the road trains. "Is that a good idea?" He couldn't bear the idea of her coming off a bike, even a minor spill could break bones though he knew her look of fragility was deceptive. She was actually quite strong.

"Heck, Daniel, we're in the middle of nowhere," she protested. "You can show me, can't you or will I get Chris to show me?" She knew she was provoking him. Chris Barrett was a good-looking, full of himself, young jackeroo who was doing a year's stint on the station before taking up a position in the family engineering firm in Brisbane. Hugely enjoying his gap year Chris flirted openly with her though the older stockmen were at pains to make clear to him he was crossing the line.

"Just let's forget Chris," Daniel said dryly. "As a rider I don't regard him very highly, let alone as a teacher. Your grandfather only took him on as a favour to his family. He'll never make a cattleman not that he was ever meant to. Please don't give him any encouragement. He's impudent enough as it is." But harmless, Daniel knew, otherwise he'd have been told to pack up his gear and leave.

"I've forgotten him already," Sandra said airily. "So I can count on an hour tomorrow?"

"Okay," he nodded briskly.

"I'd like to be able to handle the dozer." She kept a perfectly straight face as she said it.

"Forget the dozer," he said, firmly. "It's by no means easy to operate, weighing in as it does at around thirty-eight tons. There's a small tractor I'll let you have a go on one of these days."

"Thank you, Daniel." She gave him a radiant smile. "I've got a lot of learning in front of me. I want to be able to fly the Beech Baron and the helicopter in time."

His answer was serious which greatly pleased her. "Flying lessons can be arranged," he said. "I thought you *hated* flying?"

"So I do and why wouldn't I?" she retorted. "But it was wonderful up there with you in the chopper before we crashed. The best way to get over my fears might well be to learn how to fly. Don't you think?" She tipped her head to one side, staring at him, trying to understand this momentous thing that was happening between them.

He nodded his agreement. "It's the only way to get around. I know a very patient and competent teacher."

"You?" she asked hopefully.

He shook his head. "Not me. I'd find that too nerve-racking."

He softened it with a smile. "This guy, Paddy Hyland runs the Hyland School of Aviation at the Alice. He's very good, gently spoken and he has the patience of Job."

"So what are you saying, females need to be mollycoddled?"

"Well gentleness makes women feel better, Sandra."

"Plus females need instructors with the patience of Job?"

"Now you're starting to get the hang of it." That engaging dimple flickered in his cheek.

"Have you failed to notice how smart I am, Daniel?"

"Sandra, I haven't failed to notice every last little thing about you," he said with such a note in his voice it turned her insides out. "Have a nice day now!" He sketched a salute. "I'll see you tonight."

Make that every night of our lives!

CHAPTER EIGHT

SANDRA HAD BEEN going steadily through paperwork since around nine o'clock that morning. It was now eleven and Meg came to the door with a cup of coffee and a freshly baked apple and cinnamon muffin. She stopped for a while chatting—Meg was always cheerful—then went on her way. Sandra had insisted Meg get more help in running the house—it was so big. Elsa did nothing to lend a hand so far as Sandra could see—so Meg had taken two young aboriginal girls under her wing for training. Sandra often heard their infectious laughter issuing from the kitchen and around the house. It brightened up the atmosphere and she was glad of it.

Elsa kept mostly to her suite of rooms—she had not shared a bedroom with Sandra's grandfather for many years—or she took her long rambling walks. The family cemetery was one of her haunts though she hadn't taken to laying flowering branches on her husband's grave as Sandra often did at the grave of her father. In fact Sandra had given instructions for a number of advanced white bauhinias to be planted around the perimeter which was guarded by a tall wrought iron fence. Immensely hardy the bauhinias would lend shade and their loveliness to that desolate place. It had been kept in perfect order but an aura of melancholy hung over it. She finished what she was doing, put her signature to the crosses Daniel had marked for her, then decided on the spur of the moment to ride out to the family plot to check on the new plantings. The worst of the heat was over and the desert days sparkled.

On her way she stopped to break off several long branches of the fluffy flowered pink mulla-mulla, a desert ephemeral that threw a blushing veil over the landscape. Some of the branches stood as tall as herself as did the desert grevillea which was one of the most spectacular flowering trees of the Red Centre.

Most of her friends from her student days thought the desert extremely arid, a terrifying, life threatening place, which of course it was under certain circumstances. What they didn't appear to know or had never seen was the desert after the rains; a wonderland on such a scale it made the most beautiful of city gardens, even the botanical gardens, look pocket handkerchief-sized by comparison. What large country garden for that matter ran to the horizon? Where else were there carpets of white, yellow and pink everlastings covering fifty square miles? Her home, Moondai, was a world apart. She had already resolved to hold on to it. Her ancestors lay buried in the lava-red earth.

When she reached the cemetery she slipped off her horse, a highly responsive mare, and tethered it to a branch of an old gum. The gum was almost a sculpture, gnarled and twisted in its endless struggle against the harshness of sun and wind. A short distance away was the iron fenced enclosure with its marble and granite headstones. No one to disturb you here, she thought a melancholy shiver running down her spine.

A great flock of budgerigar, the phenomenon of the Inland, winged overhead drawing her eyes. They were flying in their curious V formation seeking out the nearest water which was maybe half a mile off at Jirra Jarra Creek, its banks graced by a magnificent corridor of red river gums. She took a few moments to watch the squadron of little birds flame across the sky, emerald green and gold, the colours of the nation, then she gathered the mass of pink flowers Outback people called "lamb's tails" and strode off. Once inside the massive gate she noted with satisfaction the bauhinias had responded well to their new home. She had expected to see one or two wilting but they showed their toughness holding their silvery green foliage aloft. Their seasonal flowering was over but come September-October they should be out in all their shining white glory. She had always loved the bauhinias as a child; the pink, the white, the purple, cerise. The aboriginals believed they were spirit people. It was a good idea to have them encircle this place where the bones of so many generations of Kingstons lay.

Carefully Sandra paid her respects to her grandfather and the grandmother, Catherine, she had never known, then moved on to the grave of her father, speaking aloud to him as she had as a child. His had been a bittersweet marriage—her mother had never settled in her desert home—but she had always understood her father had deeply loved her, his only child. The happiness and security of her childhood had been destroyed by his death. Her mother, even now, had not apologised for saying her husband's own brother had had something to do with it. She stuck to her claim that Lloyd Kingston was *evil* but though Sandra kept her uncle under constant close observation she couldn't see it. In fact it was starting to seem *unthinkable.* Perhaps her mother had wanted revenge for her brother-in-law's harsh criticism of her own lifestyle? Whatever the reason her uncle should never have used her, a child, as a weapon in their war. *That* had been truly unforgivable even if at some stage he'd believed his claim she wasn't a Kingston. It had only recently struck her, her uncle and her cousin had laboured all their lives for her grandfather's love and approval without ever getting it. Small wonder it had caused such bitterness and driven a wedge between them and her. The great irony was the grandfather who had banished her had made her his heir. Should anything happen to her, her uncle Lloyd would inherit the entire estate.

* * *

Daniel found her an hour later, sitting in solitude on a stone bench. He tethered his horse beside the mare, watching the animals acknowledge each other with companionable whinnies, before walking towards the enclosure.

"Sandra," he called gently.

She lifted her sunny head that always reminded him of a lovely flower on a stalk, holding up a hand.

How do I withstand her? he asked himself, unnerved at the speed with which she had gotten not only under his skin but right into the deepest cavern of his heart. Sandra Kingston was a dream he had been hankering after all his life. She was also, like a dream, out of reach.

Close to, he could see the track of tears on her satin cheeks. He was deeply moved, thinking he would always hold that little picture of her sitting here, weeping gentle tears.

"Hi, come sit beside me," she invited, moving along the bench a little so he would have room.

"I feel I'm intruding," he commented, his eyes on her poignant profile.

"No, you're not." She gave him a reassuring smile. "I was talking to Dad."

"Does he ever answer?" He yanked off his hat, relishing the cooling breeze on his head.

"Sometimes." She dashed the back of her hand over her eyes. "There's so much I'm desperate to know, Daniel. Living with my unhappy family these past months I just can't believe Uncle Lloyd had anything to do with Dad's death."

"I've *never* believed it." Daniel's eyes rested on her floral offering, his own wounded heart contracting. "Apart from anything else, he just doesn't have it in him to take any sort of violent action. As I see it, your mother was expelled from the family home in disgrace. She retaliated by accusing your uncle of a heinous crime. She would have been shattered at the time.

Your uncle had poured endless scorn on her. There's a limit to what people can take."

"So it *was* an accident?" she asked with a profound sigh.

"That was the result of the inquiry."

"So I've spent more than half my life believing a terrible lie?" Her blue eyes sought his.

"Some people use up *all* their life believing lies, Sandra."

"And our accident in the chopper? You had your suspicions, Daniel?" she reminded him. These moments they spent alone were becoming oddly intense as though it wasn't permitted for them to become too intimate.

He shrugged, not wanting to increase her sense of hidden threat. "It just seemed like one accident too many. I jumped to conclusions."

"You don't sound too sure?" She watched his face, wanting to turn his chin a little towards her so she could stare into his eyes.

"Money creates an environment of suspicion, Sandra. In your case a great deal of money."

I've got money for both of us, she cried out inside but couldn't possibly say it aloud. Daniel was fiercely independent and proud.

"Money and passions coexist," he continued. "Anger, bitterness, resentment, shameful, violent thoughts."

"So it would serve my family's ambitions if I didn't get to celebrate my twenty-first birthday?" she asked bleakly.

"Which is fast approaching." He traced the perfect oval of her face with his eyes. She had put a little weight on her fragile frame. It was immensely becoming, the woman emerging clearly from the young girl. "I'll have to start thinking of a present. By the way I have to fly to Darwin, this coming Friday. Joel Moreland wants to meet me."

That name beat against Sandra's brain. "Joel Moreland, the man with the Midas touch? You're not going to leave me for him, are you?" she asked, reduced to near panic.

"Hey, he only wants to meet me, Sandra." For a breathless second he almost pulled her into his arms to comfort her. "A man called Bill Morrissey set it up. He's a member of the Northern Territory Administration."

"Yes, I know. I've read about him," Sandra said, dismissing Morrissey. "So *why* does a man like Moreland want to meet you, Daniel, unless it's to offer you a job?" Her voice was unsteady with emotion.

"If he does, he does." Daniel shook his head, struggling to retain his own role of employee, friend and mentor. "I have to think of my future, Sandra. Let's face it by the time my year's up, you could either decide to sell Moondai or find yourself engaged to one of the drove of guys who've been calling. Don't for a moment think they haven't got their eye on Moondai as well as the fair maiden."

"Thank you, Daniel," she said crisply, tilting her delicately determined chin.

"Sandra, I've no wish to offend you. As lovable as you undoubtedly are, your rich inheritance would only make them love you more."

"You've made your point," she said acidly. "Or am I supposed to feel flattered they might want *me* at all?"

His mobile mouth twisted. "I just want you to be fully aware of the disadvantages of being an heiress."

"Don't worry. I'll have the lucky man vetted by you."

It distressed him just to hear her say it even in mockery. He locked his strong muscular arms behind his head. "What I started out to say was would you like to come along for the ride? I don't expect to be more than a couple of hours over lunch. You could do some shopping; visit an art gallery. We could meet up later. Actually I'd like you to meet Moreland. It's very handy to know a man like that. He could be a big help to you in the future."

"Well I'll need it, won't I with you planning to pack up and leave," Sandra burst out, startled by her impulse to throw herself into his arms and beg him to stay.

"What did you think was going to happen?" He turned on

her, on the surface calm, underneath battling his own complicated needs and wants. Sandra Kingston coming into his life
had exposed him to new and overwhelming emotions. Falling
in love was the last thing he had seen coming.

"Oh, I don't know," she said. "The two of us surviving that
crash entrenched you in my mind as a friend and protector, not
just Moondai's overseer which you're determined to be."

"Well that's my job, Sandra," he said tersely. "We're both
aware of that. We inhabit different worlds."

"We inhabit the *same* world!" She levelled him with an electric blue stare.

"Don't, Sandra," he said, deliberately using his position as
employee as a shield.

Her cheeks flushed with anger. "Don't what?"

"Don't go where you're going."

She jumped up, a small fury, blazingly blue eyes smarting
with her own lie. "I have no idea what you mean."

"I think you do."

"And you've decided to put me in my place?" she asked raggedly.

"That wasn't my aim." He stood up quiet, but commanding.
"What I'm saying is I've decided to remain in *my* place."

"You have a hide!" Her voice trembled. He towered over her
with those long legs but for once she didn't find it comforting.

"I'm sorry. You *must* understand."

"Well I don't!" Her vision was blurring with tears. She felt
sick to the stomach; ashamed, humiliated. Furiously she blinked
the tears away.

Daniel felt his heartbeats thudding like hammers. He was
trying so hard to do the right thing. Did she know how much
discipline that took? She couldn't, because it was her tears that
tore at him and pushed him over the edge.

One moment he was standing stalwart, battling to suppress
the emotions that were devouring him, the next he had hauled

her headlong into his arms, his blood glittering, passion gripping him like a vise.

He took her mouth hungrily, his arms imprisoning rather than enfolding her. He was smothering her, he thought desperately, perhaps bruising her for days to come but he couldn't seem to loosen his hold much less let her go. Here was beauty, softness, sweetness he had never known. The perfect prize he could never win. His hands began to range over her body, down her back… smoothing, caressing. He had to stay them but his burning desire to know her body was driving him on.

A kiss, one kiss was never enough, but so *precious* because he might never get to kiss her again. He could feel his groin flood with blood, feeding a need so powerful it scared him. What might it feel like to surrender to such desire? To let the force of his passion for her sweep him away?

Her little moans fell audibly on his ears…little expiring breaths. He took it as she was *begging* him to release her. She had placed her hands upon his chest, powerless to push him away.

Immediately Daniel came to himself, afraid of his own strength.

"Sandra, I'm sorry. And in such a place!" With near superhuman control he drew back, setting her free. "Now you know me for what I am. A man like any other."

She shook her head, quite unable to speak. She was stunned by what had passed between them. It had far exceeded even her imagining. When she spoke, her voice was a husky murmur. "I provoked you, Daniel." She brought up her blue-violet eyes.

"I tried to warn you of what might happen." His body was throbbing painfully with denial.

"Do you fear it?"

"I wouldn't do anything in this world to hurt you," he said, his expression strained.

"I know that. But you're so high minded you won't let yourself be attracted to me, will you, Daniel?"

"I *can't* be. You know that." Daniel tried to rein in a sudden impotent anger, a railing against the world.

She threw out her arm. "So all this bothers you? Moondai, my money?"

"It's a pretty dazzling legacy, Sandra," he rasped. "You'd have to be one of the richest young women in the country."

"So my inheritance stands between us?" She too was struggling for composure.

"I'm not the man who can ignore it, Sandra. You're so young. There's much for you to see and do. You'll meet plenty of guys. Guys with fine respectable backgrounds. The right man you can trust to stand alongside you, with the strength to help you keep Moondai for yourself and your heirs. You only have to give yourself time."

"And you're *not* respectable, Daniel?" She gave a laugh of sorts.

He sighed deeply. "Of course I am as far as it goes. If you were an ordinary girl…"

"You'd do what?" Sandra challenged, raising her arched brows.

"Let's face it. You're *not!*"

"What if I gave my fortune away?"

"That is totally out of the question," he said with a fierce frown. "Your grandfather gave you the responsibility of holding on to Moondai. He knew you better than you know yourself, because you do *want* it, don't you?"

"I don't want it if it means losing you, Daniel," she said. There, for good or bad, she had come out with the simple truth. Daniel had invested her life with real meaning.

For an instant Daniel was seized by a feeling of joy that carried him right up high. Up, up into the wild blue yonder. Then he fell heavily to earth again with a pronounced thud. All he could do was ram his hands into his jeans pockets lest he reach for her again. "I shouldn't have kissed you," he said as though he took shame in his own weakness.

"I know," she agreed wryly, "because now I'm absolutely *sure*."

He raised a hand as if to refute it. "You're not sure of anything, Sandra. God almighty, you're not even twenty-one. Maybe *any* guy could have kissed you."

She breathed a great sigh of frustration. "I'm going to forget you said that, Daniel. I might still be a virgin—and that's a little secret between the two of us—but let me tell you I've been kissed plenty of times. The earth didn't move. It moved a few minutes ago."

It was more like an earthquake for him, but he wasn't at liberty to tell her. He was trying to guide her, not take advantage of her. "All the more reason to slow down, Sandra," he advised. "You need to give yourself time."

When I know right now.

A wry little smile formed on Sandra's mouth. She turned away from him. "You're not going to leave me until your year is up?"

"I'm bound over not to," he replied. "I wouldn't in any case until you felt you were ready. I want the best for you, Sandra."

"But you'd think about it if Joel Moreland made you some kind of offer?" She swung back to face him.

"I don't know *why* he wants to meet me, Sandra."

"Come off it," she said shortly. "You don't have to be too modest. Obviously he's heard good things about you. Every visitor who comes here has nothing *but* good things to say about you. You turned Harry Cunningham's station around. Grandad who was as tough as they come held you in high regard. You're not a *nobody*, Daniel."

"I'm not a fortune hunter, either," he said bluntly.

"Ah, the root of the problem!" She sighed. "You think if you and I grew closer people would think you were?"

He gave her a straight look. "Of course they would."

"No need to sound so outraged." She feigned nonchalance, deciding the smart thing to do was to cloak her emotions from now on in instead of emblazoning them on her sleeve. "All right, Daniel. I can see the wisdom of what you're saying. I'm going to take your advice. I'm going to give myself plenty of time to meet lots of eligible guys. Establishment families of course, stuffy old money, reeking arrogance like Berne. The right blood lines are important apparently. No others need apply. And I *would* like to go along for the ride to Darwin. You can introduce me to Joel Moreland while you're at it. Okay?"

His eyes distant he leaned forward and picked up his akubra shoving it on his head as though he had a dozen pressing reasons to be on his way. "Whatever you say, Ms Kingston."

It was a major shock for Daniel to meet Joel Moreland. For one thing Moreland seemed *familiar* which Daniel didn't think had all that much to do with the fact Moreland regularly got his picture in the papers. It was more a real *frisson* as though he'd met up with someone he'd known in another lifetime. Moreland too seemed overtaken by the same force. He put out his hand with a charming smile, but his eyes behind his dark framed glasses had an intensity far beyond mere interest. "I thought we should meet, Daniel."

"Good to meet *you,* sir." Daniel shook the outstretched hand, responding to the warmth and firmness of Moreland's grip.

"Let's go straight into the dining room shall we?" Bill Morrissey suggested, himself looking faintly puzzled.

What was this really all about, Daniel wondered, aware Moreland kept looking at him as they walked to their table. Joel Moreland was a splendid looking man. In his early seventies he was even more impressive in the flesh than in his photographs. Over six feet tall, he had a full head of silver hair and classic features that looked eminently trustworthy. His accent was cultured. He dressed with casual elegance. He looked what he was, a dignified man of real consequence.

Although his interests were huge Daniel was soon to discover Moreland had no hint of elitism or arrogance about him.

It wasn't his reputation in any case. He put Daniel in mind of a wise elder statesman, even a revered grandfather, kindly and genial but Daniel couldn't fail to miss the high level of concentration that was being levelled at him. What was it all about? He wasn't a candidate for high political office with Moreland the backer.

Lunch, however, started out well and continued in that vein. Moreland and Morrissey were friends over many years, each comfortable in the other's company. The conversation ranged over a wide number of topics: became focused on the areas of importance to the Northern Territory, its economy and its future. Moondai worked its way into the discussion; Alexandra Kingston's unexpected inheritance over her uncle and cousin, Daniel's position as her overseer.

"She doesn't want to sell then?" Moreland asked, his eyes keen.

"Why, sir, are you interested?" Daniel met the inquiry head on.

Moreland smiled. "As a matter of fact, Daniel, I'm delighted to hear Ms Kingston wants to hold on to her heritage. I knew her grandfather of course and the whole sorry business. It was a tragedy about Trevor. He and my own son were actually friends. Both gone now leaving their families bereft. Rigby changed a great deal after he lost Trevor. He became very bitter. As for his young granddaughter, I'm looking forward to meeting her." Daniel had already mentioned Sandra was in Darwin and had expressed the desire to meet Joel Moreland which seemed to please this great man.

Bill Morrissey excused himself after the main course, having told them he had an important meeting with a Federal Minister, leaving Daniel and Joel Moreland alone.

If it's coming, it's coming now, Daniel thought. An offer of some kind. He'd be a fool if he hadn't cottoned on to the fact Joel Moreland was extraordinarily interested in him. In fact Moreland did nothing to disguise it. It was very flattering and almost but not quite, alarming. Their personalities seemed to be in too much harmony.

"I'm unsure how to begin, Daniel," Moreland said, sounding oddly uncertain for him.

"I find that hard to believe, sir," Daniel commented. What could Moreland possibly say that could cause a moment's awkwardness?

"Do you know why I wanted to see you? Lord knows I've heard enough about you."

"To perhaps offer me a job?" Daniel flashed his engaging smile.

"I'd offer you a job tomorrow, Daniel," Moreland replied. "But that's not the reason. I'm looking into your background."

Instantly the smile was wiped from Daniel's face. "I don't exactly have a background, Mr. Moreland," he said, wondering if the meeting was going to end right there. "My mother is dead. I have no idea who my father was. I know one usually knows but my mother couldn't bring herself to tell me."

"Don't upset yourself, son." Surprisingly Moreland put out a large hand, tapping Daniel's reassuringly much like a father figure. "I know the terrible thing that was done to you and your mother. However, I believe there might be a connection with *my* family."

Daniel's silver eyes flashed as though Moreland had made a cruel joke. "That's not possible, sir, I'm sorry."

"Nevertheless I've been looking into it," Moreland said, a discernible tremble in his self-assured voice.

"So this is what it's all about?"

Moreland looked down at his linked hands. "Sometimes guilt or the perception of guilt can cling to the innocent. It's only recently been suggested to me my son may have fathered a child. Imagine the shock, Daniel! I had great difficulty taking it in. I thought I knew everything there was to know about my wife but my sister-in-law tells me otherwise."

Daniel's eyes were like ice. "Why would she wait to tell you now? Forgive me, sir, but your son has been dead for many long years."

"Twenty-eight and I've grieved for every day of it," Moreland said heavily. "My wife died eight months ago. She never got over the loss of our boy. I have a daughter and a beautiful granddaughter, Cecile. They live in Melbourne. They visit me on all the right occasions but I have no one who can step into my shoes. That was Jared's role. Rigby and I always thought there was a parallel. I lost Jared. He lost Trevor. There's Lloyd, I know and Lloyd's boy. Rigby had grave misgivings about leaving Moondai to them."

"He spoke to you about it?" Daniel couldn't keep the shock from his voice.

Moreland nodded. "There was no great friendship between us. Rigby wasn't an easy man to know or like but there was a bond. All he could think of was a way to keep Moondai going."

Daniel sat back in his chair looking highly wary. "I hope the plan didn't involve *me*."

Moreland spread his hands. "Who knows? Having said that most would agree his young granddaughter couldn't possibly run it without a good man by her side. Young as you are, you managed to win Rigby's respect. No mean feat. He spoke at length about you on the last occasion I saw him which was shortly before he died. I would have been at his funeral only I was in Beijing at the time as part of a trade mission."

"So what did you read into it, Mr. Moreland, if I dare ask?"

Moreland searched Daniel's eyes. "That his granddaughter had to marry well. I'm not talking money here. I'm talking marrying a man eminently suitable to take over the running of Moondai."

"Well there's a sort of logic about it," Daniel said, his attractive voice turned unnaturally hard, "but like all things hard to pull off. For one thing it's not the sort of thing *I* would be party to."

"You mean marry a woman to take a giant leap up in life and control of one of our finest cattle stations?"

Daniel counted to twenty before replying. "That's exactly what I mean. I'm no fortune hunter."

"I can see that you're not, Daniel," Moreland spoke soothingly. "But the Kingstons aside, I want you to look at this." He reached into the breast pocket of his linen jacket and extracted a photograph which he handed to Daniel. "Do you know this young woman?"

"Should I?" Daniel's brows knit.

"Have a look."

Daniel took the photograph into his hand, staring down at the young woman's face. For a moment he almost gave way to anger. This wasn't happening. Why was Moreland doing this? Clearly he too was distressed. That fact alone made Daniel get a grip on himself. "What is this?" he asked in a tight voice. "Some skeleton in the cupboard you've let out? This is a photograph of my mother when she was young. The eyes are unmistakable." Large, beautiful dark eyes filled with more sadness than laughter.

"And her name was?" Moreland persisted, his fine face creased with emotion.

Daniel forced himself to answer, memories like importunate ghosts crowding in on him. "Annie Carson."

Moreland nodded, his expression very sombre. "Johanna Carson was a maid in our household for a period of about eighteen months. This was in the late 1970s."

"She obviously had a double," Daniel said his eyes flashing. "My mother was born in England. She came to Australia as a child with an aunt, her guardian. Her parents were killed in a motorway pile-up. That was the story anyway. Her aunt reared her but they split up when her aunt married someone my mother didn't like. My mother was on her own from a young age. She never travelled outside Queensland. She never travelled anywhere. She didn't have the money. She certainly didn't visit the Northern Territory. She is *not* this Johanna Carson. She *can't* be."

Moreland waited until Daniel finished his quiet tirade, before producing another photograph. "Look at this."

"I'm not sure I want to see it," Daniel said. "I'm sorry."

"Please, my boy," Moreland pleaded. "This was my reason for meeting."

"Very well then. I can't say…" Daniel froze in midsentence. Moreland's face had gone from handsome to haggard in a matter of moments. "Are you're all right, sir?" he asked in alarm. "Can I get you anything? You've lost all colour."

"Maybe a brandy," Moreland suggested.

Daniel didn't wait to signal a waiter; he fetched one. The waiter bolted away and reappeared with a brandy on a small silver tray in under twenty seconds.

Moreland took a slow draft then straightened his shoulders which as a young man would have been as wide as Daniel's. The blood rushed back into his face. "Ah, that's better. This isn't easy for either of us, Daniel, but we have to get through it."

To calm him, Daniel took the much newer looking photograph that Moreland had set down on the table.

He pored over it, recognising his own face, albeit the subject was a young woman. "Who *is* this?" he asked, casting a troubled glance at Moreland.

Moreland looked at him in the kindliest way possible. "It's my granddaughter, Cecile."

"She's very beautiful," Daniel remarked, not considering for a moment it followed he had to be very handsome. "How old is she?"

"Twenty-four." Moreland smiled, looking much better. "She's in Scotland at the moment and loving it. She's chief bridesmaid to a close friend who's marrying into Scottish aristocracy if you please. A whole week of festivities is planned."

"One can only wonder at how different her life has been to mine," Daniel said not without a certain bitterness.

Moreland leaned forward, his tone gentle. "I came to ask you Daniel if you would allow a blood test?"

Without giving himself time to think, Daniel shook his head vehemently. "I'm sorry, sir, no. What does it really matter now? My mother was a tragic figure. She's dead now. Personally I don't give a damn who my father was. Whoever he was he didn't want me."

"Have you considered, Daniel, he might not have known about you?" Moreland asked with a sad smile. "Your mother mightn't have been given the chance to tell him she was pregnant?"

"Whomever *he* was," Daniel answered with a harsh brittle laugh. "I don't think we should continue this conversation at the moment, sir. It's causing you great upset and it's certainly not helping me. In any event it doesn't change anything. We can't rewrite history."

"We can remake the future, Daniel," Moreland said with such a hopeful expression on his face Daniel turned his head away abruptly not wanting to be moved by it.

It was then he caught sight of Sandra, his dream and his desire but as far away from him as the moon. He felt the hot pulsing beat of his blood. She looked absolutely *beautiful* in a summery outfit he had never seen before. She must have just bought it he realized. She hadn't worn it on the plane, nor did he think she had it with her. She was walking buoyantly as a dancer does, threading her way through the tables, a lovely smile on her face.

It was difficult to take his eyes off her but Daniel turned back to Moreland speaking in an undertone. "This is Sandra now. She's looking forward to meeting you. Is someone waiting for you, sir, your chauffeur?'

Moreland laughed softly, correctly interpreting Daniel's look of concern and glad of it. "I've had a shock, Daniel as you have, but don't worry, I'm quite all right. In fact my doctor tells me I'll live to one hundred. Such are the ironies of life. My chauffeur is out the front, yes. We'll talk again when you've had more time to absorb what I've shown you. Meanwhile I want you to take those." He indicated the photographs on the table.

Not quite understanding why he did it, Daniel quickly thrust the photographs into his inner breast pocket, a little embarrassed by how vehement he had become about them.

Both men stood up as Sandra reached their table, looking lit from within. A lot of people in fact were caught up in watching her. Daniel introduced them, Moreland clearly enchanted, but as Sandra sat down for a few moments, she said in fascination, "Surely I've met you before, Mr. Moreland? Perhaps when I was a child?"

Moreland smiled back. "I couldn't possibly have forgotten *you,* Sandra."

"Then how do I explain it?" Her dark blue eyes were full of wonder. "There must be something in this other life business." She laughed.

Moreland stroked his chin. "Millions of people believe in it. Your observation interests me, Sandra. I know your uncle Lloyd of course and your cousin Bernard but I've always thought I should have met you, Trevor's daughter, Rigby's granddaughter. Perhaps you can visit me at my home some time soon. We should get to know one another. Who knows I may be of service? Daniel can bring you."

"Why, I'd love that, thank you." Sandra said, giving Daniel several quick questioning looks. Daniel was looking extremely sober, even upset, as though the meeting hadn't gone at all the way he wanted.

They sat talking pleasantries for ten minutes more. Eventually Daniel and Sandra accompanied Joel Moreland to his car, a stately Bentley. His chauffeur who had been in casual conversation with a hotel employee sprang to attention. "But you have a dimple just like Daniel," Sandra remarked in some wonder, turning to Joel Moreland as Daniel momentarily moved off. "The *same* side of your face. You have silver-grey eyes as well. One sees them rarely. Is there some connection? Is that possible?" She stared into those eyes. "There is, isn't there? I feel it in my soul."

Moreland simply smiled. "Women never cease to amaze me." He continued to hold Sandra's hand.

It wasn't just the eyes and the dimple, it was the *charm,* Sandra thought, all sorts of thoughts whirling through her head. A question was about to tumble out only Daniel, who had been stopped by a passing acquaintance, was about to rejoin them.

"Don't forget my invitation now," Moreland said, relinquishing Sandra's hand.

"I definitely won't." Sandra was still rooted to the spot. Just like Daniel, Moreland towered over her in the same reassuring nonthreatening way. "Is this *our* secret?" she asked, her mind racing with powerful intimations.

"We have to work on it, Sandra," he told in a sober voice.

CHAPTER NINE

DANIEL WAITED FOR the Bentley to pull away before he turned to Sandra to ask, "Have you had something to eat?"

"You're always trying to feed me, Daniel." She tried a laugh, a little daunted by the gravity of his expression. "I've been shopping actually." She looked down at her dress, hoping that he liked it. She'd bought it to gain his attention.

"You look like a ray of sunlight," he said, but unhappiness touched his eyes.

"You're upset about something, aren't you?" Sandra didn't care what he thought. She took his hand. She *was* his friend, wasn't she? Even if he wouldn't allow anything more. She was still working on it.

"Does it show?" He gave her a wry glance.

"And Joel Moreland has something to do with it? Why don't we have a coffee by the water?" she suggested. "It's a beautiful day. I'd forgotten Darwin Harbour is so immense. The deep turquoise of the water is amazing. You can fit in another coffee can't you?"

"Whatever you want." He made no attempt to let go of her hand. In fact to Sandra's tremulous joy he continued to hold it while they crossed the street and made their way to a harbour front coffee shop where one could sit outside beneath big blue and white umbrellas. Sandra ordered a cappuccino and a sandwich. Daniel settled for an espresso.

"Are you sure that's all you want?" he asked, sounding concerned coffee and a sandwich weren't substantial enough. She was still light enough for a zephyr of wind to blow her away.

"That's plenty," she said, anxious to get on with what was troubling him. "I want to hear all about your meeting. Please tell me."

"You *know,* don't you?" He leaned forward abruptly, slipping off her sunglasses so he could stare straight into her eyes.

"I don't know *exactly* what it's all about, Daniel," she said carefully, "but I can see a resemblance between you and Joel Moreland."

"Moreland?" Daniel asked in a voice that cracked in surprise. "Then you're seeing a lot more than I can."

Sandra's expression softened. "Whether you can see it or not, there *is.* Don't be distracted by age and the silver hair. I bet his hair was once as black as yours. He has the height, the shoulders, the manner, the charm. You both have a dimple in your cheek and extraordinary silver-grey eyes. They're fairly *rare,* Daniel." She broke off as their order arrived.

Thoroughly unnerved, Daniel took a quick gulp that burned his mouth. "He wants me to take a blood test. I imagine one that establishes DNA."

"Good grief!" Sandra, about to take a bite of her sandwich, put it down again. "This is serious."

"I'm not taking any DNA test, Sandra," he said with considerable firmness.

"Okay." She soothed him. "I don't blame you."

"I know *nothing* for sure," Daniel said, wanting to reach across and take her hand. She offered such comfort. Since Sandra had come into his life he realised he no longer felt he walked alone.

"Well what you *do* know don't keep it to yourself. He must believe you could be family?'

"Who cares!" Daniel said shortly, then made an effort to collect himself. "Once, to have had a family would have mattered a great deal. It doesn't anymore."

"You can't forgive the fact the man who fathered you abandoned your mother and his unborn child," Sandra observed, in an understanding voice.

"Would *you* forgive it?" Daniel threw down the challenge.

"No I would not." Sandra picked up a sandwich and bit furiously into it. "So if you and Joel Moreland are related as it does appear, your father would have been his son who was killed. Jared, wasn't it?"

Daniel's eyes flared as though he couldn't bear the answer. "Here, take a look at these." He withdrew the photographs Moreland had given him passing Sandra the one of his mother first.

Sandra held the photograph in her hand, studying it with intense interest. It was of a very pretty vulnerable looking young woman with haunting dark eyes. "This is?" She guessed it had to be his mother although Daniel bore the young woman no easily discernible resemblance.

"It's a photograph of a young woman who worked for the Morelands in the late 1970s," he said in a strained voice. "Her name was Johanna Carson. My mother was known as Annie Carson."

Sandra kept her eyes on the old photograph. "You're Annie Carson's son. You would *know* if this was your mother."

"I'm afraid it is." Daniel sighed deeply as though he didn't want to talk about it. "Everything she told me, I believed *all* of it. I think now, most of it was probably not true. My entire childhood and my whole adult life I've believed what little my mother told me."

"Believing one's mother is an article of faith, Daniel," Sandra pointed out gently. "My mother too dealt in fantasy."

"Maybe it's a problem with mothers," Daniel said. "Tell me what you make of this?" He passed her the second photograph.

Sandra found herself looking at a beautiful young woman who could be Daniel's twin. "How extraordinary! Who is this?" She eyed Daniel cautiously.

"Moreland's granddaughter, Cecile."

Sandra acknowledged that piece of information in silence. "Why produce these photographs *now*?" she asked, tapping the photograph with her finger. "This Cecile could be your twin. What's going on, Daniel?"

Daniel's broad shoulders tensed. "How the hell should *I* know."

"Why decide to acknowledge you *now*?" Sandra frowned.

"Exactly."

Sandra fell into a thoughtful silence. "Do you suppose if Jared Moreland were your father he simply didn't know about you? Maybe he was killed before your mother told him or he was killed before they could do something about it. Maybe they intended to get married?"

Daniel gave an off-key laugh. "My mother worked as a domestic in their house. Moreland has always been a rich powerful man. It's highly unlikely he would have looked on such a union with favour."

"I like him," Sandra said, her blue eyes burning bright. "He seems the nicest, most trustworthy man. I don't want to feel badly about him. I'm sure you don't want to, either."

"No, I don't." Daniel admitted. "He said his sister-in-law only recently suggested the possibility Jared had fathered a son."

"Did you believe he was telling the truth? You're a good judge of men, Daniel."

"I was very taken with him," Daniel said. "I had this strange feeling I *knew* him right from the minute we shook hands. Both of us were upset. In fact he had a bit of a sick turn which shook me up as well. All the colour drained from his face. I had to get him a brandy. I got the feeling he wants to make things *right*. Oh

God, I don't know, Sandra." Daniel looked away over the glittering marina with its splendid yachts. "Even if he is my grandfather I don't fit into his world. He just can't walk into mine and think I'm going to do anything he wants. I'm not stooping to any DNA test. Not now, not ever! I'm someone else entirely from that. I'm going to make my own way, thank you, not become Joel Moreland's illegitimate grandson, for God's sake. I'm *me!*" he said wrathfully.

"Could I dare put a word in here?" Sandra asked, staring into his taut face.

"Best to stay out of it, Sandra."

"Sorry, Daniel. I'm *in* it, remember? Maybe Mr. Moreland is trying to steal you away from me? It's not on. You're *mine* until your year is up or you've had enough of me."

His stormy expression lightened. "I couldn't ask for a better boss," he said, hoping his smile was on straight.

"You're the boss, Daniel," Sandra said, "but I'm learning."

"You haven't wasted a minute. You're really smart, Ms Kingston."

"Then can you let Mr. Moreland explain?" she urged. "He wants us to visit him some time soon."

He gave her one of his long glittery-eyed looks. "I'll take you any time you want, but the other has nothing to do with you, Sandra, so don't get in the middle of it. If Joel Moreland thinks he's going to recognise me now—subject to a DNA test of course—" he added caustically, "it's all too late."

Sandra put out a hand and grabbed his wrist. "Daniel, will you listen to me for a second?"

"No, I won't," he said in a dangerous voice. "You find it too easy to twist me around your little finger. Eat your sandwiches, Sandra. Your coffee must be cold. Mine is." He put up his hand to signal the waiter. "I'll order fresh."

The sun rose higher. The bush was quiet except for bursts of unrivalled merriment from the blue winged kookaburra perched on the sturdy limb of a red river gum. These majestic trees soared to one hundred and twenty feet and more forming a marvellous corridor of green along Jirra Jarra Creek. It was one of the favourite haunts of Sandra's childhood. Scarcely an inch of the great gums went unexploited much like the multistorey apartment towers in the city. Ravens, hawks, owls, magpies and even the great wedge-tailed eagles nested on the upper branches; brilliant parrots, laughing kookaburras, bigger birds and magpies underneath; bats, possums, reptiles in the hollows. Even the fallen branches and thick leaf debris protected ground nesting little birds, insects and tiny reptiles like the fierce little horny lizard. There were more lizards in Australia than anywhere else in the world, the most spectacular of them in her desert home.

Away from the brilliant glare of the plains the peace and cool of this green sanctuary was exquisite. The creek's deep dark green waters were said by the station aboriginals to possess healing powers not only for the health but behavioural problems as well. She and Berne along with the station children had swum here all the time with a stout rope tied to a high branch of a river gum allowing them to *fly* into the water or across the stream like Tarzan and Jane. Berne hadn't benefited much from the sacred waters. He appeared to be the same as he ever was, causing Sandra to believe he would be a whole lot better off starting a new life elsewhere. Her uncle was a lot easier to get on with these days, mollified no doubt by her genuine interest in his encyclopaedic knowledge of Australian wildflowers. He was presently getting ready for another field trip to a remote pocket of Western Australia, a State renowned for the magnificence and sheer abundance of its native flora. A man who loved flowers and plants with a passion couldn't be all bad she reasoned. She was an adult now and thinking like one. Her father's fatal plane crash which her mother had claimed was *murder* had to have been an accident. Only Fate had been responsible.

A little wind blew up, skittering along the green corridor, loosening the olive green leaves and the petals of some dusky pink wildflowers that grew in cylindrical clumps in this oasis-like area. The aboriginal women made a paste of these succulents using it to protect and soften the skin of the face. Sandra knew for a fact the paste was wonderfully soothing on cuts and scrapes. There was so much that was really effective in bush medicine she thought. Arranged around her were the striking dark red sedimentary rocks and boulders that littered the ancient landscape. They formed such a contrast with the cabuchon waters of the creek, the lime-green of the aquatic plants and reeds that shadowed the creek's banks and the smouldering blue of the sky.

She had been sitting there daydreaming for some time now; carrying on a lengthy inner dialogue. There was so much that was problematic in her life. Daniel's life too was as mixed up as her own. Now he was confronted by revelations that had stunned and angered him. Daniel had carried a very bad image of the man who had fathered him. That wasn't going to go away in a hurry. She knew as well as anyone what it felt like to be *unwanted*.

A commotion on the high ridge—the unmistakable sound of a motorbike—made her turn her head. It was approaching at speed. The unwelcome din in such a peaceful place caused a flight of iridescent painted ducks about to land on the creek's surface, to skim it for a few feet before soaring steeply up again; up, up, over the tops of the red river gums seeking quieter waters. The kookaburra held its position, giving way to ribald protest, cackling away for all it was worth without deigning to move off its perch.

"Shut that bloody kookaburra up!" Chris Barrett, the jackeroo, yelled to her. He rode down the track, braking to a flamboyant stop a few feet away from her. Never mind the fact the wheels of the bike tore up scores of wildflowers releasing their faintly medicinal smell. "One of the boys told me this was the likely place you would be." He gave her his cheeky grin; a young man who thought he could always talk his way out of trouble.

"Did they now," Sandra said, watching him dismount. A real show-off was Chris. "So why aren't you working with the rest?"

He took a seat atop a red boulder. "Give me a break. I've been chasing a flamin' stallion all morning. A real stroppy devil."

"I take it he got away?"

"Yes, he did," Chris said ruefully, "but we got the mares and yearlings, even a few foals. It's a fantastic sight watching those wild horses run. I'm going to miss it. Mind if I come and join you for a few minutes?"

"Sure," Sandra nodded, pitching a few more pebbles into the deepest part of the creek. "But you're looking forward to going home, being with your family—surely?"

Chris laughed. "Well yes and no. I've had a great time here. Dan is a marvellous bloke. All the men look to him. No mean achievement when he's so young. These guys are really tough, but Dan has earned their respect. He often used to stand between us and old rubber guts—sorry—" he flushed "—your grandfather. Every other day I expected to be sent packing even though Mr. Kingston and my grandfather knew one another from school days. Dan stood up for us all. By the same token we've all got to pull our weight. Even lightweight old me though I reckon I'm a lot less stupid now. I'm not exactly looking forward to knuckling down in the staid old family firm. I've grown used to all this wonderful *space,* the excitement and adventure, the company of my mates." He stared into her face, hoping he was hiding his tremendous crush. "You're not going to sell the place, are you, Sandra?"

"Almost certainly not, since you ask." Sandra glanced back at the motorbike. "Daniel has been giving me lessons. I'm pretty good, if I say so myself."

"That's the word around the traps." Chris grinned. "Want to show me?" His bright hazel eyes dared her.

"I might another time." Not that Daniel would actually *see* them, Sandra thought, sorely tempted. She loved the bike as a

means of transport and she happened to know Daniel was working at the Five-Mile.

"What about I give *you* a spin?" Chris suggested eagerly.
"You're game to get on with me, aren't you?" He pushed to the
back of his mind Daniel had cautioned him never to take Ms
Kingston on board as a pillion rider.

"I don't see why not." She responded to the cocky grin. "Ten
minutes following the stream, then back again so I can collect
the mare. Don't dare take off like a bat out of hell, either."

Chris rolled his eyes. "The last thing I would ever do is cause
you fright. Daniel would kill me. Climb on. Just don't tell him
about this. I couldn't predict what he'd do if we took a tumble."

It was Berne who drove into the Five-Mile holding camp, his
handsome face wearing an expression that could be interpreted
as I-told-you-so.

"That fool Barrett has come off the motorbike at the creek,"
he yelled to Daniel as though it was entirely *Daniel's* problem.

Daniel strode over to the four-wheel-drive. "Is he hurt?"
Daniel was both irritated and concerned.

"He's broken his arm," Berne offered with little sympathy.
"Sandra is with him. She's all shook up."

"What do you mean, Sandra's with him?" Daniel's face
twisted into an expression of alarm. "She wasn't riding pillion, was she?"

"You know Sandra." Berne shrugged with a flicker of grim
satisfaction. In their childhood Sandra had always been the favourite, Number One. "She's the same reckless little devil she
ever was."

"She hasn't broken anything?" Daniel asked, his voice deepening in dismay.

"Settle down," Berne said, not unkindly. He hadn't wanted
his cousin to actually *break* anything. "She's got a few scrapes
and bruises but she's okay. She's worried about Barrett of all
things and I suppose she got a bit of a fright."

"I'll come back with you," Daniel said, realizing afresh how jealous Berne was of his cousin. He moved swiftly to the passenger side. "I've *warned* Chris never to offer Sandra a ride."

"So I guess he's in contempt," Berne observed, wryly. He'd disliked that smart alec jackeroo from day one.

"You're mad at me," Sandra said as soon as she saw Daniel's taut expression.

"That's correct," he said in a clipped voice, going down on his haunches and feeling for her pulse. She was very pale but not clammy. "Do you feel giddy, any nausea?" It was time for Chris to go back home. He'd make sure of that.

Sandra couldn't fail to pick up the vibes. Anxiety for Chris's job begin to gnaw at her. Not that Chris didn't need his comeuppance given the reckless way he had handled the powerful machine. Showing off, of course, but they had taken quite a spill. "I'm fine," she said, when she was feeling anything but fine.

Daniel's eyes flashed like coins in the sunlight. "Well you can thank your lucky stars for that," he said crisply, turning his attention to the ashen face Chris who was doing his best not to faint from the pain. "How's it going?"

"Bloody awful," Chris murmured in a hollow voice, aware of Daniel's contained anger.

"Why don't we shed a tear?" Berne chimed in sarcastically.

"Ah, shut up, Bernie." Sandra gave her cousin a weary glance before addressing Daniel. "I've made him as comfortable as I can."

"Good." Daniel had already noted with approval she had padded Chris's lap with their hats and her rolled up cotton shirt to support the injured limb. Now she was left wearing a blue cotton singlet that showed off her delicate breasts.

"It was the best I could do with what was at hand," she offered apologetically, thinking it a miracle she had escaped more serious injury. Fortunately she had been thrown off onto the sand whereas Chris's body balanced the other way had fallen on heavier ground with the bike half on top of him.

"That's fine." Daniel spoke quietly though he felt a mad urge to let off steam. "We'll have to get you to hospital, Chris," he said. "What about the chest area, your ribs? Have you any difficulty breathing?"

"No," Chris gasped. "Look I'm sorry, Daniel."

"Forget that now." Daniel rose to his feet. "You'll need an X-ray to be sure there's no other damage." He looked at Berne. "Give me a hand to get him into the back seat, will you, Berne? We'll try to limit as much movement to your arm as we can, Chris, but be prepared for some pain."

"I deserve it," Chris mumbled, blinking several times to shake off the faintness. "I was pretty well showing off."

"I figured as much." Daniel nodded curtly before turning back to Sandra. "Sit there until I come back for you, Sandra," he said. "You've had a shock and there's a gash above your elbow."

"It's nothing," she said, twisting her arm around to look at something she scarcely felt. "Just bleeding a bit."

"Using up a fair bit of your luck, aren't you?" Berne asked her. "A bloke over on Gregory Downs was killed only the other day when he came off his bike. Broke his neck."

"Would you mind holding those stories for now, Berne," Daniel said, his sculpted features drawn taut.

"I doubt if she'd take any notice anyway," Berne said. "And Chris here is just a big-time show-off."

It was hard to argue with that.

Chris was airlifted to hospital where the fracture to his arm was confirmed.

"Why did you do it?" Daniel asked Sandra who was slumped tiredly into a planter's chair on the verandah. He picked up the cold beer Meg had brought him and downed it. It was a short while after sunset. The world was for a short time enveloped in a beautiful mauve mantle. The evening star was out. Soon it was joined by a million diamond pinpricks that quickly turned into blazing stars.

"Maybe I have a problem with authority figures?" Sandra suggested, very much on the defensive.

"You mean *me*."

"Yes, you, Daniel. I can see you're angry with me for breaking the rules."

"I'm angrier with Chris," he answered. "I told him not to take you on."

"Surely that's a lot to ask?" There was a slight quiver in her voice.

"No it isn't," Daniel said. "I'm in charge of the men, Sandra. I'm running this station for you until you're ready to run it yourself. Maintaining authority is important. I told Chris not to offer you a ride because I've learned a lot about him since he's been here. He's careless, he's cocky and I can't trust him. It's imperative to wear a helmet yet neither of you had one on. This is rough country, not a country lane. What if you'd sustained a head injury? What if *he* had? His mother was upset enough when I called her about his broken arm."

Sandra was mortified. "Okay we made a mistake, Daniel I'm sorry. We won't do it again."

"No, you won't," he said with emphasis. "When Chris is well enough he's going home. He's fired."

Sandra sat forward, aghast. "Who do you think you are?"

He drained his beer and set down the glass. "Sandra, I have to have my say out here unless *you* want to fire *me!*"

"Is that an ultimatum?" Her blue eyes started to blaze. She hated falling out with Daniel.

"It is," he said without hesitation. "It's for me to call the shots, Sandra. I'm responsible for the safety of the men and consider how many more times I feel responsible for *your* safety. I'm not objecting to your getting on the back of a motorbike *with* your helmet on. I'm objecting to your doing so with Chris Barrett who thinks he can do as he pleases because he's only fooling around for a time before he goes home to work for his rich old man. I'm not at all sympathetic to the way he acted even if I'm sorry he broke his arm. And you didn't answer my question?"

"What was it?" She sighed, resting back again. How could she possibly fire Daniel. He was everything in the world to her.

"Are you going to let me run things as I see fit?" he asked.

"Next question?"

"How do you feel?" His voice changed and a different light came into his eyes.

"Like a bad, bad, girl. I don't like it when you're disappointed in me, Daniel."

"I don't like it when you give me a fright," he pointed out, remembering the force of his reactions. "The damned fool could have killed you and himself. Berne is quite right. There was a fatal accident on Gregory Downs. All the poor guy did was hit a pothole. His helmet wasn't on properly...it rolled off. Life on the land has its hazards, Sandra. I don't have to tell you that."

"As long as you still love me." She pulled a face at him. "And if you say you *don't,* you're fired!"

A look of amusement crossed his mouth. He allowed his eyes to rest on her as she lay back in the high backed peacock chair. One slender, silky fleshed arm was thrown lazily over the side, the injured arm he had cleaned and bandaged for her resting quietly in her lap. The glow from the exterior lamp mounted on the wall behind her, turned her hair to a glittering aureole. Her skin had the translucence of a South Sea peal. He could never tire of looking at her. *Never!*

"That's blackmail, wouldn't you say?" he asked, managing to sound casual.

"Whatever it takes, Daniel," she answered.

CHAPTER TEN

LLOYD KINGSTON HAD to seek his niece's permission to have either Daniel or Berne fly him to Perth, the capital of the adjoining vast State of Western Australia where he would be staying with a long-time friend, the well-known botanist, Professor Erik Steiner who was going to accompany him on his expedition. Daniel couldn't afford the time, so it was decided Berne would fly the Beech Baron into Perth.

"I wouldn't mind staying on for a week," Berne remarked to his cousin rather tentatively for him, "that's if you can spare the Baron. I know you can spare me. I've always liked Perth. I've got quite a few friends there."

"You'll have to check with Daniel, Berne," Sandra said in a calm, helpful way. "If it's okay with him it's okay with me. A week mind. We've got the helicopter but one never knows when the plane might be needed."

"True," Berne acknowledged. "Daniel's got to be very important around here, hasn't he?" he added, almost sadly.

"Well he *is* running the place, Berne." Sandra was careful to answer reasonably. "*You* don't want the job."

"No way!" Berne threw up his hands as if to show that was way beyond his ambitions.

"What would you like to do?" Sandra asked, sounding like she really wanted to know and perhaps help him.

For once he saw her sincerity. "Something to do with aircraft," he said. "I'm a good pilot. Ask Daniel. Maybe not as good as him but good all the same. I love flying. I'd love to captain a jumbo jet flying all around the world."

"Can't you train for that?" she asked, surprised he wasn't already doing it if that was his ambition. "Heavens, you're young enough. You have the money to support yourself through your training. Seize the moment, Berne. Make enquiries in Perth. Jumbo jets aside, you could start your own charter business if you wanted to. Elsa could help you there. Surely she and her first husband were among the first to pioneer Outback charter flights?"

"Yeah." Berne thought for a minute. "She can fly, did you know? She's let her licence slip for years now but she can fly a plane. In fact she knows a hell of a lot about aircraft. She's very secretive, Elsa. She likes to act the dotty old lady. God knows why. I was trying to think the other day when it started. Dad reckons after Uncle Trevor was killed."

Sandra stared at him. "Of course I knew about the charter company, but she never flew the Cessna that I remember."

"Maybe not, but she could. There are a lot of things you don't know, cousin. Why would you? You were only a kid when you left. Your sweet mother did everything she could to paint Dad in the worst possible light. You can't imagine what it did to him, her claiming he sent his own brother to his death. If your mother could have had Dad convicted she would have. No wonder he hates her."

Sandra could see that would be the case. "I'm sorry about that, Berne," she said, all sorts of emotions swirling around inside her. "In many ways you, me, Uncle Lloyd and Elsa too have had a tough time. Elsa must have gone into marriage with

Grandad thinking she was going to get something out of it. I
don't mean material things, but whatever she craved, she didn't
get it. Looking back I'm sure it wasn't *all* Grandad's fault. I've
never acknowledged that before but I can see now it might have
been true. What happened to Elsa is a mystery. But I want *you*
to know if you'll let me I'll be your friend."

Berne had a sudden overpowering need to believe her. "You
really want that? We never got on. I was jealous of course. You
got all the attention."

"Didn't last long Berne," she sighed. "We were both deprived
kids. Neither of us got enough love or attention. We suffered in
our own way. But there's no need to be jealous of me any more.
You can have your own life. A different life, one that suits you.
Spend all your energies on becoming an airline pilot, as that's
what you want. Shake on it, reconciliation?"

"Sure." Berne gripped her outstretched hand, drawing a deep,
shaky breath. "I guess it is better to have you onside, Sandra."

"You bet it is." Sandra smiled.

They were on their own! Sandra couldn't believe her good fortune. Elsa and Meg were in the house of course, but essentially
they were on their own. It was a *sumptuous* feeling and she
was determined to take full advantage of it. During the day
she joined Daniel as often as she wanted. The evenings were
spent over a leisurely dinner, a short walk around the grounds
afterwards, then they retired to the study where the intensive
but stimulating learning sessions continued. There was so much
to learn about the business and Sandra was anxious to make
her contribution.

Midweek something strange happened. Sandra awoke with
the unnerving feeling *someone* was in or had just left her room.
Not only that there was a faint rattling noise. She sat up quickly
in the bed, her eyes trying to pierce the gloom. There was no
moon to send its illuminating rays across the verandah and into
her room. She desperately needed light.

"Who's there?" The words were on her lips before she even got to flick a switch.

She stared around the room, her body trembling though she wasn't cold. Not the slightest sign of disorder. She was a naturally tidy person. Everything was in its place. Just a bad moment she thought. Some lingering dream. She'd had a full day joining in on a muster for clean skins the men knew they had missed in dense scrub. She'd enjoyed the experience but in the end the heat and the physical exertion had gotten to her. Before bed she'd been forced to take a couple of painkillers for her headache. Elsa had rustled them up from her stockpile.

Her accelerated heartbeats were slowing. She breathed deeply, punching her pillows a few times to get them into the right shape. A glance at her bedside clock told her it was 3:00 a.m., the witching hour. The temptation to get out of bed and go across the hallway to Daniel was so acute she groaned with the pain of it. She could tip toe across his room, rest her hand upon his sleeping shoulder.

"Daniel, it's *me!*"

He'd awaken; recognise the scent of her, draw her wonderingly down onto the bed. He would gather her into him, his body against hers, telling her he wanted her urgently. His beautiful mouth would unerringly find hers. She would open it to him… His hand was on her breast. She's holding on to him, clutching him. One of her arms is locked around him, the other is buried in the raven thickness of his hair. Delicious shudders are passing through her. She's guiding his hand, wanting his fingers to slip inside her. God, she's been thinking about it all the time, wicked girl!

Only it wouldn't happen like that at all. She sobered abruptly, ashamed of the illicit pleasure she was taking. Daniel would bundle her up and escort her back to her room. No seduction scenes for Daniel. If it were ever going to happen he wouldn't let it happen in her own house. Daniel had *huge* problems with making love to her. She knew that. It was almost as if he were up against a serious taboo or he was heeding lots of signs tacked up everywhere saying, Keep Off. It is just stupid, she thought, when we both want it. She wasn't such a fool she didn't know how he watched her.

Better check the door.

She knew perfectly well it was locked. She had gotten into the habit of locking it even with Daniel in the house. If it looked like she didn't trust her family, she didn't care though these days her anxieties seemed absurd. Her mother's perspective had been warped. She slipped out of bed and padded across the room, listening for noises in the house. Not that she would hear them. The old homestead had been built of stout timbers, mahogany and cedar.

She was halfway across the spacious room when she paused, staring at the floor. There was something on the rug. Little beads. Sandra crouched down to pick them up. The beads were scattered, six in all. Jade beads. The fact someone really had been in her room hit her like a punch in the stomach. She turned on the chandelier flooding the bedroom with light. She found one more bead closer to the door. They had poured off a necklace. Sandra reached for the brass doorknob. The door was still locked. So how then had someone come to stand in the deep shadows watching her?

She started to think of an intruder coming by way of the verandah. There was a white lattice door at the end of the wing, usually locked. The other day she'd found a tiny scrap of fabric impaled on it but hadn't thought much of it. It could have come off one of Meg's dresses or even one of the house girls' Meg was training.

When a dingo's mournful howl carried on the desert air her nerve broke. Sandra unlocked her door and fled across the hallway to Daniel's room, assuming it too would be locked but it wasn't. She burst in. She couldn't help it, not doing anything appalling like screaming but rushing towards the bed, calling his name.

"Daniel, Daniel, wake up!"

Something *huge* was in her way. Hell, a damned chair! She swore fiercely, holding a hand to her throbbing shin. "Daniel!"

"Sandra, what the hell!" Daniel sprang to his feet, straight as a lance. He had thought that voice belonged in his dream. But no, she was *there,* in his bedroom swearing her head off.

"Where's the light?" she was yelling. "I don't want to run into another great hulking chair. What's it doing in the middle of the room anyway?"

Immediately he switched on the bedside lamp seeing her standing in the centre of his room *irradiated.* She was wearing the flimsiest little nightdress he could ever imagine. No concealing robe. Not even slippers on her feet. She was clutching something in her hand.

"Sandra, what are you doing here?" he asked, all his senses instantly raised to the nth power. "Do you know what time it is?"

"What's time got to do with it, Daniel?" She looked at him with highly critical blue eyes. Not that there was anything to criticise. He could have posed for a Calvin Klein ad for boxer shorts for that's all he was wearing. Brief navy boxer shorts with a white stripe down the side.

"It's the only few hours I get to sleep," he explained.

"When you promised me you'd be on call." She moved to close the distance between them and he sprang back.

"What's the *matter* with you?" She eyed him sternly. "Anyone would think I was going to give you an electric shock."

"Allow me to put some clothes on would you, Sandra?" he asked tightly, circling a finger so she would turn away.

"If you must." She gritted her small teeth.

"I must." Swiftly he pulled on a pair of jeans and zipped them up. "I don't mean to criticise your behaviour in any way—you are after all my boss—but is there something you want?" They faced one another again, Daniel's dark polished skin gleaming in the light.

He had a light V shaped mat of dark hair on his chest that disappeared into his low slung jeans.

"Well it's not *sex* if that's what's worrying you," she snapped. "I mean would I do anything so crass as to jeopardize our friendship?" she added caustically. "No, the thing is, Daniel, someone was in my room just now."

"You're kidding!" He was in something of a daze. This *was* happening, wasn't it? She was in his bedroom in a sheer little nightie with her tousled cap of buttery curls and her eyes blazing like sapphires.

"I found these beads on the floor. Look."

Now she moved right up to his shoulder. His heart leapt. She might be pocket sized but she packed such a powerful sensual punch unless he was very strong she could defeat him easily. "Show me." Daniel forced his breath to stay even. "Jade, aren't they? Or nephrite." He stared down at the small polished olive-green beads. "Maoris use it as a talisman of protection. The Chinese believe it blesses all who touch it."

"I'm not trying to *sell* them to you, Daniel," she said testily.

Such a tart tongued glowing creature! "Let's take a look in your room then," he suggested. "You might like to put something on."

"Anyone would think you had to fight off my advances," she started muttering as she stalked into her bedroom, making a beeline for her yellow Thai silk robe. "There, feel safer now?" she asked tartly, tying the sash with exaggerated movements.

"You aren't the sweetest girl in the world, are you?" He looked around, frowning in concentration. "Where were the beads?"

"On the floor, just about here." She moved to the spot rubbing the pile of the Perisan rug back and forth with her bare toes. "I woke with the panicky feeling someone was in the room or just leaving it. I thought I heard a rattling sound. I knew my door was locked. I must have been dreaming. It wasn't until I decided to double-check the door when I saw them. They certainly weren't there when I put out the light. Someone was in the room, Daniel."

"You don't think you could have missed them earlier? They blend in with the rug strangely enough."

"Then how did I miss not *walking* over them?" she asked as if she'd produced the trump card. "One was actually near the door."

"And it was locked?"

"*Yes,* Daniel."

"The only people in the house are you, me, Elsa and Meg. I can't think the house girls would meddle. You'll have to leave *me* out of it."

"Because of your vow?" She stared at him with huge challenging eyes.

"What vow?"

"The one you made as soon as we met. *Never lay a finger on her!"*

"So you know about that, do you?" he asked dryly.

"There's no logic to it, Daniel."

"Really? I consider to break it would be more like men acting badly. Now, shall we get back to the problem at hand? Your nocturnal visitor could only be Elsa or Meg or the resident ghost. I can't see Meg or Elsa paying you a call unless one of them sleep walks. Come to think of it, it does happen."

"Yes, like once in a blue moon," Sandra scoffed. "I didn't imagine any of this, Daniel."

"Hang on." He hesitated for a second looking down at her, then strode out onto the verandah.

She raced after him. "I found a scrap of material pinned to the lattice a few days ago," she told him breathlessly. The door was unbolted. She watched him as he shot the bolt home.

"It could easily have come off Meg's dress. Go back to bed, Sandra. I'll leave my door open and a light in the hall. No one is going to bother you."

"Well I *am* bothered," she said huffily.

"We'll leave it until morning to ask questions." They were back in her room, staring at one another. "Meg would never do anything to cause you concern. Elsa genuinely cares for you. You're sweet to her."

"I feel sorry for her, that's why. But she's just the type to do spooky things," Sandra felt a sudden chill. "No mouse could be quieter, though I can't think she'd wish to harm me. Can I ask you a question?"

"Fire away." He gave a single abrupt nod of his head.

"Do you wear jade beads?"

He didn't deign to answer.

"Just a thought. Would you like to stay with me, Daniel?" For some reason she had the wicked impulse to taunt him. "It's an awfully big bed. Our bodies wouldn't have to connect at all."

"Impossible, Sandra."

"I know, I'm ranting. I'm sorry." She stripped off her silk robe and threw it around one of the bedposts.

"You're not at all self-conscious of your body, are you?" he said, desire for her lashing at him like stockwhips.

"Well I'm not exactly a glamour model," she answered tartly. "What's to *see*?"

"Are you completely mad?" he rasped, astonished she could say such a thing.

Sandra spun around, furiously hurt. She rushed him very fast, hitting him in the chest. "How *dare* you say something like that to me, Daniel!"

To Daniel it was the straw that broke the camel's back. "That *does* it!" he ground out. He got an arm around her lifting her half off the ground and pitching her onto the bed with such strength she bounced.

"Daniel!" She sat up in astonishment and gulped.

"You have to stop playing games with me." He was breathing hard through flared nostrils, his powerful body tense, a vertical frown between his black brows, luminous eyes stormy.

"I will. I will," she promised. Fear didn't come into it. She wanted to *calm* him. "I'm sorry, Daniel. I wasn't trying to turn you on. Not *then* anyway." She couldn't lie to him.

"Well you did!" He knew it was wrong, but he was too tanked up with desire to be able to turn off the engine.

"Come here!" He swooped on her, dragging her up against him feeling her fingers sink into the mat of hair on his bare chest.

"Daniel!" She made a soft yielding sound, pressing herself against him.

For an instant he was worried his beard might rasp her lovely skin. "Little *witch!*" he said hotly. "You should be using those little fists on me not urging me on." He clamped her small slender body still closer against him, revelling in her female softness and the alluring scents of her hair and skin. He wanted to know the *whole* of her...so badly...so badly. With a shudder he speared his fingers into those buttery curls pulling back her head so he could take her mouth. It seemed like an eternity since he had last kissed her. He had never stopped thinking about it, how beautiful it was. He had her *now!*

His mouth covered hers, not hard but voluptuously. He found the touch and the taste exquisite, to be savoured. A primitive adrenaline was pumping through his blood, assisting his sense of mastery. His hands had a life of their own. They strayed over her throat and delicate shoulders, moving towards those small tantalizing breasts. The V neckline of her nightgown had fallen low; low enough for him to fondle her naked flesh. Her nipples came erect under his urgent fingers while a little moan came from the back of her throat. She arched her back making it easier for him to take first one then the other into his mouth. He lifted his head. Watched her face. Her eyes were closed but the lids were flickering with sensation.

He pulled her in tight, wanting her wild and wilful on the bed. She had a little wildness in her. He *knew* it. He wanted to strip that lighter than air nightdress from her. He wanted her to feel his hands all over her, exploring that sweet tender body that gave off a million sparks when touched.

She was making sounds, little kittenish *mews* he found incredibly erotic. There was a heat inside him he had never experienced before. Did she know those little mews were pushing him further along the hot narrow path of temptation? By now his need for her was so fierce he couldn't be pushed *one* inch further. Every nerve in his body was *electric* for her. There was nothing he didn't want to do to her. All was permissible between lovers.

Wasn't that what he wanted to be, her lover? Her *only* lover.

"Daniel!" Bright little explosions like stars were going off in her head. She was literally swooning in his arms.

Daniel misread her ecstasy. To him it sounded like the fevered gasp of the tortured.

He recoiled sharply. What the hell was he doing? Ravishing a virgin? Ravishing this slip of a girl he had sworn to protect? That jolted his heart.

He released her so abruptly, she pitched forward, her head whirling while she tumbled to the floor. "Sandra!" He was stunned; sick with shame. He picked her up bodily, embracing her, before he laid her on the bed. "I hate myself if that's any comfort to you."

"It isn't!" Her voice was shaken, the sound vibrating inside her head. "You're a caveman."

"I don't doubt it. But you've made me. You're an enchantress."

"Daniel, do you *mean* that?" Suddenly she was full of hope. If she could enchant him she was really on to something.

"Listen, I'm going." Daniel read the swift speculation in her huge blue eyes. "I wanted to *ravish* you. I stopped just in time. Don't you realise that?"

How to convince him she was ready? "Wherever you want to take me, Daniel, I'm prepared to go," she said, mind and body flooded with love for him. "I never thought I was going to fall in love. I didn't even think I would *want* a man too near me. I thought the way my creep of a stepfather behaved towards me I was somehow damaged. I hated being the object of *lust*."

"Did you now!" Daniel was breathing fast, thinking if he stayed any longer he would really unravel. Her loveliness, her desirability was overwhelming. How was he supposed to combat all that? "I have to tell you, Sandra," he gritted, "*I* lust after you, too. There's a warning in there somewhere but you don't want to hear it."

"Then get out of my room if that's how it is!" She felt bitterly rejected.

"Don't worry, I'm going." He speared his fingers through his thick pelt of hair, dragging it back from his tense face. "It's damn near daybreak anyway. I'll leave my door open. I won't leave the homestead in the morning either until we find out exactly what went on here. Okay?"

"Morning can't come soon enough," she cried and punched the pillow.

CHAPTER ELEVEN

SANDRA SLEPT SO heavily she might have been drugged. In the morning Meg had to wake her to say they couldn't find Elsa. She wasn't in the house, nor anywhere in the home compound. Daniel had already sent out a search party to scour her usual haunts.

"She's getting on you know." Meg pleated and repleated the edge of her white apron in her agitation. "Never sees a doctor and she should. She's often short of breath. Occasionally she wanders in her mind. You must have noticed that."

"Of course I have, Meg." Sandra was out of bed, fishing out clothes to put on. "She likes to visit the family cemetery. I hope Daniel will try there."

"I don't know about *likes*." Meg looked dubious. "More like she's *driven*. She does go there a lot. I'll let you get dressed, love. I've got a bad feeling about this."

It was when Sandra was halfway out the door she spotted out of the corner of her eye, a dark grey envelope that lay on top of the highboy.

"Wait a minute," she said aloud, though no one was listening. She retraced her steps reaching for the envelope. It was addressed to her.

"Oh, God!" Sandra knew at once it was from Elsa though she wasn't familiar with Elsa's handwriting. A sudden wave of nausea rolled through her, which was odd. She took up a position on the nearest chair opening the envelope and withdrawing its contents; two handwritten sheets of a lighter grey paper embossed with Elsa's initials EGK. Sandra found herself slumping back against the chair overtaken by a peculiar feeling of weakness and fatigue. She knew now from the bitter taste in her mouth and the unfamiliar sluggish feeling Elsa had given her not painkillers but some kind of sedative, maybe sleeping pills. It had been Elsa in her room, Elsa's broken beads. Elsa gliding around the house like a ghost.

What she read in stunned horror and disbelief was Elsa's *confession*. Her last words to anybody.

Alexandra, my dear, I find I can no longer continue. I know you will hate me now you learn the truth. I deserve your hatred. It was I who was responsible for your father's death no matter Trevor was the last person in the world I intended to harm. Trevor was always kind to me as you are. It was your grandfather, my husband, I wanted to see punished for the uncaring way he treated me. I wanted love. I got rejection. The pain and the humiliation became too much. He never loved me. I wasn't his beloved Catherine. I wasn't what he wanted at all. My first husband had all but destroyed me; your grandfather did the rest. It was Rigby who was to visit the outstation that day. Rigby sent Trevor at the very last minute. I had known what to do to the Cessna to cause it to crash. I did it without a qualm. Not much of a motive I know, but I was different then. Afterwards I was changed forever. The guilt stripped me of my sanity. I've suffered terribly for my crime, Alexandra. But there must be an end. Scatter my ashes far away from Moondai. Far away from your grandfather. I never belonged here. The sea might be the place. I never meant your father harm. I've visited his grave countless times begging his forgiveness. But my crime is unforgivable. I'll be made to suffer for it in the next life I'm sure. There's no escape.

Elsa.

Lloyd and Trevor returned to Moondai the very next day, the family closing ranks on the sudden death of a senior member. The cause of death was given as myocardial infarction or more commonly heart attack. It was noted, had Mrs. Kingston received emergency medical assistance or been close to a hospital she might have survived but she had chosen to take a long walk that day without telling anyone where she was heading. That alone had greatly lessened her chances of survival. It seemed Elsa had ignored many of the symptoms of heart disease for some considerable time without seeking help.

Whether Elsa had helped her death along, given her stated intention, Sandra would never know, but she couldn't withhold Elsa's secret from the family. They had a right to know.

"Poor Elsa," Lloyd said afterwards, without any sympathy at all. "She started going to pieces from that day on. As well she should. Her problems were all of her own making." He looked in a kindly fashion on his distressed niece. "My father did his best but pandering to a neurotic woman wasn't in his nature. It was the first husband leaving her that really destroyed Elsa. At least *I'm* in the clear," he added ironically.

"Tell me you forgive me," Sandra begged.

"Nothing to forgive." He patted her shoulder. "You were a child. You believed what you were told. Forgiving your mother is another matter. Are you going to tell her?"

Sandra shook her head. "I can't see any point in making this public, either. Elsa had her secret. I think as a family we have to keep it, otherwise we start up another pointless scandal. Elsa is dead. It's all over. Shall we take a vote on it?"

"Does Daniel know?" Berne asked.

"We've nothing to fear from Daniel," Sandra said.

"All the same…"

"Leave Daniel to me, Berne," Sandra said.

"Well that's it, I guess," Lloyd Kingston said. "To the world we've lost a dear family member. We're all sad which of course I'm not."

"So much of life is sad," Sandra said, thinking she would never get over the shock of it. "Elsa wanted her ashes to be scattered at sea."

"I'll take care of that," Lloyd offered. "She was my step-mother though she never took the time to be one. In many ways she was quite simply, *mad*. I'm going back to Perth as soon as I can. Berne can come with me. The trip will do him good. I understand he wants to be an airline pilot."

"Sure do." Berne smiled across at Sandra.

"Then good luck, my boy. You'd better get on with it. You'll have a lot to learn."

"No problem!" Berne appeared entirely comfortable with the idea.

There was a memorial service for the late Mrs. Elsa Kingston in Darwin. Dying so soon after her husband, people acquainted with the family shook their heads in sympathy prepared in death to overlook the fact the marriage had been a disaster.

Outside the church people pushed forward to introduce them-selves, or reintroduce themselves, offering a word of condolence or respect. From time to time Daniel touched Sandra's elbow, dipping his dark head to murmur the names of people she didn't know. The healing process with her own family had started, but Daniel was the one person Sandra wanted beside her.

"It's Joel Moreland coming this way," Daniel alerted her, easily spotting Moreland's distinguished silver head among the crowd. "He has a lady with him. Seventies, beautifully dressed. The sister-in-law I'd say."

They approached, a handsome couple. Moreland looked even

more impressive in his dark clothes. He certainly was a splendid looking man Sandra thought as introductions were made and respects paid. The lady *was* Moreland's sister-in-law, Helen, widow of a younger brother who had never enjoyed good health and died prematurely at fifty-six.

Helen Moreland tried, but couldn't conceal her shock at meeting Daniel, indeed her expression crumpled into tears.

"Now, Helen," Moreland took her hand in a comforting grasp. "It's all right, my dear."

"I just can't believe it that's all," Helen Moreland said, staring into Daniel's eyes. "He looks *exactly* like you at that age, Joel."

"I'm not sure I want to speak about this, Mrs. Moreland," Daniel said, very quietly.

She put her hand on his arm. "But you must, my dear. Not here, I know. But you *must* hear what I have to tell you."

"Perhaps you could join us at home," Moreland suggested. He looked from Daniel to Sandra, his eyes resting on her as though she were a powerful ally.

"I'm sorry, sir," Daniel said, courteous but firm.

Sandra turned to him immediately. "Perhaps you should, Daniel," she urged. Secrets turned into terrible burdens. The best thing Daniel could do was let Mrs. Moreland tell him what she knew.

"*Please,* Daniel." Helen Moreland lifted her gentle eyes that nevertheless missed nothing to his face. "Did you know Joel was christened Daniel Joel Moreland? His father was Daniel too so somewhere along the way to avoid confusion Daniel got to be Joel. Jared was christened Jared Joel Moreland."

"Where is this leading, Mrs. Moreland?" Daniel asked, intensity in his voice.

"Why don't we follow a bit later on?" Sandra smoothly intervened. "Any taxi driver will know where you live."

"If that's your wish." Joel Moreland inclined his silver head. "Or I could send my man back for you."

"I don't seem to have much choice, do I?" Daniel turned away from an intense scrutiny of Sandra to ask in an ironic voice.

"It's all *for* you, Daniel," Helen Moreland said.

"Perhaps an hour, Mr. Moreland," Sandra said quickly, linking an arm through Daniel's and holding on.

Moreland, the man with the Midas touch, nodded, seemingly content to let a twenty-year-old girl handle things. "As you wish, my dear."

The fact they had reached a decision gave Sandra a new sense of purpose. Resistance, however, was coming off Daniel in waves. She knew and sympathized with the intensity of conflict going on inside him but she trusted her feminine intuition. The crowd had dispersed and the two of them had wandered off finding the same coffee shop they had visited once before.

"You don't want to go, do you?"

Daniel had removed his dark jacket in the heat. The dazzling white of his shirt made a striking contrast with his tanned skin. "You know damn well I don't," he replied, tersely, thinking he had done nothing but drink coffee over the last few days. "Though I've taken great note of the fact you seem determined to get me there."

"Maybe it's where you *belong,* Daniel," she said. "Ever thought of that?"

He dismissed that with a cursory wave of his hand. "I don't exactly belong anywhere. Most certainly not with the man with the Midas touch."

"Even though he could be your grandfather?" she asked, covering his hand with her own.

"Why are you doing this, Sandra?" He stared into her beautiful eyes, his own filled with emotion.

"Because I love you, that's why," she said briskly.

"Sandra." He bent his dark head over his hands without looking up. She couldn't keep telling him she loved him otherwise he could never go away.

"No need to be embarrassed," she said cheerfully. "You know me. I rush in where angels fear to tread. You don't have to love me, okay? I can see you're obsessed with standing alone, but you need a little bit of a hand with this. I'm the right woman for the job."

He lifted his head again, finding those electric-blue eyes. "And a *little* hand is what you've got." He raised it to his lips and kissed it.

"People are looking, Daniel," she pointed out, love for him invading every part of her body.

"Fine. Who cares?"

"I thought you did?"

His eyes glittered. "How many people do you think know you're the rich Alexandra Kingston, mistress of historic Moondai station?"

"You want to pretend I'm not?"

"I wish with all my heart you weren't," he said, with intense feeling.

"Then I wouldn't be *me,* Daniel, would I? I know you care about me."

"I wouldn't be heading for the Moreland mansion if I didn't," he told her a shade harshly. He was lashing out in frustration when he loved her. Hell he knew it, but it was impossible to say. What could he offer her? Maybe in a year or two when he had time to get going. Hope reared its head. She looked so beautiful, so exclusive. She was wearing a little black suit with gold button detailing, a white silk blouse beneath the jacket, sheerest black stockings—he had never seen her in stockings—with a pair of high heeled black shoes on her feet. The shoes matched her handbag. No hat. Just her radiant curls that were growing longer and thicker by the day. He knew the outfit had been air freighted in. She'd told him she had nothing she could wear to a funeral in her wardrobe. Well she wore this outfit with considerable chic. She looked what she was: a lovely, fashionable heiress and thus way out of his league.

* * *

The meeting with the Morelands passed with far less difficulty than Daniel had anticipated. Helen Moreland who recognised Daniel was there to please Sandra more than anyone else, lost little time telling her story while Joel Moreland and Daniel, sat forward in their respective armchairs, their heads bent at *exactly* the same angle.

"I want to tell you the truth, Daniel," Helen Moreland began, "you know, the truth, the whole truth, nothing but the truth as I know it. The story is as old as time. A secret arrangement between two women. One powerful, one of lower station. The young scion of the family falls in love with a pretty young woman employed as a servant in the house. It was Jared's mother, Frances, who became aware of this attraction and found it utterly *unthinkable*. She sent the girl packing while her husband was away on business and her son was enjoying what should have been a fun week with his friends which took in the Alice Springs annual rodeo. What tragic event happened next pushed all thought of a dismissed servant out of a wildly grieving mother's mind. For almost four years Frances was literally off her head with grief. She adjusted to the harsh reality of life in time but had never fully recovered. Frances adored her only son. She had such plans for him. She genuinely believed no blame could be attached to her for getting rid of a girl she considered little more than an opportunist. It wasn't until Frances lay dying that she told me she had a feeling—just a *feeling*—the girl could have been pregnant. She said she did try to trace the girl—this was some five years after Jared's death—but Johanna Carson had simply vanished with the money Frances had given her to disappear. But that *feeling,* remained. It must have haunted her, particularly as she kept it all to herself. After Frances died it took me quite a while to work up the courage to tell Joel. He'd had enough to bear but what if there was some truth in this feeling Frances had? Joel set an investigator to find out. The rest you know."

Joel Moreland looked up as his sister-in-law's voice faltered. "We have ample reason to believe you're Jared's son, Daniel," he said. "The son he never knew about because you were in your mother's womb. Knowing my son the way I did he would have stood by Johanna no matter what. As Helen said, my wife had great plans for Jared—she worshipped him almost to the exclusion of our lovely daughter—she already had a girl picked out for him. She would have been determined not to allow Johanna, your mother, to ruin those plans. God knows what would have happened only Jared was killed. It was all too late. And it *would* have been only Frances couldn't keep her secret to the end. She knew not to tell me. I would have been shocked out of my mind. We're talking my grandchild here! She chose to tell Helen."

"I tried to get her to tell you Joel," Helen said, emotional tears springing into her eyes. "But she was adamant you should never know. You would never have acted as Frances did. I believe Frances had *more* than a feeling Johanna was pregnant but she was already condemned as not being good enough for her son."

"A *nice, compassionate* woman," Daniel observed grimly.

"Your grandmother, Daniel," Joel Moreland reminded him, sadly. "I know how you feel, son. I understand perfectly. Perhaps if Jared had lived Johanna would have found the courage to tell him she was pregnant. Had I been at home more often; been more aware of what was happening in my own household I wouldn't have permitted my wife to sack her. I don't remember Johanna all that well, I'm sorry. I was so busy all the time, travelling around the country and overseas. Nothing worked for your mother, I'm afraid. Nor for you because of it. My wife's punishment was not only the loss of her son but her only grandson. That's *you,* Daniel. I know I asked you to allow a DNA sample but I didn't really want to anyway. I *know* you're my grandson."

"So do I," Helen Moreland added with untrammelled joy. "You're the image of Joel at the same age. You also have a look of Jared, though you have Joel's eyes. Cecile has them too. No one seeing you and Cecile together would doubt you were family."

"So what *is* it you expect me to do, sir?" Daniel addressed Joel Moreland directly.

A look of agonised longing passed over Moreland's distinguished face. "I want you to take your rightful place as my grandson, Daniel. Be in *no* doubt I would never have let Johanna go, knowing she was carrying my grandson. Your father would never have permitted it either. If you doubt it, you don't know me," he said emphatically.

Daniel believed him without hesitation. "How many people know about this?" he asked.

"For *sure,* only the four of us. Sandra—" Moreland turned his head to smile at her "—recognised the resemblance right off but then I sense she's very close to you?"

"Aren't you forgetting something, sir?" Daniel asked bleakly. "Sandra is the Kingston heiress. I *work* for her."

Joel Moreland nodded. "I understand your feelings, Daniel. Your sense of pride and decency, but *you're* the Moreland heir. Don't you *want* to be?"

The question saw Daniel on his feet, obviously upset. "I'm sorry, sir. It's too much to handle." He shook his head.

"I understand that as well." Moreland rose to his full height, laying his hand on Daniel's shoulder. "You need time, Daniel. Time is on your side. Unfortunately it's not on mine."

"You're not ill?" Daniel asked with a rush of dismay.

"No, no," Moreland reassured him swiftly, "but I'm not young anymore. I'm not even middle-aged even if I don't feel so old. I'm a septuagenarian, Daniel."

"Like me." Helen Moreland smiled at them both, wondering how *anyone* could fail to see the resemblance. "I couldn't be more thrilled to meet you, Daniel. It's like a dream come true. Thank you so much for bringing him to us, Sandra." She reached out to take Sandra's hand. "Now that we've met, you can't go away, either."

A lot more than the words said was communicated through the women's eyes.

Just as Sandra guessed, Daniel, with a fixed determined look in his eyes insisted on moving back into the overseer's bungalow.

"We're in the middle of nowhere, Sandra," he told her as they rode out to the holding yards. A road train was due in around noon to transport a mob of prime cattle to market. "There's not a single soul on the station who would harm a hair of your head. Your uncle and cousin have left for Perth. They were never any threat even if they've been damned unpleasant up until very recently. It was all in your mother's mind, sad to say although she was right about one thing. The crash was no accident. Meg is in the house and I'm near enough for you to yell if you want me. I'd be with you in a trice. I can't stay in the house, you can see that?"

"Certainly," she answered mockingly, watching a small group of nomadic emus feeding on some dry seeds in the ground. Emu oil had been used for countless centuries by the aboriginals for a variety of ailments. These days it was having great success easing the pain of arthritis. She had to think about that one. Lord knows there were enough emus running wild on Moondai. "You're scared I'll barge into your room." She turned her head back to Daniel. He looked marvellous in the saddle, all lithe athleticism, a superb horseman.

"You bet I am," he said. "I'm scared what I might do."

"Could I believe...consider having sex?"

"It's okay for you, to joke. By the time you got around to yelling *stop,* you'd have pushed me right over the edge."

"There's a cure for being a virgin, you know. I think that's what's worrying you."

"You want to stop teasing, Sandra," he warned. "In my book there are certain rules of behaviour."

"Does this mean you're going to keep me at arm's length until we're married?"

"You can stop that right now," he admonished, noting the cheeky mocking look on her face. "Besides, did I ever mention I love you?"

"If you had any brains you would," she answered, smartly. "Sandra, I love you more than life itself!" She assumed a melodramatic voice, quickly reverting to her normal tones. "*That* would be nice. And that's not *all,* as any good salesman would say. There's an added incentive. The house comes with me. There's tons of room for future kids. Try to see it my way, Daniel. There's only one word for us. It's *soul mates!*"

He gave a short laugh. "Then this soul mate has a lot of soul searching to do."

"I know," she sighed, riding her mare in closer. "Daniel there's nothing wrong with admitting to being Joel Moreland's grandson. He's a lovely man. A lovely, *lonely* man. You could think of him."

"I expected you to say something like that, Sandra. Thing is, I'm thinking of my mother."

"I am too, Daniel," she said with utter sincerity. "I could never be insensitive to what your mother went through. But had she lived long enough I don't think she would have told you to deny this relationship. In a way it's a vindication of all the sacrifices that went before. Frances Moreland paid for what she did. I just don't think you and your grandfather should have to suffer her mistakes any longer. It's not as though I'm doing myself any good, saying this. You become a Moreland, where does that leave me? I'm sending you off to join the competition when I desperately *need* you."

"I'll be here as long as you need me, Sandra," he promised, a flash coming into his eyes. "When I get my life straightened out we can talk."

Well at least we've got *that* cleared up, Sandra thought. She knew she only had to sit still and she'd get her way in time. She *loved* this man, this Daniel. She was more than prepared to put up a good fight for him.

EPILOGUE

HER MIRROR TOLD her she looked dazzling. This was the eve of
her twenty-first birthday. A big party was being held downstairs
in her honour. Moondai was a much healthier, happier place than
it had been for many long years. Daniel continued to manage
the station wonderfully but the time was rapidly approaching
when she felt in her bones he would go to his grandfather. For
Daniel with a good bit of coaxing from her had cemented his
relationship with his grandfather. She could take extra credit
for the fact Daniel had bowed to his grandfather's dearest wish
to allow Moreland to be added to his name. These days Daniel was known as Daniel Carson-Moreland but everyone knew
it was only a matter of time before the Carson was dropped.
Maybe Daniel C. Moreland she'd suggested to him? She was
after all, a terminal do-gooder.

The entire Outback had taken in its stride the revelation that
Daniel Carson was actually Jared Moreland's son. Stories like
that might have happened all the time for all the lack of fuss.
The great thing was, Jared lived on in his son. Most were pretty
sure a fine young man like the late Jared Moreland would have
married his young love had he not lost his life so tragically and

needlessly. Such a waste! But Daniel was universally liked and approved of, a fitting heir for his grandfather.

Neither Lloyd Kingston nor Berne resided at Moondai anymore. Berne was continuing his intensive training and doing extremely well. Lloyd had taken up residence in Perth, a city he had always liked, close to his academic friends. He had also acquired a lady friend he brought back with him to Moondai to celebrate Sandra's twenty-first. Festivities were to last the entire weekend. Sandra had invited all her old friends, especially those who had formed the hospital entertainment group. Vinnie, her former next door neighbour was invited, too.

Several members of the Moreland family had been invited, Sandra having met them on previous occasions. Sandra had taken to Cecile Moreland at once as Cecile had taken to her. It was very heart-warming to have such glad-hearted acceptance. It established them as friends who wanted to carry that friendship further. But then it was difficult not to be drawn to Cecile when she was so much like her cousin, Daniel.

Time to go downstairs! Sandra took one last look at her reflection, aware there was the sheen of tears in her eyes. Excitement was running at full throttle, fuelling every fibre of her being.

And always and always... Daniel. If I'm beautiful, I'm beautiful for you!

Her cloud of hair had been tamed with exquisite, star shaped diamond pins, heirloom pieces from her grandmother, Catherine's, collection which was now hers. Her dress was truly lovely, very romantic, white chiffon hanging from shoestring straps, the bodice tightly draped, decorated with glittering beads, crystals and sequins, the skirt dreamy for dancing.

She inhaled deeply to calm those tumultuous nerves. *Oh, Daniel, please say you love me!* Didn't he know his name was written indelibly on her heart?

When they were together love seemed to be all around them, but still he hadn't spoken, true to his own standards. She knew his mother's trauma, left pregnant and quite alone to rear a fatherless child had affected him deeply. Responsibility was Daniel's middle name. She quite liked that really.

She was almost at the door when someone outside, knocked. Probably her mother. Her mother and her stepbrother, Michael were staying at the homestead, but she had gotten in early telling her mother she preferred it if her stepfather didn't come. Her mother had expressed dismay but Sandra had remained firm. Her stepfather would never be permitted to cross her threshold.

Only it was Daniel who was standing outside the door, looking marvellous but strangely tense.

"Oh, it's you!" Wherever he was, whenever he called, she would fly to him.

"Only me." He stared at her for the longest time, then barely containing his feelings breathed ardently, "You look a dream come true, birthday girl."

"Thank you, thank you." Colour bloomed in her cheeks. She smiled up at him, her eyes a burning violet-blue. "You look splendid too. How much did that dinner suit set you back?" she asked lightly, aware they were both highly emotional on this special night.

"I hired it."

"Did you really?" She studied the perfect fit, the set of his shoulders. "You didn't."

"Of course I didn't." He gave her his marvellous lopsided smile. "But I won't be able to afford another in a hurry. May I come in for a moment?"

"Certainly." She stood back to let him pass.

He paused in the centre of the room; turned to face her. "You've turned into a beautiful woman right in front of my eyes."

"You're saying I wasn't much to look at when you met me?" She adopted a teasing tone.

He laughed softly. "You were the prettiest youngster. But *not for long!*"

"I put my heart into getting beautiful, Daniel," she said. *All for you.*

"Well you made it," he said, with considerable feeling, thrusting a hand inside his dinner jacket.

"What are you doing?" Her voice wobbled.

"I'm giving you your birthday present now, okay?" He looked up, a silver flame in his eyes.

"I just hope it cost a lot of money," she tried to joke. "Just fooling, Daniel."

"I know. That was one big fat cheque you wrote for the Childhood Leukaemia Foundation."

She nodded her satisfaction. "Joel has agreed to match me. I really love him, you know. My grandad didn't inspire a lot of affection. Your grandad is the kind of man one loves."

"He is," Daniel agreed with obvious affection, then with sudden intensity, "What about *me*?"

"I've told you I love you a number of times. I won't be tempted again."

"So I'll send this back then?" he asked, waving a small velvet box about.

"After I've seen what it is." A swarm of butterflies took flight in her stomach.

He moved towards her with his characteristic athletic grace, going down on one knee. "I've got to do this properly." He looked up at her with half smiling, but deeply serious eyes. "Alexandra Mary Kingston," he said with burning formality, "would you do me the great honour of becoming my wife?" He didn't wait for an answer but put out his arms and gripped her slender body to him. "Darling Sandra, I never had a life before you. You have to marry me."

She couldn't answer at once, literally speechless with joy. "Oh, Daniel, you're going to make me cry," she whispered, her two hands cupping his beloved head. "I dare not. I'll spoil my makeup. Oh, Daniel, I never believed you'd ask me."

He rose to his feet, bending to kiss the creamy slope of her shoulder. "How could you not?" he asked gently. "You know how *I* feel just as I know how *you* feel. We love each other. We were meant for each other since we were born." Swiftly he opened the box in his hand. "Here is my gift to you, your engagement ring. It comes with my solemn promise to love, honour and protect you all my life. Give me your hand, sweetheart."

Sandra raised it, but overcome by emotion, squeezed her eyes shut. Precious metal slipped down her finger.

"You can open your eyes now," Daniel said in a gentle loving voice.

"Oh, Daniel!" She stared down at her precious ring, a glorious sapphire flanked by baguette diamonds. "I feel like I'm going to bawl my eyes out."

"Not now, you can't," he reminded her. "You can cry in my arms when the party is over."

"Is that a promise? I don't think I can contain myself so long."

"Well we have to. I don't dare muss you, you look perfect. Tears, lots of cuddles and kisses are allowed later, but though it's *excruciating* and a real test of my control, we're not going to bed together. Not until the first night of our honeymoon which I personally guarantee will be the most wonderful night of our lives. Do you trust me?"

She smiled radiantly. "Trust in you wraps me like a security blanket. I've always trusted you, Daniel. From the moment I laid eyes on you at the airport. Now, having said that, I don't want to pester you, but *when* is this honeymoon going to be? It's a good time to put pressure on you because I don't mind telling you I'm in an agony of longing."

"You think *I'm* not?" He linked his arms around the waist. "I'm ready to start it *immediately*, but what I want even more is to see you as my shining bride. The woman I love and honour. That said, what about as soon as possible in the New Year? Would a few months give you enough time to get organised? I don't think we're going to get out of a big wedding, do you?"

"The biggest!" In an ecstasy of joy she started to whirl around the room all the while holding her beautiful engagement ring up to the light.

"Like it?" He caught her to him, commanding her to a stop.

"Love it. Love you."

"That's what I want to hear." He allowed himself several kisses that trailed from behind one small ear, down the column of her throat to her shoulder, all the while inhaling the lovely perfume she wore. "There couldn't be any question as to the stone," he said huskily. "A perfect sapphire outmatched by your eyes."

"Are you going to kiss me anywhere else?" she whispered.

His brilliant eyes rested on her mouth. "Don't tempt me. One kiss and it would all get out of hand as you very well know. We'll store the kisses up until the early hours of your birthday morning. Meanwhile I'll kiss those delicate fingers." He brought her hand to his mouth, running the tip of his tongue over her smooth knuckles.

"Daniel," she said weakly, just about ready to dissolve.

"This is *nothing* to what I'm going to do to you," he told her in a low thrilling voice.

"I *know!*" She gave an expectant shiver. "I'm going to pieces already."

"Me, too!" Ardently he touched a finger to the little pulse that beat in the hollow of her throat. "We'll have a lifetime together, Sandra." His voice was full of the wonder of being deeply, truly in love. "Just think of it!"

An enormous lightness of being seized Sandra. She linked her arm through his as they walked to the door. "From this day forward!"

"From this day forward," he repeated, looking down at her with his spirit, exultant, in his eyes. "You and me on life's journey."

For a long lovely moment they were sealed off in a world of their own.

I'm getting what every woman prays for, Sandra thought,

an expression of utter bliss irradiating her face. I'm getting the thing in life that really matters: Having a wonderful man love me as I love him.

Only with Daniel could this happen.

* * * * *